03731026

D1740528

THE BELL-WETHER

THE
BELL-WETHER

F.I. Linfoot

UNITED WRITERS
Cornwall

UNITED WRITERS PUBLICATIONS LTD
Ailsa, Castle Gate, Penzance, Cornwall.

British Library Cataloguing in Publication Data:
A catalogue record for this book is
available from the British Library.

ISBN 1 85200 079 1

Printed in Great Britain by
United Writers Publications Ltd
Cornwall.

To the memory of my parents
James Arthur Hyde and Mary his wife.

Chapter One

"Here we are. God's house done in ebony!"

The church stood in the middle of a row of small shops and houses that pressed right up to its walls on either side, giving the effect of a careful teacher about to safe-convoy a line of children across the busy arterial road. Like the cottages, the church doors opened almost directly onto the pavement, unhindered by garden, pillars or long flight of steps. Between the two porches a low wall topped by railings made a narrow cavity into which the casual passer-by tossed tickets and chocolate wrappings, but which suggested no other purpose in life. The doors themselves were studded with large nails as though to withstand assault, and as a further protection against anyone breaking in for any reason the iron gates were heavily padlocked. A row of stained glass windows stretched across the entire frontage and above these a tall 'five sisters' group led the eye upwards to the sharply pointed roof where, topping this example of Methodist Gothic architecture rose a short tower with a tapering spire, slightly cockeyed as if the finger pointing to heaven were not as steady as it used to be. The whole edifice had been gently sifted with soot by time and industry as evenly as a black bridal cake, regularly touched up again by the railway engines passing with audible gasps of astonishment over the bridge a few yards away. Nobody would call this building frozen music unless it was one of those freakish little tunes played on the black keys only.

On the pavement beneath the notice board two men paused, glancing up, for the name of one of them was there displayed.

"I'll get the key," said the older one, making for the other side of the road where, after scrutinising a few numbers he knocked on the caretaker's door. There was no response but after some moments the door of the next house slowly opened and a small boy gazed at him.

"Mother's out."

"Is she? And have you been left in charge?"

"No. I'm not there either. I've come in here."

"Well, do you know where the key of the church is?"

The child deliberated and then ran indoors where his piping voice could be heard.

"Antella, he hasn't got a proper collar."

"I'm getting the worst of this," said the man and knocked on the second door.

"Please come in. Don't stand on ceremony."

In the ground floor room a woman sat propped up in a cushioned chair.

"I'm Ella Kershaw. My husband is Poor Steward across the way and the key is left with me when Mrs Ginnell is out. I'm always in. I expect you're Mr Garner, our new minister. Ernie, my love, give the gentleman the keys, there's a good boy."

"My son and I are going to look round the church, Mrs Kershaw. Then, may we call in for a few minutes?"

Back by the church he studied the bunch of keys.

"We can get in at the main entrance by using three keys or we can slip round to the rear and effect an entrance with only one key. Can you make anything of that for a children's address?"

"Only if I were giving instruction at Fagin's school."

"We'll go round. I've just met one of my flock over the way. An invalid, I'm afraid, and I'd like a chat when I return these."

They let themselves in by a stout back door and passing several vestries walked down a stone passage leading to the body of the church, entering it on one side of the choir. They strode down the nearest aisle to the far end where they turned to survey the whole scene.

The dominant feature was the high pulpit with its glowing fall-cloth and below it the Communion table enclosed by an ornamental rail, behind all of which were the partly obscured choir stalls and the upper part of the organ, where the coloured Roman-candle pipes always made a fitting background for the preacher's head.

The plentiful woodwork had the dark patina of Old English humbugs and the serried pews were softened and enlivened by long deep-toned cushions and the shining brass umbrella holders affixed to each pew end. The gallery, stretching along three sides of the church, had its front panels edged with gold and the September sunshine also picked out the gilded names within the sombre wreath of the War memorial as if to make amends for the absence of sparkling ornaments that are the traditional furnishings of the traditional church.

Only an empty flower vase stood on the Communion table, but on either side there were ornate chairs similar to stage thrones that flank a stage banquet consisting of a single flagon. No one contemplating that bare week-day board would say in awe, 'God is here', but its very lack of candle and cross scorned the implication that He could be held captive here or anywhere.

Along the high chancel arch above the choir was painted a text in illuminated lettering: 'Praise the Lord O my soul and forget not all His benefits'. The light from the western rose window opposite threw a delicate warmth of tone into the place.

"Dignified, cheerful and without ostentation," said the Reverend Robert Garner.

"Let's hope the members take after it," replied his son. "Personally, I should like to see a plain empty cross in evidence somewhere, signifying the resurrection. At least it would give a clue to Macaulay's New Zealander if he came this way. But perhaps once we begin . . ."

"We have the Word," answered his father quietly. "I'll try the acoustics."

The young man took a seat and watched his father mount the steps and enter a boxed rostrum of fair size that did not cramp the preacher but allowed him to step back a pace, or take a turn to either side and shift his weight easily without the feeling of being caged. There were no books on the desk this day, as the great Bible was brought in with reverence for each service, so David waited for the verses to be spoken by heart to the empty pews.

Robert Garner's eyes now swept round the shining desert of the galleries. He turned and surveyed the untenanted choir and silent organ and finally gazed at the pale blue roof where, faintly seen among the high supporting framework, sparsely grouped stars gleamed silver.

"Howbeit the Most High dwelleth not in temples made with hands; as saith the prophet. Heaven is my throne and earth is my footstool. What house will ye build me? saith the Lord; or what is the place of my rest? Hath not my hand made all these things?"

A moment or two afterwards Robert descended the steps.

"Does the voice carry?" he called.

"Yes, Sir, the voice carries."

Robert smiled. They then toured the few tablets that more or less adorned the walls under the gallery. They were few because not many families could afford the cost of marble. This austerity kept the walls free from that clutter of draped urns and frenzied laudation that detains the visitor in more ambitious communities. The small homely church,

9

however, does not attract the casual visitor and becomes something in the nature of a private chapel for a district. The stranger was made welcome when he appeared, but since there was no stately tower or ancient window, wizardry of vista or vaulting or a chained Bible to gaze at, there was seldom a travelled stranger to drop an offering for the Fabric Fund or the new heating system.

"Look at this," said David, reading from one memorial ending with the simple tribute, 'His life was a rich blessing to many'.

"Yes," answered Robert. "Being where it is we can assume that it means exactly what it says. That was the type who upheld the old-style prayer meeting and raised up our local preachers by encouraging the young men to study and loosen their jaws in debate. There's no doubt they taught coherency to the faithful and gave the gift of tongues to what would otherwise have remained a silent witness. And it all depends upon leadership, fellowship, discipleship."

David drank humbly from the parental fount of advice.

"Another thing," continued Robert. "Don't get into the habit of gazing at the empty pews when delivering a sermon. We may all come to that some day, but don't anticipate. Some men deliberately preach to the pillars and windows, but a man must not be afraid to look and if necessary to look hard, at his congregation. It does them no harm to be made slightly uncomfortable now and then and it has been my experience that their facial expressions are less apt to decline into the merely bovine if the preacher consciously directs his words to them and does not leave his message to amble aimlessly up and down the aisles like an unclaimed kitten that's somehow got in."

The unheated building was beginning to strike chill and they thoughtfully strolled up the aisle, took a final glance round the place and departed as they had come, locking the back door.

They crossed the road and were admitted by the child Ernie into the house that was always accessible and Ella Kershaw made them welcome.

"For years our front door has only been on the knob and anybody can get in by just turning it. Mrs Ginnell says she would be afraid of somebody coming in and murdering her, but nobody has done so yet and I don't suppose they ever will."

David's eyes had gone very dark with feeling as he watched her. He and his friend Warner often discussed whether hospital visiting or prison work was the greater test of one's nervous powers. Warner contended that ministering to the sick was a fairly simple work, as they generally met one half way, whereas a criminal was sometimes no more receptive than a blank wall forbidding posters.

Ella was glad they admired the church.

"You'll be meeting the other ministers in the Circuit at your At Home. Little Mr Hunt is very jolly and the people round about call him Father. He does rather look like one of the monks in that picture 'Fish on Friday'. Mr Sylvester is very different by all accounts. He reads a lot of science and ought to have been a doctor as he's always illustrating his theme with the wonders of modern surgery. He makes it very real, and there's a marvellous operation that enables the deaf to hear, in which a hammer is used! He never sees any connection between his enthusiastic talk and the occasional fainting fits amongst the girls. I do hope I'm not telling tales out of school, only so many people call and tell me things."

"It sounds a very happy community," said Robert.

Mrs Kershaw smiled somewhat regretfully.

"Ah yes! We haven't had any real upsets for a long time. When the chapel was decorated three years ago there was some argument about the new text to be painted round the chancel arch. Finally they decided to let the minister choose one and abide by what he said. Even so, some did complain that the scroll-work made it difficult to read and one of the young men, Mr Sinclair's son very likely, said the last word looked more like 'beanfeasts' than 'benefits'. Not that it matters, as it comes to the same thing."

"What a delightful storm in a teacup," said Robert smiling, "only strong enough to stir up the sugar."

Mrs Kershaw reached out a hand and touched little Ernie's head.

"He spends a fair amount of time with me, but of course not as much as before he started school. You're Antella's company, aren't you, dear?"

When the men rose to go, David, pleased by the child's sitting quietly with a picture book, bent down to look at it.

"My word! What's going on here?"

"It's an elephant, squealing like mad because that lion has jumped on his back."

"I think that lion might regret it," observed David. "You've been very good. Have you a money box?"

"I've got two," answered the boy proudly.

"When a man uses two banks I always feel my confidence shaken a little, in him for being too clever and in myself for not being quite up to it. What do you want with two money boxes?"

"I have a red pillar box for myself and a globe for Foreign Missions," explained Ernie. "Where have I to put this?"

"I'm being placed in a false position. Tact would suggest the pillar box, but conscience urges the claims of our more needy brethren. The Ernies of this world force the issue. Here is another penny."

"Ernie ought to go far," Ella said with satisfaction.

"With expenses all provided. He'd make a successful touring lecturer and fund raiser."

They took a smiling leave-taking of the child and a more serious one of the invalid.

When they got outside the two men walked a little way together down the road.

"We don't get very far without coming upon some remarkable souls," said Robert.

"No, indeed," replied David glumly. "Almost the first sight of your new flock is a sick ewe."

"Only in a manner of speaking, of course. Full of spiritual health if ever I saw one. Now then, can you come back and have tea with us?"

"No, thank you. I must be getting back to the Old Ship," and so after another word or two they turned about and parted.

Chapter Two

"Is he married?"

This is said to be the first question asked by a congregation when their new minister has been appointed. They like to be informed of the fact early, so that they can welcome their shepherd purely as a superman and not speculatively as a man.

Ah yes, came the vaguely calming answer, he had been married a long time; for so long that he had a grown son, a bachelor of marriageable age. Interest raised its shining head. There was also a daughter, about twenty, studying in Switzerland. The inquirers gratefully felt a tempered wind. And the minister's wife? Did she take a very active part in church work? Oh, certainly. The Circuit Steward in Leicester had hinted that her ideas were up to date in most things and she expected ministers' houses to be like manses in the skies. She had an all electric outlook.

Alfred Sinclair, as Circuit Steward, had met the Reverend and Mrs Garner at the station to accompany them to their house.

"I'll call a taxi. I would have run you up myself but my son wanted the car for a University match. He takes three or four friends."

When seated, Alfred craned forward, booming out the names of the streets as they came into view. He worked steadily through several more or less precious stones and then started upon the commoner stalwarts of the English woodland. He jerked his eyes away to the other side of the road and promptly chanted the name of a hostelry, after which he was truly thankful to change the subject.

"We are now approaching the scene of your labours. Just past this bridge."

They stared at it in silence.

To the Methodist minister in his long pilgrimage, each circuit is a Jerusalem which during his three years sojourn he tries to gather as a hen gathereth her chickens, after the example of his Master, with the constant reminder of the great work once performed in so short a time. This system does not allow a man to settle down too comfortably in some pleasant rut. If he is exceptionally gifted, his work is spread over a wide area and if he finds a place uncongenial, his ministry there is shorter than his own and the Church's long-suffering. He is continually aware that he has come not to write a parish history or catalogue its flora and fauna, but to win souls.

The Oldham Road goes on and on, taking the main stream of traffic with it, but after about three miles the Moston route has had enough of it and suddenly darts to the left, hurries over the railway bridge, past the gates of the Carriage Shop fast closed during working hours, and at the bottom of the hill swerves, as though about to be tackled, to the right, to avoid a grey ravine such as might appear on a half-cooled planet, down the slopes of which a lorry was at that moment unloading a dry chute of ashes.

Alfred waved towards it and said spontaneously, "The Tip." Grace was filled with curiosity and excitement. Her home for the next three years was somewhere about here and at the moment she could not see anything to which she felt particularly drawn. Upon rounding a corner the travellers saw first, on the other side of the road, a fair sized Anglican Church with its typical manse close by, a large and old-fashioned house standing apart from neighbouring houses like a wealthy woman opening a bazaar.

The taxi stopped immediately opposite and here, a few yards back from the road, stood a pair of semi-detached houses, their doors side by side for sympathy and separating their respective windows which looked out upon a rectangle of garden common to both dwellings. The low outer wall, topped by the usual wrought, almost overwrought, iron railings, was screened by neatly trimmed privets. The flower bed or shrubbery was skirted by two little paths that started at opposite ends of the hedge and pointedly avoided each other until with a little rush, they suddenly met and embraced at the feet of the two front doors.

Alfred was speaking meanwhile.

"My wife has not been able to get across town today. We live some distance on the other side, but I'm sure Mrs Martland will have everything in readiness here in your own house. She is our organist's wife and lives next door here."

Just then the door was opened by a woman some years younger than the minister's wife, with a clear complexion and a welcoming smile. After the introductions and assurance by Mrs Martland that tea would be ready by the time they came downstairs again, the travellers found their advance luggage upstairs.

"Don't let's be long, Bob," said Grace.

"No, I'll just see what the study is like. I shan't stay."

The study was a small converted bedroom at the back, past the bathroom and along a passage, and being over the kitchen should be dry for the books. He would attack those packing cases as soon as possible. Thank goodness there was a gas fire, since the shelves were mostly open. Also, he hated to see a maid or charwoman lugging a coal scuttle into the room. He would prefer to do it himself, but never thought of it until they appeared at his door, so a gas fire served that involved mechanism, the conscience.

Downstairs, Mrs Martland was brewing tea.

"I've set for you, Alfred. You'll stay and have tea, won't you?"

Alfred didn't know. It was now getting on and he'd told Ada that he'd be back early. He'd let the taxi go and if he just missed his Didsbury connection, Ada would wonder where he was. He was still rumbling doubtfully even as they all seated themselves round the table.

"I'll tell you what I can about the domestic arrangements later," said Mrs Martland. Mrs Garner was grateful. She hated being told during her first meal in a new abode that at present the day woman was ill and there was something wrong with the hot water system. She exclaimed upon the prettiness of the tea service.

"Ah," said Mrs Martland. "You will have to thank our good Circuit Steward for that. He has been over everything very thoroughly."

"And what I missed, you pointed out to me, my girl," he responded gallantly. "And you chose this tea set, you know."

The minister was craning his neck. Chimneys could be seen from this window, but at some distance. There was a bit of garden at the back.

"Thank Heaven for it, such as it is," said the new tenant. "I'm not a particularly keen gardener myself but I like to have a plot of grass where I can take my book on a fine evening."

Alfred became expansive. "Now if you want to see really handsome modern houses, you should walk round Didsbury and Cheadle way. I've built several there myself, all with good sized gardens. I employ an architect who knows just what people will want when they see it for the first time. Bank managers, heads of firms, aldermen, are all after them. I live in one myself. Extra special wood has gone into the fire surrounds there! When you've settled down you must come across one day and see us. My wife will be delighted to show you the garden, too; she takes great pride in it. She might have been across here today if she hadn't wanted to make sure the man didn't slip away early."

15

"There, Alfred, you're a clever businessman and Ada is a very fortunate woman," said Clara sincerely if with reservations. "True, a garden is a place for young people to sit and read and enjoy the fresh air, as Mr Garner just said."

"Oh," Mrs Garner smiled across. "Then you have some family?"

"Yes, two daughters to point out my faults; Sybil and Kerry. Sybil is secretary to a land and property agent who was once a member of our chapel before he married and went to live at the other side of town. Quite unspoilt in spite of his wealth and his wife, although I didn't mean to put it like that."

"Sam had tremendous luck," observed Alfred sagely. "Demobbed; offered a junior partnership and in five years was the sole survivor."

"And your other daughter?" queried Mrs Garner.

"Kerry is still at school, with no particular career in mind."

Alfred looked up. "I thought she wanted to drive a dog-team in the far North?"

"That was some months ago, Alfred."

"Is Geoffrey coming up tonight?"

"Sybil hasn't said, but he might be. Since it's so fine, I suppose he'll want a game."

Robert Garner looked up.

"Ah! Your young people play tennis, do they? David is very keen, too. It's a fine exercise for townspeople."

"And may I ask who David is?" Mrs Martland asked, guessing.

"David is *our* boy," replied Grace gently. "It's a great stroke of luck our coming to Manchester just now because he is studying at Didsbury Training College as his father did before him. This is his last year and we are looking forward to seeing quite a lot of him."

"How lovely for you all."

"Yes, it is, really. As perhaps you know, we have worked for years in the China Mission Field, so this opportunity of being near to David is doubly welcome."

"Margaret, our daughter, has just returned to Switzerland," broke in the minister. "She is studying infant training there. It seems to be such an important subject nowadays with children so very much in the limelight. Scarcity value, I suppose, now that cars and American style kitchens seem to be a home's first needs."

Mrs Martland was about to ask further questions about the minister's ewe lamb when Alfred interposed a comment on his own ram lamb.

"My son is at University here. Doing very well by all accounts. History is his special subject but he seems to be good at most things judging by the time he spends away from home. Always something to see to."

Mr and Mrs Garner inclined themselves with a deferential air and Clara wondered if there were Chinese overtones in the polite gesture. Very expressive.

"I'll tell him to call one evening when he's up this way. He might be up this very night if he feels like a game, you said?"

"If he feels like it," Clara responded somewhat drily, "but if a party of them have gone to this match, they might make a night of it. So your daughter is studying in Switzerland, Mr Garner. Have you ever made a trip to see her there?"

"Not as yet. She was home for a time with us at Leicester during the summer. She sends very happy accounts from Lucerne with some good snaps. The air is so clear."

His wife reached for her handbag and was looking into a small leather case as Mr Sinclair took up the conversation.

"Lucerne! We nearly went there a year last Easter, but my wife couldn't bring herself to cross the Channel. In the end Geoffrey went with a friend. He says she wouldn't have liked it. Too much up and down."

Clara Martland, having taken a few snapshots from Mrs Garner's hand, was engaged in looking them over whilst the other gave such directions as, "That is Margaret there. There she's with a party of holidaymakers, second from the end. That shows her with someone in the garden. He's taking a bit of a liberty but she wouldn't have sent it if she thought so herself."

Clara glanced across at Alfred but the two men had got on to the subject of church membership and, pushing back their chairs a little, were turning towards each other, deeply attentive, so she handed back the snaps with the remark that their daughter was a very attractive girl and they must be very proud of her.

"Well, it's a mistake to expect to be always proud of one's children. Sometimes they do things that make one blazing or they hold views with which one cannot possibly agree, so the best thing is just to pocket one's pride and try to avert any falls."

She found a quick response in her companion and they fell into easy talk over their final cup of tea.

When the two women rose, Alfred declared that he must be getting off now. He didn't know that he had done right in staying so long. Ada might even be keeping something warm for him, as the evenings were now too nippy for cold meats and salads. Clara piloted him steadily to the door after the Garners had thanked him, and her

17

own kindly squeeze of gratitude on his arm sent him well satisfied on his way.

There was a friendly altercation over the washing-up, but Mrs Garner was adamant and set to work while Clara gave her some domestic information.

"I suppose you've been used to plenty of help in the house, but the last girl left and went back to the mill; she missed the company and noise. However, Mrs Ginnell comes in two mornings and hasn't to be told what to do. She just takes one look! She and her husband are the caretakers, too. Wonderfully energetic. And they've a large family for these times, but only two at home now."

"For these times! Yes, times have changed since Susannah Wesley's day. Strange how one century's virtue can become a later century's vice. A large family once indicated that people weren't afraid of work, but nowadays we'd suspect them of being too lazy to get up and too backward to learn. The habit of going to church on a Sunday morning would be of immense benefit to women in many ways, if only they'd see it."

Mrs Martland concentrated on drying the cutlery in startled silence.

"But small or large family, I do respect a woman who has arrived at conclusions. I hate to hear women who have joined the never-again club hiding behind such tags as, 'You can do so much more for one'. Even if the tag is true, don't tell me women are as much in love with truth as all that!"

"Don't you think so?" murmured Mrs Martland cautiously. "But wait till you meet Mrs Sinclair! She's a great believer in the one and only, the pearl of great price."

She turned to the cutlery drawer.

"By the way, you heard Alfred mention Lucerne, didn't you? Well, rather surprisingly his son Geoffrey appears on two of your daughter's snaps."

Mrs Garner swung round from the sink in astonishment.

"What a coincidence! She doesn't mention the names of all the friends she makes, but she'll be so much interested to hear of any connection with our people here."

She was looking quite pleased but suddenly a thought occurred to her and she hurried back into the middle room. Her husband had gone up to the study. Clara had dried several dishes before the minister's wife returned with a few snapshots fanned like a hand of cards and held them out for her scrutiny.

"Yes, I'm sure that's Geoffrey. It's a very good one, too."

Mrs Garner replaced them in the leather wallet and resumed her rubber gloves.

"Of course, youngsters on holiday always link arms or clasp waists and so on when having their photographs taken. It helps them to keep still, I suppose."

Clara agreed.

"He's very good company and very handsome as you can see. I can't think where he gets . . ."

She stopped in confusion and Mrs Garner dropped an offering into the cavity of silence.

"It's the same in art. Mix two colours and you get something quite unrelated seemingly. So, he has an understanding with your Sybil?"

"They've been engaged for over a year."

"Then he's made his final choice and won her. There doesn't seem to be any romance in the air with our two."

The subject faded out naturally and the minister's wife turned her attention to household matters again.

"I don't mind a bit about a maid not living in. There are only the two of us and electricity is woman's best friend, making all things possible. Personally, I shall hail the day when we can do without domestic help and hindrance altogether and another generation ought to do the trick."

She was on her hobby-horse. After experiencing Circuit houses before and after overseas work, she had met and endured and occasionally mastered every conceivable domestic anachronism and every form of unintelligent toil. She had slept in beds with high canopies, beds with tarnished brass knobs and beds with carved wooden spindles. She had dealt with kitchen grates all blacklead and brass, or all blacklead and steel, which was worse. Most of these had sunk into the sands of time, but she was still a connoisseur in smoking chimneys and had known fireplaces that belched continually when the wind was in a certain direction, or that puffed unexpectedly when a door opened or closed, or smoked gently and persistently from the entire framework.

"Is your Mrs Sinclair interested in labour-saving devices, do you know? Some Circuit Steward's wives never seem to go to a Brighter Homes Exhibition or look out for modern aids."

"Well," said Clara with some caution, "everything at their house looks beautifully cared for. Alfred would see to that. And they always have a resident maid; sometimes two sisters or two friends. Of course you know what I mean when I say always; that means when they can get them."

"Give me watts and therms and the slave of the amp every time. Now, you seem to be the power behind the throne with our Circuit Steward . . .'

"Indeed I'm not. It's just that Ada leaves everything to him."

"And he leaves everything to you. I can see he's a very old fla--
friend of yours."

She had stumbled over the word, but Clara Martland only laughed.

"You know as well as I do that in the Methodist Church most of us
are. We all grew up together."

"Then will you please use your influence to get me an extra electric
kettle for the bedroom only?"

"Of course I will. If I may use your 'phone the request will go in
this aye night."

She rinsed out the tea towel and went into the yard to hang it to dry,
Mrs Garner following to survey the little lawn beyond.

"At any rate, it's free from tin cans," she commented tolerantly,
"although it has never had the tender enthusiasm of a Mrs Sinclair, I
should say."

Clara nodded.

"You'll be meeting her and all the rest of the membership at the At
Home. Sybil will be singing."

"Oh! Taking after her father, musically, I suppose."

Clara was silent. She herself had been a choir member and soloist
at one time.

"And your other daughter?"

"Kerry? She could do quite well but she hasn't much patience; she
says there aren't any songs written for her, whatever that means. That
will be Kerry home from school now. Watch is barking and he doesn't
seem to take any notice of strangers. And now, Mrs Garner, if there is
nothing more I can do at the moment I will be getting back.

Mrs Garner accompanied her new friend up the side passage to the
front communal plot.

"This is in trim. Who attends to this?"

"When our privets need clipping, Len goes right along you know,
and Jimmie Northcroft from the farm comes and turns it over every
year. We find the shrubs so much easier to maintain than flowers. What
with music and tennis and homework to be done, the garden cannot
hope to look more than merely tidy."

Mrs Garner then took her hand and thanked her cordially for all her
kindness and trouble in making their arrival so comfortable.

"It was a pleasure," responded Clara, "and I hope that you and your
husband will have a very happy and successful ministry amongst us."

She returned the pressure of Mrs Garner's hand and they regarded
each other pleasantly, already well disposed without the need of
Christian effort. Then with a parting smile, the two women made their
way by the side passages to their respective tradesmen's entrances.

Chapter Three

Hailstones pelted the window as if an army of pygmy warriors were hurling javelins at it. Sybil opened her eyes, yawned and stretched and kicking back the bedclothes sat up and lay down again, hands on hips several times with the greatest ease, then swung her feet to the floor, managing to retain balance and an upright position in one swift movement. The gusty rain at the window gave a louder huzza at this performance and Sybil looked out. No tennis tonight at this rate! The prospect roused no particular rancour. Perhaps in a country like England, and especially in a county like Lancashire where so much play is postponed, so many matches rained off and so many garden parties transferred to the Hall, a certain amount of resignation is taken for granted.

Some families all sit round the breakfast table together, but not at the Martlands. Sybil always started first and had a glance at the newspaper afterwards. When she heard her father go into the bathroom and lift up his voice not in song but in some wordless composition, she took a cup of tea to her mother. Still having a little time to spare, she went into the drawing room to sing and play for a few minutes. It was a clear voice lacking any affectations, her highest notes or loudest volume being achieved without that cavernous, distorted rectangle that spoils the features of so many singers in action.

"Not bad, Sybil, not bad at all," called Mr Martland when she had finished. "They'll like that at the Welcome."

He was proud that she was a member of the Hallé choir; but pleased she let matters rest there when so many chits who could jig and chirp a little were aching to go on the stage.

A city girl is more observed than a rural beauty and although the countryside makes a better frame, the town provides a larger audience, and when a man looked again as many did at Sybil, with her quiet tones of a Greuze portrait, he felt a vague hopelessness as though viewing a picture beyond his usual purchasing power. Perhaps modern taste favours Diana rather than Venus and as Sybil surveyed the hoardings on her way to town that morning, she saw many Dianas but she noticed them idly as a woman who possesses pearls would glance at moonstones. All the shampoos were blondes, likewise the toothpastes, and they all smiled out over their super-fatted soaps or whatever they were holding, but not one of them showed a super-fatted arm or leg. One girl with a tennis racket was drinking lemon-barley through a straw, which made Sybil smile to herself, as she and a tenor voice sometimes sang a trifling little encore entitled 'Sipping cider through a straw-haw-haw'. But September was here and any day now the girl on the hoarding would be obliterated by a young giant in mud-stained white pants; a poster with some kick in it.

It was still raining of course, for Manchester believes in rainy days and not just shilly-shallying, when Sybil walked quickly to her place of work in St. Peter's Square. She enjoyed being there. Mr Buckley knew her mother and father, for at one time he had brought a creditable tenor voice to church; but that was long before she had joined the choir. When he married, however, he had gone to live at the other side of town and latterly at Chorltonville where his wife played lawn tennis, so he was seldom in his old haunts. But the Stewards kept track of him and he regularly received notices of Anniversary Sermons and sundry Special Efforts, which mute appeals he had not the heart or the pocket sufficiently stony to ignore.

"I don't need a frightfully efficient typist such as you see at Business Efficiency Exhibitions, who can dash away blindfold. I just want someone who can spell correctly with her eyes open. How does this machine suit you? Just type a few sentences for me, will you please? Anything you like."

When Sybil handed him the sheet of paper he glanced at it and then read it steadily to himself.

Yes, these things ought to mean something, 'or let me die'.

"Are you fond of poetry, Sybil? Do you read the modern poets?"

"I haven't caught up with much modern poetry yet."

"It needs a lot of catching up with, I'm afraid. But my wife is rather keen. Well, this is very neatly typed."

That was how Sybil started to work for Sam Buckley, to their mutual satisfaction. He called her Miss Martland before strangers when he remembered, but he thought Rainbow suited her better.

Two years had passed when he showed considerable surprise and consternation upon first noticing her new ring.

"Hello, what's this? Are you actually engaged to be married, or is that the only finger it fits?"

A glowing affirmative being given, he emitted a groan.

"Well, well! I suppose you think you ought to be congratulated. Heaven knows why! I loathe engaged secretaries. First their work suffers if it's a short engagement and their tempers if it's a long one, and neither does the poor employer any good. I suppose it's no use my offering to raise your salary? Who is this interfering young man, anyhow? Oh, Mr Sinclair the builder's son! I remember the father well; one of the more portly pillars. Perhaps I'd better congratulate you after all. You must get me to buy you a piano."

But another comfortable year elapsed without disturbance.

On this particular day, Sybil paused in her work to watch the rain swishing down on the stones of St. Peter's Square with such force that the drops rebounded inches high. Drenched macintoshes and umbrellas shone like fishermen's oil-skins on a wave-swept deck. The Midland Hotel and the offices opposite Buckley's were burning their electric lights and between Sybil and those other buildings lay a small oasis of quiet, the level foundations of a long demolished Church of St. Peter, on whose broad pavement now stood the Cenotaph, where generally at its feet lay the large official wreaths and small bunches that mark public salutation and private grief on certain fateful anniversaries. In the daily life of a great city men still raise their hats in passing that severe memorial. From below, only a corner of a great-coat can be seen over-lapping the flat summit, but from her vantage point at the office window Sybil could see the sleeping warrior there with his accoutrement laid down, his spread coat shielding his body from the weather and his face calmly exposed to the elements.

Sculptors, like the greater number of people, had grown weary of chariots and horses and avenging angels pushing their way through trophies, palms and trumpets. For the terrible calamity of war, calamitous however justified, the modern artist has stripped away all false decoration, to expose the reality of a plain sacrificial block on which lies, unmoving and unheeding, a generation of the world's manhood.

In moments of idleness or rest Sybil looked out upon that representative of slain men, withdrawn from the sight of the hurrying crowd of those who remained.

Sam Buckley, at his desk in the next window, saw her eyes fixed upon the recumbent figure, as indeed his own eyes were often so drawn.

"I was through that as a lad," he said curtly, and Sybil nodded gently.

"In the Pals," he went on moodily. "I volunteered and was probably constipated as well. Strange that I should have to sit here and look at *him* every day of my working life. I sometimes wonder if some of those chaps would care to be in my shoes, or whether they're better off where they are."

He saw his secretary's eyes switch over to his with a pained look, but he continued.

"I mean that. If some of my old pals came in here now, would they be much impressed? Or would they say, 'What! Still sitting there? At least we got away from that.' I don't know. But there, my dear, don't look so shocked. I sometimes get this way when the damp gets in my artificial little toe."

But Sybil protested.

"You don't want to be marching round singing and fighting all the time, or rushing up Mount Everest, even in peacetime. I think daily life would get terribly out of hand."

"I dare say, Sybil. Very much so, I can see now you've pointed it out. But wouldn't you like your young man to do something heroic for you, such as laying Everest at your feet?"

"Oh, not if it meant his going away," she replied earnestly. "Speaking as a woman, of course, deep down we think a man has got his sunrise over the Himalayas and his Taj Mahal by moonlight if he's got *us*."

"You've left out Sydney Harbour Bridge by torchlight," responded Sam. "So modest women think along those lines deep down, do they? And I'm sure they are right. I take back any aspersions upon Commerce by the Irwell."

His face cleared to its usual tempered good humour.

"Rainbow, you're a tonic. Not a cocktail, mind you. But your sheer common sense is guaranteed to tone up the system and make up any deficiencies or whatever it is that the best tonics do. Perhaps not many people whisper in your shell-like ear that you are very sensible? It may not be the popular idea of a bouquet, but coming from your middle aged employer it is the high water mark of praise. And now let's get on with our work before you ask for Saturday morning off."

On this wet day the luncheon hour crush got off the streets at a smart pace and the basement café which Sybil used was well filled, the hurried waitresses advertising the obvious by serving the courses with extra verve on to the green tiles framed in a deep band of dark oak that were a special feature of Kardomah table tops. She sniffed the pervading aroma of freshly ground coffee beans appreciatively. The businessmen who brought their clients here for a mid-morning cup did not usually return for luncheon, but their lingering cigar smoke wreathing with the eastern scent of coffee blending, whispered of divanned ease to the people who came in later for their one hour's break. Of course, there was four o'clock tea. In thousands of offices junior clerks put on the kettle each afternoon at the same time, and the accumulated steam as they all came to the boil would have driven a mighty locomotive from London Road station to Alderley Edge 'and beyond'. But tea was taken on the premises; it was respite, not freedom.

Sometimes she walked down Princess Street to look at furnishings, pictures, china and all the fine arts, occasionally wondering as she admired them, about her own house in that misty future when she and Geoffrey would actually have a home of their own. Such a future seemed remote and unreal, but because of it, the present slipped by almost incognito.

Hurriedly returning through the rain after her exercise round the shops, Sybil was passing the Cenotaph when her eye was held for the moment by the splash of colour made by some fresh flowers there and in that moment she came into violent collision with another pedestrian legging it furiously in the opposite direction. Sybil's handbag flew from her clasp at the impact which was sufficiently unexpected to have caused her quite to over-balance if the irresistible force had not grasped her elbows firmly and so steadied her. He had nearly knocked the girl over! A passer-by on Sybil's heels at once picked up her bag, which the stranger took with a word of thanks and commenced to wipe clean upon his fair white handkerchief, rubbing the leather industriously as Sybil remarked that it was fortunate that neither carried an umbrella as the damage might have been more personal.

"I haven't an umbrella now," replied the young man. "Kind friends have on certain anniversaries pressed them on to me, but a discerning providence mysteriously removed them to what I hope turned out to be more appreciative homes."

"I have quite a decent one," confessed Sybil, "but it slows one down in a crowd."

The young man stole another look at the perfect complexion before him and wondered if the soft rain had aided and abetted it.

"Would you mind looking inside to make sure that the contents are intact? I once sat on my sister's purse and broke the mirror!"

"Well, you can't repeat that shattering experience here," replied Sybil smiling, "because my mirror is a steel plate." She flicked open the flap to show him the immunity from ill luck that surrounded them both on this occasion.

25

b

"How extremely sensible," exclaimed the young man.

Sybil felt her face warming a little under the praise which had failed to be prosaic and, uttering a further word of thanks, she hurried on.

When Sam came in some time later he found her with her hands resting on either side of the typewriter and her eyes focussed on the Cenotaph.

"You mustn't dwell too much on that young man," he said heartily and she turned a startled look upon him. "That was the war to end wars, you know. Your generation won't be short of boys, never fear. You, my dear, are more likely to be spoilt for choice if anything. But I was forgetting! My error."

"Oh yes, Mr Buckley. And I wasn't really looking at him. I was looking at the flowers below."

"That's more the spirit," he rejoined as he seated himself at his own desk. "But why they chose to carve the words 'Lest We Forget' and then make the poppy, the emblem of forgetfulness, our buttonhole for November the eleventh, beats me. Now don't tell me! I saw them growing."

Sybil made two spelling mistakes in the course of the afternoon and was annoyed with herself because Sam discovered them first and said he put the blame on her bottom drawer.

During the afternoon the rain ceased, the sun shone forth and to crown the day, Geoffrey came with the evening amendment. It is astonishing how such golden evenings can emerge from an unpromising cut-you-off-with-a-shilling sort of day.

It was just after seven o'clock when Sybil opened the door to him as one flinging wide the portal to a flourish of trumpets. He embraced her with a young man's natural self help and her left shoulder gave a twinge of pain so that she winced.

"Oh, I bumped into someone in town today with such force that I've hurt my arm just a little. Do you mind if tennis is off tonight?"

"Of course not. The great gorilla, whoever it was! And I bet he would let more softly than you would, too."

Breathing indignation and commiseration, Geoffrey massaged the arm and shoulder for a minute or two before going into the middle room and joining Mr Martland in a final cup of tea. Mrs Martland greeted him with cordiality. Kerry slid hurriedly downstairs to tell him the worst of her new Form Mistress with a few brief sketches of other members of the staff thrown in.

Then Mr Martland took his evening paper to the sofa in the front room while his wife and the girls cleared the table so that Kerry could spread her books for the homework that would be a nightly affair now a new school year had begun.

Such was the healing in Geoffrey's magic touch that Sybil already began to feel that her arm was much better and when later he stretched his long legs and looked out at the sky and wondered if she might manage a game if she served underhand, she complied eagerly.

Then Geoffrey looked about him for some light activity and found it. Always in the Martland home, the wall by the door leading into the kitchen was decorated by what in some religious communities would have been reckoned a sacred picture. In Russia it would have been an icon; in Italy a Madonna or other saint; in parts of Africa a coconut mask; in Scotland perhaps a portrait of the Moderator or of the poet Burns. But nothing more fulsome than a grave respect was shown towards the photograph of the President of the Methodist Conference which was posted up each year as the new president was elected. His humane, intelligent face looked out upon them at the beginning of his tenure of office. At its close his most intimate friends would never have recognised the likeness.

It was Geoffrey's practice to paint the lily with a few added touches at almost every visit as opportunity allowed. The canvas grew too crowded in time to hold with any touch of plausibility the pirate's hat and large earrings, the excessively bushy eyebrows, side-whiskers and Chinese mustachios; likewise the check tie and diamond pin, the cowboy's lariat and Lord Mayor's chain and latterly the Maori markings, Cromwellian pimple, horn-rimmed spectacles and pugilistic plaster strip.

It was a point of honour never to be caught at work. When taxed, Geoffrey protested that in England a man was innocent until proved guilty. Tonight, as Kerry went to fetch her school case, he contented himself with the swift insinuation of a few coarse hairs sprouting from ears and nostrils.

Then he retired to wait for Sybil in the back garden, where he found Watch advancing towards him in a deprecatory manner as one anxious not to give offence, but whose tail quivered wildly like an unhinged metronome. He handled the dog with easy familiarity and spent some time in ascertaining the progress made by that patient animal in the sport of wheelbarrow racing.

Upstairs, Clara Martland was saying a few words to Sybil who had appeared on the landing in a white tennis frock.

"He should rearrange his plans for *you*, now. You don't want to strain your shoulder muscles. Mark my words, there will be plenty of scope for self-sacrifice *after* you are married, without starting before."

Clara was really displeased with Geoffrey on this occasion and in consequence, Sybil was displeased with her mother. For how could anybody criticise *him?*

Chapter Four

Miriam Crumps was a widow and looked it. The wonder was that she had ever been a bride, for even with half closed eyes it would be difficult to visualise her in anything but the clothes she stood up in.

Some women put up with the married state for the sake of one man. Some put up with almost any man for the sake of the married state. To have a husband was a very uneasy honour, but to have *had* a husband was a matrimonial felicity that suited her constitution.

Edgar had softened the blow, or rather parried the feint, by leaving her in possession of a tiny income just sufficient to preclude the need for ever having to think hard. Her sister's husband, Alfred Sinclair, invested her money for her and all she had to do was to express gratification or pique if the interest varied at all. She lived alone near the Catholic cemetery, not within sight of that institution but near enough to mention as a guide to visiting friends instead of their having to ask for such rollicking abodes of the living as The Thatched House or The Blue Bell.

She had been very much put out when Ada and Alfred left the north side of the town where the air had a good reputation, and settled in one of the most imposing of Alfred's latest houses. Her usual expression of stodgy calm gave way to that of a pouter pigeon receiving an unrepeatable proposal, but it did not affect Alfred. However, the sisters kept in close touch, as in some families blood is not only thicker than water but is positively coagulated.

Surprisingly, Miriam was a seeker after light. Unfortunately, she sought it in such unlikely places that the prospect of her ever finding it was itself a poor lookout. Also, she chose to follow so many different guides that she got very little distance in any direction before she decided she was on the wrong track and at once switched to another leader and a new path, most of them from across the Atlantic and backed by dollars, and a few from Asia with no visible means of support until they arrived in London.

Between shilly-shallyings with other churches Miriam always came back to the one where she had been christened and married as her jumping off place, which represented a faithful and long-suffering husband to whom she returned, fault finding, after attending a new musical comedy featuring a rising matinee idol.

Alfred poured cold scorn on Miriam's flickering lights, therefore Ada could not always agree with her upon the authenticity of her most recent revelation, so their triangle was not always equilateral and Miriam occasionally found herself far out.

If the swan would be a proud bird but for its feet, so Ada Sinclair would have been the veriest backyard hen but for her really noticeable hair. It was not so much her crowning glory as a shock of surprise. Elsewhere all her features looked as if they had run in the wash, all the primary colours drained off to nourish the all-consuming fire on the roof and her energies concentrated into one prime duty, the cherishing of an undying flame.

When she betook herself to the bathroom to wash her hair, the ritual took place behind locked doors even if she were alone in the house. There was an accompaniment of musical glasses and the whisking of richly lathered potions. By the time Alfred came home Ada looked as if she and the Mona Lisa had been asking each other riddles, with the game drawn.

Twenty-five years ago Ada and Miriam had peered out at life. They had peered out but life had found it difficult to peer back, they were so discreet.

"Look! There's Tom Kershaw bringing Ella Cawdor back. They've only had time to walk as far as The Brown Cow, so he must be going to supper. And there go Fanny Crossley and Joe Cawdor. He never signs the Pledge on Temperance Sunday as he says he needn't swear not to touch, taste nor handle to keep from making a beast of himself. I shouldn't be surprised if Fanny has trouble with Joe some day."

Here, both sisters would crane a little over the maidenhair fern to savour more fully a situation likely to give trouble some day.

"Here's Alfred Sinclair back. Clara Crossley never asks him in. I think all the Crossleys are stuck up. Old Mr Crossley says Alfred has an inventive mind and Pennine Gas keep putting his wages up."

"Pooh, Miriam, there's nothing about him at all."

Twenty-five years and more had not greatly altered the sisters' attitude to life, but they had modified their criticisms of Alfred. He had made no headway with Clara and another young fellow had cut in as if Alfred did not exist; Leonard Martland, smart and sociable, who had taught himself to play the piano and organ as a surprising number of young people did. At one affair Clara and Fanny Crossley and Ella Cawdor had sung 'Three little maids from school are we', dressed in kimonos and with flowers in their hair and often afterwards these young men had worn those flowers in their buttonholes for the rest of the evening. Alfred had not been favoured with so much as a leaf.

It was at a subsequent Whitsuntide outing that Ada Tipping had played quite a wild game of rounders and had afterwards sat on the grass and asked Alfred to hold her hairpins while she combed and rearranged her brilliant locks. No Lorelei combed to more purpose. She complained of its weight and the length of time it took to dry, but she had been told it would be a sin and a shame to cut it short; not that she cared! What did *he* think? Alfred sagely advised that ease came before elegance.

"Oh! Do you think me elegant? What a flatterer you are, Alfred Sinclair! Now hold up the pins one by one, quickly, as some of the others are coming near us and I don't want everybody to see me looking such a sketch."

The idea that he alone was allowed to see her thus gave him a peculiar feeling of daring intimacy, making him feel quite reckless.

"You don't look a sketch at all," he said almost defiantly.

"Aha, quite an oil painting in fact? Alfred Sinclair, I didn't know you were a bit like that."

"Well then, you don't know me very well," he rejoined with an air of great mystery.

Yes, Ada Tipping married the shrewd yet simple Alfred and he did actually do well in gas fires until he became interested in the houses in which they were installed and then he did better than ever. The money began to come in very steadily and the flow widened and strengthened, engulfing their old way of life and floating them comfortably higher up the bank to a very fair prospect.

The Tippings also received his friend and best man, Edgar Crumps. Edgar was constantly seated next to Miriam, both at the Tipping's and the Sinclair's, and the poor man hardly realised what had happened until too late. It was a wonderful illustration of mass hypnotism. The family assumed that he was going to marry Miriam, and in time he did.

The Crumps had no children. Miriam had been 'above that sort of thing'. The Sinclairs had one.

Alfred was honestly jubilant when his son was born. He promised to go and sin no more, or words to that effect and Ada forgave him.

Forgave but did not forget.

Even Miriam looked pleased, although she would have preferred it to be a girl. She felt that a girl would have been more delicate.

Geoffrey had known from his earliest years that 'he had cost his mother a great deal', which used to mystify him at one time since it was so obviously his father who had the money. He was under the impression that his mother left all money matters to his father because she had impoverished herself to buy *him*. When the coal-house was filled to capacity, the man would knock at the kitchen door and count aloud the folded empty bags while the little boy and his mother watched, but no money changed hands. A bill was handed in 'for father to pay later'. He was touched that she only had enough money to buy little things such as cakes and cream for his tea. The butcher, who called daily, was quite beyond her. Oh, dear. He must indeed have cost her an awful lot!

As the years went by he got into the habit of giving sympathy rather than expecting to receive it, and he chatted away to her from his southern wall only.

He learned much sound sense from Alfred, along with the knowledge that women must be kept in a special pigeon-hole entirely different from any other of life's compartments. The world of commerce was fairly predictable on the whole; politics had their defined aims and so had religion; sport had a great deal to offer if you weren't such a fool as to bet; but women did not come into any of these categories and must not be confused or mixed with them. They were a race apart. It was also better not to entrust them or harass them with money matters. Once they got hold of money they moved from the pigeon-hole to the pigeon loft and could fly round and develop a defective homing instinct.

When Geoffrey got himself engaged during one of those brainstorms of independence that sometimes overtake the most carefully nurtured, the sisters were greatly disturbed. Ah! Clara Crossley's daughter was also a singer and had doubtless been getting herself up in a kimono and a flower.

"It's not right to tie a young man down! He might not really know his own mind!"

"He's not a fool," replied Alfred. "If people don't know their own minds, there isn't much mind to know as a rule."

He might have been speaking to Miriam, returned from a flutter round the wrecking lights of British Israelites.

The sisters glanced at each other.

What would this man Coué do that Miriam had been hearing about

31

lately?

"Every day and in every way . . . "

Thereafter, they always discussed this subject in undertones as if to raise their voices would give it substance, whereas it was likely to fade away altogether on their thin whispers.

Chapter Five

The long summer holidays were over. For weeks the thought of school, like death, had been very remote, but it crept nearer and nearer as the gracious evenings shortened and the shadows lengthened. No more reading in bed all morning. No more evenings all to oneself until Christmas, three months ahead. No more sunsets over the sea until next Easter. That was hardest to bear. Nobody knew with what anguish she watched the last evenfall over the Irish Sea the night before they all left the coast. Nothing could tempt her from that vigil on the deserted shore, where she sat on the stones and watched the life-blood of another day gushing unstaunched into the sea, while cloud palettes and ray pencils were stretched forth to catch the molten gold needed half a world away to enrich the dawn. She would stay until all colour had been diluted and lost in the grey waste, searching the exhausted sky for some last wandering beam, and then she would walk slowly back to the house, a pain in her chest as if her breast-bone were breaking, like that advertisement depicting an arrow pointing to 'agony after meals'.

Now it was Black Monday again. There was her sombre gym dress hanging by its wooden shoulders on the key of the wardrobe. Goodness! She hadn't read *The Last of the Barons*. Did anybody? She toyed with the idea of getting up earlier this coming term. Her late heroine, Mary Queen of Scots, had been a late riser, 'bringing habits of luxury from the French court where she used to lounge in bed for days at a time'. But Miss Cassell had raved at Kerry all last year for dreaming; she said a dreamer was a dupe, anybody's cats-paw. Yawns made pawns. Kerry blanched at the thought that this term Jacky was only taking her Form for French and not English, alas. Jacky would drag her unmercifully through the scrub of irregular verbs as usual, but this term there would be no pain relieving balm in the next English period. Perhaps it would be as well to start imitating Queen Elizabeth, who got up at 5 a.m. to study under Doctor Ascham. What about maths? Maths! Well, I ask you! Je vous demande! Anybody who got up early to swot maths wasn't human.

The smell of bacon was stealing upstairs. The house was awake.

Sybil was already breakfasting when Kerry appeared and begged for a glance at the *Manchester Guardian*, just the back page. Any of the mistresses died suddenly? No luck. Any got married just as suddenly? What a hope! So they would all be about the place for another year.

"Is Geoffrey coming tonight?"

"Possibly."

"I hope he does. It will be something to look forward to on the first day."

"You talk as if you were going back to prison."

"There are similarities. By the way, that's rather good. I'll start that idea at school. The building can be Sing-Sing, Miss Harrison can be chief warder, and we can be doing time. I wish I wasn't going back today to do another stretch."

"Oh, I wish I'd never mentioned the word. And make up your mind to listen this year. They find you out in the Fourth," Sybil added darkly.

When Kerry left the house she called upstairs, "I'm going," and a bedroom door opened and her father's voice answered, "Good morning," and then "Good luck," for some reason.

Seated in the upper deck, she glanced out of the windows. She knew this journey by heart and it was the most familiar thing in life. Wherever she went or however long she stayed away, school was lying in wait.

She opened her case and took out *The Last of the Barons*.

The school, in the heart of the city, was really a very good building, large and airy and with a look of being free from frills both within and without. Kerry entered the main doorway in company with a steady stream of girls, which increased in speed as it poured down the stairs into the basement cloakroom, where it spread out in delta formation along the numerous rows of pegs and lockers. Here it was Bedlam. After the separation of six weeks, greetings were shrill and boisterous. Most of the girls were tired of the undisciplined languors of the summer holidays, even if they didn't know it, and now they surged back into this place of rules and regulations with all their combatant spirit refreshed and invigorated. The excitement of tourney prevailed and bright eyes looked round for old rules to mock and new rules to question.

34

The first day clamour was indescribable and the mistress on duty, with senses all delicate from her vacation in the Tyrol, shrank from the noise of what now seemed unrepentant savagery.

"Come along, girls. Hurry upstairs and wait for your friends in the hall. We want the basement clear."

Her black gown billowed behind her as she darted here and there, managing to sweep the sluggish tide more quickly between the grille gates.

Kerry sat fastening her slippers and surveying the sloping tiled wall many feet in thickness, that marked the depth of the basement below the level of the canal outside. Wouldn't it be awful if that wall ever burst? She remembered reading a play once about an Egyptian queen giving a feast to her enemies in a place something like this, and then opening the sluice gates of the Nile and flooding the banqueting hall. Wouldn't it be pandemonium? Kerry idly swung her shoe bag and continued to gaze at the massive wall. She could see the guests starting to their feet, knocking over the carved chairs and spilling the goblets and dishes and drawing their futile swords at the first cry of treachery. What a howl of desperate fury would arise! Then they would stand on the tables among the wine cups as the water rose higher and higher and the cold fruit from the golden bowls washed clammily against their bare legs. Later, empty flagons would drift unheeded amongst the upturned faces and threshing arms clutching at floating scarves; and all the time men would be hurling themselves against the inpouring flood and dying with an iron grip on the relentless iron grille.

A small dark cyclone bore down upon Kerry.

"Wake up, Kerry, it's morning."

Kerry grinned and thrust her shoes away.

"You look nice and brown," went on Jacky cheerfully. "Had a nice holiday?"

"Yes, thank you, Miss Cassell. Have you?"

"Yes, thank you. I haven't seen rain for over a month, so I find this weather most bracing. And that's the effect I should like to see it have on all of us. Now, all in this row, march."

They marched. Kerry got between Gwen and Freda, her special friends.

Upstairs in the hall nearly all the school were assembled. The three entered this bear garden and immediately fell back with gestures of surprise and horror. It was not the noise that staggered them, for they contributed to it themselves in a moment.

"Oh, I ask you! Je vous demande! What have they done to the bathing belles?"

35

Scattered about the school in hall and library and corridors were many classical statues of heroic size. New girls were apt to gape at these figures in amazement until they recollected themselves and guiltily averted their virgin eyes, for most were undraped and the sort of thing that their parents hurried past if they came upon them. Here, however, the naked forms of nymphs and athletes were a commonplace, and in a surprisingly short time were taken as much for granted as the hot water pipes. Wistful glances were sometimes thrown at the Apollo Belvedere, but nobody associated him with the man in the street. These Apollos and Hercules were a departed race, mere relics of a dead age and to be admired openly as such, but it occurred to hardly one girl in a hundred that they represented works of nature, too.

All these wonders of Praxiteles and Pygmalion were referred to by names other than those given to them by the original artist and would not be found in any catalogue, but although lacking reverential regard, the Percys and Di's and Polly dears were held in high affection by all, and were greeted hilariously at each new term's beginning.

"What have they done," cried Kerry aghast, "to the Fast Girl and Caught Napping?"

"They've *whitewashed* them!"

For many years the plaster casts had been the colour of old piano keys, the rounded limbs of dryads and the muscular torsos of wrestlers having the faint amber flush of a nicely mellowing meerschaum. Their surfaces were beautifully polished and little accumulations of dust accentuated the delicate nostrils and threw into relief the orderly rows of curls. They were perfectly adapted to the city background, shining coolly but not coldly in the summer and on foggy days appearing through a haze of incense as in a temple.

Outrage had been done. The statues had indeed been whitewashed. The hard unglazed surfaces glared starkly and the sweet calm faces of goddesses and heroes had no soft light and shade.

The desecration was hotly discussed at the back of the hall. Diana could hardly have witnessed such partisanship since the hey-day of her temple at Ephesus. Glorious Apollo, pallid as a leper, was mourned with a great lamentation and 'Boy with a corn on his foot' received the sympathy due to his having fallen into a chalk pit.

It was noticeable that the noise of laughter and talking that battered the ceiling was subject to a gradient like the water in a large swimming bath. At the platform end by the Head's door, the noise was barely perceptible. Here, the little new girls squatted tailor fashion, waiting to be told what to do. The clamour deepened as it shelved to the

36

back, where individuality was lost in a sea of navy-blue tunics, and none was less or more guilty than another. A few girls near the windows eventually caught the sound of nine o'clock tolling from the police station nearby, but the assembly heeded it not. A moment later, however, a tiny click, very slight but quite distinct, was heard, and a silence slow and sure as an ice age began to creep from the shallows at the foot of the platform, spreading its chill over group after group, freezing animation as it travelled, until it reached the buoyant souls sporting in the safety of anonymity at the rear, who suddenly becoming aware of their isolated revelry, fell silent and abashed, as might a carousing felon in an American backwoods saloon, at the touch of a heavy hand upon his shoulder.

Miss Harrison quietly emerged from her room by the platform steps and surveyed the scene, casting a glance of sympathy and affinity towards the statue of Hercules resting on his club. Perhaps it was a mistake for anybody to rest at all! She ascended the steps and took up her usual position at her table.

By this time all the mistresses in their black gowns were lined up along the wall by the door and the sixth form girls faced them from the windows across the hall. Their ranks were immediately scrutinised for grand passions and pet aversions. Every detail in dress and style of hairdressing among the mistresses and prefects was infallibly noticed, some to be copied most slavishly during the ensuing weeks, to the bored irritation of the adored.

The music master, the only male in the place, took his seat at the piano. Music mistresses had but brief sojourn in this school. In their lessons spirits were high and rampant and a music lesson was counted as good as half an hour's break. So Mr Miller came, quiet and efficient, and at the last Speech Day the singing had been highly commended in high places.

Miss Harrison bade the school "Good morning." There was a subdued response. They were now at the beginning of a new school year, she went on. There were new girls to welcome, new resolutions to make, new goals to strive for. There were also a few new rules and these were read out. Then she glanced at Mr Miller, who struck a pleasing chord or two, and paused. This was the signal for the Jewesses and the Roman Catholics to leave the hall while the Head made a short prayer and the school sang their inoffensive hymn. Miss Harrison frowned slightly as this little procession filed smugly out. She felt that if the parents approved of the education meted out by the school, it was carping to withdraw them from such a brief and general service. She could see no harm in RCs singing 'Jesu, Lover of my Soul'. However,

37

march out they did and really the line of Jewesses seemed to grow longer each year. Most of them were brainy, and Esthers, Sarahs, Rachels and Leahs were liberally sprinkled in the scholarship lists and passed easily into College or University. Now, incongruous in their short gym tunics, they moved with their mature poise, lustrous eyes and forty-inch busts, in the wake of the fervent RCs, and the heavy doors were closed.

Mr Miller played the first line of the hymn and Kerry was filled with gloom and foreboding. What a hymn to start a new term! She was glad now that the Jewesses and RCs had gone out. They *would* think us a browbeaten lot! Although perhaps they were indulging in their own private kow-towings in the library. Wouldn't it be queer if some girls were confessing their sins at one end, and the Jewesses wailing against the glass partition at the other end? The statue of Shakespeare was in there, too. It would be rather difficult to do anything outré in the calm presence of one who continued to lean negligently on his elbow.

During the singing of the hymn something else had arisen on the morning air besides the youthful voices. A barge was slowly passing on the canal outside, and the great wooden lock gates had as usual stirred the noisome depths, so that a fearful stench arose, permeating the hall with noxious gases. The sixth form girls lost their poise, and springing upon the hot water pipes hurled their weight at the windows, so that the last verse of the hymn was punctuated by resounding crashes.

Miss Harrison now made a short prayer. Some of the little twelve-year-olds carefully placed their palms together and closed their eyes tightly. The continuance of the hand clasping practice depended upon the time elapsing before the children began to peep during the prayer, Some soon discovered that they were in a minority, while some kept it up for weeks. The back rows were content to stand very much at ease with eyes more or less downcast as they twisted and fumbled with their tunic belts.

After the Lord's Prayer, Mr Miller struck up a loud and lively march and the assembly left-turned and began to march quickly out in twos. At the door each Form was joined by its Form mistress and as soon as they were out of ear-shot of the music, the girls broke into an exuberant dash up the stairs. That was another thing that ought to be stamped out; that wild pace, two and three steps at a time, which they could keep up to the fourth floor, finally bursting into their Form room panting and laughing and about as much prepared for calm study as a herd of wild colts rushing into a corral.

IV C were now on the run and Miss Fridgely followed protesting.

The little hooligans! Up she sped, black winged like Dracula and as thirsty for blood; but surprisingly as she got nearer no hoydenish row swelled to meet her from the demure procession now disappearing through the doorway.

Only a couple of yards away, standing about eight feet high and composedly erect, was the plaster cast of a completely naked athlete regarding his own biceps with an indulgent smile of admiration. His had been the golden age when the laurel for the brow had been the only leaf worth wearing and even Miss Harrison with her scholarly freedom from embarrassment, had considered the top corridor the best place for him. He had knocked the wind out of Form IV C and Miss Fridgely, herself very pink possibly from exertion, entered the room to find twenty-five girls modestly looking down their noses, strangely silent and amenable in their temporary but highly advantageous sense of the proprieties.

Chapter Six

"It might have been worse," commented David, looking round.

"My dear, it *was* worse," replied his mother, "but there's a wardrobe drawer in the second bedroom full of pictures and china that will never see the light of day while we are here; and when we go, the Circuit Stewards will say how very careful I have been with the furnishings! At first it looked as if this room was expecting a deputation, but we cleared out several chairs."

"The second bedroom?"

Grace nodded.

"It *is* a business, this periodical upheaval, but each time we decamp I try to take a little less with us, not a little more. I can see that I'm the opposite of a born collector; I'm a born dispenser."

"But *this* will always have a place in the saddlebags," and David moved across to the mantelpiece and stood regarding the central ornament. He had seen it often before but its appeal was immediate. It had been a parting gift from Robert Garner's Chinese friends and always had pride of place in their drawing room. Where most people put a clock, here was timelessness. When anybody glanced for the time of day they were confronted by an age.

David turned it slowly round. A heavenly blue background was portioned into slender panels in which were drawn with fine lines and delicate colours, little pictures of Chinese family life. Children stretched out their hands towards tame birds and sprays of blossoms and a polite girl was listening to a youth playing a musical instrument erected upon a small table. Still further round, a boating party had launched out imperturbably in a frail craft festooned with flowers, taking with them for the day's enjoyment a small supply of fruit and wine and a cage of singing birds. They viewed with nonchalance an impending cataract.

"I suppose," said David slowly, "we all have moments in which we hesitate to teach such people how they should live."

"I know what you mean, my dear. Perhaps in the past it has been one of our mistakes to give without having the grace to receive. We said 'Sup with me', without the courteous 'And I with thee.' "

"Yes, the old method was to throw in the seed with a flourish and it promptly got thrown out. Then it was thrown in again with holy fervour until the garden became a battlefield. We've learnt to prepare the ground a bit now by paying courtesy calls."

"Presenting a new idea is always dangerous work, David, but it is more acceptable if presented with humility. Energy does not always meet the requirements of a situation."

The Chinese vase had come full circle and David straightened himself.

"I expect that is the most beautiful and the most valuable thing in the house."

At this moment Robert Garner appeared in the doorway and he came forward and put an arm round Grace and a hand on his son's shoulder.

"Ah, my boy, if you've been shown round the house we'll tackle the books. Very kind of you to offer."

"But I haven't been round the house. I've only been round your Chinese vase. I'm all agog to see the second bedroom. I may have to sleep on top of the wardrobe sometime."

"Come and see my study instead. I want to show you my extensive view of the local backyards. All the dustbins here live in a sort of dolmen or stone kennel by the back gate. The effect is of a row of shrines and all the women go down during the morning with cabbage leaves and carrot tops, like charitable villagers taking offerings to hermits in caves."

"Yes, go along," urged Grace, "and help your father. If ever you have to sleep in the second bedroom I'd rather lead you in blindfold."

They went upstairs where the gas fire was rallying the September warmth against the damp.

"It's quite a nice study," said David, "and anything seems palatial after our cells at Didsbury, though you haven't so good a view, certainly. Books stand the journey all right?"

"What a job! It's the corners, you know. Your mother and I wrapped them in batches of a dozen in newspapers we'd saved for months; but a removal is terribly hard on the corners."

"Let's get them on the shelves now. I'll unwrap and hand them to you. You'll be glad tomorrow."

David made a vigorous start and soon one packing case was out on the landing and Robert had to admit that his books really seemed none the worse. Soon he lowered the gas fire and David took off his coat. He had all the stooping, lifting, unwrapping and refolding to do while his father was gauging the comparative heights of shelves and books and tentatively trying some for size. A few books for immediate use were placed in a trough on the writing table; those in fairly habitual use were graded for convenient reach as near as possible, and prizes, presentations, the rare and the old were encased behind glass doors, to be caressed by the eye more often than by hand.

Neither his studies nor his experience had nurtured depression of spirit in Robert Garner. He believed that the death-fruit is not the knowledge gradually unfolding to man's research, but a curious and premature hankering not so much to do God's work as to steal His job; always a dangerous ambition.

As Robert Garner turned over the tumbled fabric of the past that, erected in hope, had in time sunk to be stumbling blocks, he searched for evidence of those stones rejected by builders throughout so many centuries, which had they been properly placed, would have upheld their wonderful but doomed temples. Always there was some indication that the stones had been present, but never in that key position that alone could give strength and durance to the whole. In Robert Garner the anthropologist merged into the spiritual explorer and this understanding of the past, which he never regarded as the 'dead past', and this faith in the future which he never clouded by referring to as 'eternity', made his work at home and abroad absorbing and worth while from day to day. He implicitly believed that God operates between the vast immensity of the solar system and the pin-pointed energy of putting breath back into a body whence it had fled.

David coughed.

"I think we'd better not start dipping now, Father. I'd like to carry all these cases down before I go, or Mother might start on them. Is there an outhouse? Not the second bedroom, surely?"

"Oh, yes, there is an outhouse. By the way, David, there's a strange idea going around that all learning, or art, or indeed any form of mental exercise, is an unworthy escape from reality; reality evidently being represented by physical toil. It's like a man accusing his immortal soul of escapism for struggling out of the pit."

Another shelf was filled before Robert spoke again.

"We all feel travel-sick at some stage of our pilgrimage if only because of occasional fatigue. Surely studying something uplifting is preferable to being sick in public."

"You've got it wrong, Father, about not wishing to be sick in public. It's considered a natural expression of criticism today. We eat the whole of the suspected bad egg in order to be the more effectively sick on the grocer's counter. That's realism."

"But there is John Wesley's moderation of agreeing to differ when peaceable conversion seems improbable for a time."

"No, you take your adversary not by the hand but by the throat, today."

"That won't do!" exclaimed Robert. "How can a man discuss reasonably with pressure on his wind-pipe?"

They pursued their own thoughts and work for some minutes until David lifted out a parcel of small green volumes and ran his eye over their titles.

"R.L.S. What an output for a short life! But it was tactless of him to say books are a bloodless substitute for life when they are such a vital part of civilised living."

"Ah, bloodless! If he meant anaemic he was wrong. I prefer Milton's 'precious life-blood of a master spirit'. And Milton reminds me of Oliver Cromwell. Now *he* knew the stern difference between beauty and truth. The problem of the times could not contain both and he let the wayward sentiment go."

"And that meant drawing the straight line rather than the curved."

"Yes, my boy, the Roman road of urgency, and that road must have a foundation to take the traffic of civilisation; a Thou Shalt and a Thou Shalt Not!"

David took out a floppy leather binding and gave a short laugh.

"Here's beauty enough with some questionable truth, although he will always draw our adolescent tears, bless him! Imagine Omar Khayyam, belly-aching that the flower that once has blown for ever dies, suddenly coming upon the author of Job in the garden, contemptuously flicking worms out of his path. Omar would about swoon."

Robert nodded at the surrounding shelves.

"How depleted our libraries would become and how much thought would be lost to us if only absolute truth were printed. Pagan literature naturally contains an element of endemic grief because all beauty seems lost irrevocably in time; not as we believe, lost to us awhile. True literature should help to ease the burden of man's long trek; take some of the heartache from the contemplation of beauty and give reassurance of perpetuity and treasure laid up. This generation lacks its poet seers."

"Even drawing an oblique line."

43

"I wish our people read more, David, and seasoned their daily fare and enlarged their mental acquaintance. When earnest Methodists were readers they were a power in the land."

"You must get to work on them. I'll help if I can. I'll give a paper if you like on the 'Ring of Words', R.L.S.'s phrase. Now take Shakespeare for instance. Supposing that instead of saying, 'It is the nightingale and not the lark', Juliet had said, 'It is the nightjar and not the cock', I expect Romeo would have left earlier. I wonder if they have a Literary and Devotional Society here?"

"I can see you'd have it more Literary than Devotional in no time," answered Robert drily.

The young man made no further suggestions towards helping to run his father's church. 'He is by nature a High Priest', thought David with sudden humility.

"Where shall I drop these Kai Lungs?"

"Don't drop them literally; place them with devotion over there," answered Robert, and David's slight unease left him as they exchanged glances. "If I have them within too easy reach, I shall reach for them too often. It's wonderful how Ernest Bramah could literally orientate himself. He is genuine Chinese ginger; not flavoured vegetable marrow."

The work progressed in silence and soon the little study was almost fully lined with books. The bare shelves now glowed with colour or showed pale with dust jackets. Long rows of the sturdily prolific authors relied on their numbers for effect; old soldiers in dark brown or maroon leather standing shoulder to shoulder by the dozen. Anthony Trollope's bindings, the colour of club armchairs, already looked as if they had been members for years. The room no longer had a hollow sound when a voice spoke or an empty packing case was dragged out, and when a bookcase door was shut and the key turned, it was done with a quiet and comfortable tone of muffled repletion.

"Now it's looking more like home," exclaimed David as he placed Minutes of Conference amongst other works of reference between book-ends on one side of the writing table. Then he carried the last empty case out.

Robert sank gratefully into what had once been the carver of a dining set. Its plush, nail-studded arms were at a comfortable height and the well sprung seat had the additional comfort of a feather cushion. The back was fully upholstered so that no draught at the rear could assail the lumbar regions. All in all, an unobtrusive, thoroughly trustworthy chair, and that was a very necessary prelude to hours of reading and writing if one was not to get writer's cramp or even underwriter's cramp. Robert Garner would spend many hours in his small study and seated in that particular chair whose duty was to enable the occupant to forget corporeal self.

David had returned and was leafing through a collection of modern plays and frowning slightly.

"You know, it's impossible to melt down this stuff and find a precipitate of modern philosophy. There isn't one; it's all diagnosis and no treatment. Authors are taking refuge in light comedy."

"And comic phraseology makes me feel I've been dead some time," replied Robert. "Some queer words are landing at the ports and trying to settle. Speech used to be expanded thought; now the thought is compressed as if for storage. Not wanted on voyage. A pity. Words should have an open expression so that the genealogy of our speech is apparent, like looking into the face of a child and tracing there the lineaments of a noble ancestry. And some of this dishonest spelling is responsible for the voice being the voice of Jacob and yet deceiving us into giving our blessing to words that are not rightly heirs."

David cast a glance at the orderly shelves. They were elder sons all right, but they were going to be hard pressed.

"I'm just asking out of curiosity, Father, but have you ever tried to sell any of your books in recent years, to keep numbers down?"

"No, I haven't felt the need. I've given a few away here and there. Why do you ask?"

"I was just thinking you must have spent pounds every year for many years."

"Some of them are gifts, of course. Your mother gave me all the Hardy works, Christmas and birthdays. Thomas Hardy was excellent at portraying the weight of convention that could bow down and ultimately blast a life, but he made his women less intelligent than in fact they are."

"Ah! You were comparing them with Mother," laughed David. "But it's very difficult to sell books today, so yours are happier where they are. And as for Theological books, it's like trying to sell them to a blind-worm! I suppose new thought is pouring in and pouring out fast. Do you miss your teaching and lecturing now you're in Circuit work again?"

"In taking up routine pastoral work again, I have rediscovered a subtle variety among the ninety and nine. There's no such person as the ordinary Christian. A Christian is an extraordinary human being; he lives according to the light and that light casts such varied shadows on the path that the possessor of a delicate conscience is a much less predictable person, given to unexpected changes of direction, than the mere evil doer who consistently does the wrong thing. I certainly enjoyed my three years in Leicester, professionally speaking."

"My friend Warner finds habitual criminals the most boring people on earth; but I'd still rather go round the prisons than the hospitals."

"That is because you are a 'modern' and so to you suffering appears to be more terrible than sin. The wards and the sick rooms have to be faced squarely and we have to find clear words where other people are let off with a silent handshake, so there has to be a great deal of clear thinking before those clear words come when needed. Much is being done, but our soul-saving is not keeping pace with our medicine and surgery. Many missionaries are expected to have some medical knowledge, but are our doctors expected to be missionaries too?"

"I suppose a few are; perhaps more than we think when it comes to the pinch," answered David hopefully after a little thought. "And speaking of dual roles, Warner can go into a public house and start talking about the grace of God! But is it fair to track people down? If the money-changers are barred from the Temple, naturally they won't want the priests offering *their* goods in the bar parlour."

"People will listen to a man of courage generally, even if he pursues them into their own peculiar fastnesses. We have to go up the airy mountain, you know, after all the strays and we have to learn the language of the region and that always makes the little flock nervous. It is very distressing when they bleat, "Don't leave us," particularly when the time comes to go after Old Adam with new truths."

"Isn't it wonderful after all these centuries, to have the old Church hasten to proclaim new truth instead of belatedly admitting it? It is the criticism from within that does most good; from without it tends to make us more chuckle-headed. Some of the Bishops are on the march, too. They're unbuttoning their gaiters and putting on their seven-league boots and coming in the direction of the Free Churches, too."

Robert looked with fraternal rather than paternal interest at the young man in his enthusiasm. Would he be more useful at home than on the Mission Field? The World Parish was so vast they couldn't afford to misplace a talent. But they would sort that out at the Ship, of course. There are men and women so much interested in distant lands and peoples that sailing away is not all sacrifice; they would be nowhere else.

There was a gentle tap at the study door and David sprang up to open the door for his mother. She had come to praise their work and suggest refreshment. She looked round admiringly.

"What a good thing that you came today. Your father practically re-reads his library when we move and he stands at it, too. Now they've been whisked onto the shelves, Robert, and you've been foiled."

Indeed, the minister was looking round as if some trick of time had been played on him and he rose slowly. Grace shepherded them downstairs for tea.

Back in the little front room David sprawled on the settee, glad to relax after two strenuous hours, while his mother passed fragrant China tea.

"I've no difficulty in getting it here," she said.

"I should think not, Mother. Manchester is so cosmopolitan that any nationality under the sun could find what it wanted in the city. Actually, there's a Foreign Field on the doorstep for anybody who doesn't want to travel."

"But you do?" came swiftly from Grace.

The young man paused, glancing at his father.

"I think there's going to be more pressure on the windpipe and vocal chords. Even the voice in the wilderness may be choked off in some places."

A silence ensued.

From his seat in the window David saw a young girl in school uniform enter the gate next door and come up the path, whereupon a frantic barking broke out from the passage alongside the house.

"Does that ever bother you, Father, when you are working?"

"Not at all. It's our organist there, you know. And I'm grateful to people hereabouts for not keeping hens."

"They're such a nice family, aren't they, Bob? And we've promised to take you in sometime. Their young people are lawn tennis players."

"Ah, I get as much tennis as I've time for at Didsbury, I'm afraid."

"You are quite right," agreed Robert, "not to devote over-much time to sport."

His mother refilled his cup in silence before uttering what seemed to be more of a statement than a question.

"You don't meet many girls, do you?"

"Girls?" he echoed, as he half rose to accept his cup. "I sometimes meet one or two when I go out to supper after an evening service. And of course I shake a few hands in the porch. And there's Margaret," he added for good measure. "They've done you rather well with this tea-set, haven't they? It's one of the prettiest I've seen."

"Yes, Mrs Martland next door chose it although she isn't exactly in office."

"Perhaps," ventured Robert, "the women who have had the greatest influence usually have been those not exactly in office. Your mother wants that altered with more women clamouring for high office in their own right."

"On the throne and not merely behind it," said David with proper seriousness. "Nevertheless, the lady next door, whatever her position in relation to the throne, shows great good sense and taste. Look at these cups, for example. Very good design. I was once out to tea at a place where they had fluted cups with butterfly handles! The tea flowed out at three separate points so you had to negotiate for the middle one carefully or get your mouth across all three. Meanwhile the lepidopteral handle bit into the fingers and it would have been a relief to fling the whole lot into the garden to fly away. There are times when one could suffocate one's hostess with her own tea-cosy!"

Grace was reassured. This was indeed her child.

"Oh yes, things ought to be simpler. We use far too many things in the west. It's an awful clutter."

"The old English way wasn't bad, Mother, when men kept their hunting knife handy all through dinner, eating the baked trencher or throwing it to the hounds at the end."

"You'd better reintroduce it at Didsbury," suggested Robert. "It would look like a scene from Beowulf, tossing your horns of pure Manchester water and boasting of the texts with which you'd been wrestling."

"Ah," exclaimed David, "speaking of Manchester water reminds me. Can you lend me a clean handkerchief, please? I dropped mine in town."

"Dropped it!" said Grace upon viewing it. "I should think you have been mopping up the streets!"

"I'll get one at once before we forget," said Robert. "Yes, I will. Don't you move," and he left the room.

David abstractedly picked up the tea-cosy and examined it.

"I say, Mother, is it complimentary or tactless to tell a girl she's sensible, when you don't know her well?"

Grace laughed outright at this.

"It all depends on the girl. If she really is sensible she'll be flattered that it has been noticed. If she's not gifted in that way she'll still be pleasantly surprised at not being thought a complete fool; and if she happens to be a pretty girl she'll be better pleased than anybody, feeling with Solomon that all these things had been added unto her."

"I see," replied David, putting the tea-cosy into position again.

Grace looked at her son coaxingly.

"Surely, my dear, you do meet a few nice girls here and there?"

Having both a son and a daughter she was aware of two widely differing maternal sensations. Her son had to be defended from the Eve hidden in every feminine skirt, and yet her daughter had to be warned of the pirate masquerading in every conventional masculine suit. But naturally their Margaret was not an Eve and David was not a pirate and some day they would meet other exceptional youths and maidens and pair off very suitably.

"Oh yes, of course I run into them . . . "

He stopped abruptly.

"Is there anyone you would like to bring home sometime? We should be glad to meet any friend of yours, you know."

"Thanks," answered David, coming out of a reverie, "I'll ask Warner along some day."

"Oh." Grace was plainly disappointed. "Is he pretty and sensible?"

David laughed, although he was somewhat awed to find with what tenacity a woman could follow a train of thought along an obscure branch line and through a tunnel.

The minister returned with the clean handkerchief and as the young man tucked it into his breast pocket his mother remembered something.

"Oh David, I got your father to have another key made. Here it is. This is your home now since it is ours."

"It's like being twenty-one again! But of course it isn't at *this* end that I shall be making an unobtrusive entry in the small hours. If anybody sees fit to wait up for me, it will be at Didsbury."

"Oh, you don't, do you?"

He pocketed the key and smiled across at his father.

"Warner and I occasionally go to the Scala and don't quite make it getting back, but they haven't said anything about having an extra key made for me."

From her handbag Grace had also taken a letter which she handed to him.

"Margaret's latest. According to her, the theory now is that when children start to smash things, you hand them a bigger hammer. The child in the western home is now placed after the fashion of Japanese flower arrangement; a single bloom instead of the massed effects we used to see years ago."

"Oh, we can get the massed effects at school and college," said David at once. "Let's have a bit of peace at home. Peace and plenty for that matter. Now take your own modest family."

"Modest only in number," interrupted Grace.

"At least we are less likely to become chargeable to the Parish. If we're cluttered up with things here in the west, at least we are not cluttered up with people as in the east. We can give our possessions to the poor and acquire merit, but nobody is commended for giving their

49

c

children away. Although look what I should have missed if you'd exposed Margaret! I suppose Christmas will be the next time she comes home?"

Robert nodded.

"Unless," said Grace thoughtfully, "she stays to see what Christmas is like there."

"Oh, she won't do that, surely," protested Robert.

"She might, just for once. It wouldn't be a bad idea."

But the two men thought otherwise and then David rose to go.

"I must be off now. I shall read tonight."

"Of course you'll be coming to the Welcome next Wednesday, will you not?"

"Wouldn't miss it for anything, Mother. What time do we descend on the fold?"

"Seven-thirty."

"I shall be there. It will be interesting to see how many D.V-ers there are nowadays. D.V-ers have largely replaced the Ameners, but I don't like the breed. I once heard a man say he was going to get his hair cut, D.V. He deserved to be singed at his latter days."

By this time they were all three at the front door and Robert stepped out as far as the gate, the better to hear an approaching tram. Grace slipped an arm through David's.

"Don't forget, that if ever you do meet someone who is pretty and sensible we should be awfully glad to meet her."

"Why, Mother, you mustn't think I've met anybody at all special, because I haven't."

"I just wondered. Perhaps you live in a more rarefied atmosphere out your way. Mr Sinclair said there was a difference."

"No, honestly, Mother. I just happened to catch a passing glimpse of someone who appeared to be above the average, but that's all. There's nothing alarming in noticing a sensible girl, is there?"

"Mercifully not, but remember, David, when the time comes, you are choosing a wife of your bosom, not a Deaconess."

Grace seemed unusually nervous and David was surprised and amused.

"I hope, like Father, I shall get the government I deserve," he said laughing, and kissed her. "Goodbye and don't worry, Mother. I've no time for that sort of thing."

That sort of thing indeed! Perhaps it is better that young people should despise love until they find themselves deep in it. They spare themselves a lot of bleating. Grace smiled as she wheeled out the trolley.

Chapter Seven

The Lecture Room, situated at the back of the chapel and above the vestries, was used mainly for the more serious adult gatherings and tonight was pleasantly filled for the official Welcome. Chairs were grouped round small tables in friendly constellations, the chatter giving way to curiosity as the Circuit Steward escorted Robert Garner and the two other ministers to the rostrum. After a few moments Clara rescued David from the group surrounding his mother and took him to meet the young people near the piano and was astonished to see Sybil overcome by an almost alarmed surprise as introductions took place. The stranger's surprise was equal but showed total pleasure.

"Why, it's my rainy day acquaintance!"

He shook hands with Kerry, Leonard Martland and Geoffrey and they made room for him at their table.

Ada Sinclair pointed out her son to Mrs Garner at her side.

"I see he's been lucky enough to inherit your - er tawny hair, Mrs Sinclair."

"He's our only one, you know." (And here those nearby waited as tourists wait for the big gusher to work.) "You see, when Geoffrey was born, Alfred was quite unnerved. Never again, he said; never again."

"It's surprising what some men go through," answered Grace politely.

Alfred now smote a large brass-domed bell to suggest that the business of the meeting should begin and since all business in Methodism begins with a hymn, he announced "And art Thou come with us to dwell." Leonard moved to the piano and struck up in heartening style, and at its close the Reverend William (Lancet) Sylvester offered a short prayer for his new colleague.

He thanked God for their church system which regularly enjoyed an intake of new blood. Mr Garner's predecessor had been a much loved

51

soul's physician and parting from him had been like losing a limb, but here was a beneficent transfusion and a worthy replacement to be grafted on and serve them as well as that amputated right hand.

When Mr Sylvester sat down, one or two men wiped their foreheads and Alfred was one of them because he now had the unhappiness of having to stand up when everybody else was seated. He had to say a few words. He often gave twenty pounds to buy off twenty words.

First a low growl started deep down in his mechanism, giving way to a humming note slightly higher up the register.

Grace half expected him to strike the hour at any moment but he suddenly decided to Speak your Weight and so found his voice.

He welcomed the Rev. Robert Garner and his good lady to this their new sphere of endeavour. He used the word sphere advisedly since as John Wesley said, the world was their Parish. He was sure that the minister and his wife would find an open door wherever they called on their people. This remark called forth much applause as if in the surrounding churches the people were in the habit of peeping through the curtains with a shotgun. They had a slight burden of debt, but things could be worse. He had been reading something by Sir James Jeans who says (here Alfred untwisted a small piece of paper from round his index finger) that all the stars visible to the naked eye are only about 60,000. We thought there were a lot more. So it is with our troubles and debts; we think they are countless and yet they are only - er - 60,000 so to speak, in sight.

Then, with relief, Alfred called upon the new minister to respond and sat down as if someone had tapped him smartly behind the knees.

The hand clapping was something in the way of 'The King is dead, long live the King', for it started as acknowledgement of their Circuit Steward's remarks and finished as a welcome to their minister.

Robert Garner rose and smiled at his flock. How interesting life in such a great city would be and he hoped to become affectionately attached to one corner of it. He was sorry to hear of their present debt. Considering the world's debt to the Church, the Church ought never to be in debt, but in Church life they had to be greatly daring. And now he believed that for the rest of the evening they were to have entertainment and general conversation and personally he was looking forward to a particularly happy time and meeting all of them for a handshake.

When Robert sat down Alfred stood up again and announced a song by Miss Sybil Martland, "My heart is like a singing bird," and after a few preliminary bars, the voice that was always so gentle and musical in speech now soared easily into song.

"So this is the fellow who barged into her. A pity he missed the Cenotaph," reflected Geoffrey.

'I mustn't take a good look at her just when she can't look at me. Hardly cricket.' David lowered his eyes. 'What trim feet and legs! I didn't mean that. Call it a no-ball. What is it all about? Ah yes. Poor Christina Rossetti. A nice slender proportionate body, too. Careful. Over. How well Mr Martland accompanies. I like the way her neck comes out of her blouse or whatever it is, with the smooth continuity of a wine glass from its stem. Come, my boy. Let's see what Father's doing. Ah, Looking at her too! Watch those corners, dear boy!'

Geoffrey and Kerry did not applaud for more than a moment because she belonged to them, but David permitted his slender hands to beat together two or three times after Sybil was by his side again and she with downcast eyes regarded the long, well kept fingers and the smooth knuckles that not by a hairs-breadth marred the line narrowing to the tips.

Conversation broke out again for a few minutes all round until Alfred was on his feet again.

"We're now to have the pleasure of a song by Mr Fred Winskill, *The Two Grenadiers*."

Mr Winskill had good command of his voice and something of the hero-worship of the Old Guard for their Emperor stirred the audience. Kerry applauded heartily as this song was a favourite of hers. It reminded her of Watch. Faithful! Like the Old Guard he never bit the hand that bathed him.

"Napoleon! How that man crops up," said Geoffrey, "and what a godsend to poets and dramatists; when they're all finished with the facts which are plentiful, they carry on with the fictions, which are legion."

Sybil cast back in her mind to the many songs she had heard.

"Now I think of it, I don't know of a single song in praise of Wellington. You'd think there'd be some."

"Ah! He didn't butter up his soldiers as Napoleon did, and on this side of the Channel we don't glorify war as do the French and the Germans."

"I suppose the war killed la gloire," responded David, "but most of us are aware of loyalties less spectacular but more rewarding in the long run."

Geoffrey shook his head lugubriously.

"In the long run! But I don't see you saying 'What a place to sack' at your first sight of Heaven."

They all laughed. Then David spoke again.

"My sister is studying in Switzerland and she loves their national characteristics, order and beauty."

"Oh! Yes indeed, but the Jungfrau must remain the Jungfrau, cool, distant and above the battle. Eh, Sybil? She must never break out in a Flamenco!"

Alfred's voice was heard above the chatter.

"Miss Ginnell will now sing *Always*."

Tonight Connie Ginnell felt pleased with life because she felt pleased with herself. She had indulged in a professional hair-wave and now all eyes were upon her including Geoffrey's and that other young man's. She possessed a full contralto voice, chocolate creamy in quality that Mr Winskill the choirmaster was coaching with selfless devotion.

During the applause Kerry leaned near to Geoffrey.

"I always call that sort of voice a goitre contralto."

From his place during the concert Robert had been surveying his people and they him. As usual, he had been able to identify many of them with old acquaintances. A very few advanced in age still cried "Amen" during prayer after the fashion of their fathers, but they were dying out. The following generation had not the art of returning thanks so simply. These were middle-aged members; the active stewards, the women bustling with such enjoyment in all the arrangements necessary to the welfare of the Church. They put in the real work of the community; in other words, they raised the money. The young ones were a nice crowd seemingly. Of course they had not that gentle retiring look their mothers had at that age; the retiring nature that had the same effect on a young man as a retreating chicken has upon a young dog. Youngsters were eager to help where they could. They were very keen as a rule on amateur dramatics and bursting to act either *Romeo and Juliet* or *The Bathroom Door* with equal enthusiasm in aid of Church funds, but somehow or other they could not go to some old teapot in a corner cabinet, or to a cash box reposing under the best tray cloths and take out five pounds to give to the Church in its hour of need.

Yes, all present had their prototype in every other church and in the next three years he would marry some and bury others and be a friend where he could. Always there was one early morning wedding. He knew those eight o'clock ceremonies where the bride was already pregnant or several inches taller than the groom. But here in the wide field of the Church was his present allotment and among these new faces there would emerge the individual magnetisms and antipathies; those members who would give him joy in his work and perhaps those who might destroy or diminish it. And amongst them there would be the friendly houses of Simon, the Marthas and Marys from whom he would be called to wrench himself in three or four years' time and who would become names on an ever lengthening Christmas card list, or occasional unexpected visitors descending on him from the past with shining faces and prolonged handshakes and news of a once familiar vineyard which others now tended.

His eyes sought his wife in the audience. When questioned about losing close friends from some especially congenial circuit, she would only admit that she missed someone to whom she could grumble her exasperation when a baked custard crust rose to the surface or her rock buns sank into rock pools.

Alfred now rose and said there would be an interval for conversation and light refreshment. He and Robert Garner and the other clergymen left their places on the dais and moved out among the nearer members to accompany and introduce the new man. The ordeal by handshake had begun.

Down in the kitchen two bright brass tea urns were placed under the boiler tap and filled. Ginnell and Tom Kershaw made for the stairs, where a shout caused someone to fling open the door and clear a way to the long trestle table where the polished, brazen symbols of cheerful fellowship were steadied into position.

"Whew!" said Tom. "This is China."

It was a thoughtful compliment to their travelled guests.

He then moved purposefully to the group near the piano and raised his voice.

"Geoffrey. Give us a hand with the big trays, will you?"

Both young men jumped up at once.

"Oh, not *you*, Mr Garner," cried Sybil with her family's respect for the Cloth, but Geoffrey demurred.

"Yes, come along and take the skin off your knuckles. Those stairs are like a medieval castle's."

Connie had seen them go off together and she approached Sybil in order to be in position for an introduction.

"What a good turn-up tonight."

She jerked her head round quickly to survey the company, her tongue moistening her lips as her eyes darted from table to table half relieved, half affronted that nobody seemed to be watching her closely. Oh. There was Mrs Crumps. She would be!

Having performed their strong man feat, the young men returned, laden.

"Here, as the anthologists say, is something for everybody. Hello,

55

Connie. Ah, Garner, Connie here is one of our star turns, as you will have heard."

The pleasant battledore and shuttlecock of harmless, necessary flirtation with which civilisation gallantly makes game, with decent rules and regulations, of the lawless warfare that nature would have us wage, is denied the religious student. He cannot indulge in the fencing and feinting that would teach him to keep his balance and his head when he passes one day into the temporal arena to fight with strange sensations that have been specially starved for the fray. He enters the lists of love a raw recruit, eager, courageous, hopeful, with all the attributes of the chivalrous knight-at-arms save that of essential training.

David congratulated her and, finding three pairs of young feminine eyes upon him, was glad to wait on the girls and be occupied. Leonard joined their table when one of the helpers brought him a cup of tea. He turned to the newcomer.

"Methodism's vocal chords are revived by tea, and I'm almost tempted to pour a cup into the piano."

"It's the real life-saver being nearer to water, but it shouldn't be adulterated with a lot of extras. Ernest Bramah's story of the discovery of tea is as memorable a classic as Charles Lamb's essay on roast pork. Both attributed, you will notice, to our friends the Chinese."

Connie gazed dreamily.

"I should love to travel. How marvellous to visit China and places like that, but I don't suppose I ever shall."

"How marvellous to sing as you do, and I positively know I shall never do that!"

Naturally, in his calling he heard much singing but if the words were nonsensical all the trilling in the world would not commend them to him, but he had no desire to say so at that moment. Connie, however, persisted.

"But you'll have to sing sometimes."

"Only when I have to, on my lawful occasions."

Geoffrey laughed.

"Artistically speaking, that sounds appalling."

"But I haven't to sing for artistic effect; only to start the ball and I lapse into lip service at the second verse. Ah! But I'm forgetting the College song. I join in that, of course."

"Let's hear it for the noble sentiments alone."

"The sentiments are all right, otherwise I should advocate changing it for an American-style college yell."

"Get on with it and then perhaps we can have a ballot on that point."

"All right, and the tune is Ripon, in case there isn't enough to go on."

The three girls looked into the distance as the young minister sidled round the note exploratively like a dog about to lie down, and then settled more or less to his satisfaction on a low range.

The buzz of conversation in the room was loud enough to give each table its own privacy, so nobody else was incommoded.

"I'm tired of living alone!
I want a wee wife of my own,
To kiss and caress me,
To cuddle and bless me.
I'm tired of living alone."

Geoffrey showed the happiest receptivity.

"You're sure that wasn't the Yankee yell you were considering? Anyway, most acceptable in the proper quarter, one feels, but your best friend would advise you not to sing it under anybody's window. If it were perpetrated under yours, Kerry, how poor Watch would resent the competition. And as for Sybil . . . "

"Geoffrey! Please get me another cup of tea."

While Geoffrey was away, Leonard questioned David about his ministerial training at Didsbury.

"One more year. It's been taken for granted that I'm for the Foreign Field, but there's a great deal to think out."

"Of course your parents' work would be remembered."

"My friend Warner thinks the home front needs strengthening and he may be right."

"Oh, but Britain has two stable exports, coal and missionaries."

Geoffrey returned with a tray.

"Any more for any more? What about you, Miss Kerry, or can I get you another Russian sandwich?"

"Oh, not you, Mr Sinclair," she answered mockingly, so that he made his way to the buffet muttering, "Drat the brat!"

Meanwhile, Robert Garner had been slowly circulating amongst his people, piloted by Alfred. He had suitably complimented the ladies at the long tables for their services and there met his Poor Steward, Tom Kershaw, busily waiting upon the more elderly members and learned that someone had slipped across the road to spend a few minutes with Ella. Tom's head was covered with innumerable grey curls which somehow predisposed people in his favour.

"Has Mr Garner spoken to Ben Northcroft yet, Alfred? Don't leave him out or the whole pan will be on fire."

The old man surveyed the new minister with some severity. When you get to be over eighty, the new man might be the one to have dealings with you in your last illness and Ben did not fancy a chicken to wave him off. However, seeing that Robert was a boiler and not a roaster, he felt easier and soon reeled off famous names that had served the church in former years, as well as Local Preachers of his own age, fast going downstream. Then seeing a favourite face he hailed it loudly.

"Clara, someone's given me a rum cup of tea!"

"Oh, Mr Northcroft, if you don't care for China, let me bring you some Indian instead."

"China, is it? They might as well pour boiling water on straw for all the flavour it has. Thank you, my dear, if it's no trouble."

Alfred moved forward to spare her this errand and Ben took her hand.

"I've been telling Mr Garner about your sainted grandfather. What a man he was! It's a pity you have no boys, Clara. You might have had sons in the ministry yourself with that strain. Speaking as a farmer, we have to produce more and from better stock, too. The world is suffering from a lack of good men from good stock. We want perfection in the cradle, not in the grave. Aye, get good stock in the cradle and the manger, and we'll prosper, a credit to earth and heaven."

So Robert Garner moved among his new church, learning something of them even at so perfunctory a meeting. He caught Ernest Ginnell about to carry one of the urns below and had a few words with him. Like Tom Kershaw, he worked at the great Carriage Shop and was a very good carpenter.

"Don't make a hasty judgment of Manchester, Mr Garner. The weather doesn't matter if you've money to keep it out of doors and out of your shoes. Our weather has made trade. Now I grant you, if our trade went and left us with just our weather, then we *should* start grumbling."

Miriam Crumps was talking to Grace Garner in company with Ada Sinclair.

Throughout this little conversation she had steadily regarded the minister's wife, not for signs of enlightenment, but for signs of superfluous hair which those powerful glasses detected in most females of her age. Mrs Garner's skin, however, seemed to be free from any prickly suggestion of musical box cylinder and Miriam reluctantly concluded that she was either very lucky or very clever, distinctions which had never endeared those of her sex possessing them, to Miriam Crumps.

Her sister Ada now wished to engage Mrs Garner's attention on behalf of the weekly Women's Class, which Grace readily agreed to preside over. Ada looked pleased at this.

"And every first Wednesday in the month we have the Sewing Meeting instead of a speaker."

Ada enjoyed her Wednesdays although it did mean trailing all the way from Didsbury, but she took advantage of these new express buses into town that cut the time considerably and were so very comfortable. She was the wealthiest woman amongst them but that hadn't much weight, because as everybody knew, Alfred was old-fashioned and although she lacked nothing that she could think of, she never actually handled much money. Clara Martland had spoken a few words to Alfred in confidence and even given him a little lecture on Ada's rights. If, as he said, Ada hadn't much of a head for money matters, that was because he'd never bothered to teach her. Any woman would soon pick it up with practice! "I'll speak to her about the Faith Teas," he rumbled. "Anything you suggest, my girl."

Leonard Martland now played a few delicate chords on the piano, the signal for a general settling down for the continuation of the programme. For the second part of the evening, however, the grouping was still less formal, the half-moon arrangement of little cliques of people being in closer formation and there was more whispering among the younger ones during the proceedings, especially in the coveted area at the back of the room.

Geoffrey radiated warmth and Sybil drew a little nearer to him as instinctively as she would move nearer to the hearth on a cool evening. He was not looking at her but had turned his head towards his other companion.

"I suppose all Methodists look alike to you, like the Chinese?"

"As little alike as they," David assured him.

Further remark was postponed by another singer stepping onto the dais. Like Sybil, he also was a member of the Hallé Choir, without neglecting to add lustre to the chapel choir and their numerous musical occasions. He had a fastidious air, holding his song sheet at arm's length as if it smelt slightly. He sang *Summertime on Bredon* and in the lull following the applause, Geoffrey was holding forth.

"Highly reprehensible conduct, not to say downright carelessness, this lying about on the grass even in summer time. By the end of the first verse a good old Methodist audience would naturally expect the girl to get into trouble of some kind."

He felt Sybil move slightly away.

"Her early demise saved the reputation of the song at least," David responded.

Soon it was the turn of their organist and teacher again. Sybil always liked Mr Winskill's singing. His voice was durable yet delicate as silver in firelight and when he sang *Comfort ye* in the annual oratorio, the congregation really felt absolved as the sweet but authoritative strain flowed calmly over them. Tonight, however, in more secular mood, he was trying to wheedle information from a taciturn shepherd as to the wayfaring of a nymph, Flora. Over and over again he urged his simple question, but as sometimes happens in sequestered parts of the country, he was forced to remain in a state of doubt and Geoffrey was of the opinion that the shepherd was either deaf or daft . . . or very deep.

Jimmie Northcroft, grandson of Ben, now scrabbled behind the window curtain near to the piano and drew forth his violin. Mr Martland gave him his notes and the boy quickly tuned up. Then they swung into the gently heaving rhythm of the prayer for the outgoing fleet of "The Pearl Fishers". Such a soothing, swinging, rock-a-bye motion drifted away the minds of the listeners to seaside and lakeland summers of long ago and there remained hardly a person present-minded in the room. Their thoughts dispersed swiftly and diversely as Titania's fairies, some to placid Rydal Water held in the palm of smoothly sloping hills; some to giggling days at Douglas and voyages à deux at Ramsey, and nearer home, the day picnics at Rudyard Lake and the more common four-foot deep perils of Boggart Hole Clough.

Then Sybil left her place and stood before them all again, cool and pastel shaded as a rainbow just appearing. Geoffrey's head was lowered but his eyes were raised to her and he dwelt with sensitive appreciation on her quiet ways. She was a long, lifelong, clear as crystal draught that a man must sip with thanksgiving after due libation to the gods, not to be roughly tossed off to slake a common thirst. Rainbows and ritual wines are not to every man's taste and Geoffrey was jealous for the fineness of his judgement and the perception that had first appraised an almost evasive grace.

And this was his, he mused gratefully, or at least his for the asking and the taking, which is the same thing really; merely a question of time and tide. Life is not a bar parlour that he should fear a slip 'twixt cup and lip as if uncouth neighbours were expected to jog an elbow spitefully. Surely in a civilised community a man may hold his vintage trustingly up to the light with a steady hand without the Fates willing that he should lose thereby, like an oaf spilling his beer.

A slight nudge on his arm arrested his reflections and he glanced down at Kerry who had moved into her sister's place to whisper to him.

"This is really a contralto song but Sybil liked it and Father transposed it for her into a higher key."

Sybil had started to sing, something entirely different from her first effervescent out-pouring. It was dreamlike, almost trance-like, and even David followed with his eyes full upon her this time. Geoffrey watched from under his lashes.

"Leave me, love, and let me go,
To see the lands where corals lie."

So that's what happens when Sybil gets keyed up! In all her love ballads she sang as if it were all sunshine and no shadow, and yet here she was pretending to throw it away and go to study under-water formations in the Malay Archipelago! A fantastic situation and mercifully nobody was expected to believe it. When she again took her place beside him, he stretched his legs easily and asked if she were thinking of going far.

"Far? Oh, I see. Well, all the way there and back."

Leonard now looked round the company, nodding decisively at little groups here and there. Once in the choir, always in the choir in the membership sense and although some might not be on the strength, they never actually resigned and for such feats as the Choir Sermons or the annual Messiah, long-married matrons made a great effort to be present. For smaller intimate gatherings such as this, there was a fair sprinkling of grandparents who now exercised their rights in the manner of country members of a club on a rare visit, or of ancient peers doddering up to cast their votes in an emergency. There was some jockeying for position on the platform and when all were ready, Fred Winskill draped one hand aloft and when it suddenly stiffened in the expectant hush, their held breath gently exhaled in the first tender line of "When evening's twilight gathers round". There were many evening faces among them, restful and meditative, and at the line "And nature's self seeks sweet repose", the bass voices settled down deliberately for the night.

Geoffrey was thoughtful. For twice three hundred and sixty-five days he had thought of his love at their close, and still they were no nearer seeking nature's sweet repose. Not, of course, that they had expected to get married while he was still at University, but somehow the peace that he had felt sure would be his when Sybil's name was ringed around with his own, had not developed. It had been there at first, but of late he found the continual going back and forth to see her a serious hindrance to his studies; and then in some moods he found that his studies provided a set-back to his courtship. He felt that one was crippling the other but could not quite make up his mind which was the loser.

It did not seem to bother Sybil at all. She never betrayed any heartache at the inevitable delay. Never a sign of impatience escaped her. True, she opened the door to him as if he were the Sun-god, but a Sun-god whom she never for a moment suspected could scorch. Always she lived in a temperate zone where the sun's rays fell delicately aslant and her emotions were akin to her physical colouring, unforced, clear and English. Yet it was within the bounds of possibility that under such a sun as shines in lands where corals lie, she might feel - and consequently radiate, a more elemental fire.

Geoffrey roused himself with a twinge of self blame. Thank God she was as she was; not by a hairs-breadth would he have her different and he remembered with a grin that of all the operatic heroines, Carmen bored him most. No flamenco tantrums for him!

The end of the choir singing marked the close of the concert.

The Minister had pronounced the Benediction and once again the groups gathered and loitered in farewell. It was still quite early, barely ten o'clock, but the electric lights had come into their own and the windows had darkened, making the room look less like a cage than when in sunlight.

The Garners were standing with the Martlands and Sinclairs.

"Have you time to drop into our place for an hour or so?" asked Clara.

Leonard was closing the piano and looked round encouragingly. "The night's young."

Alfred consulted his watch and hesitated and hummed and ha'd, but Ada declared that it would be late enough by the time they got home.

"Come along," Ada said to Alfred. "They don't want to miss a tram."

"I thought it a remarkably good service," said Robert Garner innocently.

People were tramping down the stairway now and past the kitchen door. Ernest Ginnell put his head out and shouted upstairs.

"Last man out switch off all lights, please."

"Do you feel like walking up, Leonard?" asked Clara. "It's such a lovely night."

"Yes. We'll walk. It will do us good after sitting all evening."

"And may we come along with you?" said Robert.

Then it turned out that nearly everybody wanted to walk. David said he would walk to town at least and perhaps Geoffrey would join him.

"Will it be all right if I come up tomorrow night," asked Geoffrey. "Kerry has an epicurean feature to introduce that I mustn't miss. She says she likes to drink coffee through a cube of Mexican chocolate clenched in her teeth. So I'll bring some along."

"Of course, Geoffrey. And if ever *you* come up and find your mother and father not at home, Mr Garner, you must try our house. You would be very welcome."

David expressed such pleasure at this invitation that his mother was surprised.

The crowd was thinning out and the main company drifting towards the door.

"There's nothing to stay for any longer, Kerry. The trestle tables are folded and there's not a crumb left."

"It sounds as if you've been asked to carry the trays down again."

Ada Sinclair looked disapprovingly at Kerry. That girl ought not to be allowed to speak to Geoffrey like that.

"Just let me try, merely out of curiosity," he said, "if I can get your plait to wind three times round your throat. I do believe that with a little pressure I could just do it."

"Come along, Alfred."

Ada vented a little irritability on her husband.

The Lecture Hall was still faintly a-glimmer when the artificial light suddenly ceased. Geoffrey sighed and Sybil gave a little yawn.

"Another turn of the social round," said Geoffrey, halting in the doorway as the retreating steps grew fainter. "This room has staged some sober festivities in its time. Look at the chairs getting into a huddle to talk it over."

"Yes, and I can hear some of them creaking slightly, glad to ease their own legs and relax a bit."

They stood awhile with their arms round each other's waists, smiling and swaying.

"I wonder if that piano ever goes gay," he went on. "People are always hammering out hymns on it, or gems from the more circumspect operas by way of light relief. I don't suppose it has heard a waltz for years. I wonder if Mr Collard senior ever reminds Mr Collard junior of that time when someone played Paderewski's Minuet when a few of its notes had fallen upon silence. That final flourish was erratic with sudden stops as though they were only playing leap-frog. That was a notable secular performance but it's been chiefly Rock of Ages. But, perhaps," Geoffrey murmured with his lips on Sybil's temple, "when we have all gone, the mice come out after crumbs of comfort and hear the old wires quietly humming to themselves a Schumann Serenade or a lullaby of Brahms!"

At the word 'lullaby' the girl turned her head and leaned it against his bosom, nuzzling the top of his waistcoat. Then she disengaged herself.

"We must go They'll be waiting perhaps."

She passed to the head of the stairs as Geoffrey shut the door.

"Do you think they've been pleased with their welcome?" she asked.

"They've been rapturously received. There was a sufficiency of enthusiasm to satisfy the most fervent old-timers or even John Wesley himself. A very successful love-feast!"

She looked at him searchingly.

"Do you know, sometimes you sound just like Mr Buckley. You're feeling quite all right, aren't you?"

"Why, doesn't *he* feel quite all right?"

"Goodnight all," Ada called.

"Don't bother to come up," Sybil whispered unnecessarily.

"Sleep well," he wished her also unnecessarily.

"Oh, I always do after singing."

The Moston and Didsbury contingents divided and moved off. In spite of Alfred's offer to give David a lift as far as they were going, the young man had decided to walk to Piccadilly, and Geoffrey said he would accompany him for the exercise. If he were as sleepy when he got to bed as he had been at some moments during the concert, he would be lucky. As they walked under the railway bridge he set a brisk pace.

"A lovely mild night," he exclaimed. "A shame to be indoors really, but a very good number turned up and at least we've advanced from Old-fashioned towns, Alice-blue gowns, Angus home from the wars and Because."

But David's praise was whole-hearted.

"Tonight's was a very good concert. I've enjoyed it very much."

Geoffrey hastened to agree.

"Oh, so have I, although we've both come more for personal reasons than mere concert attendance. Did you note that the room where it was held is called the Lecture Room? If anyone goes round the world or on a tour nearer home, they are expected to 'give a little talk' when they come back. They nearly got me . . . "

"That's what I like about our system. It believes in sharing. We inch along like any nation seeking the Promised Land, with our women and children, our flocks and herds. It's slow work, but Democracy has to strike camp and pitch tent and water its flock by the way."

"Unless," said Geoffrey, "it's the brand of Democracy that reaches the Promised Land overnight with a few million dead, as in Russia."

The two walked in silence awhile.

"Um," said David glumly, "that's the snag in little men having big ideas; they want too much result seen in their own lifetime and at all cost."

"True," agreed the other. "I don't foresee much future in brotherhood at the point of the sword, or being clapped into Utopia as people were once thrown into prison, at someone's whim."

David looked about him as they walked and saw a brilliant entrance over the road.

"The Osborne. That looks gay enough. I wonder if they can make a theatre pay in the suburbs; though this can hardly be called a suburb; it's just a main road out of town."

"It relies a great deal on its placards, as you see. Those ought to fetch 'em! But I'm told it puts on a very good pantomime in the winter. There was a bit of fuss a year or two ago when the Ginnell daughter wanted to be in the chorus. I think she'd have done jolly well myself but one of the Misses Leat dissuaded her finally. I think the placards had overdone it a bit."

"Plenty of people coming out," observed the young minister, "and they've paid to go in. No Silver Collection there."

"And as well as the placards there's a chappie outside when the doors open, calling out what a treat there is in store. He gets the casual strolling couples and idle passers-by, with his loud voice and air of absolute confidence in the goods he's advertising."

Geoffrey was grinning as he finished but David gave a long sigh.

"Perhaps we shall have to come to it, but even my friend Warner might jib at that."

Geoffrey straightened his face. Of course these people with vocations were never far from the main job.

"Down that street over there, Francis Thompson lived for some time in a religious community. Poets have rather a thin time in Lancashire! 'The Hound of Heaven' isn't a very good title, at least in my opinion. Hounds are associated with warders on Dartmoor or Uncle Tom escaping from slavers. And there's the 'Hound of the Baskerville', not at all the patter of little feet one would care to hear overtaking one. If one is to be pursued it had better be a comfortable St. Bernard, with suitable restoratives."

Nearer to New Cross he indicated three buildings on the other side of the road.

"That's a queer lay-out. A little school and a church with a pub in between. They're known hereabouts as Education, Temptation, Salvation. They're in darkness by this time."

"All in darkness," echoed David. "I like the Church of England habit of keeping a sanctuary light burning at all times. I wish all denominations had it. No superstitious nonsense about never letting it go out, even by accident, but just a small reminder glowing through the hours of darkness."

"A very good idea and it wouldn't cost much," agreed Geoffrey. "It would certainly appeal to the non-churchgoing public because of its easy symbolism. Like famous landmarks and respectable relatives, we like to know they're there even if we never trouble to visit them."

They walked quickly in the direction of New Cross at the Manchester end of Oldham Road where, not high enough to be easily discernible among the swiftly passing traffic and the outmoded drinking troughs round its base, stood rather diffidently a stone shaft topped - not by arms to form the expected Market Cross - but by a wind vane.

"In all my life," David exclaimed, "I've never seen anything like that!"

The other looked in that direction.

"Do you mean all that mêlée in the middle? It would be more than your life's worth to try to cross there."

"I mean the decapitated cross with, of all things, a veering, changeable, this way that way, weather-cock stuck on!"

Geoffrey's lip curled.

"Pragmatism versus dogmatism. Showing which way the wind is blowing rather than how it should blow. People like to know."

But David was irritated by it.

"A straw, a feather, a man lighting his pipe in an idle moment could tell us that. But here they've done away with the one thing that can tell us how the wind of the *spirit* blows. I didn't think a great city like this could be so crass!"

It was Geoffrey's turn to be irritated and he defended Manchester as best he could, enumerating virtues that he had been at pains to deride when put forth by others. He praised its numerous museums and galleries, its great libraries, Rylands and Chethams that attracted students from every civilised and would be civilised country in the world. There was its genuine musical reputation fostered by the Brand Lane and Hallé orchestras and concerts, the Opera season, Drama (hadn't we the Gaiety?) and its still kicking music halls such as the Ardwick Empire and the Osborne which they had seen disgorging only a short time ago. As for such cultural plankton as the Zoological Gardens at Belle Vue, they too had their aesthetic value, for the set pieces on the island, the scene of nightly sieges and attacks, were painted with all the precision of a Canaletto and the vigorous colouring of a Gaugin.

So Geoffrey talked on with a civic patriotism that surprised himself, until his new friend's mood quite changed.

"Yes, we're all very lucky to be at grips with such a place and such people. I'm sure you find it so. It's a really exciting opportunity. Do you do any youth work?"

"Er - no."

"It's absolutely vital. They say the home wins in the end, but there are too many homes that mustn't win, and the greater the city the greater the risk."

By the time the two young men had reached Oxford Road at their good pace and were heading for home or duty, the elder Garners and company had made rather slower progress in the opposite direction, for the minister often paused to scrutinise side streets and separate rows of houses with some architectural characteristic as he spoke of the desirability of every man living under his own vine and fig tree, speaking figuratively.

"When I retire we shall have to buy because houses are simply not being rented any more. I used to calculate that if we saved a thousand pounds for a house when we 'sat down' it would be enough, but as time goes on I'm beginning to doubt it."

"Of course you don't know as yet where you'll eventually settle," answered Leonard, "but it might be worth while having a word with Alfred. Owning one of his specialities at Didsbury could mean having something to bargain with when the time came."

Clara turned to her husband admiringly.

"That's a thought, Len. He'd build a gem for a thousand pounds."

Grace Garner showed keen interest.

"I've never lived in a gem of a house. It would be something to look forward to; even a semi-precious detached."

"In that case, my dear, I'd better broach the subject to Mr Sinclair at some convenient time. He would advise us, taking everything into consideration. A very practical man, I should judge, more used to making profits than making speeches."

"That reminds me," said Leonard.

They had reached Grimshaw Lane where on the corner a large sweet-shop was still open with its glittering glass jars in the windows catching the front lights shining across the broad pavement. He nodded towards the bright interior.

"As lads we used to go there for lemonade in summer when walking up from chapel. We waited until the coast was clear, then slipped in and sat chatting perhaps for half an hour or so. It's still the same family business. There was hardly any Sunday trading then but we were glad to quench our thirst after evening service and we didn't always want to go home straight away. People must have known but no one said anything. However, time went on and Alfred Sinclair reached his twenty-first birthday. His mother and father gave him a very nice walking stick with his initials engraved on a silver band. He was very proud of this stick. One night while we were sitting in there someone got hold of it behind his back and when we were ready to go, Alfred turned for his stick and it was covered all over round and round with yellow sticky paper. Oh! He was disgusted! No hesitation for a word that night."

"Who did it, Father?"

"Oh, you're there, are you?"

"It sounds," the minister said, "as if you've all known each other a long time."

"We have really. The place has hung together remarkably well on the whole. Naturally it isn't the centre for everything that's going on, as it was for us. There's a strong cultural interest outside nowadays that was beyond our scope. It was a big event for us to see and hear the best artistes of the day; something we saved up for and we got our money's worth. But in between times we entertained each other and didn't ask for anything better, and I'll go so far as to say that there wasn't anything better to be had amongst amateurs."

"But what about the outsiders? Did you bring in any new members?"

There was a note of urgency in the minister's voice that for a moment halted the organist's reminiscences, but he resumed with decision.

"It was pretty rough outside the church in these parts a generation ago. Poverty was more hopeless. If a man or a woman 'drank', the whole family seemed to go down in ruin. That's why we could never afford to be polite about drunkenness. Our Sunday-school teachers dared not speak tolerantly about it to the youngsters; there was too much at stake. And the truth is, Mr Garner, there's an element that hates decency and order. You can't compel that kind to come in."

"Perhaps the word should be urge them to come in."

"Well, we've urged many to come in and they've refused. We've got to let the Salvation Army tackle those to whom respectability has no appeal. I've heard one or two young ministers sneer at the Methodist Church for its respectability. That shows they've never lived in a community that had none! You know, I've worked for many years in a very large firm, but I've seen some firms try to expand too quickly. They got to the stage when they talked big about their assets, but those assets were only on paper. That is what some young ordinands are trying to do with the church today; to blow it up into a huge bubble, all expanding surface and no hard core! When I looked round our Lecture Room tonight I couldn't help but compare our people there with some of those outside whose only contribution to the Church has been to throw a stone or a cob of mud literally or in kind. Our folk looked self-respecting and happy, and they're not stone deaf to the arts, especially music. The children are healthy, with not so much as a stammerer amongst them. And for these blessings we can thank the hard core!"

Robert Garner was delighted to find his organist so sure of his ground.

"Indeed, I agree with you, Mr Martland. It is clear that here we have a church of fine quality, not uncaring for the needs of those by the wayside but anxious to bring them in as brethren in truth. We don't want just the expanding bubble as you say, but we do work for the consolidating snowball, growing as it rolls along."

So the sextet, occasionally pausing and then hurrying to catch up with each other, drew within sight of home simultaneously and grouped themselves around the newcomers' front gate before separating.

"It was a lovely Welcome," said Mrs Garner. "We've both enjoyed it, haven't we, Robert?"

"We have indeed! You all have singing hearts as well as singing voices. We know these sociable evenings mean nine-tenths of preparation below the surface and I hope you sleep well after it. And good-night, young ladies. You obviously enjoy your beauty sleep, even if others are wakeful on your account. But I feel sure your consciences are clear. Thank you all for your company along the way. We shall travel it together many times I hope, and with as much pleasure."

Then for a very little distance their ways curved apart, in the sure and certain hope of a speedy reunion.

Chapter Eight

A great arterial road wakes up very early in the morning, if indeed it has slept at all during the night. Perhaps the traffic may be said to doze a little between two and four a.m. with certain organs such as the all-night trams, late taxis and the ever increasing number of motor transport lorries functioning automatically like the human heart and the respiratory system. But before the first peep of day, the traffic is out and about again in full vigour and to a town dweller the night watches cannot honestly be called long watches.

Ella had never acknowledged the night as her declared enemy. She dared not. Seeing so much of it she endeavoured to learn its good points and avoid arousing its cold hatred. She found it kind when she was in most need of respite from pretence. She knew that many other women came to see her when they were depressed, so that their low condition might be seen to be positively elevated when compared with hers. She had no enemies - but at a terrible price. No one envied her. So she was glad of darkness at a time when she saw her life all too plainly and could cease for a time from all pretence. At least in the night hours she wasn't expected to set a Christian example! And the night offered no platitudes. But the morning sounds rose early in the day when there was an unbarring of doors and undoing of chains to flood the place with fresh air.

Running feet were heard and a lad flung the morning paper through the open front door, right down the lobby to the foot of the stairs. This was not just roughness on his part, but a rough kindness, calculated to save Tom the walk to the door and while Tom was in and out getting their breakfast ready, Ella reported on how the world wagged. Later she heard Mrs Ginnell bringing her accoutrement for cleaning the front step, which she did with all the noise and bustle of Tweedledum and Tweedledee preparing for a battle and then tapped on the window by way of greeting, for she never entered the house in a morning until Tom had gone.

Tom carried in their breakfast and put his own plate on a little folding table that he'd made himself. His work was very good and the things that Ella used every day were all of Tom's design and craft.

"Thank God for gas," he said, pronging the first of his eggs so that a slow flood of molten gold was loosed over the smoked ham. "It's quick and clean."

"Yes," said Ella complacently. "But they say Mrs Garner is mad on electrical gadgets."

Tom remarked how nice the bacon was this week. Ella nodded.

"When we were courting, Ben's farm was flourishing with a lot more cattle, pigs and poultry than they have now. Fancy! Three generations at Northcroft's with young Jim coming on."

"It would be better for him to clear out."

"Don't you ever say that to his mother, Tom! We've had many a field-day up there with games and milk and buns among the buttercups and daisies. Then we always finished up with letting off a big balloon with a candle inside. Old Mr Crossley did that for years, didn't he? D'you remember that time when the children ripped his coat right up? And when the lorries drove back with the infants, they used to pile some of the bigger ones in as well, they were so dead tired with rushing round. And the road home could be traced by those coming after, by all the daisy chains let fall on the way. Northcroft's farm was considered a good way out in those days and now it's only a twopenny ride on the tram."

"It'll soon be more," prophesied Tom. "I think everything will soon be more." Breakfast proceeded leisurely and thoughtfully. "Now, I'll be getting off. Are you all set?"

"I don't want the gas fire yet. It's quite warm. Nurse is coming today to give me a good bath and I'll have it on then for her coffee. I should like to finish turning a corner of my crochet this morning if possible, and there always seem to be a few letters to see to. I wonder how I'm going to get through it all, especially if I have visitors."

"Don't you do too much," admonished Tom as he leaned over to give a parting kiss. Ella slid her fingers into his thick grey curls and held his head against hers.

A tram was slowing down outside the house and the driver, looking for such a regular passenger, hammered with his boot on the iron knob by his feet and raised such a clamour that Tom and Ella unclasped with a start and Tom rushed out, seizing his cap from the hallstand in passing.

71

When Mrs Ginnell came in, Ella was already at work on the intricate pattern. Mrs Ginnell started to dust round and she put a newspaper on the stand.

"I never look at the morning paper; there's no time. But Ernest brings the evening paper in and I like to look at that. We always take a newspaper, as you need something for the ashes, but I say that Sunday is my time for catching up with the news. On Sunday afternoon I go and lie down for an hour or two with three Sunday papers full of pictures. Between them they pretty well cover what the human race is up to. And that's what I call peace, when Ern is listening to speeches round by the Ben Brierley and young Ernie is at Sunday School and our Connie's gone for a walk. She's fallen out with going to Sunday School now and dolls herself up for the parks. And not even the Clough always. She says 'Oh, the tulips are out in Fox Denton Park', or 'It's Rhododendron Sunday somewhere else', and off she goes. I don't know why we always think we'll do better where nobody knows us."

Thus Mrs Ginnell held forth until she went into the kitchen.

When Tom and Ernest dropped off the tram again, soon after twelve o'clock, Ella was freshly bathed and propped up in her armchair.

"Have you turned that corner yet?" asked Tom, when he had bent over his dinner for some moments.

"Not by half. The morning has gone in no time."

"You know," said Tom after a while, "it's becoming to look a bit serious about the Dean and Chapter raising the rent of the Shop. They're after more money and I think our folk have dug their heels in."

"Well, one side will have to give way somewhere," said Ella. "They'd never close a great place like the Shop."

"It does sound a bit far fetched," admitted Tom.

"Why," said Ella, big eyed, "who would throw thousands of men out of work? It would be downright wicked!"

"That's true," said Tom, with his eyes turned to his dinner, "but we must remember that sometimes downright wicked things *are* done."

An hour later, the house and even the road seemed very quiet. Such moments were uncommon and Ella rested her hands and looked out of the window. The sun was shining now and the room suddenly flickered with a darkling flash as a bird darted between the sun and her window.

So it was serious at the Shop! But it couldn't be! How could anything go wrong with a great concern like that? Of course things had gone wrong with the big cotton mills, but that was through foreign competition. Then there were the coal mine stoppages, and yet people wanted coal. The Carriage Shop turned over a vast amount of work but the owners could not make big increases in wages *and* pay higher rents, they said.

A dog fight in a side street caused an immediate outcry from many sources, and shrill howls of involvement came shatteringly on that brief silence. Then the barking ceased as suddenly as it had begun and a neighbour's canary could be heard trilling away high above the cheerful limitations of the sparrows. Ella listened eagerly to that other voice in a cage and then the peculiar break in the traffic ended and once again the Oldham Road became its rolling rumbling self and footsteps trotted briskly by and active life surged before her window in endless energy.

"Oh! They'll never stop the Shop," she said with a revival of conviction and turned her attention to the crochet corner again.

At the early hour of a quarter past two, Miriam Crumps came hesitantly into the narrow lobby. She always sang her prim warning of "Hello . . . hello," on exactly the same notes used by the cuckoo.

Ella smiled as the door carefully opened, for Miriam took no chances with an invalid's room, entering cautiously.

"Do come in. I'm ready and waiting," Ella said gently. "You are an early bird!"

Miriam seated herself and explained that she was meeting Ada in town at three o'clock and was just looking in. As she spoke, her eyes took stock of the little room severely. It always looked clean and bright. Somebody came in every day, of course, but that was not the same as being up and doing oneself.

On one point she always burned with curiosity. She longed to know what Ella's gas bills amounted to. It must be a pretty penny. Miriam worshipped economy with passion; her own gas bills were meagre and she felt that she could indulge a feeling of positive triumph if she could catch Ella in an extravagance on that point.

"It's quite warm enough without the fire today, isn't it? I suppose you last without it as long as you can, since you have to burn so much in winter."

Ella agreed that the weather was delightful and that town would probably be full this afternoon. That reminded Miriam of another matter.

"Oh! I've found such a wonderful man," she said with so much earnestness that Ella looked up startled. "He explains the gift of tongues beautifully. It's somewhere down in Blackfriars and I'm taking Ada this afternoon. You've no idea! The gift works all in a moment, as if a person had been tapped on the head with a hammer and suddenly gets up to tell us all about it in his own way. Last week a man

d

had been sitting quite quietly with his arms folded, when he leapt to his feet and looked round at us in a most excited way. 'I've got it! I've got it!' Then he preached most vividly for five minutes, but not having got the gift yet I couldn't tell what he said, but the Reverend Brother listened very keenly and when it was over, he went to the man and asked him if he knew what language he had been speaking. The man looked dazed and said he only knew English and had been hearing his own voice in English, so we all knew that he had been under the influence of the gift. The Reverend Brother said it might have been Fiji, and then he gave the more earth-bound of us the message."

"And what was that?" asked Ella, truly interested.

"I can't remember much of it, except that it was about prophecy. He said that if we wanted to know anything, we ought to turn over all the stones of the great Pyramids, where everything was written down."

"Everything?" asked Ella in amazement.

"So he said," responded Miriam impressively, "and we must remember that he was speaking under the influence."

There was silence for a few moments.

"Well, I must be going now. I felt that I should like to call just to leave that thought with you. It's a pity you can't come with me."

Ella thought that if she had the use of her legs she would find something better to do with them.

Miriam rose and looked at the cream gas fire.

"I've toyed with the idea of having one of those in my front room, but I think it might run rather dear. About how much do you think it would cost me a quarter?"

"I don't think it would cost you much if you didn't use it much. There is the outlay of the rent for the meter of course, but after that you just burn what you want, much or little according to what you can afford."

Miriam tried to look as if this information was what she had hoped for, but did not succeed very well. She liked people to answer innocent questions simply and not put her in a false position.

"Perhaps when all is said and done, a coal fire looks better and seems more natural. When I've sifted the ashes and cleaned the brasses and blacked the bars and the kettle, remade the fire, washed the hearth and filled the coal scuttle, I always feel that it's a good job done."

"If you feel like that about it," said Ella kindly, "you might as well continue."

"I'm sorry I can't stay longer," said Miriam, picking up her black bag and gloves. "Are you expecting anybody else this afternoon?"

"It's Mrs Garner's class at three o'clock and one or two generally run across later."

"Oh, yes." Miriam felt that Ella considered that she ought to be there. "I wonder if they will like her as time goes on. You know, she's not really my idea of a minister's wife."

"Isn't she? What is your idea of a minister's wife?"

"Oh, it's just that she isn't," she replied vaguely but with disapproval, just as Ella was not her idea of an invalid. "And she says peculiar things. When I went to her first class, she said, in the course of her address, that she ranked cheerfulness as a virtue even above industry. She said laughter was man's badge of courage! Don't you think that's a strange remark for a minister's wife to make?"

Miriam cast a parting look of severity round a room which obviously made a point of cheerfulness and then said goodbye, stealthily closing the door after her as if Ella had been falling asleep before her eyes. As she went out she wondered doubtfully how often Mrs Ginnell dusted behind the pictures.

Not long afterwards, Ella saw the women of the Wednesday class passing the front of the chapel. Mrs Ginnell hurried into Ella's to see if she was all right.

"That's good. Well, I'll toddle along. It's a real treat for me at class. D'you know Mrs Garner's latest? She's fished out some old hassocks from a vestry cupboard and if we want to put our feet up, we take one. Sure you don't want anything? Ernie will be along just after three."

Little Ernie had started school now he was five and so Ella did not see him much during the week.

Ella was left to her own devices and once more picked up her work, pondering on the women who had just now entered the chapel. She knew them well and all the incidents of their youth which some of them hardly remembered themselves by this time, overlaid by the changing scenes of life.

We are accustomed to the habit of stags fighting for the docile doe, but Ella remembered the long, silent, bitter combat that was fought out by two young women for the possession of a man who had not really made up his mind to have either of them, but who found, when the struggle was finished that he could no more resist the champion than could a silver cup retire from the knock-out winner's grasp. The loser, as often happens, consented to be chief bridesmaid.

She was the first and only one to hear the personal woes and trials of women who trusted their secrets to no one else. Only Clara Martland, her lifelong friend, was ever allowed a discreet peep or two at matters not for public commentary, for Ella herself sometimes felt the need to impart unusual knowledge and to be assured that her advice could not have been bettered.

Ella's fingers hovered over her crochet with the irregular movements of butterfly wings not quite ready to fly away. It was beautiful work and although she gave much to the chapel sales and the endless bazaars, she had no difficulty in finding good custom elsewhere.

She and Tom had weathered it. They were independent as far as money went; dependent on each other and upon friends for all else!

Little Ernie was soon pushing the front door.

"I've come, Antella," he called as he squatted on the hall floor to put on the red felt slippers that he had been trained to assume before entering the clean room. He came in and beamed at her with his white milk-teeth.

"You're home quick today, Ernie. Have you walked all the way?"

"Oh no, I ran some. Can I light the kettle?"

"All right, but be careful. There! You're a little expert, aren't you? It's early yet, so I want you to turn it quite low for now. Well, well! It went plop. Gently does it. There, you've done it perfectly this time. Now you can look to see if the King's got a biscuit for you."

Ernie headed unerringly for an old purple and gold biscuit tin, which was constantly replenished.

"What have *you* been learning today, Ernie?"

"C is for corn, crows and clouds."

"Indeed," said Ella, smiling. "When I went to school, C was for cat, but this modern education seems to be giving itself airs."

Ella's remark was not of sufficient interest to Ernie to steal any attention given to the delicious dryness of the shortbread biscuit. As a change from licking it, he let the biscuit lick him, by rubbing it along his tongue, and decided it must be great fun being a kitten and being washed all over with a tongue like a shortbread biscuit.

The last few crumbs dissolved eventually and Ernie rested his right ear on his arm and gazed along the tramlines towards Oldham.

"What have you been learning today, Antella?"

There was silence for a moment or two.

"Well, Ernie love, it's like this. Some days Antella does what's called revision. That is going over a lesson you've learned some time ago just to make sure you really do know it and haven't forgotten bits of it."

Ernie brought his head round to look at Ella.

"I know about visioning," he cried triumphantly. "You have it before a test."

Ella sighed.

"Now you can have a biscuit from the Queen's side of the tin if she hasn't eaten them all herself."

This time there was the ecstasy of sucking round a blob of icing sugar in the middle of the biscuit, which Ernie prolonged until Mrs Garner's class emerged from the chapel.

"Mrs Martland and the new lady are coming over here," Ernie informed Ella. "Shall I turn up the kettle now?"

When Clara and Mrs Garner entered the room, after exchanging a few words with Ernie and seeing him across the road to find his mother, the first steam was issuing from the freshly boiling water and Clara moved about the preparations for brewing tea almost as easily as if she were at home.

"I've done it for years, Mrs Garner, and could do it blindfold."

"So you say! But we're always boasting of the things we could do blindfold. I thought I knew our street in Leicester so well that I could find my way home blindfold, but one foggy night Robert asked me to try. I was all over the place. It was his part to keep me on the pavement but even so I'd no idea where I was. The loser was to put half-a-crown in the Missionary box, but we both went past the house. So don't you be tempted."

With her emphatic manner and direct look, she had the air of a mature seraph coming with striking news straight from high authority, so that to Ella it was rather an anti-climax when her buoyant visitor sat down and accepted a cup of tea gratefully.

"Ah, thank you both, ladies. Tea warms us in winter and revives us in summer and manages to do the right thing even in autumn and spring, when our needs are not so easily defined."

"It's also been called the char-woman's solace, to bring it down a peg."

"Well, anything that can do that, Mrs Martland is fairly potent, I must say, and tea has the advantage of not drowning us along with our sorrows. Life looks better even if we're only looking through tea-rose coloured spectacles."

"Was Mrs Mossop there today?"

"The blind lady," Clara explained to the newcomer. "Yes, and she's staying to tea over there. We excused ourselves because I wanted you two to meet and this was a good opportunity."

"Mrs Mossop can do a great deal for herself," said Ella, "and she really can find her way about the house in the dark. Sometimes I wonder . . . well, I wonder if, given the chance, I would change places with her."

Clara glanced at her friend. She would not brush aside the remark as if it were foolish or unimportant, impugning Ella's right to occasional melancholy. Neither did Mrs Garner hasten into panegyric on the blessing of sight.

"It appears to me," said the latter after a pause, "that Mrs Mossop is a very intelligent woman and knows a great many people. I gather that she is a widow, though."

Instantly, Ella's cloud threw back its cloak.

"Oh! By the way, Miriam called on her way to town. She's found a wonderful man."

"What!"

"Yes, a wonderful man somewhere in Blackfriars, so we shan't be seeing her for a bit."

"Blackfriars sounds rather suggestive," said Clara disgustedly.

Ella was now laughing.

"She was in class last week, wasn't she, Clara?"

"Yes. She joined us last Wednesday."

An embarrassed silence fell.

"Ah well," said Mrs Garner composedly, "it is part of our feminine education to learn that however wonderful we are, we can't compete with a wonderful man in the eyes of other women."

"Poor Miriam," Ella said quietly. "If only she *had* found a wonderful man; how different her life would have been."

"What happened to the late Mr Crumps?"

"He died a year or two after they were married. I fancy that marriage - at least Miriam's brand of it - didn't suit him. In old-fashioned terms, he languished."

They all observed a brief compassionate silence for the demise of passion.

"Does your Sybil ever mention Sam Buckley?" Ella continued, with a seeming lack of continuity, but which made Clara Martland start a little.

"Not very often. That's one of our old members, Mrs Garner. He married years ago and they never come to our place now. Perhaps they don't go anywhere, but he was a likeable young man and clever."

"I have met his wife," said Ella. "Ada Sinclair brought her once. She bought a crochet bed-spread of mine. She's rather reserved, but very stylish."

The minister's wife was now looking at a photograph on the wall opposite Ella's bed; Three Little Maids from School very dear to Ella.

"Isn't that a photograph of you two ladies there? Do I know the other one?"

"That was done the year before we married. We'd had such a good time rehearsing that song. The other girl is Clara's sister Fanny who lives at Southport."

"Ah, a Fanny Crossley that was, I suppose."

"Yes, and a Fanny Crossley that is and is to be, I'm afraid," answered Clara, sighing and looking at Ella. "I've got one of those at home over our bedroom mantelpiece."

Ella smiled. "I've noticed lately that errand boys can whistle very tricky tunes quite accurately. There's one about a girl loving a butcher-boy with a beat I've never heard before, but the errand boys have got it pat. It's not easy."

"Well," said Mrs Garner, "people want a change from supreme works of art. We need the daily newspapers as well as the twenty-third psalm. Your daughter has a particularly good voice, Mrs Martland. Has she no desire to take it up professionally?"

Clara became rather serious, as lively matrons are apt to do when suddenly reminded of their families.

"Of course I don't know how she might have branched out, but under the circumstances singing will remain just a useful hobby; useful socially I mean, not financially."

"A pity to let marriage become the cemetery of talent. David was very much taken with her singing and usually he doesn't say much. I do think it necessary for women to have some interest that gives them private pleasure, because after all, the need to amuse ourselves comes round more often than the call to entertain others."

"Yes, indeed," said Ella softly. "Not," she amended hastily, "that *I* have any cause to grumble. Clara, didn't Kerry shape at all with her singing?"

"Well, she hasn't a bad voice really, but she led Fred Winskill such a dance with her definite notions. She wouldn't sing anything about religion, love or flowers, and when you come to think of it, that does narrow the field. Fred says the kind of thing she likes is only written for baritones; songs about ships in storms being lost with all hands, or the eve of battle and such like. It was very awkward, so after a term or two we just let it drop and neither Fred nor Kerry appeared to be sorry."

Mrs Garner laughed.

"Very wise of you. I have known homes to be turned into a sort of hell for the sake of an inferior piano rendering of the *Blue Bells of Scotland*. No, I'm not at all in favour of flogging dead donkeys in the pious hope that they'll be resurrected as racehorses. There ought to be a place in our scheme of things for donkeys as they are."

"Dear little things," exclaimed Ella rather unexpectedly. "I love the way they put their feet down. I shall be very sorry when donkeys go out altogether."

"It will be a long time before human donkeys go out altogether and they don't mind how they put their feet down as a rule."

Mrs Garner had just recollected something she had read recently and her indignation boiled up again.

"I know you give to the Work Overseas, Mrs Kershaw, so what do you think of this? The *Methodist Recorder* called it a charming story; I don't! The Chief of a tribe in one of the hottest parts of Africa was converted to Christianity and one day he brought his twelve wives to the Mission and asked that all should be received into the Church. Wasn't that wonderful? But wait! He was told that he could only bring *one* wife with him into the Faith, so the whole party had to go back. Then a few days later the Chief returned with one wife and explained that he had sent all the others back to their native villages. And, to crown all, the girl he had kept was the weakest of the household as she would have been least likely to find another husband."

Here the minister's wife rose from her chair in agitation and addressed Ella and Clara as if they really were a public meeting.

"A charming story! Do you know what would happen to those women? They'd never hold up their heads again after being sent back to their father's house. And as for the poor creature who was kept as the only wife, can you imagine the work she would have to tackle, and in great heat? She would have to produce a large family towards her husband's status, since *that* attitude isn't got rid of easily, and on the whole that unfortunate girl would rue the day that her husband had set eyes on a Christian. She would soon be dead! And then the Chief would take another wife. In that climate he might run through half-a-dozen, one after the other, instead of all travelling happily along together, sharing the work as the custom was. A charming story!"

Mrs Garner was very near to angry tears and the two other women stared at her in consternation.

"But, Mrs Garner," began Ella - and then stopped.

"Surely you can't mean," said Clara - and then she also stopped.

"I mean this much," answered Mrs Garner vehemently. "That if a baker's dozen of sincere people come and ask to be taken into the Christian Church, they should get a better reception and response than that!"

They were all busy with their own thoughts for a time, then, since Mrs Garner did not sit down again, Clara rose also.

"You stay and talk to Ella, Mrs Garner, while I clear away these tea things."

That evening when Tom was busy with some pieces of neat dove-tailing, Ella told him about her day; Mrs Ginnell, Nurse Fielding, Miriam and her later visitors.

"I think we are going to like her very much when we get used to her. I've known some lovely ministers' wives in my time."

"Yes," agreed Tom, "our itinerant system was a good idea from the very beginning."

"I sometimes remember them as 'ships that pass in the night', and I'm grateful that they do pass this way. I think of them, some graceful and mysterious, other-worldly, coming to a humble port of call. Then they set sail again. No exchange of addresses and hopeless promises to keep in touch. They pass, as they should, going their busy ways."

"Well, remember my lass, that this isn't my port of call; it's my home port and I'm not thinking of passing in the night yet awhile."

Tom concentrated on his woodwork while he cogitated this mood of Ella's. If she were dispirited he would pack up and read something lively to her, but he would give her a few more minutes; it might blow over. He spoke with head bent near his hands.

"Before we know where we are, it'll be time to be choosing our Christmas card again. I'll get the sample book soon. You and your passing ships! I'll have to beckon one in home to pay for all your correspondence as it is!"

"You'd better light up, Tom. You can hardly see that wood. But the evenings are beginning to draw in. I'm very sorry. It makes the night very long when we've to light up early."

"Well, let's enjoy the twilight for a bit. The lamps will come on any time now, and the trams. My word! The old place opposite looks drab enough when there's nothing going on. It's all right saying those coloured windows come to life when seen against the sun, but really they should be lit up from the inside. That's what the Church is for - to shine out. Here's a tram, thank goodness! All lit up. Did you see Willie Briggs wave from the upper deck? He knew you'd be here. Chipping at stone lettering might not be so good for his lungs, but there's nothing wrong with them judging by the way he runs after the ball. Willie's going to do very well. He'll be a footballer yet."

When the street lamps made their impulsive leap into brilliance, Ella herself lay in deeper shadow behind the curtain folds, and lying parallel with the window wall could only watch the approaches from the Oldham direction. Three or four times a year Tom and Ernest moved the bed to another position to give a slightly different outlook so that at least she had another set of front doors and windows to watch on either side of the church.

"Tom!"

"Um?"

"How would you like to be an African Chief with several wives, then if one fell ill, the others could share the work?"

"I thought there was something! Which of your visitors has started this? I certainly don't want to be an African Chief, but if I were and my wife fell ill, the work could be shared out by slaves. No call for more wives."

"But they'd work all the better if they were called wives. I think that would be only fair to them."

"You don't marry a woman just because you think she deserves a medal. Or even a consolation prize! What are you driving at?"

So Ella recounted the 'charming story' in full.

Tom remained silent at his work for long moments.

"A right mess all round, wasn't it? So many people getting hurt through no fault of their own. And our Lord did say a man must not put away his wife except for adultery, so that makes the chief a wrong 'un for putting aside eleven innocent women. Heck!"

"Perhaps he shouldn't have had them all in the first place," ventured Ella.

"He'd got to start from where he was. You can't argue that he shouldn't have been in Oswaldtwistle at all. He was there and it's beginning to look as if he should have stayed there. I think your Mrs Garner was right. It *was* wrong!"

"Oh! Poor man."

"Poor missionary, too! You know, I can't see how Christianity can be quite the same all over the world as it is here on Oldham Road. There'll have to be a fine sight more of the spirit and less of the letter as time goes on. I wish the Chosen People had done as they ought, blazed a trail and then the others could come along at their own pace."

"But all people are the chosen people now, Tom. No more Ishmaels."

"Some would be better behind the door for a bit. If the world is to be turned upside down, then a lot of people are going to be shaken off and I don't believe God wants them to be."

Now it really was lighting up time and the curtains were drawn and Tom found the library book from Newton Heath, about travel, but not in Africa for a change. There were other places, praise be!

"Now then, are you all set? Well let's get on a bit further with *Travels with a Donkey*, shall we?"

Chapter Nine

Sam Buckley was not particularly interested in his domestic mail. His business post was what really mattered. So he opened the little box behind the front door in a desultory manner, like emptying an ash tray, and carried the meagre contents to the breakfast table.

"A circular for you and nothing for me, except this invitation to their Harvest Festival from Alfred Sinclair. I don't suppose you want to go?"

"Not unless you specially want to."

"Then I'll send a couple of guineas; they'll take up less space."

"Oh! Mine's an appeal for something called 'Woman's Work', a sort of Missionary effort. They won't get far with a title like that! Woman's Work sounds very unglamorous. It has an aura of potato peelings about it - an un-manicured atmosphere!"

"By the way, the Sinclairs will be sending a lot of thick background stuff. Is there anything you can spare? It would be appreciated, you know."

"I can look something out."

Why wouldn't they leave Sam alone! They were always sending appeals. Would they have kept in touch so obstinately if he had been a poor man? She deliberated awhile and then spoke carefully, keeping any peevishness out of her voice.

"You know, I do think that if a church can't pay its way, it is in the wrong place, to say the least. There may even be something wrong with it."

"Oh, come, Elsie. On your argument, if the Hallé Orchestra didn't pay, it would have to disband or play jazz. There's nothing wrong with Beethoven, but he doesn't appeal to everybody and yet that isn't a sufficient reason for pulling down the Free Trade Hall."

"More coffee?" She adroitly changed the subject. "The newspapers are late!"

"We got them at half-past seven, years ago, but I suppose in a district like this it's difficult to find a kid who'll get up to deliver papers. Mrs Ginnell coming today?"

"Oh yes. I shall be informed on many subjects in which I have no interest." She gazed out onto the garden with raised eyebrows. "How do people get that way?"

"What people, which way, or vice versa?" asked Sam.

"The people at that place," nodding towards the circulars. "Mrs Ginnell talks about them."

"What's wrong with them?" Sam spoke lightly.

"Well, there's the Crumps woman for one, always spring cleaning and suspicious of other people's methods, and Ella Kershaw, resigned to living in one room, year in, year out. You'd think she could get into a Home of some sort; and that husband waiting on her all the time he's at home. It must be positively soul-destroying!"

Sam remembered the Kershaws. It was a situation to make one sweat, if one thought about it.

"People like to manage in their homes as long as possible, I suppose. And we shouldn't play about with our health. I don't think *you* eat enough breakfast under the circumstances. What have you had this morning to build you up to full strength again? A bit of toast and marmalade!"

Sam tried so hard not to fuss, but now and again his anxiety overcame him. He knew he had irritated her now.

"Oh, I don't like a full breakfast. Breakfast has been spoilt for me for ever, I should think."

Sam stole a furtive look at her with her gaze intent on the garden outside as if to ignore the room. The french windows were not open this morning and the panes had been faintly steamed for the first time. Soon the breakfast table there would be abandoned for the centre of the room as the days grew cooler and the garden faded; a sad move as if they were embarrassed at the sight of a sick friend.

Perhaps she was feeling the unrest of the changing season. People did. And everybody had occasional outbursts of discontent whether they were married or single, uncluttered or knee deep in toddlers.

What a fool the matron in that nursing home had been! It wouldn't have been so bad if *he* hadn't been there, but as they shook hands in the hall, she'd said smugly and all too cheerfully, "I should start another straight away!" He remembered Elsie's look of dismay turning to anger at the woman's tactlessness. But for her, everything would have slowly righted itself, whereas the recoil had jerked Elsie further away from health, perhaps, and from happiness, certainly. Poor girl!

Sam pushed back his chair.

"Looking quite autumnal this morning, isn't it? Now don't go standing about in the garden and getting cold feet. The best planning is done with an illustrated catalogue in front of a good fire. Have any come lately? Little Hans ought to be a lot taller than any of his father's tulips by now. More likely to be standing on his father's foot than on his hand!"

Elsie nodded and went to bring Sam's coat from the hall cupboard and held the lining towards the electric fire until she helped him on with it. She could do things like that for him with smiling friendliness, especially in a morning when he was going out of the house. She felt safe in showing a little tenderness when he was on the point of leaving. Sam kissed her on the cheek. He had been wise enough never to stop the habit. He kissed her also when he returned in the evening. She had grown accustomed to his leave-taking kiss and to one upon re-entering when she had to hasten away to the kitchen. But he never attempted a kiss when they were at leisure. It made her uneasy.

He thumped his ribs where his wallet was pocketed, not ostensibly to deflect bullets, although a wad of notes did stand between a man and certain slings and arrows.

"All right for money? Got quite enough for anything you want?"

"Oh yes," she answered with slight impatience, and at that warning note he put on his hat and went out to the garage.

He had gone! He had gone before she had actually screamed! Or pushed him off the step! But really, he ought to have more sense than to dawdle. She took a long drawn breath and then drifted back to the table. She had heard women say that the final cup after everyone had gone in a morning was the sweetest of the day. The coffee-pot was still hot and she poured herself another cup, knowing that relief would come in a moment. And as she sipped slowly, the tears welled up. Come on, let's get it over. Fall!

She washed up before Mrs Ginnell came. Mrs Ginnell must have a clear field. Elsie Buckley preferred the American ideal of using all labour saving devices and so cutting out the unsatisfactory human element, but Sam had put his foot down firmly there and Mrs Ginnell had been approached. Their place was a dream. The kitchen shone like the inside of a biscuit tin, Mrs Ginnell reported later to Ella. Mind you, you wouldn't put a rocking chair with a crochet wool antimacassar in there; and, as *you* say, a rocking chair gives a kitchen a finishing touch, same as flowers on the window ledge. Instead, there was a chromium stool with a round top where she was supposed to sit for her elevenses, but she found standing more comfortable.

Elsie had not really taken to Mrs Ginnell. Her glance was too sharp, but she could not put it that way to Sam. Although Sam allocated a generous sum to the housekeeping, she was very careful Sam could never reproach her there. What did she mean, reproach? Sam never reproached her for anything. He had no need, for the house was beautifully kept and she could cook. He got value for his money. But she wished he would not offer so much. Sometimes she wanted to throw it back; she didn't know why. She wanted to make some sort of sacrifice, but of what nature she could not decide. When he thrust more money at her she wanted to reply, "I'm good but *you* know and *I* know that I'm not as good as all that!"

Mrs Ginnell arrived very wide awake from looking at shop windows on her way by tram and bus.

"I'll tackle Little Filthy and give it a good cleaning after this drink, Mrs Buckley. I will say it gets the water nice and hot. Oh, those fancy magazines are no good for wrapping up ashes, ma'am. You could do with some of our Sunday papers; they're worth it for the rubbish alone. And another thing, if any woman wants to think ·better of her own husband, she should read the Sunday papers and see what some poor souls have got. I'm always pleased to see my Ernest back at Sunday teatime. If it's all the same to you, Mrs Buckley, I'll take these magazines for our Connie to look at. Eh, just look at these adverts! Low lights, perfume and soft music to make a man pop the question. Some women work hard for a pair of trousers round the house." Mrs Ginnell broke off with a derisory laugh. "My husband didn't need all these things, I can tell you. The perfume round the Rochdale Canal may have been a bit niffy when he asked me, but at least he asked me with his eyes open."

Elsie managed to interrupt the commentary and then she escaped upstairs to do the beds. Machines couldn't do everything but they had the virtue of keeping their life history to themselves.

It was nippier this morning, as Mrs Ginnell had said upon arrival and Elsie rummaged for a cardigan. The house was only a few years old and it would not take much to make it independent of outside help. Some day she would be self-sufficient, Elsie told herself. This was only their second house since marriage and she was well satisfied with it. She buttoned the cardigan as she surveyed her room. It was her room now, but it used to be the guest room. When she came back from the nursing home she had promised the doctor to stay in bed for a whole week, so she had come straight into this room. Sam had offered to use the guest room for a time but she said she would rather have it;

it was warmer, facing south.

She had read that French women make great use of their bedrooms as boudoirs, reading and writing rooms, and the idea appealed to Elsie. Gradually it had become a comfortable bed-sitting-room and the large square-bayed window was her favourite retreat. It had more of a bird's eye view of the garden and it received the afternoon sun. Here she brought her tea tray and came nearer to peace of mind and body than she had known since . . . since that affair.

As she trundled the vacuum cleaner over the carpet, its hum shut out all other sounds, including Mrs Ginnell's metallic assault downstairs. There was only this satisfied purr of an efficient engine and it soothed her. It was power without fuss, something spinning round evenly and humming to itself like the music of the spheres, gentle, self-centred, eternal. Inanimate nature was controlled, admirable in every way. Only at very close range do we become aware of the force, the tumult and the strife of creation.

The strife of creation! The music of the spheres was only bearable at a distance after all. She would never let it come nearer again. She switched off and went into Sam's room.

As always, there wasn't a thing out of place, not a garment or personal possession to be seen. This might have been the guest room from which the unobtrusive visitor had stolen away. There was little to indicate what manner of man used this room, except that he was tidy. The dressing table was bare. Elsie slid open a drawer. Even his military brushes were put away so that dusting the table meant neither dodging an article nor picking it up. The few pictures of the Lake District he had bought before she knew him. It could have been a bachelor's room, for everything feminine had been removed except perhaps the pastel shaded carpet. She opened the wardrobe. Until recently Sam had crammed his clothes into his own smaller wardrobe, but now his winter overcoats were sharing the larger cupboard with her fur coat. So he was not expecting her to use the cupboard for her everyday things again! It was a significant and reassuring signal.

Quickly she made the bed. A well flung sheet knocked the bed-light askew and as she straightened it she tested it. Quite in order. She idly wondered if Sam read in bed. If so, he put his book away. Tentatively she pulled at the bedside drawer. It held one clean handkerchief and a light handbook, *Invest Your Assets*.

Sam was contented enough, as of course he had reason to be, she added quickly. He seemed to have no worries, but of course men's nerves were less sensitive. Their skins, like their clothes, were thicker and impervious to brambles. Men spent on their brains all the care that women lavished on their emotions, and how unequal were the results!

She returned to her own room. Summer was indeed over and opening her wardrobe, she pulled out the frocks that would not be needed again. While engaged on this sorting out she heard a rap on the door, Sam's door, and looking out on the landing, saw Mrs Ginnell with a tray containing Elsie's mid-morning tonic wine and a couple of biscuits.

"Mrs Buckley, you've forgotten your pick-me-up. Your husband did just mention that you had it, and as *you* say, strength goes in at the mouth!"

"Oh," answered Elsie, rather annoyed. "I was just coming."

Mrs Ginnell saw the annoyance and misinterpreted it. "You can still call yourself a teetotaller, you know, if you only take it medicinally, and Doctor Bedser always says if you're going to take the stuff, have the real stuff while you're about it. My Ernest makes no secret of his stouts and so on and he keeps very fit on the whole. Sometimes when he's had a drop too much that's noticeable, I say to him, 'One of these days Nirvanah will overtake you', but I think he's sensible really."

"Well, thank you Mrs Ginnell, and I'll take the tray," and Elsie waited for her help to retreat before entering her room again. "Anything to look in cupboards!" she muttered unfairly.

Then as she sipped she reflected that after all Mrs Ginnell was a warm-hearted person and probably only obeying Sam's orders. But husbands and servants sometimes took too much on themselves. However, she resumed the scrutiny of her wardrobe in a more generous frame of mind.

When she got downstairs she was much more affable.

"Perhaps your Connie might make use of this, Mrs Ginnell. I've heard you say she is clever with her fingers."

"Oh, that's lovely. Are you sure you've done with it? It will need very little altering as she's a well built girl for her age and you're very slim for a married woman." A comprehensive George Robey glance swept over Elsie.

"How is she?" asked Elsie quickly.

"Our Connie isn't the sort of girl to throw herself away. And her brothers have done well for themselves, too. I told them, 'Don't marry for money, but fall in love where money is.' If they catch the girl first, when her people see she's bent on having him, they'll see he gets on. Both are in their in-laws' family business. They've no regrets."

Elsie bent down to a drawer for paper and string.

"Going out into the world to seek somebody's fortune!"

"Though I say to our Connie, don't *you* try any tricks on. *We've* no jobs to offer any young man. But I think she can take care of herself."

Mrs Ginnell put her finger obligingly on the knot that Elsie was tying and continued.

"We were at the minister's Welcome, you know, and your friends the Sinclairs were there with their son. He seems in no great hurry to get married but perhaps he's been a bit hasty already. I think he really needs someone to stand up to his mother, someone more like our Connie."

"I thought he was engaged."

"Yes, he is, but she doesn't go up to his place much. Of course there are wheels within wheels, before your time."

"My husband knows Mr Sinclair through business."

Elsie finished the parcel and went upstairs again. She did not wish to hear what had happened before her time, that is, before she came on Mrs Ginnell's scene. Really, that woman saw mankind as animals just emerging from the ark. Life to her was one long pairing off. It was the only interest in her life except for accounts of their killing each other off. That Mrs Ginnell was of the opinion that her family gave her some sort of superiority over Elsie Buckley was obvious, but it was very primitive. Many ancient religions had tried to do away with that sort of feminine competition by levelling all women in temple rites. Even the worship of Priapus had a spiritual basis in belittling the importance of carnal experience. If all women were equally the bride of a god, then they were equal in each other's sight. There was a great deal to be said for it.

She actually ran downstairs and into the garden. The sun had come out strongly and she could not be thoroughly discontented in its glow. When she had been ill, she had longed for her garden.

Burning hot all over, she had imagined herself lying naked on a bed of flowers with a clump of cool daffodils in the small of her back. She had a vivid memory and imagination, but some people had neither. Mrs Ginnell had no memory at all to cool her passions and experience taught her nothing as she went along. And what were children but the dunce's immortality!

She had other ambitions and Sam was contented enough. Romance had drained away from her during her illness and Sam had evidently outgrown that immature idealism of her as part Queen Guinevere and part Queen Bee. She was now just Elsie Buckley, an excellent housewife, keen gardener and worthy of her place in the social scheme.

She walked along a path, looking at the plants to be taken up. She would choose an entirely different colour scheme, divergent even in temperament from the ordinary, a garden that would surprise with a triumph of warmth in an unexpectant wintry waste. Content to be no better than its neighbours in their common heyday, it would take on rich life as the others faded, slowly gaining ascendancy in beauty until it dawned on all surrounding ritualists that here was a winter queen indeed. Summer was lavish and slap-dash in its poster colours, but this soon to be sunless garden would be royal in old masterly depth of tone, creating its own blaze in defiance of the empty sky.

She stood still.

"If only I can keep my health. I ask nothing else of life but that I can keep my health."

Fervently she began to pull up some of the dead flowers. She had not stayed to get her gardening gloves and now in her eagerness she was starting work without them.

Looking out of a window, Mrs Ginnell saw her kneeling on the stones, wrestling with the stalks and tough leaves.

"What's she doing out there? Is she burying herself in that garden?"

A rat-tat snapped out from the side door which Mrs Ginnell answered. It was the butcher's boy and after some conversation with him, Mrs Ginnell came down the garden.

"I've put the meat in the larder, Mrs Buckley, and what do you think? First he handed me a great packet. I said, 'Surely Mrs Buckley hadn't ordered all that! She isn't the old woman who lived in a shoe, you know.' He said, 'Oh, I thought this was the nursing home. I'm new and yesterday when I came along there was someone sitting reading in the bedroom window.' He's gone now. I told him there's nobody ill here."

"Of course not. The nursing home is further along and much bigger than this house."

"Although this house is very big for just two people. Don't you and Mr Buckley think so? But if you're going to dig in that damp soil, I do think you ought to put on some thicker shoes. You'd soon get cold feet in those and you don't want to go digging your own grave, do you now?"

Elsie sprang to her feet and, unable to conceal her distaste for the conversation, moved quickly away in vexation and walked in silence into the house.

Chapter Ten

The morning sun was as bright as it had been on any fine day for a month and the shadows were as sharply contrasted, but the year could no longer dissemble; it was getting older and although it retained its vigour, shrewder. There was a crustiness underfoot that belied the distant hills gently steaming as if the earth had just been drawn fresh from the oven.

Ben Northcroft's farm had lost many of the sweeping draperies of his father's time, but the closer-fitting home fields were rich enough. On the outskirts, the surrounding pack of new houses yearly grew nearer and nearer to the farm, threatening to gulp the Red Riding Hood basket that had gone to feed the district for so long.

A field sold to a building prospector brought a good price and Alfred Sinclair had paid handsomely for his plots of ground; but the building site brought its good price to the farm only once, whereas the wheat and barley field or the sugar beet made a habit of it.

At one time Annie Northcroft had not wanted young Jim to stay on the farm. She had other ideas for him which had not escaped his notice. He had once brought home a pamphlet headed 'Join the Navy and see the World', and strangely his mother had destroyed it quite openly and casually as if it had been an election leaflet from an unpopular candidate. On another occasion he had remarked that there was good money in a dance band - so he'd been told; but this time his father and grandfather had given him identical stares for a moment that were somehow a parallel to his mother's movement to the fireplace. Then he reported having heard from a friend who had been up for a flip in one of Alan Cobham's circus planes and was full of the experience. It was at this point that Annie quite dropped her hints of a different way of life for Jimmie.

"The promise of thy days being long in the land," the old man impressed upon him, "has nothing to do with one man's mortal span, but with family continuity. If a man attends to his father's business the name becomes established thereabouts. And our name is known for good products. No one spits in *our* milk."

This morning the cows had already strolled to the far side of the yard, waiting to go down to the field, when Annie Northcroft came out to remind the three men that the minister and his wife were coming to tea that day. John wanted to cry off.

"Another time, but not this first time," replied his wife firmly. It had once come to her ears that John was like the bull; people knew he was about but were not always introduced to him.

Her strong characteristic was a love of order and in such a place it was natural that one should pass remarks. Because the farmhouse was squat and old-fashioned, all the residents of the new houses round about stared in as they passed as if it were a Folk museum. Its way of life was different from that of its neighbours, so it was regarded curiously. It had the attraction of an oil painting on a wall of Town Planning drawings or of a Christmas card among a batch of circulars.

For woman's beauty withered before its time, for ceaseless toil and unrewarding years, architects even more than false lovers and neglectful husbands must take the greatest share of blame, especially when the architect was an exhibitionist and his house cried "Look at me!" instead of "Come and live in me!" Then ornamentation was crammed into every cornice, doorway, window-frame, hearth and stairway. There was more than enough to amaze the eye before a curlicue of furniture was taken in. But nowadays the architect had recanted in somewhat abject fashion and the little brittle shells of houses that had silted up around the farm were temporary rest rooms in which a fagged generation might recover strength and having done so, would draw breath once again to revile the architect, this time for neglecting the spirit as once he had overburdened the flesh.

The farmhouse, however, had escaped the lavishness of the early fashion and the meanness of the present and there was much in it to warm a certain type of woman's heart, even if the style was what Mrs Ginnell called "granite with knobs on". Annie had been brought here years ago by John to bring order and comfort which had temporarily fled the scene when Mrs Ben Northcroft died. John had already been in a fair way to becoming an uncomplaining bachelor until physical distress changed his mind.

One wet night Ben had looked round the kitchen with disfavour.

"The place is beginning to smell mouldy. It needs a proper mistress, not just someone for a few hours. What about looking for someone to twist thy tail a bit?"

John had been startled but not frightened.

"Perhaps I'd better," he agreed.

"And this is no place for a killing, mind," advised Ben. "We'll need someone strong enough to lift the lid of the chest in Peover Church at least."

When Ben announced loudly that their place needed a new mistress and that John was under orders to do something about it, the chapel went into action. Older members held Whist parties and asked John and Annie "to make up a table". Many small front rooms barely accommodated three card tables and the number was reduced to two. Then intimate foursomes were arranged. "Just you two and ourselves - nothing elaborate." When the hostess withdrew to muster the refreshments at the ready on a larder shelf, the host, preparing to engage John in agricultural talk, found himself instructed that his presence was required in the kitchen.

"What's the matter? One of the cakes turned out heavy?"

At last, after one of these intervals, the conspirators, or rather host and hostess, with the tea tray wheeled on a trolley squealing like one of John's young pigs, found their guests bursting with secrecy. In silence, an embroidered cloth was placed over the card table and cups of tea poured and placed before them, but they could not eat or drink, replete with news as they were.

"Well," - began John heartily - and stopped, glancing at Annie.

"Oh, Mrs Crossley," said Annie, beginning to tremble.

John looked round at them with some defiance.

"I've got Annie to say she'll be my wife."

"Good for you, lad," exclaimed his host, while Mrs Crossley patted Annie approvingly and kissed her.

"I can't say I'm honestly surprised, as I've thought you suited to each other for some time. Now drink your tea while it's still hot and we'll wish you happiness."

Matchmaking is a dangerous pastime but a kinder one than matchbreaking.

When she took possession at the farm, to her astonishment Annie found hardly any room in the many drawers upstairs and down to house her own trousseau. The wardrobe drawers were full of paper parcels containing enough bed linen for years to come, and the dressers in kitchen and dining room were stocked with long damask table cloths. It was a housewife's Aladdin's cave; a linen hall more acceptable than any baronial hall; cotton fields folded small with lavender stalks between the layers and yards of crochet in snowy rococo and arabesque patterns guarded by ice-blue tissue paper against long years of disuse. The lavender and mothballs could be smelt fighting it out together.

"Did you know all these things were here?" she had asked John incredulously.

"I expect I did at some time."

It was the same with the china. The ring of the crockery had been faintly heard during careful spring cleanings and even less often were the polished glasses raised to any lips.

Nothing here had been for the common touch and so it still lived, or at least it was still preserved.

Annie had brought these treasures into the open and as youth receded, she gave to them and to the house the extra care that less philosophical women give to their own physical attractions in the teeth of time. She polished the furniture as regularly as more sophisticated women buff their fingernails. There was not a nook or cranny in the whole house that she had not at some time scrubbed or brushed with her own hands. She knew the graining and every knot in all the woodwork better than a captain knows his quarterdeck. Familiarity had bred content and now, standing at the landing window overlooking the yard, she heard the raucous shout of seagulls. The day was fine but there must be a wind freshening on the coast over thirty miles away Annie knew that freshening wind. She had felt it after her parents' death when she had been living with her only brother in the parental home which was as much hers as his. To her consternation he had been clapped in the bonds of matrimony first and she found that a sister-in-law was an even greater incentive to marrying than a brother who had taken her for granted. The wife never took Annie's presence for granted and the phrase "until Annie gets married" lost its first cheerful tone and became shrill with annoyance.

Annie craned to follow the wheeling and swooping gulls. They too were thankful to shelter inland when their old haunts blew inhospitably.

When the front gate clicked, Annie heard it distinctly through an open bedroom window and she hurried down.

Yes, it was a lovely day, though there was a tang in the air and really it was to be expected now the harvest was well in, and we shall be thinking of Christmas before we know where we are. Perhaps Mr Garner would like to look round the farm before tea? John and Jim would be busy for another half hour but Father would be at liberty. Oh, certainly, if Mrs Garner wishes. We can all go outside this way through the house and out at the back. That is the dairy of course, facing north.

Yes, indeed, those rag rugs do keep out draughts where there's a gap under the door. Oh, we all help. This step is very much worn. Like a temple's is it? Really? I've never been abroad. Be quiet, Clover, good dog. Yes, those are the Pennines you can see, or at least the moors. Are you there, Father?

Jimmie was there too and came along to chaperone the visitors when they were taken to inspect the bull, with the curiosity that must have drawn many Philistines to gaze at Samson in captivity. But here was a Samson whose Delilahs were entirely without guile and yet his temper seemed to be permanently soured.

"Does he live indoors always?" asked Grace of Ben.

"Not always, but we know just where he is when he's here and other folk like to know he's indoors too. There's never absolute peace of mind for anyone when a bull is loose."

"And could that tumulus of flesh really run?"

Ben laughed shortly.

"It would be like an express train thundering after you."

They all looked at Samson with respect.

"Perhaps," said Grace, "if he were in a sort of stockade with grass and fresh air, he might feel more composed."

"I doubt if liberty would make him sweeter tempered," returned Ben.

"I think," went on Grace, "for their size, cows are the most insipid creatures. They ought to pose a few questions of life."

Robert regarded Samson thoughtfully.

"We have managed to domesticate the horse, the dog and the cat without making them utterly imbecile and yet cattle and poultry seem to have suffered great mental deterioration at our hands. Perhaps dogs sense that we do not eat them as a rule and the knowledge gives them confidence. But cattle and poultry seem to be descending from the animal kingdom to the vegetable, a retrograde step. Their functions have been narrowed down until they are mere seed-cases and pulp. The animals that can, if desperate, abscond, even though to perish, retain individuality more than the stalled ox. The bull, to his credit, voices his perpetual rebellion against fate, alias mankind."

"Now, Mr Northcroft," the minister's wife broke in, "where's your theory in favour of large families now? See what intensive breeding's done to some part of animal creation."

"It's what they're here for," answered Ben shortly. "It was ordained that man should have dominion over them."

Grace was shocked into momentary silence but Robert continued with his own theme.

"Where there is defiance, there is hope. The cock and the bull, the gander and the boar, still display indications of assertiveness."

"That they do," exclaimed the farmer, reaching over and slapping Samson. "Never trust a bull even if he was born in your best bed and reared accordingly. As a calf, this one here would follow me about like a dog, but I never let him get ideas in his head."

"I can see," the minister's wife said glumly, "that the female is less enterprising and I can understand why."

"Ay, she's got something else to think of," agreed Ben. "You know, when we bring a new calf up from the field, we don't bother to put a lead round the old cow's neck; she just follows the calf."

"What a life!" exclaimed Grace. "There's a lot to be said for vegetarianism."

"Not all that much," countered Ben. "Remember we can use everything but the squeal or, in this case, the bellow.

"That is Chicago's boast," said Robert gently, "but I do not think even the squeal is utterly wasted. It may be that in some other sphere where perhaps we are hoping to hear a heavenly choir, we are surprised to find that first we have to listen to the squeal, a terrible sound, wasted by man but cherished by God. A civilisation that ignores the squeal is in danger. The squeal that goes up from any hidden barbarism can drag a man or a nation down to hell."

Here Jimmie turned to the speaker as if he would say something, but after a moment he muttered some words about work not quite finished and walked away.

Annie Northcroft, however, smelt burning words and hastened to change the subject, if only slightly.

"Now, if they are going to inspect the pigs, Mrs Garner, you and I will go indoors, shall we? Will you kindly remind him, Mr Garner, if he keeps you more than ten minutes!"

"I don't think my husband is quite the person to remind anyone of the time either," said Grace.

"I'll run out again later then. Would you care to see my jams and bottled fruits? In here."

She unlocked a door and, stepping through, Grace at once saw shelves filled with glass jars, showing dark or golden with preserves. Some had little white mob caps frilled round the edges. On the higher shelves were ranged the bottled fruits in tall jars with their paper coverings reaching to their shoulders, like so many Lawrences of Arabia with their Desert Corps. The latest preserving sets had dispensed with such dishabille and stood in elegant rows with gold bands encircling their brows; the new élite. Incorruptible, they would make the last stand and endure until bottling time came round again.

Grace gazed wistfully. This sort of larder was utterly beyond her.

"It must be wonderful," she murmured, "to see the results of your labours."

The farmer's wife was touched.

"Only for a short time, you know. The fruits of this sort of labour are soon gobbled up. Yours must be . . . "

Annie stopped as her companion had seemed to be about to speak again, but Grace apologised.

"No, do go on. I was only going to say what an interesting life yours must be."

"But that's exactly what *I* was about to say," exclaimed Annie. You are always seeing fresh places. Did it seem a bit tame when you settled in England again?"

"It's always lovely to come home," said Grace, "but perhaps there isn't the excitement of opening up an entirely new district, nor are there quite the extremes of enthusiasm and rejection, but out there it is still possible to die for one's faith and of course some do."

"Of course, here you are always moving on."

"Yes, and perhaps it's as well. Moving on sometimes saves a minister from heartbreak."

Annie regarded her solemnly.

"Yes, I suppose we do look set in our ways."

"Oh, but yours is a beautiful setting and I'm sure you live your life to the full and the weather and the seasons mean such a great deal on a farm; you can't ignore them."

"No," said Annie, "I couldn't bear to be shut in by rows of houses again after this. I work with the kitchen door open for the greater part of the year, and rain or shine I love to see an open view before me. Let's go into the kitchen. The menfolk won't be long now."

Grace looked about with interest. It wasn't an up-to-date kitchen at all and it had what is not expected in a kitchen, an air of charm. At ordinary times it was used for meals and all its furniture and fittings being made of wood, it looked warm and dependable, with not much to go wrong.

"Of course, in a place like this," said Annie, pushing the kettle nearer to the blaze, "you've got to keep the fires well up, even in summer. These thick walls keep it cool, but the place is never left."

"Do you never go away?"

"I've not been away for years and I see no likelihood," responded Annie in a matter-of-fact voice. "I've got to look after the men just as they've to look after the livestock."

e

"But don't you ever feel like a change?"

"Well, I won't say never, but it doesn't last long. You can't say to men and beasts, 'Shoo and feed yourselves for a week!' Not to domesticated ones, so called."

Annie looked round her kitchen and back to her guest.

"When I feel like a change, I think of Ella Kershaw cooped up year in, year out."

"But, Mrs Northcroft, we must think of the more fortunate and not only of the less fortunate, to keep a balance."

"Oh, like the Buckleys going to Iceland, if you can call that being fortunate! But she's very house-proud, too. Being a housewife is skilled labour if it's done properly."

Annie had spoken defensively but Grace warmly agreed.

"Most women are fond of housework, within reason, only with my visiting and classes, I can't linger over it as some do. I have nothing of the curator in my make-up and people, not things, are my business; mine and my husband's. Labour saving devices give me more time for people."

She looked round the farm kitchen with interest. It was usually a scene of great activity but it had its moments of peace for the woman who worked in it. She found here all the solace, quiet reflection and wholeness of mind that she needed. This kitchen was her convent. It could be dangerous never-the-less. Even the Englishman's castle could become a prison, a sort of house arrest.

At this moment old Mr Northcroft came in and, sitting down, started to unlace his boots.

"John's out there. Did Jim pump that water for the trough?"

"No," said Annie. "I told him to leave it till later. It makes his hand tremble, you know, and he might play us a tune later."

"It would have stopped trembling by now if he'd done it earlier."

At this moment Mrs Garner started visibly as a loud shot was heard.

"Oh, he's starting that," exclaimed Annie with real annoyance. "They really must come in now. Excuse me. I'll go and tell them."

John was not a man with a great spate of words. Perhaps he had spent too much time listening to his father and had been held down as under a weir. He was aware that his wife would like him to shine more in company. It wasn't that he disliked company, but he wished she wouldn't expect him to take more part. It is a pity that a woman cannot bear to leave a man as she finds him. If he is quiet, she tries to draw him out; if he is boisterous she tries to tone him down; if he is a sinner, she must reform him and if he is a saint, she tries to rouse the only bit of devil left in him.

98

John was a mild man, but he dearly loved a gun; not so much for sport or pot, as for marksmanship. A tin on a gate post would do in passing. There was, however, one happiest hunting ground that afforded real sport - the manure heap. This was a hillock by the out-buildings that grew in size, variety and odour through the months until it and the time were ripe for it to be spread abroad on the land. Onto this melting pot of Gehenna were thrown the sweepings from house, stable, sty, stall and shed.

"Chuck it on the muck heap," Ben would say.

"Throw it on the midden," said John.

"Put it with the refuse," came from the one most influenced by Annie.

This olla-podrida was the magic pot for all the rats in the neighbourhood, who over-ran it, tunnelled and catacombed it in their pursuit of unimaginable titbits. Greed and the unfailing gratification of greed made the vermin bold, so that even in daylight, shadows heaved and slid unobtrusively over the moist, melanic, straw-pricked mass. Here and there a large bone, picked clean by voracious incisors, was churned up, and about these the scavengers played 'in and out the windows'.

It was these flickering, elusive targets that drew John's sudden fire. No shooting range at any fair afforded anything like the macabre excitement and skill required here as at the first shot the quivering surface stilled, melting into teasing camouflage, to return after a few moments to furtive, restless life.

The men had been on the point of going to the house when John had noticed the mound showing signs of liveliness and detaining his guest with - "Watch this", he had fetched his gun.

At the crack, all movement stiffened and John scrutinised his distant target to see that it would never take cover again of its own volition. He waited for the stealthy reconnoitering to begin again and then fired a second time so that now two stealing shadows became tangible additions to the integer from which they had formerly filched.

"Like a shot?" asked John, holding out the gun.

Robert took it.

At this moment Annie appeared hurrying round the corner of the stable.

"Oh! Mr Garner, what's he making you do, and you a pacifist?"

"Is he?" said John, surprised. "Well, there's no harm done."

"No," said Robert, laughing. "As a marksman, I'm a very good pacifist," and he handed the gun back to John.

But Annie was looking exceptionally vexed and the two men

followed her to the house, John apologetic.

"You'd hardly got it pointed at the midden."

"Never mind. Perhaps some other time when the ladies are not wanting their tea."

"Many years ago, before I married and my father was still a youngish man, we used to have regular rat hunts in the stables and cow houses after dark before the stock went in for the night. We'd all have a good thick stick and we'd stand still as posts for a minute or two, hardly breathing, with a sack held over the storm lamps. Then the covers would be whisked off and there the beggars were, and we'd lay about us like mad while any were to be seen as we kicked the straw about. When all was quiet we'd line up by the wall again to get our breath and let the vermin regain confidence, and then suddenly the performance would be repeated. It was warm work I can tell you."

"But you would keep a few cats about the place?"

"Oh, yes, but you can't get a cat to work a twelve hour day and at night they're on the stable roof, not on the floor. Cats work for themselves, not for you."

John remembered that he was delaying the whole party.

"Ten minutes will do the trick," he called.

When all were seated, the prospect looked very bright. Annie had a vague knowledge that people who had lived 'abroad' always felt the cold in England for the rest of their lives and so the Garners were placed with their backs to the autumn fire.

Grace enjoyed going out to tea where the honours were so well done, and knew that the depth of the crochet border on a cloth was indicative of the occasion. There was something abiding about the atmosphere of this place; perhaps the three generations round the table gave it an air of continuity like a royal succession.

After Robert had said grace, his wife sat there appreciating the picture. Annie was pouring tea and the gentle sound from the first plash to the filled cup was very soothing with its suggestion of ritual and reward. Mrs Garner had said that she did not collect things, but she was a collector of perfect moments. In her life of movement she fastened certain pictures of still life in her memory by taking in all the details of a scene with a keen self-conscious scrutiny. This must go in, she thought, her mind painting avidly as the filling of the last cup tinkled to a diminuendo, a sound which did not so much disturb, as adorn the silence. If time stood still, what moment of the day would one choose to prolong for all eternity? Perhaps the Mad Hatter had made the sanest choice when he cried happily, "It's always teatime here!" Alice and the other creatures round that woodland table could come and go. They were free, but the time and place were for ever static, to be stumbled upon delightedly. It was always teatime there. Or here. As one journeys through wonderland and paradox one comes to these oases of eternity, these eternities of oasis where of course there is always room, as Alice sensibly affirmed.

Annie glanced at John. It was Ben who spoke.

"British farming can go under for good and all and no one's going to raise a finger, Mr Garner. People just want their fresh milk put on the doorstep and everything else can go to pot. Foreign bacon, foreign butter, even foreign eggs! It's bringing up a country on the bottle like a motherless child instead of being breast fed from its native soil."

"Are you going to be a farmer, Jimmie?" asked Robert.

"It looks like it."

The boy at least did not sound aggrieved.

"The farm will about last John's time," said Ben, "but I don't know about Jimmie's unless something turns up to make it more worth while."

Grace was admiring the crochet border of the cloth.

"Is this some of Ella's work?"

"No, it's not as new as that. That was done by John's mother. Hasn't it kept well?"

"That'll be above a good fifty years old," said Ben, "like somebody else I could mention."

"It does us good to use our nicest things," said Grace smoothly, especially if it is something that can be washed. Perhaps some afternoon, Mrs Northcroft, you might find time to come and look at my Chinese embroideries. They're nearly all white, too. You've to look very closely to realise the variety and the neatness of the stitches."

"Thank you. I'd love to come," said Annie.

Robert was paying special attention to Jimmie. In this household Jimmie's character was his destiny in that he could crush or be crushed. It is very trying being the hope of one's side, as the weight of expectation can be a crippling burden. Jimmie might turn out silent like his father or assertive like his grandfather. So Robert asked questions that could not be answered by a monosyllable and drew the lad out. How was the formation of the concert party going and was there enough variety of talent? A funny man was essential.

Annie listened, with pleasure.

Then what was Jimmie saying?

"Farming seems to be all I know, but if this place is petering out, I'd like to try my luck in Canada."

Robert, to whom the world was a parish, replied without

excitement.

"Oh yes, youth is the time for experiment."

Annie interrupted sharply.

"There seems to be enough work on this farm to take up all our waking hours. It isn't the young blood we can spare."

Ben snorted but said nothing.

Annie was ill at ease. If it hadn't been cutting off her nose to spite her face, she'd almost have liked to see them lacking Jimmie's help.

John pushed his thrice emptied cup away and waxed communicative.

"When I was in Belgium that time, the woman of the farm where we stabled our horses made a fortune just from that. Manure, you know. They know how to work it there."

He had shot his bolt and left it to sink in.

"We know how to work it here," thundered Ben. "It's low returns that are killing us. People want their food dirt cheap, even if those that grow it work all round the clock. Now look at coal. Coal's been going up for years and is still going up and people pay it. Pity the poor miner! Nobody says 'Pity the poor farmer'. Yet how many people know what processes milk goes through before it's considered fit for us to drink! A good clean life, they say to us, washing cows down on a dark morning. I don't know where they get the idea of its being clean!"

"Am I really listening at first hand," said Grace, "to a real farmer's authentic grumble?"

"There'll be plenty more to follow," went on Ben. "It's putting too much faith in human nature for a country to depend on others for its food. Anybody knows that if one hand holds the full spoon, the other is the whip hand."

Robert now asked how many times a year Ben preached.

"Perhaps only twice a year at our own place," he answered ruefully. "But I go round the district a bit you know, filling vacancies. I expect most of us here work seven days a week at one thing or another."

"Like our horses," murmured Jimmie.

"And I suppose, Mrs Northcroft," said Grace, "that just as the miner gets unlimited coal, you get an abundance of good things for the larder! You all look so very healthy and so does this table."

Before Annie could reply, Ben broke in.

"What we eat we don't sell. What I should really like to see is a fair and decent wage for everybody and no perquisites. I think it would strengthen human dignity and brotherhood if miners got a good wage and paid for their coal like the rest of us; and likewise, if railwaymen had a good wage and no tips or free tickets. The same in other walks of life, such as waitresses, telegraph boys, taxi drivers and all else."

"I agree with you entirely," said Robert.

"And further," went on Ben, "if you don't mind my saying so, why should ministers not pay rents and rates like everybody else?"

"The houses are church property," said Annie quickly and anxious for her guests.

"Yes, but what happens when ministers grow old and retire? They've had no experience of these things and the world suddenly seems a terribly strange and expensive place. I've seen it happen. We've all heard of the Worn Out Minister's Fund. Well, that'll help to wear 'em out more!"

"It's an awful name for a fund, isn't it?" said Annie.

"Perhaps you've never seen the type that have really worn themselves out," answered her father-in-law. "I have, and there were plenty of 'em when I was young. They believed they were their brother's keeper and would have to answer for other men's ignorance. That kept them sweating under their collars!"

"Well, please don't start," Annie cut in, "on Mr Stormalong and the others whose collars were limp and wet after each service. They were old fashioned and have gone out."

"I'm old fashioned and I'm not out!"

She was terrified of anything he might say that would seem to criticise the quiet style of the new minister and so after making sure that even Jimmie would not accept further sustenance, she rose and ushered the party from the feast.

When they were seated in the more spacious front parlour across the passage, Grace looked about her with enjoyment.

"This is a room where anybody trying to recover from a nervous breakdown would find peace."

"Whatever made you think of that?" cried Annie laughing.

"Well, you know how some rooms react on you if you let them. They could get on our nerves. This is different. And fancy the sampler coming back into fashion again!"

Grace turned her head to admire the embroidered pictures.

"The sampler with a difference, Mrs Garner. There's nothing about early death or vale of tears about these. I take a magazine that makes a special feature of royal occasions and so on. They're rather cheerful to do in the winter evenings."

"I don't know how you find the time," said Grace, "looking after three generations as you do. And you've kept the old stone fireplace, too. It does look well. Sometimes inherited furniture is just the sins of the fathers visited upon the children, but all this is absolutely in keeping. I don't go in for ancestor worship myself but I must admit that I like to be invited to tea at an old house."

"There's a bit of history attached to this place, Mrs Garner. In this very room my grandparents held the prayer meetings and services for Methodist folk before the first chapel was built in these parts."

"Cottage meetings must have been very friendly and comfortable. We have them in the villages in China, you know," said Robert.

"We have more expensive premises now but we don't fill them."

"Why not, in our particular church?" enquired Robert anxiously.

"Not many of our members live near the chapel. It's as if people like to *go* to church. It's a walk; somewhere to go. But if it's on their doorstep they walk away from it."

"And then," said Annie, "too many of the old members moved right away, right out of the district. They'd helped to build the place up and then in their later years they moved further out where it *wasn't* built up."

"Is much visiting done?"

"We have house to house canvassing. Dollie and Jenny Leat have walked miles knocking at doors in all weathers."

"What about the young men?" asked the minister, glancing at Jimmie.

Ben made a throaty sound as though about to spit, but refrained.

"We try to keep a connection between the school and the chapel. The good voices are brought into the choir and the older boys and girls encouraged to become full members. When a young man has been an efficient school official, he's asked to take some form of stewardship. Sometimes he prefers to stick to teaching. That's what I did. I had my vote in the Leaders' Meeting and so on, and I preached as a Local, but my real work lay with the school. That was our only chance with some youngsters before they broke away and never came back."

The minister nodded sadly. Then Ben added a more cheerful testimony.

"But many a poor dying soul has croaked a verse of a hymn he learned in Sunday School, even if he'd never been in a place of worship since. Ask the Salvation Army!"

"Between the stirrup and the ground," quoted Annie with a look of satisfaction.

"I'll tell you something else," went on Ben dramatically; "You know all this talk of church unity? Well, I'm agin it. A team, yes! But one unit, no! Little differences of opinion are healthy and natural and they form individual nesting boxes for souls. As a farmer, I've noticed that, in nature, things are always joining together and then breaking up again. It's the same with church denominations. Lump them all together and funny little offshoots will start sprouting again. It's a continuous process and I'll never hold with any legislation that tries to stop, speed up, or in any way interfere with such a sensible airing of the parts."

"Indeed," exclaimed Robert, encouraging the old man to enlarge on his opinions.

"Ay! Let's all belong to *the* Church by membership of a church."

"Quite," the minister nodded. "The whole includes the parts."

"And we don't want the parts all alike. These differences satisfy someone's conscience who might stay outside a dictatorial church. Better to agree to differ than that all hell should be let loose in an endeavour to agree."

"An agreed church may not be a dictatorial church," argued Robert mildly.

"There'd be doubt all round the fringe and that fringe always being sat on. Let them non-conform with each other's respect if not with each other's blessing."

"Truth certainly owes a great deal to the doubters and even to the heretics," began Robert.

"Time was," interrupted Grace with a smiling aside, "when all the best people were excommunicated."

Robert inclined his head to acknowledge her remark and then went on.

"But even so, Mr Northcroft, I should always look towards the time of a united front. In the world parish, facing great religions such as Islam, Hinduism and Buddhism, we can't much longer splay out in a delta of denominations. Traffic gets trapped on the mud flats. We must conjoin in a mighty river of faith that keeps moving."

"And I think John Wesley would strongly approve," said Grace with some emphasis. "Things have changed so much for the better since his long working day, and whenever I read the marvellous all-embracing Liturgy, I think we ought to get those prayers back into our worship even if they come in gaiters."

"But we mustn't force it," argued Ben. "We're like children in matters of religion; we sometimes fall out amongst ourselves, but if a child flings itself out of the room that's not so serious as rushing out of the house and getting lost. That's where the denominations score; they keep plenty of rooms aired for the children feeling a bit out of sorts."

The minister was delighted to talk with the old campaigner who had spoken with great feeling and he nodded sympathetically.

"And how," asked Annie, "are you liking *your* house? You're not wanting to rush out of it?"

"Oh, it's quite compact, thank you. Not too many rooms to keep aired! And electricity is the answer to practically everything in these days."

She glanced aloft and stopped short. There was no gas or electric fitting pendant from the ceiling, but from the cream painted beam hung a capacious oil lamp. Her jaw dropped slightly and Annie followed her gaze.

"It hasn't begun to answer anything at all here yet. My father-in-law thinks they charge too much for bringing it into the house."

"But it's worth every penny," urged Grace, quite scandalised. "Look at the work and dirt it would save."

"I like lamps," commented Ben stubbornly. "Good for the eyes. And the best cooked meat's been fired. My wife managed this way and very well too."

"But if it's there for the asking," went on Grace, "it seems a shame not to take advantage of it. It would halve the work of the housewife."

"While she's doing that, she's doing nothing else."

Grace flushed with annoyance and looked rather hard at Annie's husband to see what his feeling was on the matter, but John had stretched out his legs and was studying his toecaps.

Annie had seen the look shot in her husband's direction and was nettled. Not for worlds would she show any eagerness for electricity, or that she noticed John's entire lack of partisanship.

"Oh, it all seems to fit in. Jimmie, shall we have a tune or two?"

The upright piano was old, but it served. Behind the fretwork grille and taut pleats of green silk, the gallant hammers sprang to attention at Annie's bidding, glad of the exercise, although occasionally one of the old gold keys, when struck firmly down, lacked the resilience to line up again without a quick chuck under the chin.

Grace watched curiously. An ardent but not rabid feminist, she was always glad to see women enjoying happiness and dignity and she understood that the best things that Annie Northcroft had got from marriage were the power of household management and the pride in her one child. The mother tried to endow him with all that she missed in her partner; demonstrative affection, consideration, mutual under-standing and social grace. That these attributes were there in part, satisfied Mrs Northcroft it would seem and if ever a woman gave value in return for her stall, she did.

Three short pieces were earnestly rendered before twilight obscured the music page and as the listeners sat in the privacy of reverie, the battle between the firelight and the retreating sun gradually resolved itself and the pastel shades faded from the room, leaving walls and ceiling flickering in a glowing triumph. The silver in the glass cabinet winked fitfully or gleamed sharp as a lighthouse beam and the raised numerals and metal hands of the clock flashed gold as they helio-graphed the passing hour.

"As charming to the sight as to the ear," said Robert gallantly as the music stopped. "To sit with friends comfortably digesting a happy meal to the sound of sweet music is one of the higher pleasures of life."

He might have been describing his Chinese vase.

Annie returned the worn pages to the cavity in the stool with feelings of elation.

"It has been delightful, Mrs Northcroft," said Grace with more than usual sincerity. "We've had a lovely time but now I'm afraid we must be going."

The usual deterrents were uttered by Annie with greater meaning on her side also, but the visitors rose.

"What a lovely sky!"

All turned to look over the intervening bit of croft to the road and the autumn afterglow above it, dusky with either smoke or cloud.

"Oh, look, and there are young Mr Sinclair and Sybil coming home from a game. We know Sybil well of course."

"Does young Sinclair do much for the church?" asked the minister.

"Nowt!" answered Ben. "His father does all that."

"Anything in the school?"

'No."

"I expect his studies take up a great deal of his time," said Annie, watching the couple go briskly by.

"Dr Bedser's a busy man but he manages to give us a sermon now and then. Alfred Sinclair's made a pile of money and a good bit has gone on that son of his. Let's hope it'll be worth it."

Grace now smiled archly at the speaker.

"Light is worth paying for, Mr Northcroft, whether it is material light or the light of knowledge. Mr Sinclair has the right idea what to do with his pile."

Annie turned sharply from the window and the others drew away.

As the minister and his wife walked home in the dallying light they were saying how much they had enjoyed the visit.

"What a wonderful old boy the grandfather is," said Robert. "I'd really like to hear him preach."

"Antiquated old skinflint!" answered Grace. "I shouldn't be surprised if he's got as much in the bank as Mr Sinclair but he doesn't want the younger ones to get hold of it. To him, money is power. That woman ought to rebel."

"Why should she rebel, my dear? She is a real queen there."

"Queen she may be but she would appreciate a king born to the purple; not a puppet king."

"Oh, we're all that where our wives are concerned," said Robert, glancing down at her. "John's a very sound man. But perhaps sound is hardly the right word."

"Isn't Jimmie the picture of health? He came in soon after his grandfather and as he stood in the doorway with two great cabbages under his arm, he looked the personification of plenty. There's one in that carrier bag, by the way, with a pot of jam. It struck me, looking at him, that Adam was a nobler creature, more in the image of his creator, when toiling by the sweat of his brow than when mooning about in the Garden of Eden."

"He'll probably go to Canada."

"Don't you say any more about that in his mother's hearing, Robert. She's frightened to death of that happening. But he ought to try being a millstone himself instead of being caught between the others. He doesn't know the strength of his position, only its weakness."

"He will in a year or two."

"Well, his mother has a good half of the realm and she'd be happy for Jimmie to have the other half if John Northcroft doesn't show any sign of wanting it. What will happen when Jimmie is old enough to marry, I don't know. I can't see two crowns or two wedding rings in that kitchen."

"But in the meantime, my dear, old Ben is still king of the castle, or in this case perhaps the term is cock o' the midden!"

Chapter Eleven

Geoffrey Sinclair staggered into the church with a huge plant pot of tall chrysanthemums, two of which were to flank the choir stalls like sentinels. They marked the limits of the exuberant masses of flowers and fruit that spread across all the communion space and surged up the sides of the pulpit like colourful pirates boarding an old wooden merchant ship. Hanging from the reading desk of the pulpit and backed by the red and gold of the velvet drape, were the most luscious black grapes imaginable, a great temptation to any preacher conducting the Harvest Festival service. It was as if a luxury market had been opened in the church as the produce piled up and the floor became littered with boxes, tissue paper, stripped leaves and broken stems. Mrs Ginnell darted round mopping up any little spill of water as soon as it occurred and enjoying it all, because she knew of old that everything would be left tidy and clear when the display was perfected.

The communion rail was topped all round with alternate red and green apples. The cushions had been removed and instead of kneeling communicants, there were flaming pot plants closely arrayed, their best sides turned towards the pews.

"A bit more that way," Clara Martland called softly to Geoffrey, waving her hand. "Hello, Alfred, how is it looking?" she added as Sinclair senior appeared at her side.

"First rate," responded Alfred. "I see you've left a space for the wheat sheaf."

"It'll be along presently. I think Ernest is wanting Geoffrey to help with the pillars. And Alfred, you might see that those doing the gallery don't cover the clock face."

"That was a time, wasn't it? He went on and on, not seeing the clock. Good evening, Mr Garner. You're going to be surrounded with all good gifts tomorrow."

"Indeed, yes. We haven't enough sick members to receive all this, surely?"

"We'll get rid of most tomorrow night," said Clara, "and then sell the remainder on Monday. Mr Sinclair is generally our good auctioneer."

There is a tendency to make Harvest Festivals as inclusive and far fetched as possible. To the glass of water representing rain have been added lumps of coal, logs and oil to signify gratitude for warmth, and coastal churches are made unbearable by fish or fishing nets, the unusual sight bringing as many outsiders as the smell keeps away.

"What about a packet of cigarettes?" asked Geoffrey, joining the party at the front. "Tobacco is a fruit of the earth."

"Geoffrey!" said Clara.

"Not so much a fruit as a weed," answered Robert smiling at the young man. "A fragrant weed, but a noxious weed. We couldn't sell that here on Monday night any more than we could sell opium from poppy seeds."

"It's all a kind of incense," said Geoffrey. "And why can we have apples but not cider, grapes but not wine? We can go so far but no further, when the spirit of adventure in us is always driving us to go further!"

"But all those avenues have been explored long ago," said the minister. "It is because those things have been taken further, to their bitter end, in other and ancient religious ceremonies, that we don't let them have even a beginning here now."

Clara smiled. Geoffrey wasn't going to have it all his own way all the time. He was not abashed.

"Look at Mrs Martland holding those grapes aloft. She would be scandalised to think of herself as a Bacchante, but she only needs flowers in her hair to look the part."

Alfred was stirred by old recollections.

"A flower in her hair suits Mrs Martland very well," he rumbled.

"Yes," went on Geoffrey, enjoying himself, "it's really just a primitive earth worship, a thanksgiving for a full crop in every sense of the word."

Robert was looking ministerial by this time.

"Gratitude is a noble emotion," he said. "Man's thankfulness is no less fervent because he has more understanding of how the miracle works. What the pagan started in blindness, we are continuing in light."

Clara was glad to see old Mr Northcroft coming up the aisle carrying a bundle that everybody recognised as the wheatsheaf loaf in

110

a startlingly white cloth.

Geoffrey ostentatiously removed the lid from the font, but at a look from old Ben, he replaced it with less eclat and sauntered off to the gallery where he found Jimmie Northcroft.

"Ah, can I help with the greenery gallery or gallery greenery? What sort of a harvest has it been this year, by the way?"

"Not very great," muttered Jimmie without looking up from his work.

"But you'll turn up tomorrow to see what a little sarcasm will do?"

They tied lengths of foliage with raffia for some time in silence, Geoffrey really concentrating on his job until his father hastened down the aisle and called up to him.

"Watch that clock now!"

Sure enough, the moon face of the clock was peeping as through the branches of a thick tree. Geoffrey sighed at having to unveil it.

Where the gallery joined the wall by the choir, the green leaves were finished off with great full-stops of dark grapes. Connie Ginnell was attending to one side with elaborate grace. Jimmie had been planning to approach her with a casual air in the sight of all the people and as he edged slowly round the gallery, Geoffrey walked over to her smiling.

"Do I see Miss Ginnell treading the wine press alone? What do you do with the stones, Connie? I'm sure these bunches have gone smaller."

Connie's chin went up.

"She can't speak because her mouth is full. Poets and artists always prefer a heroine who has a full mouth, so they say; perhaps so she won't talk so much. Is the other cheek as rounded as at this side? Just look this way, Connie."

But the cheek at this side only went a deeper pink and Connie would not turn from her tying of raffia.

He stood looking at the scene below. Mrs Ginnell was folding up flower wrappings and occasionally retreating through a vestry door with a pile of paper. Miriam Crumps was waiting to see exactly what would be done with her grapes so that she could look at them occasionally during the service next day. Leonard Martland had long ago resigned from active work with the plants and was now at the organ playing over the voluntaries for the morrow, the tilted mirror above the keyboard reflecting an unwonted green from the pulpit sides. He had the electric light on there behind his little curtain, but the choir stalls in their ingle-nook behind the pulpit were rather dim, and then came the blaze of slanting evening sunlight on the banked flowers and fruit, some of them with an added depth of colour from the rich stain of the windows, others looking unrealistic in a wash of unfamiliar sea-green; fruit offered by mermaids.

The wheaten loaf was now reclining on a sloping bed with a white crochet worked cloth of Antella's as an under-sheet. The sheaf was thirty inches high and took pride of place. At first sight one might think it a marvellous imitation, a romantic artist's ideal of what a wheatsheaf should be. It was, however, made of bread; a baked loaf. Perhaps it had been set in a mould, its symmetry was so perfect? No. Every stalk and ear had been laid on separately before being placed in the oven. This beautifully crusted brown and cream bas-relief was daily bread proved and put to rise and tried by fire, emerging in artistry; the staff of life, richly carved, flowering into beauty as Tannhauser's staff had budded and leaved on his pilgrimage.

The workers in the body of the church had almost finished and were gazing at the general effect. Round each slender pillar supporting the galleries there was loosely twined a green snake of foliage, a reminder perhaps of the serpent that once wrought havoc in Eden. Swags of hydrangeas festooned the gallery frontals.

"A lot of that stuff came from the Buckley's," said Geoffrey to Connie.

"Are they here? I don't know them."

"No, they're not here. The lorry called at their place after leaving ours. They've certainly got a lovely garden."

"So mother says," said Connie, and then stopped - red and uncomfortable. But Geoffrey had not noticed anything. He looked down at the communion rail. There his parents had been married. There he had been christened. Some day he would stand there with Sybil. She would come up this nearer aisle below him now, gift-wrapped on her father's arm, to music from this organ, although her father would not be playing it that day. Heaven only knew when that day would be! Perhaps only another year?

A faint sound of footsteps approaching on the iron grilles and patterned tiles caused Geoffrey to glance down as Sybil with David Garner came slowly round to the centre of the front pews, murmuring words of admiration apparently and gently agreeing with each other.

"I've seen it every year for as long as I can remember," Sybil was saying, "but it always gives me a new shock of pleasure. It isn't really autumn yet, is it? The Harvest Festival always seems to catch me when I'm not looking."

"Oh, no. You'll get lots of tennis weather yet. The summer's only looking over its shoulder, so to speak, at the pleasant way it has come.

It's not saying goodbye."

"Good," exclaimed Sybil. He was touched at her brief dismissal of the subject. Only that morning he had noticed the virginia creeper darkening on the walls of the College, with patches already smouldering here and there, not quite aflame, like burning string preparing to touch off a firework. But of this he said nothing.

Clara Martland turned and caught sight of them just as Mrs Ginnell also gave them a glance, and both mothers involuntarily turned their eyes towards the gallery where Geoffrey and Connie were standing immovable, gazing down, caught in one of those unaccountable, helpless silences.

Other eyes, looking round the floral decorations, had come to rest on the two standing at this garden gate in all the vulnerable indiscretion of innocence.

Miriam Crumps withdrew her gaze from criticising the placing of her grapes and bent it sourly upon her nephew's sweetheart. It was just like Clara Martland's daughter to be so thick with the young minister. Like her mother, she always seemed to have the opposite sex somewhere around. She herself, and Ada, thought but poorly of the opposite sex, who never seemed to appreciate where true merit lay. Sybil Martland ought not to be gossiping there for everybody to see, but ought to run up to the gallery to find Geoffrey. Miriam wouldn't have looked any the less acidly upon the girl for that, but at least a Martland would have been running after a man of Miriam's family instead of the men of Miriam's family running after a Martland or Crossley, generation after generation. And running after was unseemly, very different from a discreet and cunning creep.

If Miriam was spiteful towards the handsome Martlands she absolutely detested the Ginnells. There was something in their eyes when they looked at her that put her on edge. When Miriam looked at anybody, she liked them to know that they were being put in the balance and for the most part found wanting. She was sure that Ernest Ginnell went for a drink of beer before putting the school or lecture hall to rights after a social evening, and she couldn't get over the shock she had received when, meeting him in the Sunday School porch one night, she had given him a hard and knowing look and he had winked at her! She didn't seem to fare any better with Mrs Ginnell either. She had upon occasion given a little homily on total abstinence and wifely exhortation. Mrs Ginnell had listened drily without argument, but at the end she had said she must go and attend to Ginnell's supper now, as she thought it was a wife's first duty to keep her husband alive and well.

113

But Connie was a different subject. To Miriam, modesty was synonymous with guilt and she could at any time raise a blush on Connie's cheek by an admonitory glance. Indeed most of Miriam's glances were admonitory, for to her mind everything and everybody was fraught with guilt unless proved otherwise, and a wisp of smoke was warning of a blazing conflagration. So she peered and sniffed around continually, ever the first - and perhaps the only one - to shout "Fire!"

Although any householder or camper struggling with ill prepared equipment to light a fire knows that there can be volumes of smoke with little or no result in his primary aim, he also has noted that flame sometimes travels up smoke. Thus a rumour can start an event and a suggestion germinate a fact.

Connie's throat had gone dry.

"There's Mrs Crumps," she remarked hoarsely.

"Ah! My sainted aunt," said Geoffrey. "Strange, isn't it, that there are worse family ties than those we get at Christmas? I wonder if I could interest her in demonology. Or interest demonology in her."

He blew her a kiss, which made her turn uneasily away.

His eyes ranging the church still, he spoke idly again to Connie.

"Are you singing tomorrow?"

"I'm singing in the morning, Sybil at night, as you'd know if you looked at the notices you were sent."

"I'm always waiting for one of those rousing drinking songs you're continually promising us."

"What on earth do you mean?"

Connie turned a face from which astonishment had ousted all suspicion.

"You know, that one where you sing 'I've songs for camp and bar and hall'. We've had the hall, but no camp and bar."

Connie turned away again.

"It's bower," she said shortly.

"How my ears deceive me," lamented Geoffrey.

Sybil had not yet looked up. When she did, how swiftly and lightly would she make her way back down the aisle to the stairs. He felt warm with well-being and a touch of veneration stirred him. This church had produced some splendid people. Some highly desirable girls, too. The throng below was indicative of the friendships matured over years of common loves and service. It explained how the money came in. This place was a part, and an important part, of their lives. His father gave generously and was glad to do so. He could see him chatting to Leonard Martland who had stopped playing and was pointing in a deprecatory manner to some of the organ stops. Alfred was nodding sombrely. Even if adequate church funds exist in the bank, a Circuit Steward hasn't to be too quick on the draw!

Just then David directed Sybil's attention to Geoffrey and Connie in the gallery. They all four smiled and raised a hand and then Sybil and David went on with their conversation.

"Ah, there's Garner," Geoffrey observed easily. "I'll go down and have a word with him before he goes."

He moved away past Jimmie Northcroft who did not look, and went downstairs, sauntering up the aisle to the others.

"Have you ever seen such a gorgeous display, Garner? I must be here on Monday night, too. A nation of shop-keepers we may be, but if we count the cost, we also count the change fairly and sell good stuff. This is a sight for the gods."

Sybil shot a half apologetic glance at David, as if asking him to make allowances for something.

"Such, I suppose, was the original intention," he said affably.

Sybil now looked at Geoffrey as if inviting him to admire something.

"Look at these fine apples," Geoffrey went on. "Brides in the bath; cheap at eight pence per pound come Monday. Oh, 'Beauties of Bath' are they? Well, one thing leads to another as the conquering Romans doubtless knew."

David turned aside his head and caught sight of the wood and bronze circular plaque wreathed with laurel and underlined with flowers, now gleaming faintly under the southern gallery.

"The War Memorial looks very well, too," he said to Sybil.

"It is a nice one, isn't it?"

There was a pause and Geoffrey gave a derisory smile.

"I doubt if there could be such a thing as a *nice* war memorial. If it's nice, as you call it, it certainly wouldn't commemorate war."

Sybil looked chastened and fell silent.

"I think," said David, "it *is* a nice design. Of course a Cenotaph represents the nation's sorrow, but these short lists of well known names are very personal and they jog our memory more frequently."

"Do you remember," enquired Geoffrey, ignoring the other's better manners, "those awful little brackets perched high upon street corners? They didn't last long. They soon grew shabby and neglected, but they pointed a terribly harsh moral; that nothing goes out of fashion more quickly than a war and those broken and forgotten pots of basil were the best all-round commentary."

"And I don't know," said David, "that I'm too keen on the practice

115

of putting money so raised to the buying of playing fields and sports pavilions. Some good is sometimes produced from evil, but it does seem as if someone's cashing in on it."

"I know," responded Geoffrey. "It appeals to the commercial instinct. We say, 'Look what we've got out of all this mess; a lovely recreation ground.' It makes it seem as if all was not in vain."

David nodded in agreement.

"I'm not a committed pacifist, but I think we should nurture our one per cent of pacifists; we may be glad of them some day. I was once talking in hospital to a masseur and his job was to keep a patient's muscles supple and so hasten mobility after an operation. Our Leagues and Unions may seem rather futile sometimes but they help to keep our minds receptive to movement after a terrible ordeal."

The three stood looking at the plaque rather solemnly until Geoffrey spoke in robust comment.

"Ah well! We are all pacifists between wars or until the other fellow hits us. And I agree that we should tolerate the fractional percentage as they keep us from being one hundred per cent unanimous, which always reminds me of the Gadarene swine!"

The young minister rested a hand on the end of the pew and continued to look serious.

"Even in the church we are divided on this subject. I think that if Christ had wanted to say something about pacifism he would have taken the opportunity when the centurion came to Him and said, 'My servant is ill: but do not come to my house, only say the word.' The response to that was 'I have never met faith like this anywhere in Israel.' Is survival the main object and shall we have to discontinue practising Christianity in order to survive to preach it? That would be unthinkable. I suspect that is why we now substitute the word civilisation for Christianity. We are prepared to defend civilisation at all costs, but we're not sure how far one goes to preserve Christianity."

"It all boils down to fair play for the defeated and the minority. You'll know the parable of the good Samaritan better than I do, but as a non-combatant he behaved admirably and left the pursuit of the bandits to the Roman soldiers whose duty it was to preserve order. Civilians should always be civil to each other!"

The speakers were addressing their argument to each other until Sybil interposed.

"Mr Buckley says that if hefty war memorials were pushed where practically everybody fell over them, in the way of traffic and blocking the best views, then people might begin to think how to get rid of them and also what they stood for."

"Who is Mr Buckley?" asked David, who had turned to her instantly.

"To put it vulgarly, her boss," answered Geoffrey. "I don't think the Buckleys show up here nowadays. They send donations and boscage, but the actual presence was withdrawn to Chorltonville some years ago."

"But he's awfully nice, I mean good," said Sybil loyally. "And so is she. She came once to the office after it had been decorated and I made her some tea."

"Awfully nice, I mean good, of her to swallow it," commented Geoffrey. "She was very keen on lawn tennis, I believe, and that's why they settled at Chorltonville. What a name!"

"Your family moved out too, but keep in close touch," said David. "It's fine when people stay and build up their community, then the next generation takes over automatically."

"Does it? I seem to be Ginnell's henchman, generally," said Geoffrey looking about him, "but fortunately for me at the moment, he's withdrawn to join the laddies."

"Don't you find that people such as ourselves, for instance, more or less follow in their forebears' footsteps?"

"If we fancy the direction in which they're going, but we don't all want to end up by Saint Agnes' fountain. Doubtless you, born with an Apostle spoon in your mouth, will go that way round."

At that moment Alfred Sinclair came out of the minister's vestry and moved towards the trio.

"Is your father about, David? I'd like to show him the registers if he's interested. There are some marriages here at which his old friend the Rev. Cyrus Stormalong officiated."

"I can see him from here," answered Sybil. "I'll go and tell him," and she obligingly moved away.

"It's very good of you," continued Alfred, "to give up an evening's study to join us tonight."

The young man flushed slightly and Geoffrey regarded him levelly.

"He's not giving up any study. We're all part of it, aren't we, Garner?"

"In a way. I'm learning church procedure at any rate and this evening has been very instructive. There must be a strong aesthetic sense in people who can arrange a tableau like that. Just look at it."

As they stood facing that small tropical island of colour, Robert Garner was approaching with his hand affectionately on Sybil's shoulder.

"This angelic messenger bids my presence here. Ah! Geoffrey. How good it is to see you young men here."

"Your son's just been pointing out how easily the mantle of leadership falls on our shoulders, but so far my hereditary duties have been scene shifting with the heavier plant pots."

"Never mind," answered Robert. "So long as we older ones can see the line of succession we are not anxious about the future, are we, Mr Sinclair? I was wondering, Geoffrey, if you would address the Senior Sunday School one afternoon in the near future? Old Mr Whitham generally alternates with Mr Northcroft but his cough is troublesome at the moment and it will be difficult for him to take his superintendent duties yet awhile."

Mr Whitham had taught in the Sunday School for over forty years. He had left day school at twelve years old, but he held the turbulent Young Men's Class in the hollow of his hand.

Sybil blushed with pleasure and Geoffrey with consternation as the minister made his request and pursued his theme.

"We look to you young men with a longer education to throw a new light on the old lessons."

"There!" exclaimed Sybil happily. "You talk to him, Mr Garner! I've asked him several times, but he won't for me."

Her face showed that if he would do it for somebody else, she would be just as pleased.

There was a stupefied silence before Robert spoke again.

"I could ask a colleague but we cannot hope for a divine to succeed where such a divinity has not. But at the moment I'm wanted in the vestry I believe."

The quintet fell apart as Alfred Sinclair turned and led the way to the vestry, rumbling something about "studies taking large part of his time, he supposed."

Geoffrey turned suddenly to the girl.

"Are you ready?"

"Are we going?" She looked round at the thinning numbers. "Well, I suppose so, if you are."

"I've stayed too long already. Goodnight," he called and steered Sybil out of reach of any handshake had it been proffered and took her swiftly down the aisle and out.

"I'll run you home but I'll have to get straight back for my father."

"Well, don't bother. I'll wait for the others."

"Oh, get in."

As he drove up Oldham Road neither spoke and Sybil unhappily wondered if he really were overworking and she and others had been making tactless demands on him.

118

"I do think," Geoffrey observed, his words appearing like a bunch of withered leaves at the end of a long, bare branch, "that a clergyman should not take his harp to a party; or at least keep it decently slung behind him."

Sybil's eyes widened.

"But they've got to. That is their job. You can't expect them to leave the hall when the harp is passed round, like poor Caedmon." Then she smiled, but for once did not share her private amusement. Would the tune be Ripon?

Jimmie Northcroft at last got round to Connie, who at that moment was leaning slightly forward over the gallery to watch the unexpectedly quick departure of Sybil and Geoffrey.

"It's all done, I think. Care to go across to the Playhouse? I don't know what's on but we'd be in time for the second house."

"Oh," said Connie, surprised. "Now? Well, I wouldn't mind. As you say, it's all done."

Since the Playhouse Cinema was only a few yards away at the crossroads, she did know what was on but forbore to air her knowledge. *Grapes of Desire* had been advertised in purple and gold on the hoardings for the last three days.

"I'll see you home afterwards," offered Jimmie, which sent the girl into fits of giggles. Looking up, Mrs Ginnell saw that Connie was looking brighter; a few minutes ago she had been looking as if she'd lost a shilling and only found sixpence.

Alfred had already returned to the vestry while Robert and David followed slowly.

"There's a great vocation for service just running to waste there," said the young minister severely and Robert nodded, not mistaking the subject of his son's remark.

Alfred had opened the safe in the vestry and the big books were placed upon the table.

"You'll find us all mentioned there," he said, "in one capacity or another."

They examined the changed styles of handwriting, the fiddle 'S' and copperplate giving way to more full-fed lettering.

Alfred pointed out his parents' marriage entry amongst the first named and ran his finger down the pages to the couplings of his contemporaries, reading them aloud of course.

"And there's Mr Stormalong's signature. He was here for Temperance Sunday that year and he married my sister-in-law and her husband on the Saturday; the last wedding before this church was registered and his first ceremony, I believe. Ah, he was a very forceful preacher. You knew when he was around."

"So I have heard people say! Yes, he left College the year before I did. His standing up for service in the Foreign Field made a tremendous impression. He'd always been such a wag. I saw him in those days manage the neatest bit of double crossing I've ever seen. He got most of us out on the lawn to watch, but of course our presence had to seem casual. Then a man within was called to his study window on the ground floor and told to observe something immediately below on the flower bed. He leaned out and from the window directly above him a man emptied a vase of water on to him. But to our joy, the window above *him* now showed a second man in readiness who emptied a whole jug on to the first offender. But at the very top was Stormalong himself with his wash-pot! We cheered and danced below while all four men hung shaking across their window-sills, their arms down like Punch knocked on the head. Someone had to help Stormalong lift in his basin, he was so weak."

"Ah," said Alfred, laughing heartily, "we could see when he came here that he was full of life."

"He would be ordained a year before I was. We always remember our first wedding, we are more nervous than the bride and groom. That would be in . . . "

Robert bent over the register.

"Perhaps you mean that Mrs Crumps' wedding was the first *after* this church was registered and a Registrar need not be present?"

Alfred was startled into silence for a moment and then recollected.

"Young Mr Stormalong was quite willing to take on all the paperwork."

Silence fell again.

Robert hung over the page a moment or two longer and then straightened up.

"Mrs Crumps is a widow and childless, is she not? Don't mention a word to her or anyone, but it's always a point to watch. Occasionally there's a slip and Stewards have to be very careful."

Robert shut the register and Alfred replaced it in the safe. After putting the keys in his pocket he stood awkwardly for a moment.

"I can't think there's anything wrong there."

"No, oh no!" agreed Robert. "After all this time nobody would be affected. Ah, Stormalong," he admonished with a tender smile, "always eager to help. Ah, here's Mr Ginnell wanting to lock up for the night. It's been a busy day for you today, but rewarding, I hope."

Clara and Leonard were ready and waiting to walk home with the minister. Clara looked at the scene with satisfaction. All was in order;

not a thing needed another touch. Ginnell flicked off the main lights and stood by the switch box in the vestibule.

"Fancy! Another Harvest Festival here," said Clara reflectively as they stood looking at the full effect from the inner door. "I'm sorry summer's over."

"Are you too tired to walk home?" asked Leonard.

"No, I don't think so. I shall be sitting down tomorrow. Another full day; full to overflowing!"

At last the place was empty and Ginnell placed the key in the outer door before stepping in to turn off the last lights. He had not minded the others loitering as he'd taken steps to make a quick survey of the local hop harvest before closing time. They wouldn't show good beer in here! Young Sinclair might. He talked a lot but some of it was sense. But people like Miriam Crumps wouldn't. Miriam Crumps! The name seemed to cause him some private satisfaction as he locked the studded door and slid the grille.

The harvest moon was huge, hidden from the street by the roof tops, but the upper windows of the chapel were high enough to meet its low set stare, and the softly luminous interior of the deserted church might have been the inside of that melon-coloured lantern.

That ancient and long venerated heavenly body, which in reality was no more worshipful a body than the sphere on which it shed its beams, now filtered its disquieting light through sainted and haloed windows so that it fell washed of all terrors, superstitions and unholiness on to the cool-toned fruit and muted flowers.

It fell on a dedicated harvest, a newer harvest of human and divine charity, working hand in guiding hand. And in the midst was set the show-bread no longer forbidden; life-giving bread that had been placed for a terrible and immortal moment in history, first on a sacrificial altar and then for all time and for all men, on a communal and sacramental table.

f

Chapter Twelve

Early Monday morning to the minister is a time of relaxation, of quietude to reflect upon the new work for the week. To the layman it is the millrace again in which he whirls until the weekend casts him exhausted on to the calm banks of the Sabbath and those same rapids the minister takes in the upstream direction, approaching the Sabbath as a salmon leaps the waterfall in spate. To the layman Sunday is the millpool; to the priest it is the weir.

It was Monday again and Robert lay with his hands clasped behind his head, while Grace switched on the electric kettle, swished back the curtains and reported on the morning.

"No smoke from the rectory chimneys yet. I wonder if they're electrified like us. I do hope so. The church isn't a Mrs Crumps and even the bride of Christ should learn new methods."

"My dear!" said Robert, unclasping his hands.

"And especially not to run into debt," continued Grace.

Robert gave a heartfelt sigh.

"And above all," his wife went on, "if she is poor, she should avoid personal display and extravagant imaginings."

"Leave the poor soul her extravagant imaginings," pleaded Robert. "What have you been hearing in the whispering gallery?"

"Just a rumour that Mr Martland thinks the organ is getting a bit past it! Everybody's horrified of course."

"Hear, hear!" said Robert. "The organ sounds quite all right to me."

"But in the choir they say he often has to wrestle with some of the stops, and repairs cost almost as much as a new organ."

"Ah," said Robert hearing an oft repeated chorus, "that's for the Leaders' Meeting to decide, but personally I'd rather listen to a hurdy-gurdy than be in debt."

"Even if debts can be dignified sometimes, hurdy-gurdies never are."

Robert was disturbed.

"If they want to have a money raising effort, I think the Foreign Missions could do with something urgently."

"Nobody wants an effort with a capital E at all, just now!"

The kettle boiled. Sometimes when Grace switched on her bedroom fire she exclaimed jubilantly, "With all its faults I love my century best!" To the social conscience, the luxury, wealth or privilege of earlier times are no more enviable than the unassuming self help of today. The modern knight no longer needs a squire to assist with the armour, and so far as trappings go, the squire is entitled to buckle on the same handy accoutrement.

Grace took her cup to the table under one window where she sat each morning to study a portion of the Scriptures. She couldn't keep at it for hours in privacy as Robert could, and in her opinion the mark of highest secular power was to pin a notice on one's door, 'Do not Disturb', and know that it would be honoured. But a woman's thought is nearly always second fiddle to action. It follows her about wistfully from duty to duty and gets trodden underfoot and pushed down into the subconscious, where it wanders about delightedly, making inspired and surprising appearances at odd moments like a coalman popping up through a manhole.

She glanced to see if Robert wanted a second cup, but he had closed his eyes and was perhaps thinking. Rodin sculpted his Thinker struggling with an undeveloped power of thought and having to harness his whole body to the effort, but as man's brain became progressively in action, thought became indigenous and ceased to ravage his countenance, no longer presenting the furrowed visage of Huxley's experimental ape, sunk in furious and baffled choice between this or that banana!

"More tea, Robert," she whispered.

"Yes, my dear."

Opinions among church members varied on the subject of the minister's wife not having a maid living in. Mrs Sinclair thought it was an inference of insufficient stipend and so was a reflection upon the church and its officials, including Alfred. Maids living in could be troublesome, but Ada would much rather be troubled with them than troubled without them. Miriam on the other hand, regarded fondness for housework as a virtue, perhaps the brightest and best, so they chewed this cud silently together although very little cream would result.

From the bathroom window Grace could see the Martland's kitchen door and there was Mrs Ginnell, her voice raised in song.

"On the other side of Jordan There is rest for me."

"Where's she got that from?" Grace asked herself as she softly closed the window.

A few minutes later, hearing a slight knock at the front door, she opened it to find Mrs Ginnell there.

"Good morning, Mrs Garner," began Mrs Ginnell rather breathlessly, "since I was doing Mrs Martland's I thought I'd give yours the once over, too."

A protective goodwill suffused her features.

"Why, Mrs Ginnell, that's too kind of you," said Grace, touched.

"It only takes a moment," said Mrs Ginnell. "If you don't care to do it yourself, I will with pleasure."

"It's not that," said Grace defending herself, "it's just that I think the clean stone is sufficient."

"Nothing looks better to a caller than a well stoned step," went on Mrs Ginnell decidedly. "I always did it for Mrs Westaway, the last lady, when the maids left."

Grace felt that Mrs Ginnell quite thought that she had given up all hope of expecting maids to stay.

"As *you* say," went on Mrs Ginnell, "it doesn't do for the minister's house to look neglected, especially opposite the rectory."

Grace felt unwonted emotions stir her bosom, but she soothed them promptly.

"Mrs Ginnell, it's most kind of you to think of us and the welfare of church property. Now, how much will that be per week?"

"Oh, don't bother about that little thing."

On this particular morning when Robert was quiet in his study, an indeterminate but piercing cry rose on the air and Grace hurried down to the back gate. In reality the cry was meant to be "Fresh green watercress, radishes, young onions, fresh green watercress", but only old customers would have guessed. It was the music rather than the words which was recognisable. Neither had the vocalist, at least in November, any fresh green watercress, radishes, young onions or fresh green watercress at all; but the cry was his trademark, his bill heading, his advertisement and the scroll work lettering on plate glass, and those are not changed with the seasons or the fashion or because goods are temporarily out of stock.

The man had been made to realise that at the minister's house they wanted salads all the year round, and on the days when Grace did not appear or after she had returned indoors, he would enliven the little group round his barrow with a new line in salesmanship. "The lady at the chapel house there says we ought to eat more uncooked food. She says it's a gross type of man who only likes meals that have cost someone's sweat. I shall have to start bringing hay round next."

Then the housewives would look curiously at the back windows of the 'chapel house' and wonder if she looked after him properly. When a man came home from Moston Colliery or the Carriage Works, what would he say to a salad? Nevertheless, the greengrocer's barrow was becoming more adventurously stocked and might mean the swapping of a donkey for a pony. Gee up! Fresh green watercress!

A fumbling hit or miss at the front door bell made Grace wonder for a moment if Mrs Ginnell was stealing back for a furtive attack on the brasses. Grace had known other 'helps' who, if anyone tried to alter their routine, couldn't get into the swing of their work but had to go back to the beginning. Like Dr Johnson returning to touch a particular post, they couldn't skip a certain job without perturbation of spirit. But Mrs Ginnell was not the culprit.

It was a pedlar with a tray of cottons and needles and such. He just stood there jerking and making shapes with his mouth, waiting for the housewife to complete the whole business transaction, choosing her purchases from the little ticketed compartments and placing her money in the tin. It was as well to make it a round sum to avoid complications.

Now Grace had a theory and practice of pedlars. She believed that if sufficiently discouraged, pedlars would cease to be. They would make a detrimental mark on the gate and gradually die out. Grace objected to answering the door every half hour throughout the day. She had explained this politely to dozens of itinerant tradesmen, and by dint of perseverance and kindly firmness, she usually got the house free by the time she and Robert were due to move on.

The figure on the step, compared with what Grace had seen in her twenty years in China, was a picture of health and well being. He wasn't being led around by a child as a spectacle in his own right. He was mobile of his own volition and doubtless could be trained to do something other than interrupt busy people. It really was too bad that the unemployed and unemployable should be loosed upon the housewife instead of being dealt with by a special body.

"No thank you," said Grace gently.

The figure seemed surprised and interested, but pushed his tray nearer to Grace and grunted in an imperious manner.

"I do not buy at the door," she went on, "because my husband is studying and the bell constantly ringing disturbs him."

She seemed to have nettled the figure in some way for it became charged with emotion and appeared to be mustering its resources and after a minute of anxious effort, was able to swear at Grace in a quite recognisable way. With an unexpected movement, the man shot out his hand and gave the door bell a vigorous and resounding twist. A look of pleasure and triumph overspread his mutable features as he turned and jogged down the path.

Mrs Ginnell shook a duster out of the window next door to see who had rung with such purpose.

"Oh, everybody buys from him, Mrs Garner. He's dumb, you know."

Grace looked round at her neighbour's bow window.

"I managed to get him to say a few words," she said, and went in.

It wasn't the work, but the interruptions to work that were such a waste of time. Life is a series of interruptions; an endless series of minor interruptions, and most wives, particularly ministers' wives, find they have married the man from Porlock.

Grace went into the front room where, if spit had been reduced to a minimum, a polished performance was still much in evidence. She surveyed it critically. That suite must go for one thing. It had a sort of floral trellis at the back of the sofa and chairs that possessed the dual devilment of grating on the spine and also letting draughts through.

She had lately pondered the idea of getting rid of that suite and buying a more useful set of chairs with one of her modest nest eggs. She would bequeath it to the house when they moved on. If Mrs Ginnell was going to look to the front step whenever she did Mrs Martland's, Grace could show appreciation by giving her the old suite. She had married children who might not mind it.

Yes, she would give it away.

Thinking of Mrs Ginnell's children brought Margaret and David to mind. Margaret's letters were full of life and enjoyment, descriptions of her work and methods. She was obviously happy.

Grace, with her energy of mind and body, naturally admired 'women who did', but she also thought that in a world of better order, there would not be the same need for certain of their efforts. Some feminine triumphs were mere admissions of men's failures. Joan of Arc, Elizabeth Fry, Florence Nightingale, Josephine Butler and Edith Cavell, were great women but were a sign of contemporary deficiency in masculine stature, whereas Queen Elizabeth, Lady Hester Stanhope, Gertrude Bell, Mrs Siddons, would have been of heroic size even in a golden age.

Grace was pleased with her children. They would be loved,

Really, Margaret's nature was akin to that of the girl next door, Sybil Martland. They had something in common. Grace paused in her

126

self-communing. So they had! She remained seated for a time in thought. When she at length got to her feet again she spoke aloud.

"The only way! Christmas in Switzerland."

By three o'clock, the minister's wife was dressed to go out. There had been a fragmentary dialogue between Ella Kershaw and Miriam Crumps a week or two ago.

"Has anybody mentioned Mrs Butterway to her yet?"

"No, not yet, I think."

"Don't you think it's about time?"

"If you think it will do any good, Miriam."

"Oh, she ought to go. Every minister's wife goes once."

Because of that short conversation, Grace had before her one of the most difficult and disappointing interviews that face the clergy. Through Ella, she had come to hear of Mrs Butterway who lived in the street behind Ella and the Ginnells. The backyard was always full of washing, but Mrs Ginnell was of the opinion that it was to screen the place rather than reveal a show of cleanly zeal. The minister's wife would be wasting time! Wasn't there enough to do in the church for its members without going after Mrs Butterway? Grace admitted that with such people breath spent on them had often to be regarded as dead loss, but the effort must be made, the offer put forward and the sign given to the carping world that no soul was left without a call to its better self.

Henrik Ibsen says that a man should not go out to fight for truth in his best trousers, but the direct opposite applies to women, and Grace gathered courage as she carefully settled her smart hat and saw two curls show themselves off advantageously under the close fitting brim.

Was there a Mr Butterway? Not now and perhaps never had been. Easily recognised; small, sallow, monkey-like, quick of eye and movement.

As she turned into Daisy Street, her opening words were still uncertain. One might just as well appeal in the name of Buddha, one name being as much a mystery as another to some people.

Grace glanced up at the house numbers. A few doors away a hawker side-stepped from one to the next and knocked. He turned as Grace approached and his face lit up like the Demon King's. It was Pins and Needles himself. If she walked on, the door might open and shut irrevocably, so there was nothing to do but wait her turn, looking politely up-street and withdrawn a pace or two from the door, which opened briskly enough.

"I could almost set my clock by you, Mr Dutton. Nippy day, isn't it? Just a card of elastic, please. Yours has never let me down yet."

127

Money chinked in the tin and Grace turned. Mrs Butterway was shaking her head emphatically at Pins and Needles, with her eyes closed and her mouth firm.

"Goodbye, Mr Dutton. I can't offer you a cup of tea today, I'm busy."

The man stepped back and scowled at Grace, then stood his ground as she moved forward.

"Nothing more today, thank you," came sharply from the doorway. The man's features prepared for action.

"She's peddling religion. Say 'Not today' to her."

The brown faced woman glanced at Grace, who now came forward.

"Mrs Butterway, I believe. If I'm not disturbing you, might I have a few minutes conversation with you?"

The dark eyes in the pinched face grew wary.

"What about?"

"This is a pastoral call, if you will allow me. Mrs Kershaw asked me to call."

"Oh, if you're a friend of Antella's."

Grace was admitted and introduced herself properly and was shown into the small parlour which smelled unexpectedly of scent. The woman darted forward and lit the gas fire.

"Everybody knows the Kershaws. Isn't she wonderful?"

"She has a loving heart, Mrs Butterway, and her concern for others less fortunate than herself is very touching."

The bright monkey face looked sceptical.

"I shouldn't care to change places with her."

"She is surrounded by people who love her. We all command some service by love or money."

Seeing that the watchful look came back, Grace changed the subject.

"That man at the door gets round the district very quickly. He was in Moston this morning as a deaf-mute until he called at our house, when he became quite informative."

"Oh! he's harmless," laughed Mrs Butterway. "I expect he could learn a trade, but he's by no means penniless. He prefers his freedom, though."

"It must be a chilly freedom in winter."

"That's when he finds business most brisk. Housewives are anxious to shut the door again but too soft not to give. He loafs about more in summer. There are tricks in every trade but ours."

The dark eyes laughed boldly at Grace.

"I have a soft spot," the woman went on, "for those who like to be independent. I'm made that way myself."

"It's a great thing to be one's own mistress if nobody else's."

The bold look gave way to one of suspicion again.

"Oh, but I am, you know. I haven't to honour or obey anyone and I can please myself about loving."

She reached abruptly for cigarettes.

"Do you mind if I smoke?"

"Not at all. Well, I don't often, but since you are so kind I will join you, thank you."

Grace did not at all enjoy smoking as it was so finicky. She thought women had taken it up solely as an occupation for idle hands in the absence of the elegant fan, or the harp, or the embroidery frame. In China, a walnut or pebble rolled between the fingers kept them supple and found harmless employment and Grace could find little commendation for cigarette smoking in her hostess's nicotine stained digits. However, declining to join her in this small matter might have indicated a moral smoke-screen which would have clouded the beginning of their acquaintance.

"I didn't guess," said Mrs Butterway, "that you were the new minister's wife, in that hat. It's a bit different from some I've seen here. I wondered what you wanted. You weren't canvassing; there's no Election coming on, and you weren't selling anything, at least as far as I could see."

"That man was wrong. I'm not peddling religion. But how kind of you to ask me in. Mrs Butterway, do you belong to any church at all? I ask because if you don't and our church is the nearest, then I'm not just the new minister's wife, I'm *your* minister's wife."

The sharp face looked caustic.

"If you know Antella, you'll probably know Mrs Ginnell and if you know Mrs Ginnell you'll know enough about me to know that I don't go to church."

"I'm sorry, Mrs Butterway. I wanted to find out if you had any real friends; people interested in your happiness."

"I know heaps of people, thank you."

"I hope you can find room in your life for one more," persisted Grace with the obstinacy of someone under secret orders. "Tell me, Mrs Butterway, are you really happy?"

"Who on earth is!"

Grace looked at her with commiseration. Mrs Butterway was a hard nut, admittedly, but there might be a kernel and not just a grain of dust inside.

Seeing her visitor's concerned look, Mrs Butterway came to her own defence.

"I should say I'm as happy as any woman in this street by the look of them. When I pass the time of day they look so solemn. What's wrong with them?"

"Not having seen them, I can't say, but at a guess I should say nothing much."

The amusement faded from Mrs Butterworth's eyes but Grace hurried on in quiet and rational terms.

"Can it be that they look solemn when you pass because you are unkind to them?"

"I certainly am not! I'd have a pleasant word with any of them if they'd let me."

"They may feel that you have damaged them in some way."

"Oh yes, they think I'm a blackleg. They probably feel that I'm undercutting them with their hankering after a soft berth and a man tipping up all his wages. It isn't what I do, but because I don't get a half-Nelson on a man first that they hate me."

"Hate you? And yet you would have a pleasant word in passing. That is very forgiving of you!"

A short truce of silence occurred during which neither withdrew. It was no good pretending that this was merely a social visit, either, now, and Grace might never be let into the house again.

"No, Mrs Garner, I have no regrets. Don't worry about me, but thank you all the same. They all come once, and now you've done your duty!"

Mrs Butterway looked thankful that the visit was so brief, but Mrs Garner did not take the hint.

"I told Ella Kershaw I was coming here this afternoon. Does she never talk to you on serious matters? Surely it isn't possible to evade them for the whole of a lifetime!"

"There are other serious matters besides religion," exclaimed the younger woman with some impatience (Why didn't the woman go?) I thought you people were not supposed to cast stones."

"I'm not doing that, God forbid. But you can't expect people to throw bouquets when they see a woman throwing herself away."

"I'm *not* throwing myself away. I get a decent living." Her voice trailed off for a moment but she rallied. "Well, what I call a decent living. It means no more to me than nursing. Some women make good nurses; some don't."

"Nursing!" exclaimed Grace, her voice betraying outrage in spite of attempted calm. "A nurse would never be subjected to the monotony of giving an endless series of - well, let's say emetics to avoid being too clinical." She was agitated and spoke again quickly. "In China I met such wonderful women who were nursing and that last remark took me by surprise. Please forgive me, Mrs Butterway."

A look of absolute exasperation came over her hostess's face.

"Oh, why do you bother? I've got my friends and you've got yours. I don't come to your house pestering you about the way you live. You ought to know by now that all those old fashioned ideas of chastity and so on have been debunked. The war did that."

"War always does, and we can't afford that. You see, in China where my husband has worked for twenty-five years, girls had very little say in their own lives; no vote, no prestige, very little education. Now that things are better it means a great deal to the modern woman. That is why it has given me such a shock to find a countrywoman of mine content to live in a state that the Asian woman is sloughing off."

Mrs. Butterway moistened her lips.

"Those women had no say in the matter. That makes all the difference."

"All the difference in the world; the difference between being sold into slavery and selling yourself into slavery."

"As I told you before, I'm independent."

Grace paused.

"Do you really like your visitors, Mrs Butterway? I'm afraid I'm asking out of curiosity."

"Well - I'll put it this way. A shop-keeper feels bound to serve any decently behaved customer who comes with money in his hand and asks for ordinary goods. Some are regulars, some are likeable chaps who send me a comic postcard when they're on holiday with their wives. Some send me Christmas cards - robins and so on," she added hastily upon seeing the other's face, "but it's just a business deal. There's no romance, no hooks, no trying to take some woman's husband away from her!"

Grace sighed.

"No romance sounds very dull to me."

"I'm not pretending it isn't, but you might give me credit for doing some good. All my clients are not young, Mrs Garner. I wish they were. Some are getting on in years and some women will take the best of a man but not the fag-ends; it's too nerve-racking. That's where I come in."

"Oh, Mrs Butterway," exclaimed Grace, "you are not old enough to understand."

"Oh yes I am," answered the other stubbornly. "Nature can be very cruel."

Mrs Butterway smiled at her visitor, feeling that she had taught the older woman something.

"My nerves can stand it because the men don't mean anything to me and consequently I'm not disappointed and don't bear them a grudge. They all merge."

"What about the young men who should be thinking of marriage?"

"All in good time, all in good time, and I *have* heard that a little previous experience is an advantage."

"Very rarely," exclaimed Grace. "Anyway, young people can happily share even their ignorance and should bring something new and shining to their marriage besides their saucepans."

The other flushed with annoyance.

"We shall never see eye to eye, Mrs Garner. I've never heard of anybody being the worse for my company and that is more than some can say."

"Professional pride is a fine thing, but it's harmful for people to believe that money can buy anything including, of course, us."

"I've told you, I'm perfectly happy."

The woman had snapped angrily with a raised voice.

"Oh, no you did not! I can't believe you are really happy. You manage to look bright at times but all women can do that."

"Well, I can't say I'm glad I opened the door. I'm sorry, but you ask for it, the way you go on. I shall tell Ella Kershaw never to mention my name again. She's no right!"

"Look, if you don't intend opening the door to me ever again, this may be our first and last meeting. Just for a few minutes let us be friends."

"How can we be friends? We've nothing in common."

"I know what it is," answered Grace quietly, to love a man. And surely you do, too. I hope so."

Mrs Butterway's face hardened but she did not speak.

"I should understand better if I knew how all this began. Can you remember who first put your feet on this path, and do you look back on those people with gratitude?"

Grace watched the other woman swallow with an effort before her reply came, as though there were no lubrication in her throat.

"That's an old tale."

"You became fond of someone?"

"Not especially. It's a long time ago and I hardly ever think about it, but a girl I knew invited me to a sing-song one evening when they were having three or four of the wounded soldiers in from the military hospital up at Lily Lane. They were a really nice lot at first, and they always brought a lot of drink with them. Very generous they were, really."

"Very," agreed Mrs Garner.

"Of course, looking back, I can see that this girl only invited me to play gooseberry with her boy's pal, but I kept on going and then he went back and got killed."

"And were there," enquired Grace gently, "any gooseberry consequences?"

"Oh, no," laughed Mrs Butterway, "they were all Government sponsored. But after the war, I'd got a taste for it, if you see what I mean."

She did see. That was the whole tragedy; a taste for *it*, not for *him*. Dehumanised.

"But haven't you ever been in love, Mrs Butterway?"

"Oh, well, you get more interested in some than in others, of course, and now and again a man talks to you about his job. I admit I was young and simple then, but that's how it is."

"But you are not so young now," countered Grace, "so why try to keep up the simplicity? Perhaps that first step years ago was part gift and part theft; it usually is. Then you had to choose between self disgust or justification and you couldn't face self disgust, could you? Oh, Mrs Butterway, the wounds go too deep for mere repentance. Isn't that what you feel?"

Mrs Butterway's eyes had something of fear in them as she returned the speaker's direct gaze as though hypnotised. Deep lines drooped from the corners of her mouth but she did not attempt to speak and Grace went on.

"But you are wrong. Whatever the world says, whatever other women say, you are wrong. Repentance will hurt but it is the only cure. Now you are older, you should be capable of making adult decisions."

Mrs Butterway took a deep breath and seemed to free herself from some painful inner struggle. She leaned forward and took another cigarette and, lighting it, inhaled extensively and threw back her head. The action gave her relaxation throughout and she returned Grace's earnest look with composed resistance.

"And I have made them. I choose my independence."

"It's the strangest independence I've ever heard of," said Grace sadly. "It's like a chain smoker or an alcoholic saying he likes his independence."

"I guess I know a lot more about life than you do, Mrs Garner. Men are much of a muchness and it's a bit of independence for any woman to choose her own downfall."

"Pooh," countered Grace, rallying at this dessicated chestnut. "You are trying to teach me about free will! This so-called independence isn't really free will; it is only freewheeling, and that is always downhill. And knowing dozens of men in only one mood isn't as instructive as knowing one man in all his moods. Even one man isn't much of a muchness!"

Mrs Butterway was silent for a moment and then she got up and moved to the door."

"I'll just put the kettle on. I'm sure you could do with a cup of tea. Do you ever get hoarse?"

"Not unless I have a cold," returned Grace affably, "and when one thinks of it, one never hears of clergyman's wife's throat."

"It's a wonder."

Grace was left alone. Conversation at personal depth had been so instant upon her entry into the room, that she had hardly taken her eyes from Mrs Butterway's face until this moment and scarcely knew what her present surroundings were. The door had been left ajar and sounds of a domestic nature now came faintly from the kitchen. Mrs Butterway in this little matter was trying to do the right, the conventional thing and that was a good sign. Grace was glad of this lull! Looking about her she tumbled to the secret of the general decor in a twinkling. The pink leather pouffe girt with a tasselled thong, the three-legged milking stool that would never see a four legged cow, and the hearth-set with handles of metal galleons, were all given by different people. There was no continuity of taste, but their bond was its absence.

She looked at the mantelpiece. Those vases had surely been won at hoop-la? Some, perhaps, at a rifle range, souvenirs of a night at the fair and the donor long forgotten. What made her man-friends bring these celluloid Kewpie dolls in feathered head-dresses? Evidently that was a feminine ideal and the Mrs Butterways of life the nearest they ever got to it.

At length her hostess returned with the tea-tray.

"Let's have a cup of tea and forget that the fools exist for a minute or two."

She was rather slap-dash and clattering as she did the honours, but if it was hospitality fortissimo it was nevertheless cheerful music. There were one or two dashes back to the kitchen for forgotten items as if the ceremony were not over-familiar, at least in the parlour, but Grace was touched at her bothering at all.

"A pretty traycloth, Mrs. Butterway. Have you made it yourself?"

"No, that's one of Ella Kershaw's. I haven't been in for some days.

How is she, do you know?"

"Much the same, of course. Busy as ever. I promised to look in after leaving here."

"Give her my love, in spite of the trick she's played me. Invalids must get a bit morbid now and then and brood over other people as well as themselves. She never complains but she must get weary to death of her bed."

As soon as it was uttered, both women seemed to look at that last remark with disquiet as it hung in the air between them as though unable to waft away. Grace recovered first.

"Ella could have been quite self-centred but she looks very far afield and she's very keen on women's education where women are treated like cattle and have only one function. It would be an eye-opener if every woman who ignored her vote and had no use for education were to live for a time where women had neither."

"I expect if they really wanted them they would get them," said Mrs Butterway with very little interest.

"Yes. The spadework comes in getting them to want those things," rejoined Grace with some dejection.

The other woman hoped that her visitor was tiring at last. Former minister's wives had been much easier to get rid of.

"Do you ever go to a church service, Mrs Butterway, or look in when it's empty?"

"No, I don't. How could I?"

"Simply by taking the trouble to cross the road and go inside. And I'll tell you something. You may think clergymen are always moaning about there being so much sin in the world, but what they say on most Sundays is 'I'm only preaching to the converted.' So there, you can see how welcome you'd be."

"I'm sure people wouldn't like it and neither should I for that matter. I'd rather be among my own sort, thank you."

"That's a lazy way of thinking; it gives nothing to measure yourself against. And why shouldn't you enjoy coming to church? There's nothing to frighten anybody nowadays, even at the cost of some evasion of truth!"

"It would be acting a lie," said Mrs Butterway defiantly.

It had been a mistake to fortify her guest with tea. She had meant to play for time, not to play into her hands and now Mrs Garner pushed her cup slightly away as if it had detained her long enough.

"Play-acting love is acting a lie."

"It is not play-acting," responded Mrs Butterway in a loud voice, "as you'd soon find out if you tried it."

"Altogether play-acting," asserted Grace positively. "A bedroom farce with mock emotions and puppet movements. Not a sincere word spoken in all the clap-trap."

Too late she became aware of the realism of the last word.

"No wonder," the answer came heatedly, "no wonder the churches are emptying if parsons' wives go round insulting people like this."

"Mrs Butterway, I am not insulting you. I am trying to get you to be a little angry with yourself. To us in the church you are not a music-hall joke, or a woman of no account; you are a person who matters."

The crinkled little face looked startled and incredulous.

Grace knew she had failed to get past the defences at any point and time was running short.

"Mrs Butterway, you are confusing the facts of life, which are physical, with the great fact of life, which is love and I fear you don't know what that is. If only you went to church occasionally you would have heard of the phrase, 'the sin against the Holy Ghost', which is hard to explain but is nevertheless the one sin which will be the hardest to forgive. Well, you know what the Sacraments are, don't you, when we take bread and wine as symbolising the spiritual strength we can draw from God? Now imagine that two monkeys have made entry into a church and, discovering the prepared vessels there, they eat and drink the contents. They might even enjoy them, but apart from finding them more or less briefly appetising, the ritual of partaking is entirely meaningless, an imitative act without understanding. The vessels are then cast aside as worthless. So it is with human intercourse without loving communion. A man and a woman carelessly use temple vessels; they go through the motions of a love-feast and yet in reality it is all as empty and pretentious as a chimpanzee's tea-party."

A sharp intake of breath followed by a little snort was heard from Mrs Butterway and then a high-pitched whoop, without any expiration of breath between, made Grace aware that all was not well with her hostess's powers of speech. Indeed, after a few surprised seconds, it was evident that the breathing apparatus was also involved and soon, as the situation worsened, the minister's wife realised that she was witnessing her first experience of hysterics. She rose in consternation.

Mrs Butterway kept it up for quite a long time, painfully drawing air into her lungs only to expel it violently as soon as her eyes rested on Grace. She crossed her hands on her bosom and rocked from side to side and when Grace hastily poured a tepid cup of tea and advanced it towards her, the eyes bulged anew, tears streamed afresh and the hooting laughter emerged time and again from the open mouth.

"Well, if you can't swallow, try to suck a lump of sugar," urged

Grace in desperation and finally succeeded in reducing the noise to the steady grunts that accompany the gaining of a high ridge by an out of condition seal.

The ailing woman wiped her eyes when calmer moments arrived some five minutes later. She leaned back in her chair, exhausted.

"Take yourself off," she gasped, "you and your long words and never come here again," and the effort of speaking brought on a fit of weak sobbing.

"I'm sorry if I've upset you," said Grace miserably, doubting if a fit of hysteria coincided with a contrite heart. "Perhaps I ought to have asked my husband to come instead."

There was no lucid reply and realising that the interview was unmistakably at an end she opened her handbag, whereupon the other woman mustered her energies immediately.

"And don't leave any of your tracts or texts. I'm not having them."

"No. But would you please accept this jar of home-made ginger? I'm very partial to it myself, having got a taste for it in China. It's an acquired taste as in some other things. I give it up each year in Lent. If ever you want to drop a habit, Lent is a good time to let go, as if you can manage forty days and forty nights without it, you can probably manage forty years."

"Like Mademoiselle of Armentieres," said the other, eyeing Mrs Garner with hostility.

Grace put down the pot of ginger on the tray.

"I could become really gluttonous over it, but it would be tragic if the order came to any of us to put on the whole armour and we simply couldn't get into it because of some self indulgence. Goodbye, Mrs Butterway. That means God be with you, you know, and thank you for inviting me in and giving me tea. That was most kind of you. Goodbye indeed."

Outside the house Grace mourned that best trousers or best hat had lost.

When her visitor had gone, Mrs Butterway sat limply in her chair, giving herself time to recover.

"Oh gosh!" she said quietly, almost with a whimper. She reached for a cigarette and derived, some comfort from it . "She'll never get in here again, that's flat."

Later she gathered the teacups onto the tray and picked it up.

"I'll wash this lot and get her out of my hair. What a holy terror! But she isn't going to make any difference to *me*, for all her hanging on. She can just forget me, quick!"

As she finished her cigarette a knock sounded on the back door.

"Who's this?" she said irritably aloud, and went to answer it.

There stood Pins and Needles.

"She's gone, hasn't she?"

"Yes, she *has* gone and you can go too. I'm busy," she snapped, closing the door again. She delayed it for a moment to put her head round it and to add one word.

"Chimp!"

Chapter Thirteen

Clara returned the letter to its envelope as she stood by the breakfast table.

"Fanny says will it be all right if she comes for her week in Manchester next week."

"Ah yes," replied Leonard absently. "Glad to see her as usual."

"Yes," sighed Clara.

Leonard looked up.

"A week's not long, you know! And she's out nearly every night for the D'Oyley Cartes."

"Oh yes. But it's the days!"

During the day Leonard had other things to think about and one of them came into his head at that moment.

"Do you remember Barton who had to go last year?"

Clara brought her thoughts from Fanny to recollect that Barton was one of the clerks at Bolt's who had been lopped during a fairly severe pruning by the heads of the firm.

"Well," went on Leonard, "he came to see us yesterday."

"Did he really? How is he?"

"He came on business. He came to see if any of us would buy a pound of tea."

Leonard stirred his breakfast cup slowly as he said this.

Clara stared at him.

"Tea?"

"Yes, tea. He was lugging a suitcase round with him. I got some but forgot to bring it home. I'll try to remember tonight."

Clara was still gazing at Leonard's downcast preoccupation.

"But Barton wasn't a salesman of any kind. He was a clerk."

"No openings," said Leonard. "I think he'd come to have a look round and see how things were doing. Of course he would see there were fewer of us than ever."

Clara had a strange and bleak feeling in her vitals. She couldn't say anything for a moment.

"But Bolt's is a big firm and has been going a long time."

"Not as big as it was," said Leonard as he rose from the table.

Soon he could be heard at the piano in the front room, playing until the time for his usual tram.

Pruning, thought Clara. Lopping!

They were rather misleading terms for the slashing and felling that was going on in the big city firms. Some of those pruned trees were stunted for life, struggling to put forth a few life-searching shoots at unexpected angles but never again growing to the stature that would provide shade or shelter for many.

And the lopped branches? What could *they* support?

As Clara gathered the plates a confusion of thoughts milled in her mind. She must get a room ready for Fanny and tell Kerry that she must make room for Sybil during her aunt's visit. Kerry would groan at having to crowd her things together. This time last year Clara remembered thinking that Sybil would be married before Fanny came again, or it would be Sybil's wedding she was coming for, but things weren't working out that way as yet. Sybil seemed capable of drifting along happily for ages, bending dreamily over her embroidered tray-cloths. Did she think married life consisted of afternoon tea?

Somehow the deficiencies of life in general and home in particular always seemed to stand out more sharply when Fanny was coming, Fanny was an unusual woman certainly and had the respect and wonderment of her own generation. They remembered the tremendous shock she had given the whole community years ago and her tale had been told winter and summer round confidential tables for a generation and was still being told; but Fanny had long withdrawn to Southport out of earshot. For as long as her two nieces could remember, she had been in comfortable and independent circumstances and had the knack of giving presents that required some further effort before they could be fully enjoyed, such as, in early years, beads to thread, pictures to colour, bricks to build and books to read, but never dolls to hold. She did not believe in life being made too easy for anyone.

Pity for Fanny Crossley had been short-lived and had quickly given way to respect and even in later years, to a sort of envy, as of a man who has been injured and gets rather high damages. The accident is deplored but the compensation pricks even his sympathisers.

The girls regarded their only aunt with curiosity.

"Always remember," warned Clara, "that your aunt is really a

140

lonely woman."

"But it's her own fault," argued Kerry. "She could have married if she'd wanted."

"She refused on principle," said her mother, "and one cannot see into the future."

"Do you think she's sorry she let her principles win?"

"Don't say things like that, Kerry. She's got more backbone than many girls today. Their feet are too cold to stand on principle, judging by some of the cheap things they do."

For although Fanny was unmarried she had actually once stood in full panoply at the Communion rail on Oldham Road, a stormy courtship over at last, to everybody's relief.

Joe Cawdor was a strong personality, as strong as Fanny, and they must needs argue to the death-blow every little variance, so that it became a great issue leading to 'principle' and internecine war. It was 'on principle' that Fanny would not countenance Joe's taking a drink with a business acquaintance over a deal. It was 'on principle' that Joe would not bother to invest such details with any importance, but 'on principle' she wished him to conform to the ways of her family. 'On principle', Joe thought that a wife must allow a man to be head of the house and Fanny was secretly delighted to agree.

On his wedding morning Joe knew that he had won. He exulted in his triumph and peacocked his sovereignty too unguardedly, and was fool enough to quaff a swash-buckling glass before leaving home for the ceremony.

He looked a fine figure of a man as he stood to receive his bride coming in on her father's arm. He looked proud as Lucifer and every woman in the building would have been glad of the chance to bring him low in her own way.

They moved together and stood facing the Rev. Gideon Stormalong, who thought them the handsomest couple he had joined, although of course this was very early in his ministry. In fact, he kept that opinion over many years for the occasion remained in his memory.

The familiar opening words of the marriage ceremony had first faltered and then ceased as Fanny turned from Joe to old Mr Crossley and spoke quietly.

"Father, I want to go home!"

It was not realised for a few moments that anything untoward was happening, but when Stormalong hurriedly suggested adjourning to the vestry for a consultation, the congregation became very uneasy and apprehensive. Minutes passed and then figures were seen faintly through the stained glass windows along the side approach, leaving the vestry. A few moments later the minister re-entered the chapel, his face pale and perturbed.

"Friends, there will be no marriage service here today. We had better return to our own homes forthwith. Mr and Mrs Crossley have much to do."

"Father was a tower of strength to Fanny during those awful days," Clara told her own girls when they were growing up. "He took her off for a fortnight's holiday straight away and in all that time he hardly ever spoke or took his nose out of a newspaper."

"But surely," exclaimed Sybil aghast, "she could have forgiven him or made allowances or got him to do better later on?"

"Girls do too much of that nowadays," said Clara. "In those days we insisted on goods being perfect before they left the shop."

Sybil had no more to say, but her sister had.

"Mrs Ginnell seems to get on all right with her husband and everybody knows he drinks. She just doesn't take any notice, they say."

"Would you like Mrs Ginnell for your only aunt?" asked Clara sharply and Kerry subsided.

There is always an expectant bustle about an arrival that is very pleasant and Fanny's greeting from them all as they came home was genuine in its warmth. Kerry had time to recover from her grousing fit at sharing a room and Clara always hoped, year after year, that Fanny would not be so observant or penetrating as last year. Leonard and Sybil had no thoughts on the visit to speak of. It affected them so little.

"Leonard's ivory tower is made of piano keys," said Fanny when he withdrew after tea.

"He has to keep up his practising of course," said Clara. "Now, don't you bother with these."

"Well, if I don't who will?" said Fanny, gathering dishes.

"Kerry's got her homework and Sybil's meeting Geoffrey."

"I thought she was practically on the point of getting married. Leonard ought to have a word with Alfred."

"With Alfred?" said Clara, annoyed. "Why on earth should we discuss it with Alfred? I'm sure young people don't want any advice from us in these days."

"Well, so much the worse for their prospects," rejoined Fanny. "I don't like an engagement that is only a 'keep off the grass' sign. If a girl is at liberty, it's still a free-for-all."

"We talked it over at the time, Fanny, as well you know, and Leonard gave his consent so that they could feel settled in mind. And Sybil is very happy."

"Yes, she has the temperament that can wait for ever; and some girls do. Men don't often trouble to run after the bus when they've caught it, I've noticed."

"And if they miss it after all, they don't let it sour their whole outlook, either."

This was only the evening of the first day and already it was far from good.

But it put Fanny in better humour that Clara had been ruffled so early in this visit. If Clara posed as the contented nerve-nourished wife then she, Fanny, would soon prove that married women could easily be irritated into showing their claws. She suspected that Clara made it a matter of prayer and real effort to keep her temper during Fanny's stay and it heightened Fanny's morale to know that she alone probably of all her sister's acquaintances, had the power to say just the careless-seeming words that could bring her defences, not exactly crashing down, but showing those leaks in the dyke that revealed the flood-waters behind. What a pity it is that woman's morale has nothing to do with morals. Sometimes the two seem to be at opposite ends of the see-saw.

Fanny's mood changed at once and she became patronisingly forgiving, the understanding woman of independence who fully appreciated the family woman's struggle against great odds. It would do Clara good to come to Southport for a week for the Flower Show. Surely the girls and Leonard could manage for themselves for one week. She herself had got to the age when she realised that there were compensations in life and that she hadn't missed much perhaps. By bedtime she was in such complacency of spirits that even Leonard noticed.

"I think Fanny likes coming to us," he said last thing at night. "When all's said and done, her native air must agree with her."

"It had better," rejoined Clara.

When she next met the minister's wife at the 'fresh green watercress' cart, and told her of her visitor, Grace gave her a swift look.

"Robert and I were both the only child. Weren't we lucky?"

Clara laughed unaffectedly. Really, that woman had a way of casually opening cupboards and flinging out the skeletons for the old moth eaten things they were and somehow or other they never got back.

Fanny was different in temperament, that was all, and would always worry the rope, however long and slack. Perhaps it was more under-standing to answer her in kind rather than in kindness. Forgiving one's brother, or sister for that matter, seventy times seven, ought to lead to an examination of the root cause of the need for this astronomic indulgence. Perhaps opportunities for giving offence were given too frequently. People lose the capacity for fleeing temptation and a morbid curiosity makes them wander repeatedly into the line of fire.

"Tinker, tailor, soldier, sailor," counted Kerry round the edge of her fruit dish next day. "Rich man."

"Splendid," said her aunt Fanny. "Marrying either for love or money would bring you much that is worth having, only make up your mind which you can best do without before you say anything rash."

There was a thoughtful silence.

"We're entering very free and easy days," she went on in a disapproving voice, "but the slackest laws in the world can't soften life for the stupid. They'll always be in a mess. Helped out of one hole, they make straight for another. Look at Hollywood with its go as you please."

"Oh, you can't call that real life," said Clara with relief.

"Geoffrey said . . . " began Sybil, and stopped.

Perhaps what Geoffrey had said was not the comment for the tea table; that Hollywood was the western world's fertility stone like those ancient ones stuck up in the middle of fields.

"What did Geoffrey say?" asked Kerry, all alert.

"Oh, nothing."

"Very forbearing of him," said Fanny, "though I should say he was not born with a bridle on his tongue. No room for that *and* a silver spoon, I suppose."

Sybil laughed pleasantly and Fanny was contrite. The girl was not touchy.

"Are you coming with me to the Sewing Meeting on Wednesday?" asked Clara.

"Thank you. What are they doing at the moment?"

"Mattress covers."

"Very sensible. Does old Mrs Mossop still come along?"

"I should think she does! It's her big day, listening to all the chatter."

The Sewing Meeting was held in two vestries at the rear of the Chapel. At first it had seemed a disadvantage that they were divided, but the system worked very well. The treadle machines were in one room and, in the other, all the cutting out and hand preparation done away from the whirring noise. As the pinned and tacked material was carried from one place to the other, so the busy bees humming there were kept informed of the buzzing of the other group.

144

There was a good attendance this Wednesday; Ada Sinclair for one and, consequently, Miriam Crumps coming to see how Fanny Crossley was wearing.

Miriam looked at the forms and table legs to make sure that Mrs Ginnell had dusted properly and then composedly sat waiting for her piece of sewing to come to her. She didn't care for machining but preferred hand-stitching. She put her feet on one of the hassocks that were an innovation of Mrs Garner's in the vestry, but made no comment.

In the other room the sewing machines were soon in motion, speeding along the seams of new covers. Each long run started like Charlie Chaplin meeting a policeman at a corner; a few tentative steps, a hesitation or two, and then away it raced.

Since Ada and Miriam did not always favour the Sewing Meeting with their presence, a solicitous little fuss was made over them like children, and they felt the glow that isolated examples of virtue give but which gets dulled in continual well-doing. Some of the regulars even grumbled a little on inclement days, but the meeting was popular and the work turned out was the fresh milk of human kindness 'from contented cows', as the hoarding expressed it.

Old Mrs Mossop was unburdening herself of some recent neighbourly criticism.

"Of course I wouldn't have said it if I'd known she was just passing, but Daisy Street isn't what it used to be. When I first married and went there it was as nice a little street as you could wish. But it's becoming known."

There were murmurs of sympathy. Mrs Mossop had been blind from early childhood but she dropped no catches and her tongue could be as sharp as her ears. A mattress cover with its tapes pinned in position was placed in front of her and a threaded needle, and she worked as quickly as the rest of them.

Grace was giving them time to settle down. They couldn't gossip all afternoon surely, and she had brought a magazine along containing an article by Dr Leslie Weatherhead that she wanted to read to them when she could find a suitable opening.

"Does anybody know how Sam Buckley's wife is these days?" asked Mrs Briggs. "Not that I know her, but Sam I've always liked."

"I haven't seen her since July when she came to see the garden," said Ada, "and she was all right then. I've heard she suffers from nerves, but I doubt it. She hasn't a grey hair in her head."

"You'd think she'd enjoy having such a lovely house to look after," came from Annie Northcroft, "and nobody tramping dirt in all the

g

time."

"I can't see that she's much to grumble at," said Mrs Mossop, her eyes focussed by chance on a large picture on the opposite wall depicting a smooth-haired John Wesley in his Oxford chambers.

"And it isn't," Miriam said, "as if she lives quite alone. Sam will see to all the doors and windows last thing at night."

Mrs Ginnell went into the machine room to see if anything was ready to bring out.

Clara Martland smiled round at her.

"They're doing well in there; soon on our tracks. Does Fanny seem at home?"

"Very happy. They're asking how Sam's wife is."

"Oh, poor soul. Her nerves are supposed to be giving trouble, though goodness knows why. Sam's position is assured."

"And she hasn't had to worry over a houseful of children. Perhaps that's why."

Mrs Lambert, long widowed and now childless, paused and looked at them gently.

"Yes, there's nothing like work to stop you from thinking."

"But why," exclaimed Clara, "shouldn't Mrs Buckley think a bit? She's enough to think about that's pleasant, surely?"

Mrs Ginnell took up a pile of calico to carry off and addressed herself to it as she moved away.

"She's stand-offish, as *you* say, and Sam was never that, but I'm sorry for both of them if she's clenching her teeth when she should be smiling."

The machines set up their chattering again.

Mrs Ginnell got back just in time to hear the minister's wife speaking.

"I called on Mrs Butterway recently, Mrs Mossop, and found her very hospitable."

"Why, is there a campaign on?"

"There is always a campaign on," responded Grace, laughing, "whether it is advertised or not."

"But I've never known her come here," said Ada Sinclair, astounded. "She'd never dare."

Mrs Mossop snorted.

"It's not a matter of daring. She wouldn't want. What did she say, Mrs Garner?"

"Well, of course, on my first visit I could not say a great deal. But she listened."

The sewing circle stitched in silence awhile.

Then Ada Sinclair erupted.

"It won't do a bit of good you know. Only the missions and the Salvation Army can do anything with them. And that's often bolting the stable door after the horse has bolted, if I've got it right."

"Yes, I know," agreed Mrs Garner sadly. "But remember the ninety and nine left to carry on. We have to go after the hundredth now and again."

"It's very dangerous, that," Mrs Mossop said with her gaze on outer space. "Sometimes the ninety and nine get so neglected they stray off and instead of one for game, the place is empty."

Annie Northcroft could not agree.

"No, Sarah. We mustn't expect the minister to be always knocking on our door when he's other work to do. That hundredth sheep left to itself would find another black sheep and soon it wouldn't be just a stray any longer, but in a black herd."

Mrs Briggs looked startled.

"Why, Annie, you give me the creeps. A black herd! Doesn't it sound frightening?"

Mrs Garner was now very solemn.

"It sounds what it is - very frightening indeed. If the church does not make converts it could become a persecuted minority again and we should not be sheep in a fold any longer, but in the common pound, strays ourselves from something, God knows what."

The women stopped sewing, looking at their minister's wife and not sure they were enjoying today's meeting so much. Those who were country bred remembered the village pound, a little enclosure for lost cattle. Not much pasturage there.

They were rather depressed about Mrs Butterway, too.

It was so nice and friendly at these meetings without bringing in *that* element. They sang the hymn *That sinner am I* without turning a hair because humility was expected of them, but they were only sinners theologically speaking. They would never have followed Rasputin who exhorted his baffled sheep to be literal sinners the more to enjoy the grace of forgiveness. Rasputin would have made absolutely no headway with these women.

"Well, do what you can with her, Mrs Garner," went on Mrs. Mossop, "but she's set in her ways."

"And so are we all in some things. Some of us are set like jellies and some are set like pig-iron, and it takes varying degrees of heat to melt us."

Then Annie Northcroft, after looking speculatively round the table for a moment, spoke up.

147

"Mrs Garner, there's something that always puzzles me a little and since we all know each other here, perhaps you won't mind my mentioning it."

At this all eyes turned to Annie, who hesitated for a moment but went on.

"It says that our Lord was often in the company of publicans and sinners and - er - women like Mrs Butterway. In a way, I can understand some men liking the easy-going ways of a public house, although the smell when I pass makes me heave."

"Me, too," interrupted Mrs Briggs disgustedly. "When our Willie has sometimes asked what's wrong with a public house, I always say the smell!"

Mrs Briggs earned much agreement with this remark and then they turned to Annie again.

"Well, supposing He got over the smell, what did He see in the women? I shouldn't know what to say to anybody like that myself."

All eyes now looked towards Mrs Garner, except Mrs Mossop who sat like Mrs Siddons in her grand moments, staring straight before her. The minister's wife stared back at the women round the table who would harbour feelings of guilt if they happened to put knife handles in hot water!

"Being women ourselves we have a little inside information, haven't we? I suppose a man would say that these women have no pretensions, no pride, and people with no pride are fairly easy to deal with and that suits most men. Now let us try to put ourselves in the place of such women. (Here Grace beamed round at the circle of awe-struck members.) At the time of the New Testament a poor country girl would not have a great deal to think about apart from the everlasting water to draw and meals to prepare, ringing the changes on a thousand and one things a bright girl can do with a bunch of dates - the edible kind. Her only hope of change is a change of home when she marries, a very brief glory.

"Boredom, injustice, drudgery, could all help to push her further from the village to the attractions of the town, where the boredom is somewhat lessened at first. She comes within the orbit of some prodigal son, tired of washing sheep, and they are drawn together by inexperience and adventure. They have both cut loose and to each the other's name spells liberty. For the man the mess of pottage eventually prevails and so he returns. The woman's return would have met with a very different reception so she stays on in the town. It would be in this period of disillusionment that such women would follow Christ, hardly believing their eyes and ears. He seemed to understand with what high hopes they had espoused freedom and to what despair it had led them. Also in those days it was very easy to be called a sinner. Break one rule of the Old Testament code and one was a sinner, and it was probably the pioneers and reformers who followed our Lord and understood something of his teaching."

Annie Northcroft breathed a sigh of easement.

"Oh, I'm so glad, Mrs Garner. I've always been afraid that God might be bored to tears with the ninety and nine."

"Nothing of the kind, Mrs Northcroft, you may depend on it. Tears in plenty, but not of boredom."

Ada Sinclair felt emboldened to speak.

"Those women haven't the excuse they had in the olden days. I have great difficulty in finding maids to live in and the newspaper advertisements are full of situations vacant for domestic work. I don't think any woman need be out of work."

Ada looked round at the Sewing Circle and then added in a hushed voice.

"You know it used to be said that Mrs Butterway's life was a fate worse than death! But the fate worse than death nowadays seems to be working for another woman."

She looked round for support for her opinion and got it unreservedly on a wave of giggles. Then the minister's wife turned to her to cheer her up.

"How is your son getting on with his studies these days?"

"Very well, I think. But of course, however clever they are, they can't afford to spend more time away from home than is good for them."

One or two women shot a scared glance at the communicating door, but the machines in the next room whirred again. Some machinery inside Fanny Crossley also warmed up.

"How sensibly my niece Sybil considers your son's studies," she said acidly. "Only the other night when I was coming home from the theatre I saw her pointing out a Didsbury tram and apparently urging him to get it then and there, which he did."

"Oh!" Ada was more cautious now. "Did she go up with you then?"

"No. Before I could cross the road I was forestalled by a young man who seemed to know her well and who turned about and escorted her, so I didn't bother."

Fanny considered the silence that followed her remarks rather prolonged and she was surprised to note the concentrated devotion to stitching on all sides.

Mrs Mossop was listening, rapt.

149

"There now!" she intoned approvingly. "Sybil's a lovely girl and there'll always be plenty of flies round a honey pot."

The meeting this afternoon wasn't so bad after all. A few of the women chanced an enigmatic glance round the company.

"Any flies on your Jimmie yet?" asked Mrs Briggs of Annie.

"Not if hearty meals are anything to go by."

"And you'll be a very efficient fly-whisk if you're like most boys' mothers," added Mrs Briggs.

Mrs Garner cleared her throat softly.

"Now I wonder if you'd care to hear this article by Dr Leslie Weatherhead? It's about nervous disorders and how we can deal with their prevention and cure to a certain extent ourselves."

It was a longish article.

As Mrs Mossop said afterwards, it was all right in its way.

Mrs Ginnell now came with news of tea.

"Thank the Lord," exclaimed Mrs Mossop. "That's one of the ways in which I'm set like pig-iron." She carried the meeting with her in this matter and purses were produced as the table was cleared and Mrs Ginnell's voice was heard crying, "You're neither milk nor sugar, aren't you, Miriam?"

Clara waited for Mrs Lambert and they came into the large vestry together. The older woman said she thought she needed her glasses changing, as threading the sewing machine needle was hit or miss.

"I suppose I've been lucky," Clara replied, "but lately I sing a queer word or two in the less well known hymns, especially at the evening service."

"I don't see you in bi-focals."

They glanced at Miriam, who was looking across at Fanny Crossley.

"November's a funny time for a holiday, Fanny. Don't you ever think of changing it?"

"Well, as you know, I like to see the Gilbert and Sullivans when I come. November suits me best."

"I think it's awful underfoot about now."

At the word 'underfoot', Clara looked rather stiff. Only that morning they had slept a little late and at the last moment Leonard's shoes had been discovered by no means unspotted from the world. He usually cleaned his shoes at night, but he and Clara had been out with Fanny. Clara had snatched them up and it was while she was attacking the November mire at the open kitchen door, that Fanny had entered with a grimace of surprise.

"My word! I've always maintained that to clean a man's boots is tantamount to licking them."

The week was only half way through and already Clara was beginning to feel slightly ill. A line from Cowper's hymn came to her. 'Where is the peace that once I knew?' She thought of Mahatma Gandhi who had warned people against anger that poured poisons into the blood. Leonard was something like Gandhi; not to outward view of course, but she could imagine Leonard studying a sheet of music and waiting patiently for his goat's milk.

She turned to find him in the doorway, shod.

"Don't bother with those now, Clara. I've put my best on."

He kissed her and since they were at the back door, he went out that way, leaving Clara feeling slightly pleased that he had forgotten to say goodbye to Fanny.

Now in the meeting as Miriam mentioned the word 'underfoot', Clara avoided Fanny's eye and raised her voice for everybody to hear.

"By the way, do any of you ever clean your husband's shoes?"

Conversation was sliced off as by guillotine and then eyes slid round the assembly to see how everybody else was taking it before anybody rushed in with any confessions.

Grace Garner took this in quickly.

"I can't just remember when I did so last, but I should of course if occasion arose. I should think we all would."

"Oh, no." Miriam cast a shocked look round. "I call that demeaning myself."

Clara looked at Fanny to inquire silently how she liked her counsel for the defence, but Fanny avoided her sister's eye in her turn. To be bracketed with Miriam Crumps!

Nobody else was in any hurry to state an opinion, but Mrs Briggs spoke up.

"Well, of course, putting up a stone in a cemetery can be muddy work and my husband keeps a special pair for that sort of thing in the workshop. If there was an emergency I expect our Willie would clean them."

"But if it so happened that a man was pushed for time," Mrs Garner said persuasively, "we should naturally help in any way we could. It isn't our normal work but in real need we shouldn't hesitate, I hope. Isn't that what Maundy Thursday teaches us?"

All were silent and then Grace went on.

"Of all the things that money can do, one of the most enviable but the most pernicious is its power to bribe our way out of the duty to wash each other's feet and all that it implies. We've all heard of the 'remittance man', the black sheep whose family pay him an allowance to keep away; to live at the other side of the world for preference. It is so much easier for us to set those feet wandering than to trouble ourselves by washing them and in this matter, the foot is comparable to the shoe."

The sewing meeting recovered its liveliness and everybody seemed to be insisting on getting everybody else another cup of tea.

That night, Clara knocked gently on Fanny's door before switching off the landing light.

"It's nothing," she apologised, "I just looked in to see if you were comfortable. What a pretty bed-jacket."

"One of last year's Christmas presents. Nobody you know."

"She must think a lot of you," answered Clara thankfully. "Are you sleeping well here? Are you quite warm enough?"

"I'm fine, thanks. I read a chapter before settling down always."

Clara glanced at the bedside table where a Boots' novel and a slim Testament lay within reach. She had knocked just before Fanny had arranged herself and she couldn't help wondering momentarily which of the two books there would provide the chapter.

"I suppose you sleep well always," went on Fanny.

"Well, yes, on the whole."

"Don't stand there while I'm lying here. Sit down for a minute; the world will still go round if you don't push it."

Clara hesitated, but turning towards a chair lifted some of her sister's garments on to the back. Fanny's things were all more expensive than hers, she observed, touching them delicately. Perhaps women also did not run after the bus!

"You always dressed nicely, Fanny. Do you remember when we used to make and embroider our own under-sets? Yours were always prettier than mine."

"Well, I spent more time at it. You had a better voice and went to more rehearsals and musical evenings. Really, you know, you ought to have kept it up more than you did."

"Oh, there was no money for singing lessons when Len and I married, but I did go on singing for years, privately."

"And I still dress well, privately," answered Fanny drily.

Her little travelling clock propped up in its leather case was the only sound heard for a minute and Clara's eyes wandered to it.

"We're not getting any younger, are we? If you had your time over again, would you do just the same? You know, about Joe?"

Fanny, leaning against her pillows, closed her eyes.

"It's hard to tell. Perhaps if someone else had come along after a year or two, just as striking, I might have forgotten all about Joe by this time. He might have been just a bad patch in my life. But because he was the only pebble on the beach I never seemed able to toss the memory of it away, even when it was caught by the tide."

"Oh, Fanny." Tears sprang in Clara's eyes.

"And," went on Fanny, "we know that pebbles when caught by the tide glow more brightly. It's when they are high and dry that they lose lustre. Perhaps it has been like that with Joe. With salt sea and salt tears, he has shone throughout my life. Perhaps longer than if I'd married him."

Clara sighed deeply.

"I'm sorry I mentioned him, especially at this time of night."

Fanny stretched out a hand for the travelling clock and started to wind it up and Clara sprang to her feet guiltily.

"No, I'm not hinting you should go. I've not had it long and I wind it very gingerly."

"It looks rather a good one; be careful. Was that a present, too?"

"Oh yes, the same donor as the jacket."

"You said I didn't know her. I suppose you've lots of friends that I've never met, in Southport."

"A few, naturally. And I never said it was a woman friend."

She made no further comment and after replacing the little clock, turned a composed face to her sister who moved away rather awkwardly and, without going over to kiss Fanny, turned at the door to say goodnight.

"And pleasant dreams, Fanny."

But her own pleasant dreams started as soon as she got outside. What was all this? Excitement prompted her to say a few words to Leonard.

"I say, Len, I've learnt something just now. Someone's after Fanny, I think. She's got two expensive presents at least from him in there."

"It's probably a business friend or a buyer from some firm. They get samples and so on and someone's let Fanny have the benefit. Goodnight again. I think I had just dozed off."

Clara had to admit the sense in her husband's response but felt rather let down. It might only be that. In a flight of fancy she had imagined Fanny comfortably settled and taken care of and growing mellow; not having to come here with her aspersions and criticisms. In fact, thought Clara with a twinge of conscience, staying in Southport to have her feet washed.

Chapter Fourteen

November in the north brings short, ill-lit days and long glittering nights. The month throbs with activity that has suddenly withdrawn indoors and fastened itself in. Earnestness and ambition confer together at the beginning of autumn as the evening classes swing into full programme, so that by November there is a low muttering of foreign languages in the night schools by people who hope to trade with the ends of the earth or at least to cross the Channel next holiday. Girls who became engaged to be married during the soft gloamings of warm days now congregate hopefully on educational premises to learn to cook and in other rooms advanced students are furthering still their intricate arts.

The bands in the park have gone into hiding in their practice rooms over side street stores. Those same rooms, on other evenings, will be let to Whist Drives and political meetings and Silver Wedding 'do's'. The great concert halls are likewise booked up and summer is shaken off almost with brusqueness, regarded almost as a foolish entanglement as popular fancy turns avidly to velvet and furs and scans the newspapers for the theatre and great indoor spectacles. The Ice Palace has many new recruits clinging with gloved hands to the barricades, hands gloved not so much against the cold, but because imagination makes figures of eight round the novice who fears that if he falls, other skaters might ride razor shod over his tender spreadeagled fingers.

By November the newcomers will be a yard or two away from the edge of the rink, arms pleadingly outstretched, either for aid or to fend off collision risks. Only when the orchestra plays *The Skaters' Waltz* does the ice clear and from the surrounding coffee tables eyes watch objectively their future and more complete selves swooning and leaning like yachts on a white sea.

Tonight Fanny and her younger niece journeyed into town together by taxi, to the girl's great pleasure.

"Are you often allowed to run about by yourself until all hours?" asked the aunt.

"I don't run and I'm home before eleven o'clock," rejoined Kerry, resenting a hint of criticism of the whole family.

"What is this play you're going to see?"

"Oedipus. It's supposed to be peculiar, but it's all in the old classical days when peculiar things did happen."

"And have you booked?"

"No. The Manchester Guardian said it wasn't very full."

"Ah, I had to book by post, weeks ago."

Kerry got out near the Prince's Theatre and Fanny went on towards Quay Street, first passing in front of the Cenotaph, where piles of poppy wreaths lay thick throughout November. "Lest we forget," she echoed silently as she went by. Lest we forget that we walk alone, that we eat and sleep alone, that alone we watch the seething pageant of life grind past, that we are the skeleton at everybody's feast.

Hoardings screened the ground floor of the new building that was to be the Central Reference Library. It was going to be a great place when finished. She turned momentarily and looked back. Somewhere on the opposite side was Sybil's place of work. A lovable girl but not sufficiently critical of her young man! Fanny's gaze dropped to the Cenotaph again and she hurriedly about-faced. Joe! Joe had been posted by his firm to America and there he had married a girl of Spanish descent and had two luscious-eyed children. So much Fanny's friends had been at pains to recount to her. But what they did *not* know was that when he became a widower after about eight years, he had written to Fanny asking her to correspond as an old friend, which secretly she did. Only his sister Ella Kershaw, through whom he had been able to do this privately in the first place, knew of it and hoped that these two mettlesome creatures would pasture contentedly together at last. Then suddenly and without warning, as it seemed to the world at large, incredulous tidings of war swept through the whole land, and the countries of Europe were at each other's throats.

This could not last very long, wrote Joe; not into the New Year. Would Fanny, perhaps in the spring, care to come out and see him and his young children and their way of life? The place and the climate suited him and he was of the opinion that it would appeal to her. The war, however, that was to be stamped out so shortly, was already beginning to show signs of becoming the Great War and when that first winter was over, men realised the magnitude of the effort called for.

"I am coming home," wrote Joe to Fanny. "I am coming home to

155

join up," he wrote to Ella. That was why the wood and bronze memorial under the gallery in the Chapel bore a further name under its list of the fallen. 'Also Joseph Cawdor, returning home to the defence of Freedom, on board the Cunard liner *Lusitania*, sunk by enemy action 7th May 1915'.

Kerry was in funds at the moment. At least, she would have thought so if Christmas hadn't been in the offing, but even so she considered that she ought to plunge for some chocolates. They gave you something to do in the interval. So she turned aside and stood contemplating a polished, rounded window. There were circular boxes, large as sofa cushions, their contents arranged in a mosaic it would be vandalism to disarrange. Other boxes remained covered to show pictures and satin bows and there was one just right for Mrs Sinclair; a soppy-looking dog almost trampling on its own ears and leering into the camera. There was a brilliant herbaceous border that would also appeal to Mrs Sinclair. In fact, all these chocolate boxes were designed to catch Mrs Sinclair's eye. Except, perhaps, the pretty girls. Here and there, Kerry was glad to see, were miniature nosegay boxes amongst the Royal Chelsea effects.

"You like sweetmeats?"

Kerry almost jumped with surprise at the soft and level voice at her side. She saw a bearded brown face topped by a saffron yellow turban, but the rather imposing figure was otherwise clad in European fashion. The girl looked at him but he was not looking at her but at her reflection in the mirror-back of the display.

"Not all that much, really. I was just looking."

"They are fit for a queen." The voice itself had a cocoa-butter richness. "Your great Queen Elizabeth who was fond of them would never see sweetmeats gorgeously wrapped in gold as these, or arranged neatly as an Italian garden."

"Queen Elizabeth ruined her teeth, you know," volunteered Kerry, thinking that he ought to know.

"But yours are young and strong and would never suffer such a fate! Which do you prefer, the hard centres or the soft?"

"Of course a nut lasts longer, but I think I like a soft centre best. It's a lovely taste when the shell collapses and the cream pours out."

"Ah! If you could carry one of those boxes away to eat in private, which would you choose?"

"Well, you see, I'm not going to eat them in private. I'm going to the theatre here and I hate things that crackle and make people glance round."

She looked dejectedly at the highly crackling materials in and around all the boxes.

"You are going to the theatre alone?"

"Yes."

"And must you go and see this play?"

"Oh no! I'm going because I want to. I'm not going with the school."

This thought cheered the girl so much that any constraint fell away and she smiled fully at the stranger before moving jauntily away and boldly entering the Prince's Theatre.

Since she had not bought any chocolates after all, she decided to pay more for her seat. The orchestra was already playing. Her row was not full by any means, and if nobody came to the place on her left she would put her coat on it later on. The women here at the front were not wearing hats so Kerry took hers off too. They seemed to be a well dressed crowd; well, hardly a crowd. She would pluck up courage to look over her shoulder later. She regarded with envy the people who boldly stood up in their places and coolly ranged the audience for acquaintances. One woman was scrutinising the Dress Circle through opera glasses, although in this theatre there were no great distances, and the audience was held within one of those old-fashioned plush-lined work boxes with a place for everything and everything in its place. The bosomy boxes and the full-bodied upper circles were beribboned and true-love knotted with painted streamers bearing the names of the better known dramatists, their gilded name and fame further illuminated by the scintillating lustre lights glistening from swelling velvet-edged balconies like orders at a mid-European soirée. Everything was so cushioned and anti-macassared that it would seem impossible for anybody to be hurt in any way. If someone fell from the 'gods' he would surely bounce into their soft laps.

The man seated next to Kerry had given her a smile as she sat down and she heard him speak to his wife after a while.

"There'd be a riot it they altered the decorations here."

"It is rather sweet," the woman answered, "but they'll have to, some day."

Soon it was half past seven and the house lights dimmed, throwing the curtain into heightened effect in the Aurora Borealis of the footlights. Orchestra and audience were quite silent at a further swift darkening all around, and with a hushed expectancy in the air, the curtain, with a little excited intake of breath, suddenly divided and rose, making a secretive whispering in all its folds.

Over in Quay Street at the Opera House, exactly the same thing was taking place on a vast scale. Here the audience were bubbling with the

157

expectancy of a good time coming. They pitied the critics who had to carp for their supper generally, but who apart from making their annual plea for a still larger orchestra, were resigning themselves to enduring a happy night out on the same level as everybody else. Only Gilbert and Sullivan could reduce the crowd here to a family party. They would be more at home in the Prince's Theatre, leaving Oedipus to cope with the distances of the Opera House, but the Greeks would never have filled the temple intended for them, and the Victorians could never have squeezed their devotees into their own macaroni's band-box.

Fanny looked at the great mouldings high along the cornice and the huge plaster faces alternately saying 'Ha' and 'Oh' all round the frieze, the masks of comedy and tragedy. Pity and terror flanked by derisive laughter, laughter with tragedy on either side.

There wasn't a gently smiling mask suitable for the particular expression of a Gilbert and Sullivan audience; an expression of tender commiseration. Such emotions came later in the progress of intellectual participation, a civilised grace. The mere force of gravity can drop the jaw in horror, so that the human mask more readily forms the 'oh' of tragedy than the 'ha' of comedy, but the highest form of comedy lies somewhere between that 'oh' and that 'ha' and draws its expression from lines modulated from both these masks.

Fanny preferred to sit alone through *The Pirates of Penzance*, for 'He loves thee; he is gone', had become the history of her life compressed into the line of a song. She brooded throughout the Overture. She was in command of her life, she felt. Did she want to alter it at this stage? She was not at all unhappy. She knew she had some rather forthright ways of showing her independence but she certainly was not soured, whatever Clara snapped in repartee.

Some decision, however, would have to be made before Christmas. Whether to go on as she was, or to take a sudden side-step from the beaten track and surprise her old friends by marrying as she once had surprised them by not marrying! No use pretending this was love's young dream, the question was whether companionship in sickness or in health was worth having for its own sake.

Her own problems played in and out of the scenes before her all the evening, as she concentrated first on the fiction and then on her own fact. Perplexed and ill at ease, she listened to the touching farewell between Frederick and his Mabel.

"He loves thee. He is gone!"

When it came to the passing-bell of that stark word 'gone', there was a hollow echo in her own heart and she was thankful to be alone with it.

At the Prince's, however, some people were telling themselves that they would never come again; no, not if army mules were drafted for the job. If this was the Greek idea of a night out they could keep it. The lights went up on rows of faces that were saying 'Oh' unmistakably.

Conversation was very slow in starting. Women supercilious as camels drew furs round their shoulders and here and there an isolated titter went up in answer to some nervous frivolity, but the general atmosphere was chilly and unsociable. Only in the gods a buzz arose all the more noticeable because of the suspension of animation below.

The man next to Kerry stole a look at her and was reminded of rough crossings to the Isle of Man. He nudged his wife.

"This youngster next to me has gone an awful colour. Euripides on virgin soil, eh?"

The woman also peeped round and nodded.

"She ought to go into the fresh air."

Kerry coughed once but it somehow came out more like a groan and she was miserably embarrassed because of it. Her neighbour threw back his shoulders and remarked for all to hear, "Well, after that, let's have a drink, for pity's sake. Excuse me, please."

Usherettes were bringing trays of tea which were to be much in demand, but the man ignored them and went out. The woman leaned across to the girl, who was shivering slightly.

"It's not very warm in here, is it? The place isn't full enough but my husband will bring something warm."

Kerry would have gone out, too, if her limbs would have borne her and if she hadn't felt as though she were sticking to the plush.

The man had been very quick. He bore a tray of coffee for three and soon busied himself cheerfully, helping his wife. Kerry's shaking fingers were taking her purse from her little best handbag for special occasions and her hat fell on the floor from the next seat but the man said at once, "This is my idea I'm grateful to you for keeping the draught from me on this side."

Steadying the cup and saucer gave her something to think about and she direly needed something else to think about.

"Tough guys, the Greeks," observed the man. "To enjoy this stuff, you've got to be so highbrow as to be practically bald."

Kerry sipped the hot coffee and nibbled a biscuit and her vitals slowly warmed to life, but not the provinces as yet.

The friendly man was dividing his attention dutifully and was a great help.

"We'd always been led to believe that the Greeks were such wise guys, but they'd never heard of the proverb 'Least said, soonest mended,' had they? They simply let things go from bad to worse, if possible, and certainly had a word or two for it."

"It's a wonder they can learn it all," replied the woman, "or forget it again for that matter."

Kerry was feeling slightly less numb and frightened and drew a steadier breath.

"We mustn't let the Ancients get us down," went on the hearty voice. "They'd no idea of forgiving and forgetting, had they? They harped too much. Have another biscuit, do."

The audience having regained partial composure were glancing casually about to see how others were taking it. They all looked as if they had heard bad news recently and those supposed to be enjoying refreshment were doing so absentmindedly.

Kerry's cup hit the saucer rather loudly and the man turned to her again.

"These Greeks seemed to go in more for gnashing tooth to tooth than seeing eye to eye, more's the pity."

Kerry was feeling slightly stronger although the feeling of nausea came in regular waves still. She found that she could speak.

"I'd rather have Shakespeare after all."

"Good old Billy Boy!"

Taking another sip Kerry gave the cup an appreciative but baffled sniff.

"This coffee has a sort of perfume in it."

"It must be the brown sugar," said the man helpfully.

"It's giving me a beautiful glow amidships."

"I think there's another cup all round in this pot if you'd like it."

"No, thank you, but it's the nicest I've ever tasted."

Tea and coffee trays were now being handed in grudgingly, men shuffled uneasily from the bars and the audience began to settle down apprehensively to face what was coming. The man attentively poked at his wife's wrap and asked if she were warm enough and she sighed.

"I expect we shall all be glad when it's over."

"There's a spirit of revelry for you," he responded gloomily.

The lights jerked out in relays, except for a final reluctant fading round the walls.

Much had happened by the time the lights came on again; much had been enacted before the curtain made its last descent in a hurried, scared sort of way to blot out, after blinking once or twice while the audience mechanically applauded, the horrors of the night.

"I'm clapping more to get my circulation going than anything else,"

160

said the man. "The acting was fine, though." Then in an undertone to his wife, "I say, Elsie, would you care to suggest that we run her home?"

Herself considerably shaken, she was glad to acquiesce. She spoke to the girl as soon as they got to the end of the row.

"I'll be all right," came the answer through set lips.

"Of course you will," responded the man briskly, "but since we've all gone through it together, so to speak, we'll see you home. It'll be no trouble."

In the foyer Kerry pulled her hat well down and followed them to their car parked at the side of St. Peter's Square.

"It's nice to see the trams again, isn't it?" he remarked as he ushered her into the back seat.

Without the slightest jolt they moved swiftly away from the cars nosing out and from the crowds emerging from all the amusement places in the Oxford Road area. The car sped warily through Piccadilly and was soon out on the wide Oldham Road. In a few minutes they passed under the railway bridge and the woman looked sideways at Ella Kershaw's house. No lights at this hour. Their lives must be all darkness. She shivered.

Kerry looked at the chapel. The meeting would have finished long ago. Poor Mrs Mossop was blind but she didn't seem to take much notice. Kerry heaved a great sigh.

"Comfortable?" called the man with a quick look in the mirror.

"Yes, thank you. I was just feeling glad we're in AD now. One of my friends at school is a Jewess and they are very proud of their literature. When they build a house, they make a little cavity in the lintel of the door to hold some of the Scriptures, and the family bow as they enter."

"Very nice idea. I imagine some of the audience would like to wall up some of the stuff we've heard tonight."

It did not take long to reach Moston. How much quicker it was, like coming home from the station after the holidays. At the top of Lightbowne Road a tram held them up while the passengers passed across the car headlights, so Kerry said she would get out here as she only lived round the corner.

"Sure?"

He sprang out and opened the door for her with a heartening air.

What a good sort of person he must be to have around. She watched him reverse smoothly and swiftly drive down the road again. What a lovely car. It was as big as the Sinclair's.

Leonard and Clara had finished supper when Kerry came in and her mother heard her go straight upstairs. Sybil had been home from the Ice Palace some time and had gone to bed. Coming out of Fanny's room after placing a hot water bottle, Clara called out on the landing.

"Enjoyed it, Kerry?"

There was a mumbled reply.

"Are you coming down for some supper?"

"No, thanks."

As soon as Clara got to the bottom of the stairs Fanny arrived.

"Was it good?"

"Very."

"Supper's ready."

"I'll go straight up, thanks. Say goodnight to Leonard for me."

Back with Leonard, Clara was exasperated.

"Eating too many chocolates, I suppose. But I think they ought to have a glass of hot milk at least."

She busied herself in the kitchen while Leonard very mildly tried to dissuade her.

"If you go in, you'll only stay talking and I'm ready any time."

It wasn't long before Clara returned to the middle room.

"I'm taking some goat's milk to the others."

"Goat's milk?"

"In a manner of speaking. See you soon, Mahatma."

Clara tapped on the girls' door and handed the milk to Kerry.

"Don't forget it's 'Ruddigore' tomorrow. Now there's no need to be rude."

She then came back with the tray to Fanny's door.

"You'll need something after the theatre or you won't sleep."

"Thank you."

Fanny had been about to get into bed and she climbed in now. She took up the glass and sipped a spoonful.

"Someone told me recently that whisky is very soothing in milk."

The sisters eyed each other deliberately but Clara remained silent.

"Wouldn't it be an irony if after turning down a man in my young days because of it, I turned to it myself now as a night-cap?"

"Don't talk like that, Fanny."

"It was just a thought."

"Well, don't have any more like it."

Fanny stirred restlessly.

"No, if I was hard on him, I mustn't be soft with myself. But time changes one's views on some things. I think one of the great curses in this world is the desire to convert others to one's own way of thinking. Why can't we let each other alone? Everybody."

162

Clara perceived that the knife was turning and she could only look miserable.

"I was a fool," went on Fanny in low tones, "but I didn't think so then. He was a splendid man and if I couldn't make allowances for him, I'm not going to start making allowances for other people now."

Clara thought she saw some light.

"I thought you'd gone by yourself tonight. Had you an appointment with someone?"

"No," answered Fanny wearily. "I had not. But I shall have one day soon and I must know the truth about myself when the moment comes."

Fanny tapped the glass of milk with the spoon morosely.

"I'm too old to offer myself as a living sacrifice. If fancied imperfections maddened me then, how should I respond to real ones?"

"So you're going to turn down another decent man because he's human?" Clara asked.

There was silence and then Clara rose and spoke with great feeling.

"I can't say how sorry I am, Fanny, as you know. I suppose if we think we're in a better 'ole, we can't help wanting to pull others in as well. You think that's a mistake though."

"I do," replied Fanny. "The idea of a better 'ole, like the many mansions, varies with each individual. You doubtless would be lonely in my better 'ole and I should soon feel cramped in yours."

Clara felt that any sympathy created by one part of the statement was smothered by the hint of offensiveness in another. Who on earth could live long with Fanny? Perhaps nobody.

"You really enjoy living alone?"

"I don't think I could contemplate living with anyone now living," Fanny said wryly.

"In that case you are wise not to try," said Clara moving to the door. "And I hope the hot milk does the trick."

When alone, Fanny raised the glass to drain the final drops. As her lips parted, she thought of the masks of Comedy and Tragedy on the walls of the Opera House. Earlier in the evening she had played 'He loves me, he loves me not' along the row, knowing full well that either outcome was not the knowledge she was seeking. They would always say 'He loves thee; he is gone'. Now she would go through the rest of her life suppressing any revealing cry behind those expressive masks of Ha and Oh, of laughter and despair, of love and longing.

She had her work and that gave more interest to life than some fools would believe. Her business was established and her good taste was recognised and trusted beyond the seaside town.

The hot milk was asserting itself and Fanny stretched herself drowsily. She took up the gilt and shagreen travelling clock from under Sybil's frilled bedside lamp and started to wind it with care. "And really I'm letting it all run down," she reflected.

Her mind had ceased to vacillate. She surprised herself with an idle yawn.

She had survived some stormy scenes in her time; friends and family watching had cried Ha! and Oh! at the part she had played and she had played it consistently and in character. 'He loves thee; he is gone'. There couldn't be any other leading man. The curtain could not go up again on an anti-climax.

She reached out and switched off the rosy glow.

As the car that had dropped Kerry at the corner of Dean Lane sped back, the woman thought her husband had forgotten the way.

"Surely we should have turned left there?"

"No, this is North Road and joins Oldham Road later, cutting out a lot of traffic. I used to play cricket over on the right there. A very good ground, too."

"Yes, I know."

The voice sounded a trifle sharp, so he spoke quietly.

"We'll soon get home; it hasn't made much difference. Poor kid! She *was* fed up."

"Well, the evening hasn't exactly been a picnic for me, either."

Once again the man put on extra speed and nothing further was said as he concentrated upon getting along as quickly as possible.

The dining room was warm but Elsie snapped on another electric bar in the rather elaborate mock fire on the hearth.

"It had better be hot chocolate," she murmured as Sam passed through the kitchen.

"I'll switch on upstairs," he said, glad to be busy.

How soothing were the trivialities of living. They put a safety zone between him and the ancient primitive instincts. The car and its upkeep, the ever mounting electrical gadgets and comforts, the food unseen until in its most palatable form, all helped to divide the cave man from the modern man. He and Elsie stood hedged in by a stainless steel fence from all that was assertive, overwhelming and crude. They ate hygienic stainless food and expressed hygienic stainless sentiments; there was no cutting edge to the stainless knives; they glittered on the table but they were only capable of dealing with the tenderest meat. They were fenced in but also separately caged, he in

164

his protected tower, she in hers.

Gosh! What a play! How one's thoughts went back to it. He'd known it would be awful, but not bloody awful!

By Elsie's bed were the magazines that helped her to make the house modern and de-nationalised. Did she read much else? Now that she wasn't really convalescent any more, she didn't need food for the mind that was just light and tempting. Of course she had not enjoyed the evening's outing, but that was an extreme case. Had she not been moved by any emotion other than distaste? Had she never in her life known agony of mind? Had she never read any of the Greek tragedies, he wondered? Perhaps terror and self-pity were the strongest emotions she had experienced; even love had been overlaid by such bedfellows!

He cast a quick glance over table and shelf.

Elsie sipped the hot sweet cup. Oh, those awful people tonight, making such a fuss about everything and being so disgusting! In these days if things got too much of a bore, people had the decency to withdraw quietly with sleeping tablets.

She rose swiftly to her feet.

"I'll take mine up. You'll switch everything off, won't you?"

"Yes. I'll just look through the *Evening News* first. Goodnight and sleep well."

Sam took up the newspaper and lit a cigarette. There was no hurry.

Elsie was glad to get to bed, if glad was not too definite a word for being heartily tired of the day. There was nothing worth getting up for; nothing worth going to bed for! She would have her hair re-set tomorrow. A woman in front of her tonight had the back quite sleek and brought to a neat point like a widow's peak. She might try it. That was something to look forward to. Better than nothing.

She lay and considered. Should she have a good cry first and then look at the latest glossies or the other way about? She decided to study the coloured interiors and picked up a magazine. It was early days to see if these illustrations foreshadowed an oriental or American influence, but there was no doubt that space was being brought in and tangible things thrown out. She would rearrange the lounge for a start.

She must have dozed off unexpectedly for she woke with a jerk that sent the magazine ski-ing over the edge of the bed. She looked at the clock, an unwanted wedding present that needed winding every day. Only one o'clock. But she had actually fallen asleep without either comforting cry or a sleeping pill. No wonder she had only slept for an hour. Had Sam come up yet?

A deep sustained rumble came from outside that could be strong wind rushing the trees or it might be the beginning of thunder. She was sure she'd been dreaming, but the thin shreds of its retreating fringe were twitched away. She watched the edges of the curtains for any momentary selvedge of lightning, but the bed light was too strong. She slid quietly from the sheets and into her slippers and then softly opened her bedroom door. Sam's door was ajar with the light showing but no sound at all could be heard. He must be in the bathroom. He had smoked more than one cigarette if he was only just coming up. She still had round her shoulders the light woollen wrap she wore for reading, so she stepped out along the carpet and looked round the aperture. Surprise fixed her.

With his back to the electric fire Sam was on his knees by the bed, motionless with his face in his hands. Elsie felt a peculiar sensation. Fancy! He still said his prayers, after all they had gone through! Men did not feel as intensely as did women. They were nothing like as sensitive.

Before she could draw back after that pause, Sam raised his head and stood up quickly.

"I was just putting in a word for the royal family," he said and waited for her to speak.

"Oh, it's nothing," she said in a thin voice. "Something woke me up and I just wondered if you were still downstairs. As a matter of fact it sounded like thunder. Listen! There it is again."

"Well, you won't want to go downstairs again, surely. You get back into bed and leave the door open and I'll potter about a bit. It seems a long way off."

Elsie went back and could hear Sam dutifully taking as much care to make some noise as a few minutes ago he'd been careful to make none. A smooth drawer opened and shut, a bar of his fire was switched off and then, surprisingly at that time of night, a pleasant baritone with an attractive suggestion of warble in it, struck up "I have a song to sing O, Sing me your song O", and then ceased abruptly as though garroted; but in a moment or two the silence was interspersed with casual humming and wordless song.

He tapped and put his head round the door.

"All right?"

"Yes, really, but after that awful play, I can't sleep. I suppose men's nerves are different from women's. It doesn't trouble you, does it?"

"I don't think it would keep me awake. Shall we have another cigarette while it blows over? I'll fetch them."

He found the one comfortable chair and switched on her fire again and put an ash-tray on her table. He was careful not to place the chair too near. Actually he had been very sleepy but now he was wide

166

awake; not tensed like a hunter who sees his prey, but pleased and excited as Ludwig Koch would be at getting within a few feet of a rare bird and anxious not to scare her. He gazed into the basilisk stare of the electric fire. There were no pulsating pictures there.

Elsie listened for thunder and then regarded Sam.

"Tell me something of your boyhood that I don't know about. There must be lots of things that I can never catch up with."

Sam shot a quick glance.

"Sort of Arabian Nights reversed, eh? There's not much to tell, Elsie. It's all flashed past my eyes pretty quickly."

"Well, surely you'd been in love with some girls at some time?"

"Nothing special."

"But you must have. What came nearest to it? Someone admired from a distance, perhaps?"

Sam blew out some smoke and looked through it where she floated as in a pipe dream.

"Perhaps from a distance, and the distance is greater than ever now."

"Both married, you mean?"

Sam reflected for a moment or two with his chin down.

"I used to have something of a voice, you know, and one choir picnic we went to a place called Greenfield where there's a hill called Pots-and-Pans for some reason. A bunch of us went up. Very stony, I remember. There was a girl called Ena who was very pretty and who sang jolly well, too . . ."

"Like your Rainbow?"

Sam looked surprised.

"Oh, I don't know. Perhaps her style. She was on the quiet side but still entered into things, you know."

Here Sam paused and Elsie said, "Go on."

"I don't know that there's much to go on about. When we were coming downhill again and had reached a place where it was less steep, we all started to run, laughing and excited you know, and after a minute Ena called out, "I can't stop." We were in the same fix as the Gadarene swine, I suppose. However, I was able to catch hold of her hand and we raced down together, I trying to brake a bit, but then we fell down over the tufty grass and rolled over and over for a few yards before we stopped and were able to sit up, still laughing but out of breath. We'd all had a good shaking up but weren't hurt. Then Ena cried, "Oh look!" and pointed, and over my trouser leg there was a little yellow fledgling scrambling for foothold and between us a nest that one of us had overturned in falling. Someone said it was a lark's nest with eggs. We'd heard some birds trilling away as we'd gone slowly up. We were all very sorry, of course. We righted the nest and put the young one in it and an egg that we found still whole, and then we all moved quietly away, hoping that the parents would go back to it later."

Sam stopped talking. After a long pause, Elsie spoke, leaning back with her eyes closed.

"How old were you?"

"Oh, I'd be about eighteen and Ena perhaps twenty-one."

"Didn't you see much of her after that?"

"Oh, she always smiled and had a word in Choir. That winter she died of pneumonia."

There was silence in the room and Elsie was so still she might have dozed off. He finished his cigarette. Elsie's had gone out and hung over the side of the bed in her limp hand and he wondered if he could disengage it without waking her. He sat quietly until she stirred.

"Do you think you will sleep now?" he asked gently.

Elsie opened her eyes with the business-like air of a shop opening its door for the day.

"No, I do not think I shall sleep now. What a time to tell me all that."

"All what? There was hardly anything of it."

"Anybody knows that love at a distance is the real thing."

Sam backed his chair slightly.

"I can't agree with you there, Elsie, if you mean it's the only real thing. The process of loving is that it proceeds, and properly goes on from loving at a distance to loving at close quarters."

Perhaps that was too forceful. She had a delicate mind, so he hurried on.

"If we admire anything, we want to look at it closely. We draw near. It·is when time and distance intervene that we tend to forget."

Sam looked at her helplessly. Like the conditioned children in a Huxley novel she had once put out her hand to touch the roses and had received a great shock. He knew that when he came too near, every nerve in her body rang an alarm. The poor girl was too frightened to relax, or if she did, she went statuesque at the first touch, a Galatea in reverse.

And what of himself, on a starvation diet of love, nibbling at a friendly word, making it last for a whole day? His watchfulness for her made him careful for himself, taking the precaution that a hungry man takes when tightening his belt. In time the stomach would shrink and subsist on morsels.

"Listen, Elsie. I shall never give anything to anybody else that you want, but we can't measure and parcel out love, this for you and this for me, a bit extra for you, a bit less for me. It's too great, like parceling out the firmament. I love you, my darling, and would do anything to make you happy. When you are strong again, you *will* be happy."

He replaced the chair. It gave him something to do.

Elsie looked at him and then away.

"I sometimes wish that you didn't and then I shouldn't have to worry about things. You are too good for me. If only you could meet a thoroughly nice woman who would look after you properly! I'm just not cut out for it."

Terror stilled Sam for a moment. She mustn't talk about it. She must not formulate such thoughts.

"But nobody could look after me better than you do. You're a wonderful wife. And I'm not grumbling, am I?"

"No." Elsie's voice was pettish again. "I suppose if a man is well fed it takes a lot to make him grumble. But think of me! What made me ill? I could play tennis for hours on end before I married, and look at me now!" (She glanced at the table and at a framed photograph of herself receiving a silver cup.) "They say that a civilisation is beginning to decay when its women are too intelligent to have children and its men too intelligent to go to war. If that is so, then give me decadence."

She flopped back on her pillows angrily. Well, she had really come out into the open, which Sam feared less than the ambush.

"I wish," he said quite heartily, "that you could make that speech to a few European Dictators. Mussolini would be surprised, for one."

"Why do men always think women ill or nervy when we face facts?"

"Go it, Mrs Pankhurst. You're winning."

Elsie laughed, rather pleased, but then hesitated.

"The Pankhursts? Didn't they . . ?" Her voice trailed off.

"Indeed they did," responded Sam with relish. "Some did and some didn't; all in the name of the Cause. Or the effect. It was just a matter of which they preferred. That's the beauty of emancipation; everybody interprets it as she chooses."

Elsie ceased to look pleased either with herself or with Sam.

"Now you're making fun again!"

"No, I'm not. You think it over."

He took a few paces away and then back to the unwanted wedding present that always needed rewinding. Two o'clock!

"Elsie! Intelligence is not the highest form of life. Sometimes a

h

higher form is the deliberate choice of a less intelligent way. Getting married isn't a sign of intelligence, as you'll agree, but we all have a stab at it in a fit of happy lunacy; and for the majority, it works, and not because the majority are intelligent, either. And as for war, don't forget that I fought alongside men who might be here today if they'd put intelligence first. And we are here because they are not; but perhaps we haven't made the most of the chances they gave us."

Sam came to the foot of the bed and leaned his hands on the low wooden board so that his shoulders were hunched.

"We hold each other's health and happiness in our hands and what have we done to each other? We're not the same people at all. We are older, and God knows we are sadder; everything but wiser; sacrificing to our grievances from the dwindling stock of the best in us until we are . . . what we are."

Elsie now began to cry quietly. She drew up her knees and rested her forehead on them above her clasped arms. It was better not to interrupt that relief and Sam stayed where he was, watching her sombrely.

"It isn't your fault, Sam." She spoke without moving. "It isn't your fault. Perhaps it isn't even mine. I don't know. There is so much about you that I like and admire. You are so patient. But it's just that I have grown to hate love."

Sam could not bring himself to speak. Then in a higher pitch, muffled because of her sunk head, her words struck at him.

"It's like a python. At first it is only a caress; an arm stealing round your waist, and then it tightens and you realise it is going to crush you, kill you."

Sam raised his head and slowly straightened up like a tired gardener.

"No, Elsie. Love doesn't kill us. We kill love. We do not grow to hate love. We do not grow at all. We shrink, we decline, we come to hate ourselves."

He left the foot-board and paced the carpet between the bed and the door. His right hand repeatedly struck at his left palm as he walked, until finally, he seized the chair again and brought it near, seating himself upon it so that his head was more on a level with hers.

"Now listen, Elsie. Listen, my dear, carefully and answer carefully. You may not even know the true answer. But do you feel you have come to hate *me?*"

Her head flung up for a moment and after a frightened look at him she let it rest heavily on her arms again.

"No! No! I only wish I could. Everything would be so simple if I

170

could. Hate is straightforward. Love is complicated. I still do love you mentally, but . . . "

"Stop," said Sam shortly. "Don't say any more now. If you love me mentally, that's fine. It's wonderful of you to tell me and the best news I've heard for a long time. But don't say any more; you'll spoil it. Let it go at that. You love me mentally! What is there to cry about in that?"

Elsie brought her head round to look at him.

"But I know now that I'm a coward. This thunder tonight and . . . other things. You were so thoughtful for that girl at the theatre. You would have been . . ."

Her mouth closed and trembled and Sam dared to lean forward and take one of her hands from round her knees.

"You are not a coward, dear. You've had a touch of shell shock, perhaps, but courage will return with health."

"No. Health might return with courage, but I know that I just don't want the responsibilities of courage."

Sam stroked the hand, limp in his.

"Not yet. Perhaps not even for a long time, but don't worry. Love has more than one side and you are giving too much importance to one side at the moment. Fancy your telling me that you love me mentally! Why, you'll be telling me soon that you love me from a distance! And here are your opera glasses that you hardly used tonight. You take a good look at me through the other end now and again and you won't know me from Clark Gable."

She had to give a weak little laugh.

"That's better," said Sam, patting her hand. "There'll come a time some day when you'll be looking round. 'Where's Sam? He was here a moment ago.' And you'll be watching the clock and saying 'Sam won't be long now.' And on Saturdays you'll say, 'I might go and meet Sam for lunch and a movie since it's wet,' and as for Sundays, you'll think it the best day in the week when we're together."

She looked at him tremulously and he released her hand.

"There, I think the storm has by-passed us. Not Chorltonville's turn tonight."

He replaced the chair and switched off the fire and picked up the fallen magazines, while she watched him with pathetic envy. How wonderful to be matter-of-fact! He wasn't soft centred; not even self-centred.

"You ought to have been a sailor, Sam. You're so tidy."

"Ah, but I lack one of their tougher characteristics; a girl in every port. Now I think I can do a bunk to my own little bunk, if you are settling down."

"Yes, there isn't going to be a storm after all. And I do appreciate it, Sam."

"A pleasure."

"By the way, have you ever done any acting?"

"Acting? Not since sketches and charades at parties and so on. Why?"

"I think you could act if you tried. You've got the voice. Well, goodnight again, what there is of it."

"Goodnight, my dear, and if ever you'd like a signed photograph, you've only to ask."

Chapter Fifteen

There were signs that December was going to play-act an old-fashioned Christmas and open the box of tricks in the wintry lumber room for the powdered wig and the keen rapier, seemingly to suggest that Christmas would arrive in a sedan chair rather than an open sleigh.

By day the sun was a tangerine orange thrown in a grey satin lap, and by night the moon, a silvered bauble, gleamed singly through the naked branches as if the tree dressing had been interrupted as soon as begun.

Men became aware that they breathed. The air, on ice before they drank it down, surprised the sluggish lungs and then escaped in a witnessed cloud. While nature lay dormant, man was reminded that he lived though he offered up his breath.

"Do you think the lake will freeze this year?" asked Kerry this cold Saturday afternoon. "I hope it does; I love it when the Clough keeps open and people go skating by moonlight. Can I have some skates, do you think, for Christmas?"

"We'll see. But I think I've still got my old ones somewhere."

"Oh, those won't do! You've got to have them screwed on nowadays. Tell her, Geoffrey, that nobody has straps now."

"True, Mrs Martland. At the Ice Palace boots are getting higher and skirts, too. People keep a pair of boots specially for skating."

"*We* never needed fancy dress," said Clara, her voice scornful as her younger daughter's. "It would have been extravagant to keep a pair of boots idle except for skating."

"But, Mother," Sybil's gentler tones broke in, "you didn't skate indoors as we do."

"You must all come one evening," said Geoffrey. "People just go to watch. They love the awful kids who are going to be champions; insufferable little beasts."

Sybil laughed.

"Oh! Geoffrey, you won't have heard yet about the Badminton Club that's going to be started down at the school. It was Mrs Garner's idea. Not just for our own chapel members but for anybody."

"Hoping that if somebody comes to play they might eventually come to pray. I doubt it," said the young man.

"Now, Geoffrey," admonished Clara, "don't throw cold water. We've got to lead the horse, you know. Young Mr Garner has promised to join and of course Sybil will go."

"There'll be a fine band of helpers and nobody wanting to be helped."

"And then," went on Clara, ignoring him, "Fred Winskill has suggested a Junior Club in place of the old Band of Hope which seems to have petered out. Last winter simply no one turned up and Fred just sat there waiting."

"A one-man Band of Hope," grinned Geoffrey.

"I told him Kerry would be glad to go down one night a week," Clara finished in all innocence.

"What!" cried Kerry in horror. "You did? I don't want to go. What could I do?"

"It's very good of Mr Winskill to find somewhere for the children round the school to go, instead of roaming the streets. I thought you might show appreciation."

"But I don't roam the streets! Except when I take Watch. I want to get on with my reading. I want to go to the library to change my books. And there's my homework," she added as an afterthought. Tears of anger were in her eyes.

"I'm sure it's all going to do a lot of good," drawled Geoffrey.

Clara looked at him with annoyance.

"Well, it wasn't my idea. Things were going on nicely as they were. It's the people next door who want new blood."

"There's young Mr Garner now," called Kerry who was near the window. "He's just got off the tram." She pressed further into the low window and waved. "He's letting himself in next door."

Geoffrey rose to his feet.

"Well, who's for a walk before it begins to get dark? What about it, Sybil?"

Kerry looked at them.

"Are you taking Watch?"

"You mean that horizontal biscuit-barrel on the wedding cake pillars? All right, if you'll come too and take charge."

Kerry flew to throw on her hat and coat and Sybil withdrew more slowly, while the young man seated himself at the piano. It was at such moments that Clara was fondest of him. He played a different style of music from Sybil's accompaniments and Leonard's church voluntaries, being one of those sprites of the piano who can make it sound as if at least four hands were playing. He crashed out a few wild bars that made the trinkets tinkle on Sybil's dressing table and then slid into a series of musical comedy hit tunes that penetrated to every corner of the house.

"Play a bit of Haydn, please, Geoffrey," said Kerry, buttoning up her coat.

"Why a bit of Haydn?"

"He's so neat."

"Neat? What's neatness to you?"

"Well, he's a pattern I can follow."

"Don't you prefer listening to a large pattern that you can't quite follow?"

Nevertheless he controlled his exuberance and embarked upon a 'neat' piece that knew its own clear mind and revelled in it.

They were roused by a ring at the front door and the girl rushed to open it.

David Garner entered and was welcomed. He had come to ask Sybil's advice on the rota of play when badminton started.

"They're going for a walk," Clara informed him, "so perhaps you would care to join them and discuss it."

Seeing that Kerry also was ready in her outdoor things he accepted readily.

"We're still only four and a dog," said Geoffrey. "Doesn't anybody else want to come?"

Sybil came in just then looking very pretty and seasonable, and after a few words of explanation, Clara managed to get them all outside.

"You ought to put Watch on the lead, Kerry," warned Geoffrey.

"But he'll have to go on the lead in the Clough."

"Well, one of these days he'll cause an accident, not unfortunately to himself. He's all misdirected energy!"

Kerry rather sulkily clipped on the lead and to dispel her aggrieved look, Geoffrey came alongside and actually bent and patted the dog.

"Read any bad books lately, Kerry? What's the Report like?"

"Pretty foul."

"What about English?"

"Oh, well, that's nothing."

"Top?"

"Yes." Here a tone of something approaching enthusiasm came into

175

her voice. "We had a marvellous choice of essays and when we got them back, Little Billee read mine to the class."

"And that made you feel pretty good!"

"Oh, Geoffrey, I felt positively holy."

Sybil, walking behind with David Garner, was not talkative, but had an air of listening for something that she wasn't quite sure would be heard by her inner or outer ear. She glanced up occasionally at Garner. Something within her struggled for utterance but she coldly ignored it as a school teacher pretends not to see a distracting hand raised in the front row when she is doing the register.

"My idea for the rota," David was saying, "is that when a latecomer arrives he should get a game as soon as the court empties, then he's sure of one game at least."

"But if the early birds took the trouble to arrive early, they'll expect more than one worm for a whole evening's attendance," called Geoffrey over his shoulder. "And a planned foursome could be split up so that neither tigers nor rabbits would think much of the idea. The people who butted in will spoil everything. As usual," he added shortly.

But Garner was not easily put off his stride.

"The list isn't so much a crocodile as a round robin. It's amenable."

"One night I must come along to referee the rota and shall probably be trampled to death by rabbits and tigers. The mourners will form a neat crocodile shedding appropriate tears and a round robin will sing on my grave."

"Have people to bring their own rackets?" asked Kerry. "Skates and a racket! What's Father going to say?"

"No, no. The idea was mentioned to Mr Sinclair who kindly offered to meet the cost of equipment; four rackets and the net." The subs are to keep the club going in feathers."

"I hope the club sub doesn't strain itself," said Geoffrey. "He hasn't said anything to me about it."

He dropped back a pace so that Sybil moved forward to join her sister.

"I wonder if the church will get anybody from outside," he went on. "What's your opinion of this move to hold services in cinemas?"

"It's a novelty but it can't last long for the simple reason that cinemas will be showing films on Sunday quite soon, but if people are used to plush tip-up seats, they might find it less strange to slip into a cinema than through a church door."

"I say, Sybil, do you see your father coming up through the floor on the mighty Wurlitzer?"

"Not really."

"No," agreed Geoffrey. "It's all going too far. Isn't there a bit in Proverbs about a girl trying to track down her lover and getting knocked about by the night watchmen and losing her veil? No good came of it."

"There certainly is such a bit," said David laughing, "but strictly speaking, it's in the Song of Songs."

"Not Proverbs? You surprise me. I like the Book of Proverbs; it puts women in their proper place, all amongst the conies. But wherever it's mentioned, it is a warning to church or woman not to lose her veil; a mystery is always more interesting. But don't you get some shocks? The year before last there was a University garden party at The Firs and I took a special peep under a wide-brimmed hat and was rewarded by the most pronounced squint it has so far been my lot to encounter."

They had arrived at the top of the 'brow' leading down to the Clough, and from here to the bridge over the stream it was by courtesy open country for dogs. Watch could only have two or three minutes of liberty but it was worth it. Of course it was worth it. He nearly turned a somersault as he rushed from the girl's hands and careered round in circles as if doing a turn on the Wall of Death. He got some furious exercise in what to the others was a short descent to the bridge. He sniffed the clean gutter and lapped a trickle of water; he chewed the grass and rolled over, writhing to ease a sensation in the middle of his back; he derided another dog prematurely enchained and jumped up joyously at Kerry repeatedly and once, mistakenly, at Geoffrey. He chased a running boy, yapped at an elderly pair of heels to hurry them on and finally arrived, a distraught snowball, at the bridge where he suddenly sat down and dragged his tail comfortingly over the scratchy gravel.

"He wants another powder," whispered Kerry to Sybil, and grabbed him and put him on the lead again.

On the broad walk she got almost as much exercise as Watch, for she tried to keep up with him on a slack lead.

They had turned to the right upon crossing the bridge, the three others walking abreast.

"I think the air is more bracing on this side of town," said Garner, sniffing appreciatively.

"Oh, it is," rejoined Sybil loyally. "Dr Bedser always says that on the Moss the air blows straight across from Blackpool."

"When the wind is strong there are shrimps in it," said Geoffrey.

They walked quickly, enjoying the keen air until they came almost to the lake and Geoffrey whistled for girl and dog far ahead and got immediate response.

The water was black and choppy but nowhere near freezing yet, although the wind was bitter as they walked round the edge out of the protection of the trees. The boats were all indoors for the winter and the little pay-box tight shut, but someone took the trouble to keep the clock going in the gable of the boat-house.

"It's surprising what a head can be whipped up on exposed shallow water."

Geoffrey was standing with his hands in his over-coat pockets. "And it can be perishing cold up here. If this wind would give the water a chance to be still, it would freeze."

"I wonder if anybody has ever fallen in and been drowned," said Kerry speculatively.

"Not unless they'd fallen into a coma first, I should think. Anybody could walk out. Where are the swans?"

They all moved to the railings at the rear of the boat-house to look for the birds on the more sheltered pond that provided bearable winter quarters among reeds and a wooden refuge on the margin.

"A boat or a bird enhances still water," said David. "Turbulent water is a complete picture and needs no addition. In the east," here he turned to Sybil, "the attraction of the watergarden lies mainly in the delicate reflections."

"Mills look well by it, windmills, that is, and palaces," said Geoffrey. "Nothing looks nobler than a broad flight of steps leading up from the water's edge. We must go to Venice, some day," he added to Sybil.

She stared at the swans without speaking.

Kerry was leaning her forehead against the railings and remembering sunset and moonrise on her summer holidays. It made her dizzy to think of the times the tide had ebbed and flowed since she watched by the sea. It was lapping on stones or sand at this moment, not bothering whether anybody looked at it or not, except that it was more petulant in winter as if perhaps a storm was its way of drawing attention to itself, its way of showing off.

She lapsed into a childhood game of trying to think of everything at once. She had discovered that if you try to think of everything at once, you find yourself thinking of nothing; like a fakir. Not that game they did at school in English; association of ideas; but her own brand, absolute disassociation of ideas. The sea, bricks, tapers, the French Revolution, chutney.

"Kerry, my dear girl, take your head away from those railings. If you got it stuck we should have to walk on without you. Then the Fire

Brigade would come and saw through a bar, and in this weather their numbed fingers . . ."

"Geoffrey led her firmly up the grassy slope to the lake-side.

They walked four abreast here and Watch was free again as so few people were about. They were legging it rather smartly square into the wind, with chins well down, and as they gradually wheeled out of its direct attack their heads were aslant to fill in any little chink between coat collars and mufflers.

David scanned the open prospect in the direction of the Pennines and Sybil asked a question rather shyly.

"Are you hoping to go back to work in China later on?"

Garner hesitated.

"I've decided nothing definitely yet. Of course there's always a tremendous pull if you've once lived there for any length of time; and my father and mother put in twenty-five very rewarding years there. I should have some very great advantages to start with if I returned; very great indeed.

"And what's holding you back?" ventured Geoffrey rather loudly over Sybil's head, as speech tended to be whipped aside on the wind.

Garner's voice came back equally loudly.

"Things are changing very quickly in the East. There are signs that our work is being resented in certain quarters, even where it was first welcomed."

"You mean," Geoffrey called back, "like teaching a man to stand on his own feet and then he stamps on yours."

"I hope it won't come to that. More like being shown the door when the lesson's over. We can't tell yet. But Communism is doing for China what Mussolini is doing for Italy."

"And the words 'doing for' will probably come to the same thing in the end."

"Well," explained David, "at least it is getting certain wheels to go round in China which will help it to move in *some* direction instead of standing still, and although Communism may be a retrograde step for a forward nation, it may be a forward step for a backward nation. Some machinery must be found to pull it out of the ditch."

"A government without a recognised opposition is a machine built without brakes and is going to have a wild career."

David made no answer but walked on gloomily.

"No, I may never go back to China," he broke out at length. "For a time we shall be on sufferance and then not suffered at all."

"And what would you do," asked Geoffrey after a moment or two, "if you did not go back?"

The other came to a standstill, his back to the wind, facing the choppy water where its expanse was greatest. The others stopped and drew together, and Kerry picked up the tremulous Watch and, like the other two listeners, gazed into the young minister's face.

He withdrew his gaze from the far side of the lake seen past the rhododendron covered island and looked at his companions quickly in turn before speaking directly to Geoffrey.

"Some people say, wrongly, that Christianity in Europe is played out, and that Africa will be the next stronghold of our faith. Even if Asia is the cradle of early man, I consider Europe to be his school-room and university. But something has gone wrong over the centuries."

David now shifted his gaze to Sybil who was regarding him with too much interest to be embarrassed.

"As a matter of fact," she pronounced solemnly, "we were brought up to respect the Cloth, and I think we ought."

"Oh, that Cloth with a capital C," said David wryly but smiling at her warmly. "Just look at those chimneys away on the moors."

The trio turned where he pointed. "Today the Cloth has to go through the mill like any other fabric."

"To be made, I hope, into immaculate gents' suitings," said Geoffrey.

"That's the general idea," responded David laughing. "It has been so easy for the shepherd's crook to be elaborated into the crozier and for the friar's simple garb to stiffen with the gold thread of the embroidered cope, until Christianity itself became encrusted with symbols. There is a big difference, Sybil, between venerating the Cloth . . ."

"She said 'respecting'," interrupted Geoffrey.

"Sorry! Yes, between respecting the Cloth and being blinded by it."

"Hear, hear," came heartily from Geoffrey.

"All these beautiful symbols," went on David, "may help some people to concentrate and even to understand, but in some religious communities the symbols have strengthened in importance from being helpful to the soul's comfort to being necessary to the soul's safety. We do not wish to wrench the Rosary from anybody's fingers. In fact a Rosary is a good idea; a spiritual abacus."

The young man spoke vehemently and it was evident that he carried his small congregation with him, for their tight quartet remained in the same position, making no suggestion of movement beyond a nod of agreement.

Watch suddenly sprang into activity and out of Kerry's arms and the four spread out again, walking on slowly, but no one ventured to change the subject and David started again.

"You see, in Europe, the priesthood of every member of the church is unknown. The priesthood is a cult, a closed shop, with dictatorial powers. Here, the priest is leader and shepherd but the man of God is a man like his flock. The flock are men of God like their shepherd. I only want to offer a choice and nobody is going to quarrel over which people choose. But I do quarrel over the fact that they are not offered a fair choice."

"That," said Geoffrey slowly, "is the church at its very highest level. And where will you get that? Even if we consider that all mankind are the children of God, we must admit that plenty don't take after Father!"

"Plenty of us," said David gravely, but Kerry, to cover her giggle, ran ahead calling the dog.

"Plenty of us," David repeated. "It ought not to be. Europe need not embrace either clericalism or anti-clericalism. It could yet choose Christianity."

"If you remember Europe's history," Geoffrey recalled, "its atheism is understandable."

"On the other hand, if you consider Europe's atheism, its history is understandable." David swung round and filled his lungs with cold and presumably fresh air and the others became aware of the biting east wind again.

"Let's go down into the walk where it is more sheltered, or better still," said Geoffrey, "we can take the path among the trees."

Between the lower walk and the top of the ravine there was a narrow path running parallel and known only to local people familiar with the Clough.

They moved in among the trees and had to walk in single file, the bare wood affording them glimpses of their earlier way. This path would continue at its present level much beyond the bridge where they had come into the Clough and would give the walkers a good round trip, sufficient for a late afternoon start.

"But you haven't said yet," began Geoffrey as they moved slowly along the rough path, "what all this has to do with not going back to China after all."

"It is this," answered the student and those in front again stopped and turned.

"I must honour without limitations all those who have obeyed our Lord's injunction to go into all the world and preach the gospel. Among them are my own parents. But I cannot but see amongst my own countrymen a pressing need for salvation. That small building between Temptation and Education."

Here he smiled at Geoffrey. What a memory the man's got, thought the latter.

"I've discussed it with my friend Warner and since he's a great one for the Barricades, I've had a great deal of encouragement. I know our people as a whole do not like to jump up and down, but they ought to look for more expectancy, there ought to be more stir amongst them. Should we not have sunk indeed if foreign missionaries had come here to fire *us* with the Good News? Back to Pope Gregory."

"Do you not think," said Geoffrey very slowly, "that if the average Englishman felt that somebody was preaching to him out of turn, he would have enough sense of tradition to acquaint him of the fact?"

"Ah, tradition. That is always menaced by ivy."

"And here," said Geoffrey stopping short in the path, "the ivy is winning."

He indicated a tree by the path showing strong parasitical stems running parallel up to branches blurred by glossy alien leaves. He seized a cord and ripped it from the bark which it left with dry spluttering protestations from myriads of tendrils. He got out his penknife and severed the stem where it clung stubbornly.

The others joined in the attack, dragging at the tenacious ropes of mock embellishment that had crept up the gnarled crevices, hauling upon them until the loosened strands hung forlorn as forgotten ribbons on an abandoned maypole. When the tree was freed the young men and their helpers stood back and looked at their handiwork with satisfaction.

"One thing we must not do," said David. "We can't put the clock back and assume old chains of superstition and myth. Having slashed the ivy, it must not take hold again, and the next storm will scatter the bits left."

They walked on, picking their way over loose stones and a canted footpath slippery with leaves not yet dried out in the shade of the bare trees.

Kerry looked about her appreciatively. What would the week be without the week-end? Every now and again from over the top of the slope on their right, came a distant concerted roar from the football ground. It was an added pleasure to hear all those people enjoying themselves, and in a different way from oneself so that they didn't jostle into one's own field. One needn't feel sorry for them, need not bother about them or have collections for them, but just forget about them until they raised those huge shouts of delight when someone

182

scored or saved a goal.

"Willie Briggs is showing them how," said Geoffrey. "We'll go one afternoon, Garner, if you'd care. He'll be first-rate some day."

Sybil was quite elated.

"Yes, you do. You'll enjoy it. And I'll have tea ready for you both when you get home."

The arrangement gave her real pleasure.

David was the first to speak again.

"Won't you girls come as well?"

"Oh no, thank you. You two enjoy yourselves in your own way. We'll be all right."

The rough little path was now among denser trees and began to lead down gently to that part of the Clough where stood the thick grove. It led to the heart of a small clearing past the over-shadowed and deserted buildings and came to the cross-roads at the most thickly wooded hollow of the vale. At the centre of this space stood a sandstone fountain, tall and solidly built, high canopied and raised on a dais of steps. Four bronze lion heads watched the approaches, spouting water on demand into graceful metal catchments and heavy captive cups which clanked their chains when anybody picked them up. On summer days school children sat on the grass borders of the walks and sketched this well known hub.

"Look at this place now," said Geoffrey. "Absolutely forsaken. Even the refreshment room is closed, but you could weigh yourself, Kerry, if that's any consolation. That's right, harness Watch in case a peacock makes off with him."

"I wonder if one of them will spread his tail," she answered hopefully, "or don't they in winter?"

"Is there a close season for vanity?"

"Not for male vanity!" Sybil remarked sagely. "I have seen them displaying in all weathers just to please the public and not their own hens, and I shouldn't be surprised if one obliged if we stood and stared."

"I feel, Sinclair, there is a reflection upon us somewhere in that speech!"

"Not at all," replied Geoffrey. "There's nothing paltry about the peacock's display and if he is exercising his art whether the hen is looking or not, he's a true artist. That the hen may be dazzled is only important to him in spring. He's a civilised bird is the peacock."

"Except when he utters," Sybil observed critically.

They stood near the grass verge where a bird was strutting and dragging his tail over the wet sward with the indifference of an elegant woman in full court dress.

"He isn't at his best," said David, "in spite of his civilisation. We must see him in his spring fancy."

Kerry looked around and eyed the fountain.

"I wish I'd had a drink before I came out. When I was little I always wanted to have a drink there but Mother was afraid I might pick up germs or something."

"These mothers!" Geoffrey sighed heavily. "Well, Kerry, now's your chance. As almost a relation, I give you permission to slake your thirst. I'll even lift you up if you can't reach."

"Stop it! As a matter of fact I've not had the feeling for a long time."

Geoffrey affected shock.

"It's a bad sign when having longed to do a thing, the desire has worn off by the time opportunity arrives. You come with me and drink from that chained cup before you forget that it's there and that you ever wanted it between your fingers and your lips. It's chained on your side of the boundary of youth and it won't stretch across. Come along!"

He walked briskly away and mounted the steps. He gave the cup the most thorough rinsing of its existence and then producing a spare handkerchief, vigorously wiped the rim. Then he filled the cup.

"There you are, Kerry, the water of life, guaranteed pure. Drink to the idiotic ideals of youth. May they never run dry."

The chain clinked as the clip changed hands and Kerry, who seldom sipped, quaffed it without drawing breath.

"Steady on!"

The girl shot a supercilious glance.

"I've read some verses somewhere about a Burgomaster who did that and dropped dead. Only his was wine."

"Yes, I know," answered Geoffrey rather nervously. "The only historical instance of a man's drinking himself to death and being honoured for it. But he saved a city. You needn't try so hard. Put your gloves on again, it's cold."

The others had remained at a distance and the peacock, seeing that he had lost half his meagre audience already, suddenly hoisted his thinning tail with an apologetic air and having stood thus for a few moments, he then in a fit of honesty or self commiseration slowly turned to reveal the artistic paucity of the rear view. Nature in her wisdom had provided no eyes on this side of his fan; only closed lids.

"Poor creature!" said David as they concealed their laughter lest further inroads were made on his pride. "He lacks the main incentive; the approval of the one for whom he makes this humble preparation. We poor men intend so much more than we can express."

Again Sybil paused to listen to muffled drums behind the words. She tried to appear unaware of them, to tell herself they were non-existent although she could not help but hold her breath to catch the sound.

David silently watched the bird's unmeritorious effort with a hidden light in his own eye.

"It's quite sheltered down here." He pulled a *Manchester Guardian* from his overcoat pocket and spread it on a nearby form. "Would you care to sit awhile? The frost won't penetrate this."

They did not lean back as the wood shone crystalline with a layer of rime. The man crossed his knees and resting his elbow thereon, cupped his chin on his gloved palm.

"The frontiers of youth! Look at those two racing Watch round the fountain! The boundaries are not always clearly defined but sometimes we can look back and see just where early youth ended. It could be the loss of a dear friend; someone with whom one has laughed and talked for years and who is suddenly taken. The remembrance stays but gone forever is that attitude to life in which fun came first, when the worth and interest of any situation was its laughter. I think when that tremendous force of mirth is suddenly checked, even though it may well up again after an interval, that time marks the toll-gate to maturity."

Sybil looked at the serious profile bent forward but she did not speak. Without moving at all, her companion spoke again.

"A character goes from the story of our life and for a time it is Henry the Fourth after the death of Hotspur, the Tale of Genjie after the death of Genjie. It seems a long time before such another comes our way. There was a man at Didsbury. He had a fine brain and all the graces. He was marked out for great work and was sent to take over a district that was ready for a great man. He wrote to us on the voyage, full of hope. As his ship entered the harbour at Madras he died of blackwater fever."

The trio at the fountain had halted their chase and strolled towards the seated couple, and Geoffrey looked questioningly at their grave faces.

"We were trying to trace what you called the boundary of youth," David explained.

Geoffrey smiled.

"Ah," he said in solemn tones, "I think I can put my finger on the last act of youth. We are truly grown up when we no longer eat oranges by cutting a hole in the top with a pen-knife, shoving in a cube of sugar and sucking for dear life. This Christmas will be a testing time, Kerry!"

Sybil rose and David folded the newspaper and carried it under his arm. Sybil pointed.

"You see that mass of bushes this side of the trees, Mr Garner? That's where the boggart or ghost of the large black dog used to run to ground years ago. Hence the name of this Clough. I expect even in these days this spot could be quite eerie on a dark winter's night. A generation ago it would be really desolate."

"There's a culvert running through there," further disclosed Geoffrey, "and it is thought that a dog hunting in the night used to run through and so disappear. Shall we demonstrate a disappearance with Watch? Come here, you little plush imbecile!"

"You're not to, Geoffrey! Sybil, make him leave him alone."

"As you see, Garner, the natives are still half wild! No desire to explode a myth. And it wasn't long ago either that people used to come here gathering fern seed at midnight to make some sort of love potion. It would affect their digestions if not their hearts."

"Did anybody die?" asked Kerry.

"The custom has died out so perhaps somebody did."

"It might have worked in one sense," argued David. "If a man dared to come at midnight to a supposedly haunted spot for her sake, a girl might be won by his far from faint heart."

"Or appalled by his superstition," laughed Sybil, "as well as the risk of poison. Girls today wouldn't like to think of anyone meddling with their purely personal decisions."

They all stared into the bushes without speaking.

"Let's be moving then," said Geoffrey stamping his feet. "And don't let Watch chew that stuff. His personal decisions are unpredictable enough as it is. If he was poisoned there would be the ghost of a big black dog with a little white one running behind and that would be fatal to the drama."

The quartet turned their backs on the fountain and moved along the main walk in the direction of home. Again the girl and the dog ran ahead and back again so that the remaining three walked abreast, Sybil between the two young men.

"Speaking of potions," went on Geoffrey, "what a variety of results have been arrived at by their use, nearly all unexpected. The friar in Romeo and Juliet seemed to have the most reliable hedgerow collection; free samples as one might say. Puck's herbal mixtures were the most humorous, but I always think that Oberon meant to spoil the fun by waking Titania himself, only Puck kept an eye on him. As for Tristan and Isolde, when they broached that bottle of Irish whiskey intended for King Mark, they shared one of those vivid experiences that bind people together in lasting sympathy. There'd be a memorable kiss in such a cup. A kiss with a kick."

"It wouldn't be like that at all," Sybil admonished. "It would have been a sort of loving cup."

"You bet! A case of love being blind drunk! That and the cruise together would do the trick; a notorious combination. Let's keep to literature. There it would seem that kings have suffered all along the line; Arthur, Mark and Oberon all had queen trouble with or without potions. The female mind is swayed by such slight things, why drag in a potion?"

"For that very reason," said David. "A potion gave a simple answer to an otherwise unanswerable problem. It saved the king's vanity and the queen's face. In a way they were lucky; they were able to rail at fate, not their own passions."

"I think that's a terrible state of things," Sybil broke out indignantly. "People ought to be more honest than that. Now supposing," she said hesitantly, "that Guinevere had married Lancelot first. Do you think she might have got bored with all the jousting and everlasting talk of sport, and longed for the more serious ambitions of the King?"

"Too late," declared Geoffrey firmly. "She mustn't make eyes at the purple and sceptre. A king must not play the part of Lothario. Cleopatra can roll on the steps of the throne, but Caesar never! The good solid fellow is best cut out for being cut out!"

He looked up the slopes of the Clough on either side, now dank and dripping, to the dark trees clutching with their bare arms at the stoles of pale mist slipping round them.

"You're right, Sybil. I don't suppose anybody will ever come gathering fern seed here again after closing time. It may appear childish to us but after all there was a touch of humility in it. The men had more faith in some outside charm than in their own personal charm. Perhaps the episode shows them in a better light, Garner, than would shine on our self sufficiency?"

"In such matters, I suppose so," admitted David guardedly.

They were passing a rustic shelter which had slender wooden poles supporting its thatched roof. Kerry was here searching for her initials, but so many others had been added that she had great difficulty in finding her own. Her sister and escorts joined her, amazed at the close patterned lettering.

"My dear girl," Geoffrey reproved her, "when everybody's hacked his name all over these props, the thing will fall as though eaten by white ants."

"I only do it where it won't matter and nobody sees it."

187

"My poor pea-hen! Never mind, Kerry, in a year or two a poet will come along and carve your name where everybody will see and make it matter a great deal."

"I don't want that," rejoined the girl furiously. "I'd rather do it myself."

"Really! Would you rather be the author of those poker-work poems, say, than be Anne Hathaway or the Dark Lady or Laura or Beatrice?"

The alternatives made her scowl.

Geoffrey seated himself on the circular bench surrounding the central pillar.

"This thing is like those Victorian contraptions for the drawing room; they're still in use in some art galleries. You three come and sit here and Garner can face the ever rolling stream. I rather like the idea it gives of being alone and yet not alone. No, Kerry! Watch will not appreciate sitting on these ridges. He'll soon jump down and let a rush of cold air in."

David divided his newspaper between the two girls and then they all, like the lion heads on the fountain, stared in different directions. Geoffrey was the first to resume conversation.

"So Kerry reckons that it is preferable to have one's own divine spark than to be any poet's flame."

"She's got the right idea," said David from the far side. "Most of us would choose to be inspired rather than be a source of inspiration, keeping as you said to literature. And not all my poet's idols have been ideal. Look at poor Highland Mary!"

"It is dangerous for a girl to be loved by a poet! Remember that, Kerry!"

"It is more dangerous to love a poet in return," came the reply from the stream side of the mushroom, so that they all laughed, "and although he can work havoc with a Bonnie Jean, he the sooner quenches the flame, whereas through the wisdom of a Beatrice, the fire survives and refines him into a Dante."

"I doubt," responded Geoffrey, "if it was wisdom so much as indifference on the part of the lady. Until a poet has made his name he has to take his chance as a man. It was as men that Keats lost and Burns won."

"And Keats became the better poet and Burns the worse man," stated David, and murmurs of assent came from the two girls.

"Just look at Burns," Geoffrey said in a contemplative tone, "whistling through his misdeeds like a boy kicking through leaves, while one wild oat plunged Wordsworth into gloom. Does a moral sense really affect behaviour or does it merely give a heightened sense of remorse? It about killed Wordsworth's poetry. It looks as if we are all sinners but a religious sinner is a morbid sinner."

David sprang to his feet. He no longer addressed the stream but came round in front of Geoffrey, who took an arm of each companion and composed himself to listen.

"We'll form the nucleus of your open-air meeting, Garner. We are all ears so you and Watch can proceed to put fleas in them."

Both girls wrenched their arms away with cries of disapproval, while David grasped one of the roof trees as if it were a pilgrim's staff but he was too energetic to lean on it.

"I'm glad you mentioned Burns and Wordsworth. They *can* be mentioned in the same breath if it's a fairly long breath!"

"Oh come," interrupted Geoffrey. "If anybody was long-winded it was wordy William. That's the only breath that divides them."

"No. Some credit must go to sustained quality in literature and in life, just as leap-frog is a less noble mode of progression than flying. But let us look at the men themselves, the clay that their particular spirit of poetry had to upheave. Un-winged, Burns rode rough-shod over the more common ways. Winged only for brief lyrical ascents, gravity soon pulled him down to his native rut."

"Very well put," exclaimed Geoffrey. "Rut is the apt word," and even David's features were more relaxed as he continued.

"But it was not so with Wordsworth. He was always conscious of his high calling as a poet and as a child of Parnassus he believed ichor ran in his veins. The hysteria of the French Revolution made his red blood flow and discovered him to be all too human. The knowledge killed his morning song. Wordsworth's is the greater tragedy, for when Burns fell he was a fallen Icarus; but when Wordsworth sank, it was the fall of Lucifer."

The girls were immensely touched and Sybil spoke with great feeling.

"But if he was a good man, he could make amends and be himself again."

"He did all those things in time, but we must remember that Wordsworth saw God in nature and since nature had betrayed him his mind became confused. When he wrote again the stream of his intellect had deepened and was less headlong."

Geoffrey had listened very soberly.

"Yes, less headlong and more long-leaded. But I don't think he ever resolved his problems throughout his long life; he only learned to shelve them. You can imagine the poor chap at first gazing round at his beloved mountains helplessly. He couldn't very well say, 'Coniston Old Man, forgive me!' "

189

Kerry now appealed to him.

"But wasn't Burns a nature lover too?"

Geoffrey laughed.

"Not in the same way, my child. A nature lover but not a nature worshipper. He wouldn't see anything holy in a nature that had made the lasses-O."

He looked round at Sybil who appeared to be somewhat on her dignity. She presented a profile of warm flesh tints against the field-grey of November chill, and in spite of slight abstraction, she was all alive-O. He turned his head to her sister's profile upturned to Garner again in absorption.

"I do hope you girls realise what an improvement present company is on much that has gone before. We do not pour dubious potions in your lemonade or sprinkle fern seed on your porridge, or abandon you in banks and braes, or even run off to France where Helvellyn can't see us. We are in fact a highly commendable generation."

He stood up and with a bow, offered both hands to assist the girls to their feet. It was now quite cold and the light noticeably fading, and while David refolded his *Manchester Guardian*, Kerry raced Watch round the mushroom to limber up. The other two moved on.

In the distance ahead a long shrill whistle warned them that closing time for the Clough was nearly due. The melancholy sound disturbed a bird settling for the night and it trilled coldly from its unseen lodging in the dim trees near by where the mist, coagulating into drops on the rough bark, now began to plop dismally on to the leaf mould below.

Hearing the late notes from the bird and unable to discern whence they came, Sybil turned towards the sound and whistled a few high notes in response, liquid and caressing.

Geoffrey gave her a droll look.

"Don't do that, Sybil. You might excite the passions of some hapless cock-bird out of season and that wouldn't be playing fair. He might at this moment be in raptures despite the cold and gathering dusk, looking and listening for that bird of paradise who just now so unexpectedly promised him all the joy that feathered nature knows. Led by delusion like many before him, hope deferred will make his tiny heart grow sick, but always his invisible ear will recall the message of those promissory notes. Meaningless, they could yet make a poet of him. You may have turned a blackbird into a nightingale by the careless deception, Sybil, such is your inspiration."

The girl was smiling faintly but she would not look at him as she answered.

"Or into a peacock, perhaps?"

190

"After that I can only say that you changed a missel-thrush into a misogynist!"

Again Sybil looked straight ahead, but the faint smile had gone.

Because it was Saturday the Clough remained open a little later, but the November light was dwindling early and the warning whistle sounded nearer as the park-keeper, having locked the far gates at the lonely Grangethorpe end, made his way down the main walk to the gates by the lakeside, and on along the broad walk, every now and again the urgent whistle stabbing the gloom as though over-anxious that no one should be night-bound among the dead and shrouded trees.

Leaving the mushroom shelter, Kerry and David were aware of another patrol far to their rear and the answering cry of a peacock clawing the twilight. Then another thin and distant sound followed from the way they had come, a shade more eerie, a repetitive peacock or the howl of a dog and Watch got almost under Kerry's feet as if it were reassuring to be trodden on.

They stepped out smartly to rejoin the other two who were by this time approaching the bridge.

"That's a telling phrase the French have for this time of evening," David said as they drew level. "Between the dog and the wolf. Listen to that!"

"A howling desolation," agreed Geoffrey looking back at the secretive, muffling fog. "How much more reasonable then to settle down between the owl and the pussycat," and clasping the girls' hands he swung them along. But again they broke free, ruffled in mind if not in fur and feather.

Upon reaching the bridge Geoffrey peered at the grass clumps growing just underneath the stone supports on the bank and he stepped down a yard or two. The others had set foot on the bridge and their footsteps drummed over his head. David leaned over the rail to watch him. Kerry let Watch off his lead and drew near to her sister and spoke in an excited whisper.

"I say, Sybil, what d'you think? Mr Garner wants me to call him David. He says I can be his honorary sister in the Lord! He has a proper one, you know. And if I call him David, you ought to; you're older than I am. Isn't it lovely knowing Geoffrey and Mr Garner - I mean David? Geoffrey's clever, but so is he, don't you think?"

"Very," answered Sybil.

"I shall always remember the mushroom. Hadn't we a gorgeous sit down there? If they both come for tea, I'll help you set the table. I'll wash up if you like. It's the nicest afternoon I've had for ages."

Just then Geoffrey came from underneath the bridge and went up to the other young man, holding something in his palm.

"Look, Garner, this is the stuff they call fern-seed, if ever you should want some."

They all gathered on the bridge to look at it.

"It's a bit like grape-nuts," said Kerry.

"I suppose it just gave some men enough Dutch courage to speak up," said David smiling.

Geoffrey shook it up and down idly for a moment and then, looking mockingly round the company, threw it contemptuously away back under the bridge.

They strolled on up the steep incline to the gate where a lamp was already lit, gleaming against the bushes like a jewel in a darkie's hair round which the mist had formed a nimbus. Beyond the gate there still lay a short distance to climb and from round the curve of this path came a child's unhappy wailing. It was not until they had rounded the bend that they perceived the infant was alone - a little boy of about four years of age, standing miserably at the side of the 'brow', too frightened to move one way or the other as Watch, always sympathetic to mood, jumped up and down agitatedly licking the child's wet cheeks and copiously running nose.

The girls sprang forward, Kerry to haul the dog away and fend him off from licking her own face, and Sybil to comfort the sobbing boy.

"It's all right, sonny. The doggy was only playing," she said, bending and taking his clenched little fist. "He wants to kiss everybody. There now, see!"

But the crying did not cease for more than a moment and then, remembering his original grief, he broke out afresh.

"I'm lost! I'm lost!"

"Sh! Sh! Don't cry," she continued, gently turning him and leading him slowly up the path towards the not very distant houses. "And how can you be lost when I've found you?"

On either side of her the two young men had listened in silence, but at these last words their eyes met over her bent head in an instantaneous recognition.

The ground was shifting under them. Sinclair's established claim to the Protectorate was to be challenged; the supposed Crown Lands were now to be viewed as a No Man's Land with himself strangely on the defensive.

Garner's reconnaissance had been completed and a state of armed combat had come into being, with the friend as the foe and hostilities no less bitter for there being no formal declaration. From now on it was war!

Chapter Sixteen

Snow had not yet fallen with all its thrill of complete social disorgan-
isation, but a thin scurf appeared on the sloping shoulders of all
buildings and everybody was prepared for an off-white Christmas with
the worst downfalls held in reserve.

Activities with a capital A had its own column in all church winter
session programmes and on the Oldham Road, badminton had made its
first appearance as an Activity, and after several demonstrations it was
agreed that it earned its description. It had caught on and become a
social draw.

When the earliest arrivals came in on this evening, they heard the
piano in the Junior room markedly picking out a tune. The rehearsal
for the infants' Christmas play was just finishing and the young voices
tagged along, some above, some below the note, Sybil at the piano
actually on the note, and Connie beating time in front of the children
forestalling the note in encouragement. The solos had been rehearsed,
those wavering monologues that draw tears from parental eyes and as
often as not from the artistes themselves.

"It would be so much easier to sing it ourselves," sighed Connie
closing her book of words thankfully.

Miss Leat who had been attending to the grouping and actions
smiled at her.

"I well remember when you two didn't hit the note so well as you
do now."

Ginnell came along the passage after looking at the fire in the cellar.
Seeing his daughter emerge he addressed her firmly.

"You're not going in there to play with nothing on your stomach I
hope."

Of course it was at this moment that Geoffrey Sinclair stepped into
the lighted porch.

j

Ginnell turned to him.

"I know our Connie had hardly time for a mouthful before coming across here and now these girls are going to rush about in there."

"I'm going home for a snack now," and Connie hurried away.

He looked sternly at Geoffrey.

"Sybil's doing too much as well. She's looking pinched."

"Well, I've not pinched her recently," he answered curtly and held open the double doors into the big room for Sybil to pass through.

"No," said Ginnell aloud after the pair had gone in, "and if you're not sharp perhaps somebody else will."

A game was in progress so Sybil decided to have a cup of tea in the vestry where Mrs Ginnell was in charge of the gas boiler with the assistance of several vocal helpers. Ginnell came to stand under the gallery between the two vestries, one given over to refreshments, the other to overcoats. Geoffrey Sinclair was emerging from depositing his coat as the minister also joined them, looking at the game afoot.

"Listen to 'em in there," said the caretaker. "Do we or don't we want a new organ? It'll all be settled over our heads if we aren't careful."

"But," said Robert, "that's to be decided in tonight's meeting."

"It could be decided round that boiler. They have far more pow-wows than we have now. It was better when the men did all the washing up and drying in the cellar, when the minister himself would take a towel. It was as good as any night school down there before this vestry here was converted. A proper education. And we held many an important preliminary meeting there away from the women. We've no natural snug for preliminaries now."

Geoffrey stepped a yard or two into the room and turned to look up at the gallery.

"What's wrong with opening that? Then we'd be over *their* heads. Men only, as it was in the cellar, then when the Tea Vestry passes a resolution, the gallery can be the House of Lords and quash it."

"My word, Geoffrey!" exclaimed Ginnell with admiration. "It just shows education is never wasted. It gives people ideas."

He produced a key and they filed upstairs, the minister being given precedence and Geoffrey bringing up the rear. They seated themselves on the front row above the great mahogany clock set in the gallery rails.

"I'd like every child in the land to have a good education," continued Ginnell. "It puts power in their hands."

"Well," Geoffrey laughed, "I've no power. If my father went broke the lecture rooms would see me no more."

194

"Alf will never go broke, lad! But under a Communist government the State would be the father who never went broke."

"But if there were any fatted calves going, they'd be for the obedient hirelings rather than for any prodigals. I stand a better chance as things are."

The minister looked with some fondness at the young man.

"We can only give the opportunity to learn," he said mildly. "The call has always been to him that hath ears."

"Now think," said Geoffrey quite seriously, "of the blow to anyone's pride if he is robbed of his great excuse in life; that he never had a proper chance. If you insist on lining up everybody for the race whatever the length of his ears, the suicide rate will go up."

"Among the fellows you meet every day, Geoffrey, are there many Communists?"

"A few, if they're the Johnnies who sit during the National Anthem, and you can't call that really active participation, can you? Of course, what we're really there for is to study rather than to air our politics."

"But the newspapers are always showing photographs of students protesting or even rioting in places like Egypt and such parts. They're interested in politics."

Geoffrey snorted.

"Let them set the Nile on fire if they want. They can't think of anything better to do with a seat of learning than to kick it! It's much better to create mayhem once a year for a charity rag as we do here."

"I'll tell you what I don't like," said Ginnell emphatically. "The mob that Fascist fellow Mosley has on the platform behind him dressed in black jerseys, folding their arms and pushing out their biceps. I saw Dr Bedser coming out of Ella's the other evening. He was mad about what had happened at a Mosley meeting. Some young fellows from up Moston had gone and just shouted a few questions when Mosley's thugs set on them - three and four to one - and threw them out. Dr Bedser said the Black-shirts have a nasty habit of shoving their fingers up a man's nostrils and tearing them. Doctor wrote to the Chief of Police suggesting that a few more Bobbies ought to be about at those meetings."

"Mosley's a scab," said Geoffrey, "to bring this on a decent city and to a place like the Free Trade Hall."

"I don't think he'll make his mark on the historical scene; not in this country," interposed the minister soothingly.

"Flicked off like a filthy bluebottle let's hope," exclaimed Ginnell loudly so that one or two people below glanced aloft. "And they don't behave at other people's meetings either. Once or twice on Sunday afternoons they've come to the Ben Brierley and made a nuisance of themselves. The folks going to walk in the Clough usually stand awhile listening to us, but when this new lot appear, all noisy and cheap, people walk on. We don't mind those nice young chaps in green jerseys who hold forth about the Douglas Social Credit System. They stand over by the Museum; well spoken lads they are, a bit after your style, Geoffrey. They get a little crowd who don't like to move on in case it looks ignorant. But that space by the public conveniences has been ours for a long time and we don't want a lot of yelling Black-shirts from the other side of town coming spoiling things."

"Ah, yes," nodded Geoffrey. "That spot is a great favourite for ho-ing everyone that heareth. There are two pubs, a church, the Co-operative shops and the little house in the rhododendrons with its two doors like those Swiss weather predictors."

There had been a few new arrivals down below and Ginnell descried John and Jimmie Northcroft. He leaned over and called to John, "House of Lords! No ladies!"

"What's this! What's this!" cried the farmer delightedly as he entered the gallery. Ernest was glad to see that young Jim had not followed his father, as this wasn't going to be for the youngsters. He would have preferred Geoffrey not to be among the initiate really, but since it was his idea . . .

"We've got a motor van for the milk and I thought I'd run in here for practice," said John.

Jimmie had no intention of following to the gallery. He had spotted Geoffrey.

"And what does Ben think of the van?" asked Ginnell.

"It'll be something of a revolution for him," said Geoffrey, "turning cartwheels into rubber tyres."

"He says keep the horse for when the engine won't start and see how the price of petrol compares with oats! Well, here's something new, too! Nice job having Men Only up here!"

"Geoffrey's idea," said Ginnell. "A talking shop and Mr Garner has no objections."

"None whatsoever if it draws men together to discuss affairs relating to God's house."

"Well," said Geoffrey, "this school is a sort of out-house."

"Not so much of the out-house, Geoffrey," grumbled Ginnell. "It's still consecrated ground, you know."

John leaned back.

"I'll tell you what! When I was in France," (and since he had only been to France in war and never in peace, his audience always knew the year and the background), "some people made a great hullabaloo about the way the Jerries used to stable their horses in the churches. Now I was always sorry to see the churches shelled but I never got excited about their being used as stables for this reason; the first church was a stable and in a manner of speaking a hospital as well in emergency. Stable into church, church into stable, it seems all fair to me."

John stared at the ceiling as if rare birds were nesting in the vaulting.

Ernest was non-plussed. They'd be saying next that all the earth was consecrated ground or none of it!

The minister rose to his feet.

"The meeting will be starting soon so I'll be going down."

"Me too," said John. "My father's not coming tonight but he has sent a message."

"And what is the old gentleman's message?" asked Robert, smiling.

"That Methodism is a nest of singing birds but not a musical box. He's dead against the expense."

"We shall see."

Ginnell rose also and saw that his daughter had returned and was sitting on one of the line of chairs below the curtained windows. She was rather noticeable in a clinging yellow jumper that she had knitted herself. She glanced round the room and then up to the gallery. Geoffrey made binoculars of his hands and stared back so that she laughed and looked away self consciously. Ginnell saw this and was of the opinion that Geoffrey ought to show more respect. He was too casual by half, smirking at Connie for all to see. But she certainly ought to have put a few more stitches on those needles.

"Are you up there, Geoffrey?"

Geoffrey leaned over the balcony to see Jimmie craning up.

"You've not put your name down and you're before me really."

"I forgot. And I'm not quite ready, so you play now and I'll take the next game. Go on, rotation of crops, you know."

"Come on, Jimmie. You be my partner," he heard Sybil say.

Jimmie had really wanted to partner Connie but there was no help for it now. He played well, however, and enjoyed it since she did actually watch and occasionally applauded.

Geoffrey watched but did not applaud as his thoughts were on another game and another player on the field. There must be no apparent rivalry; only two people must know of its existence and even they must not openly acknowledge it to each other. It must be an understanding rather than seem a misunderstanding. Ideally it should

197

be all over before Sybil heard so much as a rumour and the ground so well camouflaged that she would walk all unsuspecting through a heavily fortified area. A ghostly war, with no ultimatum, no beginning and its end the status quo.

He heard the deep voice of David Garner immediately below greeting some of the spectators. So he had come again! He was talking to John Northcroft who had paused to watch play. Geoffrey slowly left the gallery.

"It's a very fast game," John was saying.

The court was now emptying and Sybil and Jimmie came towards them.

"Mr Northcroft, Jimmie's going to be very good. He's one of our best men players."

John looked pleased.

"If the meeting's over before play finishes I'll wait for you with the van. I was just saying that cricket is the real game. That's the game to draw the crowds."

"Oh, on a summer's day," said Sybil, "I must nave a deck-chair. I can sit and watch for hours but I wouldn't stand and watch as some do."

"It is impossible," chimed in Geoffrey, going to her side to help put on her cardigan, "to look deeply caring from the depths of a deck-chair."

"Ah, but you never saw Hobbs," said John.

"I suppose, Garner," drawled Geoffrey, "the main gulf between you and the rest of us is that to you OT means Old Testament and to us it means Old Trafford."

There was laughter at this and some eyes turned in their direction. So good of those two to come so regularly with all their studying to do!

"No gulf at all," replied David quickly. "With like passions, you know, and not always conflicting."

Over by the rota someone called Geoffrey's name and he strolled onto the court.

"What about it, Connie! Shall we take them on over there?"

As she divested herself of the canary coloured woolly, he spoke in a lower voice.

"Is that what is called a hug-me-tight?"

"No, it isn't. It's a polo jumper."

"Ah, that's why they blinker the ponies, is it?"

There was no more chat on the court. Connie was a quick learner, and she concentrated all her efforts in the contest.

"Let us sit down," said David, "although I cannot offer you a deck-chair."

They moved away, leaving Jimmie leaning against the partition by the vestry door. Mrs Ginnell was heard shrilly within.

"Is our Connie playing, Jimmie?"

He poked his head round and nodded.

"Who with?"

Jimmie growled an answer and withdrew out of range.

Silence followed the information but two or three looked meaningly at Mrs Ginnell and compressed their lips.

"Yes," she sighed thoughtfully, "young men are all alike. They think their mind's made up until they want to change it."

That was going rather far and a few eyes and mouths opened at this, but she had her allies. Mrs Mossop, with her sightless eyes seeming to sit in judgment on the gathering, had come just for such company and knowing all the voices present, was not afraid of speaking up.

"If it comes to changing their minds I can't see that anybody is going to object, from all I hear."

Miss Leat flew to Sybil's defence.

"There's no reason for starting these hares and red herrings as I'm sure they are all very happy with things as they are."

"Of course," nodded Mrs Ginnell sagely, "in these days perhaps there's more binding a couple than a promise."

Miss Leat opened her mouth and then shut it again and Mrs Ginnell continued.

"If a girl's waiting for a doctor or a minister, she knows where she is and that's bearable, but if people keep asking her when she's getting married it's like being asked at the front door who you're going to vote for. If you say you don't know they think you're not going to vote at all. But it's flaming hard on a girl's nerves, as *you* say, Jennie."

Mrs Mossop stirred restlessly as she listened.

"No, I think it's worse for the man. A girl can get on with her trousseau and a year or two can pass and she'll never miss 'em. It's the man who always wants a little something on account."

Mrs Mossop's delphic calm was of course totally undisturbed by the facial expressions of her companions, and she continued to scan a far horizon.

"It's this new Hire Purchase that's coming in, you know; take it home and pay later. I think I'd know what to say to a fellow who thought he was getting me on the instalment system! Speaking of long engagements, who remembers Minnie Gray? Some of us older ones do. Twenty years she was going with Will Naylor and then he suddenly married a girl in Douglas."

199

"And what happened to Minnie?"

"She sued him and bought a little dog."

"A fair exchange I should say."

"No, I'd rather have a parrot."

"What, after listening to him for twenty years?"

"Well, I couldn't abide a dog pawing me. And why have four feet to wipe up after because you can't get two? But I think Minnie had the best of it. The girl in the Isle of Man would find Will a bit of a stale Manx kipper by then."

The opinion of the vestry was divided, but many were in favour of the little dog. Some people of course had husband, children and pets to feed. Look at Clara Martland.

"We all know who has to feed the blessed things. That Watch of theirs has worms something awful at times. Leonard would have it destroyed but their Kerry always makes such a fuss, I'm told."

"Ada Sinclair's fancy Peke, Sun Tan, is a funny little beast. I saw it at their garden party last summer."

"Lord, I thought its eyes were going to roll on to the grass any minute. When it had a yapping fit I had to look away for fear it shook 'em out."

"Have you heard that Ada wants to go away for Christmas for a change? She fancies a hotel at Southport. Alfred prefers Llandudno."

"I expect she's no maid again, and it's a big house."

"I wonder if Miriam would go as well. She's always with them for Christmas."

"Perhaps they'll ask Sybil to join them. Alfred would like that. He's fond of company."

"Ada wouldn't though. Not she!"

"Sam Buckley and his wife always go away, as well as Easter, Whitsun and any time you like to mention."

"They say she's never really well."

"Not even yet? She's had time to get over quads! There's nothing wrong with her but nerves."

"Well, I wouldn't wish my worst enemy that. Give me something I can put a poultice on."

The company inclined to agree on this matter but there was a dissentient voice.

"If she worries over nothing, how would she go on with something?"

"Much better."

Jennie Leat, after listening to this conversation, now spoke up again.

"I've known some real invalids with lovely natures. It's as if all life's troubles have been rolled into one big handicap and when they've overcome that in spirit, nothing else seems to have any power over them. Look at Ella, for one."

They all murmured sympathetically at this and someone nodded in Mrs Mossop's direction. That oracle was wagging her head sombrely.

"That's very true, Jennie. I know one instance when worry nearly killed the cat, or at least the kitten, poor little thing. Now who remembers the Yaphams who lived in Grimshaw Lane before he got promoted to another bank further north? Very prim she was, the mother. The girl hardly ever spoke, such a scared looking shrimp she seemed. Everybody said they'd never known a girl so painfully shy; blushed if you looked at her. Well, you've heard tell of the Rev. Gideon Stormalong? Those of us who were members then will never forget him. One year he said he would organise a trip to Belgium if anybody would like to go. Those who said they'd go were saving up like mad and it had a very bad effect on the missionary boxes that year, I remember. They've never gone in for a trip abroad since. However, the Yaphams must go. Big stuff, he was. Quite a lot of the older folk went."

"My father went," said Miss Leat, "but only in his capacity as Superintendent."

"I heard," said Mrs Mossop darkly.

The women looked at each other. A trip to France, or Belgium which was just as bad, was rather risky for a minister to organise. There was some excuse when men had to go to fight.

"Well, one day, they got inside one of those art galleries, so called, and there the first thing they saw in the entrance hall was a huge painting of a woman with hair as black as night lying there casual like, showing all she'd got and smiling straight out of the picture."

"Just push that vestry door to, one of you, please," interrupted Mrs Ginnell. "You were saying?"

"They hurried inside away from the porch, where worse befell them. In France it's not like here. They don't go in for accidental done-on-purpose bits of drapery or sitting circumspect, and although Mr Stormalong was reading bits of the lives of the artists and telling them what school they belonged to, and very forward schools they must have been, no one was really listening. They got outside as soon as they could and your father, Jennie, said for all and Mr Stormalong to hear, 'If ever I come here again may I be kicked.' He never thought the same of Mr Stormalong again. But they found the Yapham girl sitting on one of the big plush seats they have for contemplation. She was laughing and part crying and all they could get out of her was 'God bless Mr Stormalong.' She was a different girl afterwards. She'd gone abroad such a timid kitten but she came back answering her mother as pert as an old maid."

Mrs Mossop's reminiscence was received in serious understanding. Many of them sighed. Mrs Ginnell was the first to speak.

"It couldn't happen nowadays, with all these advertisements for perishing sepoys. There's one thing to be said for magazines and hoardings; no orphan need be ignorant today.

The figure of the minister now appeared in the doorway.

"Ah, the conversation of godly matrons. It's very good of you to take this trouble for the club. Does it pay at all?"

"Well, it's like this, Mr Garner. Games make you thirsty and the young men might go out and not come back if there was nothing here."

It was embarrassing to explain but Robert understood.

"Of course it pays, if not in one way then in another. So the Leaders' Meeting is in the far vestry, Mrs Ginnell?"

"Yes, Mr Garner, we didn't heat the chapel, if it's all the same to you."

"I'm sure the church finances are much indebted to you and your husband. You are excellent organisers."

"Oh, that reminds me. Is the organ coming up at this meeting tonight?"

"Ladies, do not look so fiercely at me! I am only in the Chair tonight and have no voice in the discussion."

"Well, Mr Garner, we don't need a new organ particularly, but if they do vote for one, for pity's sake don't let anybody suggest a bazaar."

Groans supported this speech.

"No, we'd sooner save up for a trip to Belgium than a new organ."

"What we have to ask ourselves primarily is whether our efforts would further the coming of His kingdom; if better music would bring it one step nearer."

Robert himself was quite unbiased. To him music was an appurtenance of worship, not a necessity, but he left the vestry not realising he had tipped the balance in favour of heavy expense and effort. Music to his hearers was not an appurtenance; it was one of the great Seraphim before the throne.

"I don't know what to think," said Mrs Ginnell, perturbed. "The Martlands aren't coming tonight. They don't want to be in it at all. Who's going in?"

Many of the older members drifted through the main room to the large vestry on the further side of the school and soon afterwards the door clicked to, dividing the generations into their divided interests.

David and Sybil were seated on a form, watching the feathers driven to and fro relentlessly across the net and plummeting at the faintest weakening of attack straight as a dead bird.

The young man had no intention of concentrating on the game before them for the whole of its duration. He too had been thinking over the position and had come to the conclusion that to allow camaraderie, pleasant though it was, to become a settled habit, would be dangerous.

The delaying tactics of patience, as Joseph who could wait seven years for a kiss or, of La Mule du Pape who could wait seven years for a kick, would not serve in this campaign. The time had come, by no means for a deafening salvo, but for a distant shot.

"Is my young sister in the Lord coming tonight?"

"I'm afraid not. Homework is sticking rather these days and I've forgotten most of my algebra. But fortunately Geoffrey hasn't and he's going to give her some tuition. Isn't it good of him?"

"It is indeed," acknowledged David without hesitation. "It's a very good idea. In some wealthy Chinese households education must have reached its most perfect flowering where an honoured teacher conversed with his pupils under the peach blossom. I suppose there isn't any subject that *you* would care to learn more about? Hebrew history, for instance, or Greek?"

She had been listening with real pleasure and then was so abruptly taken aback that he almost pitied her. He had hoped for a little shy confusion to become apparent, a vague trepidation as to that out-of-the-way report, but she had started visibly as though his final words had been grape-shot flying past her ears.

She sat still, nervously turning the ring on her finger and his conscience forcibly reproached him at the sight; but if he was sorry for the girl's plight, he was also sorry for his own. His position was perilous. One false or untimely step on his part and her perplexity would end in flight, irretrievably to the familiar camp.

Yet if the balance was to be transferred from one side to the other, there would be an agonising period when the scales slowly drew level and dallied in equal weight before the emotional content readjusted and caused the scales to crash down or lower gently into contrary positions.

What suffering was he to cause her sweet nature? It was all very fine telling himself that Sinclair was over-riding and thoughtless, but was his own love less selfish and demanding?

In spite of his mother's unbelief, many girls had somehow swum into his ken and carelessly out again and he had not been jolted from his scholarly orbit, until that tender collision with a heavenly body in St. Peter's Square. So might a man finger the leaves of a book of ballads, murmuring their braggart or plaintive stanzas under his idle breath, until he turns the unforetelling page and suddenly is stilled as Poetry itself speaks to his soul.

He could not now gainsay the star that drew him or the idyll that absorbed him. His whole purpose now would be to track the star and know the verse by heart.

So the conversation by the badminton court was by no means continuous but had short bursts of speech, sporadic firing to show that neither side had withdrawn.

There is no more touching expression than resolution on a young face and her wavering gaze at last moved slowly, gathering courage as it went, to meet his own. She needed to prove that she was not helpless although she knew the power of the slight, courteous and sympathetic smile waiting for her. It cost an effort of will on her part not to allow her gaze to shoot right past and for a moment her glance trembled this way and that, as a compass approaching the magnetic pole vacillates before coming to rest.

She looked firmly, questioningly and rather accusingly at him; a singular flash, but he had been waiting for that very tryst and she quivered as the prism struck fire. He on his part, and as he thought ready for this challenge, found his eyes unaccustomed to the facets of this new found jewel and was alike startled as it sparked electric blue stabs of light through his whole system.

The moment was released from further tension by the thud of the feathers, smitten by one of the players, coming to a dead stop at their feet. David stooped and flicked it in one action to the base line and then rose. It was not going to be easy he acknowledged to himself. But at least she knew and had stood the shock of realisation with dismay but not actual repugnance.

He made his way quietly to the vestry and returned in a moment or two to her side and proffered her a cup of tea. At one stage of courtship it would be easier to touch flame calmly than to touch hands; the brushing of a finger is too exhilarating to be borne without tremor, so David, conscious of the voltage, was elaborately careful in the handing of the cup and saucer and it was received with equal caution.

The game ended and Connie went to retrieve her jumper, and Mrs Ginnell who had been watching from the doorway, held up a cup invitingly.

"Oh! Shall we?" asked Connie.

"If you like," answered Geoffrey who was not a great tea drinker and as he helped Connie haul the second skin on to herself Mrs Ginnell advanced with two cups and they all drew near to Sybil beyond the sideline.

Sybil reflected that Connie would handle a similar situation if not with ease, at least with self esteem.

"Did you two win?" asked Mrs Ginnell.

"I believe we did," answered Geoffrey airily, "and that is always a mixed blessing. The losers can always swagger off the court having obviously enjoyed the game, but the winners have to curb their high spirits and assume a mousey modesty and generally deny their own personality. I rather detest winning. Let the other fellow do the smirking and shrinking."

"It depends what you're winning," said Mrs Ginnell fondly. She bobbed happily back to the vestry leaving the quartet sipping tea together - not for the first time.

Sybil placed her empty cup on a vacant space.

"I've had enough for one night. I don't want to play again."

"Oh, I'm quite fresh," exclaimed Connie. "Aren't you too, Geoffrey, in spite of a ding-dong battle?"

"As a rainbow after a shower! But don't you really want to play again?" Perhaps Ginnell was right. She did look a bit strained.

"No. We had the infants' rehearsal earlier. I'm rather tired."

"If you were thinking of going this minute," offered David, rising, "I had intended looking in at my mother's briefly."

"No," said Geoffrey promptly. "Don't you desert the rota, Garner. It might get out of hand or bite the hand that fed it."

When the two had gone Connie looked round the room as she sipped her tea, and Jimmie Northcroft catching her eye, came over. She sat between him and the young minister, not really satisfied with her position. Fancy those two leaving early. Was Sybil becoming afraid of her!

David also sat ill at ease. Of course he had considered all this weeks ago in sleepless hours and long sessions with his conscience. He knew his own life would be richer or poorer by his success or failure in winning Sybil, but supposing woman's nature was fulfilled more by marrying where she loved best rather than where she was best loved? Well, so was man's nature best fulfilled and the golden mean had to be found where loving and giving flowed perpetually from heart to heart. He felt that he had made her absent-minded for a time. The princess was in a high tower and he had got her to look out between the bars, but by no means to let down her hair! His knightly intention, he told himself, was not abduction but rescue. Under the circumstances he had done the best possible thing.

The faint smile came back to David Garner's mouth. It was well for him that Fanny's niece was not there to see it.

Outside in the street, Geoffrey regretted that he had not got the car. They had just missed a tram and so started to walk until another one was due. A very slight rain was in the air, apparent only on the face and they hardly noticed it. So deep in thought were they that they forgot to keep a look-out for another tram and it overtook and sailed past without their seeing.

He remembered a little boat he had at Clevelys when he was about eight years old. "Tie a string to it," everybody had advised. "Tie a string to it and pull it along." For days he had trailed it behind him as he paddled at the sea's edge but after a time it seemed rather tame and he got tired of doing that, so he took the string off and played cat and mouse with it as it bobbed about in the shallows. Then someone had called to him from the family party on the sands, probably Aunt Miriam, and when he turned back to his boat a moment later, it had sidled out with a retreating wave, ridden over its crest and gained the trough on the far side. His father would have waded out and got it if he'd been there, but he wasn't. "Throw stones at it!" The idea was that stones flung beyond the little craft would create waves to drive her home, but many had fallen short and the ebb tide was too strong. Then they said "Fancy! It's going to the Isle of Man." He remembered the feeling now. They were trying to tell him it was quite a good thing for his little boat to sail away to the Isle of Man, they spoke so heartily. "But all the same, you should have tied a string to it."

Whatever had made him recall that episode now? He smiled unseen against the thin rain.

He had never known a girl with less coquetry in her makeup than Sybil. On the other hand, compliments implied, if not spoken, lay round her feet numerous as sea-shells on the shore, so he must not express chagrin that others added continually to the heap, but ignore them or adroitly kick them aside. What had brought him to sharper and more critical observation was her grave attention to Garner's serious talk. It was the unthinking inclination of the daisy wheeling with the sun and its innocence was its strength.

Geoffrey came out of his silent depression to find Sybil in like mood. She had not spoken a word.

"If I'd started pushing a barrow at sixteen," he stated bitterly, "we should probably have been married by now."

"We are very happy as we are," she said quickly.

"Are we?"

At his tone of voice she looked at him anxiously, but he was gazing straight ahead. After a pause, she spoke again.

"Well, it would be our own fault if we were not."

"How so?"

"We spend plenty of time together."

"You mean waste plenty of time together."

Now he had hurt her feelings. She wouldn't forgive that insult, for insult it was, but before he could start an apology she was speaking very quietly.

"You don't really mean that! But something has been bothering you. There's no need to go into it, but there's no need for either of us to give it another thought. I shall not."

"You darling!"

Gratitude and relief made utterance difficult and he looked about him. How much of a curtain did this drizzle provide? None at all. There were hardly any people about but one naturally did not wish to provide a Roman holiday. They walked in a happy daze round from the Oldham Road and when they reached the bridge all was deserted, so between the well calculated lights of the lamp posts Geoffrey turned to her and thankfully took her in his arms.

"Sybil!"

A kiss can hale the heart through the lips as expertly as Egyptian embalmers could eviscerate their dead through the nostrils, and the young man purged himself of fear and near hatred and all tumult during that kiss. For him, his sweetheart summed up everything that was good in life and on woman man can lavish all the outward manifestation repressed between himself and other loved objects. For the noblest Roman she is the most complete holiday.

When they reached home they found all in darkness except for the hall lantern showing a low voltage light from one of its twin lamps.

"I don't want anything to eat or drink, Sybil. Don't go away."

How slim she was; it was like clasping something that could melt out of the grasp whatever the willingness of submission.

"If only we could get married at once and I could take you out of all this."

"Why out of all this?"

"Oh, out of all this work you do; the everlasting singing practice, the rehearsals for this and that."

"I enjoy it all. I think we have been worrying too much about each other and everything's all right really. I believe we are so much in love that we are not content to be one half of a perfect whole; we are trying to be the same half as the other."

She bent away to look up at him to laugh, but he could not laugh. They were trying to understand each other so thoroughly that they would have agreed to change souls.

"My darling Sybil."

Like other lovers struggling with spirit they were obliged to use the symbols of flesh and they flung their arms around each other anew. He glanced at the clock with conjecture.

"Don't let's stay here. Let's go down to the Clough or - where else is there? Let's walk amongst the trees."

He was speaking with his lips in her hair above the temple and she laughed happily and excitedly.

The crash of the front door was loud enough to bring them - not so much to their senses, they were fully aware of those already - but to the sense of time and place.

"Damn!" said Geoffrey with fervour.

Kerry burst into the room.

"I say, I've only just got home in time!"

The others gaped at her.

"Listen! It's absolutely pouring."

So it was.

"Mother and father not in?"

"No," answered Sybil; but Kerry wasn't asking for any specific reason.

"I couldn't finish my homework so I went to hear Pachmann. Geoffrey, do you know this one of Chopin's? I can only hum the opening bars and I'm frightened of forgetting it. Do come into the other room and try it."

"I daren't touch the piano if you've come straight from hearing Pachmann."

"Oh do try, please. Just the air will do. My mind can make up for any deficiencies."

"Thank you, Miss."

"You know what I mean. Come on!"

Geoffrey followed her slowly.

Sybil stayed in the middle room and heard the cascade of notes as if she were indeed out in the rain, the drenching rain, shower upon shower hammering upon her, numbing her thought. Chopin, the genius of the golden shower!

Geoffrey played with a set face. The little boat had sidled out of reach. He must plunge in to recapture it and tie a string to it. But when?

He had nearly succeeded but for the downpour outside. The sharpening from drizzle to downpour had made success imperative.

Kerry listened and nodded gently.

"Do you know what I saw tonight at the Free Trade Hall?" she asked in a low voice. "When the concert was over he played on to a little crowd of people who pressed up to the platform. He looked down at us and laughed for joy and went on playing and playing. I looked at a man beside me. He was tall and had red hair, and do you know, the tears were pouring down his upturned face."

The girl looked intently at Geoffrey who looked intently at the keyboard.

"I didn't know men could cry," went on Kerry. "I thought a man's way of crying was swearing."

"Sometimes."

When he and Sybil parted at the open door in the dim light, they hardly murmured to each other. They were sad and listless. Sybil was weary and Geoffrey conscious of the dragging journey across town. Mr and Mrs Martland had returned, their presence a considerable stone that had rippled his little boat quite out of reach for the time being. Something would have to be done to alter this situation which had quickly grown so irksome. The vacation started soon, thank God! But she would be at work all day of course, and as for Sundays!

"The rain has eased off," she said mechanically and yawned.

"Don't stand here if you can't keep awake," he answered with so little softness in his tone that she felt quite dashed. She was confused again and so soon after they had been on the crest of emotion, when explanations hardly needed had erased problems hardly hinted at.

The sound of a tram was heard and without any further word he hurried away. She closed the door as if there were a competition for quiet and went back into the middle room.

"Geoffrey all right?" asked her mother.

"Oh yes. But perhaps he's doing too much. It's the end of term of course."

Kerry, who perked up at the end of term, tra-la'd a tune.

"He's fixed that Chopin bit for me. I've got it now. It reminds me of when we were over at their house once and the gardener had left a sprinkler working on the lawn. The spray was fine as cigarette smoke and I walked right into it holding Sun Tan, like being immersed in a silver cloud. Geoffrey played it awfully well, but Pachmann was divine!"

She spun off to bed and soon lay thinking of the concert. That young man moved to tears! His expression had shown extreme gratitude and the new-born innocence of absolution that one saw in pictures of saints. Fancy looking down from a platform or a tower and seeing such a face gazing up at you! He had looked as she had felt and all that group of listeners, spellbound by the white-haired gnome smiling down at them. How clever some people are! A talent is a suit of armour, a protection and a weight. He had looked so happy and yet how he would have to practise! Sybil could sing and her father could play, and her mother - well, *they* were Mother's career. Less gifted people, to be happy, had to nurture a talent for gratitude like that young man. But only if the talented smiled down at you. Kerry bethought herself of her mathematics home-work not done. The Fridge was talented but she would not smile down at her tomorrow! But after Christmas Geoffrey was to shed light on the subject. She wasn't sure that she wanted him to know she was such a fool but at least he would not broadcast the fact. She lay and pondered the day, with her hands folded under her chin and her legs straight down like an effigy on a tomb, with her feet resting not on a couchant stone dog but on a soft hot-water bottle.

Leonard and Clara were not very talkative at bedtime. They had been to visit an elderly cousin of Clara's and it hadn't been a very lively evening. Then the minister had got on their homebound tram and had told them the results of the General Meeting. The members had voted for a new organ much to Mr Garner's surprise and they could see no other way of raising the money than by a series of Sales of Work culminating in a Grand Bazaar! Leonard had looked as near exultation as he'd shown for some time. Of course a church on the main road should have a good organ; one never knew who might come to a Service expecting music above the ordinary. Nevertheless, it came as a surprise to him also. Someone must have spoken in its favour with some telling argument, but for the life of him Leonard could not guess who. He fell asleep giving a recital fit for a cathedral.

But Clara found the news disheartening. She didn't want to see another cushion cover in the making, or another embroidered table runner for years. Besides, if Sybil were to get married next year there would be preparations enough at home without any bazaar to think of. But if Leonard really looked forward to a new organ, then she must support the project. But it was ill-timed to say the least.

Sybil was the last of all to go to sleep in spite of earlier fatigue. She was seeing the state of things all too clearly in quiet solitude and there was nothing of cheer and she changed her bodily position at every turn of her mental exasperation. It had at first seemed exquisite nonsense on Geoffrey's part suddenly to want to go out again into the moist night air and if there had been starlight and a field path not water-logged at this time of year, she would have agreed blissfully. But upon reflection the madcap fancy was seen to originate, not in a spontaneous wish to prolong their time together, but from some outside influence. If it had been some other night even, she would have been drawn into it. If they had come from some other place, from strangers, she would have seen nothing to reprove in the extravagance of his feeling. She could have matched it.

Love's fool she could be possibly, but not nature's pawn and the light rain that had turned to downpour might well have turned to deluge if the springs of action had been love alone and they two had found sweet shelter under a night sky however clouded. She would have been the bow within the cloud, bending to fulfil a promise.

But it had not been love alone. From a source they pretended was unknown, fear had prompted the urgency, fear of an enemy who must not be named but whose presence was astir; an enemy whose threat must not be owned but because of whom they instinctively felt the need to make a more secret alliance.

The shower had descended but had been rejected and unrewarded and the question that kept the girl awake and anguished hourly and which she dared not answer, was "Who - who - had been the real and powerful rain-maker?"

Chapter Seventeen

The week before Christmas was taken more calmly in the ministerial home than in many agitated institutions. For one thing, the greetings cards had been posted betimes, chosen from charitable organisations since the season called for charity rather than judgment.

David and Margaret Garner went through the motions of charity but had other ideas and used to send each other the least aesthetically acceptable reproductions they could find and by paint brushes held in the most unorthodox way, so that upon reception they were opened fearfully, both brother and sister gritting their teeth and by telepathy each imprecating the other.

Two days before Christmas a parcel was taken in just as Mrs Ginnell was arriving at the Martland's front door.

"Hello, Mrs Ginnell. It's a busy time for everybody, isn't it?"

"It is indeed. Sometimes I wish it was all over."

"Come! It's only an anniversary, not an actual birth we are expecting."

"Well, the anniversary seems to cause more fuss every year. Still, as *you* say, Satan would find some mischief still for idle hands."

"No, I do *not* say it, not at my age. I can be idle very cheerfully when I get the chance and feel so kindly disposed to everybody that Satan wouldn't get a look in. It's fussy hands that suddenly knock the milk over."

"Mrs Garner, perhaps you won't have heard that our Connie's being stopped on Christmas Eve?"

"Good gracious, no! How's that?"

"A real stumper! The Daisy Mill is closing down. They've been struggling on for a long time but it's finished now."

"I'm so sorry. All those people! What on earth will Connie do now?"

"As *you* say, Mrs Garner, it's a flaming shame. She'll have to do something, even if it's only temporary. Mrs Sinclair would be glad to have her as a companion help after Christmas. As family, you know; a flowered overall instead of a cap and apron."

"Oh indeed," exclaimed Grace as varying thoughts rushed through her mind.

Mrs Ginnell's gaze wandered away and there was an uncomfortable silence.

"Do you think," began Grace slowly, "that it might be better if *you* switched over to Mrs Sinclair and let Connie go to the Buckley's? Their house is very easy to run, I've heard."

"No," answered Mrs Ginnell emphatically. "Sinclairs want someone to live in. I couldn't do that. And I don't hold with a girl going to a household where husband and wife aren't quite . . . you know."

"Well, I must say I'm very sorry; that the mill has closed down, I mean."

"I thought you would be. I've heard your Margaret isn't coming home for Christmas."

"No. She's staying on with friends, to see it amongst the mountains."

"I don't blame her. She'll do better for herself there than here, I expect."

Inside the house again, Grace was more disturbed in mind as she thought over the news. When she had made coffee at eleven o'clock, she took her own cup on the tray as well.

"You're not deep in, are you, Bob? Well, I'll stay and have mine with you. What do you think the latest is?"

She told him.

"And it puts poor Connie in a very difficult situation. Her mother is pushing her into Geoffrey Sinclair's arms."

"But surely they are firmly clamped round Sybil?"

"Now, Bob, some young men's arms have a spring action and although he treats Connie very casually, I see nothing but hurt coming from this move, to Connie, to Geoffrey and to Sybil."

"Why to Sybil? She has the least suspicious nature of any girl I know. I like Sybil very much."

"You are not the only one, Bob."

"Be more explicit, my dear."

"Mrs Ginnell is a great believer in the strength of proximity and she thinks she can work it with Connie."

"I didn't know you were so much concerned for Connie," said

Robert in surprise. "I had the idea you thought her a very self reliant girl."

"Robert, you must have seen that David is getting very much interested in Sybil too! I've never known him show anything like it before."

"Are you sure you're not exaggerating, my dear?" said Robert incredulously. "David is helping the church here in every way because *we* are here. Sybil just happens to be one of the best workers in the younger set."

"And she just happens to be the best looking and the most eligible girl in sight. Nothing may come of it if Geoffrey sits tight and holds on, but if he weakens his grip for a moment she may slip out. He won't actually fall in love with Connie but he's very free. He won't really want her and yet might be foolish and lose Sybil as well."

"What about David, in that case? He might see his opportunity."

"Sybil's too soft, too vulnerable to make a good missionary's wife. The life wouldn't suit her at all."

"But that is not for us to say! Unless our boy is a complete fool, he'll choose the girl who suits his taste. I thought that was your opinion too."

"Yes, of course it is, but remember that Sybil and Geoffrey are engaged. It won't occur to her to find fault if he remains attentive, and David is too honourable to try to come between them."

"Well, if he's so honourable, how come you to think he is showing interest?"

To vent her feelings, Grace picked up the Minutes of Conference from the book trough and slammed it down on the table. Robert understood that it was acting as whipping boy and held his peace.

"Do pay heed, Robert. This is important to David. There is not the slightest chance of Geoffrey Sinclair's ever marrying Connie Ginnell! You do agree there?"

"It you say so, my dear."

"But if there is a rumour of doubt about Geoffrey's engagement to Sybil, David might allow himself to hope. Then when the doubts and rumours have faded away, he will have been hurt for nothing."

Grace's emotion had lost all indignation suddenly and she turned to the study window and looked at the few lifeless trees.

"Fancy the poor boy travelling half round the world to meet a disappointment in a place like this."

They were so quiet that only the undertone of the gas fire could be heard.

"I'm glad I advised Margaret to stay for the winter sports and not come here. There's enough unrest as it is."

This last remark of his wife's was beyond Robert's following but he was wise enough to remain patiently lost. Of one thing he was certain and that was the conviction born of long human experience that a healthy young man preferred to do his own wooing in his own way.

"Is there anything I can do, my dear?"

"No, but I just wanted to tell you what was happening."

"Thank you; and I don't think we need worry about David unless he leaves his Christmas dinner untouched. I will notice especially."

Grace turned from the window. Robert's lack of apprehension was very comforting.

"You see, I came straight to you as soon as Mrs Ginnell told me and it seemed quite disturbing then. I wish I knew somebody to whom I could talk confidentially, then I shouldn't be always wasting your time."

"You never waste my time, Grace. Perhaps you do too much and should rest more from *my* labours."

"Oh no! I enjoy the work of the church."

"But you're not really called upon to do it."

"After all these years," exclaimed Grace incredulously, "you wouldn't have *minded* if I'd not helped you at all?"

"Of course not, my dear. It would have been wrong to count on it."

"The work would have killed you," she answered vehemently.

Robert shrugged his shoulders.

"I undertook that risk when I was ordained."

But Grace was annoyed.

"I have just as much right to kill myself with work as you have," she said and withdrew.

When he was alone again Robert's reverie was shattered by a terrific ringing of the front door bell. Then he leaned back in his chair with compressed lips. That would be Pins and Needles as Grace called him. Ever since she had spoken to him three months ago, he had revenged himself by giving their door a resounding alarm in passing. He had no particular day or hour, so that his explosive interruption was always effectively startling. The minister now smiled to himself. It was a bell to remind him of the work-a-day world and the goats straying amongst the stony ground, managing to butt when one was looking the other way.

In spite of these differing vexations that cropped up, rejoicing was in the air. David, naturally, was spending Christmas at home and the white elephants in the spare room had been herded into confined quarters. What a wonderful family gathering it would have been if only

Margaret . . .

Grace had ordered a turkey from the farm and she would be calling there today on her round of seasonal visits. Robert undertook the sick visiting by himself and the rest they divided as they thought best.

Annie Northcroft was in the dairy when the minister's wife came round to the back of the farm and they stood looking at all the fowls laid out there in readiness for the oven. Annie gently poked a fat one.

"Jimmie will deliver yours tomorrow."

"Thank you very much. We don't mind eating fowl, you know, especially if reared locally."

"If you investigate every mouthful you eat, Mrs Garner, you're going to spoil your appetite."

"I suppose so, but I fear this tendency towards all work and no play for our domestic animals is going to make our food dull in the end."

"That's what our Jimmie says. He reads the *Farmers' Weekly* and so on, but he doesn't hold with all modern inventions; only some."

"I suppose he won't make his fortune by his own humane methods!"

"He certainly will not, but he says quality goods will always sell so long as there are quality people."

"Does he ever mention Canada these days? I hope not."

"No, he doesn't," answered Annie sharply. "Such nonsense with so much to do here. And now this game's started down at school, he spends a whole evening there."

"Ah! that reminds me. Mrs Ginnell told me that Connie is being stopped on Christmas Eve. The mill is closing. I wonder if you could find something for her to do here for a time? She's a fine girl."

"What!" exclaimed Annie, wide-eyed. "Does Connie want to come here?"

"No, not at all. That is, she knows nothing about such a suggestion. Her mother happened to say that she might take a domestic post for the time being."

"Surely her mother didn't suggest Connie came here?"

"No, I'm afraid it was my idea, but I haven't said a word about it to anybody. You see, Mrs Ginnell made some allusion to the possibility of Connie's going to Mrs Sinclair's after Christmas; living in."

"Well, by all means let them have Connie's assistance and welcome!"

"I'm really sorry I mentioned it, but it was only a passing thought. I felt that perhaps Connie would be happier here than at Didsbury."

"There are others to consider as well as Connie. You may not know, Mrs Garner, but our Jimmie has been following her like Mary's lamb for some time and she's not his type at all. Not even for the time being," Annie added sarcastically.

Grace spoke with true contrition now.

"I see your point of view perfectly. But they are both fond of music and that may be all they have in common, really."

"Our Jimmie doesn't stand a chance there, I know, but even so I'd rather he went to Canada than brought a girl here who'd never fit in."

"We mothers are over-anxious, aren't we, and they don't like it. Well, I'll go and hunt out your father-in-law if I may, but I won't disturb Mr John and your Jimmie in their routine. If this place doesn't alter much, Mrs Northcroft, at least you know where things are."

"I'm glad you looked in. I don't see many women I can really talk to. My brother and his wife will be coming for the day, so we shan't be at the concert on Christmas night unless Jimmie goes with the younger end. There's always been a concert for those who want it, so no one need sit alone on that night of all nights."

The two women exchanged affectionate farewells and then Grace made her way to the yard and to Samson's shed where old Ben looked none too pleased to see a caller in the doorway. If she really did stay only a minute, he knew nothing about women!

"Oh, Mr Northcroft, it's so dark in here, and working in a poor light is dangerous, don't you think?"

"I'm used to it and Samson here doesn't want to read the newspaper."

"Well, if he did, he might learn something; that Delilah is studying for the Ministry, for instance."

"What do you mean?" he inquired sharply.

"The men aren't coming forward in sufficient numbers, so the priesthood will be shared with women as in ancient times."

"God forbid!" said Ben solemnly.

"I don't see why He should. Priestesses, vestal virgins and women prophets kept the temples long ago and consulted the oracles."

The old Local Preacher was incensed.

"You're talking of the heathen," he shouted. "That wasn't the Christian religion."

"Someone has to keep the lamps burning. In the parable of the wise and foolish virgins, note that all were women trimming the lamps."

The old man looked so dropped on that Grace relented.

"Think how much the church would benefit if you left this sort of work to Mr John and Jimmie and went indoors and studied your Bible. The outlying chapels need you. Old age should be the Sabbath of our days, and there's a great deal of mental health in you that could be put

k

to better use. Your son and grandson haven't the gift of tongues as yet. Don't waste yours while you're still strong."

"Why, Mrs Garner, fancy your noticing! I'll think over what you say. I will admit that I enjoy nothing better of an evening than to get my Bible and Peake's Commentary under a good light . . ." His voice trailed off.

"I'm going to call on Mrs Crumps next," said Grace, "so I must leave you. But how dark it is in the stall. Suppose some of those terrible rats are about." She peered around fearfully. She would scream if she put her foot on one.

"If I saw one of them," answered Ben simply, "I would soon put my foot on him."

"Don't say that," exclaimed Grace.

"Why, Mrs Garner," cried the old man delightedly, "don't tell me you're afraid of such things."

Finding such a silly weakness in the adversary restored Ben's kindlier feelings. He was glad to know she was afraid of mice if not of men, and with great gallantry he led the way to the gate, stamping and kicking at bits of straw and otherwise assuring her that the path was clear. Once more their good wishes rang out in the frosty air of mid-afternoon and Ben returned to his work chuckling.

Having got a little way from the farmyard gate, Grace stopped to rub her shoes against a clump of grass. A figure shuffling behind her came alongside and overtook her, turning to mouth a few uncouth words. Pins and Needles on his lawless occasions! Grace sighed. It was nearly two thousand years since Saint Paul neatly described 'some lewd fellows of the baser sort', and they were still around.

She walked smartly along in the dull wintry light. There were not many fire-lit rooms as yet, while frantic last minute preparations were being made in the back rooms. In some of the windows the plants and vases had been moved from their pedestals to be replaced by Christmas trees, and bunches of holly and mistletoe perched on picture frames to over-balance at odd moments. Tinsel glittered in the forest green of the little trees and any light that remained was concentrated in the coloured baubles. Grace tried to see whether there was a star or a fairy on the topmost spike of the trees and experienced a slight disappointment when it was a fairy.

After twisting and turning among several streets of snug houses she came on to the main road again where the shops were preening themselves like a girl before a party. Windows exhibited great slopes of smoothly packed boxes of tangerines edged with silver Vandyke collars, alternating with green apples in red paper mufflers and red apples bonneted in green. The Jaffa oranges were so big that some people said they had been boiled to make them swell.

At the top of the glowing banks of familiar fruit, a row of pineapples brazened it out in exotic minority, mystifying the children who only saw them in slices or chunks from a tin, and plentifully scattered around the display were transparent packets of flattened figs which were eaten by adults in a spirit of morose bravado, knowing that they would have trouble with seeds loitering in subtle hiding.

Tender Brussels sprouts stood modestly in barrels in the doorway. They could afford to be modest for nobody would forget the sprouts. All the best and berried holly and mistletoe was in the window too, and being so near to the Catholic cemetery, a whole row of holly wreaths were suspended from a rail as if they were part of an obstacle race. Boxes of dates showing a peep of white lace petticoat were arranged in a procession across the width of the plate glass, their pictures of desert scenes suggesting a leisurely camel corps on the march or, quite appropriately, a series of wise men all travelling in the same direction.

Grace stopped and bought some huge chrysanthemums so much like snowballs that there was a strong temptation to close one's hands round the flowers. If Miriam Crumps were at home she should have them. Grace moved on, passing the stonemason's shop by the cemetery with its life-size up-pointing angels and marble wreaths, and soon she came to the neat row of houses, flat fronted and holding somewhat aloof from the road at the top of long and narrow gardens, also very neat, with no shelter for unwelcome surprises on dark nights.

Miriam was at home.

"I'm just calling with my Christmas greetings in case I don't see you on the day," explained Grace as she was shown into the polished middle room. She knew it would be like this, with the furniture, probably her mother's, gleaming like black marble. "What a lovely fire to come to, Mrs Crumps, after a walk through the December streets."

Miriam simply could not help stealing a look at her visitor's shoes.

"It's a very cosy room," Grace went on. "Have you a cat?"

"No, Mrs Garner. I don't hold with animals. They bring germs in amongst other things."

Grace was over by the mantelpiece.

"Ah, but I see you have your three wise monkeys at any rate. Perhaps some people manage not to speak evil, but I don't think we can avoid seeing and hearing it. Perhaps it means we mustn't be touchy; not seeing or hearing evil that's not intended."

Miriam thought otherwise. To her the three wise monkeys meant not saying anything unusual when the clothes-line broke, averting her

219

eyes from the postcard stands at Blackpool and trying not to comprehend what the boys in the street were singing. So she contented herself with remarking that she'd had the little ivory trio for a long time and always tried to abide by it.

Grace at first demurred against tea being made, but seeing that Miriam would be happier in light employment, she switched from dissuasion to gratitude.

The firelight made the outside scene look darker and Miriam had carried the kettle, warming on the hearth, into the kitchen to boil up and had shut the door to keep the steam in. It was only four o'clock and yet daylight had gone. Grace leaned back in her comfortable chair and it rocked slightly on springs that gave out a sound of a clock gently ticking. Mrs Crumps would enjoy her hearth as much as any cat; there was warmth and not too bright a light and she had reached an age when weather gave as much pain or pleasure as anything.

In a short time the door opened and the kitchen was darkened as the middle room took its turn of light. Grace blinked. This was her second tête-à-tête with another woman this day, but at the farm they had been standing in the cold dairy since she would not hinder the farmer's wife. This was very comfortable.

"Are you looking forward to the next few days?" she asked.

"I'll not say looking forward exactly," replied Miriam. "I'd rather think about it than actually have it, you know. I always go to my sister's on the day but this year they're going to Blackpool. Ada has no maid again and Alfred's got a stiff neck. So I've to be ready on Wednesday afternoon and we stay until Boxing Day afternoon; just the two nights."

"Is anybody else going?"

"No. We just fill the car nicely."

"So Geoffrey will be there as well?"

"Yes. He has to drive since Alfred has a stiff neck."

Grace took her cup of tea and held it thoughtfully.

"It's soon over, really," went on Miriam composedly. "Some people make an awful upset at this time of year; cards flopping all over the place and needles dropping from the tree on to the carpet, and I have known paper streamers to harbour spiders. But I put it all in my parlour and lock the door. Have you ever bought any of that imitation holly and mistletoe, Mrs Garner? I've had mine for years. I'll take you in there before you go. There won't be a thing extra to sweep up after Christmas."

She was speaking with as much missionary zeal now as if she were recommending a wonderful man in Blackfriars.

"You keep your furniture in peak condition, Mrs Crumps. Of course you'll be keeping some of it for the young people when they set up house. I expect they won't be long now. You must be very proud of your nephew, Mrs Crumps?"

"Why, what's he done? I didn't know of any examination results yet."

"No, no. There's nothing immediate. I meant you must be proud of your sister's son."

Miriam bridled. Her eyes rested on a brown card hung at the side of the fireplace. It bore one printed word: ATARAXIA. It meant 'undisturbedness', a frame of mind that she cultivated daily. Along with the three wise monkeys it helped to counteract a discovery that the newspapers had recently brought to her notice. This was a very disturbing element that had come to light called the 'sub-conscious' and it was now bandied about for all to see like waving your underclothing in the air. It had been explained as an underground store house of old loves and hates, not merely personal but racial, and if you lowered a bucket into this cavern a lot of queer stuff would come to the surface. She was mortally afraid of that blessed bucket. Geoffrey had said it would help if she drilled a hole in it.

"He's had every encouragement," she said without enthusiasm. "Perhaps too much."

Grace perceived that Mrs Crumps was not an obsessively devoted aunt.

"Your son is a great church worker, I hear," continued Miriam. "I really don't know how these young men find time for so many outside interests, although if *your* son doesn't get through his exams, it will be because he does too much, not too little."

The minister's wife did not want to be drawn into any commentary on that particular pair, so she made her customary half bow that acknowledged the speech without committing herself.

"How very refreshing this tea is, Mrs Crumps."

"I expect it's an improvement on some you've had. Ella Kershaw was telling me that in heathen parts you've drunk it with butter in."

"Yes, indeed, and also we have been offered tea of such high quality that it never leaves its country of origin. There are extremes of every kind in China."

"And there's a right way and a wrong way in everything," said Miriam solemnly, "even in making tea."

Miriam never put her own way first; it was a providential coincidence that the right way always happened to be her way too!

"Mrs Crumps, have you ever given a little talk to one of our

221

meetings on these fringe movements that you go and investigate for yourself? Some of these American born or Topsy grown movements will seem very peculiar to us, but I'm sure you could make it very interesting."

Miriam's expression, changing through surprise, disapproval and fear, gave her pasty features the fluctuations that a barm-cake might undergo in a too cool oven.

"No," she protested vehemently. "No, I never talk. Never."

"A pity," said Grace. "When we were in China, my husband made a study of some of the smaller native sects, partly as a hobby and partly to understand the local mind. I thought perhaps that if you wrote down what you've heard on your little trips it would be very . . . not exactly entertaining, but instructive."

"If they would come to the proper source," replied Miriam primly, "they would understand far better than from me."

"But we don't want to lose you or anybody else from our membership."

Miriam graciously promised not to be quite lost to them.

"Of course, Mrs Crumps, these things only become dangerous if we take them seriously. The symbol of knowledge as a tree is so helpful. The nearer we are to the trunk, the firmer is our foothold and the higher we can climb, but along those branches mankind can crawl only so far. At best we join up with those rather pathetic little monkeys."

Miriam looked up at her inoffensive ivories and then at her visitor.

"It's easy to see, Mrs Garner, that if you had to be one of those monkeys for a whole week, you'd choose not to be the dumb one."

She reached calmly for Grace's empty cup.

"I suppose you've heard about the new organ, Mrs Garner? I was very much surprised myself, but I can only think that your husband's word would go a very long way."

"Robert has no strong feeling on that subject at all," said Grace easily.

"But I know several people who voted for it because of a lead from the minister; even against their better judgment I was told."

"But that's almost impossible, Mrs Crumps. I have never heard my husband say one word in its favour. He couldn't influence anybody when the issue doesn't affect the work. We'll be gone by the time it is paid for."

"That's just what I said, but when it came to the point they voted as their minister thought best."

"And in a Methodist democracy," rejoined Grace with some warmth, "that's almost impossible too!"

The Ataraxia card did not jump off its nail but it could not have been less conducive to undisturbedness if it had simply stated 'Piccadilly'.

Grace put her cup, saucer and plate together and rose.

"That's a most comfortable rocking chair, Mrs Crumps. It must have provided many soothing hours in its time."

She took her peep at the parlour decorations and agreed that they were labour saving. Yet Miriam spent hours on possessions that would never become the antiques of tomorrow, only its throw-outs.

Useless to explain the lack of imagination in imitation holly and mistletoe; the imitation blood and passion. She had taken the wonderful magi from imagination in setting up an angular little tree whose needles would never fall and scatter and prick the memory weeks afterwards. But in spite of this barren foliage Grace's love flowed out to Miriam, for at the fuzzy tip of the tree there was bound a star. Fixing her gaze on that, she said in all sincerity, "It's beautiful, Mrs Crumps."

Then she picked up the chrysanthemums from the hall-stand where she had placed them upon entering and handed them to Miriam with best wishes for a happy Christmastide.

Outside again the air seemed very cold after the warm room and it was quite dark, the street lamps showing that the gentle rain was in fact sleet. In front of the greengrocer's a man was throwing cork crumbs from the barrels of grapes. All the shops were very bright now and the drapers so be-sprigged and tinselled that many people would be cajoled into buying handkerchiefs, so romanticised were these usually plain sisters.

She was glad of the walk after Miriam's rich fruit cake. She went by the small chapel called Street Fold, an attractive name that made her smile in friendly appreciation. The trams coming from town were full, the windows opaque with steam and when passengers alighted they were laden with parcels from every finger almost. There were plenty of children, too, since they were on holiday, their faces alive with the expectancy of the season.

As she passed the day school she thought of its time as a military hospital and its effect on Mrs Butterway. Grace had sent her a Christmas card; no robins, just to lend a touch of variety to the Daisy Street mantelpiece, nor a Madonna as a moral smack in the eye. Even holly and mistletoe would contrast with her counterfeit fire and tenderness, so Grace's card showed just an open stable door through which a light shone.

Northcroft's farm seen from the road seemed to be in darkness, but at the rear there would be great activity until a late hour. If only the old man would have the place electrified, what a brilliant light would shine from the stable doors there, to the comfort of all but the rats!

As she neared home and was about to cross the road, Grace paused and decided to go into the church that she saw every day from her own windows. A few lights were burning to show that entry was invited, but the place was empty and she advanced to stand before the gaily dressed Nativity scene put up each Christmas for the children.

Here in this little scene was enacted the beginning of the second volume of human history, the great Anno Domini, and the story unfolding after these opening chapters had brought peace and war, solace and prick to nations and souls.

Grouped around the figures of the Holy Family were the cattle whose lodging it was, the shepherds kneeling and looking and, coming from afar, the three kings. What a cross section of all creation met there.

To the dumb and helpless the gift appeared in their midst unsought; the simple had been guided by joyful witness, and the wise by the wandering star of ancient and eternal probity.

Standing at the crib, Grace offered a prayer for all the pagan world, those whose proud but insufficient knowledge has left them out on a limb, trembling over a void in static negation. She prayed for those whose sign is the three wise monkeys with such a vast stretch of evolution between them and the three wise men, toiling and seeking in faith.

Without travail and tears there would have been no child on earth, no star in the heavens: nothing to find, no light to guide. Here at the crib there was nothing of labour-saving but everything of love. This was creation.

Chapter Eighteen

Methodists are rather fond of kissing. It is a natural outcrop of their feeling for each other. Even Dr Johnson took a couple of young Methodist women on his knees, which makes a picture of delightful freedom and confidence.

The Sunday School superintendents encouraged a certain amount of romping among the young folk at the seasonal parties. The elders themselves led the revels, choosing as partners not the shy or even rampageous fifteen-year-olds, but to everybody's merriment drawing in someone who might otherwise have been left out of the fun. Loud and philanthropic were their cries of 'sugar' and 'all mix' in the merry-go-round known as 'Making the Christmas pudding', where all the participants were the different ingredients. When sugar was added, as happened frequently, partners kissed and at the command 'all mix', everybody else's partner got the treatment. The stand-offish youth, the reserved girl, were espied by these experienced leaders and dragged kindly but firmly into the maelstrom so that no one remained aloof, either through sinful pride or lack of opportunity.

Although the older members preferred to sit and watch the revels, there was always much laughter when one of their number was carried off, her protests that she was no longer sugar and spice met with the hearty query, "What's a Christmas pudding without a sprig of holly on the top? All mix!"

In a lively church, no woman ought to be able to reflect on the sad fact of never having been kissed. At some point in her youth, she had surely known the warmth and gaiety of 'Rise Sally Water' wherein if the kiss was swift, so also was its recurrence as the locked ring tripped about. Did these old games smack of pagan licence? Perhaps the age-old games more nearly approached Christian charity.

On New Year's Eve the games started late after a concert. They

225

were not the main fare of the evening and a more sober air was noticeable. Even the girls' dresses showed that the occasion, although important, did not call for the sparkle and daring of Christmas Eve.

Excitement kept some of the youngsters lively, but eventually the games petered out and the younger children sought their parents to loll against them until it was time to go. Again the company were watching the clock, but not this time to flock out and tell the good news around the neighbourhood with carols and greetings, but about half past eleven they began quietly to walk in little groups away from the Sunday School towards the church.

As the first arrivals stepped quietly into their pews, Leonard Martland was already at the organ. He had not intended to play anything funereal for the departing year but the season had affected his own spirits and his music was more nostalgic than he knew as he thoughtfully improvised, as he loved to do now and then, blending into the chords and airs compatible tunes from other sources as they joined the procession of his thoughts.

Perhaps by this time next year a new organ would be installed upon which he could perform grander Amens and more reverberating bass notes! He tried out a few there and then. He thought back to musical evenings and concerts in the past. There was a very good song he hadn't heard for years although Fred Winskill had been fond of it at one time and it was worth preserving. *Good Company* had three verses; 'When I sit by myself; When I sit with a friend; When I sit with my darling,' the company increasing in superiority through good to excellent to heavenly! Leonard fluted through this song to the pleasurable surprise of many friends present and Clara heard it with a sudden repining for the days when she too sat in the front row with the other musicians waiting their turn at a concert, listening to each other with critical appreciation and surreptitiously passing throat pastilles along the line.

The choir did not assemble. All were in the body of the church, grouped in families. Even the young couples who had sat together throughout the concert had by silent agreement, separated and joined their own families. Love and courtship, new adventures in living, were put aside for the moment while each family banded itself as if for strength against the rigours of self-searching; against the disappointments and failures of the old year; against any weakness in facing the new.

Clara and Kerry had walked up with Mrs Garner and some of the friends. Leonard had gone ahead with the minister and David. Sybil and Geoffrey had come up the aisle together and then divided. Alfred and Ada had not been to the concert for some reason but had come by car straight to the chapel and were now moving into their pew. Clara glanced their way and then took a second more fixed scrutiny.

The Northcroft pew contained its three generations but Jimmie looked glum and sat gazing at the book ledge. The new calf had been a bull, no use for a dairy farm, and Ben had decided to sell it straight away. Jimmie, however, had upped and spoken strongly. Tessie must be allowed to keep it for a time after all that! The others were aghast at the waste of milk and said she would forget it more quickly if the calf disappeared at once, but Jimmie stuck out that he'd heard bereft cows going like fog-horns all night in the past and this time they were to be left together for a bit. Surprisingly, his father and grandfather had given way.

He had got a new instrument, a saxophone, on approval, and when he had first tried it, his grandfather had put his head in the room inquiring if Tessie had lost her calf now! He himself thought the sax sounded fine and his mother would get his father to buy it if he pushed.

The chapel was filling up and soon the service began. The minister knew that the congregation would not be satisfied without Charles Wesley's *Come Let us Anew* to greet the in-coming year, but it was still the old year with all its memories crowding. In a close fellowship much is shared, their church was their second home and many of the experiences of the people assembled here tonight had been common to all. So since these friends had gathered in the familiar building to speed the old and welcome the new, Robert had chosen *O Light from Age to Age the Same* for the first hymn, and at the lines 'Vanish the mists of time and space, They come, the loved of yore', some voices abruptly ceased for a moment or two and only the scattered choir trained in upholding art above emotion, sailed triumphantly on among the weaker brethren.

Waiting for midnight, the minister spoke of their reasons for gathering here. What drew them to their church, he asked, rather than to the public houses to launch the new year on the tawny foam of beer and strong drink? Why were they not congregated in Albert Square waiting to sing *Auld Lang Syne*, clasping the hands of complete strangers? There were many people now abed to whom the moment passed unheeded, deliberately ignored because the excitement of new beginnings and the cancellation of old failures alike, had long ceased to stir them; dead souls, deaf to ambitions and regrets, at best doggedly plodding on their way; at worst dessicated with cynicism. But what had brought the present company together at this solemn moment was the joy of shared beliefs and the strength of shared certainties.

Now Robert dared to tread on delicate ground. He reminded his people that many amongst them were disturbed in mind because of the shadow of unemployment darkening over the land, over the county and over their city.

But calamity ought to be and could be averted in a righteous land by the energy and example of its righteous communities. Whatever the coming year might bring, of one thing they could be certain; that it was the will of God that man should live more abundantly and therefore advance his neighbour's joy in life also.

In the few moments now left, all the people knelt in silent prayer. A few hitherto frivolous resolutions were hastily pushed aside and rather more aspiring intentions were hopefully paraded before the private conscience now in its most tender mood. Such was the solemnity of the hour and the deep sense of reverence that it did seem as though a patriarchal and enfeebled Eli were passing from this world leaving a young, untried but well favoured Samuel to stride into his place.

Then the quick of hearing caught the sound of midnight chimes and somewhere a hooter gave its whooping cough note. A goods train passing over the railway bridge nearby whistled piercingly and a tram clanged more noisily than usual. The town, never fully asleep, was saluting the new day that was also the new year. Behind the red curtain Leonard started the bold strains of 'Come, let us anew, our journey pursue', and the congregation straightened its spine and squared its shoulders.

"The arrow is flown," sang Geoffrey, "and eternity's here." He wondered if the Methodist church hymn book would be the same if its founders had not been Oxford men? Charles Wesley sauntering up and down the garden paths at Epworth as he composed his hymns, brought great chunks of philosophy and theology from his studies and compressed them into the neat nutshells of his verses. "The arrow is flown, the moment is gone". Geoffrey knew that arrow of old. It had been going a long time and he used to quote it as one of the best efforts of fuddled after dinner reasoning that the ancient philosophers could produce. He liked to describe Zeno and his friends reclining, mellow and replete, round the convivial table and discoursing on the full fed moment swift as an arrow in its passing. The subject would affect them to vinous lachrymosity. But stay! They could remain here for ever. Hoisting himself up on to his elbow with a happy cry, Zeno waved his other hand back and forth. "Like an arrow!" he insisted. "Lishen! At any given moment of itsh flight, an arrow ish either where it ish, or it ish where it ishn't. If it ish where it ish, it ish not moving, sinsh, if it were, it would not be here, and it cannot be where it ish not. All itsh

228

moments are at a shtand-shtill. Time ish like that. Letsh shtay up all night."

Geoffrey brought his thoughts to heel with a jerk. That arrow had not confused Charles Wesley. "The fugitive moment refuses to stay and eternity's here." The arrow was flying to some purpose taking the moment with it through time and space; the here and now into eternity.

What had Robert Garner once said to him and to that other who might have been his friend? "We look to you young men of education for our new leaders!" He had spoken with quiet satisfaction as if there were no obstacles. Geoffrey now wriggled his shoulders at the remembrance as if to throw off some old man of the sea. When he was through University he would have more time to think of these things. When he was earning, he would give his donations and subscriptions as his father did now. But in the meantime, was he going to make any resolutions? No, except one. Sybil must come more often to Didsbury. It would be better for many reasons. There must be an end to these casual and frequent meetings with David Garner for one thing. Resolved!

On his left side were his mother and then his father. He was aware of their singing, Ada's rather surprisingly accurate contralto and Alfred's droning like a hive of bees beyond. There were dozens of married people singing in this church tonight, a Dante married to his Beatrice, many a Keats settled down with his Fanny Brawne and carrying the Protean fire to the domestic hearth where it blazed without searing, a creative heaven in control. Only small and private worlds know of these silent poets, but they are geniuses nevertheless, for falling in love is the genius of every man.

Do we want to hear of Dante and Keats settling down, like dust? Creative genius has done much with a little dust and when two lovers marry they do not settle down, they are stirred up, they take their dancing places in the terrific movement of the spheres, for love is an expanding universe.

Was there any expanding universe in the Sinclairs' life? Ada was thankful to be Mrs Sinclair. Her ambitions had been realised.

Alfred, having hens like Ada and Miriam to look after, expanded in his own estimation so that he gave serious thought to his opinions and actions. They mattered. Alfred would never be able to found a library as the Rylands family had done, or give large tracts of land for public parks, but according to his way of thinking, he was 'well off' and all sorts of charities benefited. He was generous to a fault, the fault being that it did not reach his wife and son in any great force, it being a spent force by the time it reached them. Money was power and they should have the over-spill but not touch the reservoir. Alfred had seen plenty of men and women with more money than sense and having had for many years more sense than money himself, he knew the relative values of both. Ada at least had been glad to supervise the loaves if not the fishes. Alfred liked to bring home a fine middle cut fresh salmon or a plump fowl; he was such a good judge of quality. Perhaps hers was not so much an expanding universe, but she had been preserved against shrinking and at the moment she was actually a little puffed up.

A fur coat has a different effect on different women, of course. So attired, some look as if about to open a bazaar, even if they're just going shopping; others look as if they're just going shopping when about to open a bazaar. In her new fur coat Ada Sinclair felt very self-conscious as if she'd been on her way to the shops and been kidnapped to open a bazaar against her will, but she knew that her coat was a badge of honour, a sign that her husband not only had good hunting but brought the spoils to her; a twofold virtue.

Clara Martland viewed Ada's latest acquisition with disfavour. If there was one thing she longed to have by the time their Silver Wedding anniversary came round, it was a grey squirrel coat. Now Ada and Alfred had spoilt it all by this premature silver fur. They weren't playing fair! Clara felt at this moment that all the Sinclairs, father, mother and son were totally inconsiderate and well on the way to becoming downright nuisances. Ada's everlasting servant problems and Alfred's stiff neck had scant sympathy from Clara just now.

Robert Garner had been at work among his flock for three months and more and judged that this present society had enough strength to remain in control for the time being, but had it enough to influence another generation now that outside forces were making some new and penetrating weapons? The humblest sinner was learning that he is always more sinned against; the proud sinner that he is another Lucifer defying the outmoded thunderbolts. The new hero is the rebel and it matters little against what he rebels so long as his antics are unpredictable and never conform to a pattern; his bit of jigsaw must not fit into any design, his personality never merge into another's even to fill the cup of happiness. If only madness can accept utter aloofness, utter rejection, then he chooses madness, remaining outside humanity's orbit, playing like Robert Helpmann's 'Rake' in his final progress, hopelessly and alone with a piece of rope's end that ties nothing together and is not even long enough to untie the conformity of soul and body.

Robert Garner felt that tonight his people were in true fellowship. Their present anxieties and their long term expectancies were in common, as were their ritual hail and farewell together at the crossroads of the year.

"I have fought my way through," the congregation sang triumphantly.

After the closing prayer and benediction the people rose, to smile round at each other and to shake hands.

Kerry glanced at her mother who seemed to be sitting longer than usual after the Benediction, looking severely at her gloved hands and making no sign of moving. Clara had prayed that she might have a sensitive conscience that would, at the first intrusion of unworthy thoughts, ring like the most up-to-date burglar alarm, but she was listening to its ringing now and doing nothing about it. But really, that Ada should have stolen her squirrel coat! That's what it amounted to!

"Are we going?" asked Kerry.

Her resolution was that she would restrain her passion for chopping wood and cleaning drains and plunging her hands along with Watch into his sheep-dip bath. She made great fun of the Four Indian Tummy-aches but it would be marvellous to have pale hands that someone loved beside the Shalimar.

Ernest Ginnell began to turn off some lights as Clara and the girls left the pew.

"One more, one less," said he as they passed.

Outside, the moon was a glittering silver lozenge on a shield of cold steel. It was considerably sharper out of doors.

"Oh, here you are!" cried Mrs Garner genially. "I've got Mr and Mrs Sinclair to come up for a glass of ginger wine with us since they have the car. I hope you will look in as well."

"It's rather late," murmured Clara.

"Happy New Year, Clara," rumbled Alfred, giving her his annual kiss on the cheek just as Leonard came out of the door; then he stood like a heavy dog debating within himself where he should bury his bone.

Leonard moved forward and kissed Ada, making quite a little ceremony of it so that her pout turned to a simper. The little groups on the pavement were rather noisy as they intermingled with affectionate salutations, but they were not disturbing the population as most windows showed lights and there were still a few householders, turned out before midnight with part of the cruet and a piece of coal, who had found a neighbour on the same errand and stopped for a chat before returning with the luck of the new year.

"We can hold six," announced Alfred presently, "so you and Leonard come up with us. The boys can walk."

231

John Northcroft came up to see if anybody preferred third-class riding to first-class walking. He had got the van. Alfred looked round to see Jimmie standing by it.

"Jimmie," he called, "can you squeeze the girls in the van?"

Jimmie replied that he'd have a good try and Kerry laughed aloud so that Geoffrey told her to jump in the van instead of jumping to conclusions, but for the first time he noticed how tall Jimmie had grown. When the two car loads had moved off, Geoffrey looked down Oldham Road for any all-night tram coming up this way. No lights were moving. He looked towards Oldham. If a tram came from that direction he would be tempted to get on it and go home. It was well past midnight now and his parents would soon guess what he'd done when he didn't show up.

"Are you coming my way?"

At the question Geoffrey turned from his hopeful scanning of the northern distance to find Garner at his elbow.

"Oh yes. I suppose it *is* your way at present. There's nothing in sight so we'll walk up and see if anything overtakes us."

Nothing was said on either side about a happy new year.

At the minister's house, Grace quickly switched on a large electric fire while her guests arranged themselves comfortably in chairs about the room, and as Alfred sat back he noticed an unusual degree of ease in the seating. He glanced at the upholstery on the arms and then more sharply at the rest of the suite.

"A new suite, Mrs Garner? I know nothing of a new suite. What's become of the old one?"

"Ah, Mr Circuit Steward," laughed Grace, pleased that the improvement had been noticed, "this is outside your province. I had a little windfall and so bought this for the house. The old one, Mrs Ginnell kindly consented to take."

Alfred looked surprised.

"Well, that's very generous of you, Mrs Garner, but of course it will have to go before the Trust and be noted; it is an addition to the value of the contents of the house."

"Just as you think best, Mr Sinclair."

"If you made a donation to a museum anonymously it would still have to be audited and catalogued."

"Oh dear. I'm sorry. Look, Mr Sinclair, I don't want a letter of thanks from the Trust or anything like that. I bought this suite for our own personal convenience."

"But you disposed of chapel property to make room for it, Mrs Garner. We should have difficulty in reclaiming if you decided to take this with you after all."

"I shall decide no such thing, Mr Sinclair."

"Well then, when you've a moment to spare, drop me a line stating this is a gift to the Circuit and giving the exact cost and mentioning how you got rid of the old one. You wouldn't get much for it, I suppose?"

"Of course not," said Grace, outraged at the idea. "Mrs Ginnell cleans our front step; she *will* do it, and I thought the old suite would just be a mark of appreciation."

Alfred did not seem to think much of this idea, either, and Clara Martland's mouth twitched.

"It's greatly improved in here, Mrs Garner, not only by what you've put in but by what you've taken out."

"What have you done with that carved cabinet?" asked Alfred in a frightened voice after jerking his stiff neck painfully round.

"Oh, that thing! It's in the middle bedroom under a dust sheet. It calls itself a cabinet, but it's all fretwork and mirrors except for a bit in the middle. A dust trap if ever there was one. It's caused *me* a lot of fret-work, I know."

Again Clara intervened.

"Alfred, perhaps there are a few little things that could go."

"You mean sell them?" asked Ada aghast. "You'd only get an old song for them and they do make the place look lived in."

"No, they make it look died in," cried Grace, full of New Year zeal. "I guess Mrs Martland here would rather have an old song than an old chore any day."

"True," said Clara, "if I had any choice in the matter."

The Northcroft van stopped outside.

"There are the girls," exclaimed Grace. "Robert, just go and bring them in, will you? I did ask Mrs Northcroft but Mr John said they'd better get off home."

The girls came in and Sybil explained that they'd been delayed slightly by Mrs Northcroft calling in Grimshaw Lane with some bottled fruit for an old member. She'd left it on the step at that time of night of course.

"And we saw Geoffrey and - er - David halfway up Lightbowne Road," added Kerry. "They'll be here soon."

"Good gracious, we've been talking," declared the minister's wife and she hurried away and by the time she came back with refreshment, the young men came in.

"Ten of us now, Mother. Shall I raid the second bedroom? Mine and the white elephants!"

"No, David. Get some chairs from the dining-room."

Soon all were seated and Crabbie's ginger wine handed round, and after coming indoors from the cold night air they found the ginger startling to the larynx and Kerry caught her breath. She choked so that Geoffrey looked at her with raised eyebrows.

"Steady there! We can't have you reeling round the place. Oh, and that reminds me. There was a little item in the *Guardian* yesterday that took my fancy. It said, 'Two men, one armed, hold up girl of seventeen.' That's what I call co-operative chivalry, although I think one man, two armed, would do better. At least the left hand has some inkling as to what the right hand is doing, which makes for co-ordination. Haven't you found it so, Garner?"

Nobody seemed to be hanging on Geoffrey's words, but Sybil found it suddenly of the utmost importance to know if David had indeed found it so.

Then she heard his deeper voice speaking easily.

"Doubtless you would scorn my limited experience, but I hold that a single mind would out-manoeuvre a force of arms however distributed."

"I guessed he would know," said Geoffrey "He's one of the dark horses of the Apocalypse."

Kerry had been grateful for the digression and had recovered from her discomposure.

"Come on, Kerry," said Geoffrey, "have one of these patties, if you're not too full of resolutions. Have you made any?"

"Well, yes, I have made one, but I don't know if anything will come of it."

"Nor I of mine. Indeed at the moment one would not guess it ever had a separate existence, as the coroners say."

The others were not as talkative; the episode of the suite seemed to have stemmed conversation and Grace turned to Ada impulsively.

"Do throw off your coat, Mrs Sinclair, or you will be too warm. And how is your new little maid doing?"

At once Grace regretted the question. Ada, however, looked more cheerful.

"She's only been with us a few days, you know, but she fits in with us very well. She likes the house and knows good furniture when she sees it. And she's very prompt with the morning tea. She even takes it to Geoffrey."

"Waited on foot and mouth," remarked Geoffrey so that Kerry giggled.

"She's different from all the others," went on Ada happily. "In fact, a daughter couldn't be more considerate."

Clara could not help but catch Mrs Garner's eye and Sybil regarded the speaker with a curious and perplexed air. Mrs Sinclair never gave *her* an opportunity to be daughterly. She turned her gaze to Alfred.

"How is your stiff neck, Mr Sinclair?"

"Almost well again, thank you."

He waggled it about gently.

Clara Martland had been following her own line of thought.

"If Connie works in every way as hard as her mother, she ought to be a success."

Somehow there always seemed to be a jolt at the end of each fragment of conversation. Time seemed not to be gliding swiftly away as in the hymn they had lately been singing, but apparently someone had got Father Time on to terra firma and sent him jerking along on a pogo-stick.

"And we give proper wages," said Ada, and Mrs Garner in her turn, could not help but catch Mrs Martland's eye.

"We mustn't be too late," Ada suddenly recollected. "I forgot to mention going to bed to Connie and I don't suppose either of *you* did."

For a moment Geoffrey closed his eyes and then with an exclamation of pleasure: he turned to Clara.

"Mrs Martland! Have Mr and Mrs Garner ever tasted your Bees' Wine? It seems to me that New Year is just the night to introduce them to it and we haven't really let the New Year in here."

"No," said Grace in answer to Clara's unspoken query. "I can't say that I've heard of it. Is it a sort of honey confection?"

"Another name for it is Balm of Gilead," explained Clara. "A cousin brought some home from Palestine years ago and I believe we have some bottles put away. Surely you have some, Ada?"

"I had once upon a time. We bottled some but there isn't any actually working now."

"Well, if you would really like to try it," said Clara, "it may be that you won't find it anywhere but in Lancashire. It mustn't be sold, you know, but it passes by gift from house to house."

"I'll come and help you get them down," offered Geoffrey. "It's a golden opportunity to try it."

"I'll wash these glasses," said Grace, "since the ginger was rather strong and might come through the taste of honey."

When the door shut again, David moved next to Sybil's chair.

"Have you learned any new songs lately, or are you too fond of the ones you know?"

Sybil hesitated. She always listened with some apprehension to his words now.

"Mr Winskill likes to give me something new quite frequently, and of course there's always the Hallé Choir."

"I prefer listening to a solo rather than to a choir. I can get the words of a solo generally. That's why I know your heart is like a singing bird."

It was fluttering slightly at the moment.

"I'll go and help dry the glasses," she responded lamely, but after opening the door for her, he followed. His mother had almost finished washing the glasses and he took a linen cloth and then calmly handed it to Sybil who took it in a sort of daze. He watched as if the sight gave him pleasure and then bent forward and flipped his finger nail against the outside of a glass and continued against them all.

"I think I could learn an instrument."

"If that's the only instrument that appeals to you," his mother advised, "don't bother to take lessons."

Sybil, with her back towards the kitchen's outer door, took a step forward as she replaced a glass on the trolley and, treading upon a small piece of grit, she stooped to pick it up in the shadow. Then she suddenly veered over to David and stood by him in unself-conscious appeal.

"It cricked and I thought it was a cinder. It was a beetle!"

"Oh, it's come under the door!" said Grace, hardly noticing.

But Sybil stood with closed eyes.

"In my bare hand!"

"Tut, tut," responded David sympathetically, and taking out his handkerchief, he dabbed at the offended hand reassuringly and led her into the middle room where, regaining composure and becoming aware of the tender shepherding, she withdrew her hand.

"I will attend to our dark stranger," he said, permitting himself a slight smile.

She also could smile now as she moved to return to the main company, but feeling that she ought to offer something in her own defence, she paused in the doorway.

"Anyway, I'm not afraid of mice!"

"Bravo!" he returned with grave respect.

"At least," her native candour insisted, "at least not in the abstract."

He bent down quickly for the hearth brush and she went out.

Soon a loud buzzing noise was heard outside the front window and the minister hastened to open the door and admit Geoffrey carrying several assorted bottles containing the Balm of Gilead.

Mrs Garner had a tray in readiness and soon Geoffrey was filling the reassembled glasses.

"It's some sort of eastern flower and definitely medicinal," he informed them. "It has a wonderful bouquet, or rather scent. It is said to sweeten the breath, dispel depression, cure insomnia and promote friendship. Fern seed wouldn't have a look in if this were put on the market, Garner."

"It's got a very nice sparkle," said Alfred appreciatively. "Shall we wait and toast the New Year together?"

"If you really think it's all right," Clara said nervously, reference to a toast making her uneasy. What would Mr and Mrs Garner think? But those two had drunk home-made concoctions up and down China for years and took their glasses on trust, as they had accepted cups with one, two or no handles at all, for a quarter of a century.

"We've had Watchnight," said Grace, looking round the company, "so perhaps you, David, will say a few words now."

They all looked at him as he smiled at his mother and rose to his feet.

"This is the first time I have ever let the New Year in, or more precisely, given it official welcome and I am especially pleased to welcome it into my parents' home to which I am entrusted with a key and so made a freeman. Home, to most of us here, is something constant, to leave at will and return to at will. But to the exile, the traveller, soldier or missionary, home is a picture that we carry about with us and in that picture are people dear to us. The spirit of home goes with us down the years through city and desert and so I wish all good to this house in the New Year. May its FENG SHIU be all beneficence."

They all raised their glasses in silence and bowing towards the minister and his wife, slowly drank their Balm of Gilead. His mother would be touched by that little speech.

"It's very nice indeed," rumbled Alfred. "You've no need to be shy about this, Clara. I should say it has matured to a nicety."

"I didn't even know we still had it," observed Leonard. "How did *you* know of it, Geoffrey?"

"Oh, I've seen it upon occasion when I've been lifting things down for Mrs Martland."

"It's really delicious," conceded Ada. "I can't remember why we stopped making it."

"Very palatable indeed," said the minister.

The Balm of Gilead was a great success and at Clara's instigation, Geoffrey acted as attentive Ganymede.

"Perhaps I ought to have got out the tumblers," said Grace.

She turned towards Leonard.

"I did so much enjoy your pot-pourri of old tunes tonight, Mr Martland. It was so unexpected and yet so appropriate."

"Yes," Robert followed. "Everybody was listening with great feeling. You touched chords outside the instrument."

Leonard's cup was full as well as his glass. He needed very little praise but the quiet beams of his wife and daughters added delight to inward satisfaction.

"Sometimes," he said thoughtfully, sipping his glass with its golden contents, "sometimes only music can rise to the occasion as on the first Christmas Eve. When words fail, music can continue."

"But words did not fail on that occasion," Robert reminded him gently. "We still know what the Word was, even though the tune be lost. But perhaps when the mind is over-charged and the body tired, music soothes with least effort."

"No, no," Len contradicted. "Music played or composed or appreciated needs faculties at fullest stretch."

"Let me help you to more honeydew," chimed in Geoffrey and refilled Leonard's glass without waiting for a reply. "And of course, Mr Martland, music is older than speech, the first wind instrument being the wind itself."

"Ah, thank you, my boy. Strange that we speak of fleeting breath as if it were of no moment, or no longer than a moment. Some day I shall catch up with, or catch coming round again, all my Voluntaries. To hear the best of them will be heaven; to hear the worst of them will be hell. The same with your words, Mr Garner. Seeming to be spent almost on the threshold of the lips, in reality they streak into the heavens to spread everlasting wings."

Leonard gazed upwards as if watching them.

"I agree with you entirely," said Robert. "We are used to the truism of Thou God seest me! And, of course, its parallel, Thou God hearest me! The old-time believers spoke of a Recording Angel and how very near the mark they were."

The minister and the organist nodded at each other in accord.

"I don't like the wind," Ada said with solemnity. "Mournful I call it, I think I should prefer any sound to just the wind howling. Except cats. That's an awful sound too, but not dangerous like the wind."

"Quite right, mother," said Geoffrey soothingly. "Cats are on the tiles but they don't blow them off. Let me take your glass."

He put it firmly on the tray and did not replenish it, but he was very attentive to the others.

"One of the hardest things to tolerate," said David, looking round on them all, "is complete silence. Blasphemy itself is a challenge, a desperate listening for evidence of life and when a man dares God to strike him dead that very instant, his fear is not that He will, but that He will not. The blasphemer is really dying to know and would welcome the thunderbolt."

Geoffrey partly agreed.

"So he has a choice of saying 'I told you so' and living unhappily ever after, or exclaiming 'He told me so' and dropping dead on the spot with joy and concussion."

Clara looked at Kerry with displeasure as the girl rocked with laughter and then suddenly yawned.

"May I have some more? It's gorgeous."

"I think not," replied Ganymede, "or we may hear something unexpected from the mouths of babes. Sybil? No? Nothing oracular from the Sybil? But speaking of babes, do prodigies ever come to anything much? Do they show anything more than promise?"

"Bach, Mendelssohn and Mozart were infant prodigies who fulfilled all hopes," answered Leonard quickly, "but of course today we are getting a lot of banging and twanging by people who only play by ear. As for all this crooning and percussion that's coming in, it comes from misguided patronage of the incompetent. Noel Coward has done us a bad turn there. Crooning! That's something to do while you clean your shoes!"

"But I love Melville Gideon," proclaimed Kerry loudly.

"And Layton and Johnson and the Western Brothers," added Sybil, looking round for her own generation's support.

"Ah! They are not pretentious," conceded Leonard. "They are saved by grace."

"I've never heard of a first class child painter," now said Robert. "His experience has no perspective."

"The same with literature," David joined in. "Even 'Songs of Innocence' were written by experience."

"Ah, experience!" exclaimed Geoffrey. "In acting, that can be most ingeniously assumed. An actress plays by ear, but not her own ear. She is an instrument played by the producer, any producer, just as a girl varies the gestures and tones of love learned from her first teacher, with every new performance in a new company."

Geoffrey refilled his own glass without being asked and David raised a warning hand.

"The bees aren't making us all honey tongued, Sinclair. And, remember, it isn't the recipient who is killed by the sting!"

Kerry looked at her adored friends in bewilderment. She was used

239

to hearing arguments on all subjects; her father and Mr Winskill sometimes shouted when going over points about the Great War. But her father's friends in their hottest differences never watched each other narrowly as these two were doing now.

"I'm sure Sybil Thorndyke feels what she says," she exclaimed vehemently. "She couldn't act like that without feeling!"

Geoffrey looked at his own Sybil.

"It is possible for some people to have an inadequate nervous system, like fish."

The minister's wife became suddenly martial.

"Not like fish," she declared stoutly. "Whatever they say, I say that if any creature is jerked out of its element into an element which cannot support life, and makes repeated efforts to return or at least escape from its present environment, and goes through motions which are so violent as to suggest the utmost strain, then I contend that those motions are connected to emotions, both so acute that they achieve the status of actual pain!"

David in his turn rose to take his mother's glass and replace it unfilled on the tray.

"But you do eat fish," Clara asked falteringly.

"Yes, I do, but I don't kid myself that the fish when caught is giving an exhibition of joie de vivre. On the whole I much prefer my near vegetarian meals. With cheese and raisins and milk and honey and plenty of nuts, I consider my diet fit for a . . . a . . ."

"John the Baptist?" queried Geoffrey.

Mrs Garner looked at him crushingly.

"It is at least an innocent diet."

"Ah! Innocence," he returned. "We used to talk about a child's mind being a clean slate, but according to psychologists, apparently that slate comes already crowded with rude words . . . "

Here Ada let out a whoop and drew everybody's gaze to herself. The others laughed rather self-consciously at her disproportionate mirth, but when Alfred stared at her she reddened and suddenly looked accusingly at the Balm of Gilead as if remembering something against it.

But the minister gravely considered what had just been said.

"What Geoffrey says may be very true. As our pilgrimage continues we may be approaching, not departing from, innocence. True, we are born with primitive, age old instincts that in the Baptismal Service we call being born in sin. I have had to explain that point to many young and indignant mothers," he added with a smile. "But we learn the law of light as we grow, for we brought that light with us as well, the glint of the flaming sword that is our conscience, our spark of true wisdom.

We have travelled a long and painful distance, but like Drake circumnavigating the globe, every further mile calls a hail and not a farewell, until at last mankind, no longer young and ignorant but with the innocence of joy, re-enters the Garden by the Western gate and finds himself returned marvelling to a state of grace and his first home."

The company here regarded their minister with great affection and Clara found herself touched to the point of tears and drew a handkerchief from her pocket to dry them.

"Travelling hopefully," rumbled Alfred, as he awkwardly observed her.

"Strictly speaking," said David slowly weighing his words, "we *have* arrived. I mean we're not like the Jews, looking for the Messiah in every new-born male child. Christianity has arrived at the knowledge of salvation and should entrench there."

"There seems to be a little doubt," remarked Geoffrey to Kerry, "as to whether or not we are in the garden. Perhaps we are just swinging on the gate, innocent problem children that we are. I think it's time we all came in out of the wet, so I'll collect a few glasses. Is something amusing you, Kerry? What's this little filly had? Only Balm of Gilead."

"Ah!" exclaimed Leonard ponderously, "The Messiah! It takes genius to cope adequately with arrival. Hence the angelic choir. But Handel runs them very close. He rose to the occasion - Wonderful! Counsellor!"

Leonard started to beat time and to keep him company the others joined in a few lines of oratorio.

"So glad it's singing rather than fighting," said Geoffrey, affably.

"Very nice indeed," Alfred commented with feeling. "We hardly ever hear you singing nowadays, Clara."

"Help me up, Alfred," said Ada unexpectedly and they all began to think of moving. Alfred did not at once spring to his feet but he cogitated on the suggestion like Mark Twain's jumping frog. Leonard, however, was always light in his movements and using more strength than was apparent in his grace of manner, he eased her from her chair and held her by the elbow until she was quite sure. She admired Leonard. Deep down, every woman would prefer a man with polish if she could get him.

Clara rallied her sense of charity.

"My word, Ada! Do I see a Christmas box?"

Leonard had picked it up from the back of the chair and was holding it in readiness.

Ada blushed.

"Yes, it is. I didn't really need it; my old sealskin would have done."

"Alfred knows what's good for you," said Clara. "And he wouldn't get the kind you pick up by its ears."

Ada smirked uncertainly.

She hadn't needed one! thought Clara. Her old one would have done! What a wife for a man who had got on, as Alfred had. If you couple with an eagle you should learn to fly!

"Try it on, Clara," offered Ada in a burst of generosity.

"Oh, it's much too big for me," protested Clara.

"Go on; just to let me see how it hangs."

Leonard swung round to his wife and held Ada's coat. She almost backed away but the others were expecting her to put it on and, avoiding Leonard's eyes, she did so. It was indeed too wide for her so she wrapped it well round and then pushed up its comfortable collar and slowly turned round for the company to see. A slight flush of pleasure and excitement heightened the flattery of the soft fur. She did not look as if she were going to open a bazaar, but she looked as if she were going to the opera as she made a few mincing mannequin steps towards the door.

"It suits you very well, Clara," said Alfred, absentmindedly helping himself to a cigar without taking his eyes off her.

"You look lovely," exclaimed Kerry, surprised.

But a sort of startled look had come into Leonard's eyes, for as Alfred spoke, Clara had turned her well shaped head in its sepal-soft corollary and smiled at him. It was a slight, almost a deprecatory smile, of the child who was not asked to the party next door but who hears the jumping feet.

Perhaps most women would rather share the chariot of Alexander than the barrel of Diogenes and the trophies would have hung well upon Clara as this fur coat testified. Perhaps many women would wish their husbands to make a fortune if only for the elementary reason that the rich man's wife dresses fashionably and dress is the untalented woman's artistry. She can't afford to be poor.

But if Clara Martland had for an instant contemplated her lot as wife of a rich man, rich according to her way of life, it was not with any other emotion than curiosity. Alfred certainly did not come into it at all. She could never have married him; but since Ada had, Clara was impatient that any woman could be so dead to her advantages. If she herself sometimes felt that she had hitched her star to a wagon-lit, the mild regrets of her life were as nothing compared with the wild remorse that she had avoided.

Watching this scene, the minister's wife understood the situation. But happiness, Grace knew, could never be gained by heeding the subconscious, that abode of the caveman. It would not be helpful but positively fatal to attach any importance to it. The subconscious rarely contributes one iota to our well being, which depends upon our realising and insistence upon, our waking and conscious choice.

And Leonard had been Clara's conscious choice. The smile that had hit Alfred would have enlivened Clara's expression had she been quite alone at that moment, and the others of her generation knew full well that if they were foolish enough to dig up those old experiences and opportunities and open the box, they would get a whiff of corruption that would wipe off any smile whatsoever.

Nevertheless, Ada's underlip trembled slightly as she took back her fur coat.

The minister's wife attentively helped her with the big fur button at the neck and kindly stroked two or three of the squirrels.

"You're very fortunate people! You are indeed. Have I ever told you of our first winter back in England here? I got a nasty dose of 'flu and Bob thought I ought to have a fur coat as I really did feel the cold. Just after Easter we paid a visit to York Minster. Oh! Did I say Minister? I mean Minster of course. How silly of me! Well, after looking at the windows, we decided to go up the tower where there's a beautiful view, as you will know. But I found coming down much more of a strain than the climb up. My knees were weak, I suppose after 'flu, and when I came onto the Cathedral floor again, I could not straighten up properly. My knee muscles had gone on strike and I simply could not get them to support me. There I was, shuffling about in my fur coat with my knees bent, looking for all the world like King Kong. Robert walked me up and down but it was no use. Actually, it took a couple of days to wear off. So we had to go outside eventually at a place called the Shambles. Very appropriate."

"You did not look like King Kong, my dear," remonstrated the minister gently.

"Well, the Queen of She-bear then," and Grace sat down again to shake comfortably at her own joke.

"Ha!" said Geoffrey very quietly, not particularly wanting anybody to hear. "And now the Queen of Beer-Sheba obviously."

Sybil rose hastily and seized her coat from the back of her chair. What if Mr Garner were offended!

"Father, some of us have a concert tomorrow," and at this there was a general bustle and mutual help with coats, and soon they all moved slowly from the warm room while Robert opened the front door for his guests and preceded them as they filed out onto the stone path before the two doorways. He looked left and right appraisingly as he breathed the sharp January air.

"The air is clear and bright like your Bees' Wine tonight, Mrs Martland. I don't think I've ever seen the street look so well lit."

Leonard inserted his key in their house door and pushed it open but stopped, for there were more hand-shakings and farewells.

"Are you driving, Dad, or shall I?" called Geoffrey, after kissing the two girls.

"Go on then. You can," replied his father after a pause.

"Not too fast," cautioned his mother.

"I'm never too fast. I'm sure I'm damaging my brake linings."

David Garner now stood in front of the girls.

"My dear sister in the Lord, may I wish you a Happy New Year?" He solemnly kissed Kerry on the cheek.

"What a lovely moon!" she exclaimed softly, looking up into the night sky devotedly, but her father caught hold of her plait.

"Now you girls come in out of the cold and never mind the moon," he said sharply, but his attention was at once diverted.

"Goodnight and a Happy New Year, Mrs Martland." Geoffrey kissed her affectionately. "And thank you for the Balm. It really oiled the works."

"A Happy New Year again, Clara, my girl," followed Alfred immediately and kissed her, droning.

David knew he could not surprise Sybil when he'd kissed her little sister; those were the tactics he had employed when trying to get her to use his Christian name. If she now put on a pretence of surprise it would be a tactical error on her part, but she made no undignified rejection of his good wishes as he bent towards her, but raised her eyes so that he slowed his movement as he met that look of appeal. Again it was he who trembled but he had sufficient quickness of wit not to withdraw in disorder, so after a lightning survey he chose an eyebrow. He was well satisfied, knowing nothing better.

"Happy!" he managed to bring out.

In another minute the doors of a car had banged and two house doors, one rather noisily. Leonard shot two bolts and put the chain on.

"That's all right outside chapel," he muttered savagely, "but there's no need to keep it up all night."

He marched down the lobby to the middle room and called out loudly.

"It's time everybody was in bed!"

He looked round with raised eyebrows, aggrieved.

Everybody had gone.

Chapter Nineteen

The front doorbell rang and two bedroom doors flew open.

"I'll go," said Sybil casually.

"Of course," answered Kerry with an apologetic grin. She went back for a moment and drew a long breath. Should she pinch a drop of Sybil's scent? She stole in and helped herself fairly sparingly. What exactly were the perfumes of Arabia? Travel books seemed to differ widely on the subject.

Sybil opened the front door just as Watch rushed into the hall barking frenziedly.

"Good evening, February fair-maid. How do, February fill-dyke. It's still snowing."

Kerry heard the drawing room door close and then she slid swiftly downstairs and into the middle room. She opened her school case and took out a magazine while she massaged Watch's recumbent barrel with one foot.

"Listen to this, Mother, In America some women are having their hair dyed strawberry blonde and their dog's hair to match. They'll look as if they've been run over,"

"Don't say such things!"

"D'you think that's what Mrs Sinclair has had done? Only it suits Sun Tan best."

Clara was folding washed clothes into a basket and seemed too busy to reply.

"It says here," went on Kerry after turning a few pages, "that vests are going out of fashion. It says they spoil the line. What line? The clothes line?"

Leonard lowered his *Evening News* and held out his hand.

"Let me see what you're reading, please."

He flicked through the pages disapprovingly.

"Can't you find anything better to read than this? Rubbish! Utter rubbish!"

He tore it across and Kerry gave a shriek.

"But it's not mine. It's Freda's. She paid fourpence for it."

Leonard produced fourpence and handed it across.

"Why, it's only a generation or so since women were pleading for higher education. They clamoured for the Colleges to be opened to them; they demanded recognition for their brains."

"I was only looking at it."

"And what have we now? Parents implore their offspring to study. We push them towards scholarship, removing all obstacles, and they respond by paying fourpence for their reading matter!"

"I didn't pay fourpence for it. I shouldn't dream of paying fourpence for it. Freda asked me if I'd like to borrow it in return for telling her about Bertran and Bimi. She doesn't read much; she's good at Maths. I don't know what she'll think when I tell her you tore it up."

Sounds of life were heard and Geoffrey came in where two of the trio were particularly glad to see him. He stood briefly to attention and saluted the photograph of the President of Conference before greeting them.

"Oh, Mr Martland, have you heard that the *Manchester Guardian* is being sold?"

"Good gracious, no!"

"Twopence a copy as usual to pay expenses!"

"Come on, Kerry; let's get down to it again, although after explaining to you last week that two minuses make a plus, I've been suffering from awful doubts myself. How's this last week gone?"

"The Fridge says my work is very uneven and it's never been that before. I don't like to tell her that the stuff I can do is what you've taught me."

"It is extremely advisable to refrain. Come on; where are we sitting?"

It meant keeping the two fires going all evening when the Maths lessons were on. One night when Leonard was at chapel they had tried sitting in one room but Kerry had hardly raised her voice above a whisper and Clara herself had felt fidgety, so now the young people sat in the drawing room, Geoffrey and Kerry at a table while Sybil at the side of the fire got on with her embroidery. It was called Richelieu work and the exciting moment came when the linen was cut away between the bars of over-stitching, leaving an elaborate tracery.

Seated at the card table, Geoffrey was aware of a tidal wave of Pacific Dream engulfing his olfactory sense. It was already familiar to him in minor ripples because he had bought it and he was on the point of remarking upon it when he managed to veer away from the subject in time.

There is a picture called 'The Education of the Virgin' which portrays an angel instructor holding an open book, but the Virgin is turning away to look at a dove; it's a way virgins have. It is difficult to make out whether the sacred page is covered with meaningless scribbles or wonder-holding hieroglyphics. It was Geoffrey's job now to show that this page was full of symbols and little by little the book held the wandering interest and commanded respect and understanding.

As she worked with pencil and exercise book, Geoffrey watched her and reflected that masculine and feminine minds do not run parallel although they come close here and there. He looked at the mantelpiece and at the ornaments flanking the clock. Yes, the male and female natures were like the lines of a vase, the combined outline graceful and well balanced. If the lines ran too closely together they produced not a vase but a tube; and sometimes a tube explodes. Just as the best glass is blown and not moulded, so does the mind best develop when influences are capable of fluctuation; a little pressure here, a breath held there so that the glass never shatters or becomes an imitative tube, but has points of distinction from its neighbours, maybe all equally lovely products.

It is when the Iron Maiden of an unnatural education closes in upon the maiden of flesh and blood that agony is felt inside.

The virgin was applying herself diligently to the book at this moment and it was the attention of the mentor that strayed towards the dove, innocently engaged upon her Richelieu work. What a marvellously equable temperament she had! He was lucky. Meanwhile she was getting on with her cardinal work in life!

Kerry finished her exercise and was highly commended. Under his words of praise she would have slavishly followed his line of life even if by so doing the outcome had turned out to be a curly glass walking stick; fortunately becoming rare. She was set upon a more difficult sum and Geoffrey leaned back and stretched his legs.

Was he going to teach eventually? Had he sufficient interest to give his life to historical or mathematical truth? Modern history was entangled with political economy as one tried to unravel the differing trends. Money came into it a great deal. People were unbalanced about money; either loving it too much or hating it too much, causing upset to those who regarded it purely as a useful universal tool. Man is a tool-using animal and without it he recedes into pre-history.

247

He could do with a bit more tool himself. As to saving up to get married, his father's allowance was quite inadequate for effective courtship even. Bills went to his father's account, so naturally he didn't need much loose cash according to parental reasoning, and when the time came, a house would be provided so he understood, and that time would be when he got a post. Or a job.

Another year and a half to go before he qualified for a remunerative post. As little time as he wished to go if he chucked it all up for a job! And got married.

He looked again at the mantelpiece and the vases and the placid clock. Next door, there stood a Chinese vase alone in its perfection, generations old, a careful and unhurried work. No, education was not a rush job, whatever the exigency of loose cash. And marriage was not a rush job, either.

"Finished!" said Kerry exultingly.

Geoffrey examined the page with appreciation.

"You've grasped that, Kerry, and having got that, you're safe for a bit and should be able to keep up. I'll just set you one more. And that's no way to treat a text book."

The lower corners of her Algebra book were adorned with tiny sketches of a ballet dancer, each very slightly different from the last, so that when the gages were flipped quickly there was enacted a very slight and elementary solo performance. He took his own fountain pen and on the top corners of the same book he drew a cat arching its back.

The lesson ended on a congratulatory note and Sybil watched from the sofa.

"He's always kind to her," she said to herself, but did not extend the reflection.

"We all say at school," Kerry burst out in pride, "that the Fridge wasn't College trained but was kennel maid at the lost dogs' home."

"That's the sort of remark that makes me feel less like teaching myself."

"I haven't put you off, have I?"

"Only for two or three weeks, if you don't mind, and then we'll start the spring offensive. I must catch up with some work I've undertaken for the Rag-Rag. I'm on the editorial staff this year."

Both girls expressed great interest and hero worship.

The Rag-Rag was the organ of the University Rag-day, published annually and with a peak sale for one week only. The cover design was signed by a name that was sometimes heard of again but otherwise no journal could enjoy a more dramatically mayfly existence. In its brief and hectic life it sold by the thousand, thereby helping to raise thousands for the hospitals; a charity that had to cover a multitude of impertinences.

Shrove Tuesday was a day of much needed tolerance. The participants worked hard. There were girls to be kissed and tycoons to be coerced into giving more pennies and pounds than the number they'd first thought of. Money was tossed from high windows into the lorries below where all manner of catchment was displayed, from children's shrimping nets to outsize and out-moded female garments.

Trams and buses were invaded and systematically levied. Private cars were surrounded and the owner drivers held to handsome ransom, unless they were discovered to be wearing Immunity Badges awarded to donors whose initial generosity spared them further molestation.

All day the heavy collecting boxes were clanked round the town and far into the suburbs. Trudging home late at night they were still at it, horseless highwaymen connived at by the public under the very noses of the police.

Even the theatres were not inviolate and the fag end of the pantomime season was enlivened by a noisy horde of pickpockets surging into the performance demanding Danegeld and altering the action of the plot considerably before they withdrew. Some of them remained with the cast on-stage throughout the performance; some were chased into the wings and after some surprised shrieking behind the scenes, chased out again. The rest settled, if that is not a misnomer, for the afternoon in various parts of the auditorium to give the benefit of their glowing opinions throughout the show on the young ladies of the chorus and the principal boy.

Such was the general tenor of the Shrove Tuesday Rag, that became yearly the much appreciated philanthropist that enriched the Manchester hospitals. It was the Rag Day and not the Flag Day that gave the positive answer to the question on the banner tied to the railings! 'Have you seen the nice new nurses' home?'

"Yes, Pancake Tuesday approaches once again," said Geoffrey blithely, "and our heterogeneous procession will defile along Oxford Road as usual."

Kerry rejoined her parents and reported that lessons were over for two or three weeks as Geoffrey was going to be very busy.

"It's the Rag-Rag. He's actually on the editorial staff this year. It's sure to be good, isn't it?"

Leonard and Clara were considerably less enthusiastic but they looked pleased, or at least Clara looked pleased.

She had been ironing in the middle room for Len's company and had almost finished, the clothes horse waiting for only a few final garments when Geoffrey and Sybil came in as well. The budgerigar chirped abominably above their voices and Geoffrey advanced upon him.

"Bedtime. Where's your cover?" He picked up something waiting to be ironed and spread it out. Then he carefully folded it again and put it back.

"Perhaps not. I shouldn't like anybody to get psittacosis."

"Here's the cover," said Sybil hastily and the cage was screened.

"Night fell with tropical suddenness," commented Geoffrey.

Just then a knock on the back door was heard, strangely at that hour, and Watch lying under the table began to bark. Leonard decided to answer such an unexpected summons himself.

"Good evening, Mr Martland," came David Garner's voice. "I couldn't make you hear at the front so I came round if you don't mind. It's still snowing."

This was the first time he had ever come in by the back door, which in Lancastrian social contacts corresponds to the difference between the use of 'vous' and 'tu'.

Clara greeted him cordially, if only because nobody else did. The clothes horse was predominantly full of feminine attire and at a glance from her mother, Sybil closed the contraption and was about to carry it into the kitchen when David sprang forward and lifted it from her hands, whisking it away so quickly that a shoulder strap streamed out and caught a button on Geoffrey's cuff in passing, leaving him in possession of a pink silk slip.

"What it is to be a ladies' man," Geoffrey said as he unpicked it from his sleeve and draped it round Garner's neck.

"Put Watch out at the same time," called Clara, somewhat flushed from her ironing.

"Out into the cold, cold snow, my lad," said Geoffrey, grabbing the dog. "We ought to have a marker-buoy; it's quite deep."

"He has a box in the wash-house. He'll be all right until he comes in for the night. Someone's sure to step on him in here."

Clara hoped her remark cast no aspersion on the company.

"By the way, Garner, just before you came in to give your demonstration of scene shifting, we were settling Gigli here for the night and your advent reminds me that Aunt Miriam has recently added to her devotional mystique with yet another cryptic printed card. For some time it has been Ataraxia, but lately the password has been altered to Paraclete."

A rather guarded expression came over David's face.

"But I was able to convince her," Geoffrey went on, "that it was mis-spelt; a printer's error. It isn't Paraclete, but Parakeet. It is really the Dove, but in the eastern hemisphere the bird would be a sort of parrot. Aunt Miriam was perceptibly swayed when I pointed out the reason why old maids keep parrots for pets. They find them a comfort."

Clara was uneasy and tried a slight change of subject.

"Gigli can only say his own name and 'pretty boy'."

"He does very well with his tiny brain-box," said Sybil compassionately.

But Geoffrey would not accept this line of thought at all.

"His speech mechanism is only the same as the starling's, imitating other birds' cries. It is only the mirror of the voice, an echo. Anyway, perhaps he's really a Yogi. Teach him to say 'Om' and then he has a perfect excuse for saying nothing else."

Leonard Martland looked up at Gigli's tented dwelling place.

"Perhaps he has the ability to say a great deal. Perhaps he is only waiting for a chance to get a word in."

Clara decided to get them all out of the way.

"Sybil, just see if the front room fire wants making up," and in a few moments she and Leonard were alone.

"Well, they watch each other so, I needn't lift my hand. When they make coffee they'll all crowd into the kitchen and there's no room for me, thank goodness."

"We deserve some slight compensation."

She surveyed Leonard out of the corner of her eye. Was his evening at home being spoilt? He went on reading the news, so evidently he did not want to talk.

"I don't know what to think," she remarked absently after a few minutes.

"Think about what?"

"Sybil and these young men. They can't drift along like this for ever; I wish he'd go away."

"Wish who would go away?"

"Young Mr Garner, of course," Clara said sharply. "We don't want a great upset, do we?"

Leonard still held up his newspaper as a sort of shield."

"I don't know. If Sybil wants to change her mind, and for all we know she may not, but if she does, we can't let the risk of an upset make any difference."

"But," and here Clara's voice rose in alarm, "we don't want the girl sunk in oblivion thousands of miles away in China."

"This is hardly the mother of the Wesleys speaking," Len answered

251

to her annoyance.

"I really don't know what to think," and after a pause she added resignedly, "Perhaps I'd better speak to Alfred after all."

A little colour heightened on Leonard's face.

"Even Alfred can't wave a magic wand over people's likes and dislikes."

"No, but he could wave a thousand or two over Geoffrey's prospects, which might come to the same thing. If they could be married next week they'd never regret it. But this drifting is dangerous."

Leonard nodded absently.

"I think I'll slip next door and have a word with Mr Garner."

"What about? Surely not . . . "

"Good gracious, no. There *are* other things, you know," and he went into the hall for his hat.

"You'd better put your coat on as well, it will be perishing outside."

Yes, thought Clara, left alone, there are other things. The Bazaar for one! A very cheerful subject for a busy and worried housewife, I don't think! Tears of vexation were not far away and then she too went into the hall. She would go and see Ella for an hour. When a tram came along, nobody heard the front door softly click.

The piano was taking some punishment in the next room. Geoffrey had not appeared to be deliberately following Sybil but went straight to the piano and dealt it assault and battery in fine style. After a slight hesitation, David seated himself on the settee next to Sybil, who picked up her embroidery again and gave it her whole attention. Geoffrey was singing "On with the motley" with affected intensity so that Kerry was in fits. "Laugh, Punchinello," he howled, and at the end took his curtain with tragic dignity before going lame and lurching round with hand extended for alms.

"Only one silver thimble," he grumbled. "Allow me, Alice, to present you with this thimble for your race against time in completing the linen feeder or whatever it is."

Sybil fumbled the receiving of the thimble and it dropped and rolled away, but was retrieved by David who held it towards her finger. Geoffrey quickly seized her hand as the thimble was about to be fitted.

"That's right, Garner. Give us your blessing. With this thimble I thee rig."

But Sybil twisted her hand away with an expression of great annoyance and he returned to the piano.

"Geoffrey, will you play some scales after all that," pleaded Kerry.

"Why scales, my dear child, and what do you mean by 'after all that?' But you're quite right. Scales are to music what corsets are to a full-blown figure. They are corsetière to Terpsichore, doing more than all else to keep her from becoming blowsy and over-emotional and generally going bust."

He began to play scales rather surprisingly well and their dependability soothed not only the others but himself as well. Notes ran out laughing, touched a boundary fence and ran straight back like playing children.

"I do wish Father would let me give up music lessons of any kind," Kerry said to him in between times. "There's nothing so humiliating as stumbling along in an alien art." Geoffrey crashed out a chord to hide his amusement.

"It isn't entirely alien. All these notes are letters which the composer arranges in a poem or an essay with written instructions to convey pace and mood. Even your old enemy Mathematics has much in common with music. These scales are multiplication tables that enable us to calculate without stopping to think. The arts and sciences aren't alien, Kerry; they are sisters, with something in common."

He flicked his little finger delicately down the outline of her nose and then turned to play some resounding arpeggios. She waited for an interval and then came in with her opinion.

"That's all very well about scales being multiplication tables, but there aren't both major and minor tables. You can have an alternative note in a scale but an alternative answer to a table is just wrong; it can't change key."

"All right then; sister arts but not always on speaking terms. Figures and figures of speech not playing since the scales fell from their eyes."

Her eyes danced at him as he spoke, but she defended her pet subject.

"I'd rather have figures of speech; you can't make jokes in things like Geometry. You're either right or wrong but never funny."

Geoffrey swung his legs round and faced the room where Sybil and David on the settee were listening in silence. She was stitching away and he was leaning back against the corner cushion with his legs stretched obliquely towards the fire so that her downturned head came naturally within his line of vision.

"Did you hear that, Garner? Kerry says that Geometry lets you make mistakes but not funny mistakes. There's no human humour in it; and I should hope not. It has its own sacred books of truth which are no laughing matter. I like the term 'pure mathematics'; absolutely no smut!"

The others were giving him their full attention, not just sitting there thinking their own thoughts.

"You can't say that of most subjects, especially the arts. Give me the subject in which you can't make a pun but which needs the highest form of wit; and that is any form of mathematics. It is the purest activity possible to the brain of man. In the arts he can stray, but in pure mathematics he cannot invent or distort but only disclose what has always been a truth. Man has not always known that if two circles touch one another, the centres and the point of contact are in one straight line, but the fact was there before man existed. And heaven and earth may pass away but the peculiar quality of those circles never varies. Mathematics always were and always will be, and a man engaged upon a mathematical problem is practically all spirit."

David was regarding him with extraordinary friendliness as he listened, just as he used to when he had first come amongst them and the young men had been so glad to know each other. Sybil bit her lip. They were always more in accord when she was out of the conversation; watching them the thought occurred to her that if she were out of the way, they would get on splendidly together. They both appeared to have forgotten her.

"After all," Geoffrey continued directly to Garner, "what are the Commandments but rules for groundlings. Moral law is that part of the law that talks down to us, but pure mathematics is, I think, the normal conversation of archangels, and man is at his purest when his mind is turned upon its wonders."

David drew in his legs and turned smilingly to the speaker, who leaned back with his elbows resting on the piano keys and looking ready for contradiction, but there was no truculence in David's reply.

"True, some physical laws are perfect and if we try to break them they may stave in our ribs. But not all physical laws are eternal and there is a moral law powerful enough to decide which physical laws shall be disproved. I, for one, accept that someone broke them consistently throughout his physical life and beyond. The physical and moral laws may be bound together more closely than we know. You mentioned scales being the corsets of music a few minutes ago. Now, consider a man like Tolstoy. He regarded the Christian idea as a formidable whalebone corset to prevent the body from becoming gross . . ."

"But he took those corsets off every night."

"Exactly. But if instead he had performed some definite religious exercises, he would better have succeeded in keeping spirit from over fleshiness. He relied too much on the physical and too little on the moral law. I'll grant you that the Ten Commandments are more for fledglings than for archangels, but progression was made from Mount Sinai to the Mount of Olives with its Beatitudes and from there to the final hill where the moral law reached its peak. Your physical laws are the whalebone corset but the moral law is the exercise with the flexibility of movement allowed by the modern girdle."

Sybil and Kerry here looked at each other and Kerry left the piano and went and sat down at the other side of the fireplace.

"I see," came Geoffrey's voice in pleased surprise, "that even your arduous studies leave you time to study the advertisements. We could do with you on the Rag-Rag staff. But you speak of flexibility. What virtue is there in flexibility when Euclid and even the great I AM boast that they change not?"

"For all we know, someone may come along and knock Euclid's circles for six and who knows what other Einsteins in other centuries will bend our light rays and do unimaginable things to all our so-called fixed principles? The fact that Lewis Carroll was, amongst other things, a clergyman and a mathematician is to me a great comfort and a great warning. He knew more than most about law and about flexibility, and he bent the law to amuse the pure in heart. Carroll knew so much of the mysteries. His lips had been touched by living coals so no wonder he stammered. He was a great modern prophet and what a vast truth it is that Alice at last became a queen after jumping the last brook."

David here smiled round at Sybil beside him, listening with hands inert.

"Speaking of Lewis Carroll," he said, unexpectedly lifting her hand and popping the thimble on it, "prize for winning the human race."

"Oh, there it is! I'd forgotten it. Thank you but I shan't be doing any more of this tonight."

She folded up the linen again and leaned sideways to open a workbox table that stood between the settee and the wall. Geoffrey stood up and moved from the piano stool and, giving Sybil's knee a pat to indicate that she should make room, he sat down between her and Garner. It was rather a crush.

David leaned forward.

"What about the girls giving us some music? I suppose I'm the least musical person in this house. Perhaps I only listen by ear as some people play by ear, but at least I make a good audience."

"Not really," argued Geoffrey. "The best audience, like Budge and Toddy, wants to see the wheels go round and those who can't appreciate the works are not of the inner circle. Are they, Sybil?"

Before Sybil could answer, David spoke firmly.

"But you mustn't despise those who happen to be outside that circle We should be made welcome in spite of our inferior understanding. The truly creative artist doesn't want merely admirers. Do you remember our peacock, Sybil? He doesn't want even disciples; he wants companions. No artist wants to win by several lengths. He would rather arrive at the winning post in a glorious bunch. The artist loves a golden age. Hence the popularity of the Mermaid Tavern."

The others gazed at him in surprise but at mention of the peacock Sybil had turned her head.

"My whole life and work," David continued gravely, "are based on that assumption; that fellowship is preferable to dominance. Hence not only the Mermaid Tavern, but the Upper Room."

They were all silent.

"You're right!" suddenly blurted Kerry and to her annoyance they all relaxed and smiled at each other. Seeing her chagrin Geoffrey rose and touched her hand with one finger.

"But murder is done, my dear girl, when the companionship turns out less perfect than expected. Hence the fall of Lucifer; hence the expulsion of man and God knows what future horrors that may cause us to think wistfully of a good old-fashioned flood!"

He turned from Kerry and faced Sybil.

"Sometimes it is better to remain alone since the search for fellowship is an awful risk at all levels."

She shrank slightly, but Garner swiftly contradicted.

"But the risk must be taken, eternally and at all levels, for the sake of the most complete and perfect one-ness possible."

Sybil now looked searchingly into her fiancé's face, but he motioned her to the middle of the sofa and he took the corner seat.

"How we talk! I could do with a drink and I expect you could too, Garner. No, don't move, Sybil, it's a real drink I want at this juncture."

"Oh," exclaimed Kerry, remembering, "Mother poured all the Balm of Gilead down the sink weeks ago."

"Lucky sink! The drains would wonder what was coming to them; flushed with wine. At this moment I need something full-blooded, ichor of the young Bacchus. Could you resist that, Garner, or do doctor's orders and Holy Orders disagree?"

"Don't be silly." Sybil was pale with annoyance.

"Or better still," went on Geoffrey as though wound up, "something that looks as warm but runs as chill as the blood of a pure girl. Perhaps you would prefer to go outside and melt some snow as no doubt a man of your iron will will resist anything, the pure or the full-blooded. Mercifully such chilly self-denial is not expected of me."

It was Garner's turn to go white.

"Now you are trying to poison the wells, Sinclair."

"No, I'm not, but they've gone stagnant, thanks to you! You keep to Dillwater's invalid tonic wine if you want but I'm going for something that wets the clay better."

"Why," said David very evenly, looking up at Sinclair who had risen to his feet with a face as red as the others' were pallid, "you're not going to paddle in it, are you?"

At this moment Kerry ran out of the room and opened the door into the dining room. There was no light there. Where were they? No one had heard them go out. Perhaps they had only gone next door since they hadn't bothered to say. She ran along the hall and left the front door wide open as she reached for next door's bell just as that door opened. Her father was leaving.

"Father! Come quickly." Her eyes were wide with fear and distress. "I think Geoffrey and Mr Garner . . . David . . . are going to fight!"

Both men jerked their heads up and the minister's mouth opened in astonishment. Then he stepped forward.

"Wait," said Leonard sharply.

"Why on earth wait?" exclaimed the other.

"Let them settle it; it'll clear the air. It might even give Sybil a chance to know her own mind."

But Robert hurried forward.

"Good gracious, we can't have this."

He sprinted round onto the Martland's step, but Leonard, his mildness dropped away, grasped the minister's shoulder and hand firmly.

"Mr Garner, please. I insist on leaving them to it."

"Rubbish!" exclaimed Robert vehemently. "We *must* intervene. I doubt if David knows anything at all about fighting or even self defence," and he tried to shake off the restraining hold.

"It'll come if necessary," answered Leonard, not letting go. "Let's get back."

"No," stoutly declared the captive, jerking his arms repeatedly.

"Yes, we must," urged Leonard. "You can't do any good," and being more than a decade younger, he propelled the minister away from the Martland threshold and into the chapel house doorway where they seemed to stick.

Of course it was only a matter of pushing and pulling and not even roughly at that, or of clinging to the framework for extra leverage, but even so, jackets were torn open and half off and buttons and buttonholes strained to bursting point.

Kerry stood between the two houses, distraught. Where was Mother? Where was Mrs Garner?

The two interlocked figures now hardly moved in a determined but silent trial of strength in which each was endeavouring at any cost to himself not to hurt the other. They swayed slightly but doggedly.

Down the passage beyond them a door opened.

"Are you there Robert? The news is coming on and you're letting the cold air in."

There was a pause and then the voice took on a slow and emphatic authority.

"You two come in here at once. Do you hear? I'm thoroughly ashamed of you both."

The organist and the minister lurched inwards and the door shut with a bang as though a heavy weight had collapsed against it.

Kerry rushed in at their own door and ran upstairs and then came halfway down again, pulling on the handrail, listening.

Were those thuds coming from behind the dividing wall or from their own front room? Her mouth went dry. No, it was her own heart pounding. She had never heard anything like it before.

Suddenly the drawing room door was flung wide open and Sybil dashed through it, her voice intense with fury.

"Am I a cow, to be fought over? Am I to stand here and watch you two behaving like cave-men as if the stronger were to walk off with me? I'll do the choosing if any choosing has to be done!"

She was rummaging on the hallstand and shakily wrenching at heavy winter coats on the highest hooks.

"We should both lose," came Geoffrey's voice bitingly from within. "Girls are such ninnies they'll accept one man and smirk at the next. And a weakness for parsons is one of those ailments peculiar to women, as the Aspros say."

The hallstand shook as Sybil strengthened her efforts and something gave way with a rip. She ran and pitched one coat out into the front garden and leaped back for more.

"I'm not a person to you," she sobbed. "I'm just a feather in your cap, or the feather from a game of badminton in which you've been showing off as usual. And as for you," and here she turned on Garner emerging from the room, a blaze that daunted him, "you think you're very clever, raising the whole game to the level of chess to show how subtle you are. But I'm not a feather and I'm not a pawn, and I've finished with you both. You're not worth having, either of you!"

Hats, coats, scarves and gloves were hurled into the night. As soon as the young men realised that their things were not being flung at them, they too rushed out into the sobering February chill to rescue their outdoor clothes. The crash behind them also shut off the light.

Scrabbling amongst the dripping rhododendron bushes which shook off their burden of snow onto the blundering trespassers, David trod upon something and finding Geoffrey's hat, kicked it vaguely in its owner's direction. Geoffrey clawed up the other's and shied it into the roadway.

Sybil had thrown at random with more passion than precision, in armfuls rather than in handfuls, and the coats would not have got so wet had they not been trodden on in the first confusion. But undoubtedly they had been trampled upon and were as much saturated within as without. Moreover, a glove crushed into the snow is, for a time, below the level of the searching fingers already losing all sense of touch, and even when found there is nothing less of the comforter than a soggy scarf, bright though it may be with one's noble university colours. As for a good theological looking hat, it has assumed a most everyday, battered and unromantic humanity when discovered run over by a crowded double-decker Manchester Corporation tram.

Chapter Twenty

Elsie Buckley read the printed sheet addressed to them both, without a spark of sympathy. So they were preparing for a Grand Bazaar now, were they? She slipped the notice under the coffee tray and said nothing about it. They weren't going to get hold of Sam's money so easily this time. He was too free with it.

He always paid the housekeeping money in beautiful, crisp new notes, got especially for her from the bank. She liked to handle clean paper money but tradesmen gave such dirty change, worn coppers that had passed through thousands of grimy fingers, that she had taken to emptying her purse into the sink when she got home and giving the silver and copper a thorough washing. Mrs Ginnell had seen her do it and Elsie had curled her lip. It would never occur to such people to be so particular.

Sam's voice broke in on her reflections.

"By the way, it's Shrove Tuesday, you know. Would you care to come down to the office and watch the Rag procession pass St. Peter's Square? It's a fine day."

She considered the question.

"I haven't seen the Rag-Rag this year, by the way. Haven't you got one?"

Sam quite jumped in his chair. He certainly had seen the Rag-Rag this year. As usual it had been opened by all the city, laughing expectantly before they'd got beyond the covers, but the laugh had been wiped off the town's face before they'd got very far. It really stank in places and someone was going to catch it, he was afraid. No, he wasn't afraid! He jolly well hoped someone would catch it, the young beggars.

No, he had not brought one home this year and he'd been careful not to let Rainbow see it either. She might see it elsewhere, but certainly not in the office of Samuel Buckley, Estate Agent and Valuer. He had said a word to that effect to the two young men in the outer office - "Don't leave it about," and they had nodded.

At his restaurant men had looked quickly at each other and, encouraged by a grim mouth here and there, had said it was a bit thick. Sometimes it got by until "Boys will be boys" was countered with "It depends on your knowledge of the world." If there is one point on which a man is more tender than on his sense of humour or his driving ability, it is his worldly sense. It began to be hinted that under the gay cover of the Rag there were hidden sores that no abandoned cur would feel tempted to lick, and that in the language of a popular monologue currently enjoyed and imitated, "Someone was going to be summonsed."

"Ah," replied Sam to his wife's query, "the old Rag Rag. 'Umm! I don't think there are so many about this year. Perhaps costs are rising. Yes. I think costs will come into it somewhere. Well, what about it? Can I expect you?"

"I think I'll come."

"That's right." He tried not to sound too hearty. "Come and throw your small change in a good cause."

While driving in, Sam noticed a pet-shop window first seen some weeks ago. It had started an idea that recurred to him now and again. How would Elsie react to a small dog, something like Mrs Sinclair's Sun-Tan? He had read that some could be carried in a roomy fur coat sleeve and that was what women liked, perhaps; something small, secret and intimate with the elaborate pretence that it was hugely important, discovery leading only to surprise and laughter. Sam had already made a few enquiries among business acquaintances as to what fashionable wives had up their sleeves these days but on the whole the men said they kept a healthy ten-bob mongrel for the kids.

Today, even at 9 o'clock there were lorries waiting by the University gates and Sam's mouth relaxed in the grin that would have been more frequent if life had not decided otherwise. The whole effort was a rummy output for a scholastic body, but it was said that some of the best bred dogs rolled in the muck. If that were so he would have to be careful if he decided to get one for Elsie.

Already a group of tall and muscular ballet girls were shaking their collecting boxes along Oxford Road and peering searchingly into cars near the pavement. Sam pulled up and lowered the window.

"I'd better have an Immunity badge; it'll be cheaper in the long run."

"Thank you, Sir. I'll fix it on if I can find my drawing pins. I always bring some to rehearsal since you never know with tights."

They patted the bonnet and stroked the mudguard and said regretfully that she didn't seem to want her sugar today. Did *he?*

Sam glided away into the stream of traffic again. He had gone into commerce at sixteen but if he had a son, he would like him to go there. Yes, their own University, Rag-Rag or no. They'd soon shake that off. Dash it all, boys *must* be boys. But not before the ladies! Well, if not before the girls, where else? There was nowhere else so worth while being a lad. He felt in lighter spirits. Other people seemed to be affected also and as he drew up near the office he saw the reason why. Long legs in football shorts momentarily revealed by a tipped up tu-tu, slid over the window and came to rest on the running board and then jumped clear.

"Thanks for the lift."

"A bit cold, wasn't it? You should have come inside."

"Oh, I wanted to float in on a Sunbeam," and with a shake of his box he went purposefully into Dingley's the florists where even in this first week in March there was, not a wild profusion, but a cultivated optimism of spring.

As Sam stepped out of his car he was immediately seized by two gendarmes, but upon catching sight of his badge they saluted smartly and marched on.

Business was brisk already and Sam knew they had a lot to make up on the losses of the Rag-Rag, but these youngsters intended to make it.

The gas fire in the office was burning steadily and Sam rubbed his hands before it for a moment. If Elsie was coming, he hoped she would be here before the main body. She was haughty looking but that would not save her from being centred in some rumbustious ring o' roses.

Sybil was opening and smoothing out the letters and he looked at her with some curiosity.

"Are you feeling cold, Sybil? We'll turn the gas higher if you are."

"I'm all right, thank you, Mr Buckley."

"Very good, if you say so. Only we must have you looking your best if any students come in. I shouldn't like one of them to complain that I was driving you."

"No one's going to complain, even if you were."

The studied unconcern mystified Sam. A shutter had come down over Sybil's usually indicative features, but even if her face was expressionless as a safety curtain, he wondered what was going on back-stage. He picked up a letter.

"Expiration of lease. Premises are not being snapped up as they were, but we'll make the most of it. Hub of city, not to say the hubbub.

We might find someone who wants to move to more commodious offices, as they say, from the big places they can't keep up any longer. If I saw a dog kennel with a good address I might take it myself."

"Why, Mr Buckley, it's only a few months since you said perhaps you might consider a partner."

"Exactly so. Somebody who has just come into a fortune and is looking for a project to lean it up against."

She did manage to smile but without looking at him.

"And here are several enquiries about the gown shop in Oxford Road. I've clipped them all together."

"What is there about a gown shop, Sybil, that most people seem to think they can run one? We'd better not call it a going concern because that's just what it is. I'll read them over."

Sybil returned to her own desk in the other window.

"Oh, and I shan't be going out this morning, Sybil. Mrs Buckley is coming down to watch the procession. I'm glad it's fine for them. They'll need all the money they can get."

He decided to say no more about that, her young man being one of the University products. Then Sam paused. Surely there hadn't been a quarrel! Presumably he *was* her young man still? Yet of late she had seemed to be just an efficient part-timer on loan from a secretarial school during the real Sybil's absence.

Leaning his chin on his hand he turned his head slightly to look carefully at her left hand. Did she wear her ring every day? He couldn't remember. He had noticed it for the first time fairly soon after its first appearance, but afterwards the little row of diamond asterisks had ceased to engage his attention. Had they ceased to engage Sybil?

"Ready for me yet, Mr Buckley?"

"Sorry. I was thinking out the wording for a rather tricky situation. Right, if you are ready to be dictated to."

The office work proceeded normally but the noises off were becoming more distracting and down below people were finding it more difficult to move along the pavement as others stood about in groups, unwilling to leave the main road and better vantage points. The sound of impatient motor horns grew more insistent and on the corridor behind Buckley's office, footsteps were hurrying from back rooms to front windows.

Glancing out, Sybil could see the steps of the War Memorial already taken and the office windows across St. Peter's Square showed onlookers enjoying the general disruption. Above the noise and chatter rising from the street below, she could hear a distant shouting. She sat still and unsmiling.

263

A knock came on the door.

Elsie would not have dreamed of just walking in unannounced. She was visiting, even if it was her husband's office.

Sam sprang up delightedly, trying not to fuss. Which window would she prefer? He opened the sash window to its fullest extent and made room for her chair. He would stand on guard.

Elsie threw back her fur and opening a handbag that had been one of Sam's more successful presents, she took out her cigarette case and extended it to Sybil who declined the offer.

"No vices at all?"

"People always say that," answered Sybil with a faint perplexity. "It must be the commonest, I suppose."

"How's Didsbury these days?"

"It's still there, Mrs Buckley."

"I haven't heard any news of the Sinclairs recently. Is there any?"

"I believe they are all quite well, thank you. Excuse me."

A woman can notice all points without seeming to scrutinise an object; indeed, if she stares at a thing fixedly it is a sign that her mind is wandering. As soon as the door shut behind Sybil, Elsie turned to Sam.

"She's not wearing her ring! You should have told me."

"I've only just noticed it myself this morning."

Elsie looked at him in amazement and he felt like a little cock bird no good at bringing worms home.

"And she's never said anything to you?"

Sam shook his head glumly.

"Well, then something's gone wrong. I wonder what. I don't suppose *she's* changed her mind."

People were now running from buildings to the pavement as a great shouting was heard. The first lorries of the Rag procession were very slowly rumbling into view by the Prince's Theatre and the onlookers clapped as the various scenes went by and continued along their route down Quay Street. The Buckleys could see well enough from the window. There were of course the various European dictators with their dark-shirted henchmen giving their familiar salutes, and at intervals they came to the side of their lorry and gave impassioned but unintelligible speeches which were received by the populace with catcalls.

"Where's the band?" asked Elsie. "Doesn't one of the local bands usually give its services for the Rag?"

"Perhaps they couldn't get one this year, and of course they don't want to pay for the hire of one. But there's enough noise as it is."

Some music of a kind was provided by a more than ordinarily mad Nero, fiddling with all the verve of a Paganini and surrounded by an assortment of fiery Roman beauties that would have given him pause. The solo was interrupted now and again as Nero doffed his laurel wreath to acknowledge the pennies falling into the decorated lorry, the ladies in waiting sometimes testing the coins in their teeth as they swept them together, while the bystanders applauded the unextravagant simplicity of the first century style costumes, well rendered in bathing towels and beach sandals.

Following came the Serpent of Old Nile on her barge with attendant bargees. Her ladies, in bead curtains and pan lids, were trained in the more elementary deportment of feminine allure and such was their jealousy of the popularity of the preceding royal entourage that they took time off from lolling about the deck to snatch up their peashooters and riddle the frenzied artist a few yards ahead.

"Sybil's missing it," cried Sam, enjoying it immensely. "But perhaps she's slipped out. Have you got anything to throw, Elsie? Here you are."

The lorries were out of range but young men and women with boxes were hawk-eyed for opportunity and canvassed all windows. Sam was surprised to see how accurately Elsie could throw.

"Let me try for that butterfly net," she called excitedly, and one after another the sixpences were lobbed into it with ease. Heads turned to see who had such an unfailing aim and she laughed unaffectedly as she attracted warm thanks and warm glances.

"Bravo," exclaimed Sam with a steadying arm on her waist that she did not notice in her high spirits. If he had done that at home she would have changed from molten to marble in an instant. This Rag was really good. Hang the Immunity badge. Let's throw some more.

The draped or flowered vehicles rolled by bearing the varied tableaux vivants, their company watchfully raking in the city's piecemeal but abundant liberality. There was a Baby Show, of necessity including the huge scales that usually weighed sacks of cattle or pig food, resounding as coins rattled on it. A few but representative yards of Blackpool's Golden Mile were exhibited, crammed with bearded or over-developed ladies, skeletons, vampires, supernaturally strong men, Siamese twins and other distressing wonders. Immediately behind came a full size replica in painted canvas of Epstein's great sculpture, Genesis, but because of the grotesques parading outrageously before her in her interesting, not to say startling condition, someone had thoughtfully bandaged her eyes.

A float that set all the girls agog was manned by Miss University

m

and her runners-up, some of whom would have been quite acceptable in Shakespeare's company of players, and by the time speculation had come to a halt as to whether Miss University herself was a girl student or not, she had been borne smiling enigmatically away.

Sam, watching the procession and also Elsie's safety at the window, saw more out-runners along the pavement below and then someone in the corridor outside the office knocking loudly and entering with a flourish. A horned Viking, cross-gartered and breast-plated, carried a battle axe covered with glittering tin-foil upon the shaft of which was slung his collecting box. He looked quickly round the room.

"Why, it's Geoffrey Sinclair," exclaimed Elsie, turning, and Sam's arm dropped away.

"Oh hello, Mrs Buckley. Hello, Mr Buckley. Have you been fleeced yet?"

"Pretty well by this time. Jolly good procession though. Sybil was here not long ago but perhaps she's run out to the corner of the Square."

"I didn't think she was all that keen on seeing it," volunteered Elsie. "Of course, it doesn't touch everybody's sense of humour. You don't happen to have a spare copy of the Rag Rag, Geoffrey? Sam couldn't get one for some reason."

The men glanced at each other.

"I'm afraid not, Mrs Buckley. As a matter of fact they were faulty, whole pages all wrong; really rather a washout this year."

"What a pity! Had you anything to do with getting it out this year? I should have thought it would be just in your line."

Geoffrey bit his lip for a moment.

"Oh, well, not much, but I was on the editorial staff."

"Wait here a bit," offered Sam good naturedly. "She might be back soon."

They watched the misleading pageant of social history glide by, Geoffrey ruminating cheerlessly on the last month. He had not been able to give an undivided fervour to the hatching of the bad eggs that had created such offence, but he had enjoyed the get-together of the editorial table; it had occurred to him that the *Punch* table would be something like theirs, but the illusion had been short-lived. So also had been the editor's panache. He might have to withdraw from the academic scene as a burnt offering to the Watch Committee. The rest of them had suffered a couple of interviews that would be remembered much against their will, the first with their Vice Chancellor who regarded them as the type of immature offenders who scribble private matters on public walls, and the second with the Chief of Police who equated them with those actual scribblings and intimated that to obliterate them all would be a Civic duty.

The *Manchester Guardian* was very discreet about the Rag Rag. It was an unfortunate lapse of good taste and best forgotten, but future editors would take the public's recoil as a warning and bear in mind that the means must not disgrace the end.

Nevertheless, Geoffrey dared not go up to the Martlands yet awhile. One embarrassment was enough without going covered in depreciation.

The last fortnight had been a difficult time to make one's peace with a girl. At first he had lain low, but when he considered that Sybil would have regained her composure and with it her sense of the fitness of things, he had written a careful, tactful and apologetic letter, not minimising the gravity of her anger but asking her pardon and assuring her of his eternal devotion.

Funny how girls harped on the longevity of love; not its depth, strength or vividness which in all possibility carried the seeds of endurance in them, but treating love as if it were a clock in danger of running down. "Will you love me always?" a contemporary had challenged him at fifteen and a half. He remembered the rough straw of her school hat catching his nose as he asked, "Do you love me today?" and she had grabbed his school cap and thrown it on the park greenhouse roof and run off.

Well, he was older now and knew the correct feed, but there had been no reply to his letter. This would not do at all.

Might not that other be seeing her to plead his own cause? Not that he had a chance. Geoffrey wrote again.

His third letter brought an answer. Connie brought it to him saying, "I signed for this; it was registered," and handed him a small parcel that he had not been expecting. It stopped his breathing for a moment. Connie had looked at him from under her lashes before turning away.

"Oh, thank you, Connie, but I don't know why they bothered to register it," and he went into another room casually without shutting the door.

Immediately under the lid was Sybil's note. His eyes raced down it and then with a sense of recovering more than his breath, he slowly went over it again word by word, just as a man sprinting across a lawn returns, thoughtfully casting about for the keys and small change scattered on the grass.

'Sir,
    I remain,
        Sybil Martland.'

Slowly the tense look on Geoffrey's face relaxed into an expression of relief. He'd had a fright but it wasn't serious. If she had really wanted to break off their engagement permanently, she would have let him down gently in a letter entirely different, full of regret and offering to be a sister to him. Let her tell Garner she'd be a sister to him, or a second cousin once removed for all he cared. Fancy darling, gentle Sybil coming out with this!

He sat awhile with the note in his hand. At least she was telling him that she wasn't changing her name for any other and that was an important key-ring. Of course she had not behaved like a darling gentle Sybil on the night of the general exodus but that had been quite out of character. Like this!

Get her back he must, since there was genuine sorrow in him now and he wanted to comfort her and make amends and also, a prick of pride advised him, she was more worth the effort after that show of rebellion. But he had learned his lesson and would show her that he could be a darling gentle Geoffrey himself in future.

Now standing in Buckley's office window, he realised that his first attempt to see her had fallen flat. He had wanted to surprise her into a look of thankfulness, of forgiveness, perhaps a look of asking pardon for herself, and instead, she had retreated. He could not stay here much longer.

"It's over," said Elsie regretfully.

Below them the crowd hurriedly dispersed, heads disappeared from office windows as the tail end of the procession was lost to sight beyond the scaffolding of the new Reference Library, leaving the onlookers to catch up with their work and make some more money.

The three moved back into the room.

"I'll tell Sybil you called."

"You look quite resplendent," said Elsie approvingly. "Will you rejoin the others now?"

"Oh, easily."

"Well, take the last of these coins. I brought them from home so they're quite clean. I washed them myself."

"The Nurses' Home will like that antiseptic touch," said Sam, but he gave her an anxious glance as she dropped the money in the box.

"I think I'll walk as far as Deansgate with you if I shan't be in your way."

"Do, Mrs Buckley. Delighted."

"Oh," blurted out Sam. "But I thought we'd go for a coffee, Elsie, and perhaps lunch after your shopping."

"I only came in to see the Rag and shall probably be home for lunch. Say goodbye to Sybil for me. Ready, Geoffrey?"

Disappointment struggled in Sam. Dash it, not his wife *and* his secretary, he thought confusedly. He was craning out of the window again when Sybil entered with a tray of tea.

"Has Mrs Buckley gone already?"

"Only just this minute. She's gone with . . . someone she knew who was just passing. Now this is thoughtful of you. Tea for two! Never mind, we shan't waste it. You must have it."

His jocular tone did not last long, however, and he sat looking out into the normal street again. Sybil carried her tea over to her desk and likewise sat silent. After finishing one cup Sam spoke.

"Their name liveth for evermore! Not really, you know. That's what they have sacrificed; particular work that might have made them famous. But they have the perfect alibi for being nonentities. Mutts like myself are left to be downed by even opportunities."

Sybil roused herself and struggled out of her own depression. It was one of Mr Buckley's bad days, and this sounded like one of the worst, strangely after he'd been in such high feather earlier.

"Well, you've done your good deed for today, anyway, by giving generously to the hospitals. And that's very useful."

"Yes, *it's* useful all right, the money. But that doesn't make *me* useful. If I died, my money would go more freely."

Sybil took a chance.

"Perhaps if your money died on you, *you* might go more freely. You could walk out and become a gipsy."

Slowly he lightened.

"You're a wonderful secretary, Sybil; you never run dry. I doubt, though, if I could cultivate a taste for hedgehog at this stage, and it would never occur to me to steal a horse. Leave the darned things where they are is my motto. I met a few in the war."

She nodded sympathetically and silently poured him another cup. He took it and became more naturally conversational.

"Chaps are still writing about the war as one way of doing something for their names. And it's a queer thing; if the language is particularly lower deck or front line, the book is dedicated to wife or mother, and if it's positively not fit to read, to the *memory* of mother."

Then he stopped as if the ground were becoming boggy. Reference to lower deck had reminded him of the Rag Rag.

"By the way, Sybil, I'd almost forgotten, but Geoffrey Sinclair came in for a moment hoping to find you here. I'm afraid I thought you'd gone out to watch the procession. I'm so sorry. Naturally he was disappointed."

Sybil, like Sam, looked steadily ahead.

"Thank you, Mr Buckley, but it's quite all right."

"Is it really? I mean, are things all right? You are quite happy and all that? I just wondered."

At the sound from her direction Sam jerked round.

"Oh, my dear girl, I didn't mean to upset you. I wouldn't have uttered a word if I'd known things were so bad. Look, Sybil, I'm older than you and Geoffrey. If you like each other and generally get on well together, as I'm sure you do, don't let a little episode like this upset you. I know it's a bit thick this year, but they are doing their utmost to raise enough money so the hospital won't suffer. Now don't you be foolish and go making yourself and everybody else miserable."

Sam spoke with great feeling. So speak all older people warning young people to patch up their legitimate quarrels and equate their serious differences and lose no time in deliberation, for time is the real enemy. Sam was thinking only of the crack in the ice which time would widen. He was urging them to stay together on the same ice-floe and not be in the terrible emergency of calling across a darkening stretch of water.

By this time the girl was sobbing quietly.

"Sybil," pleaded Sam, "you won't let this silly Rag Rag come between you?"

She raised her head for an instant.

"It's not that. It was something else."

Sam was taken aback.

"Nonsense!" he blustered. "It can't be much, I'm sure; and in any case, don't be too hard on a fellow. Men feel these things more than women often realise; at least let's hope they don't realise. The world would be a happier place today, Sybil, if we stopped falling over backwards to forgive our enemies and tried forgiving our friends for a change."

Sam walked to the window and sighed heavily.

"We're not having a very good morning, are we? But just take heed of this, my dear. If you find one man you can trust absolutely, bind yourself to him with hoops of steel and if he can afford it, as your young man can, with hoops of gold. Don't waste valuable time in quarrelling."

Sybil sat up and drew a querulous breath.

"At the moment, Mr Buckley, I can't be bothered any more, We're so differently made, aren't we? Lions and lionesses, tigers and tigresses seem to be more or less alike, but men and women seem to belong to different species, don't we, as if nature had made an error in expecting us to get on together?"

Sam was very guarded.

"I've never reached that conclusion at any time. A little co-operation, a bit of give and take and I think we should do fine, and whatever we think, by the circumstances of creation we have to go through with it together. I once read an article by that chap Bertrand Russell. He's taken a lot of punishment in his time, but he said that a man trying to please a woman was like a gorilla trying to play the violin. Well, I personally think the gorilla deserves some credit for trying, which the lion and tiger would never bother about. Just one upper-cut with the paw, you know. Well, well! Perhaps you'd better remove this tea, Sybil, thank you very much. By the way, are you fond of animals?"

"I used to be before humans came more into my life. Why?"

"I was thinking of getting a nice dog for my wife and I wondered if you would help. I was thinking along the lines of a Peke."

A Peke! All roads were signposted to Sinclair.

"Since she hasn't been so well," Sam hurried on, "humans haven't come into her life so much and I don't think she gets out enough. She might go for the dog's sake."

While Sybil removed the tray, he reflected on the real reason for considering the purchase of a dog. One mid-day when he was alone, he had telephoned Dr Bedser after some hesitation.

"It's about Elsie, you know. Nothing much but she's suddenly taken a scunner against money; the hard cash we handle, you understand. I believe she actually washes it in soap and water. Just hypersensitive I should say, but I thought I'd mention it to you."

Dr Bedser had been most cheering and after some explanatory chatter, he ended with advice.

"She's got over that mishap by this time and she wants something more to do. She's bored. The happiest solution would be to start a family in earnest and she'd soon lose that pernickety fad."

"Simple, isn't it?"

"Quite. It would do you good too."

So when Sybil came back to her desk he decided to go out then and there. It would make a point of interest for her too on this miserable morning. He put his head in the back office and told the two young men that he was going to look over a little property not far away.

"I don't suppose I'll be much help," she said as they walked up Mosley Street. "Our Watch's pedigree has veered here and there according to . . ."

She stopped as if in an old fashioned maze she had come to a dead

271

end for the fiftieth time.

"Yes, of course, but you'll know a nice dog. They are getting one or two possibilities for me to consider."

"And we'll look out for that kennel with a good address that you mentioned."

Good girl, thought Sam. If she couldn't wag her tail at least she didn't whine.

They were making for Tib Street on the other side of Piccadilly, an area well known for traffic in household pets of all kinds. There were established shops that paid rent and rates and were connected with respectable kennels, but a quick trade was done on the edge of the pavement in barely weaned and probably wormy puppies carried inside men's coats, their heads bobbing uncomprehendingly from bulging lapels. In Tib Street, dogs changed hands at guineas as well as shillings and were borne off to homes with lined baskets and long gardens as well as to homes with small backyards and a friendly welcome under the kitchen table.

As St. Peter's Square quickly regained its natural composure, the stream of Shrove-tide joviality poured down Quay Street and along Deansgate and up Market Street with Elsie still alongside and not having gone into any shops yet. The Viking gently swung his battle axe.

"Thank you. Thank you. I shall be in hospital myself at this rate; it's a frightful weight. Are you all right, Mrs Buckley? The crowd's very thick here; don't get carried away."

Expertly, if absentmindedly, he clasped Elsie's waist and guided her along, but she was no more aware of it than when Sam held her as she threw money from the window. She was enjoying the excitement and action and the noise of people applauding as they did at a tennis tournament. The wildness and high spirits here were all controlled and harmless, girls could shriek and giggle, young men could seize and kiss, but it was all within bounds. You could let yourself go in a crowd, with masses of shouting people round you and everybody flirting with strangers.

A flower from a passing lorry hit her cheek and she snatched it and flung it back. Some of the tableaux had been patiently decked, people staying up nearly all night to trim the floats, but sooner or later a Battle of Flowers developed. The transport would be needed for work again after the Rag, so instead of waiting until they returned to base, the crews started to strip the flotillas on the homeward run. It was a crazy mercy killing of flowers that would be dead from thirst the next day; if human nature did not destroy them, impartial nature would lay them waste overnight. So the revellers forestalled decay by pretending to enjoy annihilation and the flowers were pelted at the crowd who sometimes caught them but for the most part they were allowed to fall to the ground and be trampled to death.

"If there's a jam we'll get on a lorry," exclaimed Geoffrey, scrutinising the procession. "This box needs horse power to carry it now. Can do?"

"I think so with a bit of help."

"There'll be willing hands."

He spotted the Viking Ship and moved into the road.

"Hi! Greenhalghe, help us aboard, will you? You take the loot and I'll take the lady."

" 'Ware wheels!"

Elsie felt herself hoisted up. Her knees were on the edge of the platform and she more or less fell into the lorry, fielded by strong hands, but losing a court shoe. Her hat fell onto the floor and several pennies landed in it at once.

"Oh, my shoe," she shrieked.

Someone obligingly threw it after the departing vehicle but it fell short and then someone else threw it more accurately, hitting friend Greenhalghe, who made as if to hurl it back when Elsie grabbed it. Geoffrey had managed to scramble on unaided and he steadied her now as she replaced her shoe. The hat lay disregarded.

" Any lady tired of standing can ride for sixpence and a kiss," roared Greenhalghe.

"Extra pretty ones let off the sixpence," amended others of the crew.

"Go on, kiss her," yelled some of the crowd.

"Let some of us come up and help you!"

"You clever Dicks don't know how to begin!"

"Boo - oo!"

"What!" yelled Geoffrey, shaking his battle axe at them. "That's what we get our Degrees in. Watch this, you landlubbers!"

The Boos turned admiringly to Oohs and further small change was lobbed into the craft by a populace in frolicsome mood as the calendar threw off this one festival in the first dull quarter of the year.

It was at this merry stage that the lorry slowly jolted past the entrance into Tib Street.

In spite of a crisp start, the late afternoon crumpled into a depressingly wet evening and rain drummed insistently on the windows. Sybil had gone into the front room to practise and Kerry settled down at the dining table to stare at her homework, feeling at cross purposes with everybody although school had finished at noon and she, Freda and Gwen had stood on the steps of Queen Victoria's monument in Piccadilly to watch the procession before going to a little shop on London Road for chocolate biscuits and lime juice. Then the three had gone into the Art Gallery for a couple of hours, looking round and sitting on the comfortable seats to talk in the almost deserted rooms. She got home at the usual time after what she considered an ideal sort of day and yet when she had tried to describe the Rag procession later, she was chalked off tersely. She sat glowering at her books.

Sounds of music came from the other room and after a time Sybil started to sing, scales with melodious chords to accompany them disguising the fact that the voice was doing exercises. These were dutifully performed and after a silence one or two songs were gone over, not very brilliantly. Then she started another and got only as far as "Would that my heart could utter", when voice and piano stopped.

Clara glanced at Leonard as there was no resumption of music but she got no response. What can parents do, she asked herself, when children's love affairs go wrong? They can do nothing, only hear the song choke on the young lips and strain their ears for further sounds, pretending to hear nothing. Hardly anything was ever said about the situation that was troubling them all. During the first week she had been aghast, but both Sybil and Leonard had been mute on the subject.

"They can't just break it off like that and nothing said," she had argued. "We shall have to see Alfred soon."

"We shall do nothing of the sort."

Later she had tried again.

"Sybil can be stubborn in her quiet way and don't forget she has some of Fanny's blood in her. Something will have to be done."

It was the thought of kinship between Sybil and Fanny that frightened Clara most of all.

"If Sybil has made up her mind to change it, she can do better," said Leonard firmly.

"Don't you be too sure. Geoffrey would be all right in the long run and with him she would be comfortable. She'd be able to keep up her music and dress well. And even if she accepted David Garner, what sort of a life would she have? Wandering on the face of the earth, ruining her good looks in unsuitable climates and most likely her health as well. I don't know what's come over you. A proper life for a girl like Sybil is looking after a home where she can entertain people who have something about them and enjoy a position worthy of herself. I don't want to think of either of our girls having to struggle all her life."

Leonard had listened with coals of fire, the best kitchen nuts, pouring on his head, for here he recognised the voice of Woman, the voice not heard when she is asking for herself but which rings out when asking for her children. Here was the authentic comment on marriage slipping out unselfconsciously.

So this evening with the rain pelting down, they were all shut away with their own thoughts. This is what it is like, thought Clara, after a war. We work and do the things we used to do, but with a difference. There are no young men about.

Clara had not lit a fire in the drawing room. It was very cosy in here and Sybil must not expect to sit apart all the time when nobody would be calling. If she did not want to sit with them night after night, the advantages of a home of her own might begin to dawn on her. At that age they all want Elephants and Castles, but if they're not careful they are more likely to get Pigs and Whistles.

Sometimes when there were kippers for breakfast or tea, Clara divided the remains carefully for the cat. Later she would hear the tinkle of crockery as Ebony softly jumped on the trolley; not content with the picked morsels, the cat was hungering after the indigestible mass. So do the young remain unsatisfied with the best that is offered but demand the full flavour of life, bones and all.

Well, this was Sybil's time for tasting the bare bones and Clara hoped that she would not have to feed on them for life. Clara had read reports now and again of cats accidentally shut in the engine rooms of ocean going liners and emerging at landfall quite unharmed, having licked the oil from the machinery and being further sustained by their own stored energy. Fanny had managed so to live. Was it to be Sybil's lot to do so too?

Sybil did not join them at the fire, but went upstairs and going into her own room, slowly approached the dressing table and opened the deep bottom drawer. Is that what love does to you? Traycloths! You sit down meekly with eyes lowered as in those pictures of the Annunciation and stitch away, waiting to be called for. Well, she had finished with traycloth love. David's coming amongst them had done that for her at least. He had stirred the pool and gone away; had been driven away perhaps, but had stayed away. That stirring seemed to be all that was required of the acquaintance.

There was a tap on the door.

"What is it?" she called in a voice more abrupt than it used to be.

Kerry sidled in, uncertain of her welcome and looked with interest at the open drawer.

275

"I'm sorting out some things for the Bazaar," Sybil offered in response. "I shan't need them."

"What do you mean, you won't need them?" Kerry stared unbelievingly at her sister. "He'll be coming back soon. He can't stay away for ever."

"No, Kerry, he won't be coming again."

"Not ever? Do you mean he's really stopped coming to our house at all? He didn't quarrel with *you!*"

"Yes, it's all over. We don't think as much of each other as we thought, that's all."

"But we do! We all like him very much; you know we do. And I hate David Garner if it's his fault. Will *he* start coming now?"

"No, indeed. Nobody will come. We've got to strike out two minuses, Kerry."

Sybil tried to smile.

"But there's no plus!" Kerry almost shouted. "What are you doing? Everybody thinks you're going to be married soon."

"Well, we must just explain that we made a mistake. We have changed our minds."

"Geoffrey hasn't. I saw those letters come. He's steady as a rock."

"Stop it, Kerry. Go downstairs again."

"But I don't understand. You've liked him for ages."

"Listen, Kerry. We've changed."

"But you don't hate each other!"

Sybil took a deep breath.

"Even that might have come in time."

Kerry's eyes opened even more widely but Sybil continued.

"I'm sorry, Kerry. We all liked him. But even if he were steady as a rock as you think, I'm not the one who can hew out the man he should be. That will take someone stronger than I."

"He's all right as he is," persisted Kerry, bursting into tears.

"Oh, don't, Kerry, do stop it. It's hard to explain to you, but I've come to see that he likes to be amused. We can all show our claws at times but we scratch down a piece of wood, like Ebony, but Geoffrey doesn't care if he draws blood. I once read of a rat . . ."

"Sybil, you're awful!"

"It's only an illustration! This rat had lost an upper tooth, leaving the lower tooth with nothing to grind on however quickly it gnawed. Wit can sometimes be like that and needs another as hard as itself to be natural and healthy." Here she paused, staring into the open drawer and then added in a whisper, "I couldn't stand any more. I was too soft."

A miserable and awkward silence fell and the younger girl made as if to withdraw. She had really come to ask about a French negative but decided not to bother; she would go into the bathroom and dab her eyes with cold water before going downstairs again. She gently opened Sybil's door just as the front bell rang. Both girls stiffened and strained their ears. They heard their father emerge and open the door.

"Good evening, Mr Martland."

"It's Geoffrey," sang Kerry, joy suddenly transforming her.

"Be quiet," ordered Sybil not moving and listening keenly, so that Kerry also remained fixed and mute.

"I regret," they heard their father's firm voice, "that I cannot ask you in. My daughter is her own mistress, but your acquaintance with the rest of the family has ceased. Good-night."

The door was shut.

The listening girls were Gorgon stilled.

An outburst of rain struck the window like a rush of exclamation marks.

"Sybil, run after him! What does Father think he's doing? Sybil, catch up with him before he gets right away!"

Sybil did not move. She was crouching by the open drawer with her head against the shut drawers above it. Here eyes were closed and she was breathing sharply. If she ran downstairs now, the past weeks and months would recede almost as if they had never been. If only she ran after Geoffrey now, all would be as before, laughter and daydreams and timeless drifting and . . . traycloths! And also, if she admitted now in her heart of hearts, smart and echo of doubt and a turning to the horizon with an undefined perplexity.

The horizon was starkly empty, dark and without a vestige of reflection of light beyond, but at least she could look to it without betrayal if without hope. If she ran downstairs and out into the downpour at this moment, never again would she be able to search the horizon, but live embosomed in the dreaming cloud; in a cloud cuckoo land. Kerry looked hard at her sister motionless and then she herself moved swiftly. The hall was empty and all the doors shut. She pulled open the front door. There had been no sound of a car. Dare she stay to seize a coat before anyone came to stop her? She snatched the nearest and, casting it round her shoulders, sped to the gate and out. The few people across the road at the tram stop did not include Geoffrey and she turned the corner and ran as fast as she could down the road, scanning the pools of lamplight ahead for the sight of a hurrying figure. On fine nights it was possible to see nearly all the road but the rain curtained the lamps, if only skimpily. There, on the other side! She almost caught up with him just before the next light.

"Geoffrey! Stop!" He halted abruptly and turned in surprise. Kerry's breath was laboured as much with agitation as by swift running and she stood in front of him panting.

"Come back, Geoffrey. You mustn't go away. It's all wrong."

"Kerry, go back at once. You'll get wet through."

"It will be awful without you. It is already."

"It's not exactly unanimous! Now off you go."

"You come as well. Sybil's crying."

Geoffrey's mouth was down curving at the corners.

"She didn't send you, did she?"

"No, but she's crying. I saw her."

"She isn't crying for me, Kerry. Now go back." The girl broke into sobs and he spoke in desperation.

"Don't you cry. She'll soon get over it! Now run straight home. Look, I'll take you to the corner."

He seized her hand and started back at the same furious pace and stopped under another lamp. They stood in a cage of light with silver bars.

"Good-night, Kerry. What a night!" he said bitterly.

But she had not finished.

"Don't take any notice of what Father said. It's like my Report. It'll blow over."

A cold left-over of mirth appeared on Geoffrey's face and she took heart.

"It's all that silly fuss over the Rag Rag," she went on hurriedly, "and I thought it was good. Gwen got one from her brother and we read it in the Art Gallery this afternoon. We laughed like anything."

Geoffrey peered down at the streaming face. He took the young jaw between thumb and finger and gazed penetratingly. The rain washed down it while the tears welled up out of the unwavering eyes.

"You thought it was good?" he queried grimly. "You laughed like anything?"

Kerry tried to nod.

"God!" he exclaimed. "Let that be my just reward," and he flung off into the night again.

The rain had held off until late afternoon but could no longer contain itself and so let fly. Pedestrians fled like matadors to the barricades and the streets became as empty as in the small hours of the morning while the first outburst spent itself. Connie Ginnell was hurrying back to

278

Didsbury and she walked quickly towards the Oxford Street traffic, when the heavens opened and the cloudburst beat on the pavement with all the venom of a virago turning on her paramour. The stones hissed and steamed as the storm-flood made rapids of the gutters, but for a few moments the pavement had to take a thrashing.

"Here, quick! Jump in here."

A man in his stationary car leaned back and opened the rear door and Connie thankfully got in.

"Any more for the Ark?" he asked cheerfully. "A minute of that and you'd have been wet through."

They watched the scene for a few moments and then Connie turned to the less familiar interior view. What a lovely car!

"Seen anything of the Rag earlier today?" asked her rescuer.

"Only towards the end," answered Connie rather dejectedly, "and I thought the bit I saw rather silly."

"Ah well, sometimes we miss something we went especially to see and see something we were not expecting."

"Do *you* find that in life?"

He laughed and then spoke seriously.

"Only occasionally. I mustn't put you off."

Connie studied the head politely inclined to her and decided to take it into her confidence, shut in together as they were in this padded cell.

"Well," she confessed defiantly, "I did go especially to see someone and I did see him . . . with another girl, or rather a woman. She was years older than he is."

The man grunted sympathetically.

"But it's a day for miscellaneous bonhomie, you know; It could happen to anybody."

Connie surveyed the rivulets jerking their way down the windows in a most uneven race, as some great drops seemed to be held up only an inch or two from the bottom and other recently hesitant trickles would suddenly dash down.

"I've had singing lessons for years and our choir master has always dinned the proper vowel sounds into us, so I'm not so bad. Am I?"

She discovered that the man was studying her in his driving mirror and he shook his head hearteningly.

"I'm sure you have nothing to worry about on that score. As a complete stranger I see a very attractive young woman, if you will pardon me, a Northerner like the rest of us in these parts, with the additional graces of being dark and true and tender, I'm sure."

They watched the pearl and silver of the raindrops on the windows, screening the outside world.

"Are you married?" asked Connie.

He started.

"Yes. Oh yes. Quite some time."

"Have you any family?"

"No."

Connie looked at the good upholstery and large folded rug beside her on the rear seat.

"I expect you have wonderful times. Good holidays and so on."

"Well, yes, we do go away occasionally."

"And good seats at the theatre and cinema?"

Again he sought her reflection in the mirror to see if she looked resentful, but she did not; only interested.

"We like more comfort as we grow older, you know."

"It sounds an ideal sort of life now."

"Oh, I wouldn't go as far as that."

"I expect you have a nice house too."

"Yes, the house is all right, I suppose." Here he turned sideways in the front seat in order to see his passenger more directly. "This is where I ought to add that a house and car and holidays aren't everything, but let me tell you this so that you will really enjoy the good house, car and cruises if ever you get them. Don't waste time trying to drag anyone along. If they don't run alongside, step for step, let go and let them go. It must be a fifty-fifty affair or nothing."

Connie regarded him solemnly and in the silence she heard a faint scrabbling sound from the left side of the front seat.

"Now don't say *you're* not satisfied," the man said, tapping the lid of a box there, and Connie leaned forward.

"Is it a dog or something?"

"Rather more of a something than a dog if you ask me, but the salesman assured me that it is uncommon but likely to become more popular. Do you think he looks at all like me?"

The lid was lifted.

"Good gracious!"

"My sentiments entirely."

"But he's sweet! Oh, isn't he adorable! What kind is he?"

"Well may you ask. A Papillon."

"Oh, a butterfly. I know. Whenever I hear that music I shall think of him. He looks very fragile. He'll have to be cuddled very gently. Are you just taking him home?"

The man nodded.

"A present for your wife? Oh, how she'll love him."

Connie extended a finger and ventured to touch the unsettled ears that looked as if they stayed awake when the rest of the dog was asleep. When the entire animal stood up and showed signs of escape, the man closed the lid again.

Connie leaned back and sighed. The rain was easing off to its customary stolid habit and the pavements were thronged again by a citizenry that took little heed of ordinary precipitation. There was nothing to detain her further.

"Thank you for sheltering me."

"A pleasure."

He opened the door for her and then resumed the driving seat and she spoke through the slightly open window.

"And thank you for showing me the little dog, and for the advice. I'll always remember them together. I think your wife must be the luckiest woman in the world."

The car shot forward and the life for which Connie felt herself to be admirably cut out, slid from her view. He had not asked her where she was going or if he could run her there or see her again some time. He wasn't a bit like the films; not one of those good men with a wife who did not understand him!

She had to bustle about well and truly when she got back to West Didsbury. Geoffrey came in and went straight upstairs to change into less spectacular costume and afterwards there was not much sound of conversation issuing from the dining room. Later, he was rather a long time upstairs before going out again, but she was in the hall.

"I saw you in town this morning on a lorry. That was a nice boy near you with the stuffed parrot."

That was as near as she dared get to remarking on his company.

"Oh, Greenhalghe! I'll tell him. He'll be pleased."

He went out.

Connie spent most of the evening cleaning the silver, a job she enjoyed, sitting in the kitchen with the smell of pancakes still in the air. She had kept the squeezed lemons to rub on her hands, of which she took great care, wearing gloves for every job where possible and she had lately bought a pair of perforated mitts for sleeping in, said to have almost magical powers. She was now wearing an old pair of wash-leather gloves that had been Geoffrey's and she did not in the least mind the continual wriggling necessary to keep them on as she rubbed the silver. The radio played softly and, seated in a big cushioned chair listening to the saxophones cooing and mooing, she thought it was as good as being in the Piccadilly Cinema.

She was not lonely. Alfred was very handy and fond of tinkering with household repairs that meant frequent passages through or busy tarryings in the kitchen. Ada was quite taken with Connie's willingness and her admiration for the house and its furnishings, so that when Miriam was not there, Ada sometimes loitered in the kitchen and chatted to Connie who was a very sympathetic listener and really interested to learn about Ada's own young days, and right up to how much Alfred had paid for a bedroom carpet. Connie thought it exciting to meet rich people like Mr Sinclair and that man this afternoon. This was the only kitchen she knew that ever smelt of cigars.

Alfred and Ada had only just gone up to bed when the front door opened and Geoffrey came in, much earlier than expected. He stood in the hall before removing his coat as if he had forgotten about it, and then went upstairs.

When Connie tapped lightly on Geoffrey's door with a hot water bottle, there was no response. He would be in the bathroom.

She opened the door.

"Oh!"

Her face crinkled as she saw him.

He was standing over by the chest of drawers between the fireplace and the window. The top drawer which was always kept locked was open and letters were lying about in front of a photograph of Sybil which habitually stood there. He was leaning with both elbows on some of these letters with his face covered by his hands.

"Are you all right?" And then she added, "I'm sorry you didn't hear me knock."

He turned slowly and she spoke defensively.

"I *did* knock."

"Oh, it's you, Connie. You can put those things down somewhere." He turned away again.

She stood there unable to tear herself away.

"Oh, Geoffrey, is there anything much wrong? I *am* a friend, you know."

"Yes, Connie, I believe you are," he replied with a catch in his voice, but went on more strongly. "Much wrong? Oh no! It's only that in the last fortnight I've been hauled over the coals for general scurrility in print; before that I'd struck a man when he was barely on his feet, and now my girl has thrown me over finally and definitely and I've been forbidden the house. Not much wrong! A cup of Bovril and a hot water bottle will soon put things right!"

Connie's chin went up.

"I didn't say they would," she retorted. "But I don't think you need worry about the Rag Rag any more. It will be forgotten in a week. But I'm sorry," here Connie's voice trembled, "about you and Sybil if she's

282

turned against you because of it. It doesn't take much with some people, I must say. But isn't it strange? Only today I was talking to a man, very happily married, who gave me some advice out of his own experience. He said that if it wasn't a fifty-fifty affair, don't waste your time. He was taking a sweet little dog as a present to his wife and they seemed to have everything. So try not to care too much, Geoffrey. There may be someone, nearer than you think, who would meet you halfway and be glad to."

Her eyes went on talking after she'd finished.

"Thank you, Connie. You are as you said, a friend, and I'm truly grateful."

"Are you sure she means it for good?"

"Yes, she means it, although at first I didn't think she did, fool that I was."

He leaned back against the tallboy, facing the room and obscuring the photograph. Connie was glad of it.

"When I was at school in Miss Leat's class, we learnt a poem about being hurt but not slain, and lying down to bleed awhile and then to rise and fight again. Do you know that one?"

"Connie, you're a Trojan. But at the moment I feel bloody enough to be Sir Pat Spens himself. I've been riding a bicycle made for two for so long that I've lost my balance now she's got off."

"Well, the sooner someone else gets up behind, the better, only, like this man I've been telling you about, you must choose someone who'll pedal a bit harder next time."

"Oh Lord! Look Connie, I don't think I could stick it here for the rest of the term and I have a great deal to think out now. Quietly."

She realised this was dismissal and grew desperate.

"Honestly, she wasn't your sort, Geoffrey. Oh, you needn't look at me like that. Others thought you weren't well matched, too. And you're not the only one to feel let down. Others know how it feels to see someone you like very much, looking at someone else. Only I would never have let you down," she now sobbed. "We could have lovely times. We play badminton well together and I could sing while you play. Your mother and father would like that. They like me. I could make you all a really comfortable home here and we could have a dear little dog to start with . . ."

"She stopped and stood there enveloped in her own total misery.

Gently and sadly Geoffrey came across and put his arms round her and thankfully she leaned her head on his breast and cried bitterly and longingly. Her nose was level with his tie and the vee of his jacket so that she inhaled a faint manly scent of good tobacco, leather wallet and fresh linen. She had never been so close to him before and through her sorrow she felt the rapture of that redemptive moment. As she wept, the cloth readily absorbed the tears on one cheek and on the other they coursed down on to her flowered overall unchecked. Here she could cry away all her disappointment, her dissatisfaction with life in general and her defiant rebellion, and here also for a few blessed moments she could breathe in strength and security and peace.

"Oh, Connie, this is where we bleed awhile," and he sank his head wearily onto her dark head. Dark head, fair head, did it matter which so long as it was a loving head? If he looked back on a fading Eurydice was there not a Daisy pedalling gallantly on the bicycle made for two? A warm flesh-and-blood Daisy, not an evanescent Rainbow! Life with Daisy would have its delights. She was a splendid armful. She had body. Abstractedly he patted her shoulder blades. Some lucky man would get her; luckier than he. He was still reeling from the shock of Sybil's desertion and Connie was trying to steady the machine, but she could not control it. It was wrecked.

Her shaken breathing was struggling for an interval in which to speak, although the tears still flowed.

"It's lovely here," she said jerkily like a child still trying to ask for something after a severe spanking, "but you don't love me, do you?"

"Don't talk like that, Connie. We're hurt. We're both hurt, terribly!"

A groan escaped him.

"Slain," whispered Connie.

They stood there locked together in sad stillness until slowly the deep shame of the unloved flooded through her and with a final tremulous intake of breath she raised her head and looked at him shyly. At her slight movement his eyes opened and at the sight of their dry lack-lustre fixedness, any self pride of her own fled away.

"I'll be all right, Geoffrey," she said quickly. "Don't worry about me. I understand."

The eyes that were parched as a snake's dying in the hot dust, focussed on hers. With one hand he took out his handkerchief from his breast pocket and carefully dabbed her cheeks. The other arm he still held about her and as he gently wiped her tears she was thankful to see some expression return to his own eyes.

"Listen, Connie. Always think of me as kindly as you can, because I think you are the best sort of girl possible. You've seen me in deep trouble and stood by me. Don't avoid me, ever, will you? Or I shall feel sorry that you know."

Loyalty sprang up in her at once. Underneath the Connie there was a Constance and it now showed.

284

"It will be a fellow feeling, Geoffrey, and I will try to smile back."

It was with a natural, uncalculating movement that she raised herself a little on tiptoe, and as naturally Geoffrey bent and kissed the flushed and still moist cheek.

There was a sound on the landing beyond the door still slightly ajar and Alfred put his head round. He looked puzzled and disapproving.

"Now then! Is anything the matter?"

Connie bade farewell to the moment and let it slide away like a ship down the gangway, its launching chains dragging as it went. She sighed and stepped back unhurriedly.

"Poor Connie's got a jumping tooth," said Geoffrey heavily, returning his handkerchief to his pocket.

"A good thing it isn't catching," responded Alfred severely. "I'll get you something for it."

"No," said Geoffrey with over-bearing decision, "she didn't want to disturb you and mother, so I'll see to it. Come along, Connie," and he took her by the arm and drew her out of the room and escorted her downstairs to the dining room. He opened a deep cupboard in the massive sideboard and rootled around at the back. He found what he wanted after some time and then got out a tumbler and filled it to the brim.

"Here you are, Connie. Drink this."

"What is it?"

"Balm of Gilead, and may it live up to its name and fame."

"What was it?" asked Ada when Alfred climbed back into bed again.

"Connie's got toothache."

"Oh, poor girl. I was sure I heard crying. Did you get anything for her?"

"Geoffrey's still up and giving her something for it."

"That's thoughtful of him. Well, I can't say I was fond of going to the dentist myself, but I'll tell her tomorrow the only thing is to have it out."

The minister sat in his writing chair by the desk and watched his son moodily reading book titles as he restlessly moved round the room.

"Are you sure, David, that you are going for love of the East and not because of any disappointment in the West?"

The young man flushed in discomfort.

"Not altogether one or the other, Father, I must confess. But I want to be off. I'm not doing any good here."

"Not always a criterion of being able to do good elsewhere. It's no good going in a spirit of self-mortification, you know. It has been known for a man to assume the hair shirt as if to say, 'Oh God, I could not love my enemies; I did not suffer little children, let alone fools, gladly, but remember in mitigation that I put peas in my shoes.' It's not enough, David."

A sound of pain escaped the young man's lips and he came forward.

"This won't do. I'm not only wasting my time and other people's. I'm wasting God's time."

"It's all His time," answered Robert mildly. "But why this sudden impatience?"

"Oh, I suppose you haven't noticed but I've been making a perfect fool of myself."

"You seem to be extremely dissatisfied with yourself but there must be a reason."

David put his knuckles on the desk, leaned some of his weight on them and spoke with lowered head.

"I thought I had met the one girl who would make every step of the way brighter and worth while. She was just right in every way, gentle, patient, an absolute fountain of self-forgetfulness."

"And unusually pretty, if you are referring to our neighbour, as I suspect. Surely that had not escaped your notice?"

"All right then, clear as a Provencal morning if you must know how I feel about her! A face to make a man believe in heaven!"

"I just wanted to know, my boy," said Robert, relenting.

"I watched very carefully before telling myself that I was entitled to cut in and try my luck."

David glanced at his father as if expecting some comment but Robert remained silent.

"At first I don't think she knew what was happening and I began to hope that I was making some headway while she was off her guard, so to speak."

Again he looked to see how his father was taking this confession, but still he drew no reply.

"Well, I was wrong. You and Mother won't know about this, but about three weeks ago the situation suddenly erupted and Sybil showed that she absolutely . . . I'm ashamed to say the word . . . despised me."

Robert got up and quietly placed a chair immediately behind the young man and indicated that he should be seated. David automatically did so.

"I'm sorry, my boy. Very sorry."

"Yes, she said she would do the choosing and of course she had done that before I came interfering and making trouble for everybody."

He got up, pushing the chair away, and went to the window, pulling one curtain aside and looking blindly out onto the darkened window streaming with rain.

"No, I'm an also ran that should never have been entered. And today I saw him . . . you know . . . in the Rag procession. If ever there was a conquering hero, it was he today . . ."

David pulled the curtain into position again and leaned his forehead against it with his back to the room while Robert drew an open book forward and appeared to concentrate upon it. He allowed a few minutes to pass before he addressed the motionless figure at the window.

"Of course you can't leave, you know that, and in any case you have enough Lenten deprivation without going any further into the wilderness. But don't keep away from all of us at this side of town, my boy; it would greatly distress your mother. Now what about tonight? Can I tell her that you'll be staying? Oh dear, that will be Watch barking next door; he must be shut out."

David nodded as he turned from the window and Robert went downstairs to speak to Grace for a moment. The young man felt that it would have been wiser to go back to Didsbury, but the desire to catch only a glimpse of Sybil in the morning when she left the house next door was too strong for him. He would remain hidden but the sight of her would surely help to restore some meaning to the day! Just as the hope of seeing her from a window tomorrow would help him to endure this night.

There is an Indian sect that repeats the name of Allah with every heartbeat and yet manages to work in the world as other men do. So he, aware of her image at every throb of his pulse, would have to live and move as did other men around him. He wandered from shelf to shelf searching for a volume that could nurse him through the dark hours and for the first time in his life he sneered with disgust at the rows and rows of failures. He pulled one or two out in a threatening manner, as though to compel them into sustaining him in this hour of need, and then wearily turned his back on them and leaned disconsolately against the writing table. He aimlessly pulled the open book lying there and took it up, automatically reading a few lines and then looking for the beginning of 'The Story of the Loyalty of Ten-teh the Fisherman'.

When Robert quietly re-entered the study some minutes later his son was standing, engrossed, by the table, but Robert remained by the shelves just inside the door in silence, for as he read, tears were coursing unheeded down the young man's face.

Shrove Tuesday was nearly over and tomorrow would be Ash Wednesday and the beginning of forty days of Lenten fast, and already the taste of ashes was in many mouths.

There were ashes in the Martland home. Clara had been weeping and telling Leonard that if David Garner had never come amongst them, all would have been well. Len answered her sombrely.

"Do you remember Barton and his suitcase of tea? We were all called into Mr Bolt's office today and told that the firm is closing down. It's finished."

"Finished!" whispered Clara uncomprehendingly.

"There's no hope of the firm's pulling round. They've held on until they're on the verge of bankruptcy trying to manage with a skeleton staff. And now they've to close down. When I've brought the books up to date and paid everybody, I'll be about the last skeleton."

Clara came slowly round to his chair and sank onto the hearth-rug at his side, clutching at his coat sleeve and gazing tearlessly up into his pinched face.

"Leonard, my darling! Don't look like that," and she hid her own face on his knees to hide from the sight.

At Chorltonville, too, the day of penance was at hand.

"But Elsie, I was glad to see you enjoying yourself. Everybody was in high spirits and letting themselves go and why shouldn't you too? You must be feeling stronger to be able to do it. Perhaps we should start going out more again, dances and so on. Soon you'll be as perky as this little chap here."

"He is sweet, isn't he? You're so good, Sam. I feel awful, sometimes."

"Now don't you bother, my dear."

"And today I felt that men are all right, really. It must be just me. If only I could be shaken out of myself; forget myself. I was so happy in that crazy crowd."

"You don't think I'm a sufficiently crazy crowd?"

She looked at him as one would coming unexpectedly upon a wounded animal that had always been cheerfully bounding about the place and was now dramatically in dire need of elementary first aid. Only the eyes begged for help.

"Oh Sam," she cried piteously, "do you think if you made me drunk, like old fashioned operations?"

If any medieval penitent had looked into Sam's face at that moment he would have had compassion on a fellow sufferer and said, "That man is in pain."

Lent. Lent. Repent. Repent.

All creation groaneth.

Watch, his limbs quivering as with ague and looking dejected as a scapegoat, was still outside in the rain. Even the wash-house door had blown shut. He lifted up his voice in protest, first in an excited fanfare of barks and then in despairing howls as time went by. Was he utterly forgotten? He drooped in silence and then roused himself to the injustice of his plight and continued indignantly in alternate yappings and wailings, in self assertion and self commiseration, like the National Anthem of a very small nation.

n

Chapter Twenty-one

March had come in roaring like a heraldic lion, storming weightily from street corners or stealthily catching wayfarers in the ribs with a penetrating iron claw. It prowled round tram and bus stops, dogging the cold feet in the queues and went rushing down the wide main streets buffeting and rending, lashing not at fingers and toes like the snow, but at the whole man, bending him unresistant as a sapling.

A room with a mature and confident fire is a refuge against frost, but not against the razor-thrust round doors and windows, along passages and down cold bedroom chimneys. The mad March wind rattled letter-box flaps and the draught mournfully shoved at hall carpets, heaving them slightly in the middle before they subsided again sluggishly.

Fires were unsettled. They hit back at the intruder and puffed out at him, and either retired sulkily and fitfully or, goaded by desperate damper pushing, flared back under the boilers fiercely and extravagantly so that the hot water boiled and belched in the pipes.

Ella Kershaw listened to the swashbuckler from the fastness of her bed. Visitors were so tactful. They would come into her room blown and untidy and exclaim, "You're in the best place today, Ella," and so she was, for that day, but when they went out from her warm room into the gusty world again they were rested and eager to stretch their legs and move on.

The winter had tried Tom's feet somewhat and he tackled those overburdened extremities with tender care. He wished he could go to the Shop in his carpet slippers, for even his wide boots pressed harshly nowadays, but he never complained.

"And what about the Carriage Shop now?" Ella enquired anxiously.

If the Shop closed, some of the men would have to be transferred to Derby, but she and Tom could hardly uproot themselves and start again in another town amongst strangers. She was feeling restless and helpless, knowing of great changes and anxieties in the area and yet not being told of them so instantly and intimately as of old. She could not remember another week when she had so few visitors.

There was a knock on the front door and the big knob was turned and someone came into the passage.

"It's Dolly. May I come in?"

The younger Miss Leat put her head round the door to spy out the land.

"Good! I'm glad no one's here, Ella, I've brought the harbingers."

She stepped back for a moment into the passage and lugged in a large white cardboard box.

"They've only just arrived from the warehouse. Do you feel like looking at them?"

"Indeed I do," said Ella eagerly and easing herself up in bed as best she could. "And is it really getting on for spring? You wouldn't think it today, would you?"

"The designers know that it *will* come some time and they've let themselves go this year."

Kneeling on the floor, Miss Leat took off the big square lid and lifted layers of sibilant tissue paper, triumphantly exposing the first consignment of spring hats. It was as if Flora herself had come in for shelter against the cold. The snowy crinkled paper formed a bank whereon were set one by one as Dolly conjured them from the hedge bottom, snowdrops, violets, primroses, lilies of the valley and other delicate prophecies; the contrived 'immortelles' expressing the artistic awareness of the perennial in nature.

Ella craned towards them.

"They're real hats again this year, aren't they, Dolly? Not just protection against falling slates."

Miss Leat held one up speculatively and sat back on her heels.

"Yes, I think we may call them creations this season."

Truly the hats were distinguishers of persons and not extinguishers. They would signpost a woman and not make her just one more traveller incognito. These hats would persuade the beholder that the ordinary face beneath was pretty and make the pretty face appear ravishing. The ravishing face beneath such a hat would become a national emblem.

"I can just see Sybil Martland in that one," said Ella and then paused, remembering that Sybil had not been looking at all flower-like of late. One would think that such a gentle looking girl would be sad and drooping under the circumstances, but nothing of the kind had happened. There was a hardness, an aloofness about her that utterly baffled people.

"She's going like Fanny," Ella whispered.

"I can't see the end of it, can you?" queried her visitor. "Clara Martland never says anything. Has Mrs Ginnell anything to say?"

"It would be a wonder if she hasn't! She says bluntly that Sybil has fallen between two stools. I can hardly think so, but why drop the bird in the hand if you're not having a shot at the bush?"

"True, but Miriam is spreading the idea that Connie is trying to ingratiate herself at Didsbury. Of course, if there was any danger there, Ada would be sure to see it, considering what she and Miriam were like."

Here Miss Leat and Ella laughed softly together, shaking their heads.

"I ought not," confessed Miss Leat, "but I can't help wondering where she gets her hats." After a pause for wonderment, she went on, "I did hear that Miriam hinted to Mrs Ginnell that Connie was over familiar with Geoffrey, and Mrs Ginnell retorted that her precious nephew read French novels in bed and Miriam ought to turn her bi-focals on *him*. I'm afraid poor Connie will be like a dog running after a bicycle if it's true."

She delved for another hat.

"Try this! I haven't seen a Leghorn for years and they're a lovely texture."

Several others were tried and commented upon.

"That suits you very well indeed, it really does. I'll hold this mirror for you to see the back."

Ella made her decision and her purchase, whereupon Miss Leat pulled out a hat box from under the bed and revealed Ella's winter velour.

"I'll give that to Connie," said Ella. "It's never been seen outside of course. Gracious! Is that young Ernie coming in? It's never that time!"

But it was a woe-begone little figure that entered slowly.

"Why, my duck, whatever is the matter?" cried Ella.

Miss Leat stretched out her hand and brought him forward.

"You tell Antella, there's a good boy."

Ernie hid his face against the side of the bed and only after much coaxing did he tell his story.

"A man came round this afternoon and said 'Hands up anybody who has a brother in the school' and I put my hand up and he said 'What class is he in?' and I said 'All little boys are my brothers whatever class they're in,' and everybody laughed."

The two women looked at each other over the boy's head.

"That's my fault," said Ella quietly.

She stroked the head laid against the bed. What thoughts was it harbouring against her at this moment? Miss Leat tried to lift him onto her knee but he fought her off.

"Listen to me, Ernie," she said, kneeling down on a level with him. "Those other people haven't been as well brought up as you. Whenever you meet anyone as badly behaved as they are, you just say to yourself, 'They don't know Antella or they wouldn't talk like that'."

Slowly they talked him round until he was persuaded to come out of hiding and turn up the gas ring for tea.

"You're a little champion, Ernie. And *you've* given up your early closing for me again, Dolly!"

When Miss Leat picked up her box of 'harbingers' some time later, she left a tranquil scene as she battled home against the wind. Ernie was licking his biscuit in a better frame of mind and was communicative again.

"My Dad says it'll be a caution if Uncle Tom gets sent to Derby and we stay here."

So they were discussing that possibility next door! She knew now that the men not transferred to Derby would be out of work.

Man has grown so well represented on this planet that he competes not against nature alone but against himself, and that is a much more inhuman and taxing contest. In his ascent, the crampons are grappled not into unfeeling ice but into the fighting flesh of his own kind and in the race, the rowel that once spurred, eventually tears at the vitals.

Some men at the Carriage Shop were already seeking elsewhere before the blow actually fell that would cut them off on the debit side. Children were quieted earlier and more harshly than usual as their noise intruded on the harrowed concentration of their parents. The groups of women shoppers were more silent in the butchers and grocers, for soon one would be taken and the other left.

It was the day after Dolly Leat's visit to Ella that Mrs Ginnell met with her accident - or rather, met with her husband's accident, for Ernest Ginnell had the unusual experience of falling and breaking his wife's leg.

"Why ever did you leave your leg sticking out like that?"

Whatever the cause of the disaster, it certainly had wide repercussions. Dr Bedser's busy little two-seater arrived and he told Mrs Ginnell that although the bones were not broken, muscles had been wrenched and ligaments torn and she must remain out of action for some time.

Mrs Ginnell took to her bed, complaining that a real breakage would have hurt less, she was sure. She was temporarily withdrawn from general helpfulness at Chorltonville, at Clara Martland's, at the Kershaws and at the Chapel. The people who had long relied on her could better have met with a change of national government; it would have been less noticeable.

Connie's instructions from her father had been brief and forceful and a subdued young woman left Didsbury to look after her parents and little brother at home.

Nevertheless, Mrs Ginnell's damaged leg would mend more quickly than Leonard's broken fortunes and of those around them.

Good humour, that comes with the modest assurance that year by year life will get a little easier, helps to keep men and women healthy. They do not mind the hard going if they can see their way clear; but now for all that stream of men who used to surge along to the Carriage Shop, the way was no longer clear and their faces had clouded with the view. Clara saw it happen to Leonard. He lacked the ebullience that can storm at circumstance and demand a better deal. Happier were the ne'er-do-wells, the scroungers and the work-shy, for they had forgotten what it was to be a man and so could not sorrow as a man.

Only once had she asked him if he was looking out for something else. He gave her a piercing glance that once would have seemed impossible from that mild face. She had a sick intuition that he was 'looking' during his lunch time and a cry of desolation and rebellion broke from her.

"Can't Mr Bolt do anything for you after all these years?"

"Clara, Mr Bolt hoped for better times and the times have worsened. If references could do anything, I could go as tally-clerk to the Angel Gabriel, but only young men are wanted now. Men like myself are on the scrap heap."

Clara stood behind his shoulder for a moment and kissed the back of his head.

"The world must be very rich if it can afford to scrap men like you," and she hurried out of the room. At the top of the stairs she met Sybil who seemed undecided whether to go downstairs or not. Clara brushed past her and then turned.

"Mooning about just because you can't make up your mind between your precious young men! You're all children. You don't know anything about love for all that you don't seem to think of anything else. If you'd seen a man work for you day in, day out, year in, year out, for a quarter of a century and then thrown on the scrap heap, then you'd know whether you loved him or not."

Clara rushed into the front bedroom and Sybil recoiled, stricken with fear at the implications of the words just spoken. Her parents never discussed their private affairs in her presence, probably because Kerry was nearly always there, but they had not taken her into their confidence at all, had not explained the half-heard rumours. Now it was all flung at her without preamble and momentarily at least her own heartache was equalled by her sympathy for her parents in this crisis and in a few minutes she went quietly downstairs, stealing a look at her father when she was certain he was unseeing. She fed Watch and Ebony and routed out Kerry to remind her of her homework, and later in the evening suggested that she might like to have supper in bed while she read a chapter. Barely emerging from her own world to say goodnight, the girl went off. She loved the fruitful inertia of reading in bed and to close first the book and then one's eyes upon completion, set the perfect seal upon the day. Coming to the end of a powerful book was an enacted death; the tears and beatitudes incited by the tale-telling and the tale-ending were a preparation of the spirit for other departures, other rewards.

This bitter March was a month to be remembered with detestation, a Lenten of canker and leanness for Robert Garner's flock. Was there anything he could do? He visited their homes and listened to the latest developments, but they were less social occasions now and more of the watchman's rounds, although he could not cry All's Well! Hearing him coming in from the wind that perpetually whistled through sharp teeth, or out of the rain that was blown off its downward course and came at all angles, Grace hurried to meet him. Seeing him tired and worried she felt angry with the world at large for not being good and prosperous and going peacefully on its way.

One afternoon over a cup of tea he made a casual observation on their neighbours, now but rarely discussed.

"By the way, I think the Martlands are having some new furniture. At least they are getting rid of some of the old, I noticed as I came in."

"Indeed!" Grace was surprised. "So few people are making anything of a splash just now."

"Mrs Martland was putting one or two articles out on the path. I'm afraid, my dear, that she did not smile."

"It's too bad!"

"But the others pass the time of day, on the rare occasions when we meet."

"I should think so! What have *you* done?"

"Well, girls can be very touchy about their fathers," said Robert rather guiltily and his wife, recollecting something, looked at him severely.

"And our son has to keep out of the way so as not to offend their sight. But I'll look in for a word with Mrs Martland, to show willing. We can't allow the young people to come between us."

When Grace opened the front door a little time later, daylight had almost gone. She stepped across to the neighbouring door and knocked. There were a few sounds of movement within but nobody hurried to answer the summons. When Mr Martland appeared he looked at her oddly and did not ask her to enter.

"Is Mrs Martland in?" she enquired, hiding a feeling of awkwardness at his unusual manner.

Clara Martland now came in sight behind her husband. She was carrying a Japanese vase whereon a warrior in an ungainly stance was putting the experience of a lifetime into a mighty overhead service with a two handled sword.

"This can go too!" and catching sight of the minister's wife she went on, "You told us to get rid of many possessions and I'm doing so."

Hereupon Clara lobbed Old Japan neatly over their heads onto the rhododendron patch. It struck the stone border and smashed, and Clara returned in quest of other objects that had suddenly ceased to have value in her sight. Now Sybil appeared and without looking at Mrs Garner, she carried back a picture that her mother had placed against the wall. From the interior her voice came quite calmly and persuasively.

"I think that's enough for now. We can consider other things tomorrow after a night's rest. Please, Mother."

Mrs Garner gaped fearfully into Leonard Martland's face, not daring to speak. His face worked a little as if he were silently clearing his throat, almost like Pins and Needles. Then he spoke.

"No, you may not see my wife, Mrs Garner. She is very poorly. I consider that you have been a dangerous friend to her; in fact a tragic influence."

"Oh no!" whispered Grace, clasping her hands. "I love Mrs Martland. Why, I stopped my own daughter . . . " Tears overflowed and drowned her words as she stood there.

Leonard's own mouth trembled but his eyes were accusing.

"You have taught my dear wife that her life of service has been a life of servitude," and with that, he very quietly shut the door.

Robert ached over Grace when she came in. He stroked her hair while she wept, for he also knew what it is to see well-meaning utterly fail.

"You know, dear, you sow a brand of seed that is particularly strong. You pop a mustard seed into every aspidistra pot you find and an ordinary plant pot can't take the strain."

"But what else is there to do?" wailed Grace with a spark of rebellion. "We have to sow the seed."

Robert gently smoothed the perplexed frown between her brows.

"Of course, but we must be especially tender towards the cramped pots and the old bottles. They deserve some consideration for services rendered and should be handled gently."

Poor Grace was quiet and depressingly humble all evening so that Robert found himself looking round for *Punch* and reading it to her instead of signing Class tickets. Only once did she refer to the sad episode next door and that was indirectly.

"It must be rather lovely to have a daughter living at home."

It was a rare domestic evening during which they spoke of themselves and their work and their children, but there was a lack of satisfaction. Failure was in the air.

When Robert was saying his prayers that night he felt Grace kneel beside him, putting her left hand over his left hand and inserting the other between his clasped palms. She had done this many years ago on their honeymoon, endeavouring to be one spirit as one flesh. Now she laid her head on one arm wearily.

"Pray for two, Robert. I'm so tired."

During the next few days Grace confined herself to visiting the sick, the lonely and the older members. Ben Northcroft had a bad cold and stayed indoors and was astounded when Mrs Garner sat so lacking in fire, so modestly unopinionated opposite his kitchen chair. He had to do most of the talking.

"You're a long way behind me, Mrs Garner, but I think your husband knew the Rev. Gideon Stormalong years ago before you left the country? We had a fine Young Men's Class in those days. Mr Stormalong got hold of that class, Mrs Garner, and he made something of it that surprised the whole city. Do you know what it became?"

"Did they become campaigners or something like that?"

Ben chuckled and made himself cough but when order was restored he leaned back with great satisfaction.

"They went campaigning all right and their namesakes still do. They were the actual beginnings of Manchester United," he said triumphantly. "Mr Stormalong started a football team that became famous over the years and it all grew from our Young Men's Class on

Oldham Road. He did a grand job did Mr Stormalong."

"Yes, indeed," agreed Grace meekly.

"Young Briggs is training for it. He's got ambition, has that lad. Ah, our place has had its great days, Mrs Garner, and produced some good men."

Since Grace was not sure whether he meant good men or good footballers, she merely nodded agreement.

"All we want is more fire. Things have been getting a bit namby-pamby of late years; dramatics and so on. I suppose it pleases the girls but get a strong football or cricket club and the young men'll come to play and the young women will come to watch."

"There is of course the Badminton Club, Mr Northcroft, and it's nice when they can all play together."

"No. A man wants to keep his spooning and his sport separate. In my cricketing days I liked to know that a girl was sitting and watching and expecting big stuff from me. Fine happenings if a man should be caught out by his own girl!"

"Don't you think a good set of mixed doubles is a fine game to watch?"

"The best match in any contest is man against man, man against devil, devil against God. If you want team spirit there's St. Michael and all angels against Lucifer and all the sons of darkness. We don't want any mixed doubles there!"

Grace meditated on the rights of old bottles and made an effort to ignore the message so transparently inside this one.

Annie Northcroft got a few words with their visitor on the way to the front door.

"You see, he's housebound and John and Jimmie have more to do than ever. Yet he'd let our Jimmie go to America! I know he can't be spared. They'd never manage, but they forget what his young strength can do."

"I'm sure your husband will see that. He's such a sensible man in his quiet way and will stand up to his father. I mean, stand up for his son."

Annie drew her into the big room, now cold and uncomfortable since there was no time for anybody to sit in it.

"Do you know what I'm going to say if it really looks as if they'd let Jimmie go?"

Grace looked concernedly into Annie's troubled but determined face.

"I shall tell them," the farmer's wife said deliberately, "that if Jimmie goes, I shall go with him to make a home for him. And I really

298

mean it."

"Oh, Mrs Northcroft, don't say that! Never let Mr John suspect it for a moment. Our children grow up and can fend for themselves as mine have done and as your Jimmie could do."

Annie hesitated and looked disappointed.

"I thought you would be the one person to understand. You know how much I'm taken for granted here."

"Trusted is the better word, Mrs Northcroft. You are what Greenwich Mean Time is to all the clocks and you must not fail them."

"I didn't think you'd take the men's part, somehow."

"I'm taking yours. Do drop such a cruel and fantastic idea. You'd be a frightful encumbrance to Jimmie over in Canada."

Annie was annoyed and did not conceal it. She had looked for sympathy in her independence and here was Mrs Garner opposing it. For days afterwards Annie turned over in her mind what the minister's wife had stated so bluntly on leaving: "Your position here is the best thing you've got out of life. Don't abdicate!"

The following afternoon Grace was in Dolly Leat's pink and white striped millinery shop with its few square yards of window display wherein hats were arranged on painted wooden stands. The white balusters segregating this exotic collection were further enhanced by pink net curtains, and anybody buying a hat actually 'out of the window' was doing something very special, for only the rare avis were kept in that cage. Mirrors with gilt frames decorated with cupids and candle holders adorned every wall, so that an unsuspecting customer intently scrutinising her head and shoulders in one mirror with some satisfaction, was put out to find herself being watched by a lumpish person over there who turned out to be another version of herself. So when it came to such an intimate transaction as buying and first trying a new hat, several in fact, in which one might descend in spirals of growing ridiculousness, it was better to choose Miss Leat's modest establishment with its convenient peephole in the passage wall enabling one to make quite sure that the coast was clear.

Mrs Garner made use of that little window before entering as she did not want to interrupt business, but Dorothy Leat was alone, stitching at a last year's hat left to be retrimmed. There seemed to be more renovations than new purchases so far this year and a quarter gone already; quarterly bills coming soon and not enough women trying to raise their pluck by getting a new hat.

"This is a pretty room, very different from out of doors today," said Grace, sitting carefully on the pink sofa that looked more suitable for some fledgling Pompadour.

"We're nearly through another winter, anyway," answered Dolly, "and if the winter doesn't get us, we stand a better chance against the three other seasons. I suppose we all feel that it's not so bad to go on a cold day."

"Well, Miss Leat, it would be a terrible time if we had to cope with the nation's funerals in one season, so it's all for the best that some of us pop off on Bank Holidays and in the Dog Days, or even like someone I knew, just when setting off on a cruise to see the midnight sun."

"We're not seeing so much of it even at mid-day at the moment."

Trade was bad all round, like the weather. Money was tight. She had not liked having to tell a gipsy woman selling the old fashioned forked pegs that the clip style were all she used now. The woman had looked very darkly at her refusal to buy.

"You'll know perhaps," said Grace, "that Connie has come home to nurse her mother?"

"I do know and I don't think it has sweetened her temper."

"Poor girl!" said Grace.

"I don't know about that. What do you make of this, Mrs Garner?"

The hat rested on its creator's knee while Miss Leat concentrated on her story.

"You won't know, but every spring and autumn Ella buys a hat, a really good one, although she only wears it in secret as you might say, and she always gives the old one to Mrs Ginnell. This time she gave it to Connie. You'd think she'd be grateful, wouldn't you? A good velour. But when I went down the yard with the ashes the other morning, what should I find near the back gate but that same velour hat!"

Mrs Garner stared at Miss Leat.

"How on earth could it have got there?"

"Thrown over."

"But why?"

"Oh, her highness evidently doesn't thank anyone for a second-hand hat, so throws it back where it came from."

Miss Leat resumed work and stabbed the needle through the ribbon with verve. But her visitor made some protest.

"Oh, but think of the wind that's been blowing for days on end."

"I know the wind bloweth where it listeth, but that hat was thrown over."

"Oh dear! I do hope Connie isn't terribly unhappy, poor girl. It might be a good thing on the whole if her father got moved to Derby and she had new surroundings and new friends."

"Oh, Mrs Garner, haven't you heard? Tom Kershaw has got the

300

offer of work at Derby and Ernest Ginnell's been turned down. I suppose they've considered Tom's case with sympathy, and of course Ernest is always grumbling about something. They say he gets orders from Russia to keep on grumbling."

Grace was much distressed at this news and they discussed it for some time. Grace said she would look in at Ella's on her way home if the information was certain.

"Yes, it's all over Oldham Road by now. But it is a mess!"

"Ella will be missing Mrs Ginnell, both now and later."

"Oh, the neighbours have got a rota. They take turns to go in and dust around, et cetera. Someone wondered whether to ask Mrs Butterway."

"I'm afraid I've no progress to report in Daisy Street. I've never got in since my first visit!"

Miss Leat stared into her pink-netted aviary for a moment, thinking. She herself did not attach much importance to Mrs Butterway, yet the minister and his wife struggled to make some impression on a nature that abhorred them and all that they represented. No wonder Mrs Garner seemed depressed today, having continually to go where she wasn't wanted.

"Mrs Garner," she said hesitantly, "you'd better know, but do be careful; we think that you and your husband have made enemies; outside the church of course."

She paused to gather courage.

"Someone has heard Mrs Butterway say very nasty things about you and they think that woman ought not to be allowed inside Kershaw's house."

"That's not very charitable," reproved Grace.

"Wait! Mrs Mossop had a terrible brainwave. She sees some things very clearly that others perhaps wouldn't notice. She said Mrs Butterway would do anything to spite *you* and might be trying to get at Tom just to mess things up. I'm not afraid of *her* so much. Daisy Street would watch that. But there's another matter."

Miss Leat paused.

"I've only kept it in case you want to compare the writing, but has Mr Garner ever mentioned getting any anonymous letters since Christmas?"

"Never." Grace's eyes were startled.

"Well, she'd not let Pins and Needles in for weeks and he swore it was all *your* fault and he'd like to get his hands round your throat and so on. Then one night he got his foot in the door in Daisy Street and there was a proper fight."

Grace shuddered.

"I always said she was the type to get murdered! What happened?"

"They say she nearly killed him! He's been very quiet since, but this was pushed through our letter-box some time ago and we're not the only ones."

Grace was handed a sheet of poor quality writing paper which she unfolded with loathing before scanning:

'I saw your Mrs Garner coming out of a shed with old Northcroft.'

She returned it quickly.

"Yes, I remember Pins and Needles passing the farm gate."

"Shall I destroy it?"

"Yes, please do and tell any others to do the same."

Each fell silent, engrossed in thought until Miss Leat held up the re-trimmed hat appraisingly.

"No one would suspect that of starting its second spring, would they? Now, Mrs Garner, if I ask a little favour, you won't take it the wrong way, will you?"

Grace watched as Dolly Leat put the finished hat in one drawer and opened another full of hats, not at all in a Pompadour or Dolly Varden style, but suitable for matrons who would take a sharp and critical glance at a spring day and suspect the worst of it before nightfall.

"I'd like you to choose a hat as a little present, Mrs Garner, because the weather at this time of year gets us down a bit. Do you like any of these?"

Grace struggled with emotion at this generosity so poignantly timed, as a snowman, stoic against winter's bleak attack and growing firmer as the cold intensifies, begins to waver when the first warm day arrives and he discovers tear-drops on his marble front.

"Oh, Miss Leat, this is thoughtful of you."

She entered into the spirit of the occasion and tried on several hats in much happier spirits, to Dolly's great gratification. They finally agreed upon a very smart and simple shape after studying the effect in profile, front and back.

"I'll make this an excuse for calling on Ella Kershaw, since I know now that she's interested in hats. There'll just be time before Tom gets home. What *can* they do?"

Outside, the rain was still being shoved around by the rough wind and the frivolous looking paper bag containing the new hat swayed in her grasp with crackling noises as Grace made her way round the corner into Oldham Road. If it whisked away, might it not hover and bounce and mount kite fashion into the boisterous air, to collapse dramatically into Miss Leat's backyard? She took a very firm grip.

For once, Ella's door was tight shut and her window curtains almost closed. It evidently was not a convenient moment for callers so she tapped on the next door, and to her surprise it was Ernest Ginnell himself who answered her very gentle summons and looking so dropped on that it was apparent that had he known who was standing there he would not have been door-keeper.

It was not a house at peace with itself by any means, but Mrs Ginnell called downstairs for Mrs Garner to go up awhile and Ginnell escorted her to the front bedroom where from a sitting position the invalid had managed to throw over the bed a cover usually kept folded upon a chair near at hand for just such a contingency.

Mr Ginnell was at home early and under a cloud, not to say a cloudburst. There had been some argument and demonstration at the Shop when the results of the negotiations had become known to the men. Closure of the Works had at first been deemed unthinkable, then recognised as possible, then probable and finally inevitable. All surprise had gone long ago but dismay still remained. Some blamed one thing, some another. Altercations arose and it was while one well known at the Ben Brierley parliament was giving his views that Ginnell inadvertently caught the speaker's eye - with his fist. Like a promising child at school he was allowed to go home early, but with instructions to stay there. He had not been taken on at Derby. Tom had the chance but could not bring himself to take it. Could Mr Garner get in touch with those making the decisions and get them to reverse this short-sighted result? If he spoke for the chapel caretaker they might take notice of him.

Mrs Garner promised to mention it to her husband at once but Ginnell himself doubted if it would do any good.

While the atmosphere was heavy with this grievous subject, Connie entered the room with a cup of tea for their visitor. The poor girl looked miserable.

"It isn't China, Mrs Garner."

"Oh, Connie, how kind of you. This will do me good, I'm sure, although I had not intended to come in. I was really on my way home, meaning to pop into Ella's just for a moment to show her something she - er - might be interested in."

"Oh, your new hat? I saw the bag in the lobby just now. I told Ernie not to touch."

Mrs Ginnell looked at her daughter meaningly.

"Perhaps if we'd known last week what we know now, some of us wouldn't have been so quick to give away what would have saved good money next winter."

"Oh that!" exclaimed Connie peevishly. "It was much too old for me and that gipsy woman meant to have something and I wasn't going to give her money."

Grace's eyes grew wide as she listened but she thought it better to say nothing in this quarter.

The girl had so far pointedly ignored her father and he now glowered at her.

"Our Connie doesn't care for the way we do things here. She's been learning different ways over there in Didsbury."

"And she could have stayed there but for you," retorted his wife. "Mrs Garner, over there she was earning money and her keep. We could have managed."

"We could *not* have managed," insisted Ginnell hotly.

"Mrs Sinclair says if I stay away long, she'll have to advertise again," said Connie anxiously, feeling that she had a friend in court.

"Did you like it there?" asked Grace sympathetically, but as the girl swallowed before replying, her father, red and blustering, broke in.

"Oh, aye, anywhere's better than here! It's poky here and we're right on the dirty road with no roses to hide it either. But what's been going on under those roses, I want to know? Miriam Crumps has her own opinions about that, if what has come to her ears is true."

"Oh, blow Miriam Crumps!" shouted Mrs Ginnell. "She's always got her ear to the cesspool."

Connie blazed up too, her face aflame.

"That woman! Some morning she'll wake up with the mange. What does she matter to me! Mrs Sinclair likes me and I'd go back tomorrow if I could."

"I don't think, Mr Ginnell," said Grace in a soothing tone, "that you need attach any importance to what poor Mrs Crumps says."

"But I *did* attach importance to it, since it was our Connie she was speaking about. Doubtless I should have listened very coolly if she'd been speaking of your daughter in Switzerland that no one's set eyes on yet. But she was speaking of our Connie out at Didsbury and she says that Alfred caught her and Geoffrey talking in his room when the others had all gone to bed."

Poor Connie, overwhelmed by the sorrow of that Shrove night's conversation, stepped back and feebly sank on to her mother's bed and burst into tears.

"Oh, come, Mr Ginnell, you're upsetting her unjustly. You'll make her feel that you don't trust her, and of course you do really. I know *I* do!"

Ginnell appreciated Mrs Garner's praise and became more

304

temperate.

"You're right, Mrs Garner. Our Connie is a girl in a thousand and I don't care who hears me say it, but she shouldn't judge me when she doesn't know all the facts."

Connie raised her head.

"I don't, Father. I'm only fed up with everything."

Down went her head again and her mother poked at it impatiently."

"I told your father there was nothing in that. You had to do hot water bottles and Bovril and so on, hadn't you? I told Miriam so."

"And that's nothing to what I told Miriam outside on the pavement," said Ginnell suddenly bracing up. "You might as well know. I pulled the door to after us and, 'Woman,' I said, 'let me hear of your giving one squeak or cheep at our Connie ever again and I'll let everybody know what *I* know about a page of *your* history. There's a blot on *your* copy book that's open to anybody that asks to peep at it.' My, but she was scared. You've heard people talk about the Reverend Gideon Stormalong, Mrs Garner?"

"Indeed I have! He left a tremendous impression, I'm told. He was the one whose collar was all wet and crumpled at the end of his sermons."

"He left something besides an impression. He left Miriam Crumps' marriage lines wet and crumpled beyond repair. Oh, Mr Stormalong would do anybody a good turn, but our chapel wasn't authorised to solemnise a marriage then without a Registrar. Not till the next year. Your husband found it out, Mrs Garner."

Connie did sit up and gazed at her father with a much brighter eye.

"Ask Mrs Garner here and she'll back me up. It's not the swearing to leave father and mother in front of a large congregation that makes a marriage legal, but the Registrar's certificate that's usually signed in the vestry. If a bridegroom fell dead on that short walk between altar and Registrar's table, the marriage wouldn't be legal. The highest in the land wouldn't get their titles and gold in a Court of Law without that bit of paper properly signed, and Miriam's doesn't entitle her to Edgar Crumps' watch-chain even."

His family drank in Ernest's words thirstily.

"So hold up your head, Connie, and remember it's a good thing to have a father behind you sometimes."

Mrs Ginnell besought them to lift her up; her transports were too great to be taken in a reclining position. Mr Ginnell found himself all at once a hero in the bosom of his family and Mrs Garner had to remind them repeatedly that this was a secret unless Mrs Crumps broke her part of the bargain. They must all play fair. The thought of playing fair had a sobering effect. What a curb it was.

"Well," said Grace, rising to go and glad to see them well pleased with each other now. "Perhaps when one of you sees Ella, you'll mention that I called but that the door was fast. She'll be missing you, won't she, Mrs Ginnell. Such a good friend to her."

But Mrs Ginnell, sitting very still, held up a warning finger which silenced the little group as they gazed at her. Her nose wrinkled suspiciously as she took in a quick breath and then she spoke sharply.

"Can anybody smell gas?"

Chapter Twenty-two

The babble in Hall was aggressive and strong as only morning assembly could be after a night's rest, yet in spite of the ebullient buzz the place looked as if it were evening rather than the beginning of the working day. The windows were misted with damp and mooned with the gleam of electric lights, and those left open for ventilation revealed an outlook as through the thin grey hair of a Yorkshire terrier's fringe.

The long line of hot water piping so conveniently edging the polished floor provided comfortable seating for grateful and otherwise chilly maidenhood, voluble and at ease in this unsupervised period. Gwen and Freda in boyhood of Raleigh attitudes watched the third member of their usual trio crossing the hall towards them slowly. They made room for her between them and eyed her.

"Is something wrong, Kerry?"

"I finished *Hypatia* last night and wish I'd stuck to *Hereward the Wake* after all. No wonder she wasn't on the syllabus."

"What happened?"

"She was torn to pieces."

"What for?"

"Lecturing."

They stared across the hall at the gods and heroes opposite, towering over the chattering groups of youthful seekers after knowledge who, although grunting slightly at the pearls daily strewn before them, recognised them as such, which is on the way to the finishing touch of the silk purse. The lectured here were about twenty-five to one of the lecturers but the mob never actually got out of control of the superior nob, even though on some days they went about wrong-doing with a sort of absent-minded precision.

"Have you ever had the sensation," asked Gwen still regarding the ancients, "that you have been here before?"

Freda arched her neck forward to view her other friend.

"What d'you mean, been here before? We're here five days out of seven."

"I mean," Gwen explained haltingly, "that the place is so familiar that sometimes I can see the whole of the school as if the walls were made of glass and know everything that is going on in every room."

Her friends nodded comprehendingly.

"It looks as if you are going to be a Head," said Freda.

"I feel that whatever happened could not surprise me," went on Gwen. "I should be half expecting it."

"Even if the school were struck by lightning?"

"That's never unexpected, else there wouldn't be so many lightning conductors on buildings."

The three pondered this fact and then Kerry offered her opinion.

"I don't think we expect to be struck by lightning as often as *they* did," indicating the disillusioned pagans. "They were always expecting something unexpected to happen, especially the girls. A god might start chasing them as well as ordinary shepherds."

"The gods must have been worse than the men," said Gwen scornfully. "Deceitful lot!"

"You know how you can't run in a nightmare?" asked Kerry dramatically. "Well, those girls, Daphne, Clytie and so on would know how that felt when they were suddenly changed into something else. They'd find themselves rooted to the spot. That frightful jump we give when we wake up would be the leap into another kind of being for them."

"How awful! And it wasn't their fault," exclaimed Gwen.

"Which would you rather have happen to you," asked Freda the realist dreamily, "to be changed into a tree or to be caught?"

This question needed serious cogitation with their eyes travelling from one to another of the plaster casts of long played dramas. Did any of them look pleased?

The question remained unanswered but Freda finally spoke.

"I think we have a better time than *they* had, on the whole."

"Even with stockings?" asked Gwen, twitching hers round so as to avoid sitting for another agonised moment on a suspender.

"Yes, I think so. They couldn't even dot somebody one with an umbrella."

"Well, what about compulsory Maths?" asked Kerry in dudgeon. "I wouldn't mind being turned into a bush during the Fridge's lessons; one with long spikes so she wouldn't come near me."

There was a pause and then Gwen asked a direct question.

"What *are* you going to do, Kerry, if you don't go in for teaching or secretarial work?"

"I don't know. Nobody here seems to do anything else, do they? I think I'd really like to go on a ranch in America and see nothing but wheat for miles and miles and miles."

They all gazed at it together.

"And what when you've taken a good look at it?" asked Freda.

"Oh, just go on reading."

"But nobody's going to pay you for that!"

"It was just a thought. It sounded restful."

"But we've got wheat in this country," persisted Freda.

"Not to ride through for days on end," sighed Kerry blissfully. "It would be like a tremendously long yawn or a cat stretching."

She suited the actions to the words.

The next moment the whole assembly rose to its feet as the teaching staff filed in and stood along the inside wall. Last hurried scraps of conversation were whispered and then silence took over in quite forceful contrast. Old Harry's door remained closed and a senior mistress mounted the platform steps.

"What's the betting," whispered Gwen, who had a brother, "that we have *Jesu, lover of my soul*? I have been here before."

"We always get it when it's raining," answered Kerry. "And remind me afterwards to tell you a joke about not caring whose bosom it is!"

The hymn tune struck up away in front beyond the rows of heads. Yes, sure enough, 'Let me to Thy bosom fly'. Yet all around them were the Greek comments on the bosoms of the gods; it behoved mortals to fly from them in terror. The Greeks for all their beauty and balance, were looking for something more than the loveliest forms in the world and they once surrounded with acclamation the two unhandsome Jews who came so austerely amongst them. Kerry's eyes roved idly from figure to figure until she came to rest at the Apollo.

Nobody even so much as mentioned him now who had come in and out of their house so freely. She could imagine him working hard with that concentrated look that came upon him sometimes when he stopped talking. She herself had tried to study more painstakingly since he had shifted most of the clouds from the middle slopes of Algebra and she admired the trickery that could prove a point and arrive at a conclusion much as one could make a 'plane journey by night, but she doubted if she could ever join in the geometrical conversation of seraphs.

And now he was studying all the time, not lounging about, not joking, never sparing a thought for old friends in Dean Lane. How could Sybil do such a thing! How could she, if pursued by such an Apollo, flee from such a bosom? He was not like all these powerful but unpitying figures that played their charades of mute warning in halls and corridors up and down the place. Why! If she were gazing at miles and miles of bending wheat and suddenly there came running through it a glorious, kind and clever Apollo, to tap her ear gently with his pencil and explain again so persuasively how the brackets were struck away and the simple answer revealed, she would not fly in panic, praying to be changed into a tree. She would stay, singing, singing with joy, "Let me to thy bosom fly."

"There's a girl by the window over there not singing!"

The school had finished the first verse and at Miss Bontoft's signal Mr Miller had not started on the next verse but waited with his hands poised over the keyboard.

"Yes, look at me. I don't know your name. Someone tell that girl to look this way."

Gwen and Freda perceived that this was directed at their companion but they both looked steadily at the platform hoping that Miss Bontoft would tire of the waste of time. Kerry, at the pause in the vocal offering, switched her attention to the here and now.

"Yes, you, girl. I don't know why you should expect everybody to know your name. Come up here and let us all take a good look at you if you think we ought to remember you."

Kerry sighed and picking up her school case, made her way forward, stepping over other people's books and bags.

"Marsden or Martin or something like that, isn't it?"

"Yes, Miss Buntuft."

Miss Bontoft was not *quite* sure but she was *almost* sure there had been a slight mis-pronunciation, and if she had worn her hair in a more up-to-date style, nobody would have shot a glance at it, but unfortunately she twisted it into a repressed little chignon that was always trying to squirm round the other way in spite of its shackles. It was not as spirited as a Catherine wheel nor was the whole head in open rebellion, but strays among the less important faction kept dodging out for a breath of fresh air until they were thrust in again and put in irons.

As Kerry came demurely up the platform steps, Miss Bontoft eyed her shrewdly.

Kerry had halted a few paces from the rear of the platform where most defaulters were told to stand and she guardedly exchanged glances with Gwen and Freda. Gwen had this brother who told them at home that if the High Master at his school met any boy on the corridor or anywhere, whether he were a new boy or not, the greeting was

310

always by name. Good morning, Jones, or whatever it was. And there were over a thousand of them!

Some of the mistresses were turning to look up at the high wall clock, resentful of minutes lost from the first lesson.

"All right. Now perhaps you will condescend to catch up with the rest of us, so please sing the first verse by yourself."

Kerry was surprised but by no means discomforted and hoped she was in good voice. Sometimes the vocal chords were smooth as treacle and sometimes knobbly as an abacus. Some of her Form grinned amiably at her from the back of the hall and Mr Miller, the soul of tact, played the first bars and waited for her to begin, which she did with the composure of slight boredom.

There had been some shouting on the canal bank just outside the hall windows and from her vantage point Kerry could see through an open lower window about half-way down the room. For a few moments it framed a macabre picture in the murky drizzle as she mechanically sang on: "While the nearer waters roll."

Two men leaned over the stone wall, grasping something heavy with water which they hauled up with difficulty. Up the dripping sides of the canal a rigid body slowly and stiffly slid, unbending even as it was drawn over the low parapet; unbelievably perpendicular as it poised on its heels before the men gently lowered it to the pavement, shining and wet almost as the dark canal. Silence fell and there were no more shouts.

"Safe into the haven guide,
    O receive my soul at last."

Kerry gave a tremendous sigh and watched the still figures outside standing quietly looking down. Then other men came into view, also quiet and unhurried until a small solemn crowd had collected, all gazing down.

The canal would be terribly cold, its surface green and slimy, especially by the great wooden lock gates where the filthy flotsam and jetsam looked solid, and yet it had seemed preferable to life as that man knew it. She had always thought that when schooldays were over, if ever they *were* over, life became more a matter of choice and liberty, an opening into unfenced uplands. Yet that man, mature and free, had chosen the canal. And such a canal! It was sickening to get a hair in one's mouth; what would it be like to gulp trailing weed and undeterrent insinuating slime? Did he too late repent his mad decision to end it all, but found he had bitten off more than he could chew? In fact could not bite it off at all, the weeds forcing themselves down and down nevertheless, unendingly in unsifted and wide mouthed gulps,

311

the choking cry for help rammed back with the swamped breath.

Perhaps he had not intended it that way at all, but had fallen into the canal when drunk. He had meant to drown only his sorrows in wine and not himself, but his drowned sorrows had become a millstone round his neck when he fell into the water and had gone on drinking, drinking, drinking beyond all thirst quenching.

The school had joined in for the remaining verses, Mr Miller trying to instill some verve into the singing by spirited accompaniment and then he quickly launched into *A Daughter of the Regiment*, which he spanked out in fine style to everybody's gratitude. As her own Form marched out, Kerry came down and joined them, but just outside the hall doors Miss Cassell reached out a thin sunburnt wrist and seized her in passing.

"Go to the cookery room at once and ask Miss Berry to give you a hot drink. Tell her I sent you."

The girl turned a wondering face but Miss Cassell had sped on like a mosquito with a busy day ahead.

"You're an early bird," Miss Berry greeted her cheerfully, dragging a light camp-bed before the huge and glowing grate. "Would you like a hot bottle?"

"No, thank you," answered Kerry, staring. "I'm all right. It's all Miss Cassell's idea, I don't know why."

"Don't you feel at all ill?" The mistress was drawing screens round the bed but observing meanwhile the girl's white face carefully. The hot bottle did the trick with most callers.

"I'm never ill," came the boastful reply. She was standing and watching these preparations with interest. Miss Berry looked like a hospital nurse in her white things, or even a Madonna. She had beautiful features and perfect colouring and she taught cookery and hygiene and physiology to the upper school. She might have been a tall and stately goddess Hygiea herself, but she did not look as if she would run from anything or anybody; indeed, in an emergency, people would run to *her*. Her white apron was a badge of neutrality, but ought there not to be a red cross on the bosom? Let me to thy bosom . . .

Miss Berry detected the first slight forward tilt and at once firmly guided her patient to the camp bed, slowly as Kerry's feet now seemed rooted although her head was soaring, light as blown leaves.

"Sit down! Now lie down and I'll soon have a hot drink ready for you. Hold this thermometer in your mouth."

Lying before the red and comforting coals, Kerry surveyed them thankfully. At her Elementary school there had been splendid fires in all class-rooms throughout the winter and the caretaker used to come round with huge buckets, and grinning at the children gaping at him as he strode mightily in. His bare arms were blue with tattooed patterns writhing round his muscles and he was strong enough to lift the great bucket high over the fireguard and empty it into the glowing heart with a following rush of slack, so that it thundered and spat out sparks that escaped madly up the chimney. The teacher would smile round at him and the children's eyes followed him enviously as he went cheerfully on his round, a liberal, competent giant, a member of that glorious grown-up world so tantalisingly ahead. His element was now fire and not sea-water any more, but at no stage of that exuberant life could one imagine him being fished out, stiff as a barge pole, from a green-walled ditch of a canal.

Her stomach now had a sensation of weeds coiling round and round in it, as Miss Berry pulled a chair near to the bed and proffered hot Bovril to Kerry's lips.

"How do you feel?"

Kerry pondered.

"Like a tree."

Miss Berry decided to hold the cup herself.

"Warm enough? Let me tuck this rug round you."

"Thank you. That's a proper fire, isn't it? When you consider that coal is really old trees, every fire is really a burning bush."

With an extra pillow supporting her head while she sipped from a spoon, Kerry's appreciation was expressed whenever her lips were disengaged.

"Going to bed in front of a fire needs some beating, doesn't it? That would be the best part of cave dwelling, I should think. I like the idea, too, of piles of thick animal skins all round the great hall where the heroes could stagger when they'd had enough, still within sight and feel of the central fire. And in Scotland they have a sort of cupboard opening off the living room, where a bed lies all in readiness. That would be my favourite way of retiring for the night; just summoning enough energy to open the door and then leaving it open to the warm air, especially in weather like this."

"Come along now and take this while it's hot. And those beds you admire so much may have been simple and cosy, but not very hygienic, I fear."

"I know hygiene is supposed to prolong our lives, but I often catch cold and start sneezing in the bathroom."

"In the long run it helps," responded Miss Berry, tilting the cup. "Probably the heroes were made more hardy by an occasional swim in the lake or river; a cold dip is very freshening, you know."

o

Kerry gave such a shudder that Miss Berry adroitly withdrew the cup only just in time and gave her patient a searching look.

"How were you when you left home this morning?"

"All right. And I'm very strong really. I have good teeth and masses of hair and I've never fainted, and Doctor Bedser says I'm one of his best babies. Physically, that is. I'm not clever."

Miss Berry felt reassured and gave a friendly smile.

"I think you'll do."

She noticed that the girl's colour seemed to be returning, but it was touch and go. She applied the cup with the remaining beverage straight to her lips and then advised her to try to sleep for a time.

"Rest your brain," she added kindly.

"My what?" asked Kerry sarcastically.

The mistress knew that Miss Cassell would not send the girl up without cause. Perhaps there had been more notices this morning and the school kept standing too long.

Kerry dozed, gazing at the red coals through half closed eyes and beginning to enjoy a pleasant torpor. The blanket added comforting weight and she felt, in Geoffrey's graphic phrase, snug as a bug in a rug. Would he really never come again? She reached out for her school case and got a clean handkerchief; her eyes were watery from the steam in the cup. She would take Miss Berry's advice and have a little sleep here in the relaxation of a private cell with screens curving round her. She put the handkerchief folded in a band across her eyes in case they surprised her even when closed and then she lay still.

If she could only tell him about this morning she was sure he would say something that would make it less awful. He would not approve of that poor man's choice of resting place; indeed, she could catch his shocked tones as he repudiated any place that did not please: "I wouldn't be found drowned there!" Found drowned! What a short epitaph and not at all biographical. Could anything be more terse? One had to believe every word of the simple statement: Found drowned.

Peeping round the screen at the still figure with its rather strangely shaded eyes, Miss Berry decided to let the girl stay there until she rose of her own accord. She evidently needed a good sleep; many of these growing girls did not get enough by a long way. First making sure that breathing was actually taking place, the mistress quietly withdrew.

It was nearly eleven o'clock when Kerry awoke in the empty cookery room. A small piece of coal was spluttering fussily, gas hissing from a small fissure. She removed her handkerchief and looked about her without raising her head. A room without people is at its best, entirely itself and at the moment this must be the most peaceful room

314

in the whole school. She inhaled a luxuriously deep breath. She was warm through and through. At moments such as this she felt she was going to live a very long time; lazy people had to if they were going to get anything done. There was no hurry. This time was calm, temperate, soft-pedalled, lingering with its self contained message. Such an hour could take its place alongside a symphony, a poem, apprehended but not heard, emerging only as a wonderment in the eyes, in a smile. It was a chance meeting of spirit, time and place prolonged as in the hidden veining of a rock stratum. Tap along the subterranean gleam and intercept the message. 'And thou, child.'

Kerry raised herself on an elbow, listening. The spluttering coal ceased and collapsed, whispering.

The Police Court clock struck eleven and she became now fully awake and regretfully aware that she must go. She stretched and then got up slowly. She stood awhile. The windows were milky with mist. She then folded the blanket and pushed the camp bed under a long kitchen table where it lived between bouts of active service. That was all she could do.

At the door she turned, holding the brass latch that seemed to be even more scintillating than the hundreds of others in the building, while she noted the homely severity of the tall cupboards and scrubbed surfaces, the air of peace and harmlessness and the quiet vividness of the fire. The atmosphere was of tranquil self-assurance like a good cake rising serenely up the tin and bringing its mixed fruit with it, as it ought.

Goodbye, calm akin to ecstasy!

There were five floors to descend at speed to find Gwen and Freda washing their hands in the basement towards the end of break.

"What have I missed?"

"You can have my geography notes," answered Freda, looking at her searchingly. "Afterwards it was only gym. We're going to start doing it barefoot."

"I liked it," said Gwen. "You can lean an awfully long way back when you haven't to consider suspenders. By the way, where've you been all this time?"

"Jacqueline sent me to Miss Berry and I fell asleep."

"Lucky you! I'll sing for them tomorrow."

French was always a brisk lesson, Miss Cassell being what she was, and she thought that Kerry had been allowed ample time to get over her touchiness at being made to sing solo and was not entitled to sit staring at the wall any longer.

"It looks nice and clean and empty now, but you wouldn't like to

315

stare at it for long. You know, that is what the Nazis do to the people they take for questioning in the Brown Houses; they stand them with their noses up against a blank wall for hours, which is not at all the same thing as being in a brown study. Now Judith, this is not the time to make a speech; not for you, that is. I am just reminding you all that an empty mind would soon bore you stiff and the only resistance to any blank walls of life is a well stored mind. So now, all of us, let us move a little furniture in, in the shape of a few necessary irregular verbs."

The class worked on, Miss Cassell hardest of all, sometimes dangling carrots of persuasion by giving colourful vignettes of her holidays in France, Italy and Spain.

She hurried on with an enviable self portrait of walking up the Grand Staircase of the Paris Opera House, then followed it by a lightning sketch of her Basque host and hostess in the Pyrenees enjoying a game of chess in stiff politeness under the great silver candlesticks. She sighed as she hitched her academic gown onto her shoulders, realising that no one appreciated these accounts more than Kerry Martland and yet no one more quickly flagged in her French grammar.

She left off her French impersonations which she illustrated so expressively and continued in English again.

"Come along now, girls, you don't want to belong to the great Don't Knows, all those people who can never meet an emergency. Can you translate this letter from the French, Miss Jones? Can you tell me what this Latin inscription means, Miss Brown? Can you play the hymn today or a little piece for the musical chairs, Miss Smith? It's a great and terrible army, the army of the Don't Knows. See that you don't get enlisted in it."

She glanced at her wrist watch, a rather large one for a woman and not really a wrist watch in the first place but encased in a tortoiseshell holder slotted into a leather strap where it looked too heavy for her thin wrist.

The lesson went on and Kerry wondered why, on some parts of the earth's surface, people pronounced a group of two or three letters so differently from others. If only one knew where and when these matters were settled, one could start learning a language but while one pondered these things, the rule of the subjunctive passed one by and one fell behind.

The sudden electric buzzer in the corridor startled them all and as books were being put away, Jacqueline lobbed another hand grenade into their trench.

"You'd be surprised to know how many old girls I see at night

316

school classes, paying fees for the very same lessons they were learning here three and four years ago. So don't waste your time."

She smiled at them without rancour and moved swiftly out to descend like a vegetarian wolf-hound on the next fold, meeting in the corridor the hygienic Miss Berry accompanied by 'poor old Joe' the physiology skeleton. Although very handsome, the first impression received by the girls was of extreme cleanliness and good health and her hair, worn in a bun, was as different from a Bontoft bun as patisserie is different from King Alfred's efforts. As always, the class stared at her, missing no detail but by no means disturbing Miss Berry's composure. Sometimes, after prolonged inventory, girls were seen moodily to inspect their own fingertips and then sink into dejection from which they were roused by a lesson on hand-care so incorporated in physiological information that instruction fired their vanity without wounding it.

Today it was the feet. Miss Berry had heard that barefoot movement, Eurythmics, was to come on the syllabus and, turning to poor old Joe, suspended by a hook in his cranium from his present day slender scaffold (for the girls fearfully believed the unfounded theory that Joe was a felon who had suffered execution) she proceeded to demonstrate the wonders of human pedestrianism.

Joe continued to grin sardonically at the girls sketching his metatarsals. Observing poor old Joe's deep-set mirth, Kerry found it comforting that underneath their faces people are grinning all the time, knowing that there was a mind within the skull and a spirit that made its temporal shelter there and could say, "Travelling light: go anywhere". That would be wonderful so long as one's friends could exclaim "Well! So you've made it after all", or one heard a voice say, "My dear girl! I was just going to lodge a small complaint!" She did not think it would be fair of God to create poor old Joe and to make him aware of his Creator and after all to deny him an after-life.

Of all the world's funeral customs, she decided, the Vikings' seemed to be the most decent and helpful; a blazing ship sailing out upon the sea with its perishable cargo, there to await its future. But where was Joe now? On the way to becoming His image! What a burden of responsibility rests on translators. They have unwittingly sent people to the stake in times past. Miss Cassell would have written something biting on their Reports if she'd caught them out.

"Have you finished your drawing, Kerry?"

"Oh! Nearly, Miss Berry. Well, not quite. Actually, I've not begun."

She was in time to join in the laughter.

"I can't think why not," said the mistress patiently. "You've got your pencil sharpened and your demonstration notebook I see. If your equipment is ready, what are you waiting for? You must have been wool-gathering enough to knit yourself a jumper."

At the end of the lesson it was also the end of morning school. It had been a long morning, in a way.

Miss Berry's voice sounded above the burst of chatter.

"Will Gwendoline and Freda please carry the figure up to Floor C and try not to shake it unduly."

Joey was really more awkward for two than for one to carry, but they got him upstairs, past the tall athlete testing his biceps, and left him shaking with silent laughter in the corridor, next to a headless Victory.

Kerry had walked behind her friends for company and on the return descent they discussed Miss Berry.

"I wouldn't mind being like her, would you?"

"Even if you're silly or lazy she still treats you as a silly and lazy human being and not a silly and lazy worm."

"She's a bit like these goddesses, I think. When she's dishing out frog's feet and bullock's eyes for dissection she might be handing strawberries."

"I think my favourite is Miss Cassell; not to look at but to be with. She's really the only one who has taught me anything - anything that I wasn't keen on knowing, that is. You know that funny story about a man who was going to be hanged next morning being asked what he would like and he said he'd like to learn to play the violin? Well, Miss Cassell is the kind of person they'd send for."

"By the way, in Assembly you were going to tell us a joke about not caring whose bosom it was."

"Oh, it was nothing," said Kerry lamely. "Let's hurry, else everybody will have started."

They entered the dining room where the clamour was not so persistent as in Assembly, for hunger concentrated their energies. The food was served really hot and any grumbling that went on was that there might have been more rather than that it should have been better. At Kerry's table the girls were canvassing for a team to play ring-ball later on if there was only a drizzle of rain and they arranged to sidle out unobtrusively so that they could play unchecked unless there was a door mistress to turn them back. Gwen passed the word along that she would get the ball from the gym and meet them outside.

The dining room was the opposite number of the main hall, forming the two ends of a dumbbell with the corridor holding them together and spanning the whole length of the school, at least of the girls' school, for on the far wall of the dining room was a small door, the only break in the long bare wall, the only point of interest in a large monochrome surface.

"I've never thought of it before," said Gwen, "but I suppose the boys' school joins ours along that wall."

A few heads turned that way.

"We never hear a sound, so it can't be their dining room."

"With a door there we should hear *something*, I should think."

The door became a matter of some speculation.

"Somebody passing ought to open it and take a look," which suggestion made some of the girls giggle and some goggle.

"Go on then, do it yourself."

By this time the whole table was curious about the door.

"To think we've been sitting here day after day and we don't know where that door leads. If there was a fire we might have to use it."

"It's sure to be locked."

"But we don't know."

"I know what we can do," said Gwen, leaning forward for those opposite to hear. "When Miss Snipe is down at the other end, you table monitors get up and walk past and when I signal that she's looking the other way, the one nearest can try the door."

"But others will see."

"Who's going to say anything? Keep in a bit of a crowd with other monitors if you can."

Gwen rose and lifting a tray with a few plates on it, she walked carefully forward, followed by Kerry with another tray and behind her Judith carrying one plate only in her right hand, leaving her left hand free. Other monitors from other tables were busy on their errands as the three filed past the door.

"Now, Judith."

Judith, with her precocious aplomb, nonchalantly extended her hand, but just as she was about to touch the knob, the door was jerked open from the other side. A boy's head and shoulders thrust through into their side of the school as he took a hasty look left and right, observing the whole dining room.

"Hello, girls," he said jauntily with a grin, and then with an audible uncontrollable laugh he dodged back and shut the door again quickly with a hurried bang.

The mistresses eating their lunch at the far table under the windows glanced in that direction, looking puzzled, and Miss Snipe spun round.

"Who touched that door?"

The girls were wavering in surprise and there were titters from the nearer tables. Then everybody listened.

"We didn't, Miss Snipe," answered Judith with composure, but now all their eyes were dancing and full of adventure. They looked as if they would all readily open that door now and give hoydenish chase after Peeping Tom. They had changed from half-fearful inquisitive girls to the Thracian horde that fell upon Orpheus, and a sort of fever had risen in the air and an expectancy of something unusual to happen. What if that door opened again and not just one boy but crowds of roaring boys charged through? The girls would have to run as they had run since time immemorial. But if that door were not wrenched from the other side, it might now be pushed open from this side and a torrent of laughing and shrieking girls surge through, far more turbulent than their youthful and energetic rush on the staircases where the mistresses were left protesting in the rear. Miss Snipe felt for a strange moment that she was an experienced priestess timing the unleashing of a Bacchante revel that was about to sweep from the sacred groves into the world of men. Breathing heavily with annoyance she glowered at the trio.

"Are you sure? Did you, Gwendoline? Did you, Kerry?" but their daring eyes remained fixed on her as they shook their heads.

"I do believe, Miss Snipe," Judith's indignant voice protested, "that some impudent boy had the cheek to open that door and look in!"

"Yes, I think that was it, Miss Snipe."

"Do you think you ought to go through and find out who it was, Miss Snipe?"

"No, no. Never mind," answered the mistress irritably. "I'll speak to one of the caretakers and see that it's kept locked."

"I wonder if they've been spying on us before? Perhaps we ought to report them to Miss Harrison."

"Now, Gwendoline, don't make such a fuss. It was probably quite an accident. Now hurry along with your trays. Why are you carrying only one plate, Judith? It isn't like you to be so inefficient."

"Ichabod!" said Kerry to Judith as they trotted quickly to the serving hatch. When they returned with helpings of pudding, their table gave a little trouble to Miss Snipe but she soon walked away pretending not to hear the silly creatures. Then normality quietly returned as to a field of grazing cows momentarily startled by a galloping horse.

A quarter of an hour later it was reported to her in the library that some girls were out in the rain playing ring-ball. She hurried downstairs but when from the doorway she saw which Form it was, she drew back unseen. The little simpletons! Let them work off some of their surplus energy and get chilled to the marrow into the bargain. Do them good!

Not that Miss Tangent the Art mistress would agree. The whole Form were hopeless in the next lesson, their hands being unsteady from slapping at the big leather ball. Miss Tangent scurried to the front of the class and addressed them fiercely. The lesson was a fiasco today because of their thoughtlessness; they must study their timetables and use their commonsense. Valuable minutes would be wasted while they massaged their fingers. Well, not perhaps quite wasted! Here Miss Tangent's face softened and then became positively loving as she lifted a large portfolio from a cupboard. The girls gently chafed their hands as the mistress laid it upon the big desk and opened it with care, explaining that last summer she had been in Italy again and now she would show them some reproductions from the famous galleries and perhaps one or two of her own attempts. The girls sat up. This was better than shading cylinders and spheres and they especially clamoured to see some of her own paintings, so that Miss Tangent cast affectionate glances first on her pictures and then on the viewers as they uttered little cries of praise.

"You see, girls, now that photography has reached such precision, there is less need for art to be so natural and detailed. It can emphasise other qualities, both in the artist and in the subject."

Several pictures were held up for inspection and Judith particularly was much interested.

"And if the camera cannot lie, is it going to be left to art to do all the lying?"

There was laughter at this and the mistress hunted in the portfolio for two or three more landscapes.

"Now I want you to compare these paintings of the same scene by different artists, friends of mine. You will see that the results differ greatly, although one can tell it is the same view . . . just! But a hundred photographers standing at the same spot would not get that variety; indeed any variety at all would be entirely technical, differences of light and exposure but not of artistry."

"That one there," pointed Judith, "has put in every detail like a photograph."

"And it took many hours; whereas this which shows great grasp of essentials, only took half the time and is really the better picture."

Miss Tangent was careful to cover her own initials with her thumb.

"But if a farmer wanted a view of his farmlands," argued Judith, "he would ask for technical skill and never mind imagination, wouldn't he?"

"In that case he would only get a coloured diagram. Skill and imagination are Siamese twins and if you try to separate them, one may die."

There were cries of horror at Miss Tangent's realism and she smiled.

"You know how some people are better raconteurs than others," she went on. "They can heighten light and shade in a story by their own telling. They are not telling white lies or black lies, but lies in all colours of the rainbow. That is what artists do."

Judith was now perched on the edge of someone's desk on the front row and the other girls kept quiet.

"So," queried the girl, "it's no good ever putting an artist on oath? Can he only tell the truth as he sees it and not as it really is?"

The art mistress gazed at her thoughtfully.

"The artist would not really understand the nature of an oath and if he tried, it would frighten him. If he put his hand on the Book and swore to tell the whole truth and nothing but the truth about a landscape or a seascape, or a portrait, he would never finish it and might go mad in the process."

The girls burst out laughing.

"The plain unvarnished truth as we sometimes call it, is a very serious thing," said Miss Tangent. "Like a strong poison, only in measured doses does it act medicinally."

While her head was bent, someone called a question.

"Have you been to see Epstein's 'Genesis', Miss Tangent?"

Someone snorted in a muffled tone and this set the class off. But Judith was blazing.

"It's wonderful, isn't it, Miss Tangent?"

"Yes, it is," agreed the mistress gently, "but we won't go into that now. We are studying painting, not sculpture."

Judith tossed her head at the others and resumed her haughty calm. The mistress had observed the interest of many of the girls besides Judith's and she spoke kindly with real concern, looking round the Form.

"It's time you were thinking of your future careers. How many of you are planning to go to University?"

Judith's hand shot up and a few others followed.

"I should have liked to see a few more. We have a very fine University in our own City, you know, and you should consider it seriously."

Then she went rather pink as the girls looked self-consciously at their desks. Oh, the Rag Rag! She had forgotten it.

322

"Of course," she hurried on, "you will get all sorts of people in a group that is based on one commodity, such as intellect, but you need not swallow the place whole. Take what will help fulfil your ambitions and reject what you know will undo them. We also have a very good Art School here and in a week or two, when the crowds have gone from the Art Gallery, I want you to go and look at some of the pictures and we will talk them over one afternoon. Some of the people in the queues at the present time will never have visited the gallery before and most likely will never go again, but do get into the habit of knowing what it possesses at all times and not just when the press is wanting to cause a stampede. Now, Judith, calm yourself!

Hands were by this time sufficiently steady to hold a pencil, but minds had been stimulated to look for something more exciting than groups of geometrical figures and so Miss Tangent, hearing their complaints, pointed to a plaster cast of a man's head.

"All right, then, try that. Take your chairs to any vantage point you like and see how you go on. Who is he? He was a musician in the ancient world who was tactless enough to gain more marks than Apollo in a musical contest, and was consequently put to death by order of the jealous sun-god himself. Very mean spirited you'll agree, but that's what professional jealousy can do!"

Kerry was deeply shocked at this revelation. It showed Apollo in a very bad light, sun-god or no. Really, she was getting a bit fed up with the Greeks after all. She said as much to Gwen and Freda and they agreed. When you were in the First and Second forms you thought they were marvellous, but by the time you reached the Fifth they were beginning to be a pain in the neck; the more you knew! Sketching the unfortunate winner and praising the improved sportsmanship of modern times filled the latter half of the art lesson and the girls finally handed in their sheets of drawing paper to Miss Tangent, modestly aware that the results of their efforts would at no point in time have by one jot or tittle endangered their lives.

When the class filed into their own Form room they were still effervescent when Miss Fridgley joined them and perceived they were not in a mathematical mood.

"Come now, come now!" she called. "Compose yourselves for study. Whatever have you been doing? Whatever it was seems to have been no preparation for serious thought. We'll have a short session of Long Tots and Cross Tots to limber up.

"Why are you consumed with mirth, Kerry Martland? Perhaps it would have a sobering effect if you cast a forward glance towards your next Report?"

"Miss Tangent has been asking about careers," said Judith rather unctuously, "and urging more of us to go on to University."

"Good, very good," responded the Fridge eyeing them in a calculating manner, "but it will mean a mighty effort for some of you. There's generally a parting of the ways at School Certificate; a Rubicon to you, Judith, a Pons Asinorum to you, Kerry Martland. Now turn to Theorum forty-eight; this is a very simple one, even to simpletons."

If all this were the conversation of archangels as Geoffrey said, wouldn't it be funny if one Sunday morning Mr Garner read out a theorum instead of a text and ended with a Q.E.D. instead of a benediction? Kerry wondered if the square on the hypotenuse would become as universal as the twenty-third Psalm and if people would derive comfort from contemplating a right angle. This study was capable of development, and she turned to the back of her notebook and jotted down a few reminders to the effect that at morning Assembly they would raise a hymn to the eternal triangle. Before she could flip the pages back, the notebook was picked up from behind her shoulder.

"What on earth is this rubbish?"

Heads were turned sympathetically at the Fridge's angry tones.

"It's a sort of joke," faltered Kerry, and alarmed though she was, she could not repress a feeble grin.

"Some people can afford to joke," said the mistress grimly, "but not you. Your position is serious in the extreme; no laughing matter at all!"

The words 'no laughing matter' are highly suggestive to the young. Risibility inevitably follows in their train and now a faint twitching showed on several faces which irritated her beyond measure. She rounded on the whole Form.

"You were in no mood for work when you came in, I noticed at once. I must see if the syllabus can be altered so that there is less frivolity in your minds when you come to me. And now our time is further wasted by the incredible foolishness of one girl."

The Form were not sure whether to sit idly listening or to get on with their work. Miss Fridgley turned back to the culprit, her eyes flickering angrily.

"Lately, I think someone has been trying to teach you the rudiments of Mathematics that others before me have failed to instil into you. Is that so?"

"Yes, just for a time. They've stopped now."

"I'm not surprised. I envy the fortunate person who could find any excuse to get rid of such a pupil."

Miss Fridgley walked back to her own desk and seated herself, her face flushed and her eyes piercing.

"I too will escape something of this fruitless effort. You, girl, must never produce any more work for me to mark. I shall ignore you utterly. That is an order, so you will in future use that end desk on the back row there. Go and sit there now."

The Form sat in shocked silence as Kerry slowly rose and walked to her new position at the end of the half empty back row, where she sat with burning cheeks and the conviction that if ever she caught Miss Fridgley's eye again she would die of hatred and loathing. In glum embarrassment some of the girls rubbed their shoes slowly on the polished floor as if trying to erase a stain that bothered them, but the rest sat miserably eyeing their exercise books.

"Did you speak, Judith?"

"I did."

Judith was leaning back in her chair, her right arm hitched over the back of it.

"And what was so important that it could not wait?"

Even as she spoke, Miss Fridgley regretted the question, for the face before her had become strangely mature with its ageless olive tint and the dark luscious eyes that gazed steadily with a penetrating judgment grown from centuries of persecution endured.

Now the full red lips curved in a half smile that held her like a half-Nelson.

"I just remarked," drawled Judith sagging with even greater carelessness in her demeanour, "that sometimes a white blouse conceals a brown shirt."

The twenty-four pairs of eyes that suddenly shot at the woman facing them were like a firing squad. With an effort Miss Fridgley gathered herself together and mentally measured the distance to the door. She rose stiffly and fixed her gaze on it and the girl nearest to it sprang up and opened it instinctively. The woman passed through with a deep breath of relief, but the breath was drawn too late, for as it expired it took full consciousness with it and she pitched forward, her fall broken slightly by the door-girl's rather frightened grab at her.

"Run up and tell Miss Berry," ordered Judith, adding curtly, "Leave her where she is," so that the door-girl hesitantly moved away and upstairs. Judith shut the door and looked so utterly unapproachable that no one spoke to her, while they watched uneasily over the glass corridor partition for the approach of the hygiene mistress. Some began to pack their cases for home-time, knowing that the lesson was over for that day, and already one or two were quietly reminding each other that no Maths homework had been set. As they spoke in undertones, shuffling noises were heard outside and the Form eyed the closed door.

The loud bell made them all start although they had been waiting for it and slowly they filed out. In the basement they looked at Kerry secretly as they changed their shoes. It had been a rotten term for her on the whole and today was not much worse than some others; in fact she had been lying down for some of the time, so what was the matter with her?

If anybody was in hot water it was Judith. Would Judith be expelled, do you think? The whispers went up and down the coat rails. No, she's too brainy.

Judith got near to Kerry, who had not spoken.

"The Fridge wasn't playing fair and she knows it, so she won't say anything at all."

Kerry nodded in silence.

"But if I were you," Judith advised, "I should tell your father. She's paid to teach and she could get into an awful row, you know, whatever you've done."

Again Kerry nodded.

"Yes, I know. But it's not that I was thinking about. It's something else. Goodbye. See you on Monday."

When Kerry had hurried away, Judith looked at the other two standing together.

"You see, I'm older than you are. As a people, I mean," she added impatiently at their stare. "You sing a hymn about earth's proud empires passing away. What happens if you let the umpires pass away? There'll be some games going on then!"

"Oh, Judith, aren't you afraid?"

"Not in the least," and giving her first real smile in the last hour, Judith sauntered out, her glance over the surrounding throng haughty as that of Mordecai.

Gwen and Freda watched her go.

"I do hope Kerry has got over it by Monday, don't you? The Fridge has always had her knife in her so she ought to be used to it by now."

When Kerry left the school building she turned as usual along the street by the canal where all was quiet, and past the basement windows where the lights showed the black surface of the water pitted all over with the falling rain which she hardly noticed. She was not noticing anything at all very much and seemed almost to have forgotten how to breathe, for her breath came and went in deep sighs with an interval of complete lack of respiration in between. She went straight home without loitering and let herself in a little earlier than usual. Her mother was not in but the middle room fire had been banked up and she mechanically gave it a poke to brighten it and stood awhile staring at it. Then she took off her wet shoes and tilted them against the fender and went upstairs for her slippers. She avoided looking at herself in the dressing table glass; the eyes looking into hers would know too much. She wondered whether to lie on the bed for a time but the feeling came over her that if she succumbed now she would never get up again and might become like poor Antella, helpless and a prisoner, waited upon by a patient Tom . . . No, not even that. That was why Antella lived on year after year, never complaining. Surely people would understand that after all, Mr and Mrs Kershaw were to be envied? She had never realised, until now. She moved away from the bed quickly and went downstairs.

Later that same evening Sybil glanced up to find her sister's eyes watching her keenly.

"Haven't you much homework this week-end?" she asked as Kerry began to put her books away.

"No. The Fridge wasn't well in class today and went out. As a matter of fact she fainted."

Clara looked up.

"Did she really? I hear there's a lot of 'flu about. Do take care, all of you," and she looked concernedly at them, but nobody made any response.

Kerry went into the front room and sat on the music stool, pondering with her fingers extended to the keys but not moving. She didn't know what to play. Ah yes, there were always scales, they practically played themselves. What had he called them? The corset of Terpsichore; corsets to keep one from slopping over. Scales it should be, then. Carefully now; up . . . and down.

So that was it! It had taken an enemy to open her eyes to the truth. Any excuse! It would never have dawned on her. But she wasn't to blame for her sister's loss.

He had tried to come back for Sybil. Up . . . now down again. Mr and Mrs Kershaw. Her mother and father. Mr and Mrs Garner. They all had something worth living for, she could see now. It was like Blake's poem, The Lamb. She had jibbed at having to say that instead of Shakespeare.

It was only a nursery rhyme, she had sneered, but Jacky had persevered last year until they saw that it was poetry. Little Lamb, I'll tell thee! Up . . . down. Try the minor scales now. It was like a turning wave when the minor scale lipped the rim of the topmost note and then sadly fell back again. When a major scale reached the top it had arrived and could stay there if it liked, playing its Hallelujah Chorus, but there was nothing for a minor scale but to turn and go back from where it came. Little Lamb, I'll tell thee. And thou, child. But you, girl!

Up . . . and inevitably down. She knew now, like that man this morning, she also was just another minor scale.

Chapter Twenty-three

For the time being Elsie Buckley was satisfied. The house looked shining, expensive and as near like a special Spring Furnishing Number as could be. No Mrs Ginnell came to clutter it with the paraphernalia of attention and it was surprising how spick and span a house could be by just keeping itself to itself and not seeking popularity; popularity that wore out carpets, took the surface from fabrics and eventually broke the springs of chairs and settees. Such free and easy houses were the places where something was always in need of repair, where things got broken through repeated use or careless jollity, but here all was in perfect order, everything was treated with care. She was careful. She always took care. Care filled her mind and haunted her eyes.

She had an unexpected visitor one morning. Dr Bedser called. He was in the vicinity, he explained, and thought he would look in and see how she was getting on. Of course that unfortunate affair was a thing of the past. It could be forgotten now and she could regard herself as being fit for anything, perfectly normal and able to do just as she fancied. No need to be nervous at all; no fear of overdoing things any more.

As he talked, Doctor Bedser moved about the room, examining a picture here, picking up a vase there, fidgeting from place to place and absently casting a cushion from one chair to another when he sat down. Elsie followed him round, smoothing, replacing a piece of pottery to its exact habitat and putting everything just as he had found it. He paused before a small cloisonné vase on the mantelpiece and, while describing one of his own, flicked his cigarette ash into the tiled hearth. He was always so much interested in his patients' surroundings, hobbies and general way of life that some people said he had no time for anything else and was out of the house without so much as a request to see their tongues.

He stood in the window and seeing him absorbed, Elsie took the opportunity to sweep the cigarette ash onto the effete little shovel, but had to leave it there since only the electric fire was burning so early in the day.

"This is your great hobby, isn't it, Mrs Buckley?" he asked, nodding at the front garden.

"It is indeed. A good day's work in it ensures a night's rest at the worst of times."

"You're not sleeping too well?"

She did not reply and he turned to look fully at her.

"How's Sam sleeping?"

"All right, as far as I know. He doesn't complain."

"I've known your husband a long time and he's not the complaining sort, of course, but you could ask him sometime. If you compared notes, you might be able to help each other. By the way, you know the Sinclairs, don't you? I know they are older than you and Sam, but you could do worse than go round in the evening now and again for a change and brighten things up, although that son of theirs is bright enough."

Doctor Bedser twisted a picture a little way from the wall to eliminate gleam and after giving it some attention he set it back, not quite straight and wandered away. Elsie barely waited for his interest to be engaged elsewhere before she crossed the room and eased the picture to the horizontal.

"Mrs Buckley, you're a wonderful housewife and you'd make a charming hostess, I'm sure, so start entertaining again. Do your husband a world of good."

Elsie extended a foot and flattened a corner of the hearth-rug that he had kicked up and he apologised.

"Very comfortable rug, that. Have you a cat?"

"No. Oh, but we have a dog. Sam brought one home only a little time ago without saying anything. We've christened him Wispy."

"I'd like to see Wispy, if I may. Evidently not a Great Dane."

"I'll bring him," said Elsie.

Doctors have the run of a house without invitation, so he followed her casually out of the lounge and into the kitchen where he could see no sign of a dog. Elsie went over to a high cardboard box and lifted the lid, disclosing Wispy looking if possible rather more ethereal than when he first arrived.

"Does he live in that box? He needs a low basket."

"He's out of the way there. He can't be loose of course or he'd be all over the place. Sam takes him for a run every morning and evening."

Dr Bedser stooped and gently lifted Wispy against his chest.

"Poor little guinea-pig," he murmured. "Cost a few guineas, this," he said more loudly. "But you know, Mrs Buckley, this kind of dog is really meant to be carried about and fondled. They get some kind of nourishment and warmth from human contact, like pearls, and like pearls, they're expensive. Here, you hold him while we're talking and remember, this little dog needs love, just as a baby or a husband needs love."

Dr Bedser admired the illustrated kitchen calendar and glanced idly down the monthly engagement memorandum containing paltry domestic notes only and then returned to the hall and took his hat.

"Our friend Mrs Ginnell will not be long before she's about again. Things are bad, I'm afraid, with this slump. By the way, if ever you feel like going to the office and helping your husband in any way, you do that. Lots of wives find it interesting nowadays if they have time on their hands, and Sam's business is growing I hear. He'd appreciate the thought. Well, goodbye, Mrs Buckley. Very nice interlude in my busy day, seeing you in your charming home."

No, again Dr Bedser had not felt a pulse, listened to a heart or tapped a knee, but as he drove away he knew she was battling with fears and being pushed back day by day, and had no intention of confiding either in her husband or in her doctor, and seemingly she had no friends.

After he had gone, Elsie stood for some time with the dog in her arms. Was that visit purely social? There had been an undercurrent in his conversation that made her uneasy and she wondered if he had meant to drop her a hint on some matter. She cogitated on his words, to find a key. Why should she fill the house with people to amuse Sam? What need to help at the office? If business was expanding there was no need to save on expense and in any case he had an excellent private secretary in Rainbow already. Sybil Martland! Is that what Dr Bedser was getting at, that it would pay her to watch the situation there? Impossible! And yet, she remembered, they had been out together on Rag Day after she had left and later Sam had joked about *her* being on the lorry with Geoffrey, but saying he'd been glad to see her taking part in the fun. Perhaps that was because he'd been taking some part in the fun himself. Even this dog she was holding could have been some sort of blind! How disgusting!

She walked quickly back into the kitchen and petulantly dropped Wispy into the box. She was sure now that Sybil's engagement was off, which made her gadding about Manchester with Sam on some pretext or other all the more suspect.

She went restlessly into the dining room. Dr Bedser was shrewd and he must have had some reason for these suggestions, but she would not go to the office. If that girl wanted to make a fool of herself over Sam, she could take the consequences of her romantic notions. She would not feel romantic for long if Elsie's own experience was anything to go by. But of course, nobody felt romantic for long, that was the tragedy. Life was a succession of disillusionments and the romantic turned into the realist some day. If this was Rainbow's turn she was bringing it upon herself. Some girls did fall for older men, both quite sure they would get from it more than they possibly could, and while Sam was good natured, humorous, generous and well off, he was in spite of all that a middle-aged man and most unsuitable for Sybil Martland, the thieving little hussy. Let her be ditched.

Much against her will but because for once Sam was gently insistent, Elsie had agreed to visit Mrs Ginnell in state with black grapes. Sam would run her there himself one afternoon and bring her back, for such a visit would be expected and much appreciated; he knew these people. She decided to get it over quickly and stop Sam fussing about Mrs Ginnell being a good soul and they must not hurt her feelings. Mrs Ginnell's feelings!

So that afternoon the car stopped outside the Oldham Road house, Sam helped his wife out and handed her the decorative box from Dingley's.

"What will you do while I'm in here?" she asked.

"Oh, I'll take a stroll round the district and give Wispy a bit of exercise. Don't worry about me; I can amuse myself for half an hour."

He just waited to see the door open and to make sure that she was admitted, but paused in surprise to see the dark girl he had sheltered on Rag Day. Connie stared at them and then at the car, and blushed deeply for no other reason than that a slight confusion does make girls blush. Sam raised his hat and smiled.

"I'm Mrs Buckley," Elsie informed her. "Is Mrs Ginnell at home?"

Mrs Ginnell most certainly was at home and quite prepared for visitors as Sam had dropped a postcard advising her of this impending visit. She was wearing a presentation knitted cape, and downstairs Connie had a tray ready with the best teacups for their visitor's refreshment.

When seated at the bedside, Elsie recalled the girl's reaction to Sam's appearance there.

"Of course, my husband used to live in these parts," she said quickly, coming out with the very remark she so often checked in him.

"Oh, yes, a very nice family they were, too. They left long before she'd be old enough to notice, but he's given her many a bright penny. You won't remember Mr Buckley, Connie, will you?"

"Well, not really, Mother, but on Shrove Tuesday there was an awful downpour in St. Peter's Square and I sheltered in his car for a few minutes. I had no idea it was Mr Buckley. He had that dear little dog with him and he told me it was a present for his wife."

"A dog over at Chorltonville?" exclaimed Mrs Ginnell, startled. "Well, I am surprised. What is he called?"

"Sam said he looked a Will o' the Wisp so we called him Wispy for short. Sam is taking him round the houses now, so I mustn't stay too long. He's rather delicate and mustn't catch cold."

"Mrs Sinclair's Sun Tan is a very well bred dog, too," said Connie, "only Mrs Sinclair was terribly upset just before I came away. She's had five puppies, Sun Tan, you know, and they're not pedigree at all. Mr and Mrs Sinclair were at the Martlands' on Circuit business early in the New Year and their Kerry asked to take Sun Tan down the brow of the Clough for a little run and got her all wet, so when they got in, Kerry put her in the kitchen with Watch."

Here Mrs Ginnell emitted a shriek like somebody's parrot being tortured.

"I'd like to have seen Alfred when he clapped eyes on 'em," she exclaimed with considerable relish. "That'll be new blood with a vengeance. Watch was supposed to be a throw-out from good stock but these little beggars will be kicked out from east and west, as *you* say, Mrs Buckley."

Elsie hastened to change the subject and turned to Connie. Really, she was a fine looking girl, marred by a rather sulky look at present, perhaps because she had been brought home to nurse her mother.

"I haven't been across to Didsbury for some time and there are so few people I could ask, but is the Martland-Sinclair engagement still on?"

Connie felt ill at ease and looked at her mother.

"No," answered Mrs Ginnell firmly. "It is not. Connie, slip downstairs and put the kettle on for a cup of tea, there's a good girl. No, Mrs Buckley, that we do know. I don't think the Sinclairs are much put out if you ask me, for Geoffrey's a bit of a spark and wants a girl with more go in her than Sybil Martland; fond of her though I am."

"Not that it is important one way or the other," mused Elsie Buckley in a bored tone. "Indeed, I'd as soon attend a funeral as a wedding judging by the miserable marriages I've witnessed."

"My word!" exclaimed Mrs Ginnell, thunderstruck. "You must have moved in some tragic circles!"

"And how long does poor Mrs Kershaw expect to be away?" asked Elsie. "That was very terrible."

"Oh, she's got over the gas attack or whatever it was and now they're building her up properly before she comes home. But it's given Tom a rest and he needed it."

"Do you know how the accident happened?"

"No, although it's been talked up and down. Dr Bedser had a little talk with our Ernie and says he mustn't be allowed to light the gas fire in future. But there, we simply don't know. You can't say too much to a child, can you? And here he is now, just got home from school. Come on up, love," she screeched, throwing her voice towards the stairs.

He was used to Antella's many visitors so was not shy at the sight of a stranger here, but he was more than usually interested just because he had never seen her before and he would have liked to touch the soft dark fur coat and sniff the bunch of violets on the lapel.

"Would you like to see my world?"

"That's his missionary box," his mother explained fondly. "He gets a book every year on prize day for the amount he collects. Go on, Ernie, you can bring it for Mrs Buckley."

Ernie scurried off into his little back bedroom and came back bearing a small globe with a great aperture cut in its Arctic regions and its base set in the Antarctic plinth with John Wesley's ambitious boast thereon: 'The world is my parish.'

A few minutes later his eyes sparkled at the sight of the half-crown dropped amongst the polar bears.

"Do you ever put anything in it yourself?"

Ernie was astonished.

"No, of course not. It's a *collecting* box. I'll show you what I use for myself," and he made another swift excursion, returning with the red pillar box which he held before her. Seeing the little highwayman so well practised, Elsie was piqued into holding him off from the usual easy victory.

"Do you want me to post you a little note?" she asked innocently. Mrs Ginnell broke in with voluble dissuasion.

"Now, Mrs Buckley, you're too generous. Ernie doesn't expect anything like that, I'm sure. A sixpence or a shilling or a half-crown at the most would be ample, Mrs Buckley."

Ernie heard the afternoon mail drop into the pillar-box with a good solid thump and raising his eyes to the donor he thanked her with the awe due to such a presentation. But the lady also was unsmiling and looking at him speculatively.

"Game, set and match to Master Ginnell! I wonder what he'll be when he grows up, Mrs Ginnell. Perhaps if he follows his father's political footsteps he'll be in charge of Party funds."

"Oh, him and his Communism! Well, he'll be away from all that talk now, for a time; that's one blessing, if the only one. And here am I laid up with this leg. As soon as Dr Bedser says the word, I'll be over at Chorltonville, never you fear, Mrs Buckley. I'll soon have the place swept and garnished, as *you* say, although come to think of it, who wants sprigs of parsley all over the place!"

"Be careful not to get up too soon, Mrs Ginnell, because health comes first and the house is easy to maintain. Take your time, do."

"And you're not forgetting your pick-me-up, I hope, and fancy, a little dog! The place won't be the same at all. I'm longing to see him, Mrs Buckley."

Connie came in with the tea tray and neatly she dispensed hospitality. Watching her movements, Elsie Buckley thought that the Ginnells might possibly win and she harboured a sneaking feeling that they deserved to do so. Geoffrey Sinclair could do worse than marry Connie, and she would keep an eye on him, too.

"Tell Mrs Buckley about the hat you gave the gipsy," Mrs Ginnell ordered, and then proceeded to tell it herself. "And whose backyard wall would it be but the Leats'! Our Connie thought Dorothy Leat gave her a queer look next time she saw her and but for Mrs Garner nobody would ever have known why. Dolly's been to see me once or twice since and we've had to laugh, but as *you* say, Mrs Buckley, a flaming coincidence."

Connie had made a very creditable batch of scones with a plain light cake to follow and handed them with confidence. Indeed, before tea had got very far, Mrs Buckley was beginning to ask herself if the Sinclairs really deserved the girl; and yet if she were aware of the ghost of a chance, Connie ought to look happier than she did. Well, if she didn't get Geoffrey Sinclair she was in a fair way to attracting something as good and possibly had every intention of so doing. She had enough intelligence to know what sort of car to be alongside in a cloud-burst!

Ernie had not returned to his mother's bedroom after taking his pillar box to his own small domain and Mrs Ginnell raised her voice more than adequately.

"Are you coming for a buttered scone, Ernie? What are you doing?"

"I'm waving to a man," answered Ernie.

"Go and see what he means, Connie. There must be somebody in the entry and we've no more velour hats to give away if anybody's begging."

"Who is it, Ernie?" asked Connie, going onto the landing.

"It's a man waving to me from Mrs Butterway's back bedroom. He's got a funny little dog with him and she's giving it biscuits."

Silence fell like a great crushing boulder in Mrs Ginnell's room so that life seemed to be extinct.

How does a man amuse himself for half an hour or so? On the Oldham Road, or at least that part of it where Sam Buckley found himself, there were no shops worth his scrutiny and over the way the chapel there was padlocked as to withstand a siege. He noticed, however, one new feature.

The 'Wayside Pulpit' was beginning to appear up and down the land. People only had time to read the headlines of the Good News. As speech and thought became more scant and jerky, following the fashion in wisecracking entertainment, people found even the shortest sermon or leading article or political argument too much of a tax, so how was the church to attract the hurried passer-by who could spare the Almighty only a grudging moment? The church hit upon the idea of having its own hoarding and bill-posting, hoping that a sample crumb of the bread of life might attract the hungry to the table d'hôte.

Often the few necessarily plain words were taken from the book of common sense and Sam paused to study the clean poster that was not yet a week old and so far had no mud-pats adhering to it, the only form of defacement that could reach its carefully placed eminence.

"This Church is one of God's lost property offices. Come and find yourself."

Sam rather appreciated that, although it did not look as if God was at the office today. It was a pity they had not built the minister's house next door or very near to the church so that strangers could easily find him for private consultation.

Supposing something had gone wrong with a man's life and he saw that notice, what could he do about it on the spur of the moment? Supposing an ordinary chap like himself had a problem . . . a very private problem . . . supposing he himself . . .

"Come on, Wispy, I've got to see that *you* don't get lost. Let us take a turn."

He put Wispy on a thin strip of leather and let him dither along by the houses and not a soul passed by but had a good look at them, the highly bred dog and the well set up man. The passers by seemed to be of the opinion that natural selection had the best of it in this case.

"I was born round here, Wispy, but don't tell the missus I mentioned it again. Round this corner. Nice corner, Wispy. You don't fancy it? Evidently you don't think any more of the district than she does. Round another nice corner and here we are in Daisy Street. Let us stroll along and see if there is a plaque to commemorate master's first seeing the light here."

They walked along the clean and empty street where there was nothing to be seen but cream-stoned window-sills and defiant lace curtains. Here was the lamp-post which had been his earliest wicket and ubiquitously, his first mast-head. The iron grids in the gutters still bore the name of the local foundry, some of the fortune from which had helped to build the chapel. That family must have given a mint. Not only money but time and energy as well, for the daughters had been Sunday School teachers and Sam's favourite wore a gold bracelet with a tiny safety chain dangling and round the bracelet was written in flowing letters, 'Mabel', and further along, 'Good Luck', all in small, even pearls. He remembered that bracelet after these many years and would have liked to buy Elsie something similar, but fancied that she would not appreciate it as much as he had. One of these days he might chance it though, for the girls of that wealthy foundry had been extremely well turned out always; in fact quite in Elsie's style and what had suited them ought to suit his wife; 'Elsie - Good Luck'.

The church and school had done some fine work in their day, but the day was declining. Alfred Sinclair was next in the line of benefactors, but he had not parted with anything like so much as the iron founders, although there were still some generous sums given. And what about himself? Not in the same street and yet well-off as present church members would account. He responded to all appeals but had never come down with a hefty lump sum. But perhaps he would. Some of the old ones used to leave the place something in their wills and he could do worse than leave his money to it when the time came. The local kids would be able to listen to the talk of honest men and kiss the right sort of girl as he had done, years ago.

Sam gave an involuntary jerk to the thin lead which quite upset Wispy's tentative equilibrium and Sam picked him up to settle his nerves and strolled on for a few yards. The street as a whole had not gone down. Paintwork was in good order and whatever the hardship of present times, the street presented a solid front and trouble did not show on the doorstep. At his old home the curtains were full length net such as his present home sported and the idea, he had been told, came from Belgium. He had better not mention that their window

337

p

furnishings had their counterpart in Daisy Street! Chorltonville would feel obliged to redress at once.

Well, when he had done with it, as the older ones used to put it, he would leave a bit to the chapel and some to the University. A verse of an old song came to mind.

"Ten men shall mow my meadow;
Ten men shall mow my meadow.
Count my rams, my ewes and lambs,
And gather my gold together."

That would be a long time off, of course, but a long time seemed to reel off very quickly nowadays. Not that it mattered much. Staying wasn't all that important. 'Elsie - Good Luck!'

"Have you lost something down there?"

A woman in a white raincoat peered down into the grid opposite the netted house and Sam hastily raised his head and lifted his hat.

"Thank you, but I used to know that family; very generous, they were. As a matter of fact this was once my home; I was born in this house here."

The woman smiled as she sized him up.

"You've travelled since then, haven't you? And you don't look so dusty! Have you come specially?"

"No, no. My wife is visiting nearby and I'm just exercising little Wispy here."

"Oh, isn't he sweet!" She came closer and touched the dog's ears lightly. "Has the place changed much?"

"I was just thinking that things looked much the same."

The woman looked at the street without much expression.

"It's a very respectable street on the whole, if rather drab. Look, if you'd care to see the house for old time's sake, I don't mind. I might find a biscuit for one of you. Is he cold?"

"No, not really, but this breed do look as if they've left their engine running."

The woman turned and let herself into the house and, murmuring a word or two of thanks, Sam entered also.

His parents' generation had been very partial to wood graining that looked as if treacle had been applied and then a comb experimentally run down it. That style of decorating had gone from Daisy Street as from elsewhere and the interior of the house was as strange to him.

"I'll tell you what I do remember," he said. "My bedroom was the little one over this kitchen and I rigged up an overhead cable with string from my window to the back window of the house opposite where another boy lived. We used to wind a little box with messages

338

and bits of things backwards and forwards. With occasional repairs that cable lasted all one summer, until my mother discovered that one tiny sweet bottle hauled in contained a flea. That put a stop to that!"

"You can go up if you like. It's only a box-room," and she led the way.

The room contained no bed but the water cistern was still there high on the wall. It used to make an awful row, especially when anybody had a bath, and ordinarily when he was in bed it still gurgled gently.

He stood at the window overlooking the diminishing scale of outbuildings sloping from the back of each house; wash house, lavatory and coal-house. He had often clambered over the roofs of their own and many of the neighbours' domestic extensions, to the resentment of any temporary occupant. He and his friends had become quite expert in finger and toe holds in their brick mountaineering days, although landlords had complained about mortar being chipped out and the necessity to re-point more often.

Perhaps that was why he was drawn to holidays in the mountains when he grew older. After he was demobbed he had scrambled up ghylls in the Lake District and up steep paths in Wales and at the summit of Snowdon he had first set eyes on Elsie.

Why do we climb mountains? Apparently we are trying to get away from people, but it may be that the real object is exactly the reverse. One is hoping to find someone, someone who is more easily recognised when the lower levels and their inhabitants have been left behind. High in the more rarefied atmosphere of the peak, the choice is narrowed and so also is the margin of error, one would suppose. That must be a kindred spirit, surely a kind spirit, breathing the same clean air!

But love is of the valley and there his carefully picked bit of edelweiss had wilted. Would he have fared better in some lucky dip in the hills? Even Rainbow had looked askance at the attempt on Everest. Innocent as she was, she knew when flowers were being placed on strange altars.

A hand touched his sleeve and Mrs Butterway was brushing away some biscuit crumbs that Wispy and she had let fall between them.

"Oh, look, that will be Mrs Ginnell's boy opposite. He gets lost for something to do now his old friend Mrs Kershaw is in hospital and his mother in bed."

They both waved to the child who shyly waved in return.

"That's where my wife is at the moment," said Sam.

"And does your wife know where *you* are at the moment?"

Sam dutifully smiled at the arch question. Perhaps it would have

339

been better if he'd not come in after all. The place was quite different.

At the top of the stairs he glanced towards the front bedroom which lay a few yards along a passage skirting the stairway. Sam's mother had been a nervous woman, frightened of lightning, cows, burglars, the dark, in the order in which they happened to occur. She always locked her bedroom door, a fact not discovered by the infant Samuel until one night when he had raced along to his parents' room after being scared by some quarrelsome shindy in the back entry.

He had been considerably shocked to find that he could not get immediate sanctuary and had thereafter planned a satisfactory line of independent action which relied on a quick dodge to the bathroom and the smooth turning of a key.

Sam now grinned a little. The knowledge had helped to make him tolerant of women's nerves. As Sybil had said, they were a different species, whose minds worked in an inconvenient and often irritating way of their own.

"Would you like to peep at the front room? Mind the step!"

"No, thank you. That was my parents' room and I hardly ever saw it."

"Just take a look. It won't be anything like your parents' room now, I feel sure."

But Sam experienced a feeling of distaste and he somehow shrank from entering once forbidden territory just because there was nothing to stop him now.

"I think Wispy is anxious to get down and I'd better not thwart him," he replied, just halting at the excuse that his wife must not be kept waiting.

Sam was glad to get out and put Wispy down on the pavement.

The street was beginning to be peopled a little with mothers and children who gave the strangers, man and dog, some curious notice, and a hawker with his tray of pins and needles stared hard as he passed. When Sam reached his car he was alarmed to see Elsie already sitting there. He had kept her waiting after all. Picking up Wispy hurriedly he opened the door and handed the dog in.

"Sorry if you've been ready to go some time, Elsie. You said about half an hour and it's just about that now. You're quite comfortable at the back?"

He felt rather put out that she had withdrawn to the rear seat and was wearing her Chorltonville face, not to say her Snowdon face. He quickly went round to the driving seat and noticed that the Ginnell's door was shut; not even Connie had stayed to see them off. Just as he was about to start, a figure appeared at the car window.

"Any use for some hooks and eyes or linen buttons, Guv?"

"No, thank you," answered Sam shortly, pressing the starter.

"Come in useful for the wife or some of your lady friends."

Sam turned angrily and then looked closely at the man, who leered back and peered in at the passenger.

"I've seen you before somewhere," said Sam concentrating.

"Just now in Daisy Street, having a word with one of my best customers. You can have this monster packet of pins for two bob."

"Before that," went on Sam, searching his memory. "Isn't your name Dutton or Hutton, and weren't you in the Pals?"

The man was considerably shaken and his right hand left the tray to make an attempt at a salute.

" 'S'truth, Sir, Captain Buckley, Sir, I didn't know you after all this time and in a soft hat. Begging your pardon for any inconvenience."

The man, who had spoken in jerks, now worked his mouth at Elsie, who looked away. Sam regarded the agitated figure for another moment and then, slipping a half-crown onto the folded pin-papers, let in the clutch and moved on.

If Elsie was pointedly silent on the journey home, for once Sam did not notice. He was silent himself. He could just remember Dutton, an ordinary man about camp, not conspicuous in any way and unlikely ever to rise from the ranks. But he was pitifully conspicuous now as a shell-shock case and probably other things. Such wrecks are profoundly pitied by men because the hale can afford to pity a man who will never cross them in love or work, whereas a woman's pity is tinged with the rue of knowing that the man is a total loss to her, unlikely ever to be husband or breadwinner. Indeed, Elsie thought it to Sam's detriment that he knew the name of such a creature.

Well, thank God he retained the use of his limbs with no road blocks from the nerve centres. And Sybil had been right; one could let one's money bestir itself in the world and do some good. Earlier this afternoon he had played with the idea that he would leave a bit to the University and to his old church 'when he had done with it'. He had by no means done with it, by golly, and he would make a lot more before he had done. The old boys in the foundry had done well for themselves and for others and there was no reason why he should not do the same. Only he had been getting rather soft lately, a trifle under the weather for some reason and there wasn't a real reason; not what other businessmen would call a reason.

Unexpectedly two or three years ago, another door, another best bedroom door so to speak, had been found locked when he sought sanctuary and one cannot take up permanent residence in the antiseptic bathroom unless it is made comfortable and interesting. That is just what we are doing, thought Sam. The whole generation seems to have rushed along the landing and found a door locked and not known how to open it; not had the sense to knock and call someone's name. Hence the growing interest in the bathroom, its use, its gadgetry, its adornment to make it appear more like the best bedroom.

"I'll call in at the office for a moment as we go through town," he said aloud but absent-mindedly without turning slightly to make sure Elsie would hear. That shop on Oxford Road was not selling as quickly as it ought, but those small premises at the top of a large block in Portland Street were much sought after. He would pop in and ask Rainbow if there was anything in the afternoon post about the dress shop. Gown shop, he supposed he should say.

He drew up in St. Peter's Square and got out, only recollecting that his wife was in the rear seat as he turned to slam the door. She had noticed the slight forgetfulness.

"I shall only be a moment or two if you don't mind waiting," he said apologetically.

"Don't hurry on my account," she replied distantly.

Sam was true to his word and soon they were on their way again in the direction of home. Neither spoke and Sam was deep in thought. After the war he had been lucky, so people said. There had been gaps in the office staff, one partner had died and Sam's promotion had been swift, his war service an asset. Later he himself had become the junior partner and within four years had found himself the sole survivor at that level. He could think of no one in the office now who was in a position to add a little capital and step into partnership, and he could do with both. Property was changing hands fast.

Upon reaching home he drove straight into the open garage as he did most evenings.

"It's because you're sitting at the back," he mumbled as he opened the rear door. Elsie brushed away his proffered hand. Twice, no, three times within the last hour or so, she had been completely forgotten. No wonder Dr Bedser had called to give a word of advice and warning.

When they got into the house he could see that something had gone wrong with the works, but perhaps she would feel better when they had eaten. Both she and the place needed warming up.

"Anyway, you've done your good deed for today," he called as he stuffed the gas poker under the coals that had died down. He wished she had banked up the fire before leaving, as the air was cold and damp, but she seemed nervous of coals dropping out. Nervousness about so many things seemed to have slowly accumulated and in a way

342

she was as much to be pitied as that poor fellow Dutton.

Elsie was busy in the kitchen so he started to lay the table, remembering to put the flowers back on the linen cloth. She was particular about flowers. On the small table by the window a few bunches of snowdrops, meek and aloof, took his gaze. Snowdrops or Snowdon? She was neither, just a pitiful, nervous woman who had 'gone over the top' and been grievously wounded. And it was all his fault. He lacked the power to warm her through and through, although perhaps the casual heartiness of a Geoffrey Sinclair could do it to a small degree.

He wandered into the lounge and switched on the fire, and as he bent down he caught sight of something unexpected in that setting; cigarette ash on the hearth. She must have had a caller earlier in the day, a careless person. She hadn't said anything about it, but then she hadn't said anything at all since they came in. He returned to the dining room where she was just then wheeling the trolley in.

"Had a caller today?"

"Oh, yes."

She returned to the kitchen and Sam opened the evening paper, his curiosity evaporating as a sizzling dish was brought to the table, but as he seated himself the question asked itself automatically.

"Anybody I know?"

Elsie's face wore an unusually stubborn expression.

"Perhaps he knows you better than I do!"

Interest between the savoury smell and what his wife was saying was by this time very unequal, but he looked at her enquiringly.

"Who was that?"

"Only Doctor Bedser."

"Oh."

Perhaps she did not wish to discuss anything the doctor said so he remained silent and took his plate with some relief.

"I notice," broke in Elsie with a harshness in her voice, "that you don't favour me with any mention of calls *you* might happen to give or receive."

She sat staring at the flowers between them and Sam felt startled and uncomfortable. He watched the steam rising from his plate. It could wait awhile.

"Oh, you mean this afternoon. Well, I'm grateful that you went this once, but once is enough. It's a mistake to put the canary among the sparrows."

"According to another of your old friends you'd been doing some visiting on your own."

Elsie was making no attempt to start eating but the steam from his own plate was abating so that now was the perfect moment to begin.

"Does this need any salt? Yes, I did walk Wispy round the corner and into Daisy Street, but I've no particular feeling for it nowadays. The whole thing was as much a bore to me as to you, and it's over. Now don't let that grow cold."

He was on the point of starting on the still hot repast when a new idea arrested his full attention.

"I've just thought of something, Elsie. You know that shop on Oxford Road? Perhaps you don't but you'll remember it when you see it. Well, it's for sale and I believe I could get it at a reasonable price. How would you like to take it on? Just as a bathroom . . . I mean just as a hobby, something to keep you occupied now the garden's a bit soggy. What do you think of it?"

He himself thought it a brilliant scheme. It was exactly the thing for her and he wouldn't be surprised if she made it pay its way!

The enthusiasm drained from his face as he heard her reply.

"Doctor Bedser warned me! But I want to know where I stand and what you've been doing. Why do you want me out of the house suddenly when I do all I can to make a beautiful and comfortable home? And think of the gardener's wages I save you! I don't understand why you've turned against me."

Sam looked at his plate. A skin was forming over it.

Elsie was working herself up into an almost violent state. He stretched his hand across the table towards her and spoke coaxingly.

"What's it all about, Elsie? Of course I don't want you to do anything you don't want to. You know me better than that. I thought the gown shop would amuse you, that's all. And what do you mean, Doctor Bedser warned you? What did he say?"

Sam looked at her anxiously.

"He just warned me," she answered wildly. "He hinted you're being unfaithful to me, and now I know."

Sam, his face red as though it had been slapped again and again, sat straight up for a moment and then rose slowly and went round the table to her.

"Don't talk like that, Elsie. It's silly and cruel. I'm sure he meant no such thing. How could he? What a terrible misunderstanding, but it can easily be cleared up. The afternoon's been too much for you after all. Now for goodness sake eat something. You're over tired and hungry."

Desperately he stirred her plate as one would try to draw a child's attention to it. She pushed his arm aside.

"Appetite! That's all men think of. Food and warmth and a welcome in Daisy Street."

"Oh, for heaven's sake!" shouted Sam at last. "Damn Daisy Street!"

It was a tone of voice that he had not used since rejoining Civvy Street years ago and it penetrated the woman's hysteria so that she stared at him and then started to sob.

"And there's the Martland girl, too. Just because I'm ill!"

Sam backed away and returned to his own chair, leaning his elbows on the table and with his hands pressed against his mouth. After a minute or so he sat up again and studied her.

"No, I don't believe you are ill," he said quietly. "Not even mentally ill. It hasn't been all plain sailing for you, I admit, and I'm sorry I've not been able to do better for you and make you happy, but at least you must have known I've always put you first. Always! You might have given me credit for that at least." He paused. "The trouble is not that you have poor health, after all. It's because you have poor vision; everything is distorted as if you'd lived in a hall of grotesque mirrors all your life."

He stood up and putting his hands in his pockets, walked round the table, while she stifled her sobs and gaped at him. He looked at her closely again.

"I thought you were over-sensitive and couldn't quite square up to the sordid details of life, such as me. You had to look at things through a screen of flowers to make them bearable."

He picked up the silver epergne with its satellites of three fluted glass flower holders that he and Elsie had chosen together at Finnegans in Deansgate on some anniversary.

"Your attitude to life is like this; people swivelling round you without getting any closer. I bet this thing in the middle says 'Keep circling, all of you, because I'm ill'. You've squinted too long through flowers, but at least I can stop that rot. No flowers by request."

He strode into the kitchen and turned the epergne upside down over the sink, flinging the empty holder on top of the broken glass and sprawling stems. He then advanced upon the snowdrops on a side table.

"I used to think you were like snow, frozen purity, but if anything did melt you, you'd only be dirty water. You pour the dishwater of your mind over everybody, over the two girls I've happened to admire, one dead and one spoken for, but that doesn't stop you. Snowdrops!"

Sam made a second journey to the kitchen and tossed the vase into the sink from the doorway, making a high pitched splintering sound as it landed on the shards of the previous casualties. He came back to the dinner table and gave it a glance as cold as the viands upon it. Not fifteen minutes ago he had thankfully seen his plate well plenished and had lowered it carefully onto the flower-painted mat, ready to do it more than justice; to do it honour. He had bowed his head over the rising vapour, but it did not look so attractive now without the aromatic haze.

"This stuff has lost all heart and soul."

Once more he made for the kitchen and dashed his plate, contents down, onto the destruction already tumbled there. Then he stood with bent head looking at the broken meats, glassware and flowers and made no further to and fro-ings but stayed where he was as if he had suddenly lost his memory or broken the mechanism of decision.

He drew a slow and querulous breath, half fearfully, such as a man might draw when at last declared free of an inherited disease.

"I've finished with all this, Elsie. Finished!"

But his face, turned from her, was grim and strained with the absorption of a man cutting out his own appendix.

Chapter Twenty-four

Most of the congregation were staying for Communion after the morning service and of the few who rose from their places to leave the church, the greater part were housewives tied to their own apron strings and to whom the Sunday joint was the solemn morning sacrifice now placed upon the hearthstone.

Flamboyance is drained out of Sunday by some people as if it were a cabbage ruined in the cooking, and what should be a love feast becomes a gourmandising, heavy with food or sleep. The women who now turned their backs on the bread and wine would partake at some other time more convenient to the sacred cow and her fatted calf, but in the meantime the gravy must be made.

It was still rather cold outside and after a handshake with Robert Garner in the porch, those going home paused to fasten up-turned collars as they left the warm chapel, which Ginnell had made very comfortable. He had been glad to put in extra time at the caretaking away from the house, and alone in the place he had dusted the pews and made the umbrella stands twinkle and the tiles shine clear so that everybody said how well he was managing without his energetic wife, who had been a lie-abed liability for longer than her temper could stretch.

Among the last to leave, hoping to evade notice, was Miriam Crumps. Even as she shook hands she avoided the minister's gaze.

"You're wanting to hurry home, Mrs Crumps, in this weather, and you have a long way to go. There's nothing else keeping you from the Lord's table? I remember you didn't stay last month."

"I haven't been sleeping well lately, Mr Garner," she answered without meeting his eyes. "In fact last night I hardly slept at all until it was nearly time to get up. That was why . . . that was why I dropped off during the sermon."

It was not a face that normally arrested the straying or the sweeping glance, but Robert was sorry that he had not noticed.

"Now, you are sure there is no other reason for not drawing up to the table?"

Miriam's lips moved and then she pressed her teeth on the lower one while the minister continued to retain her hand. After a time she looked up at him.

"I don't think I ought, under the circumstances," she murmured.

"Now, Mrs Crumps," protested Robert kindly but with pastoral firmness. "Perhaps Mr Sinclair happened to mention something to you, but . . . "

"But he hasn't," broke in Miriam. "Does *he* know, too?"

"I thought he was the only one besides myself who did," answered Robert, much surprised.

"He hasn't said a word, Mr Garner."

"Well, it isn't of the slightest importance by this time, and we agreed it was not to be mentioned. Believe me, Mrs Crumps, to all intents and purposes and in the sight of God you are just as you have considered yourself to be all these years past."

"Perhaps so," faltered Miriam, "but what am I in the sight of Mrs Ginnell?"

So that's how it was!

He got her to return to her pew where she went over in mind what the minister had said. A minor legal quibble, but the actual ceremony had been quite perfect and the church's registration had followed immediately.

What a mercy she and Edgar had no family as it would have provided a heavier stone for the Ginnells to cast. Indeed, if she had a girl like their Connie, she would have thought it a judgment! Ernest Ginnell could get on with his Communism; he had nothing to fear from her now. He was what her Psychology column called a Depressing Maniac. Free love, indeed, according to the newspapers! At least Edgar had paid his seven and sixpence *and* the organist!

Miriam, her yoke suddenly eased, decided to draw out her Divi. She was entitled to sign her name Crumps and would continue to do so, but still she would draw out the accumulation of years. Alfred would be surprised to learn of all that money mounting up, but he would advise her. Unless she thought of something herself, of course.

Only the habit of a lifetime kept Clara Martland in her seat after morning service. She had come near to leaving the chapel along with the gravy makers but Kerry might have been alarmed. Clara had told Dr Bedser that this was the opposite of a breakdown; in fact it was a rush of common sense to the head, a conversion of the intelligence. It was only the old obsolete household gods that Clara was throwing out, but if she had broken with them earlier, she would have had more time to serve better gods in better ways. And Doctor Bedser had shaken his head at her, observing that converts were notoriously misrepresentative, exaggerating the follies of the past and inflating the virtues to come. She had always enjoyed life and even the hours spent in polishing silver and wood and tricking out her little drawing room had satisfied her at the time with no sense of sacrifice.

The severity of his tone had been softened by his using her Christian name and the sigh he had given as he finished speaking.

"If you want to face facts, don't invent facts that aren't there, but remember the fact that you made your world in love."

Clara thought of all this as she automatically turned the leaves of the Communion Service. The real discontent that bites deep is not the lack of new worlds to conquer but the knowledge that one has not conquered those that were available.

Women build as the Israelites in captivity had to build, against unexpected odds, making bricks without straw, but the means will be wrestled with uncomplainingly if the end can somehow be achieved. But if the end is not achieved, then some of those unsatisfactory brickbats are flung at fate and this was Clara Martland's brick-throwing period. And what more natural target is there than a husband, who is for most women their recognisable fate? But Leonard himself had been subject to the cruel impact of brickbats from other quarters, so Clara had perforce to change her aim and she built up a barricade between herself and the act of worship now proceeding.

Why should a man such as Leonard be brought low? He was silent for most of the time, his face was thinner and his shoulders appeared to feel an east wind more than formerly. Things must get better soon, or this might be the turning point in their lives, the point where they began to go downhill - to grow older.

Clara struggled with panic. They must get over this, she and Leonard. Tears suddenly gathered in her eyes. Doctor Bedser had been right. Such happy times. All along the busy years, happy times! It was she who had turned traitor and denied them.

The choir always came into the side pews for easier summons to the Communion table and to hear more clearly the quiet reading. Sybil also would have left if her going could have been unremarked, but she stayed as usual. She felt cornered. If only her mother were not ill, (Sybil could not but think her mother's present ways part of an illness, and if only her father were not caught in this plague of unemployment that scourged the North, then with what relief would she turn from home and toil and kindred, leaving all . . . for what? For all the wrong reasons; for weariness and impatience, failure and for the sake of self. But she would stay. When a ship goes down it seems natural for the little boats to keep together, to remain at least within hailing distance. There is the hope that what could rescue one might rescue all. Her father, her mother, Kerry, Mr Buckley and many of their lifelong friends, were all at sea; something in all their lives had foundered. But she would stay. She would not row away on her own. To see the lands where corals lie!

The side pews opposite were occupied by those among the contraltos and basses also staying for Communion. Sybil did not glance across but she heard Connie's little nervous cough now and again. Connie had not gone back to Didsbury. Mr Sinclair had decided against it although Ada was wailing at the prospect of interviewing again. She would have raised no objections at all to having Connie for a daughter-in-law, especially if they all lived together. Indeed she liked her very much better than Clara's rather self-contained girl, but if Geoffrey did not really want to marry Connie, he must not run the risk of being trapped into it. Such things were not unknown!

Connie looked about her dejectedly. Really, it was hardly worth belonging to a church in these days; when the better weather came she would join a hiking club.

She caught sight of the Misses Leat, heads bent over their books, waiting. Miss Dolly had been sweet about the velour hat! Had they always been like this, unselfish and uncomplaining, or had there been a time when they too felt as she felt now, cheated and hopeless?

Mrs Lambert only half succeeded in stifling a sneeze, thus locating herself to her friends in front and it was her presence that chastened the company. The Psalmist knew what he was talking about when he deplored the fate of the widow and the fatherless, but Mrs Lambert, long widowed, had also been bereft of her only child, that well remembered Ena who had been lost to them all as soon as she had reached perfection and was drawing the eyes of all who had a view of the choir. Mrs Lambert had never seen any reason to discontinue regular attendance at church, and was of the opinion that the church would not have been instructed to pray for deliverance from evil if evil did not exist. Now her friends, hearing the sneeze, were glad that they too had stayed, feeling all the stronger for her unassuming presence.

It had turned out to be a good thing after all that Ernest Ginnell had been at home on the day of Ella's accident. He was first on the spot when suspicion arose that something was amiss next door. His wife's shouted instructions of "the back door, not the front," showed great presence of mind, else a crowd would have gathered. He hardly needed reminding of these things as his foot was already against their neighbour's kitchen door, by the lock.

Doctor Bedser had ordered Antella into Crumpsall hospital, where she was making good progress. Would it have been what is glibly called a happy release if Ella Kershaw had slipped out? It was rumoured that Alfred Sinclair thought so, at least for Tom, but Ada had not at all agreed with this opinion and so Alfred had not repeated it in the bosom of his family. Tom would be able to rest while his wife was away and get his feet in working trim again before going off to look for lodgings in Derby. Heads turned carefully towards Tom's usual place in chapel. He was staying for the Sacrament.

Some, outside the life of the church, had described Tom Kershaw's life, consisting of work at the Shop and then more work at home, as soul killing.

Soul tending is an unpredictable self employment. A man who maintains that his soul will flourish only in special soils, only in handpicked circumstances chosen by himself, may find that soul mysteriously withering season by season, whereas a man who does not put the safety of his soul absolutely uppermost and sometimes loses sight of it, so forgetful of it has he been while cherishing others whose happiness depended on him, at the end enjoys a fair prospect of finding that somewhat neglected soul of his held carefully in the hand of God.

While waiting by her mother in the pew, Kerry had been trying to lighten the interval before the minister's return by turning over the hymn book pages at the section headed 'The Lord's Supper', choosing and rejecting the likely choice. Mr Garner had a good sense of words and she guessed he would not announce that one mentioning 'For thy flesh is meat indeed'. Here she glanced up at the stained glass windows on her right where a sheep was clearly marked out by lead strips across the flank and head; leg, shoulder, thick end, à la Mrs Beeton's illustrated guide for the young cook. She hastily looked away again.

The Martland family all had tune books and she noticed that a favourite was called *Sicilian Mariners* and was a melody of that island. What a gorgeous name! *Sicilian Mariners*, she repeated lovingly as she saw sun-burnt men rocking in their fishing boats on the blue seas. *Spanish Chant* was another old tune but there was nothing of the sea in it; it brought a vision of religious processions winding slowly through hot streets, the shuffling progress delayed by embroidered vestments and the load of images.

The swinging doors at the rear of the church had ceased to creak and the minister came from the vestry and entered the Communion rail to stand before the table from which the Steward had removed the white cloth humped over the bread and the tiered rack of small individual wine glasses. To Kerry's relief, *Come Thou everlasting Spirit* was announced and her father played it through once as the congregation stood.

The hymn sung, the congregation sat and opened their copies of the Order of Service, to follow the well known and mighty words now being read, fine language to which they had been long accustomed. They needed no interpretation of the vocabulary of their faith, and its high flying strength lifted them as no earth bound images could. Brotherhood can speak with cheer, expressing its shared passions and understanding, but the deep speech of creative fatherhood implies and employs a power that can do all things well, subject neither to world nor time.

Robert Garner's voice read steadily on until he turned and knelt sideways in front of one of the heavy armchairs and his utterance dropped to a murmur as he took up a small cube of bread and in a moment or two a tiny glass of unfermented wine. Having ministered to himself, he rose and waited by the table while two Stewards moved quietly down the aisles, opening pew doors to indicate who should go forward to the Communion rail. The organ piped the strains of a far away shepherd boy watching his flock safely graze, until the semi-circle of red cushions was filled with kneeling communicants. The minister then took up the platter of bread and worked his way from one end to the other along the row of upturned palms.

"Feed on Him in your hearts by faith, with thanksgiving."

Mrs Ginnell, with well scrubbed hands had herself cut the loaf and made those little pieces after breakfast that morning. Young Ernie had munched the crusts for the sake of his teeth and any bread left over after the service would be thrown to the birds.

The congregation trusted Mrs Ginnell's goodwill and accepted the bread's wholesomeness unquestioningly. Had she been unworthy of their trust they would have suffered accordingly.

"In your hearts by faith" went the phrase over and over again as the minister moved along the line.

Returning the platter to the table, he lifted the upper tray of wine glasses and again moved along the waiting hands, deliberately placing each slender vial in the expectant fingers.

"Drink this in remembrance," he said, repeating the historic words again and again as one by one heads were raised and lowered until all had participated and the empty glasses placed in the holes pierced in the top of the rail for that purpose.

In the many mansions looking towards a green hill, people enjoy the grace and favour of both the giving and receiving of a special hospitality, and friends visiting from adjacent mansions ideally should expect to gather at the table, and the casual wayfarer also be sure of his knee-room and bread and wine. In some houses the bread is broken at need; in others it lies ready and waiting. Likewise, the wine in some company is passed from lip to lip in a loving cup, while elsewhere it is handed severally in individual vessels; but all these variants conjoin in one purpose, the symbolising of spiritual largesse to those who call.

In Hans Christian Andersen's story of the Snow Queen, an icy splinter pierced a mortal breast and numbed the freezing heart to all love and goodness. There is such another fragment of chilling forgetfulness in every human heart that can only be melted by the penetrating warmth of the Holy Spirit.

The chalice used in that farewell communal wine-taking at the Last Supper is the prototype of the loving-cup used throughout Christendom in all Communion services. The cup that once touched the lips and destinies of a chosen few is for all men everywhere, and in the necessity to reach all men and the desire to serve each several need, the Holy Grail shattered into innumerable fragments, one for every human heart and each holding within itself the ruby glow of divine compassion and companionship.

"In remembrance!"

As the lens of a burning glass concentrates the sun's rays, so at that moment of searching out and acceptance there is complete recognition between creature and creator, a culminating passionate remembrance.

"Go in peace."

After a silence, the first line of communicants rose slowly and filed back to their pews, the Stewards again went down the aisles, opening doors, the invitation conveying the assurance that a place was prepared. When the semi-circle was reformed, the minister took up the platter once more and the organ music ceased. Robert Garner paused at the beginning of the row of bent heads, but there was no movement from behind the red curtain and Leonard Martland did not climb down as was his custom, to take his place at the nearer end of the kneeling figures. The minister hesitated and after glancing towards the choir stalls he took a few paces back, then quietly mounting the shallow steps he approached the side of the organ stool.

"Mr Martland," he called in a low tone.

Leonard turned his head sharply and encountered the minister's inquiring look. He flushed and faced the open music books on the rack.

"In love and charity with your neighbours!" he reminded the minister curtly.

"That is your true nature," responded Robert, standing there waiting. Time seemed of no importance.

"I'm coming," muttered Leonard and got down.

The recital over the bread and wine was continued.

"Drink ye all of this."

Leonard swallowed his. What sort of cup was he having to drink? No work; his family all sixes and sevens, and the crippling slogan: too old at forty. Every day he saw men around him with broken springs, like himself in the middle forties. If this went on much longer their savings would dwindle. It was no use calling this a rainy day; it was a flood and not an ark in sight. Th'Irwell, as Stanley Holloway said, were fifty mile wide! As he placed his glass in its receptacle he could see from his vantage point at the tip of the curve, his wife staring at the polished floor between them. He lowered his own eyes immediately and clasped his hands on the rail.

"O Lord, in Thee have I trusted. Let me never be confounded."

Connie dodged past Mrs Crumps and got between the Misses Leat who smiled and made room for her.

Surely life had something more to offer than just wiping up after men's big feet had been trampling all over your life? But she would not try to go back to Didsbury, after all. Geoffrey did not love her but she would keep what she had got. He had been different since that night. What was his attitude? Chivalrous, that was it. He had talked to her more than he had ever done before, but there was less chaff.

Connie took the proffered bit of bread. It was very dry. Difficult to feed on with thanksgiving when you could hardly get it down. She supposed she and her two companions had all been crossed in love, as the saying is. Three of them in a row. Three of them in a row! That reminded her of something . . . of somewhere. Connie clutched the Communion rail with bare fingers, ungloved for the service. She wasn't the only one by any means. If anybody had ever been crossed in love, literally and spiritually crossed in love, it was He. Do this in remembrance! He must have known there would be plenty more coming after and in their extremity they would remember and come close. As she heard the familiar words drawing near she reached out and accepted the cup.

"O God, help me to keep up my singing whatever I feel like."

The Misses Leat, one on either side of the girl they had known from infancy, remembered their 'dear parents, John and Eliza Leat', and they also gave thanks for each other, Jennie especially remembering

Dollie's touch of rheumatism and Dollie putting up a word for Jennie's occasional fatigue at the end of the school day, for she had headaches every now and again, an aftermath of receiving a short letter towards the end of the War, enclosing a War Office telegram with the mother's request for its return.

"In His steps" and "Yes, in remembrance always", the silent words went up as the two sisters drank. Tom Kershaw was glad to be on his knees. He had been beautifying Ella's room and meant to do as much of the rest of the house as he could before she came home. No need to let the place become a disgrace just because they might have to leave it. It must be fit for her to come home to. "O God, I thought I was going to lose her!" He bowed his head and gave thanks.

Ernest Ginnell, Tom's immediate neighbour here as at home, waited for the almost noiseless steps of the minister to come into view as they worked along the row and he noticed as they came in sight that Mr Garner's boots were as highly polished as the floor. Ernest received the piece of bread and watched the boots move away to the left. He had stayed to Communion chiefly because of Mr Garner's words in the vestry that morning.

"The bread of idleness tastes rotten mouldy, Mr Garner," Ernest had said when asked how he did.

"Well, don't miss the opportunity of eating the bread of life later on, my friend. There will be others in as great a need of it as yourself, you know."

There was that about it; he wasn't alone in this mess. If you did happen to catch anybody's eye, you saw fellow feeling there. They'd all been let down. He softened the bread into a moist pellet behind his teeth. To do any good at that size it would have to be full of vitamins.

"In remembrance," the quiet words rose and fell.

Yes, those men eating that supper would have been badly let down before suppertime came round again. All that they'd worked for betrayed, not really for money but on principle, like the Carriage Shop and the Dean and Chapter.

Now the wine was being handed out and Ernest Ginnell took his. Unfermented raspberry wine it was, because of those whose undoing might lie in wait for them even here. Well, in remembrance of the real thing! He swallowed it. This raspberry wine or whatever it was, rasped on the teeth like Parish's Chemical Food. "The world is my parish". That was John Wesley, not J.C., but strangely this stuff was having a fermenting effect on his thoughts. The world parishioners must all be served alike of course, entitled to their bread and wine, but that was thought of long before Karl Marx; but people didn't remember.

"This do in remembrance."

Ernest Ginnell put the empty glass in the place appointed. At least he had the caretaking of this place and the Sunday School and had the chapel house rent free. Also his wife was on the mend.

"O God, I'd be glad if you'd do something for Tom here, and his wife, or of Thy tender mercy give us some good ideas."

Grace Garner was thinking of old friends in China. Word from them was infrequent and vague. Surely in the stronger districts there would be teachers to carry on, but would there be enough local leaven to work that great mass? Grace recited the names of companions over the years who had responded so sympathetically to the idea of the pearl of great price. May they stand firm. The thought floated inconsequentially to her mind that perhaps the Chinese vase was too vulnerable on any suburban mantel-shelf and that maybe it ought to stand enclosed somewhere. Perhaps she and Robert, or David whenever he came up, might carry down the banished cabinet from the second bedroom and place the vase in one of its rococo cupboards, like the Luck of Eden Hall raised above trifling accident if not beyond evil intent. And she would find opportunity to let Mrs Sinclair know, as it had only lately come to Grace's knowledge that the Sinclairs had bestowed the cabinet on the minister's house when they moved to Didsbury.

"O Lord, help me to water the aspidistras more carefully!"

Not peace but active hope rose within Clara Martland, effervescent as a glass of fruit salts. One word to Alfred and she was sure that he would find an opening for Leonard somewhere, or even make one. Leonard with his knowledge of figures would be an asset to any firm, not only in a great cotton business.

Why pretend, why try to hide such a disaster when it was engulfing so many? They weren't jungle animals, frightened lest a weakness should expose them to enemies.

Yet she realised Leonard would never consent to any appeal to Alfred, and with this broken engagement between the families, it was more difficult now than ever. No, she could not do anything to hurt her husband's self-esteem even with the best motives in the world. Knowing the already wounded spirit, the added slash must not come from her and they must lick the festering flesh in silence.

The effervescent fruit salts subsided, the fizz died down, leaving her cold, flat and dejected. She had cried "I thirst" and the response had been a spongeful of vinegar, a bitterness that seemed bereft of any medicinal value, gone sour like life itself and even her own memory.

She steadied herself in terror on the Communion rail. What had come over her? How could she think so treacherously in this holy place? The vinegar had not quenched His love, had not soured His view from the high cross. She lowered her head in shame and repentance and with tears crowding under her eye-lids. In all her years of church membership she had never before knelt on this spot with such a contrite heart, such a broken spirit.

Clara opened her eyes to see the minister covering the Sacraments reverently. They had done their work once more, had touched an icy splinter and again warmed a chilled spirit to life. Her heart began to revive and her memory to be restored, washed clean of falsity in this act of greater remembrance that flooded out all resentment and bitterness in its wine-red course.

She was aware of Len across the arc of the rail, still kneeling with bent head. There could be only one response for them to make, even in the desert.

"We'll praise Him for all that is past,
And trust Him for all that's to come."

Kneeling next to her mother, Kerry placed her glass carefully, thankful that she hadn't choked over a crumb or a sip. She was careful about other things as well because once, from her seat in the pew, she had seen one of the first line of participants tilt her head too far back when drinking the wine and her hat had fallen off. That had taught Kerry a lesson. She hoped she would never disgrace her family publicly, whatever happened.

Miss Cassell had said to her one day with a sigh, that she was a bit lop-sided; not structurally like the leaning tower of Pisa, but that she tended to push all the furniture of her mind along one wall. She ought to spread it out a bit; be more of an all-rounder.

"O Lord, please let me be ordinary."

Sybil was taking a firm line with herself. She must just forget him now. Forget the way his brown hair shone quiet and unruffled; forget the calm brow and the dark deft brush strokes, perfect by chance. She had been so violent that night, no wonder she had disgusted him and he would soon forget her and go far away to toil for many years among people who perhaps would not love him in return. But for her it was over now, the loving and hoping and despairing.

"This do in remembrance."

Yes, that was what happened. When she enumerated the things to forget, the serious expression, the waiting smile, the watchful courtesy, they were all more strongly remembered and the ache more difficult to hide. But he had never come again after that snowy night and for all she knew had bitterly struck camp and gone on his ambitious errand that would fill his life henceforth.

357

"But, O Lord, let him not die in the desert quite alone."

Ada and Alfred Sinclair, side by side, took up the room of at least three people with their own bulk added to by Ada's fur coat. They had taken Sacrament very devoutly. After chasing the bread round his artificial palate Alfred had be-thought him of the church finances and the new organ. It would be something of a saving if the position of organist became purely honorary after the new instrument was installed. Leonard Martland would have the pleasure at least of playing on a superior organ and the chapel funds would benefit to the tune of thirty pounds per annum.

The minister moved in front of him.

"Do this in remembrance."

"Heck!" thought Alfred suddenly. "Thirty pieces of silver. That's no good!" and he shut his mind firmly against any further ideas on the subject, remaining with bowed shoulders and his mind a pious blank. He replaced the glass absently.

"Monday tomorrow."

Ada was in some distress of spirit. In spite of lengthening hours in the bathroom, her hair had inexorably lost even the tints of a tempestuous and erratic autumn and was now unbeautifully streaked as if a man chewing tobacco had spat on it. She had noticed people's eyes straying towards it in conversation. And Connie had said, "You've got lovely hair, Mrs Sinclair. Why don't you go and have it set in St. Ann's Square for a treat? They might give you all sorts of hints." Ada had been startled. Hints! Tints! Oh dear! Ada considered that time and money spent at the hairdresser's was extravagant as against the innocence of a whole afternoon in the locked bathroom. But her hair was her life-line. While she had that to hold on to she felt safe in a changing world, so it was worth some sacrifice to keep her hair unchanging.

She drank the small token of wine with pouting perplexity. The wine of life, what was it exactly? Her mind returned comfortably and easily to Didsbury and home, but unaccountably went searching in the big sideboard cupboards for the Balm of Gilead.

"Drink ye all of this." The wine of life! But was there a corkscrew in the house?

Robert Garner had covered the remaining bread and wine with a fair white cloth and prepared to dismiss the kneeling men and women after giving them a little space to speak their hearts. All were very still and silent and the minister knew the portent of that seeming vacuum.

A great pianist's hands when in their most furious activity are nearest invisibility and only when they slacken to the tempo of mortal flesh do they again take mortal shape before our eyes. So when we crave a vision of things eternal we may be touching upon some stupendous angelic flight and only the condescension of pure grace condones the momentary limiting of the illimitable.

"Go in peace."

The minister watched them go. He knew that among such people, earning a living had never been their only way of life, but he prayed that the anxieties of the time would not crumble the fine edge of their self respect. They were fully aware that the privations of unemployment or dispersal were less destructive inwardly than the rapacity of a guilty conscience, but still he prayed fervently for them. They never complained that the irritant thorn in the flesh was more grievous than the pressure of a thorny crown, but still he yearned over them watchfully so that whatever personal harassments assailed his flock, it would not break up into so many lost and solitary sheep but remain held in the larger unity of the church triumphant.

Chapter Twenty-five

When Watch betook himself to a corner of the garden and died without fuss one Sunday, there was the question of disposal. At first Clara was going to ask Leonard to dig a grave under the front garden rhododendrons but later she decided not to bother him. Just after dinner he had drifted into the kitchen with the *Methodist Recorder*.

"You remember Stoke Poges?" he began. "We had a choir picnic there once with Mr Stormalong just after we were married, and he recited Gray's *Elegy* all through. It was very impressive, but some grumbled all the same."

For the first time in weeks their eyes met squarely and they intended to smile, but it did not come off for some reason and after a moment Leonard turned to the paper again.

"Well, they've got a Garden of Remembrance there. If anyone wants to reserve a plot or niche they write to Church Cottage which is evidently near by. It sounds rather attractive, doesn't it?"

"Very restful," agreed Clara.

No, she would not ask Len. He might blister his hands. She would send Kerry with a message to the farm.

Kerry had discovered the little dog and covered him with a sack before telling anybody. He was not old, only about nine years, and his short legs had twinkled many a gallant mile on Kerry's long rambles. And now like Herod, he was consumed of worms. He had been dosed with powder the previous afternoon and Kerry gazed at the strong, shifting parasites, uneasily winding themselves up taut as watch springs in the unfamiliar light of day. There was an old sack in the wash-house and she slowly went to find it.

Dinner was a silent meal by common consent.

It was not Sybil's day for teaching in the Primary department and she was thankful. She was glad to take herself out of the house at the earliest opportunity and although there would not be very many people about at this time of year, she avoided the direction of the sheltered Clough and instead crossed the road by the Anglican church and made her way to the new road, wide and empty, that stretched its macadam hygienic length through unpopulated fields devoid of any buildings save an occasional collection of farm sheds. Stark concrete posts threaded with stout wire bordered the road mile after mile on its desert way in preparation for a great housing scheme that at some future date would utterly reverse its present solitude. Only a few cars sped along the open road and the concrete slabs of the smooth pavements alongside were deserted as far as the eye could see.

This was City planning on a vast and progressive scale. By the time the new houses and shops were built there would be no mean cat-walks or duck-boards providing shanty town communications between them, but always the new road forging ahead along which the new materials would travel easily and at speed.

Sybil now stepped out quickly along the ringing pavement, her light footsteps amplified in the desolate scene. Far in front were the rising moorlands which she would not be able to reach that afternoon unless she intended to miss evening Service, but she had no definite thoughts on the subject as habit, even habit to the point of automation, had lost definite track in this new need for limited but essential escape. Like children tobogganing down a familiar slope and being suddenly spilled out of the old groove, she would go back to it again, but was momentarily and confusingly out of the rut.

It still felt very strange to be walking alone. For the past week or so she had fancied that people looked at her in surprise to see her by herself and she had blushed at the reminder. No Geoffrey, no trio or quartet with David and now not even a dog to whistle up. Poor old Watch!

Although she moved quickly she could not out-distance the shades of former happy excursions and, looking about her, only her boredom had any touch of novelty. She hurried as if late for an appointment and had met no one as she arrived at the flat expanse of crossroads at Victoria Avenue where the new roads intersected without a sign of recognition or interest in each other, lifeless as concrete canals.

There was just one exceptional futuristic token, the only string to remain intact in Hope's usually mishandled lyre, which struck an unexpected note in such a solitude. Set well back on the near left-hand corner of the crossroads there rose in Osymandian vacuity a red brick public house, large, gleaming with plate glass, wide porticoed, wistfully welcoming as a maiden in a moated grange, the lonely

q

'Gardener's Arms'.

Osymandian only in its isolation, not at all as a ruin, the Gardener's Arms was a monument to a time yet to come, patiently, patently waiting for customers to discover it and come to the rescue and stir it into life.

Sybil stared across at the building, like herself standing uselessly in a vacuum, only for herself there would be no more stir of awakening. The princes had come and gone, the road was empty and although she looked all ways, there was no sign. They had ridden away to other adventures, other wars.

One or two of the rarely passing cars had slowed down as they drew near the pensive figure immobile on the pavement, but receiving no sign of interest they slowly accelerated again, as if the retardation had been an optical illusion, and Sybil decided she had better move on. Even the presence of Watch would have indicated that she was walking for pleasure or at least exercise, whereas only she knew that there was no purpose at all in this restlessness but to get out of the house and then to return again in a couple of hours having satisfied herself that as far as she was concerned, the great open spaces were truly empty.

Sybil strode on hurriedly along the road that seemed to be as meaningless as her perambulation on it. Of course he knew. He could not be a fool. He had always been too clever to be deceived, as she knew of old. When he spoke he was not just blowing bubbles. The balloons came from his head, 'Thinks!' and not from his mouth, 'Says!'

Of course he knew!

He had wearied of the situation and, piqued at her show of temper, had gone away. And if he had not yet gone right away, he had kept away. But he knew! There could be no deception, and if he was waiting for a brick to be thrown through his study window with 'S.M. loves D.G.' chalked on it, he would have to wait a long time!

She also would have to wait a long time and it would not really be waiting, for the word implied some goal, some object and now there was none. Was it possible actually to die of boredom? When all curiosity and hope had gone from life, was it possible suddenly to roll over in one's tracks, beyond the reach of lure or whiplash?

She was putting one foot before the other in mechanical rhythm. Hope and curiosity were hard to kill. Supposing this approaching car were the Sinclair's Humber and Geoffrey were to see her and spring out! Sybil looked at it with misgiving and saw it race by, unknown, with relief. She had finished with making allowances. Either a man is worth while or he is not, and when the bluebird has flown, it never makes the round trip. Right up to the moment of its flight, Geoffrey had kept her love at an arrested stage, like a Japanese dwarf tree, watering it just sufficiently to keep it alive but not to make it grow.

Today, being Sunday, the distant mills were dark, but she had often seen them like so many palaces en fête. The uneventful towpaths had seemed bright and exciting as the primrose path, the canal bridge had been a Bridge of Sighs on which they lingered, and the gently climbing field paths had led to a temple of Venus and then dipped back to the Grand Canal again. But Sybil now knew that the glass palaces had only glowed for the night shift working at the mill; that the foot-bridge over the lock gates was only balustraded by an iron handrail; that the top of the windy ridge was surmounted by the stark War memorial, and the paths curved down to the Nag's Head where men noisily forgot. She had done with pretence and the bottom had fallen out of her bottom drawer at last.

There is a fakir trick of hypnotism that can make a broken vase appear whole. There was nobody to caress the back of her neck and murmur incantations any more. The pot lay in pieces and that pot was her heart.

Only a few weeks ago she would have believed it to have fallen into two aching halves, familiarity and hope on the one side and new ecstasies and despairs on the other, but the leaden pain had passed from one to add its burden to the other. When her undoubting love for her girlhood sweetheart had waned, a long chapter in her life had ended. With David gone, the book was closed.

After a few dreary miles Sybil turned her steps homeward and looked about her deliberately. She had lived for so long in a haze of happiness and then for some months in myopic misery that she had lost touch with the visible world. Now she forced herself to recognise the forgotten scene. She surveyed the wintry sky of late afternoon as it stretched palely tinted westward, a magician's shop ceiling hung with long stuffed alligators and hunched toads. Already the smudge from teatime chimneys was mounting in the distance, the quiet air unresistant as the smoke issued lazily, tentatively perpendicular for a yard or two before drifting vaguely, like the clouds, in the direction of the declining sun.

A foal, all by itself in the rough field beyond the wires, was expecting to be taken in for the night at any moment and seeing the figure on the roadway, cantered over and walked eagerly alongside, putting his head inquiringly over the fence at intervals. He had long eyelashes as thick and artificial looking as a film star's and Sybil finally paused to inspect him and show some reciprocity of interest. An artist could have drawn him with a pair of compasses, the haunches providing one of the most perfect arcs in the animal kingdom, then the barrel rising to the flying buttress of the neck, its high-held pride engentled by the inquisitive eyes.

He did not wish to be admired, like a peacock. He wanted to hear a voice and feel a series of smart slaps on his flank or have his nose stroked, so Sybil took off her gloves and pulled a tuft of grass at the foot of the post. The fare was no better or worse than that to be found in the middle of the coarse vegetation, but it was proffered with a few soft words and accepted as from an improved menu.

When she moved on the forlorn creature followed his benefactress to the limit of his domain where he was given a last bunch of grass.

"Goodbye, young Woodley," she said, stepping back from the surprisingly strong nudge of the upflung head. "I hope someone comes along for you soon."

For a few minutes she could hear his whinnying remonstrance as he watched her go. He was more reluctant to part than some people who were by no means fenced in, the acid thought intruded.

What did the landscape offer now that the appreciative foal was out of sight? Very little. Then all the more precious little, to be observed with every mark of attention. The few trees for instance. Most of them were hawthorn hedges, their black branches sharply angled and entangled as though crushed by huge hands impervious to the trees' barbed wire similitude. Here and there the taller trees stood clear above, bare and upsweeping like Old Testament candlesticks, unyielding in contour although perhaps inwardly yearning for the return of that great candle, the sun.

Cleanly cut through the unrolling fields with their ankle-twisting tussocks and gateways arbitrarily become barriers by wheel and hoof-churned mud, the road went on with Roman steadfastness of purpose. Roman and yet romantic, because such singleness of mind showed a dedication to a settled course of action from which it would not be swerved although the wasteland mocked.

That road was like David the modern churchman, driving through untilled facts and wild fable, confident that the road would be used and lead somewhere worth the journey. He was only one of many, he had said, that the ministerial training colleges were sending along these new roads. Their whole generation was moving, he had claimed exultantly.

For a visionary moment she had dreamed of being caught up with him in this new life, of being in company with other like minds on the same glad employment, even if her own part had been that of modest and barely audible cheer-leader to one. But now she would have to find her own way over this glutinous track and it must not be evident or hinted that she had bogged down or petered out on a path that led nowhere. Some day she would try to launch out on some larger ambition. The prospect of strange pastures drew her, although perhaps like the foal she had recently condoled with, she would only be getting the same sort of grass at the stumps of any frontier.

Meanwhile she was useful to the people she knew, at home, in the church, in the Hallé Choir and at the office. Yes, although her typing had shown a few absent-minded mistakes lately, she was very useful to Mr Buckley and he to her, for that matter. She would never find anyone so considerate, whatever work she chose to do.

Only once of late had he been so low in spirits that she became actually frightened for him. Sitting at his desk and looking out at the Square he had been motionless for several minutes before speaking quite loudly.

"*He* bivouacs in the open, rain or shine, and is no worse for it. It's being a prisoner that wears us away, not rough living and fresh air. Do you remember saying once there was nothing to stop me from walking out and becoming a gipsy? Well, I think I could stomach hedgehog pie better than humble pie any longer. Perhaps I could stock up a van with china and hearthrugs and set off touring the villages still off the bus routes. Some isolated housewives might be glad to see me for a change. If my salesmanship is any good I'll tell 'em it's a magic carpet, guaranteed to travel on a polished floor. I could have a thick sleeping bag and make a space for myself in the van at night and sleep sound, with nobody wanting me just when it thundered and lightened. In the empty lanes I could sing at the top of my voice, 'I have a song to sing-O' without disturbing anybody in any way. That's Jack Point's song, you know; the one he sings to Elsie . . ."

He folded his arms tightly against his chest and leaned forward to the desk with a sort of gasp.

Sybil sprang to her feet and stood beside the tall wastepaper basket between herself and her employer. She clasped her fingers and fixed him with a wide gaze.

"Go on, Mr Buckley, go on and do that! Get out and away, as I would if I could. Don't just say it and do nothing. Hire your van and collect your stuff and get off if it's only for a week or two. You can afford it easily. We can manage here as we did when you went to Iceland. There's nothing, absolutely nothing stopping you."

His look of misery did not pass altogether but another expression began to take over as he listened to the girl's outburst.

"Go on," she said again. "You're a free man! Act like one!"

He gaped at her and unfolded his arms slowly.

"I suppose you wouldn't like to come with me? You're free too. I'd take great care of you."

Sybil's hands went up to her face and she started to laugh or sob.

"I know you would. I'm sure you would. If I thought it would do either of us any good, I'd come. But we both know it would not. We should get about as far as Knutsford before one of us ran. But you go, do! At least try and find a hedgehog pie."

That was only three days ago and Mr Buckley had not been to the office since. She had told them in the outer office that he would be telephoning sometime and she managed to sound very casual as she went through, but she was anxious and mystified.

Now Sybil glanced back along the way she had covered. It was very flat. The village that voted the earth was flat had been deceived by a local illusion. This boredom is a local illusion, she told herself. It is parochial to think the world is flat. It must be visualised in the round and she must see life in the round too, with people doing all sorts of things. There was discovery and striving and mastery if one could find the right objective and only last week Mr Buckley had pointed out that she too was free. She had not considered her freedom properly. There must be some great virtue in freedom since men were willing to die for it. And women too. There had been the Suffragettes in her mother's day. They would most likely have approved with cheers the casting out of Geoffrey and David to outer darkness, as of course she was bound, or should she say free, to do so? On the other hand, those militant reformers would not have advised her to chain herself to the railings of Didsbury College. The Houses of Parliament, yes. The abode of love, no. But she could not allow herself to become the object of fisticuffs. She had refused to be clawed and fanged over!

In the Ginnell's house there was a picture that was quite enough to put anyone against such a situation. 'Two strings to her bow' showed a bouncing young woman between two sulky gallants. Well, that might satisfy a Connie, thought Sybil, increasing her pace through anger, but preserve me from that! Freedom. She would learn to love it yet.

Only, perhaps women do not so much die for Freedom, as of it!

She continued with her quickened stride in the fading light.

When she reached home in the dusk there was an acrid smell coming from the back of the house and smoke was filling the side passage. There were no lights at the front of the house, as of course her father and mother would have gone to chapel by this time, so she opened the gate hurriedly and went forward just as Jimmie Northcroft came through the side door, carrying a petrol tin.

"Hello, Jimmie," she greeted him with relief. "Whatever is it?"

"It was for Watch, Sybil. I would have buried him easily but Kerry wouldn't hear of it for some reason. She wanted him to have a Viking's funeral and this was the nearest I could manage."

"Oh Jimmie, how good of you. Poor old Watch. And you've missed evening Service to help us. We're all very grateful to you. And how's your grandfather's cold?"

"He seems fine again. Doctor Bedser says we'll have to shoot him, but it's all right talking. Who'd dare! Well, good-night, Sybil. She's still in the back garden but there'll only be a bit of wood left burning now. I'll put these things in the van."

After waving him off, Sybil went round by the passage quietly. The smoke came in slow gusts and there was not much to see in the deepening twilight.

Kerry was standing well back, her hands thrust in the pockets of her dark school macintosh, gazing at the dull centre of the dying fire. Occasionally she nodded her head very slightly.

This was the best way of dealing with death; wipe it out and leave no trace. Commemorate life, but not death.

She had left Watch's collar on and Jimmie had wrapped the sackcloth closely round before carrying him out. The collar with its protective brass studs and his personal rug were in lieu of the ornaments, weapons and other properties that the ancient world would in courtesy have sent to accompany the austere departed.

There was a lot to be said for departure, thought Kerry, crinkling up her cold toes and stretching them again in an absent-minded effort to warm them.

Insect life saw more departures than did higher animal life; more complete changes. Insect life accepted so many more staggering metamorphoses, that death was only yet another, hardly more surprising than those experienced before.

Animal life was not so volatile and therefore much more impressed with its one dramatic change after the slow and almost imperceptible preparation of the years.

During the last hour Jimmie had been very helpful. He had brought wood and petrol from the farm and every now and again he sent her into the house or across to the van for something he needed. She knew that he wanted her out of the way at such moments and since he was so considerate she did as she was told and did not hurry back again inquisitively.

"Leave things to me, Kerry. I've always had to do with animals and such."

"I think the animals on your farm are very lucky, Jimmie."

"Do you really?" He seemed pleased. "I like to think that our beasts wouldn't turn and kill us, given the chance, and that they somehow connect us with food and whatever comfort they get."

"Do you think, Jimmie, that animals," here she inclined her head towards the well lit fire, "go on? You know, as we're supposed to do?"

"Well, I should say if *we* do, they do. I don't see where anybody could draw the line. And a green pasture would look incomplete to me without a good herd of cows in it."

He looked down at her to see how she took his remarks and she in her turn seemed gratified.

"I'm so glad to hear you say so, Jimmie. Perhaps some day you'll be a local preacher like your grandfather. I bet you'd be good. Anyway, whatever the universal system is, it must be a very intricate one, everybody and everything being in it. It's an overall affair, I think."

"I've never really studied the actual system, Kerry, as you seem to have done, but I do think that anybody who talked of sheep as much as *He* did, wasn't going to drop them out of sight and out of mind altogether, if you see what I mean."

Kerry was then requested to stand away where sparks would not reach her while Jimmie gathered the falling brands together, standing with his back to her, silhouetted against the glow which made the late afternoon sky look prematurely dark. She turned her face where the last light was sinking and the tender day being led, yet another bride of a tyrant Sultan, doomed into the palace of night.

Yet not doomed beyond the morrow. At some point the doom fell away as palace, sultan and bride went forward. But where the system drew the line, as Jimmie put it, was hard to imagine. Perhaps there was no line after all.

The Greeks did not know everything by any means, but at least they credited everything with having a soul, a spirit. Even inanimate objects which form environment had it, a celestial scenery, so that the soul of man might be accompanied by the familiar spirit of the climate that had contributed to his life.

What was that her father had once told about some silken goods that their firm had shipped to Portugal? The voyage had encountered storms and the cargo, tightly stowed, had been battened down. Even so, the heavy seas had penetrated the hold and when the silks had been unrolled at their destination, they had been changed from plain to that dazzled pattern known as 'watered silk'; not what had been ordered by the customer, but astonishingly beautiful.

Perhaps that is what happens to us all. Life comes down with pressures that we would never dream of ordering and when we are released we have a new pattern, a unique pattern all our own, personal as fingerprints. And being watered silk was an improvement upon being a minor scale!

A few stars were now pricking here and there overhead and the last of the sun could be stared at as through smoked glass during an eclipse. There are about forty million stellar universes, Kerry had been reading in the *Guardian*. It sounded an awful lot, but doubtless there would be time to match. So long as there was anything to see there would be time to see it, and so long as there was time there was a happening! Perhaps time and space were identical twins and we sometimes confused the two. Perhaps they were really the same thing.

So although life had its dull stretches, such as the present time, one could look forward to some quite alarming excitement under that very special overall system.

Jimmie turned from the fire and leaned a long-handled rake against the wall.

"There's just a bit of wood left now, Kerry. It'll soon die down. Now please don't touch it after I've gone and I'll come and put some of the ash on your front garden in the morning. It'll be good for the soil. I only wish you'd gone to Chapel this evening."

"No, Jimmie, I'm more satisfied now. And I've thought of another thing, standing here. I've decided that it is quite natural to believe in For Ever; but I can't quite believe in Never!"

"I expect you're right, Kerry. Grandfather does most of his thinking when he seems to be just standing about."

So when Sybil had seen Jimmie drive off in the van with his implements and had gone round to the back of the house and found Kerry watching the smoke rising and swirling half-heartedly, she went over and stood by her without speaking for a little time. Then Kerry seemed to rouse herself and her shoulders went back as she took a deep breath.

"Well, so much for the worm that dieth not! Though strange to say, they too have their rights."

Smoke billowed spasmodically in a passing breeze and some boards that had slithered to the edge of the fire glowed fitfully as though swarming with fiery maggots. Sybil touched her sister's elbow gently.

"I've just had a word with Jimmie. He's very understanding, isn't he?"

"Yes, he is," replied Kerry in a suddenly sprightly tone. "He's quite wonderful really. I know he's very practical, being a farmer, but I was surprised at some of the things he said."

"Oh!" exclaimed Sybil, a little taken aback. "What sort of things?"

"Oh, we were just talking, but he said one or two very helpful things."

"I'm very glad," murmured Sybil, realising that no further explanations were forthcoming. Kerry seemed to have emerged from the sombre atmosphere of the afternoon's work and had started to whistle *Home in Pasadena* in a soft undertone, Really, one could hardly keep pace with her moods.

"I say, Sybil, have you ever noticed Jimmie's hair? I've never seen such thick hair on anyone. It must grow furiously, like mustard and cress on flannel."

"Ah! Perhaps Samson has taught him a thing or two."

"And another thing, Sybil. I've been looking at the stars just now. Crowds of them. If I wanted to bother, I could count them or at least make a start. But if they all put their gaseous heads together, they couldn't count me, not even me by myself. The nincompoops couldn't even make a start. I feel immensely cheered."

"Come on, Kerry, let's go in and have our tea now, it's getting chilly. Then we can have a long, comfortable evening together."

Strangely, Sybil felt that she meant it.

"Yes," came a hearty agreement. "Let's poke up the fire and have crumpets. And I say, you know that funny story about God loves you and you can sit on your hands? Well, it's true!"

"Let's hope you're right." Sybil's voice had an uncertain catch in it.

She gave her sister's shoulder a quick pressure and moved away, opening the door into the kitchen and switching on the light.

"And afterwards, if you'll play, Kerry, I'll sing."

It was going to be difficult and the choice would be hard, too. Nothing about love or roses according to Kerry's stern decree. Even *Wayfarer's Night Song* went soft at the end, she had complained.

Not that Sybil herself wanted to raise her voice in praise of love or gifts of flowers, but there was rather a dearth of subject matter. *The lands where corals lie*? She could not, yet.

"Right, Sybil," called Kerry above the noise of filling the kettle at the sink. "It's a long time since we sang a duet. Let's try *The Two Grenadiers*, shall we?"

Chapter Twenty-six

Elsie Buckley was so very thankful to see Mrs Ginnell that she broke down and wept as soon as she opened the door. Mrs Ginnell bustled into the kitchen. How was Sam? Mr Buckley she meant, of course. How was he? Just the same; very poorly. Dr Bedser was coming again in the late afternoon. Sam had caught the most terrible chill the other night. She did not know how . . . he hadn't said anything. T't, t't. That wasn't like Sam, Mr Buckley at all. Elsie flopped down hopelessly.

"Oh, Mrs Ginnell, I'm absolutely sick of myself!"

Mrs Ginnell came near.

"If you're going to have a rest, rest properly on the settee, not on that silly stool. I don't suppose you've had much sleep. If Sam goes into hospital you must get Doctor Bedser to give you some sleeping pills."

"Oh, I've got some already."

"You have?"

"Yes, but they're not much good. I've had them ages."

She trailed into the dining room and in a few minutes Mrs Ginnell approached with a cup of creamy coffee.

"Just you sip this, my dear. Mrs Buckley I should say. When we're sick of ourselves it's a good idea to forget ourselves for a time."

"But I'm sick with worry."

"We must trust in God."

Elsie's head jerked up in irritation.

"Don't talk like that, for pity's sake! Whoever made this world, if anyone did, made an absolute mess of it. Ask anybody!"

"Mrs Buckley, you shouldn't talk like that. It may be a flaming wicked world, as *you* say, but its maker died for his creation, which is more than some people would do. Some folks wouldn't dream of risking their lives or even their comfort for their creation, so I've heard."

Elsie was startled into politeness.

"You've known Sam a long time, haven't you Mrs Ginnell? Would you mind going and having a look at him and telling me what you think? I've tried to get his pills down, but couldn't."

He had gone out the other night without his overcoat. And why? Because he had rushed out, not staying even to snatch at a hat or scarf.

(Elsie put down the half-empty cup on the floor.)

He had run from her as if she had the plague! No, that was wronging him again; if she'd had the plague he would have stayed to help. He had run because she was herself the plague. That was it.

"O, weary wives."

The lines persisted in her head although she rubbed it to and fro on the cushion to rub them out.

When he had come back to the house later he had not spoken until she went to put the kettle on and he brusquely told her not to bother about him; he would mix himself something to fend off a cold. He felt chilly.

The cold had not been fended off. The next morning found him flushed and restless. He subsisted on liquids all day but towards evening he was obviously light-headed. He spoke of driving along country lanes and finally he had asked her brightly if she could do with a magic carpet; he had a wide selection in the van.

She had been biting her nails with fright when she telephoned Dr Bedser, who barked that he would come at once.

"Anything on your husband's mind, Mrs Buckley?" he had asked after the examination. "He's not said anything about business, money or trouble of any kind?"

She had confessed that Sam did not worry her with his business affairs.

"Well, he should then! Any wife worth her salt should at least ask if her husband has had a good day. This looks as if he's been having a run of the reverse. Any relatives near to give you a hand?"

Elsie had shaken her head.

"Any friends then? Even if they're not very intimate friends, it's surprising how they come forward in a crisis."

At that word her eyes had widened in terror and Dr Bedser changed his manner.

"I think our good friend Mrs Ginnell has recovered from her strained ligaments sufficiently to help you. I'll get her, but if you want me urgently, don't hesitate to telephone."

The possibility was a solemn warning.

Last night she had slept on the ottoman in Sam's room, although it had not even been the attitude of sleep for long hours as she lay propped on her elbow listening to his heavy breathing and the tumbled words. At intervals he would exclaim "Carry on", and sometimes he would rouse from sleep and mumble the words quickly so that it sounded like "Carrion!"

"O, weary wives."

Elsie now heard Mrs Ginnell coming downstairs and into the dining room. She looked awe-stricken.

"I don't like the look of things a bit, as *you* say! His breathing's awful. I'll just take him something to ease it. Some of the simple old remedies still work."

Elsie heard her fill the kettle and then return to speak to her nervously.

"Go and lie on your bed while I'm down here, Mrs Buckley. You'd be nearer if he . . . called or anything. And look at that little Wispy there; he's trembling something terrible. You'd better take him with you. He'll be an expensive dog, too."

"I can't be bothered."

But Mrs Ginnell brought the tiny animal for Elsie to warm and she took him listlessly.

"It's no good taking on man or beast if you can't be bothered," said Mrs Ginnell and returned to the kitchen while the woman on the settee shivered with the scrap of life on her lap.

He had been neglected in his box for hours on end over the last two days. She had fed him and opened the door into the garden, but had hardly spoken; certainly she had not given him one caress. He was Sam's gift and he'd had the same treatment that she meted out to Sam.

"O, weary wives."

She dragged herself up to her own room and, switching on the fire to full strength, kicked off her shoes and lay on the bed with the eiderdown over herself and Wispy. She heard Mrs Ginnell go into Sam's room. Both doors were open but Elsie could only hear a low murmuring, sometimes Sam's voice, sometimes Mrs Ginnell's talking as she would to a sick child.

Wispy fell asleep and about half an hour later Mrs Ginnell came on to the landing and after a moment's hesitation, stepped into the guest room doorway. She had heard a moan from within and the thought came to her that perhaps she was going to have two invalids on her hands. She was not very familiar with this room as Mrs Buckley seemed to prefer doing it herself. She stood quietly looking towards the figure on the bed and pondering the situation when the woman opened her eyes.

"Sit down in here for a moment if you can, Mrs Ginnell, I just can't settle. Do you think you could stay overnight for a day or two until things get a little better?"

"Yes, I think they could manage while our Connie's at home."

She gulped and hurried on. "I'd be glad to do anything that will help Sam . . . and you as well, of course."

A deep sigh came from the bed.

"It's funny how everybody likes Sam and nobody likes me, Mrs Ginnell."

"Oh, I wouldn't say that, Mrs Buckley."

"No, but you'd think it. You couldn't help."

Elsie reached out and took up a framed photograph from the bedside table and Mrs Ginnell gave her a puzzled look. Fancy having a photograph of yourself in your bedroom and nobody else! She almost laughed.

"D'you see this, Mrs Ginnell? That was taken at the tennis club at home years ago. I keep it there to remind myself that I'm the same person."

"But you wouldn't expect to look just the same as you did when a young girl, with not a care in the world. I'm sure you've got nothing to grumble at as far as appearance goes, for a married woman."

Elsie stirred impatiently.

"But who would have thought the girl there would be reduced to this? Miserable health, nerves all wrong! It's not fair! Life's a terrible injustice and I don't know how some people keep going."

Mrs Ginnell replaced the photograph and sat down on a chair near the fire. What a sad house it was.

"Were you very fond of the tennis club?"

"Oh yes, I had a lovely time, especially on Sundays. Not everybody played then so a group of us had it all to ourselves."

"Have you kept in touch with any of them?"

"No. Some used to send Christmas cards but they dropped off. I've not heard anything from them for a long time now and I've never been back."

"A pity to lose touch when you had so much in common," said Mrs Ginnell with private sarcasm, "but you joined another club surely, on this side of Manchester?"

"Yes, but not for long. You know what happened, I think, and my health gave way. Everything has changed now."

The voice sounded very weary.

"But," answered Mrs Ginnell, stung into giving her personal

opinion, "marriage and your own home's a mighty big improvement on any tennis club!"

"But everything has gone wrong, Mrs Ginnell. Nothing is as it should be." The head moved uneasily on the crooked elbow resting on the pillow and Wispy snuggled deeper under the eiderdown where vibrations were less disturbing. There was silence for a time and then Mrs Ginnell looked guardedly across.

"If you don't mind my asking, Mrs Buckley, was anything ever said after your disappointment about it being a boy or a girl?"

"No, indeed. I didn't want to know anything about the whole miserable business. I was content to forget the episode entirely."

Elsie Buckley thumped her pillow and put her head down again without much expectancy of comfort, while Mrs Ginnell regarded her with surprise.

"You don't seem to have managed it, I must say. I can't help but think, Mrs Buckley, it would have been better to face misfortune, yours and your husband's, and get over it together in time. It wouldn't have hurt so much as this, feeling you're the only one let down."

The other looked at her broodingly but made no reply and after a pause, Mrs Ginnell spoke again quietly.

"I once lost a little one at birth."

"Did you really?" The tone showed genuine interest. "Were you very sorry? I mean, you've had others to take your mind off it."

"It's many years ago now and of course being so busy with the others, as *you* say, I never had much time to grieve over it. There was no funeral or anything; they said it wasn't properly finished. But to this day, if I'm just waiting, perhaps for a kettle to boil or for a second table at Communion, I think about that little thing. I just think of him. I'd never been able to do anything for him, not even bath him just once, and this is the least and the most I can do. I just sit and think of him for a few minutes."

The room was very quiet and soon Mrs Ginnell gently be-stirred herself and went into the front bedroom and then downstairs, leaving both doors ajar. Elsie got up slowly, pulling the eiderdown over Wispy, and went on to the landing and then, stealthily pushing the door, stole in and approached the bed.

She had never seen anybody so ill and she quailed at the sight. It was not like Sam to be helpless; a victim. He always made an effort to master the situation and tried to laugh away awkwardness. It was very different now.

Now he was making a tremendous effort to breathe. The one bodily function that is taken so much for granted, the most elementary sign of life shared with the humblest creature, the unthinking drawing of breath, was now for Sam a labour of Hercules. It was the utmost stress, an Olympian athletic feat, a crowning ambitious exhibition of manly talent against terrible competition. It was a desperate wager against fantastic odds; just Sam struggling to breathe! Could that sound be a man's lungs filling with common, necessary, all-pervading air? Could anything that drew breath find it so impossible?

She withdrew furtively and went in search of Mrs Ginnell in the kitchen.

"It must be time for his pills but I'm sure he won't be able to swallow them."

"I'll get them down," came the decided response. "I'll crush them in milk as we have to do for children sometimes."

Elsie winced.

"I'm no help to anybody, am I?"

They went back to the sickroom and she sat tiredly in a chair while Mrs Ginnell busied herself very efficiently for several minutes.

"Stay in here," Elsie pleaded when the other made as if to depart. "He seems easier than he was."

"I'll just drop these things in the bathroom and then return."

The two women sat watching the electric fire throwing its machine-made shadows from artificially pulsating coals that never needed refuelling or riddling out and whose scenic caverns and cliffs never varied but gathered a faint volcanic dust over the years, only noticeable when the current was turned off.

Elsie Buckley glanced up nervously.

"Am I interrupting your thoughts, Mrs Ginnell?"

"That's all right, my dear. Mrs Buckley I should say."

"You've had a very happy married life, haven't you? In spite of not having much . . . in spite of setbacks of various kinds."

"Well, yes, I suppose I might say I have on the whole," admitted the other grudgingly, not wanting to boast. "Not that there haven't been times when I've felt like leaving him to catch his own fleas, as *you* say. But he's been a good husband to me even if he does look in at the Whip now and again; although to hear Miriam Crumps talk you'd think he was as shaky as old Pins and Needles himself. That's a chap who comes round our way. Shell shocked. Anyway, you can't call Miriam normal herself. Her veins run dolly-blue! But I wanted Ernest Ginnell and I got him and I paid the full price, which is more than a lot of people will do today."

"Were you rather young?"

"Yes, we married young then when boys started saving as soon as they began to earn. Someone said at the time, they didn't know what I'd do without my mother behind me. Well, things were queer at times, like the oven being stubborn or the boiler smoking like a fiend and smuts all over the place. I remembered those early days again when that queer looking Mr Gandhi said 'Give us chaos.' I knew what he meant."

Mrs Ginnell nodded at her own words, understandingly.

"And you've always been connected with the chapel on Oldham Road?"

"Always, and my father and mother before me. Up the left aisle to be married and up the right aisle bringing the children to be christened. Our family's done as much as most folks to wear out the vestry carpet. My mother sent us to Sunday School as soon as we could stand. Oh, but we had some fine men and women who weren't too high and mighty to stay round Oldham Road even when business had turned out well; and they came without fail every Sunday to teach us kids. Your Sam would have made a Superintendent as good as the best of them if he'd stayed on that side of town. It was a lively place and Monday was a big come-down after Sunday then. The one thing we were never allowed to do was to moon about. Some *did* go wrong, but they never drifted that way; they had to be mighty sure they wanted to paddle their canoe that way. You'll know Clara Martland, Clara Crossley that was? Of course, their Sybil works for Sam, Mr Buckley I should say. Well, her grandfather was one of the Superintendents of the Sunday School many years ago and I've heard my husband tell how old Mr Crossley called at their house to congratulate him on his twenty-first birthday. He was on the doorstep before six o'clock to catch him. A pity so many of the old customs are going out. Nothing so good comes in. Now there's one I've not seen for many years and it's gone right out now. There used to be a really sweet girl in the choir called Ena as I remember. She died when she was about twenty of . . . oh dear me! Yes, I've forgotten what it was exactly. Anyway, the night afterwards, all the choir and many of the congregation assembled outside their house to sing hymns, and people came to their front doors to listen and show respect, of course with their hats and coats on or they might have got their deaths of cold too. But that was how the street showed sympathy. They don't do that sort of thing nowadays, more's the pity. You're supposed not to notice there's anything amiss."

Mrs Ginnell paused in her talk and Elsie Buckley, rather sinking in her chair, glanced towards the bed and away again.

"Was this Ena a very pretty girl?"

"Indeed she was, something after the style of Sybil Martland, you

377

know; still waters that can drown, the kind of young woman who when she breaks a heart, breaks it for good."

"What was there about her that people remember?"

"I think it must have been that they felt better in health when they were near her and they wilted a little when they separated. I think she would have done well. She was open in her ways. She would join in the kissing games at the parties, but she was never one of those who went missing with the boys as one or two of the others did, although you'd never guess it of any of 'em if you saw them now," finished Mrs Ginnell with a short laugh.

Elsie sighed.

"Your parties seemed to know when to start and when to stop. I never liked things that go too far."

"It was like keeping a fire in but never letting it burn the place down. But don't think it was all parties at that place. We had to raise money, and at some of the big bazaars the stuff was so valuable that the men used to stay on watch all night. They didn't mind that at all when the billiards table was installed after a previous bazaar, and always there was a good hot-pot served just after midnight and then an early breakfast. Of course if you want quick money you can't beat a Jumble Sale. The youngsters love them. It was always a lark to be on the Flat Iron stall with the white elephants; Panama hats, old clocks, worn parasols and pipe racks that had belonged to someone's uncle who had passed on. Of course the mainstay of the Jumble Sale is the cheap outgrown clothes, particularly children's. Women from streets around used to queue for doors opening, an hour before time, knowing that at our school everything had been gone over, washed and ironed, buttons put on and tapes stitched. There were times, Mrs Buckley, when I could have done with some of those well mended clothes myself and I've known Clara Martland put by some beautifully darned vests for me privately. "Go on, Emma," she used to say, "I know where these have come from;" but I wouldn't, although as *you* say, Mrs. Buckley, people who have no children don't know the meaning of the word poverty; or wealth either for that matter. But I always say that servers mustn't take advantage of pickings and however hard the times have been over the years, I've always managed to *give* something to the Jumble Sale."

Mrs Ginnell ruminated awhile.

"And now all's to do again for the new organ, bless me. Still, if Mr Garner's set on it, let him have it, I say. He doesn't make such wild suggestions as Mrs does. They've only been here since September and already some are dead against her. Although some of ours need a pinch of gunpowder, I think she went too far about missionaries letting their converts in very hot countries keep all their wives. Mr Ginnell was shocked, I'm glad to say, though not so much at the idea itself as its coming from her. He's used to that sort of talk among the Reds at the Carriage Shop where some of them wouldn't want to keep it just in hot climates, but he couldn't get over a minister's wife saying it. Anyway, we don't want it here, whoever says it."

She got up and softly approached the bed again while Elsie Buckley stared at the revolving spokes of shadow from the electric fire.

Sam seemed to have fallen into a quieter spell of sleep and she listened intently, too much afraid to turn her head before a sidelong look at Mrs Ginnell's figure assured her that she might venture. He looked very red, not white as she had feared.

"O, weary wives!"

Mrs Ginnell came and went and then told Elsie to go downstairs and have something to eat; she had found enough in the larder to keep body and soul together for today. Elsie shuddered but after further persuasion she went slowly from the room, fetching Wispy and again pausing at the door.

"What about you?"

Mrs Ginnell laid a private bet that Mrs Buckley had not asked that question many times in her life, but she only said she would soon get something for herself.

Elsie now stared at the dining room fire, lit by Mrs Ginnell and now burning vigorously. She could not eat.

There were other things that Dr Bedser had said that she desperately pushed from her mind, not to be admitted. "I have that most difficult of patients to deal with; a man who has no incentive to go on, no fight left in him." And again, "Unfortunately, there is a type of woman who once she gets a man down, cannot refrain from kicking him." Dr Bedser had not looked at her as he uttered these words, walking up and down Sam's bedroom with impatient steps, but they had fallen upon her like bludgeon strokes, knocking her nearly senseless. Alone in the dining room now with no other voices to shield her, the contusions agonised her consciousness.

She had killed Sam. She had slowly done him to death.

She groped to her feet and weakly made her way out and upstairs again into her own room. Where had she left her handbag, up or down? Her face puckered with tearfulness. Ah, here it was. She impatiently tipped the contents on to the eiderdown and picked up the key to a small bureau which she now opened eagerly, quickly shaking several little white packets lying in a pigeon hole all to themselves. The sharp rattling sound seemed to give her satisfaction. Plenty! More than enough.

Mrs Ginnell appeared in the doorway.

"Now you've not had time to eat anything, I know."

"Never mind. It doesn't matter. Mrs Ginnell, do you agree that people should be shot for cowardice?"

"Now that's a big thing to decide," the other answered as she slowly advanced into the room.

"I mean men at war, you know. People who let the enemy in, or are traitors to their homeland, or who run away. Shouldn't they be shot?"

"I suppose it has to be done if they are a danger to other people's lives, but why bother about that now? You should be trying to keep up your strength to nurse Sam."

"I've been a danger to him. I ought to be shot."

"Now, Mrs Buckley, it's not pills you're wanting to keep you going, it's proper food."

She was now standing close to the open bureau and peering at the collection on the shelves within.

"These things are not for playing about with, Mrs Buckley. They're not tennis balls; they're dangerous."

She looked searchingly at the restless woman.

"Mrs Ginnell, have you ever been frightened, been terribly afraid?"

"Of course, lots of times. I know how you feel, but he'll be all right in a few days."

"I mean frightened for yourself; trembling with fear of something."

"Now, let's see. Not since I was a youngster that I can call to mind exactly, but there's sure to have been something, only I've forgotten. Let's shut this flap and keep the dust out."

"That's what's wrong with me, Mrs Ginnell. I can't forget. Oh, if only I could die and leave Sam in peace, I owe him that much. He deserves it. He's really a saint, you know. He's always done the right thing and said the kind word, but now he's past doing any more for me. I've heard him talking."

"Sit down for a minute in this chair. Of course he's only wandering in mind, poor man. He's wandering all over the place, perhaps back to his earliest days."

"And I've sent him wandering, anywhere now to get away from me, and he'll never come back."

"Now don't talk like that. Sam's always done the right thing, as *you* say."

"But *I* haven't. It's my fault. Oh, Mrs Ginnell." The sobs were so strong that in pity the standing woman began to stroke the hands clinging to the Lloyd Loom sides of the chair. "I've never told anyone, not a soul, but in that nursing home; you know when, they put a pillow over my face! They said I was disturbing others! They held it down! I can't forget it. I'd been alone for ages first and kept ringing and nobody came, and finally when they did come . . . They've smothered my life. They've smothered my love. I can't forget it. I can't forgive them. And poor Sam!"

She pressed her head against Mrs Ginnell's waist while compassionate arms went round her even as the indignant voice broke above her head.

"Oh, you poor girl, my dear girl! Now, now. Oh, the flaming fools. I'd a good mind to go round and tell them so this minute but I expect they've left. But why didn't you tell Sam? Why didn't you tell the doctor? Such people need a telling off and both your husband and Doctor Bedser could let it rip if stirred. Oh, I wish I'd known. I wish anybody had known, because talking about it would have eased your mind and helped you to forget."

"Nothing could make me forget!"

"You're wrong there. Talking wears it down and soon it would have been dead and buried and not just dead and won't lie down as the song says. Now, don't start again. You're shaking with weakness I should think."

"Mrs Ginnell, do you remember last Shrove Tuesday, and how it rained? On my way home I went into that church near the University, the Holy Name, to shelter for a time. Then when I was coming away I turned round and by the light of all those candles I saw the figure on a large crucifix with its face turned towards the door and something in the expression reminded me of Sam. I keep thinking of it."

"Better to remember that than those other things. Much better to remember that."

When Elsie Buckley seemed calmer in mind and body she also showed signs of such utter fatigue that Mrs Ginnell spoke with dictatorial persuasion.

"You really must eat something nourishing or you'll make yourself ill and we've both got some busy days ahead. Just you hold Wispy here while I take a peep at Sam first."

In a minute or two she was back again, on tiptoe.

"He's opened his eyes."

She helped Elsie to her feet and led the way to Sam's bedside, still holding her by the hand.

Elsie came timidly forward. Yes, the eyes were open but that was all that could be said in favour of them. She tried to focus herself in the untaught gaze that had no recognition or heed. Putting her hands on the edge of the bed and leaning over carefully so as not to startle a patient whose thoughts might be out on their own somewhere in unknown territory, she called him very softly.

"Sam! Sam dear." Not for a long time had she looked so gentle, so eager and so young, unaware of the tears falling on the sheet.

Slowly Sam's eyes came to rest on the face above his own. After a while the cracked lips moved and after another painful minute a throaty whisper came through.

"Hello, Ena."

A darker flush, brick red, such as rises suddenly on the heads of infants now overspread his features.

"Don't cry."

A look of distress came into the eyes and then the face softened at a tender recollection, bringing its attenuated shadow of long ago regrets.

"Remember the broken nest?"

Chapter Twenty-seven

Robert Garner had been on the way for an hour and the journey had not been very enlivening in the steamy windowed tram and bus. At first he had taken a more leisurely look at the *Manchester Guardian* and then swept it in windscreen wiper fashion to clear his view of the street scene. Passing his own church he saw that Ernest Ginnell was taking advantage of the soaking that the poster board was getting to tear off the old Wayside Pulpit notice in long stalactic strips.

Ginnell was a willing horse and earned the small caretaking wage and rent free house, even if some of the earnings went in leading the horse willingly to drink, but there would not be enough to live on now that the Carriage Shop was closing down.

As for Tom Kershaw, it was out of the question that he could be transferred to Derby. That had been turned down flat. The dole was an ugly word but was now in everybody's mouth, being discussed, criticised, joked about and sung about, and it kept those mouths from an uglier word; starvation.

Past Butler Street a large church had gone beyond the Wayside Pulpit stage and had closed its doors behind its last congregation. It was no use being sentimental about redundancy if the population was stretching out its arms to garden suburbs.

From the bus taking him on the second part of his journey he saw an experiment in letting the dead past bury its dead somewhat prematurely in favour of the future. The great church of All Saints, a huge edifice, had its surrounding graveyard flattened and flagged over to provide a playground for children amid the city streets. The children, it was hoped, would revere the generous thought and eventually take an interest in the beneficent building and some day be moved by gratitude to help towards its maintenance and life. In spite of strong wire mesh over the ornate windows, the stained glass was henceforth perseveringly and persistently smashed and the expense of wilful destruction rose continually to embarrass the faithful who in time, saddened at the needless desecration of their forbears' monuments within and without and harassed by the growing burden of debt, left the place that had sheltered their worship for so long and retired wistfully to new ground. The church building having severed its connection with the past and levelled its honoured memorials to accommodate the future, now found itself completely exposed to the aim of unbelievers and within a short time died a martyr's death.

Now, instead of a Wayside Pulpit there were huge posters flanking the main doors, advertising brands of paint, great drums of which were stored inside and were also stacked on waiting lorries to be delivered to businesses in and around the city. Heavy lorries were turning and backing in the old graveyard all day long, so there were large notices displayed at the exits and entrances. Danger! Children keep out! No games allowed here!

Robert Garner's lips were pressed in a grim smile as he craned his neck round at this sight. If his own chapel on Oldham Road was in exterior a decent body doing her valiant best, then this church now in view had been very much the grand dame, with a good income and a regular stream of fashionable callers. The upkeep had been enormous and when the carriages ceased to roll up, the children in their motor cars could think of other objects on which to spend their money.

The children not in motor cars had made short work of it. The neighbourhood that had produced this solid building was itself crumbling, the pedimented doorways and well proportioned windows of the houses in the square now looked into blistered halls and un-pretentious offices, so that the noble church became as useless, as irritating and as unloved as an aristocrat halting her carriage in a revolutionary alley.

Let us see, thought Robert, what the suburbs on this side of Manchester are putting up in place of the obsolete down-town buildings. From the wayside Bethel to the cathedral landmarks, a church has to serve its generation, its style reflecting the need of the hour, the pressing necessity or the consummated faith. The upstart mission is in time replaced by the dignified proportions and solemn mien of established supply to an old demand, and the tin tabernacle, stark and functional as a simple shepherd's crook, serves the same eternal purpose as the more aesthetic temple, that same crook elaborated by reverent artistry into the fronded curling fern of the crozier.

What will satisfy this generation? He pondered as the bus sped on past the vast plate glass fronts of shops trying to boost the declining sales of a great slump with the bogus economies of a drug on the market. The desperate warehouses put out a marvellous show of health with linen sufficient to furnish the hospitality of palaces, when most housewives were 'sides to middling' all but the sheets for the guest room. There were huge garden swings on splayed tubular frames for leisure hours which bore no resemblance to the idleness of weeks and months. The windows teemed with luxury, the finest china, the latest wall coverings, tall harlequin rolls of inlaid linoleums and kaleido-scope carpets offering roses all the way, to the jagged designs of broken stained glass and the similitude of wood and stone. From such store places both a merchant prince and a Robinson Crusoe could have furnished a suitable dwelling.

Perhaps these great glass emporia were the new cathedrals of the people. Instead of the glow of ancient and honoured banners there were draped the shimmering and voluptuous falls of silk and velvet. Beauty pervaded, subtle in the tinted distance, flashing to hand on jewellery glittering on mock bosoms of jetty plush, and the dazzled brain was made languorous with scents that floated everywhere in slow swirling hark-back to lost or forbidden Edens.

These were the temples to which pilgrims flocked daily in their thousands, eagerly seeking the water of life and the elixir of youth, breathing the sensuous incense of the newly accredited holiness of beauty. The big churches were going down and the big shops were going up as people craved for the things that would clothe their bodies in delights and being so clothed, their minds would enter into an unspeakable bliss.

It may be that a sense of well-being could develop into a realisation of joy and so rise by lark ascent to lyricism and beatitude. A fortunate section of humanity had attained the starting point of the climb and might soon be dissatisfied with a region so slightly above sea level.

Robert ran his inward eye over the Haves and Have-nots met with in his own working life. The Haves are not only the go-getters, the tramplers, the smug and the easy money boys; they include the careful, the patient, the wise, the deservedly rewarded. And the Have-nots are by no means all the exploited, the vanquished and the weak; they include the insatiable gambler, the shiftless stone and the determined sloth. Robert could bring to mind saints in both camps of Haves and Have-nots.

What should he call that perpetual irritant, Pins and Needles? A mean-to-have! Only recently Grace was just ready to go out to her Women's Class as the laundry van drew up at the gate and running

385

r

downstairs she had picked up the money from the hall table and hurriedly opened the door to thrust several shillings at the astonished but quickly receptive Pins and Needles, who made off at once.

Robert smiled. The poor had always been very expectant and in the early days 'Bread before Beatitudes' would be their motto. They demanded signs and they got them. It would be the illiterate who took that early teaching literally and without signal results those early audiences would have melted away. Man's nature is proof positive of that first and consequently subsequent miracles.

If only, reflected Robert, there were more simple people about today. Nowadays people hate to be thought simple, even simple hearted. They choose to be complex and such complexity has brought them perplexity and the curse of trying to be all things; and in being all things they have lost identity and found only a sense of grievance, hence the abolition of the hard stool of penitence and the introduction of the padded couch where guilt is a forbidden, not a forbidding sensation.

What would old Ben Northcroft say if told that any defaulting on his part was due to heredity or indigestion or a secretion in his glands? He would feel deprived of a personal set-to with Old Man in which he himself had a fair chance of ultimate victory. If a man believed that his glands have the initiative he would be as fearful as an epileptic of an impending seizure.

Men such as Ben Northcroft would not thank anyone for suggesting that man is as guiltless as seaweed trailing in the unavoidable cross currents of life. The flower's innocence, the unreasoning obedience of the planets, are not for man. He does not wish to be classed among efficient but inoffensive creation, without conscience and without guilt; rather would he plead guilty to bad navigation and take the consequences. And if the pleas of guilt and non-guilt are alike too dreadful to express, his very presence at the place of judgment proves that he is a man and not a mollusc, or a thing unfit to plead.

The minister's journey had now reached the edge of the town where streets had been gentled into avenues, crescents and gardens. He was making this visit at the instigation of some of the members who said that Sam had always been a giver and would still come but for her! No family, but owning one of these deus ex machina kitchens and all other mod. cons. feasible to suburbia. They were very attractive houses with crazily paved paths running fussily in all directions, playing ring o' roses round the bushes in the centre of tiny lawns and then sweeping expansively round larger ones and showing the way to successful borders and rockeries. Everywhere the grass had been strictly brought up and carefully trimmed with embroidery scissors.

The rain had stopped before he left the bus and he walked on with pleasure.

The houses themselves had broken rank and were standing at ease, some nonchalantly half turning from their neighbours either from indifference or consideration while some held quite aloof in cliques of their own in banjo shaped cur-de-sacs with warning notices at the entrance; No through road. A few were in quiet backwaters with grassy unpaved ways with name plates bearing the sad little apology: Unadopted.

Nevertheless, the whole district had the air of usually being seen with a bunch of early violets pinned to its fur coat and since it is meritorious to alleviate poverty in others, it cannot be blameworthy to alleviate one's own. If water generally finds its own level, some, pumped high enough will find and maintain an altitude far above the sea's, while other, heavy water indeed, rises only as the pumps heave. That element produces no teachers, leaders or innovators and is incapable of attaining a civilised way of life from a low condition. Poets and visionaries are by nature mountain lakes. Here at least in this suburb, unadopted or not, through-road or not, something had been achieved in material advancement and Robert Garner was of the opinion that hereabouts everybody could well afford to join the 'envelope system'.

Although he glanced this way and that he could not see a church. Probably these people motored into town . . . but no, the town churches were closing and the superseded giants of the last century were being replaced in the suburbs by more suitable modern designs less expensive to build.

Perhaps there was a new church just round the next corner.

Round the next corner was the road from which Rondel Avenue, his destination, branched and the minister scrutinised the gates and porches of these well kept houses where all fashions of name plates were used. Apart from the simple announcement in black lettering on white wood and vice versa, there were cross sections of log dangling from the beams of elaborate vestibules. There were stout miniature gibbets rearing up in thick hedges with a lettered board swinging in chains, and elsewhere it was necessary to lower the gaze to the ground where the top of a well malleted easel supported an artist's palette signed with the house's name. It was a wonder that some householders did not miss these wooden signs prior to fifth of November. As for the names themselves, the whole area was strewn with some of the most popular bays and beaches of the Channel Islands; St. Brelade's,

Portelet, La Roque and, sometimes misunderstood, Bonne Nuit. A few Scottish and Irish beauty spots and some idyllic scenes from the Lake District were also present.

Robert turned into Rondel Avenue to find Snowdonia at the far end, written in black wrought iron-work against a pale pebble-dash wall. Not content with one mountain, he observed half smiling, but must have an entire range! The gates were closed since the owner was at home indisposed, so he unlatched one half and advanced, mounting two shallow steps to open a partly glazed door into a sturdy porch. He pressed a white bell push and heard not the strident response that Pins and Needles provoked at the ministerial home, but a soft, two-tone chime dulcet as a convent clock.

The door opened and there stood Mrs Ginnell, who quickly drew back to allow him to enter. Robert turned to place his umbrella in an earthenware cylinder decorated with painted flowers. He was prepared to listen indefinitely if the invalid wished to extol his husbandry in garden or greenhouse or, if Sam Buckley's bad cold impeded talk, Robert himself might interest him in some of China's horticulture. There was a very pretty Gingko tree near the gate.

He stepped inside.

"Oh, Mr Garner. I hoped it was the doctor. He *is* ill. He's much worse than she realises although I think it's dawning on her."

"I'm sorry to hear that, Mrs Ginnell. I'd no idea. Is there anything I can do?"

"I doubt it. I don't think he would know anybody. He doesn't know *her!* And she's in a state. Perhaps you could have a word with her, Mr Garner. Just step in here and warm yourself. Some of these showers seem to have been kept in the fridge until the moment they're served."

She showed him into the dining room and looked up into his face with all her anxiety undisguised.

"Mr Garner, it's an unhappy house. I don't know what's going to become of them."

As she went back into the hall, Elsie Buckley appeared at the top of the stairs and catching sight of Mrs Ginnell, came hurrying down to grasp her by an arm and gaze fearfully at her.

"He's going. He's going, after all."

Robert Garner came to the open doorway and Mrs Ginnell turned to him helplessly. Elsie looked at him too, taking in his face and his white clerical collar gleaming above his dark clothes like a ruff in a Rembrandt painting. Her expression changed as she stared at him fixedly and suddenly out of the depths of terror in the eyes, Robert saw leap up a frenzied hope. It was an unbalanced, unpractised and pathetic hope with absolutely no solid ground under it. It might fall back into the abyss straightway but something had given it momentary leverage.

She spoke sharply, almost commandingly.

"You're a man of God! Do something!"

Robert Garner stared back at the woman in sheer amazement, completely taken off his guard by the shock of her utterance following what had gone before. 'I doubt it' had been Mrs Ginnell's response a moment ago. Indeed, whenever he had said "Can I do anything?" a cool sluice of polite doubt had been thrown over his intentions. People were brave, people were stoical, grim, obstinate; their utmost thought a furtive hope, but underneath that hope was a stupendous doubt, a dour, uncomplaining unexpectancy. Even among his own people he had seen a Job-like determination to keep faith without signs, without having seen. "Though he slay me!" Can anyone live on reputation alone? Even God? Now this woman whom he had never seen until this moment, had turned and looked at him and like a bandit had guessed that he carried concealed gold and without a moment's hesitation she had demanded it.

What had given the woman's sudden hope its leverage; what solid ground was there to provide a fulcrum and so move the earth, or at least a mountain? This poor, almost bankrupt soul had caught an inkling of spiritual wealth and she would plunder it as the poor had seized upon it whenever it had come to light in any generation. Daring to plunge both hands into it was a sign that underneath the hope there was not doubt but solid ground at last, the one place as faith, braced for the pressure of the fulcrum, squares its foundations.

Robert Garner could not misunderstand her. He knew that faith cannot be faked and he would not question her as to whether she required him to prepare her husband for what she would call death or for what he would call life.

He also could not misunderstand the origin of her hope and faith which was in reality rooted in ignorance and superstition although she did not know it. Once again the idea of religion had been confused, even in the current mind, with the medicine man, the dealer in magic and spells, and now the plain white collar of the Methodist preacher meant to the desperate woman all that the panoply of ritual garments had suggested to the awe-struck Israelites in times of peril. She thought of him in her panic as a bridge between man and Divinity, whereas there is no bridge at all but just one door, one unique, direct access door, without duplicate or substitute or the need for vicarious presentation, a door to which all the priesthood guide their flocks in the humble knowledge that every prince of the church is one with and brother to, all the sons of the blood.

The minister handed his hat to Mrs Ginnell and divested himself of his coat.

"Shall we go to him?"

As Elsie Buckley led him upstairs and Mrs Ginnell followed, he asked himself what would be the divine will on this matter and how it could be expressed, given the chance. Obviously a chance is needed, for daily it is seen to be contradicted and defeated, but if the will is done in heaven and that kingdom is also within us, then, Robert averred, it was in him now, to interpret or misinterpret.

They approached the door that the wife had left open in her flight downstairs. Open even before he knocked, but here the struggle would be to expel an invading enemy. Had he the right? Had this man been living so abundantly that his leave-taking would be a tragedy? According to rumour, not.

Why then elongate this span of life? Longevity has no great virtue in itself except as a sign of tenacity and Robert knew that the vital thing is not the length of our time and experience but its depth, since on the intrinsic merit of the moment lies the possibility of its extension in futurity. Was there anything in the present life of Sam Buckley to compare in worth and felicity with any past hours treasured for him in perpetuity? For there is a length and breadth, a latitude and longitude of time. The moment of bird song, of silence, of fluorescence or fall, of energy or idleness, can slip aside from the onward stream of change and glide upon a cross-current that advances only along its own unchanging degree. Continuity here might only add to the sum of time that would hereafter be judged as worthless and consigned to oblivion.

Then faith was now to work not for the man's sake, but for the woman's; really for the sake of the woman's own faith.

Had he the right? Yes. For if we are created for God's glory, then now and again we must do something glorious.

The minister went up to the bed and looked down at Sam Buckley's flushed head and inert form, while Elsie Buckley lingered at the foot of the bed and laid her hands very gently on Sam's feet under the satin eiderdown.

"I wish I could go in his place. He's worth something. I'm not."

Mrs Ginnell hurried to her and put a thin but strong arm round her shoulders.

"Now, Mrs Buckley, you're not to talk like that. And look who's here! Things are looking up now."

The words cut through the pondering of the minister and he turned towards the speaker.

"You are right, Mrs Ginnell. Look who's here indeed when two or three are gathered together with a purpose, namely to look up. Come, let us all kneel."

The two women remained at the foot of the bed side by side, while the three knelt with eyes closed to see, with hands inert to hold and with feet halted to journey along the way.

Robert Garner considered the man lying there and guessed that he might be perhaps about the same age as Lazarus, in the prime of his manhood. He decided to allow that recollection to be his guide and sense of permission if he could lay hold on the power to reveal the will.

"It can be done. It has been done. Thy will be done," he said aloud.

"Amen," whispered Mrs Ginnell.

A sudden emergence of utmost goodwill is generally termed miracle and can be a physical conversion akin to a spiritual conversion; there is the same speeding up of dominion over nature that may appear to be done on the spur of the moment, and to the person pricked by the spur of the moment the change is speedy. There has not always been time set for the careful preparation of mind necessary to gain that dominion, so it has become wise and of proved advantage to cultivate the knowledge of medical science with its own special method of preparation. But at this moment of crisis the man of healing is not present and whatever skill is available must be used immediately; so now it is the moment for the talents of faith and simplicity and a firm human will to offer themselves to the supreme will. It is the moment for a woman with her newly sprung faith, for another woman with her simplicity and for a man who has earnestly studied the ways of the master creator and learned much.

So at this moment for Sam Buckley worldly knowledge has sunk away, as the seaboots and oilskins that protect a man from spray and wind are useless when he is swept overboard into deep water. But Sam, deeply asleep, was unaware of both danger and attempted rescue.

Robert's lips were moving above his clasped hands and the women caught words towards which their ears were strained.

"When we have naught but Thee, we are very near to victory, as all our deficiencies are more than compensated by Thy power, which is always around us and present in us, so that we come from Thy presence into Thy presence. We pray for this needy child of Thine, Samuel. We do not ask for mercy, for that has been poured out for untold years, time known to us and time unknown to us, when it has been sought and when it has been unsought. It is because of this unstinted grace that we dare ask for further knowledge, for the key to Thy saving power, the power that can surely save our dear brother to dwell with us according to man's allotted span. We know that the places prepared for us all infinitely transcend what we have made of Thy world and we make this prayer not so much for the sake of our brother here, but for the joy and thanksgiving of this other child, the burden of whose heart is known fully only to Thee. Our fearful understanding would tell us that it is the eleventh hour; but what is the eleventh hour to Thee, to whom the night is as the day? The eleventh hour and midnight itself can be the veriest cock-crow of the spirit! What is time to Thee but a toy for our childlike imaginings and in this hour, which is neither early nor late to the Eternal, we ask that this helpless bark drifting beyond our reach, may be touched by Thy hand and turned again towards us. We remember those who toiled all night on Galilee and caught nothing; now we, like them, will cast again and by faith draw in the temporal life of this man beneath our hands."

As the murmured words ceased the minister opened his eyes and reaching out both hands, laid them upon the recumbent form and also looked towards his companions who turned searching eyes upon him at his movement. At his guiding nod they too leaned forward and tremblingly took hold of Sam's feet where they made a bulge under the covers.

"We ask," continued the quiet tones, "in the name of our Lord and Saviour Jesus Christ to whom all power is given."

Silence that was heavy with individual nervous effort pervaded the room. Elsie Buckley's breathing was rapid and her closed mouth quivered, while Mrs Ginnell's face was taut with concentrated repetition as she inwardly called for help in almost physically pushing against the shadow that she felt so stealthily closing in upon the sickroom.

"Get out!" she threatened savagely from behind tight lips. "Begone in the name of the Lord. Get out! Get out! Get out!"

Robert saw that battling visage and rejoiced. She had the winning spirit. Shall Hercules in ancient times wrestle with Death and win; and not the Christians? Shall our Father Jacob wrestle to gain a blessing and win; and not the Christians? Had we only as much faith as the pagan and the Jew, we should be victors.

Elsie Buckley's head was bowed on one of her outstretched arms and tears forced themselves out from her closed eyes, tears of weariness and weakness but also of relief. The others were in the thick of the fray but she wasn't fighting.

She was only filled with wonder that help had come so unexpectedly and opportunely and she just gave way to it, waiting upon a power she had never troubled to explore but had instantly recognised, to work its will.

But whatever the will, whatever the plan, there is always an opposition; there is an opposition to good and an opposition to evil, and at this juncture the clash of wills raged in this small space. For many years Robert had prayed for all mankind and for his own immediate flock; for Matthew, Mark, Luke and John and for Tom, Dick and Harry. He knew what it was to suffer with the victim, to feel kinship with defeat and on such occasions he had gained comfort from the knowledge that although death can be a sneak-thief, God claims the booty; the only honest receiver of stolen goods. If, however, this woman's faith were to be justified this day, the thief must be intercepted.

But how?

Was the outcome a foregone conclusion in some sphere? Was the end known somewhere if not here, and human striving vain? Robert Garner believed that God drew not one but many conclusions, considered many possibilities, allowed for all answers. And the answer to human striving would be worth the knowing.

More strength! Strength enough to hold back the stone from rolling into place. When a man prays he is not appealing to his better self but to a terrific force which is always available if he can get through to it, and the key to the situation hangs round his neck against his heart. Only when his head, like his heart, is bowed down almost to the earth, does the chain slip and the key fall to hand.

With that key in his possession Robert Garner strove against nature with the valiant help of one companion and the seemingly passive but assertive trust of the other. Nature does not always heal. She heals if we can work for her ends but she would as soon cast us, dry and barren, aside. Nature does not teach that we are immortal but that we are expendable in her sight and can be abandoned without a sign of regret. Nature has neither morals nor mercy and can shrug her shoulders and leave a man to blind chance, caring not who wins, man or worm, since whatever is left is still here. Nature has so much, she can afford to be careless, can afford to lose lavishly because of effortless duplication. More grass, more flowers, more men. Do not halt the endless procession or get out of step. Identical replacements are teeming in, so make room!

The object sacrificed is nobler than that which demands the sacrifice, so however necessary it may have been for man to invent a god, he could never have invented God, as can be deduced from the nature of the gods that he did invent. Man was more impressed by a god who certainly could save himself if not others and it was an attitude easy to understand. Complete self sacrifice at first engendered not gratitude but incredulity. It was not natural.

But nature occasionally receives a shock. She is actually pushed around.

There came a time when she was thrust hurriedly aside and in an unexpected direction. There came a day when a man who did not worship nature but whom nature came to worship, put his hands on the wheels of death and dissolution and slowed them down; halted them. Then after a breath-giving pause, slowly and surely they began to turn again, but now the other way, gaining speed and flying faster, to accomplish in minutes as many revolutions as had turned in four whole days and nights; to redeem in a fraction of the time the natural destruction accomplished in those days.

Lazarus! Come forth!

Man's worship of nature had come to an end.

Time and time again nature is proved fallible and mutable and the knowledge gave new strength to the man now seeking to link himself to that spiritual force that had broken the old laws and made stupendous new laws. He felt that he could claim the mastery by virtue of those laws; further, that he had been called upon to do so and that in implicit obedience lay absolute victory.

Robert Garner's hands remained clenched in supplication as he laid hold of the power that exists throughout existence, bonded together inextricably. He called incessantly on the name signed on every part of time and space as their maker and in his own locked hands, holding the key, he held the assurance that the submissive mountain would move as the fulcrum of the spirit bore down on the corner stone, which stood its ground.

The human spirit hailed its parent; the lesser claimed some attribute of the greater and found kinship and blessing as promised. A voice was uplifted and a voice replied and in that hour the wind of the spirit, the dove that is the carrier pigeon of God's word, by its commanding presence checked a human soul in its imminent flight; stayed it in the terrestrial home which it had thought to abandon and where it now folded its wings and abided.

When Dr Bedser sounded the discreet chimes of Snowdonia, he was heralding his approach too modestly. It would cause surprise if a medical man entered his surgery, hospital ward or sick room crying "A rescue! A rescue!" like a knight galloping against an enemy held castle, and yet no one would be more entitled to such an exuberant and determined show of championship.

There was no portcullis raised for him today but the door was opened by Mrs Ginnell, looking rather peaked he thought, and who strangely said not a word as she closed the door after him and then promptly returned to the kitchen. He would prescribe a tonic for her. As he went upstairs he saw the minister come from the patient's bedroom, bow in response to a brief greeting and also go silently downstairs. The doctor's spirits sank. Things were as bad as that, then? He entered quietly and found Mrs Buckley standing at the foot of the bed gazing at her sleeping husband. He led her solicitously to a chair. It was not his business to like or dislike people; it was his business to help them and he feared that she had a sorrowful time ahead of her. Whether her nerves had spoilt her marriage or her marriage had spoilt her nerves, life would be harder if she were left alone. At the moment, the pupils of her eyes had expanded enormously and she was possibly suffering from shock.

He snapped open his neat black case, deadening the sound with his fingers and turned to the bed, at once deftly pulling back the sheets to feel the pulse before proceeding with other examination. He was struck motionless first with astonishment and then with anger. What on earth! He had not ordered that thing he was certain, and he fastidiously peeled off a rather messy bread poultice and then nearly wept and swore at the sight underneath. He smothered his exclamations of horror because of the woman present, but he hastily dropped the offending dollop into the tiled hearth and leaned over his patient to inspect the dire injury. This man was desperately ill and would be in the gravest danger for three or four days at least; he had been suffering in mind and body and had lost interest in the struggle for survival, so offering no resistance whatsoever to the forces attacking him. Yet someone had been trying to parboil this helpless invalid alive, if only barely alive, treating him as though he were at some dreadful Red Indian initiation ceremony. Why hadn't whoever had done this, lit a fire on the man's chest while they were about it! That skin would need immediate treatment and yet Dr Bedser was almost afraid to touch it. He felt the pulse and at least found some satisfaction there, but he would have something to say later to the persons responsible. It would have been better to risk removal to hospital than to leave him to the ignorance of such people. So the doctor was engaged for some time, seething with indignation as he worked with butterfly touch and concealing his wrath and anxiety over this probably toxic condition.

He stood back and surveyed the light dressing and decided that only one sheet should be replaced to avoid pressure on the tender skin, and as he shook his head over the ill treated chest he came to realise one more mitigating circumstance. The thin layers of gauze were rising and falling rhythmically and calmly as the breath came and went in normal respiration without effort or sound of painful obstruction. Dr Bedser dived for the stethoscope and upon further examination the lungs proved to be free from any congestion whatsoever. His patient was not so much in a coma as deriving benefit from deep and healthful slumber.

Dr Bedser picked up the bottle of pills from the side table and counted them. The prescribed dose had been taken. Something new, they had acted beyond all belief, performing in hours what the full dosage might have been expected to do in three of four days at the most optimistic calculation. This was amazing.

Mrs Buckley seemed still not to be noticing anything, so he moved across to her and felt her pulse while he spoke a word or two of encouragement.

"I do believe your husband is holding his ground. I feel I dare go so far as to say that."

"Yes, I know, doctor."

"You do?"

"Yes, I'm to have another chance. I don't deserve it."

He returned her hand to her lap since her arm was quite limp and unresponsive. The whole household seemed to be tired out, he remembered. He decided to go downstairs and have a look at them since strenuous work of some kind had been taking place.

He went into the kitchen and found the occupant stirring soup. He went right up to her since she did not look round.

"Mrs Ginnell, what have you been doing to my patient?"

"Why, doctor, do you mean those poultices?"

"I do mean those poultices!" he replied severely. "A lesser constitution wouldn't have stood such drastic treatment. Whatever possessed you?"

She shot him a challenging glance, but answered very meekly.

"I know it's a bit old-fashioned but I've never heard anything against a poultice."

The doctor's voice rose in fulmination.

"A poultice! If you'd put hell-fire in a warming pan . . . "

"Sh! The minister's here," and she indicated another room. "Mr Garner has been doing . . . what he can."

The doctor frowned slightly and looked displeased.

"Anybody else?"

Mrs Ginnell caught the tone of resentment.

"Well, doctor, Sam's no worse for it, is he?"

He went round the shelves, picking up lids and looking into containers as if the answer were hidden there.

"I think he's maintaining strength," he admitted cautiously.

"In that case we mustn't grumble."

She glanced sideways at him as he absently looked in the bread bin, and turning abruptly he caught an obvious gleam of triumph in her eye.

"Although there is an undoubted improvement, we must not crow. It may only be a flash in the pan," and he replaced the enamel lid rather clumsily. But Mrs Ginnell faced him squarely now.

"It was something better than a flash of hell-fire in a warming pan, doctor. Sam's been helped from the other place."

"So that's why his wife thought she was to have another chance! What's been going on? I can tell something unusual has been happening."

"Only something that's going on all the time; the power of God. Only sometimes we get in the way."

She busied herself with collecting plates to put in the oven warmer and the doctor bent down to peer into Wispy's intelligent face watching his movements from a box near the warmth and he put out his hand and stroked the little bat-like head with two fingers.

"Perhaps better times are coming for you too, little chap."

"Oh, doctor, he's all of a doo-dah, as *you* say! He's the only one in the house who's had any of the soup that's been on the go for ages, and he still looks the most starved of the lot."

"Mrs Buckley must have some quite soon, you know. She's feeling the strain, obviously."

"Oh, that reminds me. I think I ought to tell you something she told me."

The doctor listened with impatient disgust, throwing up his hands in despair.

"Some of these places haven't enough supervision, but a few more instances of *that* nature and they'd soon find a big drop in their bookings. Poor woman. I'll have a serious talk with her when things are more settled. Everybody's not like you, Mrs Ginnell, more's the pity. Fear can do such terrible things to us."

He regarded her with curiosity.

"Not much daunts you, my dear. I've known you for many years and I'd really like to know what *would* put you out, if you don't mind telling me in confidence."

Mrs Ginnell showed a little confusion at the request.

"Oh, well, you're a doctor! You'll understand. I *can* say that I've never been one to pander to my digestion; it's had to take what was coming to it and it's done me proud on the whole. But ever since I was a child, when I read it in the newspaper once, I've had a horror of a coroner's verdict that a person had died of an over-loaded stomach. It's bad enough to be a mystery and have to be opened up; but for them to find that! I'd die all over again of shame!"

The doctor turned quickly and opened a wall-cupboard.

"It won't happen to you, by the look of you, don't worry. I'd stake my reputation on that. Now what about our patient? He ought to have a little nourishment since he's made some progress and I think you'd better give it to him yourself to avoid any emotional rise. I'll be having a word with Mr Garner while you attend to those two upstairs."

"Yes, if I can only get this down them, they might have strength to have another course or two. At least Mrs Buckley should. Come on up again Wispy, and give a sign of life."

When Dr Bedser crossed into the dining room, Robert Garner was resting on the settee with his eyes closed. The doctor was perturbed. Can intensive prayer cause loss of weight? Perhaps.

He returned to the kitchen and himself ladled out a generous helping of soup. The minister was grateful for it and drank it all at the doctor's request, feeling revivified quite surprisingly soon.

Meanwhile, the doctor eyed him without appearing to do so. He had corresponded with him on matters touching sick or bereaved members of the church, but he had never been in his company for any length of time. He did know, however, that he was a man of wide knowledge even outside his vocational training and that at home, additions to his library were made at the expense of some economy at other levels; floor level in fact, for the shoes that Robert Garner was wearing today, neat and well polished though they were, had what the doctor did not often see on a man of his standing; a patch on the outer toe line. The cobbler was a craftsman taxed to his utmost skill, in order that the book-binder might use fine leather also, tooling and gilding with artistry so that the tabulated thought of man might be fittingly, that is splendidly, housed.

The doctor had a great respect for any line of conduct that the minister would take, but he was impelled to ask questions of him that he might resent or think downright impertinent. He was glad when the minister opened the subject first.

"How do you find your patient, doctor?"

"Astonishingly improved, Mr Garner."

"Good. Then I'll be on my way."

"If you can wait another fifteen minutes or so, I can run you back with me."

Robert was glad to avail himself of this courtesy.

"By the way, Mr Garner, what time did you get here today?"

"About one forty-five, I should think."

"And what did you think of Sam Buckley's condition then?"

"He seemed very poorly, I'm afraid."

"I ask particularly because I wish to report on the medicine he's been taking."

"Just so."

Dr Bedser looked dissatisfied.

"You're guarded as a hedgehog, Mr Garner. I don't think it was just so. To me, those women looked a bit above themselves when I came in."

"Naturally they're very much relieved and you yourself must be very highly gratified."

Dr Bedser sat down on a dining chair at the table and turned to face the minister on the settee.

"Look, Mr Garner, please be frank with me. I'm on the Plan, you know, and I preach my four sermons a year and am not just a man of science. But I must know; it is my job to know why an illness worsens or abates. Yesterday and first thing this morning my patient upstairs was seriously ill and rapidly losing ground. Now, the expected crisis has not yet been reached, has been by-passed or has been encountered and dealt with. Please tell me, was our patient in a coma, or appeared to be so, when you first saw him?"

"I might say that he was."

"And while you were in the room, no more pills were administered?"

"None. But he might have had them just before I came."

"And you were in the room all the time, until I saw you leave it?"

"Yes, all three of us were there."

The doctor here showed surprise.

"Oh! She didn't put one of those simmering messes on the poor fellow while you were there, by any chance?"

"No, no, he was not disturbed at all."

"Nobody laid a hand on him for any reason?"

Then Robert looked very gravely at his catechist and Dr Bedser, springing to his feet, paced the room.

"I thought as much, I know it! There has been interference if you don't mind my putting it that way."

"But surely, if our friend Mrs Ginnell's poultices were so drastic that Mr Buckley was lucky to survive them, all the more credit to medical knowledge."

"Mr Garner, why do you hedge? Why do you not make some claim outright? Did you or did you not save this man's life? I know he was sinking."

"I did nothing of the kind; but three of us prayed that all things might work together for good and apparently they did. I arrested his leave-taking. I see no reason for disapproval."

"God forbid! But I see the danger of giving rise to hopes where perhaps there are none."

"You mean where there are none otherwise than in the power of the Spirit? And Spirit is the only thing that permeates and has cognisance of the whole. Spirit leaves no gaps, and faith, hope and love are a very powerful trinity, Doctor, sometimes only reached by man straining at the very end of his tether."

Dr Bedser was ill at ease.

"As I said before, Mr Garner, I give my quarterly sermon at your church. I am not without faith. But what's going to happen if all clergymen behave like this? It would be a terrible state of things. We should all be getting in each other's way."

"Surely science isn't a dog in the manger! Mangers have known better contents than that and I fail to see why the church's triumphant appeal should lead to a terrible state of things. If St. Luke did not think so, why should you?"

"Once people begin to think there's any easy short cut to health and healing they'll get careless about research and medical progress. I don't suppose you are typical of your calling; leaders are not typical and others may not have your rallying powers, so that after their failures people will fall back into apathy and ignorance again."

"I think it takes about seven years to become a doctor, but it takes longer than that to become an effective Christian."

"I apologise if I gave the impression that I thought your work here today had been easy. Quite the opposite, I'm sure. But there are so many sick people needing help and it isn't even ethical if it shows favouritism to a chosen few. Why have you chosen Sam Buckley, for instance, instead of a long term invalid like Ella Kershaw? Why leave her out?"

Robert Garner raised his hand to interrupt the doctor peremptorily, which was unusual for him.

"I have not left her out, Doctor. And Tom is the miracle in *her* life. She has borne with her thorn in the flesh with great patience, but perhaps she's been a church member for so long she has forgotten its privileges. Mrs Buckley suddenly remembered."

400

"And what if Mr Buckley relapses?" (The doctor was plainly aghast at the possibility.) "Supposing his condition has been improved by an exercise of will and then subsides again; what has been gained? It would be an irony if while we were discussing what exactly pulled him through, he sank again."

"He won't do that, Doctor. God is not mocked, but neither does He mock."

"You're as sure as that!" exclaimed the other in wonder.

For the last minute or so he had been twisting a small vase on the mantelpiece as he carried on this conversation. He now turned from it.

"That's not bad. Mrs Buckley has excellent taste. By the way, I hear you've got a very fine Chinese vase that's quite a rarity and insured for a considerable sum. A present from your friends out there, I believe."

Robert bowed and the doctor spoke point blank.

"What did they give it to you *for*, Mr Garner? You know exactly what I mean. Please be frank with me, a man as I said, not without faith. Was it from a scholastic body or given by a grateful family?"

There was a short silence and Robert sighed.

"You are very intuitive, Doctor Bedser. Amazingly so. But let me say this. Just now you said that perhaps I was not typical of my calling. To me, the phrase 'Priesthood of all believers' means this: that the Spirit works through all of us if we will let it and the great thing is not to deny each other's vision but to rejoice in it, whether it comes to a woman in some Yorkshire dale or to a young man in a Welsh village or to any soul the world over who has a perceptive ear for the wind that blows where it will."

The doctor stared into the garden moodily for some time but when he turned again his whole bearing had changed.

"I appreciate that, Mr Garner I hope you will forgive me. I see now that it would be unethical for you not to use your special insight as it would be for me to ignore my observations. I'm a General Practitioner and I don't meet a special emergency every day, but I hope I should rise to the occasion if it arose, as you have."

"And I'm a cure of souls," rejoined Robert, "and today our vocations have - not trespassed - but overlapped a little."

The doctor ascended the stairs in a lighter frame of mind. Mrs Buckley had eaten something and Mrs Ginnell, by nodding towards the bed with her eyes closed indicated that the patient was still sleeping. Dr Bedser went over and stood by him to satisfy himself that the natural breathing and better skin colour and humidity were being maintained and then scribbled a few notes.

"There, Mrs Buckley, just a few instructions. Simple human

401

kindness with as little talking as possible, will serve him best, and when he's really on the mend I want to see you on a very urgent matter. It concerns your health and happiness, and of course your husband's. Now, goodbye, and don't be afraid of sleeping soundly; he'll not want much for a time and I'll be here again in the morning."

He patted her shoulder, which he had never done before, and she blushed with pleasure.

"She looks all the better for being human," was his mental comment as he went downstairs.

Mrs Ginnell was in the hall.

"Mr Garner's in the car. He thought it best not to see her but he'll come again in a day or two. She wants me to stay, you know; they half expected it at home, but if you *could* just pop in. Our Connie will be mad, but at least she'll be cock o' the midden."

"Ah, yes, your Connie! I want to have a word with her, too. I need a new receptionist and a fine girl like Connie would be the very one if you think she'd come."

"She'll come," promised the mother with decision.

As the doctor went out of Snowdonia gateway to the car a woman on the pavement hastened her step.

"Excuse me, but you *are* the doctor? How is Mr Buckley please."

"There is every sign of improvement, ma'am."

"Oh, I'm so glad. Everybody will be delighted. In the avenue here we've missed him, *and* the little dog. Such a pleasant pair! Thank you."

She bowed and passed on.

As the doctor's car sped in and out of quiet side streets, shortening the homeward journey considerably, Robert was thinking that Dr Bedser had no objections to short cuts of this kind.

The doctor's chuckle burst out.

"Such a pleasant pair, Sam and Wispy! Snowdonia's under-dogs and yet the best of their kind."

"I've never met Mr Buckley until today," said Robert. "Or, of course, Mrs Buckley."

"You haven't? Oh, then emotion doesn't come into it at all. You're as objective as we are. In a way, Mr Garner, the situation might be compared with the airman who goes up to destroy the enemy; the emotion is the decision to join up in the first place."

"Yes," agreed Robert, smiling, "you might well put it that way. Or if I might trespass on your territory," he added with a hint of mischief, "a colleague of mine, Sylvester, who reads *The Lancet* for pleasure, has been telling us that the maternity wards are trying out a capsule

402

that the mother holds in her hands during labour. Only at extreme need is her grasp strong enough to release the fumes that will come to her aid. Even the power of prayer may need that further effort."

No more was said on the subject but they went along very cheerfully, calling to inform Connie of her unwonted and unwanted status.

"I'll drop you at your door, Mr Garner, and I prescribe a light meal and a good night's rest."

Reaching home, Robert, instead of opening the car door found that he was lowering the window.

"I'll leave it open," said the doctor. "It's going to be a fine evening. I don't think our trees are quite so advanced as on the other side of town, do you?"

It was so, but in the garden of the church opposite they were in bud, as if the diamonds left from the last shower had turned to emeralds.

"And look at the birds over there, flying with bits of building material. It's evidently time to be thinking of making a nest again, good luck to them."

Chapter Twenty-Eight

Geoffrey Sinclair came out of Sherratt and Hughes' to find the rain slackening. He had spent half an hour browsing there after picking up a book he had ordered some days before, which put him in as mellow a frame of mind as he achieved anywhere these days.

Coming into Mosley Street he glanced at the Art Gallery. That girl coming slowly down the steps as if she might try Mosley Street with her big toe and perhaps even then decide to go back . . . yes, it *was* Kerry. He quickly crossed the road and met her at the gates.

"Kerry, my dear girl! Can't you tear yourself away from Genesis?"

He was troubled by the sudden gladness in her face. It reminded him.

"Oh, Geoffrey, it's you! But it wasn't Genesis I've been to see, it was 'The Lark Ascending'. A wooden carving of a lark ascending," she added.

"I'm beginning to follow. But I don't know this masterpiece. Have you time to introduce me to it before it descends for the night? If so, let's rush the doors before the daylight fades altogether. Any more for the skylark?"

Delightedly she rejected the wet pavement and returned.

Back in the main hall they surveyed the slim carving on its pedestal, tapering to a height of several feet above their heads, drawing the eye naturally aloft as the upward fluttering was conveyed by the wing tilt and dip of a mounting series of diminishing birds. It was Shelley's chain of song stretched taut and vibrating.

The girl searched her companion's expression anxiously.

"This is very clever," he remarked appreciatively. "How to be in several places at once! Really, it's our old friend 'The arrow is flown' again, taking the moment along."

"I suppose," she said, going right up to it. "It could have been called

'The Lark Descending' just as well, except for its purposeful little head."

"And that buoyant head makes all the difference. Descending, it would have been plummeting, spent and ready for breakfast and skip Matins for once."

They stood and admired it together and then he glanced down at her upturned face, so full of pleasure, faintly smiling. Yes, faintly smiling, not laughing like anything as when, she had told him, she and her friends were reading that confounded Rag Rag on Shrove Tuesday afternoon in this very place. His face darkened at the remembrance so that when she faced him again she saw the difference and checked the words she was about to say.

"How are things, Kerry?" he asked quickly. "How's your mother?"

"Mother hasn't been too well," she answered sombrely. "The weather's been rotten, too."

"I'm sorry to hear that," he said with genuine feeling.

There was an awkward silence.

"And Watch fell ill and died."

"What! My old friend Watch! Oh dear, that's sad news. He was a very likable animal, was poor old Watch, and he had some good blood in him somewhere. Quite good points. He was just the right size for a house dog, too; not big enough to get in the way but not so small that one fell over him continually. He showed up well in a poor light, being white; motorists could see him, and a bath paid big dividends, didn't it? Very good natured, very tolerant, I always found him easily adaptable to his company. I hate a yapping, snapping dog, and Watch was very likely one of those dogs who would let a stranger in on trust but wouldn't let him out again with any swag, if occasion arose. I've had some happy moments with Watch. A dog on his own, really one in a thousand and absolutely a member of the family. We shan't forget Watch easily."

He stole a look after this funeral oration, and saw that the tribute had softened the severe expression that had come over her features when she first broached the subject. There was no hurry, so he indicated the gallery above them with the smooth portraits of the permanent collection.

"They're not closing yet, so if you're not on time, shall we go up?"

They moved up the shallow stairs that were slightly worn off centre in two gradual depressions as if most people went up by the handrails. They went up the middle, two steps at a time, Geoffrey carrying the girl's school case.

They walked round the portraits and Kerry noticed their waxen fingers with envy. They had no knuckles at all, and nobody bit their nails or broke them or knocked the skin off at gym.

"Do you think all these women honestly had such long tapering fingers? I mean, didn't any of them get scratched gathering roses or anything, even if they didn't turn the garden over?"

"I bet they didn't even wash them as often as we do, Kerry. Those white hands are not so much ideal as idealised. The artist was paying them a rather exaggerated compliment since he knew it was expected of him."

Kerry was much relieved to hear it and they continued their inspection.

"You get the same idea," Geoffrey went on, "in some of the Spanish Old Masters, where the hands of Christ, for instance, are shown in the affected pose current in Court circles, with the third and middle fingers slightly overlapping, like this, to narrow the less artistic full spread. Only the best was good enough for such a subject, so the carpenter's hands were copied from some nobleman who wouldn't know a saw from a modern instance! They wouldn't do it now of course, and rightly so."

"It was rather sweet of them, since they couldn't really know. The artists thought that good manners were as important as truth, and I must say I get a bit sick of the truth myself at times."

"Ah! That's bad! With you, my dear girl, a thing proved does not always meet with your approval. You prefer theories to theorems because one is always open to argument, the other not. That is why the arts demand tremendous moral responsibility; they can be caused to stumble. But all these artists, all the best ones, even those who painted these impossible hands, couldn't ignore theorems; their work is full of them and they outlast the theories."

Kerry laughed up at him.

"What about our President of Conference! You made the arts stumble there with your moral responsibilities! He's still there," she added shyly. "No one's taken him down."

With some constraint they wandered slowly past all those people who had so solemnly composed themselves to be seen in a good light.

"I don't suppose anybody ever deliberately pulled a face, as some boys do in photographs," Kerry speculated.

"They wouldn't have been able to hold it for hours, sitting after sitting, and the mood would change."

"They were marvellous at satin and velvet, weren't they? At school I prefer to draw the draped figures because of the folds. You know, at the ends of all the corridors we have statues, gods and so on and we

406

have to draw them for Miss Tangent. Then there's Miss Berry, who says Poor Old Joe the skeleton is a thing of truth and beauty because he is perfectly functional; but I couldn't gaze at him for ever. Wouldn't Assembly hall look queer if all the statues were skeletons? You couldn't tell if they were supposed to be happy or not, except perhaps the Laocoon; they'd still look frightfully dramatic, wouldn't they?"

Geoffrey thought that the modestly screening gestures of the Venuses would be the most baffling and meaningless, but he was content to be privately amused. It would be equally embarrassing if she did or did not, laugh like anything. The girl paused at the corner to continue her line of thought.

"The most pathetic would be on Floor E, the athlete gazing at the biceps that weren't there; and the happiest would be the boy grinning because the thorn had dropped out of his foot. But for all that Miss Berry says about Joe, I prefer the skeleton clothed in flesh and then the flesh draped in lovely garments like all these round this gallery, and artists can paint clothes in so many different colours more than human skins have."

"Perhaps so, but there are men at the University here and elsewhere who are busily reducing Poor Old Joe to the perfection of his component parts, neutrons and electrons. The scientists and artists are galloping in opposite directions but all looking for the same thing; the essential Poor Old Joe."

"And the artists," said Kerry persistently, "have found Joe's coat of many colours well worth the painting."

"My dear girl, you're beginning to want the last word already. Do you always use a fruit-knife now?"

"Of course not! Oh! Look at that sad face. Cardinal Newman. Why on earth have they put him next to Gracie Fields?"

"To liven him up a bit. He looks absolutely disillusioned, doesn't he?"

The girl looked directly at his profile. "But *your* mouth looks like that sometimes."

"Ah, indeed." He pulled her plait. "Ding dong, we gallop along."

She dodged a step or two away and they left the gallery and moved up into one of the large rooms which had leather covered benches placed back to back at intervals down the middle, but the exact centre was taken up by a ponderous sculpture cordoned off with thick red ropes threaded through brass holders. Here one or two last visitors were roaming round.

"I'm told," said Geoffrey not very quietly, "that editors of pictorial newspapers are tired of readers sending in freak potatoes that look like modern art. Now here we have a perfect illustration of a modern sculpture looking exactly like a freak potato."

"That's Genesis!" shrilled Kerry.

"Mine eyes dazzle! I say, you'd never suspect the presence of a Poor Old Joe inside that mass, would you? The bones are not so much clothed in flesh as had a Jumble Sale heaped on them. Is this your expansion into perfection, Kerry?"

Nevertheless, criticism died in them as they stood under the brooding shape that huddled in foreboding discomfort gazing into an unforeseeable future. It had not been taken into the Creator's confidence, and could never have said 'Behold the handmaiden of the Lord'. Itself was in the womb of time; the first experiment.

"They had nothing to go on, had they, in the beginning?" whispered Kerry.

"Only the intention that somehow Poor Old Joe, here crying 'Let me out' should eventually assume the image and other likenesses of the one who set the experiment in motion. Joe has a long way to go, but he'll make it."

Geoffrey smiled down at her but inwardly he had startled himself, having come out with words that he had not known he believed until this moment. He regarded the sculpture with increased respect.

"It's a very imaginative piece. Epstein has consulted high oracle and remembered the early vow, 'If I forget thee, O Jerusalem, may my right hand lose its cunning'. To the artist it is a matter of life and death; if he forgets, the hand not only may but surely will, lose its cunning. It is a dead hand. Come on, let us explore the other rooms and see if we can find anything to prove it."

They backed away slowly, looking at it as they moved on and into the next room.

"Miss Tangent our art mistress has brought some lovely Italian cornfields home, all different. She says that photography has reached such a high standard that art is now struggling to find a new level where photography can't follow."

"She may well be right," conceded Geoffrey. "Look at this, Kerry. The artist has dodged the photographer there, all right, but no ambassador would dare take that along to show a foreign court what the royal bride elect looked like. Perhaps we shan't have portraits catalogued 'Cardinal Newman' or 'Gracie Fields' any more, but 'Down in the Mouth' and 'Saucy'."

Kerry was amused by the idea.

"No one would fall in love with a picture any more, especially if the portraits are going to be all wart and no Oliver Cromwell. 'I certify that this wart is an exact copy of the Great Protector'. I say, Geoffrey, what would these walls look like? Fancy coming to see a view of London from Westminster Bridge and only finding the illustration of a great wen signed by the King's physician! And in the catalogue it would just have the title 'Say Wen'. It might be rather fun after all."

"Hold it, Kerry, hold it! You're letting your imagination run away with you, not to mention me. And that's just it; when people chase theories they rush hither and thither torturing their imaginations and then naturally those imaginations start pulling funny faces and it shows. And yet artists have to break out into new styles and new subjects, and new ground is increasingly hard to come by. I think artists deserve our sympathy in these days for that reason; they are cramped like Alice in the tiny room and they thrust out a giant hand which Bill the Lizard sees is an 'arrum', but what it signifies escapes him, and tragically the hand sometimes can only make futile snatchings in the air."

"That must be awful for them," agreed Kerry looking round at the contemporary paintings with a more tolerant eye. "I shall always try to find out what they are really getting at before I laugh at anything again and I shall make allowances."

"And earn their undying hatred," said Geoffrey. "Any artist worth his gift doesn't want allowances made. He wants his work to be good, not just good under the circumstances. He doesn't want Robert Browning sneering from the wings, 'So that's what you were driving at! Ah well! Down there the broken arc, up here the perfect round.' Any self respecting artist wants to say, 'Look, Browning, I brought it with me!' Otherwise the hand that has lost its cunning might as well go and shell peas."

"It could do worse. I'm very fond of shelling peas."

"A very rewarding occupation, but not one to which you would draw Browning's attention if he happened to be passing. No, the artist's visual world has been explored and exploited and he needs new substances, new colours, that only a new revelation can provide. Discovery lies with the fact finder and science will have to come to the rescue of the arts and lead them out of bondage."

Kerry looked up at him with great interest. There would be plenty of people to talk to at University. It must be a glorious place for talking and she was sorry the Fridge had told her she hadn't a hope now. But it was lovely having him all to herself like this.

"I say, don't laugh, but do you ever get tired of going up and down stairs in the same old way?"

Geoffrey perceived that this was a serious question and so admitted

S

that occasionally he did, but regretted that the banisters at home were not suitable for sliding down; one fetched up too soon against odd newel posts.

"I'm thinking more of going up, ascending you know, but I ring the changes on going down as well of course. You can go up slowly, noticing the pattern of the carpet, or you can run up two or three at a time or even haul yourself up five at a time; but you arrive on the same landing always. The stairs don't go any further."

"I'm hot on your track so far, my dear girl. Proceed with caution."

"Well, all these pictures that have recently come in here." She swung on her heel and waved a hand at the exhibits which they had scanned. "Are they just putting new carpet on the old stairs?"

"For the most part, yes. And for many people that situation cannot be improved upon, but there will always be somebody coming along and sitting thinking on the top stair. He'll see other fellows breaking their necks and their hearts tripping on the worn frayed parts or doing quite well for themselves stepping softly up the new carpet and he will ask himself what the next stage is to be in the absence of another flight of stairs."

"Flight!" exclaimed the girl excitedly. "That's why the Lark Ascending has been placed in the entrance hall here."

She started to run back the way they had come and Geoffrey hurried after her and joined her leaning over the gallery wall looking down on the wooden sculpture.

"They've put him there," she went on, "to show us that he'll hurl himself up against the skylight and break it and soar into the upper air. He's trying to discover something in his own way, his little wings beating, here, there, here, there, like his song, everywhere."

Geoffrey studied the high roof with its stretch of resistant glass reinforced strongly from the outside. Then he looked down at the impassioned instinct of wings.

"Do you know what will have to break through there, Kerry? The big guns of science. The great telescopes challenging the firmament. Then we shall see something new. Then the skylark will lift himself through the rent in the known to the unknown and sing of a new heaven and a new earth. But only Science can break the barrier and release the Arts! The questing howitzers will lead them."

The girl leaned with the palms of her hands pressed on the stone parapet and gazed concentratedly at the sculpture. It didn't matter! It was vulgar to scrap over precedence in such matters and if the arts were the handmaidens of truth, then let truth lead and let the arts attend her. Why, some of the Virgin Queen's ladies-in-waiting had more

410

admirers than she had herself and were probably better looking.

"Where are your gloves, Kerry?" asked Geoffrey, noticing the pallor of her hands. "It's not all that warm."

"They're in my case. They got wet this morning."

He put her school case and his book parcel on the parapet.

"Let's give them a warm up," and he took each hand separately between his own and rubbed vigorously. "They're as pale as any in these gilded frames. 'Pale hands I love beside the Shalimar-ar'."

"Sh," warned Kerry, giggling. "We shall be thrown out. Ouch!"

"What have I done? Is that a burn mark?"

"Yes. I threw a fallen stick on to Watch's funeral pyre that Jimmie made, and it was still hot."

"Oh, I'm sorry. Let me kiss it better."

"Why, is saliva good for burns?"

Geoffrey straightened up quickly and then gathered the case and parcel.

"Perhaps we'd better be moving. Have you a favourite picture here? We might get one from the reproduction stall by the door."

"Well, yes," answered Kerry, rather impressed at his guessing. "I suppose it's quite ordinary, just like the real thing, but I like to sit in front of it."

"Don't apologise for the old stair-carpet; there's years of wear in it yet. The present cult of mystery and symbol is a version of the secret writing that children do, passing notes that are indecipherable to those outside the group. The artist draws attention to himself, but at the same time wishes to seem an enigma, a member of a more secret society that meets in the attic or even the belfry. The landscape or still life is a friendly message to us all."

"There's another that I go to look at, but it's rather horrible. It shows a mountaineer just sliding over the edge of an icy precipice. His hands are clutching his head as his hair stands on end. It is awful, Geoffrey. He's staring at death down below."

"Very vivid, I'm sure, but we'll give it a miss today. You see, the artistic imagination is a pendulum. Like a Walt Disney cartoon, it can swing from fairies to demons, from the bottom of the garden to the bottom of the pit. But come on, we'll try to find your less shuddery favourite."

They made their way downstairs to the stands where anything from postcards to large sized pictures were on sale.

"I don't see it here," she said disappointedly after close inspection. "It must be sold out. It's called 'In the minister's garden' and it's got beehives and things and huge hollyhocks. Not at all like next door's!"

411

She broke off with a laugh and then stopped, aghast.

"We won't discuss the minister's lovesome plot, whatever it is," said Geoffrey drily and walked to the revolving door which he held in readiness for her. She passed through without looking at him and went silently down the steps. On the pavement he took her elbow and guided her through the traffic.

"This way," he said. "I wanted to get you a little memento of our visit here today, but I've thought of something else."

They walked along until he stopped in front of a large china shop.

"Do you fancy any of these little figures here? Rather pretty, I think."

"Oh, thank you very much," exclaimed Kerry admiringly, scanning them carefully. "I don't see a skylark; too small I suppose, and we've got a real budgerigar, although there's one there the exact image. Oh, look, there's a marvellous peacock! He'd remind me of that walk in the Clough we all had. Oh!"

She stopped in sheer misery again.

"When you drank from the lion fountain," Geoffrey said, trying to sound hearty. "Perhaps we'll get off birds. What about one of those dogs over there?"

This time it was his turn to want to kick himself. Watch! Kerry's mouth opened slightly and by common consent they turned their heads to see how the other was faring.

"Never mind, Kerry," he said rather forlornly. "Let's go inside and try to find a little glass pterodactyl or something else a bit before our time."

At this a quick laugh escaped her and she saw his mouth slowly widen and remain smiling as they went in at the shop door.

The lights were already switched on, sparkling on a vast array of cut glass vases, jars and bowls, tea and dinner services. At the back of one of the large windows a table had been laid for two and wine glasses glinted in the splendour of a deeply cut glass lamp in the centre.

"They're expecting us, it seems," whispered Geoffrey.

He asked permission to inspect the ranks of animal creation that would have baffled Noah to identify. They moved along carefully, spoilt for choice.

"I think after all, I'm going to choose a blue budgerigar, it is so very much like Gigli."

"You mean to have the substance as well as the shadow, lucky girl. The reality and the dream. Some fortunate people manage it. They slake their thirst at a pool reflecting the stars."

He picked up the blue bird and glanced round for the sales girl who advanced again and took it from him, quickly making a nest for it with tissue paper in a small box. She noticed Kerry watching this neat fingered operation and smiled pleasantly.

"It must be nice for you working amongst such beautiful objects all day," said Kerry enviously.

"Do you think so? I've certainly enjoyed being here, but I'm leaving after Easter, so you had better apply for the job."

She took Geoffrey's money and on her way to the till, repeated this conversation to her employer who looked towards the couple discreetly and then went over to them and bowed.

"Yes, we shall have to advertise for a young lady to take Miss Heath's place after Easter."

"Oh, a young lady!" answered Kerry sadly. "Then perhaps a girl wouldn't do. I'm still at school."

The man bowed again.

"A very young lady just leaving school is *exactly* what we want. If you are at all interested I'm sure that any application from you will be given every consideration."

Kerry was astounded at the unexpected vistas opening out before her. She'd never dreamed!

"Of course it all rests with Father. I don't suppose he'll let me leave school yet."

She was flurried. Leave school! She had never thought about such a thing. The Sixth did of course, but she was still a whole year from such a state of blessedness. Her eyes strayed to the brilliant cut glass on the intimate table for two. It was like a stage setting, everything was in order but nobody came on to seat themselves at the impending feast. There were no characters as yet, which seemed a waste of a good scene. What kind of people would enter and casually touch the fine china with alabaster hands and fill the wine glasses with red and gold fire before taking up the waxen fruit which at the touch of the pearl and silver dessert knives and forks, would change into the tempting apples of Eden and of the Hesperides?

"It is quite usual for a young lady's parents to come along to make enquiries."

Kerry switched back.

"Oh, is it? Well, Father's very keen on asking if a position leads anywhere. Has it any future? He's sure to ask that."

The man chuckled.

"Well, it could lead to an assistant with a reliable artistic sense becoming a buyer, but in Miss Heath's case it has led her to the altar. She is to marry one of our customers."

Geoffrey touched Kerry's arm.

"Come along, we'd better be going."

She gave an apologetic smile to the man and pretty Miss Heath as she moved away. Evidently Geoffrey did not want her to waste their time.

"I'll mention it at home."

She walked in silence for a time before she bubbled over.

"What do you think Father will say? I could have my plait cut off."

"And have it made into a bell-rope. It serves a better purpose where it is. Anybody at home?"

"Don't do that! But honestly, this little blue bird has brought me luck already. Such a thing had never entered my head until just now."

Geoffrey ruminated as they turned in the direction of Piccadilly. What would be the best for her? There was something radically wrong with women's education, he felt; either with the system or the teachers.

"How are the Maths getting on? How is the secret, black and midnight haggis?"

"Well, the Fridge leaves me alone now and never bothers me at all, which is more restful."

Geoffrey was startled.

"Leaves you alone? Does anybody else know on the staff or have you told them at home?"

"No, I haven't bothered to mention it to anybody."

"But my dear girl . . . " and he stopped helplessly.

"I was all right when you taught me," said Kerry and then stopped in dismay.

He noticed the words but not the sudden break.

"Yes, those were happy times when I used to come up and help you."

She nodded but remained silent as they made their way through the afternoon throng.

"We were getting on famously," he went on. "I only hope you enjoyed the lessons as much as I did."

"What?" she almost shouted, coming to a stand-still.

"Oh! come on, Kerry, you seemed glad at the time."

"Oh, I was! I was! And I wasn't wasting your time after all?"

"Time happily spent is never wasted, I think," he replied seriously and looking at her suddenly rapt face. "Now, what about school? You've another year to go."

She sighed at the reminder.

"Do you know what I think would be the ideal way to learn? Just a small group of friends together with a really sporty tutor, going for

414

rambles in fine weather and talking. Mr - er, somebody told me that wealthy Chinese families do it."

"I expect that some wealthy English families do it, too, but it isn't just a question of money. I suspect there wouldn't be enough philosophers to go round."

A century ago education for women had not been considered a matter of urgency, but it had now become so. Left to blossom without some learning in a modern world, they would not grow into bright flowers but would turn into less admirable forms of animal life as their resentful ignorance became more noticeable, more despised. That was how the secret languages, the mysteries, the brotherhoods of the abyss started. Not that Geoffrey loved the career girl with all his heart, but neither did he regard himself as an old Turk; he was definitely post Ata Turk for liberty of mind and the rent veil, but the female company that had always delighted him most was that of girls who had taken a few bites of the apple and had then stopped chewing, to sing.

He looked down at her. He could not help her any more, however, pleasant as being a sporty tutor as she called it, had been.

"But don't you want some sort of a career?" he queried. "Content to be a bul-bul in a china shop?"

She considered for a while.

"There is a great big office building on Oxford Road with huge high pillars in a courtyard which would be a marvellous place to stage *The Merchant of Venice*! I wouldn't mind working there."

"No merchant, Venetian or otherwise would take you on the staff with those ideas."

"And sometimes I feel I wouldn't mind being a missionary," but she stopped as if the words had scalded her lips.

Geoffrey took it very well.

"We can't have a mass exodus from these parts so you'd better stay at home and convert me. My good angel seems to be hiding his head under his wing, poor thing. But you'll have to do something and you can't stay at home."

"That would be terrible, having nothing else to think of but your relations."

"Your mother and mine have been very happy and with plenty of friends I'm sure they've had a very full life. Home is Gray's Elegy *and* the Heights of Abraham to fortunate people. Nothing wrong with that at all. By the way, Kerry, when you get home will you remember to give your mother my love? Please don't forget."

He had spoken so urgently that she was curious.

"I'll remember." Then after a moment, "Just her?"

'Well, we weren't talking about your father, and in any case he wouldn't be interested."

He had begun in some exasperation but was grinning as he finished and she laughed back.

"Easter isn't far away so I'll try and think it all out in the holidays when there's time."

"Will you be going to Blackpool again?"

The girl paused.

"It's a funny thing, but it's never been mentioned once. Whoever is living next door always looks after Ebony so I suppose Mother will ask Mrs Garner." She rushed on unthinking after mentioning the trouble-making name. "And of course Watch always goes to the farm."

He saw her woebegone at once and he spoke lightly.

"About ten years ago I had two goldfish which were rather a liability at holiday time. You can't take goldfish for walks like a lobster on a silver chain. Then I had Dutch rabbits for obvious reasons and later guinea pigs to drive the lesson home that some mickles make an awful muckle, or words to that effect. But the rarest pets I had were a couple of grubs I'd found when shelling peas once. Like you, it's a job I enjoy. We never became really 'intime', but I can remember their sharp black eyes to this day. One day they ran away, and Aunt Miriam was uneasy for days when she came over. Unlike Queen Victoria, she always looked before sitting down."

By this time Kerry was regarding him sideways as if not wishing to miss the slightest shade of expression as he recited this tally. After a minute or two another idea struck her.

"Speaking of grubs running away, how does one go abroad?"

"Abroad? Whatever for?"

"Places like America or Australia, to work in."

"My dear girl, the secret of the good life is to realise that foreign parts are for holidays; not to work in."

At this rate the girl would end up washing tin plates in some lumber camp! He felt that he could personally have wrung the Fridge's neck. If only somebody would find out what she could do happily for the next few years until . . . well, until being occupied with relations of some kind appeared more attractive than it did now. Suddenly he stretched out his arm and seized her plait as she threaded her way in and out of the pavement crowds of shoppers, and then drew her aside in front of one of the great windows of Lewis's shop where they could talk without his having to step off the pavement at intervals.

"It's just occurred to me. Have you ever been inside the Art School in All Saints? Students learn all sorts of things besides drawing and painting. There'll be lectures on appreciation and criticism, too, and it's the very place for you, Kerry. Why didn't anybody think of it before? While you were there, I'm sure something for the future would suggest itself. Your father is quite right, Kerry. It *is* important. Mention it to your Art mistress or your father and mother and . . . when all the family are there. They'll see it at once."

His enthusiasm was so strong that she was quite overcome and her sudden interest in the china shop and the Antipodes swung right over to this new inspiration. She was asking eager questions as they crossed Piccadilly, so that he had his work cut out to get her across and when they reached the pavement of Oldham Street she was overwhelmed with the prospect.

"I say, Geoffrey, it has been marvellous seeing you today. You've put all sorts of ideas into my head."

"I assure you it has been reciprocal," he responded gravely, although it was with an effort. As a matter of fact he felt an impulse to laugh aloud for some reason. The stir of the busy shopping street now seemed full of interest and not so much full of people getting in the way.

At one time he would have flattered himself with some cause that he lightly skimmed the cream of life, but later, by failing to protect it with a mesh of fine judgment, he had taken with it sundry foreign bodies and smuts that had turned it sour. The taste of it was in his mouth for weeks and months and was shown in the expression of the mouth. But perhaps lately; even today; particularly this afternoon if one wished to particularise, the bitter taste was not there and instead he felt a susceptibility to laughter, shared laughter.

"Kerry, if I tell you something in confidence, you'll keep it under your hat, won't you? But I, too, had been considering going abroad, for a time at least."

"Had you really, Geoffrey. Where?"

"Spain."

"Spain? I thought people were giving up going to Spain for holidays just now because of the rumour of a Civil War breaking out."

Geoffrey coughed non-committally.

"There is that, of course."

Kerry stopped dead in her tracks.

"You weren't going to *fight?*"

The stream of pedestrians divided and flowed round them unheeded.

"Can't you see me in the bullring, flapping a cape and side-stepping something like Northcroft's Samson?"

Kerry was puzzled.

"But why Spain? I wouldn't fight for either side unless they gave up bull fighting."

"I wouldn't put it quite so succinctly as you, but that is more or less my own attitude in that I find a certain inability to choose between them. The first reaction is to want to knock their heads together. (Let's move on, Kerry, before the crowds sweep us back.) It is the sort of situation that arises in personal as well as in national affairs and it seems to be catching. In either instance a democratic vote is better than resorting to the old-fashioned fern seed or grape shot, if you follow the horticultural terms. It's a solemn thought, Kerry, that the more one surveys the international landscape, the more one is drawn to Daisy Nook. I think I shall go cruising on Rudyard Lake this summer."

They had now come to Stevenson Square and Kerry paused, holding out her hand for her school case, but he retained it.

"I'll see you on to the tram. And do remember what I said about the Art School, won't you? And don't forget to give my love to your mother."

"Yes, thank you. And I've enjoyed today since a quarter to four. Give my love to Sun Tan."

Geoffrey's eyebrows shot up and she thought no doubt there had been some social lack in her leave-taking, but she couldn't very well send her love to Mr and Mrs Sinclair. Did anybody?

She took her case rather awkwardly and jumped at once on to the stationary tram, casting a parting glance at him before ascending the iron stairs. Perhaps his eyes seemed especially blue because she had not seen him for a long time and had partly forgotten. Halfway up she turned her head and looked again to make sure. Yes, they were very blue; not like the sky but like the sea.

Geoffrey caught the look and raised his hat, forgetting to smile as he watched.

"I stared too hard," Kerry accused herself regretfully. "He must think me very rude. He blushed for me."

418

Chapter Twenty-nine

No Methodist minister in an industrial area expects his church to be filled with worshippers over the Easter weekend. There is a great and thankful exodus to the coast, and to the Lancastrian the coast means not the Côte d'Azur or the Costa Brava with their torrid heats and chilling mistrals, but the bracing airs and social whirlwinds of Blackpool. The question "Where are you going for your holidays?" referred to the summer. At Easter the question was simply "Are you going away?"

At the ends of streets joining the Oldham Road the charabancs waited each morning for those making just the day trip, those who did not like sleeping in strange beds, those who did not care to leave their homes unguarded, those whose work or home tethers would not allow them longer rope. Some boards propped against those charabancs bore the tempting invitation to stranger delights, 'Over the Yorkshire Moors', but for the first delirious breakaway after the cold, the one word 'Blackpool' was all sufficient.

There were also the precious minority who timidly preferred the fringe of the fiery mantle, those who could not let themselves go in the saturnalia that covers positively square miles of roistering. Blackpool? Well nearly! We generally go to Southport or Morecambe; not quite so crowded, you know. The pressures of life there, the ecstasies and the ruinations are watered down somewhat. There is less gambling and recklessness and consequently less remorse and less drama; but Manchester appreciates poetry and drama and even melodrama, so for the most part the choice was Blackpool.

In the Methodist church on the Oldham Road the flowers on the Communion table and on the War memorial were in readiness and all were white. On Good Friday both the Communion table and the ledge below the bronze laurel wreath had been bare, and today they were alike laden; for they had much in common, those gilded names of men and the Name high over all.

Only Jennie Leat was in attendance there on Saturday afternoon. She stepped back to appreciate the general effect. People always said how well the flowers looked on these occasions. At Harvest Festivals when nearly everybody helped, there was a great Hallelujah Chorus of colour, massed bands of primary reds, blues and yellows which almost reverberated along with the organ pipes behind them. But the effect of the Easter flowers was quite as striking albeit so very different. The lilies on the Communion table, so pale and still with an avowed and dedicated whiteness as if holding their breath waiting for something to happen, were the essence of all whiteness, causing a visual amazement as might have assailed Adam's sight at the initial revelation; Behold purity!

Jennie sat for a few moments on the front seat where the fathers of brides retired from public notice after 'giving this woman away'. She thought of an article in the newspaper recently by a high-minded person who held the opinion that virtue was an end in itself and he fairly glowed with renunciation of all the promises made in solemn covenant to labouring humanity. Jennie remembered the parties enjoyed in childhood, with intervals between romps for cool drinks and crystallised fruits in round boxes with a tiny gold wire trident to dig them out. Sometimes in the games of hide-and-seek a door would be found locked or, if not locked would disclose only an exciting outline of a feast spread under a protecting cloth. Or the son of the house, seeking pencils would enter and open a drawer while a friend or two looked on. The children would fastidiously close the door afterwards, smiling and whispering prophetically of favoured delights. They would try to forget for another hour or so the elegant supper prepared for them, but no one was ignorant of the good-will of their host and hostess. No one, now reflected Jennie staring at the flowers on the Communion table, no one was so lacking in experience and hope as to doubt the solid reality of the feast under the white cloth; especially those who had been with the son of the house.

She turned to look again at the round plaque of the War memorial. Although without her spectacles she could not at this distance make out the lettering, she could correctly name each entry in that gilded roll of honour. She belonged to the generation that had been taught not to snatch, and habit had been too strong for her even when all the world was snatching. She and Ted, young as they were, ought to have realised the mischances of waiting. You can't put youth and beauty in the bank and draw them out just when you want to spend them; sometimes they are stored in the vaults for ever.

Just before dusk on that Easter Eve there was an urgent knocking on the minister's door. It was Jimmie Northcroft, very pale in the fading light.

"Can you come at once, please? Grandpa's been shot! I've been for Doctor Bedser."

Robert reached for his coat.

"Do you know what happened?"

"Father was passing through the yard with his gun and thought he heard rats in the manure heap and without thinking he fired; you know how he does. It looks as if Grandpa had just come out of Samson's pen and was standing there, perhaps looking at the sky for tomorrow's weather. I got on my bike at once and I'll be getting back now."

"I'll come as well," said Grace, hurrying into her outdoor things. "You know, poor Annie's had a trying time with the old boy; they get on each other's nerves rather."

"Perhaps so," answered Robert, "but she wouldn't get John to shoot him!"

The doctor's car was at the front gate of the farm when they arrived. They went round to the yard door and Jimmie let them in.

"It's not so bad. Doctor says it was only blast and surprise that knocked him down and he's suffering from shock. So is Father."

Robert turned to Grace with relief but she was looking towards the stairs at Annie coming down.

"It was an accident," said Annie in a casual voice.

"Of course it was," said Robert soothingly. "Jimmie told us."

Grace looked at her very keenly and went forward and took her hand.

"Perhaps not altogether an accident. I don't say your husband would let fly with a gun purposely . . ."

From the other side of the kitchen she heard Robert's gasp.

"I don't say that for a moment, but the thought that it must *not* happen wasn't uppermost in his mind, else he would never have fired in the first place. Really, some accidents seem almost providential."

Robert moved forward resolutely and laid a firm hand on his wife's arm. Annie already seemed more buoyant.

"Please sit by the fire until Doctor comes down. I must go and hear what he says," and she returned to the bedroom where she stood behind John's chair with her hand on his shoulder.

"Have a day or two in bed if you can bear it and you, Jimmie, do what you can to save your mother the running up and down, there's a good lad," the doctor was saying and relief showed on all their faces. "He has a sound constitution and this is where it tells."

They trooped onto the landing where the minister was waiting.

"Quite a shock at his age you understand, Mr Garner. Don't say anything to excite him," and Robert acquiesced with a sudden smile.

"Your other patient's recovering, John," continued the doctor as they went downstairs, "but he's very sorry for himself. A particularly nasty accident."

"Oh him!" exclaimed Annie contemptuously.

"Well, Samson's no pet dog," said John, and seeing Mrs Garner's look of mystification he went on to explain. "You see, one afternoon Pins and Needles came looking for my father and for some reason went straight to the pen. He must have leaned well over the half door as it's dark in there you know, but suddenly the great brute swung his head round and caught Pins and Needles a tremendous crack. It broke the poor fellow's jaw."

"Poor fellow!" scoffed Annie.

"I heard the racket," said John, "and ran to find him lying outside the door in an awful state."

"Was he swearing?" asked Grace with a shudder.

"You can't really tell with a broken jaw, Mrs Garner. I got him in the van and it's a good thing you were home, Doctor. But I don't think I'm liable. He was trespassing."

"May he be forgiven," said Grace. "But it's a wonder I hadn't heard since he's so well known."

Annie appeared to be considerably embarrassed.

"It was mentioned at the Sewing Meeting the following Wednesday but it must have been before you came, because it was certainly discussed. Mrs Mossop was in favour of a silver collection . . . you know, for a tit-bit of some kind for Samson."

Doctor Bedser gathered his gloves hurriedly and assured John he would call again on the morrow After seeing him out, John still looked scared and glum.

"I could have sworn it was a rat; I've shot dozens there."

Annie took down the tea caddy and paused with it in her hands.

"I'm content to thank Providence for its good intentions. I couldn't really expect it to do more. Now we'll all be glad of a cup of tea."

"It reminds me," said Jimmie, "of that time the Guild acted those scenes from Shakespeare. You know, Hamlet said *he* thought it was a rat behind the tapestry and it turned out to be the old man who might have been his father-in-law if he hadn't fallen out with his girl friend. Then he was sorry when he saw what he'd done and said 'I took thee for thy betters', meaning after all he'd thought it was actually the king hiding there. So really rats didn't come into it at all, but the thought of them had caused a lot of trouble."

"I do detest rats," confided Grace with horror.

"I don't mind them," said Jimmie easily, "but what I meant to say was that Father has been a lot luckier than Hamlet."

The comparison certainly had a cheering effect on John.

Then Robert, who had been ministering to the man luckier than old Polonius, came down to join them and the conversation widened in scope.

"Everyone's glad the bazaar is off," said Annie. "Not that it wasn't in a good cause, but it's nice to know we needn't be taking in each other's chair-back covers again. It was wonderful how the money seemed to pop up. Sam's offering I can well understand but the other is a bit of a mystery."

And a bit of a mystery it had to remain. Miriam had sincerely wished to make some kind of return to the church that had stood by her and shut the mouths of her enemies, but as an additional muffler round them she drew out the accumulated 'Divi' of all her widowed years and brought it to the minister as a thank-offering. She wanted to get rid of it, she said, as her brother-in-law did not approve of that Society. It was her guilty secret!

"A very happy turn of events for the Martlands," went on Annie, talkative since the family mouthpiece was helpless upstairs, "because although Leonard hankered after a better organ, Clara didn't relish the work of another bazaar. When do you think it will be installed, Mr Garner?"

Whitsuntide would see it in position and if it could be dedicated on Whit Sunday after the 'Walk', he would suggest that invitations be sent out and so make a special occasion of it.

"That will mean tea laid on in the Lecture Room for friends coming from a distance. It's going to be a big day I can see. I suppose there'll be special singing as well as the children's piece and, of course, Connie and Sybil as usual."

Annie stopped short. Those two wouldn't be wanting to sing together. She saw Jimmie flush deeply. Grace, however, was reminded of better news.

"I knew there was something! Yes, Connie's heard from one of the Pierrot troupes in Blackpool and if she satisfies them over Easter they're taking her on for the summer season and *that* ought to lead somewhere. She just needed to get into her stride, I've always thought. Have you ever watched cars trying to race a train just outside a railway station? Lorries and motor cycles all fancy their chance until suddenly the train clears the points and pulls ahead. Connie will be like that, I think."

"See if Grandpa would like another cup, Jimmie," said Annie with spirits further lightened. "We shall be rather thin on the field tomorrow, I'm afraid. The Martlands have gone as usual."

"I suppose you know how well things have turned out there?"

"Clara told me herself, Mrs Garner. They were passing after a walk in the Clough and called in. Len didn't say much but he looked pleased in his gentle way. They'll get on well together, both he and Sam being patient men. And what about the Buckleys? Surely they'll go away too."

"They were going to Southport," answered Robert, "but Doctor Bedser specifically ordered Blackpool."

"Yes!" laughed Grace. "A brisk walk along the cliffs each day and a show at night. Gracie Fields if they can get in."

John came out of a reverie.

"I'm glad Sam's out of the wood when everybody feared the lid was going on. He was always dependable. I expect they'll be staying in one of the big hotels."

"The Metropole, I believe."

"The Martlands," said Annie, "always go where they've been every year since the girls were little, near the Gynn. They'll be singing their Easter hymns at Adelaide Street tomorrow."

"Do we get many people from round about who don't come normally?" asked Robert hopefully.

"I doubt it," answered John. "They'll just about know that Monday is Bank Holiday. What I don't hold with is this singing of *Abide with Me* before a football match that they've started. I'd sooner it was *Old Macdougal had a farm*!"

Just then Jimmie came downstairs and reported that his grandfather had enjoyed the tea and had been talking.

"D'you know what he's on to now? He says he's going to make some alterations and take things more easily. He says Mrs Garner put him up to that. He wants to pull down some of the old sheds and build a long glass-house to grow early flowers! Can you beat it?"

Consternation and incredulity filled the air for some time and then Grace voiced her opinion.

"I don't remember putting him up to anything beyond a suggestion he might ease off, but this idea is worth considering. He'd be under cover and at least you'd know where he was."

"But even if the old sheds have to go," said Jimmie firmly, "Samson is staying as long as we keep a herd. They're having Samson to serve them and not just the vet with his bottled sunshine."

"Jimmie!" exclaimed his mother, very red, but he was very red too.

"If we are running a farm let it be a proper farm with the animals getting some sort of return for the living they give us. I've never forgotten what Mr Garner said once about the Squeal."

"Yes, Jimmie," said Grace softly. "Let that be Samson's tit-bit; his life."

"Ha! It looks as if the new boss has come!" Nevertheless, John gazed at his son with pride and without loss of self esteem.

A stick knocked on the ceiling, obviously banged by an uninjured personality. Jimmie sprang up and the minister and his wife also rose.

"Now that we know everything will be all right, we'll be getting back home. Thank you for the tea and the lovely cake."

"And thank you both for coming so quickly. You've been a great comfort."

Jimmie appeared leaning over the banisters with the bedroom door open behind him.

"He says will you all please sing a hymn before he settles for the night."

"That will be the best night-cap he could have. Jimmie, get your violin and we can stay in here where it's warm. What shall it be?"

In a few moments the big kitchen had slipped back in time a century or more to a scene that had its counterpart in candle-light and oil-lamp glow, when a small company of neighbours had met for a prayer meeting and the singing of hymns accompanied by a fiddle.

"Come ye that love the Lord and let your joys be known," said Annie quietly, and Jimmie thereupon played the first two lines and held the note for them to take up.

As they sang, each felt something of continuity and communion, making the occasion solemn and wonderful. Robert sang with his head raised, conscious of the poetry and truth held in Wesley's verse and responding with a heart grateful from long experience. As they sang the familiar hymn, new life welled up from the old phrases which time had strengthened and in no way diminished. For the duration of their singing young and old were a united congregation and a church.

"Then let our songs abound and every tear be dry."

When it was finished they bowed their heads for a few moments before making any movement, and Robert gave a quiet benediction. After the visitors had made their adieus, Jimmie put his violin away.

"Don't you go up, Mother! I'll ask him if he wants anything more. He's tough, isn't he? The stuff centenarians are made of I should think."

"It's nice for you to know you come of such stock; the thought ought to cheer you and your father at least."

"So it ought. I never thought of it like that," and he went off grinning.

The incident was to have merit after all. The boy had spoken as if he had a personal interest and say in the farm, and not a mention of America! John's gun had fired to good purpose as it turned out in the end, scaring off the birds of ill omen that had darkened the air for many months.

When Robert and Grace reached home they found David in the middle room waiting for them, much to their surprise, and they were also surprised to find that it was still quite early, just after half-past eight.

"No, Mother please don't get me anything; I'm not staying long."

Robert stirred up the fire.

"How is study going?"

"Oh! As well as anything goes; probably better."

His face made a sort of sneer at life in general that discomposed Grace.

"Now David, you've been overdoing it, that's easy to see. And you are having something to eat right now."

Robert looked at his son with concern when they were alone.

"Anything wrong?"

"Anything wrong?" David returned his father's gaze incredulously. "Well, it's not exactly right, is it?"

"In what way?"

The young man was silent awhile. Did it mean nothing to them?

"It may be what the Middle Ages called accidie." He stared at the fire and then at the deep purple window and sharply round at the wall behind him as if daring it to block his view, which it did. "Do you . . . do you see much of . . . next door?"

Amazement and relief struggled in Robert's face. Is there, perhaps, a greater simpleton than a scholarly, celibate young man? Frightening his family with his accidie!

"Oh, quite! They've come through a period of great strain; you know what the times are like, but things will be better for them now. Mr Martland has gone into business with someone he's known for a long time. Mrs Martland wasn't so well for a couple of months and your mother used to read to her in the afternoon quite often, *The Forsyte Saga* I think it was; your mother says it's the most aspidistral

426

work she knows."

Robert fell silent. If the boy wanted to know, he must ask.

After a while it came.

"And the girls?"

"Oh, the girls! Let me see, now; the girls! No, I don't think we hear so much singing as we used to. In fact, I should say *that* almost ceased at one time. And no laughter either. We heard both in plenty when we first came here, but with their mother not very well of course . . ."

David looked again at the passage wall.

"It seems terribly quiet tonight."

Grace came in with a tray.

"Now draw up to the table. I'll let you sugar your own."

He could do that yet, thought Robert, if he tried!

"Have you told him about Tom Kershaw and Ernest Ginnell?" she asked.

"Not yet, my dear. Those two are going into partnership, too, as makers of invalid furniture. Ella has plenty of ideas to keep them going and they hope to get orders from some big shops as they'll need some display of course."

"The goods will be rather pricey," said Grace, "but some production costs will be cut, working at home, and they'll have to be patented, but Mr Sinclair is helping in that direction."

At the name of Sinclair there was an uncomfortable pause.

"Not a sound from next door, is there?" burst out David.

"Oh, they've gone away!"

"What!"

"They always do at Easter."

"Where have they gone?"

"Blackpool. They've been to the same place for years, near the Gynn. Everybody says the Easter services at Adelaide Street are packed to the doors and you have to go early. Isn't that wonderful for these days?"

"You'd better take your mother," said Robert. "I can manage."

Grace shook her head. She would not let her husband get his own meals on that great day.

"But *you* go and report to us afterwards. It will be an experience. And you need a change of air, I can see."

David certainly showed more animation than when they had found him waiting there.

"I suppose it is an opportunity."

"One to be seized," said his father gravely.

Grace looked intently at her son. Puzzled, she glanced at her husband, whose gaze was fixed on him too.

David broke the rather prolonged silence.

"By the way," in a tone of voice that gave the matter the middle of the road, "I was passing the Prince's Theatre the night before last and I caught sight of Kerry going in to a performance of *The Co-optimists*! She wasn't alone. She was with . . . Sinclair."

His mother sat up very straight.

"Was she really? Just the two of them?"

He nodded.

"Well, of all things! Mrs Martland never mentions his name. It's an extraordinary thing."

"Not so very," said Robert. "I've known that happen before now."

"I'm sure he never comes up this way as there's nothing to interest him here now."

David in his turn was giving her his full attention.

"The fact is," she went on, "there was too much of the virgin martyr and the lion about that alliance."

Robert smiled.

"Are you suggesting, my dear, that he is now preparing a thorn for his flesh? That perhaps the paw might fester, even?"

"I only mean that this one will tame him a little."

"Ah, that is the function of love and music."

David was not enjoying their conversation and yet he gleaned some inspiration from it. He stood up as though jerked by strings.

"She distinctly said she'd do the choosing."

He sat down as if someone had let go.

"Perhaps she has," said Robert gently, "but no one has come forward with the winning number, it seems."

"Is it possible?" exclaimed David, pushing the tray from him. Then he sprang to his feet with limbs full of purpose.

"I'm sorry to rush away but I must look up some trains."

He shook hands with his father rousingly and hugged and kissed his mother and made for the door. They followed him.

"Don't read in the train tomorrow, dear. Rest your eyes and your mind."

"Tomorrow? I'm going tonight. By taxi if there's no train."

He disappeared hurriedly round the corner, evidently intending to walk until overtaken by a tram and Robert and Grace, still looking surprised by unexpected events, returned slowly to the dining room.

"What an evening for shocks! Perhaps we'd better drink some of this good tea. I wouldn't mind resting my own faculties for a few hours, but I'm afraid they've been set in perpetual motion for the night.

I shan't settle to anything. What on earth is going to happen now?"

Her whole attitude was a vast rhetorical question and Robert composed himself in his chair to listen to all the answers.

Forty minutes before Easter morning service at Adelaide Street, Blackpool, David declined to be shown to a seat immediately but stood in the vestibule looking at the backs of the congregation already forming, and then he went outside again.

He crossed the road and took up a position where he could watch the approaches. People were arriving early and it was not long before the stream widened and quickened. Finally it was in spate as family parties that had needed some organisation if not coercion came along. The Martlands were certain to come. Or could anything have delayed them, Kerry for instance, and decided them to go nearer North Shore?

Then he saw her. Mr and Mrs Martland were stepping briskly and several paces behind were Sybil and, yes, it was Kerry, almost as tall as her sister. Sybil was looking like a spring morning, but an early spring morning, before the sun was well up. Her colours were pastel, rain-washed, rainbow. Virgin martyr, his mother had called her; he felt angry at his mother's misunderstanding. He strode across the road with his eyes on her retreating form as they turned in at the gates and he overtook them just as they were being handed their hymn books, Mr Martland bringing up the rear. The busy sidesmen were looking left and right, counting empty places and signalling to each other.

"Four seats," said Len clearly, then became aware of a young man appearing at Sybil's elbow and saying to the sidesman:

"Two, please."

Clara touched her husband's arm.

"Come along," was all she said and he followed his wife and younger daughter.

"Mr Garner - David - is here," whispered Kerry when they were seated. Clara nodded composedly and opened her hymn book.

Sybil and David were upstairs in the gallery.

Sybil did not remember getting there, but her feet had evidently gone through the necessary motions. She sat looking straight ahead until the organist had finished the voluntary and the full choir had sung their opening introit. Then the congregation rose to fill the church with a great uprush of song.

"Love divine, all loves excelling,
    Joy of heaven, to earth come down."

Here were a people exulting in unison. They sang without restraint in the knowledge that in the universal shout they would hardly hear their own voices. The organ pealed out and each singer felt quite disembodied by that deep throbbing, as if they were a vast cherub choir.

The hymn held together a crowd of people from all over Lancashire and beyond as if they were a well rehearsed choir. They all knew the tune; they all knew the words, and the fervour of the singing was not just that the tune was loved but that the words were believed. A Christian congregation, here well-dressed, prosperous looking, pleased with life; any who might say that these people were pleased with themselves, complacent and hidebound, would be blind in spite of their over-keen scrutiny.

Any sense of satisfaction was not self-satisfaction but a repletion of spirit. Any sense of assurance came from an assurance inherent in their belief and gave to their faces and bearing on this Easter morning a felicity, an added strength that the unbeliever could only misunderstand and misname.

Sybil had no hymn book and so shared David's, which made them turn very slightly towards each other. She was aware of his voice not always quite hitting the note and sometimes abandoning the chase for a whole line. She looked at his hand and white rim of cuff, the edge of the jacket sleeve and it all seemed very familiar as if she had studied it before and it was important that she should recognise it.

He regarded her unsinging profile. She was not yet sufficiently collected even to move her lips. She had controlled her breathing after her first gasp of surprise but amazement was still with her. Not a word, not a sign, for weeks and weeks! Not a hint of anything but interest withdrawn and then suddenly to appear beside her in the aisle below, assuming control and partnership as if they had arrived together by mutual arrangement. The hymn swelled as if the windows would fly out.

"Suddenly return and never
Never more Thy temples leave."

If only he could get her to look at him just once, so that he might know where he stood. Perhaps he had been a little over-bearing downstairs, without a by-your-leave, but she had not shaken him off or walked out. She continued to look towards the Communion space filled with flowers to remind humankind of that other garden, where a girl had come before it was yet day and made that marvellous encounter with One whose swaddling bands at human birth were symbolic of the constrictions of earthly life and which were not in reality put off until once and for all they were discarded and folded in finality on that renascent morning.

David looked at her, flower-like, early one morning just as the sun was rising, as the song went. How could he get her to look at him? He must know before the prayer.

"Sybil," he said at the end of a line. She had heard because she inclined her head a little as though listening albeit doubtfully.

"Sybil."

He slid his other hand over the printed words so that in astonishment she looked up at him.

His eyes were waiting as they had waited upon other occasions and again they transfixed her shy glance with their steady gaze. She looked at him and her eyes were held although her lips were tremulous. Why had he left her for so long? Because she could not answer her own unspoken question, her head gave two or three infinitesimal shakes. But even as she looked and saw the undoubted meaning in his face the sad little shake wavered and stopped, the tremulous lips parted and light swept over her features from warmth within. Almost imperceptibly, her head gave two or three acquiescent little movements and at that, both of them exhaled their breath in a sigh through lips that smiled at last. The sun was up and it was day; not just any day, not even a glorious spring morning; but Easter morning and all the bells ringing.

Leonard did not rise at the end of the service; he wanted to hear the *Trumpet Voluntary* to the end and wondered how it would sound on the new organ to be built by Whitsuntide on Oldham Road.

If small church choirs can sing the *Hallelujah Chorus*, then small church organs are entitled to play the *Trumpet Voluntary* as fully as their pipes permit. He hoped Fred Winskill had enjoyed playing at home today.

Outside they found Sybil and David waiting.

They shook hands with him and asked after his parents.

"I think Mother would have come but for leaving my father. The singing was magnificent, wasn't it?" He felt he was on safe ground there. They walked down to the promenade in a haphazard group all talking together and then turned north.

"When did you come?" asked Leonard.

"Early this morning. I thought a breath of fresh air would be beneficial after all the wet we've been having. It has been fairly miserable, hasn't it?"

No one answered as each thought back to his own fairly miserable time.

Leonard and Clara and Kerry fell behind.

"It's a queer situation," said Len, "turning up out of the blue like this."

"Never mind, if Sybil's pleased."

The pair ahead took the middle promenade so Clara, followed by the other two, went down onto the lower walk. They stood and watched the children who had built their castles on the sands during the morning and who were now being called away. The children were loth to leave their work to jealous and hostile tribes, people who came along and jumped on unguarded castles, but they had to go as already the tide was coming in to wipe the sands clean - a lesson in history and geography.

The family did not meet again until they sat down to lunch. Leonard came to the conclusion that Sybil was pleased.

"What are we doing this afternoon?" he asked briskly. There was no reply until Clara spoke.

"Oh, I think we'll walk along towards Norbreck. Are you coming, Kerry?"

Kerry sawed at her meat intently.

"No thanks. I'd rather walk along the sands."

"Well, watch out because the tide will be coming in. You will be in for tea, I suppose."

"It will be all right if I'm not, won't it?"

"Don't fag yourself out, that's all, and don't go on the sands in your best shoes. Did anybody catch sight of any more of our folk in Adelaide Street? It's hard to tell in that crowd. Ada and Alfred are at Lytham so Southport will have to look to its laurels."

"Hydrangeas rather," corrected Len. If a man lives by a stream he may not always be listening to its chatter but he misses it if he should be out of hearing. His family were Len's stream and he was glad to hear it again, having almost forgotten that for a time he had been deaf to it when another deluge filled his ears.

"I must get my postcards written before I go out," said Clara.

"Your holiday will be over," said Len. "I know someone who writes a whole lot of postcards before he leaves home, such as 'Just arrived, pleasant journey', or 'Nice place to stay; comfortable bed', and then he posts them when he gets there and is too busy to write. He's done it for years."

"I don't think that's a proper attitude at all," said Clara. "I'll go and get mine done."

Before she had finished more than two there was a knock on the bedroom door and Sybil appeared. Clara felt her eyes prick with near tears. What numbskulls men were!

"He's calling for me at a quarter to three so I'll go straight out when he rings."

"Where is he staying?"

"I don't know yet; somewhere quite near." She came forward to kiss her mother.

"Well, you've got a most unexpected Easter egg," Clara said laughing, "so off you go to eat it."

By the time Clara had rejoined Len downstairs there was no sign of Kerry either.

"I suppose you didn't notice whether she had changed her shoes? Did she say anything before she went off?"

Len folded his newspaper, the flamboyant kind with pictures that he only read on holiday, and looked at Clara with a faint smile.

"She just said 'Having a lovely time; comfortable bed of roses!" Well, my dear, I am ready if you've finished your postcards."

It was breezy at the top of the Tower and David was supporting Sybil as if a tornado were blowing. They were standing in one corner and other people circled round slowly enjoying the view.

"Sybil, darling, I have been through hell."

"It's funny you didn't see me, then."

With an exclamation he got a further grip on things and she gazed through the curving bars at the hills beyond Morecambe and seawards at the three piers, from this height looking like resting ukuleles. He spoke almost accusingly.

"But you distinctly said you would do the choosing."

"I thought you didn't care any more. Father knows a man who collected china figures and one of his favourites was a shepherdess, quite an expensive thing. One day one of her fingers got broken and he couldn't bear to look at her again, so he put her in the dustbin. That is what I thought you had done."

David was incapable of speech for a moment.

"But you practically threw us out! I never felt so utterly cheap and worthless in all my life, small enough to go out of the gate without opening it. You made out I was less than the dust and now you talk of dustbins as if I had been doing the sweeping. You flung me so far it has taken me weeks to crawl back."

They lowered their eyes to the great rollers thumping against the stocky walls five hundred feet down. The tide was now well up and spray was flung high into the air. The sea was in pantomime dame

t

mood. It would suddenly give a flippant slap and lob a few hundred-weight of pebbles and seaweed onto the road and then subside for a moment, waiting for a motor car to pass and surprise it with a salty douche.

"People look small as insects down there," said Sybil lazily, for although the Tower was vibrating she was leaning comfortably against a strong support and was prepared to rest there indefinitely. Other people were descending and new ones coming out on to the platform, but these two were dawdling there as if it were midsummer.

"Yes, that is the danger of heights. We'll go to Paris one day and see the gargoyles of Notre Dame. They show perfectly how easy it is to have an Olympian scorn of all creatures there below."

"I didn't mean . . . "

David laughed and gave her a reassuring squeeze.

"As a minister's wife, which you are going to be, of course you didn't mean."

She pondered awhile.

"Do you think I will make a good minister's wife? We don't know each other very well really, and I never got round to calling you David, did I?"

"Would you do better with Frederick? Perhaps if you called me Frederick for a week you might slip into calling me David more easily? So long as you get it right in the marriage service."

"Marriage!" echoed Sybil.

"That is usual with people in love, isn't it?"

"But we've only just found out, for certain that is. Let's hug it to ourselves awhile."

"I'm all for hugging it to ourselves for as long as you like but still I must tell your father. Could you be ready by August?"

"August of this year?" queried Sybil faintly.

"August of this year, or at the latest September, until death do us part or rather 'us depart' as one rendering has it."

"I don't like that part," said Sybil.

"No, we none of us like that part but marriage is rather like a Shaw play; it's not the beginning and end that matter so much as all that interesting talk in between. The end is only a small walking off part. Which appeals to you most, Scotland or Cornwall?"

"I think I should like to climb a few mountains."

"Good! Pack a stout pair of shoes whatever else you have to throw out."

They stayed mute for a time and gazed into the distance. Could she be ready by August - not a tray cloth in sight! She didn't even know where on the face of the earth she would have to live. China? Portugal? But she wouldn't be taking tray-cloths along; there would be mountains to climb.

When he spoke again he was smiling.

"Do you know, you have never met my friend Warner! He must be the one and only best man. And Margaret will come, of course. The reception is the worst part. The dazed couple stand while all the guests file past opening their mouths like goldfish and congratulations float out like ants eggs. Relations appear who haven't been seen for years and nobody knows them and some well loved friends are unavoidably absent."

"I want you to meet my aunt Fanny. Mother was afraid I was going to be like her. I'll tell you about her some day."

"It's wonderful to think there will be plenty of time for telling each other things."

After a time she moved her head slightly to study his profile. He was looking far out to the horizon and was very still. Perhaps he would always do that when voices ceased and pressing demands were eased. When she saw him thus, she would keep silent and still too, waiting for him to fly back to her side and tell her where he had been ranging. And in time she would learn to fly alongside, to see the lands where corals lie, with him.

When Ada Sinclair was fully convinced that her son was quite out of danger from Clara Martland's girl and had evaded any flank attack from Connie Ginnell, she made a very sensible suggestion to Alfred that she would never have contemplated on her own behalf.

"I suppose Geoffrey has enough money on him to do things properly?"

"I don't know that he needs much money to do what he is expected to do properly, that is study."

"Yes, I know, but is he in a position to mix on an equal footing with them all? Now that he hasn't much temptation to throw it about he can be trusted with a bigger allowance."

Well, yes, Alfred could see the point. It looked as if it was all off with Sybil and what with the fuss about the Rag Rag! Too much fuss altogether. Why, at his elementary school - never mind that now, but perhaps Geoffrey would be feeling a bit low. What the boy needed was some cheering up and good money was a wonderful tonic. A great pity about Sybil. She would have been pleasant to have about. Well, money talks, so he would let it say something cheerful to Geoffrey this week-end.

On Easter Sunday afternoon Geoffrey alighted from the tram that had brought him from Lytham to St. Anne's and he crossed the road to meet the traffic approaching from Blackpool. The trams each way were crowded as people were making excursions to the places where they might have stayed, to see if they were missing anything. From the wide and flower-bedded square more holiday strollers were crossing to the promenade and the pier, neither to be compared with Blackpool's for size and popularity but claiming perhaps more personal and tender fidelity. Older visitors remembered that long before Blackpool went in for myriads of coloured lights along its wide front, St. Anne's had heightened the summer dusk with modest clusters of lights hidden among the trees and shrubberies of the squares and gardens. On the promenade where the water gardens were such a dainty feature of the landscape, the council's imagination had been given romantic rein and at every turn of the pebbled walks a delicate picture presented itself of tinted stream, glowing lilies, green leaves intensified and emboldened, and the waterfall, gushing crystal by day, at twilight was transformed into a tumbling rainbow with its foot in a crock of golden foam.

In St. Anne's, lovers were not lost in a crowd of other hugger-mugger sweethearts but had to seek out hiding places in between the lights and on forms placed discreetly in leafy alcoves. The bolder ones walked out to the sand hills and in their little Sahara, with the sea grass rustling and the blackberry thorn pricking, they found solitude and sweet privacy away from the all-seeing holiday folk. There they ceased to be just any 'Arry and 'Arriet but found themselves to be Troilus and Cressida, Lancelot and Elaine or Jacob and Rachel, each with a personal history and a personal strength or weakness of purpose.

But in the early afternoon sunshine the decorous crowds took their ease in the gardens, watched the promenaders and chatted to casual acquaintances alongside on the public seats, while the contented tobacco smoke ascended with the pervading buzz of talk.

Geoffrey was looking in the furniture shop windows in between watching each tram approach and he decided that he did not care for bogus Tudor tables with lumpish legs and housemaids' knee. Perhaps they were all right with the pewter tankards of their day banging down on them and all that was meant by a groaning board, but their lustiness mocked at the bijou residences that were to house them now. People were clinging piteously to a semblance of ye olde England among so much that was gimcrack and new. They were chucking out the gilt-framed pictures, the flowered wall-papers and mirrored overmantels of the parental home, and shuffling in came the drab devils of monochrome, the tiny etchings in a waste of white mount with funeral card edging, the staring frameless mirrors, the oatmeal walls, the plain lampshades thonged at the seams and the carpets with their sad autumn leaves. A new style would evolve but it hadn't arrived yet and the present one was mousey, refined, and timid.

He glanced away to the road and watched several people alight from a tram, one girl reminding him of graceful Sybil. Kerry! He moved forward quickly.

"Hello! For an instant I didn't recognise you. In that hat you look positively unconverted."

"It's my new costume, and you're the second today to say that. Mr Garner didn't know me at first."

Oh bother! She hadn't meant to mention him. She was starting early today!

Geoffrey looked questioningly.

"Garner here?"

She would have to explain.

"Yes, he came to Adelaide Street this morning."

"Did he sit with you?"

"Oh, not with us. He and Sybil went upstairs."

"Did they indeed."

She stood awkwardly, hesitating to move before they had agreed which way to go. Then a thought struck her.

"If you'd like to go back to Blackpool at once, I don't mind."

He stared for a moment uncomprehendingly and then he suddenly smiled.

"Oh, them! I expect they'll soon be going to the Holy Land and coming back with their little bottle of Jordan water."

Kerry felt lighter hearted at once.

"Where are we going? In the gardens or on the front?"

"Let's go and see if the sea is within hailing distance here. Have you heard of the man who jumped off Southport pier and got stuck in the mud?"

They crossed the road and walked towards the pier-head. The sea was unbearable to the gaze where each wave turned over in the sunlight and gleamed like tinfoil.

"I don't think I'd better walk on the pebbles in these shoes," said Kerry apologetically. "It's different in summer when I'm wearing sandals."

"But you are comfortable for a good walk?"

"Oh, of course. And you've got a nice suit on as well. You look quite like an advertisement."

"I say, if you talk like that I'll go and roll in the road."

There were plenty of people about by the pier-head but the crowds were not dense, moving with the placid unity of pacing kine.

"I know St. Anne's much better in August, of course, and even then it's never so crowded as Blackpool."

"Little snob!"

"Well, I like that! You've said some awful things about crowds in your time. In fact you've said some awful things about most things."

"You mustn't take any notice of what I've said, Kerry. In fact, it would be a good thing if you forgot everything I've ever uttered."

She looked up at him. He had his 'Portrait of Cardinal Newman' mouth on.

"I think I know how you feel, Geoffrey. You're like the people who are always searching for rare editions. Well, I'm not a bit interested in first editions. I like to see on the opening page '13th impression. 300,000 copies sold'. It gives me an exciting feeling that I have 300,000 friends really. The fact that I haven't met any of them doesn't alter the fact that they are knocking about the world somewhere."

"You have proved yourself not stand-offish and I apologise. Some day, Kerry, I hope you will visit Versailles near Paris where the mood was at its least democratic. Now, which way shall we go?"

"There's more to see this way. Further on we can just see the remains of an old wreck if the tide is not too high. I like wrecks, don't *you?*"

"I'm so glad," answered Geoffrey.

"Although it wasn't a proper wreck. Everybody escaped."

"I'm still glad."

They paused to look at the memorial to a 'proper wreck' which had taken place many years ago and then they walked on, Kerry pointing out the designs in pebbles which adorned the garden walls of all the houses, neat panels of grey and white stones sunk into the burnt brickwork giving the most casual visitors the lasting impression that here was a small town that had been carefully built with local pride as well as with local material. Wind-breaks of stone topped with long sand-grasses sheltered the promenade gardens from the sea breezes on one side and from the road on the other, and between them twisted and turned the flagged paths playing touch and go with the stream winding through well tended flowers. Passing an alcove set well back, Kerry loitered.

"I read *The Cloister and the Hearth* there last summer, day after day. I could usually stretch out on the form, it's so well hidden."

"I should think it got rather hard, didn't it? When it comes to making a choice, Kerry, remember the hearth provides more comfortable seating than any cloistered bench."

Before crossing the stone bridge they stood admiring the pebble pictures of a ship and a windmill set in its paving.

"Well," said Geoffrey, "there is an Itinerary of Lancashire written in the last century that speaks of this region's 'unprofitable and wearisome sands', but the author would have to admit that out of their stony griefs the inhabitants have raised some delightful little follies; stone tapestries, every stitch a well-matched pebble."

Kerry was proud that he was showing such appreciation. Rounding a bend they came across a clump of tall lilies so white that people in passing exclaimed in admiration. The two strollers decided to sit and view them for a time.

"Where did you go this morning?" she asked casually.

"I'm afraid I didn't go anywhere."

"Not on Easter Sunday?"

He shook his head, keeping his eyes on the lilies in order not to meet her rather shocked gaze, so he missed the fact that it was also a rather envious gaze.

"It was such a glorious day for backsliding."

"Well, where were you then?"

"As a matter of fact I stayed in bed."

"Gracious! Father got me up to go for a walk before breakfast. What time did you have yours?"

"I didn't bother with any."

Kerry was scandalised.

"But they give you such gorgeous breakfasts on holiday, porridge or fish as well as eggs and bacon if you want it. Even Mother has a bigger breakfast on holiday."

"I had been reading late, you see, Kerry, and so slept late."

"Oh, history?"

"In a way."

"What part?"

"It's an account of a famous young French woman."

"Joan of Arc?"

"No, much later, and rather older."

"What was her name?"

"She was called Emma Bovary."

"And I suppose you are reading it in French."

He nodded and she fell silent and he took advantage of her silence to change the subject completely.

"I'm not constitutionally an early riser, but I have ceased to regard that disability as a vice. It is a misfortune like being born with a squint. I used to waste time in idle resolutions but it's not important and I just happen to be Pip Emma rather than Ack Emma."

"I've never heard of Emma Bovary," confessed Kerry as her thoughts were switched back. "Was she at the time of the Revolution, like Charlotte Corday, or was she with the no bread and eat cake crowd?"

"Nearer our times. She had her private revolution and preferred stale cake crumbs to bread. They choked her. Now, Kerry, if you've considered the lilies for long enough, shall we move on?"

"All right; but aren't they a passionate white?"

She went close and stood as it were eye to eye with them. She turned to seek his agreement and found his look pessimistic. He also came nearer and inspected the lilies with her.

"Passionate whiteness as you call it is a considerable achievement, but be careful not to touch it or a brown stain appears. But we can't leave well alone, can we? We paint it and produce tiger lilies. Whiteness can be so sterile, it can look so anaemic and lifeless, like my sainted Aunt Miriam . . . " He broke off as Kerry pealed with laughter.

"To you all aunts are aunt Sallies. I've only got one and she's awfully nice, really. Aunt Fanny lives in Southport, you know, and we shall all be trooping across to see her tomorrow I expect. She never married on principle, and lives quite alone except for her dog. Mother is rather sorry for her but I think it's an ideal life myself."

They walked on musing upon this until Kerry added after some thought, "Well perhaps not absolutely ideal."

Geoffrey smiled.

"I expect you'd be glad when one of your 300,000 friends called."

The gardens were now left behind and the promenade, like certain stretches of the Nile, disappeared into the sand.

"What's that white tower gleaming over there? Is it some sort of municipal baths?"

Kerry was deeply hurt.

"It's a lovely white church, a Congregational church, and it has windows like illuminated manuscripts. In summer I walk out there sometimes to sit and enjoy the solitude, especially in a heatwave. It doesn't look a bit like a swimming bath."

"I could only see the top from this distance. Shall we walk that way and have a closer look?"

They made it their objective and when they got up to it, Geoffrey conceded that it was an unusual and very pleasing exterior, very fitting for a seaside atmosphere. They sauntered to the porch where Kerry slapped the white doorway briskly.

"This doesn't stain. If anything shows a bruise, it's one's hand."

It was considerably darker inside with no lights on and the windows glowed richly high on the walls, every picture telling a story, the religious heraldry of the simple.

"It's a cool place now," whispered Kerry, "but I expect it lends itself to Christmas very well with this dark wood and the fire in the glass. It's all a bit unexpected inside and out."

"It's strange how the stained glass magic lantern survives in a century when everybody can read, but Shelley's white radiance of eternity without and within might have been too blinding for us. So we have concealment by adornment again, the eye fogging the mind."

"Oh no!" protested the girl. "I think of all sorts of things when I'm sitting here alone. It's Joe's cloak of many colours again."

"That artist's cloak has many functions, by the way. It can sometimes be a time and money saver, and can cover innumerable omissions. Suburban poverty is to cut one's coat according to one's cloth, painfully, with some idea of fashionable line, but the artist does not waste time and material cutting his cloth; he flings it round his shoulders where it hangs usefully but as gracefully as the cloak of poor Clare."

Kerry had always fancied a cloak herself since that man holding a glass of port appeared on the hoardings.

Their ways parted for a time as in silence each made a separate circuit of the aisles and as Geoffrey got round to the porch again Kerry was gratified to hear a quite heavy coin dropped into an unobtrusive box.

They came out blinking into the sunshine.

"Where now, Kerry? Would you like an hour on Fairhaven Lake?"

"No, thank you. I'd rather walk back on the other side of the road."

They went along, eyeing the comfortable detached houses facing the sea and looking as if Didsbury had taken a flying leap and landed here a little self-consciously. Here lived the men who filled the club train to Manchester each morning and who still liked to be at their desks by nine sharp. Their places of retirement were already settled and the harness was eased off gradually, or so they imagined until they had actually exchanged the pen for the garden roller and cutter.

"I try to spot the houses where I should like to be asked to tea," said Kerry. "The people might turn out to be awful really, but I do feel we have something in common where there's a garden swing."

They walked slowly, criticising or praising the architecture and the gardens until they got back to the town. Geoffrey looked at his watch.

"It'll soon be tea time, but would you care for an ice first?"

"It's Sunday," she reminded him.

"The better the fruit sundae then. If you don't mind having your tea at a café on Sunday, you can't mind having an ice, surely."

"We shall have to get some tea sometime, but an ice is a luxury."

"My dear girl, the waitress on duty doesn't care whether she provides you with a pot of tea or an ice. I remember at one time my mother wouldn't use the car on Sundays; it was a luxury we could do without, so we had to make use of public transport. It was some time before she realised that she was employing Sunday labour unnecessarily and also perhaps taking the room of people who would have to walk in the rain if the trams were full. So she went back to the luxury. Now, would you care for an ice?"

"No!" said Kerry and as an afterthought, "Thanks!"

They walked past the primly closed shops towards the Ashton Gardens, she walked quickly as if she did not mind whether she was accompanied or not. She went through the gates with an air of being quite alone and when he addressed his next more careful remark she raised her eyebrows in surprise at finding him still at her side. His manner, however, was most conciliatory.

"I suppose this place is even more lovely in summer than it is now."

The remark was received with a graciousness that quickly warmed into the confidential again and she slowed her pace.

"I once ate two pounds of Victoria plums in that tree."

"Do they allow people to climb trees here?"

"Of course not!" impatiently. "There were more leaves then."

They passed the empty Sabbath tennis courts and bowling greens and she led him to the rose garden, a sheltered area sunk below the level of the surrounding terrain. Here again there could only be a promise of coming glory as all the opulence and over-bearing abundance of summer was only just stirring. They went by easy declivity to the paved expanse below and in front of a grottoed fountain Geoffrey paused to declaim a verse carved in the flagstone underfoot.

"The kiss of the sun for pardon;
    The song of the birds for mirth;
    You are nearer God's heart promenadin',
    Than anywhere else on earth."

"It isn't," laughed Kerry, glancing down at the familiar words almost in doubt.

"And I suppose you've put in some hours of reading here, too."

"Oh, rather! In there when it was blazing and over there when it was cool. I remember once when my legs were so scratched by brambles on my sunburn that I could hardly bear it, I came here and stretched out on that form at the end of the arbour to read *The White Company* and I covered my legs with rose petals. This garden was like a great bowl of pot pourri and I just helped myself to handfuls and let them drop in a soft shower. It was heavenly."

"Let's go and sit there now," Geoffrey suggested, and they toured the sheltering wall to where it passed a gentle arm round the last bower. Seated on the form they looked out upon the well-behaved scene, the borders and angles of the bush-filled plots being geometrically clear.

"The flower beds are neat as a school dormitory as yet but in a couple of months it will look like a pillow fight," said Geoffrey, leaning back contentedly.

Immense seasons of time pass and generation follows generation as primrose follows snowdrop, the daffodil and tulip giving place to the rose, each knowing nothing of the past and future save what can be remembered of a green pillar of stalk with its capital of petals in ruins at its base, or of a dying glance at some strange new bud with its secret still unfolded.

Kerry had spent summer after summer in this place and now, looking out from her favourite arbour she wondered if people's ghosts or shades or whatever they are ever haunted a place even during their lifetime. Mine would come here, she thought. Books and roses! Could there be lovelier company? To be reading and have the scent of roses wafted so strongly into one's consciousness as if something were trying to draw attention to itself and then, after leaving the book and gazing at the roses for a time, the eyes returned as the story asserted its own drama again so that one alternately read the printed page and the illuminated vellum of the flowers.

She had forgotten him it appeared, not out of pique but from remembering a time and a scene in which he had no part. He closed his eyes and left her to dream again in this place where she had so often dreamed alone. Some time later, softly and without a word he got to his feet and very deliberately strolled back to the centre of the garden and paced slowly round the square pool, looking intently into its shallows neatly overhung with flat stones.

Kerry watched him move away with some surprise, wondering if he were going to look at some striking bush that had suddenly caught his notice. She continued to watch him. How gracefully he moved. He had thrown his light jacket over one shoulder where it hung like a short Elizabethan cape or the cloak of Apollo; certainly not the cloak of poor

443

Clare. What was he so intent upon? At the far side of the pool, beyond the central ornamental figure, he paused and faced the way he had come, reflectively taking in the scene. Then he waved lightly to the watching girl. It wasn't beckoning but just a wave of recognition and she smiled and shyly raised her hand in reply. He at once started to walk towards her again.

"I just went to see what life, if any, was in the pool. With the naked eye only newts, water lilies and a few water beetles who seem to have lost their sense of direction momentarily, sculling around trying to remember where they were supposed to be going. They'll probably find out before the day is finished."

"I hope they'll be pleased," answered Kerry, rising, and they walked slowly and in silence towards the far end of the garden where she turned and stood looking back along its length. Books and roses and . . ?

They wandered through all the deceptive convolutions of the gardens and after another half hour were as thirsty as if they had been for a very long walk.

"Nothing in this place is as the crow flies," said Geoffrey, "perhaps because there don't seem to be any crows about. The layout of these paths has been designed on the flight of a drunken bee; one of your mother's Jerusalem bees. I think we'll go and look for tea now."

The Pavilion was empty after the afternoon's music, tea tables were already in use on the pavement outside where hanging baskets and lavish arrangements of early flowers glowed with spring energy. Eating in the fresh air is an innovation for city dwellers and they looked about them with pleasure.

Geoffrey ordered tea while Kerry was studying the menu and she asked for green salad. When the waitress had withdrawn Kerry made a sort of game guessing how many differing comestibles there would be.

"Lettuce, cucumber, cress, perhaps parsley."

"Olives and gherkins," suggested Geoffrey.

Kerry hoped not; skiddy things.

Geoffrey invited her to pour the tea. There was no need to ask how many lumps; she knew, and inwardly thought this one of the most exciting moments of her life.

The green salad did not take long to prepare and she was confronted with two lettuce leaves and nothing else on the plate. She stared at it perplexed.

"Hard luck," sympathised Geoffrey. "You'd better order something else to introduce a little colour."

"This'll do for now."

"All right and we'll have something after."

Kerry thought a knife and fork was overdoing it for two lettuce leaves and even taken in shreds with thin bread and butter they were finished very quickly, before Geoffrey's more robust fare. It was very pleasant sitting there, however, and a little subsidiary orchestra of three, piano, violin and cello had now struck up just inside the big open windows. How brightly the geraniums pulsated in the light. They reminded her of holidays at her elementary school, when favoured children took home a classroom plant to tend. She had liked best the fuchsias with their pendant Japanese lanterns which had to be carried so carefully and if, on the returning Monday she hurried, they all dropped off. But she nearly always got a sturdy geranium as experience had taught her teachers that her care was erratic and in summer the whole family went away leaving the ferns and aspidistras submerged like the brides in the bath and with similar results.

"Now then, Kerry, what shall it be now?"

"I'd like French plums, please."

The waitress gave her an enigmatic look and took Geoffrey's order and retired.

"Delilah's still going it in there," he observed. "If one were going to the opera one wouldn't wish to hear it first on three instruments, but in cafés a little scraping of gut doesn't sound amiss. If people don't want to talk they can pretend they're listening to the music and again those with weak digestions find the cello a great ally."

Kerry's mirth was cut short as the French plums were placed before her. Prunes!

She stared across at Geoffrey as the girl hurried away.

"What do you think I'd get if I asked for apple pie?"

Geoffrey called the waitress back.

"The lady would prefer a fruit salad; you know, just get into a frenzy with the tin opener; open the lot and then bring a sample of each. And some cream, please."

That was better. If life started playing practical jokes, people like Geoffrey just re-ordered in a masterful way. Only the best and with dollops of cream.

"What's that lovely tune they're playing now?" she asked while they were waiting.

He listened for a moment. 'My snowy breasted pearl'. In April? Probably, so early in the year. She followed the direction of his eyes and raised her hand to brush away any crumb that possibly had been visible a moment ago.

"Oh," he said, "I think it comes under the heading of Old Song.

There's an endless range, known to God, as the War memorials put it."

While she was enjoying her fruit salad she looked up into the trees to see if she could spot any electric light bulbs.

"I wonder if the lights will come on before we leave. They won't show up yet, but they switch on early and you can see them first very faintly and then gradually you see moon clusters all around in the foliage like giant mistletoe. This was the first place to have them."

"Southport was the first, I think, and then the fashion spread along the coast."

"Oh no, they had them here first."

Geoffrey paused. She had spoken very positively. "I've always known this place was the first," she asserted.

Again he hesitated, then spoke up.

"I read history, Kerry, as you know, and even the smallest truth is important in building up the whole. You once said you got sick of the truth yourself occasionally and I know what you mean when it comes to human criticism; it's rude to point, especially the finger of scorn, but this is Social history and I believe I am right in stating that Southport was the first on this stretch of coast to indulge in such cosmetics. Not St. Stones."

"It's not St. Stones," said Kerry furiously, "and we'll ask somebody."

"The Town Clerk would know," answered Geoffrey. "But one doesn't want to patent such a good idea. Let everybody have a go at it and somebody will improve on the first try in everything whether it's coloured lights or French plums."

She fell silent but was obviously ruffled, and Geoffrey turned his attention to the menu.

"Shall we lay a good foundation of cherry cake and then build a memorial cairn of meringues on the top? Or have you any particular favourites?"

"I'd like some 'maids of honour' if they happen to have them."

The attendant girl approached with a cautious air and the request was very soberly made.

"Are there any 'maids of honour' left? I'm very glad to hear it." Then he added a suggestion of his own for 'melting moments'.

"One lends piquancy to the other," he explained to Kerry, "and the other lends tenderness to the one. They should be assimilated in pairs."

"If you could only have one, which would you choose?"

"But I've every intention of having one of each."

"Well, which will you have first?" she persisted. "Which is going to be an improvement on the other?"

446

"You're certainly a keen listener, Kerry. Perhaps the order of felicity is to have the slap first and the kiss to follow. It suggests living happily ever after."

Happily ever after, he repeated to himself. I suppose people do. He looked at the girl opposite him. She didn't exactly follow him like the daisy wheeling with the sun and yet in a way she leaned on him. His glance fell on the combined salad oil and vinegar bottles on the tablecloth. Two bottles with necks crossed in gentle proximity. If they were forced apart both would cease to function; each was dependent on the balanced caress of the other. That was living happily ever after.

His line of vision was disturbed by the cake-stand being placed between them and he roused himself and asked Kerry for a second cup of tea. Then he rotated the dish before her.

"I've never heard of 'melting moments' before," she said. "When did you discover them?"

"Oh, I've known about them for some time."

"I may have two of those instead of one of each."

"Well, don't let them lead you on to painful moments."

She looked at him and laughed.

"Are you speaking from experience?"

He did not reply but sat back and seemed to be absorbed in the musical trio as he waited for his tea to cool.

Kerry looked about her in utter content. She had enjoyed the afternoon walk but was glad to sit here and gather her thoughts among the flowers. A song came to her that Mr Winskill sang at concerts occasionally.

'Glorious Apollo from on high beheld us,
  Wandering to find a temple for his praise.'

Why! The Pavilion was shaped like a temple and music was issuing forth sweetly and she was listening here with Geoffrey in the bright sunshine, after wandering together all afternoon.

They had come unwittingly to his own temple, dedicated to his praise; and as for her, in her eyes and ears he would for ever out-sing and outshine any other dweller in the spreading empyrean.

Meanwhile in Blackpool the evening was calm and the sea had been whistled off its attack and was lying low with its head on its paws far out, waiting to wriggle forward again, flat and insidious under cover of night. The clouds also like tired cattle were drifting towards the sunset as to a warm byre, the light of which reddened the sky watched from afar by a few small and teetering stars, while a slip of a debutante moon hung pale and self-effacing in the pastel shades of dwindling day.

On the promenade people were also herding slowly towards one object, a hotel standing alone, the only one on the land side near the north pier. Strollers were halted by the groups scanning the upper windows overlooking the sea and curiosity brought others to a standstill and to crane their necks likewise. Newcomers paused hoping to catch from stray conversation the cause of the gathering and others, not dissembling their ignorance could be heard asking "What's going on? What's everybody waiting for?"

"Gracie Fields! They're waiting to see if she'll come out on the balcony."

"Why should she?"

Why should she indeed? Except that she was home in Lancashire and all the family wanted to see her. Had she had her supper yet? Which of all those windows with little balconies was hers? She might be tired, poor girl. Leave her alone. But it would be a thrill if she just looked out and waved for a moment. Standing with their backs to the sea and the westering clouds, the crowds stared patiently and hypnotically at the hotel. The evening light already had tiptoed out of doors so that in some rooms the lights had been switched on. People not attending the Sunday night orchestra were coming off the pier now the wind blew cold and the crowd packed more closely as its growing perimeter pressed forward.

"Her parents are in California, you know. It's warmer there. And she keeps that orphanage going on the South coast somewhere. She's very easy with her money. Of course she gets a lot from records as well."

So the scattered remarks were made, but the crowd was quiet. There was no impertinence, no slow hand-clapping or cries of "We want Gracie."

Here and there a young man guffawed or a girl screamed without a trace of fear and set the crowd tittering. A few coat collars were turned up and couples drew closer.

Dead silence as a french window was opened and a glimpse given of a man's evening dress and then a shout went up: "Gracie!"

Cheers of self congratulation came from the crowd. They had won. There was no light in the room behind her so that a pale keen face framed in almost shoulder-length auburn hair was clearly seen. Through the iron tracery of the balcony her full length was visible when she stepped out alone, slim in her leopard-skin coat over an evening frock. She was not smiling, but looking away above the crowd, over the sea and beyond.

448

The crowd respected her silence and moment of preoccupation as her eyes took in the sweet young evening and the purpling flush of night, and the vast stretch of desolate sand where long channels and pools lay slashed with colour as though a celestial scene painter had swished his brushes in them before using the fringes of the distant clouds as paint rags.

Her gaze lowered and encountered the uplifted faces between her and the darkening sands.

"Oh, you! Surely I can come to Blackpool like anybody else to work and have a bit of fun without having you under my feet all the time? I walk along the prom to see what's going on and what do I see? You! I open the window here to have a look at the view, and what do I see again? You!"

The crowd shuffle their feet somewhat. After all, fair's fair; but most of them begin to chuckle. The shrill voice goes on.

"What's the matter with you? Why aren't you at the Fair enjoying yourselves? If all you skedaddled, I was just thinking it was as good as Capri."

A deprecatory laugh rises, but she raises her hand to emphasise her point.

"Honestly, it's a wonderful stretch, only you're facing the wrong way."

"How's Fuad?" cries a voice and the crowd genuinely try to suppress their mirth, and somewhere another voice calls angrily, "Shut up!"

"Well, now you've had a good look at me, I'll go and have my supper."

She half turns away and the people groan, looking to see where the first voice had come from and there are growls of "Chuck him in the sea!" The crowd's anger is its apology. She appears to be struck by an after-thought and faces them again.

"Will you go if I sing to you?" she asks casually.

Instantly they burst into laughter and cheers. Everybody turns and grins at his neighbour. She's a good lass and she can take a joke.

"Sing something straight, Gracie."

Banter on both sides had gone. Her head is now slightly raised and instantly the crowd is hushed. What will it be? Very softly it starts, no louder than a humming, just the bubbles that a deep-sea diver sends up before surfacing with his pearl.

"Because I love you."

Then the clear voice strengthens.

Strollers out of sight under the great sea wall halt, listening eagerly, while nearer, as the song continues, arms steal round waists now unresisting that aforetime had avoided coddling against the cold. Permanent waves subside gently against manly shoulders and arms. Gracie is saying it all for them, as her voice expands and fans out into the dusk.

"Because I love you!"

The first verse ends.

"I see Fred Phanakapan has plucked up courage," she announces suddenly, surveying them. Then she glances down at her leopard-skin.

"Do you like my coat? I hope you do because you've really paid for it. You don't think it's too quiet for me, do you?"

"It's lovely, Gracie."

She turns slowly to show it off.

"Look well, oh wolves!"

She jerks her head in the direction of indoors.

"I don't half make some of the waiters jump. They've nearly had me in the zoo twice."

A girl standing alone in the crowd is watching Gracie's every movement. That's how it's done when you know they love you! And today she herself had won the first round in a long contest. Last night she had sung well and had been well received, and at this afternoon's rehearsal she had spoken up.

"This dress is too low here, Mr Mogson."

"Not it, Connie. People like to see a bit of healthy flesh."

"Well, they're not seeing an extra pound of my flesh. I can't afford to catch cold if I'm to stay on the coast this summer."

"All right! All right!"

Then Connie knew she really could sing! Someday *she* would stand on a balcony in a fur coat and her mother would live in a modern house with electric fires like castle beacons.

"Because I love you."

The song caught at her throat. No, it mustn't do that. She must learn to keep her vocal chords vibrant and ungarrotted by emotion. Her throat was now the most important organ in her body. More important than the heart whose outrageous claims could pull one down.

She'd seen him in the crowd. He was with Kerry. So that's how it was going! It must be, as the others were around and nobody seemed to be looking for anybody else. Nor was she. They all belonged to the dead past, and she was going to zoom ahead on wings of song. There were competitions, prizes and scholarships to be won, but she would get there and once there, she would stay for the best part of some time. Her mother had once accused her of being like a cat climbing the curtains to get out. It wasn't curtains but a strong ladder she'd got her feet on now.

"Why, Connie!"

She came out of her neck-cricking dreams to see Mr and Mrs Martland as she turned her head round.

"Perhaps we shall be looking up there at *you* some day, Connie," said Clara in a friendly whisper.

"Never neglect your practising," urged Len. "We've turned out one famous singer from our place, and it looks as if you're going to be another. Keep it up, Connie."

Connie bit her lip as she faced the Metropole again. They had all helped her at times and they really wished her well. She tiptoed again to get a better view of the balcony.

Kerry and Geoffrey were listening critically. Kerry had Geoffrey's raincoat round her shoulders. He had insisted.

"Do you think she sings a bit down her nose?" she asked after the first verse.

"A little, perhaps."

"They say she could have been at Covent Garden if she'd wanted. I think I'd rather please the critics than the cabbages if I had the chance. Do you think she's good enough to please both?"

"Yes, I do. I say, I'm afraid this thing keeps slipping."

"It's all right."

"You mustn't risk catching cold."

"What about you?"

"Well, since you're so thoughtful, perhaps we could share it, just while we're standing here. Comme ça. Comfy?"

She gave a slight nod. While we're standing here, he had said. She wished they could take root. Was that the reason why that other girl had been turned into a tree? To be steadfast and not foot loose? Ah! She's going to sing again.

Sybil's eyes were downcast. David didn't seem to remember that he was wearing his clerical collar and several people had looked at them in some surprise. They had come late to the outskirts of the crowd.

"Can you see?" he had enquired, and seeing her head slant sideways for a better view, he picked her up and held her in the crook of his left arm like a child, with his other arm pressing her knees to his chest to help support her. She put her hands on his shoulders and was too

451

astounded to speak.

"Because I love you."

The words reached the edge of the crowd easily. Sybil looked at the top of his brown satin head. She'd never had such a bird's-eye view of it before, with the parting narrow and immaculate as ever, the smooth hair unruffled even in the cool breeze that had sprung up. Dare she just touch it casually? Strange that he was so much less self-conscious than she, although he was new to it all, so he said. He had said it was the Dark Ages brightening into the Renaissance. To her it was rather like going for a walk with another companion and finding his preferences, his comments and explanations entirely different, so that the whole landscape took on an unfamiliar and exciting aspect as if it were another country. In the morning, that afternoon and now again this evening, she had been lifted above the common level and each time been drawn nearer to him. She felt she was being lifted and placed high to see this new world and to be seen by the world as his!

"I think you'd better put me down, David."

"But she's going to sing again and you don't want to miss that."

Yes, the woman on the balcony after several minutes of one-sided conversation with the crowd, drops the comedienne and addresses herself to the front rows.

"Well, now I've rested my voice, I'll sing another verse."

Her head tilts back and the voice slides effortlessly into the purest vocalisation.

"Because I love you."

The colour has drained from the sky and there are only a few meaningless grey brush strokes and here and there a clear-cut star.

Gracie is nearing the end of her song and everyone is very still. Will she in this pure night air finish with a touch of magic? She exhales the last line softly and the final note emerges faintly rippling to the edge of silence. She is looking out into the night sky dreamily and almost as if she had forgotten she had been singing, but the voice suddenly stretches and lightly leaps a full octave, shivers for a moment at its own audacity, reaffirms itself and then continues, humming like a spinning top high over the heads of the crowd. The last silver bubble of sound floats out towards the sea's rim and the whispers of night, and far out it soars, trembles, and steadies itself into a star.

The crowd wait. Behind her a man is dimly visible and the windows are quietly opened wide. Her face lowers from contemplating the horizon and rests on her silent audience. Then she smiles. A deep roar of pent emotion is let loose. She did it! Just to show that she could, she sang in a way impossible to imitate, almost impossible to believe.

452

Cheers ring out, clapping and laughter come from the women. Their Gracie! The whole crowd is Romeo to her Juliet.

"Good-night, Gracie, and thank you."

"Good-night to you all. Get off home now, mind you!"

"Good-night and sleep well, Gracie."

"I'm promising nothing. Please may I go in and have my supper now I've sung for it?"

Another roar of admiration goes up. She waves both hands and the french windows close again and she is lost to view.

The crowd slowly disperses, north towards the Gynn, south along the wide promenade past the Tower, east into the hinterland of boarding houses and a night's rest and westwards to the firm dark sands, not unprofitable or wearisome to youth, and along to the shadowed wooden breakwaters, the steel interlacing of the pier props and the cold support of the stone sea wall. And wherever they go, north, south, east and west, they take with them snatches of a song. "I wish sometimes we'd never met," one couple will be murmuring as they walk entwined, and another couple passing them will take it up involuntarily. "I try so hard and can't forget." The sweet waltzing tune catches on easily and other fragments are heard far into the night.

It is the nearest thing to an Easter message that many of them will have heard, and they take it singing under their breath into public and private ways, to interpret each according to his desires and understanding.

Chapter Thirty

Flaming June earns that title more by her colourful apparel than the actual warmth of her blood, for although there are hotly leaning roses to be gathered, often the arms extended to them are goose-fleshed. When nature assumes more clothing we conversely look forward to casting a clout, but warily and with a sharp eye for caprice. June is sufficiently early for hopes of a fine summer to be strong; a badly behaved season hasn't come of age and may yet reform and all will be forgiven. But a truly flaming June shows such lively intentions that all hearts and purses are open to it and there is reckless credit on a supposedly golden future. We are sure there is to be a superb midsummer when time will fall into a doze and forget to send any bills.

One whole week of June is of great importance in the churches of the northern counties. The great festival of Whitsun brings a week of high days and holidays for those free to treat them as such, to some not too distant fields, which at the special request of the organisers have been out of bounds to Lightfoot, Whitefoot, Jetty & Co., for some days past.

The choir members go jaunting off to the Dukeries, returning late to some country railway station where, assembled in good time on the platform they raise their practised voices in hymns which sanctify the night for nearly a mile around. Then there is the general outing which of course includes some children who cannot be left at home, but which outing nevertheless ranges from Weston-super-Mare to the Isle of Man. So on the whole a flaming June is ardently desired for these glad days, worthwhile even if children are heavy as lead before their fathers carry them inside the house from which they had run so mercurially at six a.m.

Whit Sunday is the day for the famous Walks. Each Protestant church musters its congregation in the early afternoon and with a brass band at its head slowly tours the district, proclaiming to the onlookers that the Christian faith is in their midst and on this day and in this manner its adherents witness to their strength. Behind the music which draws people from their afternoon sleep, comes the silken banner with its Biblical picture and message borne on two stout mahogany poles sunk in leather holders strapped round the shoulders of young men. Four ribbons attached to the lower edge of the banner lead to four young women, two in front and two following, which prevent the wind from lashing it out of shape; and it takes more than a lax and casual hold to restrain it on a boisterous day.

Then come the children dressed in white, many bearing fanciful baskets of flowers, their ranks kept in order by an interspersion of teachers for whom this is no day of rest. After them walk the 'big girls' looking as pretty as May Queens and blushing slightly as they parade so closely to the scrutiny of the pavement throng, where the women exclaim over the children and the men's eyes silently follow the girls. The next part of the procession is made up of the mothers and matrons, gowned in great distinction. They are perhaps the only section of this public witness who make no criticism of it. The bandsmen may grow thirsty, the little ones tire, the girls look bashful and the men feel slightly pharisaical, but the women make this public display in all sincerity. On this day with all the members of both church and family in attendance, they solemnly pace the roads of their district with heads high and glances straight to meet the flinching or mocking eyes of Vanity Fair.

Processions in China for one reason or another are a common sight and the Garners were not at all put out at the thought of joining one themselves.

"Do you think you will be free to join us in the afternoon, David?" asked Clara one evening.

"Most certainly, Mrs Martland. I've never done anything like this before, as I seem to be saying rather often lately, but I'm prepared to add another foot to the crocodile."

Clara was pleased.

"I can't think what some people have against it."

"You can in a way," said Len. "Some people don't care to parade their religion just as some don't like to discuss their politics. The Whit Sunday procession is our way of wearing a rosette and advertising our man, if not exactly booing the opposition! But it doesn't suit everybody."

"The procession goes a long way back in history," observed Robert. "Treks for food and water and better conditions and then later people went up to the sacred groves with offerings. That would be more like our idea of a procession. It seems a strange custom and yet we appear always to have done it and always it has had some significance."

"In modern times," said David, "perhaps we are trying to show the onlookers that we are surrounding them, to bring them inside our fold, or even throwing a symbolic lasso round straying cattle."

Kerry was impressed.

"It doesn't seem such a bad idea when you put it like that, but I've always thought it an awful bit of showing off."

Clara was not looking forward to the probability of back-chat about walking this year. She feared that in the past the girl had been influenced by Geoffrey's attitude.

"Geoffrey said," Kerry began and then stopped.

They all looked but said nothing and Sybil recollected occasions when she herself had begun just so and ended as abruptly. The girl was sorry she had spoken but David quickly saw the advantage of a casual reference if not exactly honourable mention and so turned pointedly to her, smiling.

"Said what?"

"He said it was ghosts that walked."

She did not add that when she suggested they were a lot of holy ghosts he'd told her not to go too far!

David laughed so easily that the others were happy to join in too.

"Indeed not!" he exclaimed with vigour. "It is not a procession of dead souls at all, but our walk in life."

The older ones smiled gratefully and Sybil felt a moment of pure triumph as if the knight wearing her glove in his helmet had unseated his adversary.

"You ought to bring your friend Mr Warner on Whit Sunday," said Clara. "We need a show of more young men and we really do want to meet him. What is he like?"

"Oh! He's a great chap. He's tall with red hair and his chief hobby is music, so you'll all take to him. But I believe he's out that day."

"Did he go to hear . . ?" began Kerry and stopped for the second time but nobody followed it up.

"When we've got Whit week over," said his mother, "you must bring him here. It's time we saw your best man."

"And I'm longing to see the other bridesmaid," added Kerry eagerly. "I think the coming summer's going to be terribly exciting. I'm going to the Art School for one thing. I'm sorry to leave Gwen and Freda but they've got each other. And fancy Mother and Mrs Buckley running a gown shop on Oxford Road!"

It was getting on for midnight when Clara drew back the curtains of their own room before getting into bed.

"There must be a block of flats or something fairly high going up right over there, Len, near the Catholic cemetery. We used to see the gravestones shining quite clearly on fine nights from up here, but I can't see anything of them at all now."

"That reminds me. Sam did mention some time ago that Alfred had bought a good bit of land about there in the spring. Mrs Garner told him that the cemetery was visible from the upstairs windows of our houses. I hope he knows what he's doing, but flats are rather a continental style for Moston."

"Alfred is very far-seeing. He'll know full well what return to expect even if it wouldn't satisfy most men."

"And I was thinking tonight," continued Len, "perhaps Sybil would rather be married from another house where there were no associations with that other fellow. Do you think we ought to move?"

Clara looked out for a moment longer before turning away.

"That other fellow? No, Len, we're staying here and when Sybil goes she must take the sad memories with the happy ones. Some day she may hardly know which are which."

There was silence while Clara settled but soon she spoke again in a whisper.

"Isn't it lovely to see her so happy? All that aloofness has gone. David's absolutely right for her, thank God."

She heard Len catch his breath and she rubbed his ankle with her foot.

"You know, dear, I could still really love Geoffrey as a son in spite of it all."

A grunt came before any answer.

"Knocking about town one does see things. But Kerry's very young and I hope she doesn't go throwing herself at him."

"Not she! Remember Fanny! In any case even if she did she'd be all right with him."

Shocked silence descended upon Len but Clara was in high feather, turning over some secret that would be of interest even in quarters where it would be unwelcome. After some time she spoke again.

"You know, they'll all find Kerry a very different proposition from Sybil."

Len now pulled the bed-clothes round his shoulders with impregnable finality for the night and with a satisfied chuckle he remarked rather strangely for a loving father and long-standing friend, "Serve 'em right!"

u

*　　*　　*　　*

Earlier in this June month, breakfasting at the table pushed right into the window to catch the sun, Elsie Buckley exclaimed aloud as she read a letter.

"They want me to present the prizes for the children's races on Tuesday of Whit week."

"Ah!" said Sam. "Is it clear whether they want you to donate them or hand over whatever prizes are on the table?"

"No, I can't say it is clear," and she handed him the letter from Fred Winskill to read.

"Do you think you could do it, Elsie? If I donate them would you present them?"

"So long as they don't expect me to make a speech. I couldn't do that."

"Don't tell me! Any woman can make a speech, especially if they let her sit or lie down. It's better to stand so there's some expectation of her finishing sometime. We used to get a great crowd when I was a lad and many's the box of pencils from Keswick I've won in my time. The runners-up got a few yards of black liquorice and there was competition for the wide flat variety as we used to make a slit at each end and button them on for braces. Very unreliable if I remember aright. Well, I must be off; Len is so very punctual always. And by the way, you might be thinking what we can give Rainbow for a wedding present. What about a picture?"

"A good idea. Something she can hang on the walls to remind her of home. A nice view of Manchester do you think?"

"The Ship Canal by floodlight! We might commission a pair as I'd like one to be of St. Peter's Square."

"I'll come down one day and we can consult Mr Martland as well. Oh, and Sam! Let me have another few pounds, will you? I've been throwing it about rather a lot this week and come to the end of my cheque book."

Whit Sunday turned out to be a fine day to the joy of the whole city and the relief of all busy needlewomen, many of whom had put in the last stitches on new frocks as late as the previous midnight and had gone to bed with the feeling that protracted labour was bad enough without its being labour in vain. Next year they fully intended to make an earlier start on Weldon's pattern books.

In the morning the early birds reported a day begun well and seemingly knowing its own mind. They didn't think it would be positively hot; not sufficiently to bring the tar bubbling up between the road-stones and so spoil the white and biscuit-coloured shoes of the children, who couldn't resist prodding those smooth, treacly excrescences.

The occasion was the northern Free Churches' Ascot and a heavy shower could be equally disastrous to hats and costumes that were the result of many hours of cogitation. Nor was the full glory revealed at the morning service always. Mrs Ginnell for instance would appear in the afternoon procession, but so as not to tire her leg she would escape some of the loops in the route and pop into Ella's house and catch them all coming back. As she and her husband got out the crockery from the high cupboard she was in an excited mood.

"My word! Our Connie's surprised everybody and she'll draw a few people here today who might not have come. The big poster looks very well, 'Soloist Miss Constance Ginnell'. She says she might change to Gynn for her professional name as Gynn means something in these parts."

"She's coming on. Fred Winskill saw something in her from the start and I think she's grateful for all the coaching and entering her for competitions."

"She's truly grateful. Fred got a postcard from her at Easter. Of course everything will be different for her now if she's going to have a career; but there's plenty of time for her to bring us something to dandle."

"Ay, let her climb a bit first. She'll fall in love with life again when the congratulations start."

"And she'll keep her head as she climbs. She doesn't forget that her great-grandfather helped to build Blackpool Tower. Be careful on those steps, Ernest! We don't want any more broken legs in the family."

"That was a terrible time, wasn't it? Everything that went wrong seemed to date from that."

"It did. Even Ella's accident wouldn't have happened if I'd been in and out as usual, and perhaps Clara Martland wouldn't have got so down with a helping hand. Anyway, she came up in an express lift when Len and Sam became partners."

"It looks as if you're valuable hereabouts, Missus, so I think you ought to start taking more care of yourself now."

Mrs Ginnell snorted.

"Wives have no Union, no settled pay or hours of work and we can't just down tools as easily as you men can. We sign on for better or worse and nobody comes out in sympathy when its worse. Any suggestions for taking care of myself?"

He ruminated for a moment.

"We could go and see the Lights in October now I'm my own master."

"You work later now you are."

"And so does Tom. We've been neighbours all these years and worked together at the Shop and now we're partners! There was just one thing that worried me while Ella was in hospital."

"Go on," urged his wife anxiously. "What was it?"

"Her at the back there. I did wonder at the time if she might try something on with Tom when he was left alone. Perhaps only to spite the church, you know."

Mrs Ginnell backed away from holding the steps.

"She wouldn't dare! If she'd done that, God himself would scourge her; not because she was a trollop but because she was a hypocrite. Pretending to be Ella's friend!"

"Take it easy, old girl. It's all right. I did drop a hint to Tom but he told me when he met her in the street one day she said she'd drop in as soon as Ella was home again but not until, as some folk's tongues eloped with their filthy minds."

"Well, it's known that her run to Gretna Green is long overdue but I'm thankful things are no worse for Ella's sake. She might have been harmed. Now I shall always think the better of Mrs Butterway for not slithering to Tom's door, serpent though she is."

"No she is not. She waits at home like a spider."

"And looks like a monkey! So we'll raise her from crawling on her belly, to be a spider-monkey, if you like."

"You just remember where you are, woman."

It was a long way for the children who 'sat up in white', the tiny ones on the red cushions round the Communion rail and the bigger ones on benches on either side of the pulpit like a human harvest festival. In the morning they were restless white flames, up and down, bending this way and that with a prim rustle from their crisp clothing. In the afternoon they were tired from their walk but rest miraculously recharged their energies, so that these fragile débutante souls, frou-frou in their new attire, grew perceptibly during the service into holy terrors. Sweet-sucking had to be allowed during the speaker's address and so even as he drew flattering attention to the picture of human rosebuds below him, the angelic faces suffered a transmogrification,

460

presenting to the congregation a collection of highly competitive gargoyles.

So at a quarter past two on this Whit Sunday afternoon the procession outside the Sunday school was beginning to form as the groups of members chatting on the pavement stepped into the road. The bandsmen were prepared, having placed their little pages of music in the delicate lyre-shaped holders attached to the instruments, when the big drum far forward gave a deep growl of warning ending in a sudden boom that made the children jump and some of the tiny ones cry, but upon being lifted up to see the splendour of the offending instrument with its draped leopard skin, they were appeased even to the extent of wanting to bang it themselves!

"So we're to kick off," said Willie Briggs to Jimmie Northcroft, steadying the banner with hands reaching well up the shafts, for the wind filled the silken sail between, bellying out strongly but tethered by Sybil and Connie a few yards ahead and by Kerry and another girl two or three yards behind. "We'll be sweating in spite of the breeze before half-time."

"Someone will take over as usual. I say! It's great news about your being signed on with United to play in September. What do your folks think of it?"

"They're pleased, of course," grinned Willie modestly. "I tell them it's because Mother's fed me so well."

"I suppose the training is very strict?"

"Yes, but we're all in it together. I'll tell you something, Jimmie. I might not have been able to play for anybody, nearly. I'd gone into the workshop to tell my father and I happened to kick the end of a big wedge stuck out along the floor and a great granite headstone tipped forward. I stepped back quick, I can tell you and that stone hit the floor . . . wham! . . . about three inches from my foot. We daren't stir for a minute but when he came over we stared down at it. It must have weighed a couple of hundredweight. I saw he'd only got as far as carving the decorative heading 'Sacred' with flourishes round it and he said slowly, "When I carve that word again, Willie, I bet it comes out 'Scared'!"

"You didn't tell your mother?"

"We did not. We waited there until we looked less like clients."

Before taking up his position at the end of the procession Ben Northcroft walked the length of the assemblage advising and giving instructions. After all, he'd attended more of these occasions than anybody else present. He was sporting the last surviving top hat and when he had left them Jimmie smiled a slow smile.

"Grandpa's given instructions he's to be buried in his topper and frock coat and if there's no room for the hat, it's to go at his side."

"Tucked underneath his arm? He's expecting something of a dressy affair when the whistle blows! How's he getting on with his flowers?"

"He's got out all the books on the subject from the Simpson library and they're ordering more. To hear him talk of cold houses and hot houses, you'd think the farm was built of gold bricks."

"All be yours some day, Jimmie boy."

"We're a long living family and I'm in no hurry. I've stuck out for electricity and a few other things and so long as I can call a new tune now and then I don't care who signs the cheques. Now then, we ought to be moving."

Sybil and Connie in front, holding the ribbons, had each been delicately complimenting the other's appearance but there was a feeling of constraint; compliments but not confidences had been exchanged. Sybil was the first to comment on future prospects.

"I hear you'll be on your travels this summer. I'm sure you'll be a great success, Connie, and I'm very, very glad."

Connie believed her and was touched. She took a deep breath and looked around her.

"The further we get from this place, Sybil, I expect we shall think the more of it. We've all had some marvellous times here."

"The duets we've sung together! My favourite was *The Bird of Passage* song."

Sybil's voice trailed away.

Connie was the first to speak.

"When you've a minute to spare, will you drop me a postcard now and then? They'll be forwarded."

"Yes, Connie, I will. We ought to keep in touch. Who knows, but some day you might be touring the concert halls of Europe."

Wistfulness vanished at once from both faces.

Little Ernie ran to his sister. He had been pestering Jimmie and Willie to let him feel how heavy the banner was.

"They say I won't know for years and years," he wailed. Connie asked Sybil to hold the ribbon while she took him back to where his mother was searching for him in order to attach him to Miss Leat.

"Mr Northcroft gave me this," he said smugly, opening his palm to show sixpence. Mrs Ginnell looked round surprised.

"I hope you thanked the old gentleman nicely."

"Not him. The other Mr Northcroft."

Mrs Ginnell turned and smiled at Annie standing near.

"John shouldn't."

"No, not him," shouted Ernie impatiently. "The strong one. Him carrying the banner."

At the far side of the school, Ada and Alfred were alighting from their car. Ben hastened forward. Geoffrey was still at the wheel with his chin lowered, deep in thought.

"Just the man we want," bellowed the old campaigner.

"Geoffrey's not staying," Ada interposed quickly.

"Not staying? It's a pity to come so far and not take part."

"I suppose so," agreed Geoffrey not moving, "having come so far." Suddenly he sprang out.

"So far and much further," he said briskly.

"Young Mr Garner's at the back of the men," informed Ben.

"Just the incentive I needed," answered Geoffrey unsmiling still, but he went forward slowly.

Ada and Alfred were received with geniality in their respective columns, and if hair is a guide to health, then Ada was in peak condition, for her hair under the satin toque that Queen Mary made so distinguished, was burnished and brilliant to a degree that would have caused Titian himself to turn and look at it even when past his ninetieth year.

Meanwhile Geoffrey had gone forward, emerging on the street at the tail end of the procession. He stepped into the road where immediately half a dozen hands were extended.

"Glad to see you," said Fred Winskill, heartily shaking.

"Why, Geoffrey, it's good of you to come all this way!" exclaimed Tom Kershaw with pleased surprise all over his face. "You've brought your mother and father with you?"

John Northcroft reached out and shook. He nodded repeatedly but said nothing.

"This is good," said Robert Garner with quiet satisfaction and looking with habitual penetration into the young man's face as he shook hands. "It isn't wise to over-do the studies, you know. A little exercise and fresh air are very necessary." For a moment he laid a hand on the other's shoulder and then walked away down the lines.

Some of the faces were almost unknown to Geoffrey but hands were thrust out.

"Alfred's boy," the voices stated non-committally. "Glad to see you."

"Why, Geoffrey!" said Sam Buckley with a smile as he held out his hand. The smile implied 'neither my wife nor my secretary' perhaps, but the pressure was there.

"Hello again," said Leonard Martland in a free and easy way.

The pressure was in all the hand clasps and Geoffrey had looked each man in the face as he shook but so far had not said a word.

There was one more.

There was one more hand extended and the eyes were waiting. Geoffrey returned that gaze unwaveringly. Neither young man smiled nor uttered a sound but after a moment the proffered hand was briefly but strongly clasped.

Nobody had so much as glanced their way.

Then the drum major raised his tasselled staff, the great drum beat rhythmically as though registering the pulse of the whole crowd and the brass brayed out sharply in unison to lead the procession and warn the neighbourhood that an army was on the move.

The band wheeled slowly into the Oldham Road, crossing the bows of two stationary trams waiting patiently. The drivers leaned forward to shout congratulations to Willie Briggs upholding the banner near the head of the procession. They were proud to salute Willie. Up United! Nobody seemed to mind a few minutes delay and when Tom Kershaw in the rear raised his hand in greeting to both the up and down line drivers they stamped on the iron knobs in recognition. They didn't see much of Tom nowadays but occasionally, as they passed the door with the miniature model of a chair swinging above it by way of a sign, they gave that noisy summons for old times' sake.

The band having carefully wheeled into Oldham Road, Kerry, after watching the tension of the banner strings and easing any strain, now looked over her shoulder at the length of the procession still at right angles to its leaders. It was quite impressive even in the open road. In the narrower street where it had formed, it had been obviously a winning majority filling eye and ear, but now it had to measure itself against the larger background of city road and city onlooker and perhaps city-sized indifference. If the Oldham Road fostered a scorched earth policy, a withdrawal similar to Moscow's at the entry of Napoleon, the procession would indeed have been a shouting at the moon, a phantom army, but the Oldham Road was willing to give anything the once-over, to listen to anyone's opinion for a time and not give the 'bird' to any show without a trial. So when the brass struck up mightily there was not much indifference pretended or otherwise, but rather a heartening disposition to stand and watch the whole length go by. The pavements were thronged and there was plenty of enthusiasm engendered by the lively music and bright colours. A considerable procession, admitted Kerry and looked for her father in the still curving line at the rear. There he was, walking with Mr Buckley.

Then she almost stumbled and turned quickly forward again and with fixed gaze she stared ahead at the slow-marching bandsmen, while amazement and a wild elation seized her. *He* had come! After all the discussion and criticism he had come and was walking with David Garner of all people; the rival whom Apollo would have slain! Only last week she had told him that this year she would absolutely refuse to walk on Whit Sunday. He had replied that he actually thought the custom had much to commend it. She'd distinctly heard him on several occasions say . . . but he had interrupted sharply to say never mind what he'd said then; on the contrary, there was a great deal to be said for the faith of one's fathers, when fathers showed sense. Why had he suddenly changed, she wanted to know? She thought they might sneak off and have a day's walk on the moors. He replied that on Whit Sunday she ought not to break the sequence of years.

Sequence of years! But he'd once said that was how ruts were made, gramophone needles grooves worn until the music became a discord. Repetition ad nauseum.

"Chuck it, Kerry!"

She had paused before making a stiff reproof.

"In our family we do not use the phrase 'chuck it' as you well know."

"What do you say in your family, if it's fit to repeat?"

"I'm telling you what we don't say. No one ever said that - even to Watch."

He quickly explained that he'd always liked her family of course and he hoped she would not give them unnecessary pain. He had spoken with some confusion at the time, but it was all topsy-turvy, she had said.

"Yes, Kerry. All topsy-turvy. In fact, head over heels!"

So after that backward review, physical and then mental, she looked steadily at the road ahead but her face must surely be reflecting the creative incandescence of a new-formed planet. She could feel the swirl and dizzying sweep in her heart and it would not take any light years at all for its beam and heat to be recorded in her eyes and cheeks for a worldly observer to see.

Let Sybil or Connie but glance round at her and they would detect without a telescope the influence of some fiery and magnetic day-star. She wished the billowing sail of silk above her could abandon itself to the wind so that she would be pulled from the ground and swung into the air after it, streamlined and obedient as a comet's flowing hair. She could not remain earthbound with such winged knowledge bearing her up.

This procession was too slow! It wasn't for children really, unless as on the old field days they were riding in carts or, more fittingly, in chariots. The girls should be dancing along, garlanded, clashing cymbals and tossing their arms while the young men crowned themselves with vine leaves and one youth came smiling to seek her out from the others, the favoured one.

Walking more sedately than ever, Kerry looped the banner ribbon round her wrist, carefully maintaining the correct play. Of course a smiling youth had sought her and this was his way of showing it, walking among the older men with their rolled umbrellas and dark hats. The hero was in that throng, and interspersing the marching hymns would be heard the songs of triumph and over the heads of the vestals all might see the victor acknowledging honours. With the length of the procession between them, these two knew without apparent sign that this was their wild running, their Bacchanal, their Thargelia.

It was not long before the Kershaws' house was reached and as the women noticed the curtain held slightly aside they waved cheerfully to the woman who lived in the purdah of ill-health. Thinking of someone bedridden is like remembering something seen from a train; it is difficult to imagine it having a life of its own that goes on when we have raced by. But they remembered now and every woman's burden whatever its nature seemed lighter as she passed that window and the woman whom nobody envied. Yet there was one possession that some could envy her, and Ella waited for Tom's approach to see how he compared with other men. Was he bearing up? Was he just as straight, as lively looking as others of his own age? Or was life beginning to tell on him? As Tom got near he squared his shoulders and lightened his step and all the men raised their hats and looked 'eyes left' as though Ella were taking a march past. The curtain quivered a little in response.

Sam Buckley's hand had gone to his hat in military fashion and on the pavement stood Pins and Needles who, catching sight of his old captain, assumed a parade ground stance. Sam knew he had only to shout a cheery "Come on in" for that leader-less flotsam to follow him. It would be a blind following without understanding, just a grateful reflex action to being noticed and Sam would not do it. He dared not do it, akin as it would be to compulsory church parade.

As Sam walked on he became more uneasy in mind. Being noticed had to begin somewhere and being grateful had to begin somewhere.

"Excuse me, I've just thought of something," he muttered hastily to Leonard and he stepped out of the procession and hurried back along the pavement.

"Dutton, you're looking quite spruce today. Why can't you always stand like that?"

Pins and Needles glanced round nervously.

"I might lose my pension."

"They won't take it from you now, believe me!"

Ella had been glad to see Mrs Ginnell and she tried to look pleased at seeing Miriam Crumps who had also decided to meet them coming back. Miriam eyed the gas-fire with disfavour.

"That's not so low it will pop out, is it?"

"Will you pop out," said Mrs Ginnell crossly.

A digression was made by Mrs Butterway knocking and entering.

"Very nice, very nice indeed! Your Connie looks a picture, Mrs Ginnell. You saw her wave, didn't you, Antella? She wouldn't want you to miss her. Now she's got going we don't know who she'll meet. Bigger sea, bigger fish; that's the way it goes. She'll sing her way up the scale in more ways than one, we'll all see one fine day."

It was impossible for a girl's mother not to show gratification.

"It's a big day for us all," she replied as modestly as she was able.

"And I hear," went on the simian chatterer, "that the new organ is a great improvement on the old, Mrs Crumps. Somebody's been glad to buy off the bazaar. I'd like to give a little present myself because we've all cause to be grateful for something, however pleased with ourselves we are, haven't we, Mrs Crumps?"

Miriam fumbled among her armoury but not finding a thing that was loaded she had to be content with looking daggers at the speaker before turning to Ella.

"Do you find the noise of sawing and hammering troublesome during the week?"

"Certainly not! It's only a bit of finishing off that Tom does in here to keep me company. Ernest has got him to join the short outing to Bolton Abbey on Tuesday. Now he's about the place all day he feels easier about having a bit of time off."

"Ah, they'll miss the Carriage Shop bell. They'll both get a bit slack in their traces, I'm afraid."

"There's no sign of it yet," said Mrs Ginnell tartly.

Mrs Butterway took her departure, pausing on the doorstep to look up and down the road before turning in the direction taken by the procession. She was surprised to find Sam Buckley and Pins and Needles in conversation.

"Why, Mr Buckley! I'm glad to see you back in the land of the living again. Mrs Ginnell told me. How's Mrs Buckley?"

"She's much better, thank you. I mean she's quite well. I was just suggesting to Dutton here that if he came into church at three o'clock

467

I think he'd enjoy this special service."

Pins and Needles hung back, shaking his head; an act of will Sam could tell. Mrs Butterway gave the man a little dig.

"It wouldn't do you any harm to hear Connie sing and some of us ought to represent Daisy Street. And Mrs Ginnell would appreciate it, wouldn't she, Mr Buckley?"

That was not the point, but did it really matter? To oblige someone was a beginning.

"I'll look out for you, Dutton, when we come down on the other side. I'll find you a seat and don't worry about anything."

Sam would find an opportunity for slipping him money for the collection. He then set off at a smart pace to catch up with the procession which had been making steady progress. The band coming to the end of a tune, did not resume as on the other side of the tramlines came marching towards them the music and following of another church in full blast; St. Jude's from half a mile up the road. The children stared across at each other, the older girls eyeing each other's frocks curiously and Robert, hat in hand, scanned the menfolk for his opposite dog-collar and the two clergymen exchanged a decorous flourish in greeting.

The band struck up again when well past.

"Not so long ago," observed Tom Kershaw, "church and chapel would have looked the other way!"

"*And* the kids would have pulled faces," someone added. The older men remembered some queer goings-on within easy living memory. Matters had improved when some young and enterprising spirits like Stormalong had negotiated for cricket and football matches between clubs from neighbouring churches.

These had been well supported. Teas had been served by the women and girls of the home teams and this had inevitably led to some occasional and daring 'going over' to the opposite camp. The girls had been all too keen on these matches as time went on and some spoilsports had even suggested that only the married women should wait on; an idea so coldly and silently received that it died of frost-bite and solitude. But after Stormalong's departure these sporting events fell into abeyance and were not taken up again.

"More's the pity," observed Robert, sighing.

"I agree with your father," said Geoffrey to David as they overheard the conversation just in front and at the rear.

"Isolation isn't good for man or institution."

"That is so and as far as we know, recorded history began with a decision for communication and participation; 'Let us make man'. A cry of loneliness if ever one was made."

"That's a favourite theme of yours and a very fertile one it is. I'd like to go over it with you when you've an evening to spare; it's got such inexhaustible connotations. But what about the old song, 'God is one and all alone, And evermore shall be so'."

"Not if He can help it," returned David smiling, "and I can certainly find time for further discussion. As a matter of fact I've missed our old companionable evenings together more deeply than you'll give me credit for."

They walked on side by side in silence, affected by many emotions and recollections. It was two or three minutes before Geoffrey spoke again.

"You know, Rutherford was working on the disintegration of the atom at our place on Oxford Road in 1918. Things get together and then someone divides them; always a disruptive activity. It's going on all the time."

David caught the melancholy tone of voice and hastened to speak with optimism.

"But it's quite possible for unimagined good to come out of division and dispersion sometimes. New and perhaps stronger links may form."

They both looked straight ahead.

"Not," said Geoffrey, "that the disruptive element thinks *that* out."

"It may have a hunch or be ruled by a hunch," David insisted.

"Some disruptions," argued Geoffrey, "like Krakatao, are senseless and tragic and catastrophic. I maintain that the disruptive element doesn't give a damn."

"In nature, not. But in human nature, sometimes. I know of one instance at least where the intrusive factor could have cursed itself."

"I'm delighted to hear it."

The other turned to him impulsively.

"Sinclair, you're a good chap and I've always thought so in spite of setbacks and also I've a pretty sound hunch why you've turned up today. I saw you both going into *The Co-Optimists* the other week and there were other occasions. There are no broken heads and no broken hearts by this time so don't let's pretend there are."

Geoffrey coloured strongly but turned his head and grinned sheepishly.

"You've got the idea! And now we don't want the same thing, I'm quite a good fellow."

"It's not just that, and you're much too rational to want anything merely because somebody else does."

Another hundred yards or so were paced in silence which Geoffrey was the first to break.

"Reverting to feet of clay for a moment, I hope I'm a bit more hard-baked now."

"We all get thumped into shape sooner or later," answered David gravely.

"Yes, you're right in your hunch if I've any real influence, but you never know with that one. It comes and goes."

Geoffrey seemed uncharacteristically nervous so that David was surprised.

"Of course you have immense influence. You always had. You can't take it so casually now it's so important to you, but it's still there, I know. Just you bring a little pressure to bear and all will be well."

Geoffrey brooded awhile and became more confidential.

"I won one round not long ago. Southport *did* have coloured lights before St. Anne's. I wrote to the Town Clerk. She was more than a bit huffy but I conceded that St. Stones had made a greater success of the idea and in the end she forgave me for being in the right! Absolute harmony was achieved, however, in disclaiming Blackpool's ham-fisted knock-out win."

"You'll be all right," responded David comfortingly. "One shouldn't tell tales, but she does quote you on most points."

This information revived Geoffrey's spirits.

"I suppose I ought to wait for a time, but I don't mean wait until Doomsday! That game is altogether too dangerous. In future I shall insist upon a clear ex libris label and no lending. It's queer, Garner, how one's taste may alter, quite surprisingly. When we've read one author who's had a profound effect upon us, we feel that no one can possibly interest us so much again and yet, between ourselves, it's out of the question to give up reading, if you follow me!"

David looked at him sideways and chanced his next remark.

"And between ourselves, I hope you are going to be content with the Bible and Shakespeare, if you also follow my meaning."

Ben Northcroft a few paces in front was of the opinion that if those two young 'uns had breath to laugh like that, which he hadn't, they could take a turn with the banner. He called to them and acquainted them with the plan.

"They'll halt before turning up Grimshaw Lane. That's the time to change over."

Ben started to walk down the procession towards its head and astounded, they followed. The bandsmen were soon marking time and in a minute or two the young men were being initiated into the regulations of standard bearing.

"This is a tricky corner," counselled Ben, "as there's generally a gust of wind coming from round there. Don't let it halt you bang in the middle of the road, but go slowly. Watch those ribbons, my dears. Pull very gently forwards, girls, and you two take care not to hold them back."

Willie and Jimmie were red with exertion and yet the newcomers were just as much flushed. The two youths retired and the later colour-sergeants stood with the banner hoisted between them with its inscription under the picture 'God so Loved' which had not been visible from their former position. Connie and Sybil in front had glanced their way to see who was taking over and were startled into turning round-eyed to each other. Then the music blared out again and they prepared to negotiate the tricky corner. Before moving forward, however, Connie turned and smiled at them so impishly that Sybil, who had thought it best not to notice them if Connie did not, felt that she also ought to acknowledge the young men's presence and taking a deep breath she turned slightly and divided a polite smile equally between them as she would from the concert platform. It was brief but it indicated a general thaw in the glacial period.

During these proceedings Geoffrey had once or twice shot a glance at Kerry a few paces behind, but she seemed to be unaware of him. He gave a grunt of amusement. She was not thinking her own thoughts. It was a self-conscious, a strictly schooled stand-offishness. He knew that expression. She was guarding a secret that she wouldn't easily part with now. It was a wonderful bit of acting, this pretence of ignorance and innocence, but it didn't fool him! She was here today because he had melted her rebellion and he was here today to make her recognise her own power. He exulted inwardly as he gripped the polished shaft. He was on the homeward run. He had caught a scent of the stable and the sweet, sweet hay at last.

Rounding the wide turn into Grimshaw Lane the bandsmen slow marched again and went all out with *Conquering Hero* to give cohesion to the rank and file as they met that cross current of wind. Some of the tinies staggered and were confused by ribbons whipped undone and swaying baskets of flowers so that they were glad to feel their teachers' hands on their shoulder blades steadily propelling them forward. One or two straw bonnets slid back as far as the satin strings allowed, to be replaced when the brief danger was over. Blown dresses were patted down to cover the cherub limbs and frilly knickers, while the music boomed so loudly that what the eye saw was quite secondary to what was filling the ear.

Now the banner, slightly tilted, was caught in a stiffish breeze and six pairs of eyes watched its every movement, Sybil and Connie half turning as they walked so that good teamwork might fairly meet the challenge. The young men gripped the poles, holding them firmly to their chests as they took wary steps to keep the going even and the uprights steady against considerable strain. The banner remained fully extended, taut and with the merest bowing to the storm that slid under its silken attestation.

"Good lads!" shouted Ben from the kerb.

David and Geoffrey were breathing deeply by the time they were in the straight again but the task was easier now. Nevertheless the whole thing was a weight.

"A good thing you two turned up," called Connie over her shoulder.

"Anything to oblige," answered Geoffrey, rather conscious that he'd never obliged before. Connie was a good sort. In fact, he was really glad to be here after all. The men's handshakes, Garner's assumption of the old footing, Connie's naturalness and Sybil's shy smile all went towards making a clear passage through the 'wait-a-bit' thorns of the quintet's restoration. These things had made more progress possible in the last hour than months or even years could have achieved in other circumstances or other communities.

Yes! These people of the Church were right to keep at it. They were familiar with some purpose that could compass in one hour more than any entirely mundane power could fulfil in an age. Sometimes the triumph of an hour was for an age. By right he belonged to these people. He had been born and baptised into this community but had stumbled out of it somehow; but in this hour he had longed to re-enter and in this same hour they had without hesitation re-enfolded him. Let onlookers think his brow was beaded from physical effort; that was nothing to the inward struggle.

Suddenly he was glad of the weight he was sharing. If his mouth dried and contorted as he walked, it was at the recollection of the words above his head, words that were the cause of this processional witness through the maze of humankind drawn from their Sabbath sloth to read a message so vital and life-giving that the church drummed it in, patiently and persistently along the years, along the ways.

The minister had said when first he had come amongst them, "We look to you young men for leadership!"

Leadership!

He'd been more of a lemming. In fact he'd behaved in a manner more likely to entice away what following there was. With Sybil he had failed utterly, thank God. She had cast him off sooner than he'd expected but it would have happened sooner or later, he knew. He simply wasn't good enough. But with Kerry he had some influence, as Garner said, but of what nature? Supposing he'd succeeded in damaging some secret spring there? Only of recent weeks had he paused to consider her reactions and then he'd stopped dead in his tracks. He remembered again the night of Shrove Tuesday and the rain.

He was less a born leader than a born fool and yet in spite of all, they had made room for him. The last procession in which he had taken part had been on Shrove Tuesday. He'd never jibbed at joining that. Next year's would be the last for him but this today perhaps the first of many. From charity to love. Was it a process of progression?

He had, he supposed, just about lived by the Ten Commandments, the moral primer for beginners; certainly not by the Sermon on the Mount. Perhaps he had prided himself on living by Queensberry rules. The people round him today would have known long ago that such rules were not enough and yet at one time in his loftiness he would have thought these people rather simple, of incomplete education if not of native understanding. In this last hour he had come to know that it is possible to patronise every virtue save that of innate wisdom; the ability to make the nobler choice.

Earlier he had placed himself at the tail end of this procession, joining it almost surreptitiously, then had been recognised and made welcome and now found himself manoeuvred into a front position. He had not wanted that. He needed more time for questioning, for talking things over with Garner, for more intellectual assent.

He was not to be given more time. Something timeless was even now communicating to his twentieth century understanding, as it spoke at all times and through all time.

He was actually carrying the Word! The effort had taken his breath and the new breath pouring in was agonising to his ribcage. He was bearing a heavy shaft of wood along the road and the memory of that earlier Via Dolorosa smote him with such force that he stumbled.

"I'm not fit!" he gasped. "I'm not fit."

David glanced across and was struck with wonder. No need to pretend that Geoffrey was alluding to his physical state; David knew the symptoms of turmoil. For the second time that afternoon he used the same simple words of comfort.

"You'll be all right! Truly, you'll be all right! Somebody thinks you're fit and that's all that matters. So bear up! Come along, march on."

The words were carefully uttered so that nobody noticed anything had occurred that natural causes would not account for.

Standard bearers changed step or shifted the weight without drawing attention. Geoffrey slogged on mechanically, grateful for the other's matter-of-fact instructions. He felt like a child waiting for some indication of what to do next. He tried to collect his confused thoughts along the lines just laid out for him. Somebody thought he was fit! Fit for what? For something more than he'd managed to be so far.

In the bleak time at the start of the year he had suffered the effects of arrogance. In the softer Easter weather he had reaped some of the rewards of humility, the best of which he was now convinced were to be gathered in today. His manly pride had been chastened and then requited. What about his spiritual pride? It had taken this despised Christian witness in which he had set an exploratory foot and then been swept into the main current, to show him his deficiencies.

All around him were people who had put their cards on the table with an assured swagger, keeping entirely calm, combining daring with common sense, knowing that they held a hand meaning 'abundance declared' in daily living. Moreover they were playing for love and desired nothing better than that all should share. This round-the-houses demonstration declared goodwill towards men shining through men's ill-will; divine integrity outliving human error. The members of this church were in a position to teach him a lesson, for with all his education he had not really been seeking an answer to life's problems, which are the world's problems too. He had been looking for an alternative to the answer he secretly knew, as these people knew, perhaps as all people knew in their hearts; and there was no alternative!

Some minutes later he turned deliberately to his companion-at-arms who like himself was dishevelled but not entirely winded.

"I say!" he called above the *Soldiers' Chorus*, "I think I might take this all the way now. What do you say? I've got my second wind."

David saw the moist forehead, the now smiling mouth less super-charged than he had ever known it and felt an assurgency of spirit such as had not been equalled since Easter Day. In this last hour his friend had shed something, had gained something; not the near equality of roundabouts and swings, but both gain and loss were to enormous advantage. David's returning grin was similarly unrestricted.

"I'm with you, partner, step for step. Keep it up!"

His amazement was as great as his joy at the turn of events.

The young minister marvelled that as promised, witness sprang up almost from the stones along the way. Again and again the Word became flesh, put on actuality. People 'on the set', the church itself, were joined by audience participation, not in a historical pageant but in a plot in which all were vastly concerned, being given startling cues

474

which nevertheless they accepted in good faith. People who had not desired to be other than merely audience were called and found themselves playing important parts as the application of God's purposes got moving.

This new man on the scene was now doubly his friend and brother, David rejoiced to know.

They kept it up, aloft and legible to the crowds, round the streets at which Geoffrey gazed with keener eyes, then back onto the main road again near their own church. Let the burden be doubled, his heart would be jubilant still. He would serve somehow. He could not lead as yet but he would follow awhile. Discipleship first.

Church and state could cover so much ground together, their common interest being in both underdogs and top dogs and the necessity for being good dogs and not absolute curs.

The church must be there, like Everest, drawing people to it because of some inner response. Remove the church as such, the visible church, and the spiritual geography of the world would be reduced, abased, that high eternal plume evaporate.

Poor Francis Thompson taking refuge in the little street leading off this very road; ill and in want but always a poet! Geoffrey decided he'd take Kerry along some time soon to look at the place, very different from the rose garden by the sea. He remembered telling Garner that poets have a thin time in Lancashire, but one would always choose to be a poet if there were a choice, to recount one's vision not on Parnassus but on Patmos.

Christianity was a way of life but also a way of thought!

Words could serve.

Now he himself was literally carrying the Word, eternal truth conveyed in a trinity of words. Henceforth he would carry it, this dayspring of creativity, central to life itself, into his own world of words and any meaning expressed to his own generation.

With a last flourish and final roll and thump of the great drum, the bandsmen who had been marking time came to a finish and began to wipe their instruments. Children broke ranks and went looking for their mothers as the wide pavement filled with erstwhile marchers re-grouping into families and couples.

Connie hurried across home to attend to her face and hair in private before going into chapel. Miss Constance Ginnell! She was singing under her breath one of her examination pieces that Fred Winskill had suggested for this afternoon. 'Let the bright seraphim in burning row, their sil...ver, their silver trumpets blow'. That'll make them sit up, in white or not, had been his opinion.

Leonard Martland also had a feeling of excitement. He had played the new organ for some weeks but today there was to be a short dedication by the minister and then Len would play *Trumpet Voluntary* under the spotlight of special congregational attention. He went in search of Clara just to have a few words with her before entering the side passage to the choir vestry.

"Not tired, my dear?"

"Of course not, Len. How do *you* feel?"

"Oh! Fine. I suppose I'd better not touch, but the wind has blown a bit of hair out of place there."

"Go on then, push it in but be careful."

He was very careful as ever and then he smiled at her.

"Isn't it a lovely day?" she said.

An amused expression came into Len's eyes.

"Yes, Miss Crossley, it is indeed. Do you come here often?"

Annie Northcroft in passing stopped by them and Len complimented her on her festive appearance.

"Crowds here, aren't there?" she exclaimed gaily.

"I must have a word with Alfred about something," said Clara and went off to find him. She wanted to catch him by himself for a moment.

Jimmie Northcroft and Willie Briggs hastened forward to help David and Geoffrey hoist the banner shafts from the leather holders and lower the standard carefully, preparatory to storing it in the Sunday School, there to await its next splendid occasion. The collars of the two latest bearers would hare done justice to Stormalong in his heyday as they unbuckled with relief and dabbed at their flushed faces.

Sybil moved near concernedly to smooth David's coat as Geoffrey turned to Kerry. Where was the young victor with the wreathed brow? His hands reached out and cupped the pale helmet of cowslips that snuggled her head and with closed eyes he bent his own head upon it with thankfulness, inhaling a faint scent of milliner's buckram that after a few moments of stillness demonstrated a profoundly restorative effect.

"Listen, Kerry," he said under cover of the general stir. "I've got the car at the back of the school. As soon as this service is over, let's slip out and go for a run on the moors."

"The moors! Today! But I thought you said . . . "

"Don't hark back so. I've something to tell you. Two things

476

actually. We'll walk into Delph and have tea at a cottage later if you'll come. You will? Fine!"

He looked up at the unhurrying geography of the sky. What time was sunset? Never mind, he'd find the shelter of some sturdy limestone wall, some rocky shoulder of hillside or quiet refuge in a curving bank, with perhaps only a quicksilver lark ascending to be heard in the early evening sunshine.

Then David seized his hand and shook it warmly, and turning to the bemused girl kissed her heartily.

"My dear, dear sister in the Lord!"

They all laughed and Sybil put out her hand to Geoffrey. He saw new understanding smiling at him and he struggled to speak but could not. He took her proffered hand and bowed low over it.

"He's learned at last," David admitted to himself with a caution that momentarily restrained his high spirits. "Another few months and perhaps I couldn't have done it!"

But it was done and there would be no undoing. The balanced guy-ropes were pulled taut and the well placed pegs driven home. To your tents O Israel! The warfare is accomplished, the flesh wounds are healed, the hurt of the spirit assuaged as the regenerating streams and the newly drawn wine erase the marks of the one and the smart of the other, so that in retrospect it will be avowed that no tears were ever shed but for present joy and no true ecstasy felt throbbing in the soul until this entry into peace.

Sam Buckley scanned the opposite pavement for Pins and Needles.

"Oh, Mr Buckley," Mrs Butterway stood beside him. "My friend here was too shy to come alone. Will it be all right?"

Sam was somewhat taken aback but recovered quickly.

"Better still, of course. Come this way."

He had meant to have a shot at educating a supply but found himself with the necessity for dealing with the demand.

Elsie Buckley saw her husband's face as the trio came across the road and she turned away half smiling. Poor Sam! Like a word or disease they had never heard of heretofore, that woman was cropping up continually. Dr Bedser was trying to place her at Crumpsall Hospital in some capacity, perhaps in the children's ward where there would be a more appropriate outlet for her too easy sympathy. Ah! There were Dr and Mrs Bedser just arriving. Elsie went to join them. Her gratitude took the form of a sociability not felt or witnessed since her tennis club days. She and Sam both played at Chorltonville now.

There were lively occasions too when people spent an evening at Snowdonia, the shyest being allowed to nurse the importunate Wispy who constantly reminded them that a pet dog expects to be petted. These days the Buckley's long car was often seen in the Oldham Road vicinity where Sam had been a boy hereabouts, you know!

He'd always been well liked and she was all right when you got to know her!

"Was there ever a Mr Butterway?" asked Ada of Miriam in a whisper. "Is she really married, d'you know?"

Miriam had a slight difficulty in clearing her throat and so made no reply but she moved to the edge of the pavement and primly spoke a few words of welcome to the newcomers. Grace Garner also refrained from making any display of pleasure or surprise, great as they were. So far, so good. If Mrs Butterway was still incapable of sinning no more, at any rate she must not go away. Grace joined them unobtrusively.

"We're very glad to see you. Mr Buckley will get you seats where you'll have a good view of Connie."

Sam shepherded them inside and into the gallery.

David sought his father near the porch.

"I say, Father, before you go in I must tell you. It's good news, Geoffrey has joined the ranks, today, during the procession. I saw it with my own eyes. He's a new man absolutely."

"Aha!" exclaimed Robert with feeling. "This is good to hear indeed. Sometimes it's the blinding shock on the way to Damascus; sometimes the warmth of recognition on the Emmaus road; more of the latter for Geoffrey because of his upbringing. Thank you for letting me know just now. It gives an added grace to the day."

They shook hands and then David laughed aloud.

"Of course, if I know anything of him there'll be a sufficiency of the old habit left to make real news: Christian bites lion!"

The Stewards were already in attendance in the minister's vestry when Robert Garner entered the ante-room to prepare himself for the service. As he brushed his hair carefully, his face in the mirror showed a satisfaction that was almost akin to rubbing his hands. He had seen his son and his son's friend struggling side by side in that rush of wind; the trained man and the dedicated laity. What a combination of strength!

The trained man there must be, not for his privilege of office nor for any assumption of greater worth or deeper holiness, but for his deeper study, for the midnight cruse of oil and dawning clarity. Yet the all-embracing flash of both infinite and self knowledge had been demonstrated today and that searching fire would warm other hearts in contact with one so markedly approached by the pyrognostic touch.

What a day for such a visitation, on this anniversary of the birth of the evangelical church.

That was the contrast between the filched fire of Prometheus and the bequeathed fire of Pentecost. Of old it had been blasphemy to steal fire from heaven, but the tongues of flame descending in the upper room in Jerusalem had been placed on man's head as a crown. Man was to be entrusted with the sacred and profane fires, with life and death, and the flames playing upon his head were now an offering of a new partnership between God and man. The thief of fire and of the fruits of knowledge was invited to the feast and welcomed to the hearth as son and heir. The former commands had oft-times met with disobedience; would the proffered keys, so weighted with responsibility, be accepted with a better grace? Choice, with latent knowledge, again lay with man at his coming to man-of-God's estate.

In the mirror the face stared attentively back at Robert as his deliberations moulded his expression. If he could persuade his people of the grace and power of the Holy Spirit this day and every day, the church would be a fruitful bride of Christ indeed and the children of God inherit the earth. He nodded slightly to himself as if in absent-minded recognition and then decisively returned the military brushes to their drawer beneath the mirror and entered the main vestry.

"It's time," Tom was saying quietly. "Len's well into his first fireworks and everybody's in I should think. A good crowd."

Alfred held the door to the chapel ajar ready to swing wide at the apposite moment and as Robert stepped from the inner room calm, alert, prepared, Alfred's voice rumbled deeply.

"Your congregation are ready and waiting, Sir," and behind the opening door as the music with its fuller range swelled out, he gave a slight bow, in honour not only of the Cloth but of the man.